THE FORGOTTEN
AND
THE FEARED

THE DRAGON QUEEN #1

EC GARRETT

Cover Art and Design by EC Garrett

Interior Formatting and Design by EC Garrett

Interior Illustrations by Reina Diaz

Copy Editing by YarnWyvern

Proofreading by YarnWyvern and Ruthie Bowles

Map by Reina Diaz

eBook ISBN: 979-8-9890690-2-6

Paperback ISBN: 979-8-9890690-1-9

2nd Edition

To me. Because for so long that voice in my head said,

"You're not good enough. You can't do this."

You ARE good enough and you CAN do this.

And to the friends (on two legs and on four)

who saved me along the way.

THE DRAGON QUEEN

Series Reading Order

The Forgotten and The Feared

The Broken and The Brave

The Defiant and The Damned

A WARNING

The Dragon Queen series is set in a Grimdark, medieval fantasy world, with a high amount of violence, gore, and danger. All incidents involving animals are inspired by the real life cruelty animals in our world experience every second of every day. If The Dragon Queen series was a movie, it would be rated R or NC-17 due to graphic violence, graphic sex, language, and dire situations. Proceed with caution and review the trigger warning list below before you dive in. If it all sounds good? Then **let the Game begin.**

Triggers that are frequent are in **BOLD** and triggers that are extremely frequent are in **BOLD AND UNDERLINED.**

HATE, DISCRIMINATION, & OPPRESSION

Bullying, Classism, Disownment, Gentrification, Hate Crimes, Homelessness, Lesbomisia, Queermisia, **Poverty**, Racism, **Religious Persecution, Religious Commentary, Sexism & Misogyny**, Slavery & Indentured Servitude, and Slut-Shaming

SEXUAL & ROMANTIC

Age Gap, Graphic Sex, Sex Work, **Primal Sex, Sapphic Sex.**

MENTAL HEALTH & SUICIDE

Anxiety & Anxiety Attacks, Depression, Dissociation & Dissociative Episodes, Intrusive thoughts, **Nightmares, <u>Post Traumatic Stress Disorder,</u>** Self-harm, Sleep Disorders, and **Suicidal Ideation.**

INJURY & MEDICAL

Amputation, **<u>Blood & Gore Depiction,</u>** Body Horror, **<u>Dead Bodies & Body Parts,</u> Decapitation, Dismemberment,** Emesis, **Eyeball Trauma, Loss of Autonomy, <u>Physical Injuries,</u> Scars,** Starvation & Dehydration, Weight Gain

DEATH & LOSS

Death of a child, Death of a friend, <u>Death of a Parent & Guardian,</u> Death of a Partner & Spouse, **Death of a Sibling, <u>Grief & Loss Depiction</u>**

VIOLENCE & CRIME

Asphyxia, Strangulation & Suffocation, **Blackmail, <u>Building Collapse,</u> Captivity & confinement, <u>Cults,</u>** Explosions, **<u>Fire & Arson</u>,** Imprisonment & Incarceration, **<u>Knife, sword & axe violence,</u> Murder & attempted murder,** Physical assault, Stalking, and **<u>Whipping</u>**

WAR & GENOCIDE

<u>Colonialism, Imperialism,</u> Massacres & mass murder, and War themes & military violence

ANIMAL DEATH & CRUELTY

Animal Attack, **Animal Consumption,** <u>**Animal Cruelty & Abuse,**</u> **<u>Animal Death, Animal Illness & Injury,</u> <u>Animal Skinning/Butchering,</u>** Animal Testing & Experimentation, Forced Breeding, and Hunting.

Important: This book ends on a <u>cliffhanger.</u>

TWYN FELLS
THE ULSTER WALD
THE PASS OF BRÓN MÓR
NORTHLANDS
ABHYANN GHEAL RIVER
EAHMOND
WESTLANDS
INFINIUM SANDS
SOUTHLANDS

THE KINGDOM OF UR DAOINE
CASTAEL LARYN
ANNAG FOREST
EASTLANDS
SUD AZYL
MIDHEYM SEA

THE LANGUAGE

CHARACTERS

Aanad: *uh-NOD*

Abeloth: *AB-eh-loth*

Achan: *AH-ki*

Amalia: *uh-MAH-lee-uh*

Carmys: *CAR-mees*

Constantus: *con-STAN-tus*

Constantyn: *con-STAN-teen*

Drayven: *Dray-ven*

Dyana: *die-AN-uh*

Fionn: *FEE-on*

Hydan: *HIGH-din*

Ireyna: *eye-REY-nuh*

Jhon: *John*

Kydis: *KAI-diss*

Landys: *LAN-diss*

Livyathin: *luh-VIE-uh-thin*

Mireille: *MEER-ee-el*

Morrigyn: *MORE-ih-ghin*

Nerasha: *nuh-RAH-shuh*

Nyall: *NY-uhl*

Ophiya: *oh-FEE-yuh*

Os: *oz*

Pfern: *fern*

Remus: *REE-mus*

Remaynd: *REY-mend*

Ryu: *REE-you*

Syska: *SIS-kuh*

Tolys: *TAH-liss*

Varas: *VEHR-us*

Vesimyr: *VES-uh-meer*

Vyktor: *VIC-ter*

Wytch: *wich*

<u>PLACES</u>

Abhaynn Gheal: *ah-VEEN geel*

Annag: *AHH-nug*

Brón Mór: *BRON more*

Castael Laryn: *KAY-stil LAIR-in*

Eahmond: *AYE-mend*

Elysium: *uh-LEE-see-um*

Infinium: *in-FIN-ee-um*

Midheym: *MID-high-m*

Österhamn: *OO-ster-hahm*

Sud Azyl: *sood a-ZEAL*

Twyn Fells: *twin fells*

Ulster Wald: *UHL-ster vahld*

Ur Daoine: *ur DANE-ya*

<u>OTHER TERMS</u>

A gahrá: *ah GAH-ruh*

Ahavah: *uh-HAH-vah*

Alle Seele: *ALL-uh SELL-uh*

Archidna: *are-KID-nuh*

Arkaydian: *are-KAY-dee-in*

Arkaydia: *are-KAY-dee-uh*

Beastkyn: *BEAST-kin*

Bloodwyng: *BLOOD-wing*

Demis: *DEM-ees*

Dreamweavyr: *DREAM-weev-er*

Ether: *EE-thur*

Lir: *leer*

Lesbos: *LESS-bahs*

Macha: *MAH-kuh*

Magyka: *MA-jik-uh*

Magyk: *MA-jik*

Neiman: *NEE-man*

Oryx: *OR-icks*

Puggō: *POO-gogh*

Truewaz: *TRUE-vahs*

THE FORGOTTEN
AND
THE FEARED

HAS FOUR PLAYLISTS, ONE
FOR EACH ACT. THE ACT PAGES
EACH FEATURE A QR CODE
LINKED TO A PLAYLIST.

HOWEVER IF YOU PREFER,
PLEASE ENJOY THIS MASTER
PLAYLIST TO ENHANCE YOUR
READING EXPERIENCE.

PROLOGUE

Year 420 PBM

The howling wind shakes the small cabin. The old wooden walls rattle and the roof groans, every worn shingle barely hanging on. The wind shrieks and moans, sounding like the screams of a thousand tormented souls in the depths of purgatory.

Winter is rough in the North. But this isn't just harsh wind, no natural storm.

"We don't have much time," Jhon says, his voice strained as he gently wipes the tears from Ophiya's red frostbitten cheeks. "They're almost here. I knew that godsdamn tracking charm was a bust." He inhales, reeling in the frantic anger and fear that threatens to overwhelm him.

He can't break or falter for a moment—not now.

"We need to do this now, my darling. We must." His dark voice cracks with a pain that's invisible to all but the two of them.

Ophiya glances to the corner of the cabin where the young child sits, having an animated conversation with her tiny pet mouse. Pure white ringlets fall into her cherubic face. Despite the situation, her daughter tries hard to stay positive.

"I thought we'd have more time," Ophiya whispers, desperate and broken. "We're supposed to be more time, Jhon."

"I thought so too. But this is the only way, you know that. My father's kin aren't coming. They can't protect her, but we still can," Ophiya leans back into her husband as her knees give out, knowing this is the last time she'll have with the ones she loves most.

"Don't worry, Puff. I'll protect you from the wind." In a small voice, quiet like a bell, the little girl comforts the tiny white mouse against her chest. The little girl has *always had an affinity for animals. Without siblings or a single friend, she turned instead to creatures for companionship. The tiny mouse squeaks and hides within the girl's white curls, the same color as her father's. She looks up, her big blue eyes wide and pure, unaware of the genuine peril of the current situation. "Daddy, the wind is scaring Puff." The girl gets up and walks over to Jhon, her ten-year-old head barely coming to his waist. She'd inherited her mother's height, unlike her father, who stood so tall that she sometimes wondered if he could touch the sky.*

"Well, the wind can be very scary indeed, sweet girl. I don't blame Puff." Jhon bends down, kissing those white ringlets on the young girl's head. Puff peeks his face out, small beady black eyes scared as he squeaks in greeting.

"But Puff has nothing to be frightened about, for he has the greatest protector anyone could ever have," Jhon kisses the girl on her forehead as she nods. "Remember the story of Puff, the magyk Mouse? I think, if he tries hard enough, Morrigyn might grant him wings." The girl's smile lights up the entire room. The mouse squeaks, rubbing against her chin as she tells him how he's going to be a mighty warrior too, someday.

Another gust of wind hits the cabin and the sound of shattered glass has them all looking to the northern wall, where the only window now lies in broken shards on the wooden floor.

"Damnit," Jhon curses, "Phiya, it's time." Jhon looks up at his wife, meeting her eyes and seeing the pure, utter heartbreak reflected in each other's gaze.

"What time is it for, Daddy?" Jhon and Ophiya daughter looks up at her parents, suddenly knowing something is wrong. "What's going on?"

"Oh, my sweet girl," Ophiya says gently, her voice shaking with emotion as she squats before the little girl until they're eye to eye. "Your father and I love you so much, my darling. No matter what happens, know that having you is the best thing to ever happen to me—" Ophiya breaks off as Jhon crouches beside her.

"To both of us," Jhon finishes where Ophiya can't.

"I know, mummy. I love you so much too. But..." the young girl trails off, "I'm scared."

"Don't be scared, little spark," Jhon reassures his daughter, "We need you to be brave, now."

The girl blinks, "Like a dragon rider from my stories?"

"Exactly like that. Now grab your stuff. It's time to play the hiding game." Jhon ushers his daughter to pick up the rest of her things, stuffing them in a small tote bag.

"I love the hiding game!" his daughter says, oblivious.

"I hate this," Ophiya whispers, hurt cracking her into a million tiny pieces.

"I know, Petal." Jhon turns, looking into her eyes as he finally lets the tears flow freely. "I want to see our daughter grow up. But now, it's on us to ensure she has a future at all." His voice breaks, and he takes a deep breath, his ice-blue eyes that match his daughter's closing briefly. He leans his forehead against hers as they take a moment to themselves—a brief moment.

"I want more time with you too, my love. I want to grow old together and watch as age only makes you more beautiful. I want to wake up to see your smile every morning—" Jhon takes a deep breath, "—but if we don't do this now, they'll kill her too. You know

this as well as I do." Jhon says, his face cold. The shadows along his sharp cheekbones grew darker for a moment, almost in reaction to his fury.

"I know. I know. You're right." Ophiya takes a long, shaky breath and steadies herself. "They won't have her." The two lovers stared into each other's eyes for a few moments, memorizing every plane, every wrinkle and freckle, each minute detail of each other. Their love is deeper than the oceans and vaster than the sky. But their love for their daughter is even greater—a parent's love burned hotter than pure, incandescent flame. And so, they would do this. For her.

The wind stops, and the forest goes silent. Jhon quickly gets his daughter hidden away under the cabinet.

She protests, trembling in pure fear, but she does as she's told, hiding out of sight with just her mouse to keep her warm. The lovers nod at each other, sparing one brief look at their daughter for the last time.

"Together," Jhon says resolutely, grabbing his wife's hand as they turn to face the door.

Ophiya spares one last glance at him, at her purpose, the other half of her soul, and then opens the door with a nod, "Until the very end."

"THROUGH ME THE WAY INTO
THE SUFFERING CITY.

THROUGH ME THE WAY
TO ETERNAL PAIN.

THROUGH ME THE WAY THAT
RUNS AMONG THE LOST...

ALL HOPE ABANDON YE
WHO ENTER HERE."

— DANTE ALIGHIERI, 1265-1321.
THE DIVINE COMEDY: INFERNO

SCAN FOR THE PT. 1
READING PLAYLIST

PART ONE:

THE FORSAKEN

CHAPTER 1
AMALIA

Year 500 PBM

They say the sky used to be full of Dragons. Every day, people from all corners of the Kingdom would look up to the skies and see great, scaled beasts soaring through the clouds. Some Dragons were the size of a horse and only had two legs. Others had four and were so large they would blot out the suns themselves, covering the world in darkness. Dragons were revered as Gods; many believed that Dragons were Gods, for they were beings of a higher order. Every Dragon receives the memories of their ancestors, giving them magykal powers beyond anything you could even imagine.

All was well in the Kingdom. Dragons lived in peace, side by side with all other species. The land flourished, ripe with magyk and life, as everyone lived in harmony. Until the day a giant portal made of a twisted, evil kind of magyk ripped into existence in the center of our continent. Until the day *they* emerged.

The fae. A greedy, righteous race of supernaturals. No one knew quite where they came from. There were no accounts of any fae in any of the scrolls. What's more, they wielded a strange, life-draining magyk. But the people welcomed them with open arms—as was their way. They trusted the fae, as did the Dragons.

If only they had known the truth of things.

The fae did not bow, nor did they see the Dragons as Gods. Instead, they looked to the skies and saw power. For the fae were a selfish race, always wanting more. In the name of their God, a great, all-knowing being they claimed was the source of life itself: Constantyn. In His name, the fae began claiming our Kingdom as their own.

The fae broke our world—broke the natural order of things.

The skies are empty now. The land was sucked dry of magyk, leaving many homeless and without work. The fae captured the Dragons, captured all rare magykal creatures. Even going so far as to create fenced-in parks where fae royals could hunt unicorns and mighty gryphons for sport. Those who live in the warmer Eastlands and even in the Southlands near the Infinium Desert would see the occasional Dragon, but now they are an omen for bad tidings to come. The Dragons that were forcibly bred were of a more domestic sort. Able to be controlled and trained. Together with their riders, they formed the Dragon Guard—an elite unit of 10 fae Dragon Riders who acted as the enforcers for the High Council in Castael Laryn.

Anything can become a weapon in the right set of hands. Even a *God.*

Vivid dreams of flying through the sky on the back of a great, winged Dragon fade away as slumber dissipates.

My eyelids are heavy, laden with thick sleep, resisting as I pry them open. For a moment there is just darkness. Then my dry eyes adjust and I take in the threadbare room, dust twinkling in the cold morning air. Outside my slight window, fog coats the mountains of the densely packed trees of the Ulster Wald, a sprawling forest and mountain range that covers half our continent. The North is the largest region in Ur Daoine, but it's the least populated.

Far in the distance, Dyre wolves howl, the haunting melody drifting across the tree line. Most in my town found the sound to be terrifying. It never scared me, though. The sound didn't give me goosebumps or set my hair on end. Instead, the howls made me feel at home.

Every day of my life is the same as the day before.

Wake up. Eat. Work. Sleep. Repeat.

There would be no sleeping in. I have responsibilities and can't afford to miss a day of work or do anything that could jeopardize it. I'm what some might consider rather unlucky. Far past the attractive age of 18, I'm considered an old spinster, too worn and torn to even be suitable for marriage or anything. Well, anything except for the desperate widowed old husband three times my age who lives a few rows down.

Sorry, Mr. Blanchard.

Not that there's anything wrong with marrying older. But I would rather be alone than in a loveless marriage. I set on this from a very young age, having seen true love in my parents. A selfish part of me wanted a love like theirs, and I'd rather wait than settle. I've seen what it is to fall deeper and deeper in love with every passing day. A ghost of a smile forms on my frozen face, recalling how every morning at breakfast, my father would swear to me that Mother was even more beautiful than the day before. Mother would titter and giggle, her pink cheeks contrasting beautifully against her black hair.

But the warmth of the memory fades, and cold replaces it. I hiss as I throw my blankets off and sit up, forcing my feet to touch the cold wood floor. A small nightstand and candle sit next to my wooden trundle bed, the mattress stuffed with hay that occasionally poked through, making me itch like crazy.

I hiss in pain at the freezing floor, rushing to put on a pair of socks. Still dirty, probably smelly, but my other pair is still drying from the day before, and with only two pairs of socks—there are no other options. I let out a sigh. Next month my book money will have to go towards some new socks instead of a new book.

Fuck.

I shake off the building frustration. There will be another month and another book at some point. I pull the clean tunic over my arms after binding my breasts in place of actual undergarments and lace up my slightly too-big boots. The left one is so worn down that I would need to get the sole replaced by the end of next spring. But they keep my feet dry during the muddy season, and that's all that matters. Working at the stables is a dirty job, no matter the time of year.

There's no mirror to check my hair, just a small washbasin next to my toilet and bathtub. Well, "bathtub" is stretching it. In order to take a bath, I had to sit with my legs tightly pressed against my chest just to get half submerged, so it's more of a sponge bath. I've certainly smelled better. But I'm so used to smelling like animals that it's never bothered me. Through lots of practice, some of it on the stable's horses through a bit of carrot bribery, I've taught myself how to braid. I quickly weave my charcoal gray strands and tie them off with a thin piece of leather before tossing the braid behind my shoulder. It's nothing special; it does the job and keeps my hair out of my face. On days like today, when the wind off the Ulster Wald is freezing, I add a scarf, wrapping it over my hair and pulling it up over my nose. By now, all the villagers know what I look like, so I only use it when it's cold out.

My oddly colored hair is one of the many reasons I'm in Twyn Fells in the first place. Our world is harsh, and most of us have suffered in some way or another. But people are still mean, and it's easy to take fears out on others—trust me, I know. My charcoal gray hair has always led to rumors and veiled insults.

"She's a wytch," they whisper alongside outlandish stories of how I eat babies alive. So we left that town, and when it happened again, we left the next. Until we'd tried out every single town in the Northlands—every town except for one.

Twyn Fells. The Northernmost town in the Kingdom, and the most isolated. It takes a tough kind of person to live here. The winters are harsh, and so is the terrain. People here leave me alone. Then again, most people can't handle the climate here. It takes a certain person to withstand the long, dark nights and the cold weather.

I yank on the patched-up green wool sweater that has kept me warm for many seasons and top it with my prized brown leather jacket—it's the nicest thing I own, and I wear it every day. Crossing the small room, I lock the door behind me and head down to the Inn's main floor. I can tell breakfast is ready from the scent of warm berries and sweet brown sugar in the air. My stomach rumbles loudly in response, already hungry. I'm always hungry.

The Westlands, the central crop-growing region of our Kingdom, is in year 5 of a drought. Food is scarce. We grow what we can, but it's too cold in Twyn Fells for most crops to thrive. The fae claim the drought is a punishment from Constantyn, but I find it difficult to believe that every bad thing to happen is some sort of cosmic punishment from a God I've never seen.

Mrs. Hunton, the Innkeeper's wife, stands at the kitchen stone stirring the berry porridge in her dressing gown and slippers. Her peppery black and gray curly hair is back in a headband, like always. In exchange for caring for the Innkeeper's horse for no charge, I get one free meal a day, and I always pick breakfast. The mornings are so cold, and the hot porridge keeps me warm for hours.

"Eating here or taking it on the road, dear?" Mrs. Hunton smiles at me from over her shoulder.

"On the road, please. I'm going to share this with Dy. You know the Bird-cage doesn't feed those girls," I grumble, the early hour making my voice scratchy—the cold air wasn't exactly helping on that front either. Mrs. Hunton made a large bowl for me in the lightweight travel bowl and wrapped a red kitchen towel around it, covering the top. Her warm smile is highlighted by dark circles under her slightly wrinkled eyes. Karol Hunton looked like a woman who had lived a life with joy—and sometimes seeing that pure joy on her face hurt worse than being stabbed in the chest. Our conversations are short, but we've developed a rather comfortable rapport these past few years. Lots of nodding.

"Careful as you walk, dear—don't go spilling it!" My eyes roll, but I snort and nod my head in thanks. Mrs. Hunton made me porridge every morning, filled the bowl a little too much, and then worried I'd spill it. Something is comforting in the reliability of it, and she means well, so I always keep my mouth shut and let my sarcastic comments suffocate, dying on the tip of my tongue and no further. She's the only person in town gifted that courtesy.

"Yes, ma'am," I say, my voice still scratchy from the cold. I grab my bowl and head out the door. The wind hits me in the face like an icy punch, and I fight the urge to shiver. Twyn Fells is still covered in darkness, most of the town asleep. The village is relatively small, 300 people at most. I weave out of the small neighborhood and across town, going to the stables. My boots squelch in the mud with each step. It's been a very wet winter so far. We've had snow, but it turns into slush, creating a huge mess. My boots have seen better days.

It rains often in the Fells, what we call the town, and the nearby forest area. We are the most northwestern village in Ur Daoine, which means we get the most godsdamned rain. I usually enjoy the rain, but this year has been worse than most. The constant downpour and endless mud makes my job particularly difficult, so while a rainy day is my favorite time to stay inside and read this month's book, it makes the horses so dirty that my muscles are sore from the constant grooming and trying to get the mud off their ever-dirty hides.

Most of the horses are still asleep, but Taran is my favorite. He's a permanent resident and belongs to Mrs. Hunton's husband, Paul. Taran pokes his large white and gray spotted horse head out the stall window and nickers at me in greeting. With a long black mane and tail and a gray dappled body, Taran looks as if he is splattered in shadows. He neighs at me in excitement, knowing my presence means food would soon be delivered.

"Taran, you act as if you've never been fed a day in your damn life, when in fact, if I'm being completely honest, you're looking a little larger than usual." His ears pin back as he glares at me in judgment. He stomps his front hoof, and I laugh, kissing his soft nose. I've always been good with animals. Growing up, I didn't have many friends, but I always had an animal to keep me from getting lonely. The other horses neigh and greet me as I get inside and get situated for the morning feeding. I can't afford a horse of my own, but considering Paul Hunton is not in the best of health and can't ride, Taran is more or less my horse. Which suits him nicely, considering he walked straight up to me on the first day and nearly shoved me to the floor in an attempt for snuggles.

The ground of the barn is muddy despite being covered. The wood structure had seen better days, so it doesn't do much to keep the water out. It keeps the horses dry, but the floor? That was a river of mud.

"Wake up on the wrong side of the bed today, eh Meryll?" I poke fun at the short chestnut mare in front of me, and she glares, yanking the bucket with her grain straight out of my hand. Her mane is sideways and covered in shavings, making her look like she got caught in a wind tunnel. Taran is last, so I take a minute and stand with him, brushing shavings off his neck while he eats.

After giving everyone their grain and hay, a warm voice comes from the other side of the barn, "Good morning!"

"Morning," I call. Dyana pops her head in the feed room, her dark mahogany eyes sparkling. "It's unsettling how chipper you are this early in the morning."

Dyana rolls her eyes, laughing, "You only think that because you're always cranky in the morning," she says before pausing, pretending to look thoughtful, "then again, you're always a bit cranky, you damn curmudgeon." Her eyes close in awe as she catches the scent of my porridge. "Oh Goddess, yes. Tell me we're splitting that."

I pause, mirroring her thoughtful face from before. "Hmm, would a curmudgeon share their warm, brambleberry oatmeal?"

Dyana clasps her heart dramatically at the mention of brambleberries, "I take it all back. You, Amalia Roth, are a ray of absolute sunshine in the morning."

I laugh at that and motion for her to follow me into the tiny room with a table just big enough for two, where I eat most of my meals. Dyana is a classic beauty.

With a heart-shaped face, inky black hair, a slender figure with tawny skin touched with pink, as if she'd just come in from the cold, she's always turned heads. But the warm smile and twinkle in her eyes always made you feel happy when she was around. It's why she's so good at what she does. Dancing has always been Dyana's passion ever since she heard music in a local pub in the first village we moved to. Then she discovered her talent in movement. Now, she entertains dozens nightly at The Birdcage with her gorgeous performances.

I grab a spare bowl and split the porridge, putting a serving in front of her as I sit down. Dyana is wrapped in a thick red wool dress with boots in much better condition than my own sticking out from underneath, and a black cloak trimmed with fur. When we moved for the second time, farther into the North, I saved up and splurged on that cloak for her. It doesn't fix things, but it's my way of apologizing for the constant moving around. Sometimes words are difficult for me. Actions are easier. Dyana cried when she unwrapped the coat and immediately put it on. She's worn it every cold day since.

"Gods, I'm so jealous you get Mrs. H's food every morning."

"Yeah, but your room is huge, and you get it completely free." I remind her. "Plus, I do share it with you when you get up on time."

Dyana sighs, "I suppose it's worth all of the creepy males leering at me. Vanas, you know, the Satyr who runs the shoeshine place? He wouldn't leave me alone last night!"

I glare as my anger instantly ignites, and Dyana rolls her eyes, "Calm down. He didn't try anything, and he tipped well. I'd just rather it be some hot woman ogling at me." She snickers and winks at me. Humor has always been her way of dealing with things. Neither of us are rich by any means—don't get me wrong, we were poor as fuck. We made okay money, considering our circumstances, but we were putting aside most of our monthly earnings to save up and buy a place of our own.

"You work tonight?" I ask as I finish off my bowl. She nods in return, eyes going a little dark at the thought. Dyana loved to dance, loved it more than anything in the world. But I could tell it wore on her sometimes.

Unsurprisingly, I was not a fan of the idea when she first told me, but it's her choice, and its good money. Dyana did make me promise not to throw any more stray punches just because one of her customers was "staring" at her too long. I get a bit overprotective sometimes and may have beaten a few people to a pulp at the establishment she danced at in the town we lived in before the Fells.

"See you tonight?" I ask. We have dinner together when we're able. Mrs. Hunton always has "extra" stew and bread some nights. Something I suspect is a lie, but I will accept it without complaint. She's a kind woman.

Dyana shakes her head no, "But I'm off tomorrow. I'm gonna be tired, so I'll be here around lunch."

"Sounds good. Be safe. And if anyone gets handsy, you remember what to do—"

Dyana holds up her hand, stopping me, "Okay, no, we're not going through an hour lecture on self-defense again. It was cool when I was sixteen, but I'm twenty-five now. I'm not a child."

I just look at her, "I know you're not. But the fae come for the Selection in just five moons, Dy."

Dyana pauses and grabs my arm gently, leaning into me, despite the fact that she's now—to my great annoyance—more than four inches taller than me. "We will be long hidden by then, Ama. It's okay. We have plenty of time."

I bite my lip, and she slaps my hand, making me groan grumpily. It's a bad habit of mine when I get nervous. "I know, I just...they can't pick you. As soon as it seems like the snow might melt, we go to the cave. Okay? I refuse to watch you get slaughtered for the fae's entertainment."

In five moon cycles, the fae will begin a tour around the Kingdom, selecting candidates for the 20th Annual Gauntlet. A tournament to the death. It's a bloody, awful event held every twenty-five years, and I've been on edge since the start of last year, knowing it's coming up.

Dyana hugs me, whispering, "I promise, Ama. We're gone as soon as the snow looks like it will melt." She pulls back, "But...we're coming back, right?"

I smile even though guilt turns my stomach into knots. "Of course. This is home. Things...work here. At least for now. We'll stay."

Dyana smiles, and it makes her look so young for a moment. Then she's back to the gorgeous, tall adult woman before me. "I have half a cabbage left and an onion. If you bring carrots, want to make a stew tomorrow? I'm off work."

My stomach grumbles at the thought of her vegetable stew. We've been making it together for ages, and it's still my favorite, "Goddess, yes. I'll see if Mrs. Hunton has any leftover bread too."

Dyana winks before heading out to get ready for the day.

A nose shoves me forward suddenly, and I turn to see Taran, who is looking back with needy eyes, "You literally just ate!" But he just continues to stare at me. I grumble and sneak him an extra handful of grain.

CHAPTER 2
AMALIA

My hair flows behind me in the wind, like a wave of shadow swelling and crashing against the shores of my back while Taran and I gallop through the edges of the forest. The braid from this morning has come undone, and my scarf now sits bunched around my neck as the cold wind slaps me in the face. It hurts, and my raw cheeks are chapped and burning, but I don't care; this is worth it.

Taran's black and white dappled body gallops beneath me rhythmically, the sound of his hooves like roaring peals of thunder. I let my eyes close, tilting my head back to the sky. This is as close to peace as I've ever managed to get. Sometimes, for a brief moment, when Taran goes all out, and his legs are absolutely flying underneath him, I like to imagine that we're not down on the muddy ground but soaring through the clouds. And my saddle isn't on a horse, but a Dragon.

It will only ever be a dream. All Dragons in our kingdom have been enslaved, kept in Castael Laryn under lock and key. The only sightings of Dragons are of the Dragonguard; the High Council's personal squadron of tamed Dragons, ridden by imperial fae. But they haven't been seen in the North for decades.

The High Council rules Ur Daoine from the capital city, Castael Laryn—their seat of power and home—to the Dragon Pit, an old temple turned prison where the Dragons are kept in cramped stables. The capital is five days south of the Pass of Brón Mór, and Twyn Fells is two days northwest from there. Seven days—if you were riding the entire time—is all that sits between the fae and us. Castael Laryn is a sprawling city right on the Abhaynn Gheal, a vicious river that carves down from the Ulster Wald and east towards the Midheym Sea.

Taran snorts underneath me and slows down into a walk. "Good job, buddy. That's the farthest we've gone in a while." He shakes his head up and down as I caress his neck. "Let's go home; it's dinner time." At the word "dinner," Taran's ears perk up, and he turns around, picking up a fast trot. I bounce wildly for a moment before I can regain my balance and start posting, laughing at his sudden hurry, but

Taran is a male on a mission, and that male is very food motivated. We trot for half an hour until Taran sees Twyn Fells in the distance. Only slightly mollified that he will actually eat hay again, Taran relaxes into a happy walk. This is always my last ride of the day. The horses all need to be ridden regularly to maintain peak physical shape. The Pass of Brón Mór is brutal and steep, so part of my job is ensuring the horses are all fit and ready for the journey at any moment's notice. Some of the owners ride their horses themselves, but I've been on three rides already today, and my thighs are aching. I always save Taran's ride for last so that we can take our time.

I've trained all the horses to always walk when they're in the town vicinity, just to be safe. Besides Dyana, most of my time is spent with the horses. You see, animals won't betray you. They won't lie to you and hurt you.

People, on the other hand? People can't be trusted.

I'm jolted from my thoughts as Taran comes to a sudden halt nearly causing me to fall off. There's a sudden tension in his body—something has spooked him. I frown and look around, having regained my seat.

There's no wind. No birds, either. Even the trees seem quieter. Stilled and sub-dued, as if they too are afraid.

A sound rises as my heart races, thumping hard within my chest.

Something's wrong. I feel it in my bones. Taran flares his nostrils and prances nervously beneath me, feeling the sense of wrongness in the air.

"Woah, it's okay, friend. I've got you," I mutter to him, running my hand through his mane and sending waves of calm with each touch. My magyk rushes into him, eager to be used. "It's alright. I'm not going to let anything happen to you, I promise," I send a little more calming magyk, and he finally settles, but I can feel his senses pleading at him to run away.

Screams towards the west suddenly echo through the valley below the forest when a large boom explodes in the distance, followed by a gust of wind so hard it nearly bends the trees back. Taran rears, almost losing his balance. Another explosion sounds, followed by more screams. That's not what robs my lungs of breath. It's the sound that rises above all the rest. A loud, multi-layered warbling screech that infuses me with such fear I feel as if I actually might die.

Which can only mean one thing, and its many moons too early.

"GO TARAN!" I shout, urging him forward with my magyk, abandoning the reins altogether. I click at him and squeeze him into a gallop, and Mother bless him, despite all his instincts urging him to run the other way, Taran, my brave Taran, makes a beeline right back into town. We race into the town limits, but another scream distracts me as I get to the stables.

Black smoke billows into the air in giant waves, turning day to night as the sky grows dark. People cry out, fleeing their houses and tripping over themselves in the mud. Fae soldiers drag several of my neighbors out of their houses, shoving them to the ground and ransacking their belongings.

Another building goes up in flames in the distance and I squint, realizing what direction it's coming from.

The Birdcage. Dyana!

Taran reads my mind as we race over to find her. He avoids the frantic crowd with surprising agility. I can feel his worry; he considers Dyana part of his herd.

When we turn the corner to the town square, my magyk recoils, making me flinch. It's just enough of a hesitation to offset my balance, so when Taran loses control of his fear and rears again, I'm tossed to the ground. I hit hard, mud splashing onto my face, but I roll into it, trying to minimize the impact. Another scream has me scrambling to my feet, but someone runs into me, knocking me to my knees. I glance up just in time to see The Birdcage collapse in flames, wooden panels disintegrating.

Through the fire, a giant green Dragon emerges. Thick, dark green bumpy scales cover the Dragon's body, meeting dark green horns as big as my own body and spikes lining down the spine before ending in a tail coated in barbs. It's at least four times the size of Taran and could swallow him in one bite.

I was so distracted by the Dragon, I didn't even see the others. Fae soldiers in dark metal armor quickly swarm us on horseback and on foot, swords raised. I'm yanked to my feet, stumbling into the other townsfolk as the fae begin to round us up. They yell, herding us until we're cramped in a circle in the middle of the town square. An older demis male I recognize as Vyktor, the town Blacksmyth, throws a punch and tries to go after a fae soldier. Vyktor is old for a demis, his hair gray and white, his skin wrinkled.

I blink, and they've cut Vyktor's throat. I don't even see the fae move. All I see is Vyktor's body falling to the mud, his head flying through the air as hot blood splatters my cheeks. His head hits someone in the face so hard she falls to the ground. The wail following has me elbowing people to get out of the way, but it's no use. Mrs. Hunton is on her knees in the mud and the fae notice. A group of them chuckle, abandoning us and approaching her. "I think we have our first candidate for the Gauntlet, lads," one growls.

"Leave her alone," Dyana's shouts.

I inhale so hard I choke. What the fuck is she doing? I try to find her mind but it's been so long since I used that part of my magyk, and there's too much going on. I can't control my emotions enough to grasp the wild magyk within me.

The old-fashioned way, then. I start shoving and throwing elbows in earnest, using my lack of height to wiggle my way through the crowd.

"Pick on someone your own size, you dick!" Dyana shouts again, followed by a sharp scream, and I move even faster.

"Dyana!" My cry is answered as she cries out again. I easily shove past the fae soldiers at the edge of the circle with a grunt, ducking to avoid their swords. I have enough magyk left to calm the horses they're on, so I brush my fingers against the horse's legs as I dive and roll, breaking past their blockade. Adrenaline makes me numb as I see Dyana between two fae soldiers on her knees in the mud. One of them shoves her face down, and something in me snaps. Before I can rethink it, I'm bodyslamming one of the males holding her. But just as I hit the fae and knock him over, another fae grabs me from the hair and yanks me around. I throw another punch and a nasty kick to his right shin, and pain explodes in my face. The fae punches me right in the nose, and I slam face-first into the mud, unable to catch my footing. Blood floods my mouth from my broken nose. I see stars and my entire face instantly aches. I smother the pain, drowning it easily with fear and fury.

"Amalia!" Dyana shouts, fighting the fae that holds her.

I groan, spitting blood and struggling to stand. The soldier that hit me shoves me back down in the mud. A rumble of thunder announces the rain, and soon we're drenched in the icy downpour, and puddles gather beneath my knees. I crawl, reaching for Dyana. The fae holding her slaps her in the face so hard it knocks her over, and she cries out. I shove harder through the mud, trying to pull myself closer and we reach for each other, hands almost touching. The fae responsible for my broken nose yanks me up by my hair, laughing as I flinch in pain.

The Dragon roars again and we all go silent as the Dragonfear kicks in. A primal, unavoidable response where your body kicks into fight or flight mode. An acceptance that you are now prey. My adrenaline soars and my muddy hands begin to tremble.

No. I can't lose control now.

The green Dragon growls, flashing double rows of razor-sharp fangs that could rip my torso in two with no effort. It paws at the ground, kicking rocks and mud everywhere with its sharp black claws. The Dragon lays down, hissing at us as its tail slams down on another house. More of the villagers scream, but it's quickly quieted as the Dragon growls again, watching us with hungry gray eyes.

A being covered in black metal armor jumps down from the Dragon—a jump that would break a human's legs. But this was no human.

Ice floods my veins, colder than the wind turning my cheeks raw. Colder than the mud beneath my knees, soaking my work pants as I feel the sharp, sour, metallic taste of magyk.

Imperial fae magyk.

Imperial fae are still fae, but there is one major difference; they possess magyk.

The imperial fae rips off his helmet, pointed ears emerging with pure silver hair, so light it's almost white, contrasting against glowing, unnatural blood-red eyes. Something else all imperial fae possess. I hear some townsfolk cry out at the sight, but we all fall quiet as the fae raises his armored hand.

"Citizens of Twyn Fells, blessed day to you!" Everyone is silent, not repeating the blessing back. The fae smirks, but I see the fury in his eyes. "Our esteemed High Council, Constantyn's chosen representatives here on this Earthly plane, have received a vision. As you know, every 25 years Ur Daoine holds the Gauntlet, where two humans from every town get the chance to compete for a boon from his holiness, High Councilor Drayven." His deep voice echoes across the square. He doesn't shout, yet it's projected. The fae continues his righteous diatribe. "500 years ago, humans committed the worst offense of our history. They tried to overthrow the fae, tried to kill the Father's chosen," the fae says with disdain, looking down at us in absolute disgust. Smoke trails out of the Dragon's giant nostrils at this, clearly feeling the Bonded's emotions. "Our Father then sent another vision. One of peace and forgiveness, if the humans repented for their crimes, accepting Sol Constantus into their heart as their one true savior."

Rain continues to fall, soaking me to the bone, but all I feel is disgust.

"But the Father is not happy. So this year, the Gauntlet is happening early, as Constantyn demands, for we are merely his servants. As such, the High Council has decreed that the human who wins the Gauntlet will receive 100,000 gold marks," he pauses to touch his Dragon's side with a smirk, "and the losers will become Dragon food." The green Dragon licks his lips and flashes his fangs again. I look over at Dyana from where I'm lying in the mud.

We say nothing, but our eyes say everything. Pure panic floods my veins as my heart starts racing.

They can't pick her. They can't. I don't have anyone else. The years of my life spent alone, before I met Dyana, play through my head, causing my panic to grow as my chest tightens to the point of pain. Dyana sees my frantic eyes, and her eyes mist slightly, not panicked but sad, knowing my thoughts.

"So, who will it be? You have two minutes to put two people forward." Nobody moves or says a word. "No?" The fae asks, but there's no response. The fae clicks his tongue against his teeth in mock disappointment. "Such a shame."

Then he looks towards his Dragon and snaps his fingers. There's no time to react as the green Dragon suddenly snaps his head to the side and jumps forward, his long neck reaching right into the crowd of people and grabbing Mrs. Hunton, snapping her in two as her legs dangle out of his mouth. A shocked noise falls from me but it's drowned out by the sudden wails and screams of the crowd. The Dragon chews, crunching down and silencing her screams. Organs fall from her chest cavity as blood sprays from the Dragon's mouth. That's when the screaming starts.

"Oh my Gods, oh my Gods," Dyana cries, spiraling in panic.

I feel the same panic, but everything slows down as I turn my head to the side, still on the ground, and watch black armored boots splashing through the mud heading right toward me.

"These two seem unable to behave, sir," the fae holding Dyana says. She fights him and spits on his face before he backhands her. At the sight, I go from kneeling to shoving up to my feet as I tackle the fae. He goes down hard in the mud and I punch him twice before arms pull me off.

"Don't you fucking touch her," I hiss, spitting blood and rain and mud as fae guards yank my arms painfully.

The imperial fae just laughs, amused.

"Oh yes, his Holiness will be very pleased. You two will put up an entertaining fight, won't you, little puggōs? Names?" I stay silent. He steps forward as if to attack me, but pauses, his red eyes calculating. "Actually, I don't care. You're going to die soon anyways, I'm sure."

My thoughts are a blur as I try and calculate a way out of this. But as I look around at the other villagers, everyone soaking wet, muddy, and covered in blood, with pieces of flesh and bone coating so many in the crowd and the ground—pieces of a woman who kept me from going hungry for the past three years—it's the pity in their eyes that sinks my heart into my stomach.

My mind races, trying to think of a way out of this, but there's nothing.

We have to run the Gauntlet.

"You have 30 minutes to grab your things, not that either of you must have much, judging the state of those ragged clothes," the imperial fae says, his eyes looking at me with disgust. "If you're not back in the square by then, Bloodwyng might just get one last snack after all." He chuckles and climbs back on the giant Dragon. "Soldiers will escort you back to whatever fetid little hovels you call homes and accompany you to the capital, so don't even think about escaping. I'll just return and burn back the whole town if you do," he says with a wistful smile, and I could've sworn the Dragon, Bloodwyng, looked wistful as well, but that must be my pain-ridden mind playing tricks on me.

"Thirty minutes, little humans," he says before putting on his helmet as the Dragon stands up, the ground shaking with each movement. Those giant green legs push hard off the ground as they make a pure vertical ascent, wings narrowly avoiding taking out entire houses.

There's a ringing in my ears as I turn to glance briefly at Dyana, who is looking around in similar shock. As soon as our eyes meet, soldiers shout, reminding us we have to hurry and pack up our things. A thought pops into my head and I force myself to move.

I spin around. "How are we traveling to Castael Laryn?" I spit, demanding an answer from the pale, skinny soldier behind me.

"By horseback, fucking idiot," the fae sneers and shoves me. I fall backward into the mud, briefly losing my breath. I choke and try to breathe, immediately going to get back up but slipping. He moves and crouches over me, getting right up into my face.

"Tick tock. Better hurry, puggō!" He shouts the last part, spit spraying into my eyes.

"If you hadn't shoved me, this all might be a bit quicker," I drawl, and he slaps me across the face so hard I taste blood and my vision goes black.

"You're a mouthy little shit, ain't ya?" He grabs my face and squishes it until my jaw aches and my lips purse. He shakes my head, and I feel mud soaking into my hair. I force my hands to stay at my sides and my body to remain still; now isn't the time to get into a fight.

"Get up and get your stuff before I beat that mouth until there's nothing but pulp left." He shoves my face into the mud again before walking away. One of the soldiers escorting us shoves Dyana. I grab her, tugging her to my chest despite the fact that she's a little taller than me.

"Ama, what—" Dyana gasps, trembling, "what do we do?"

"Go get your stuff and meet me at the stables," I say in a low voice. Dyana blinks, looking at me with confusion. "We'll figure it out, but right now we need to stay alive, and if we try to run, they'll catch us. Trust me." The resentment in my voice makes Dyana pause. But she nods, taking a deep breath to steady herself.

"Right, okay. I'll meet you at the stables," Dyana's words are confident, but her eyes are terrified.

"Any food you see? Grab it. Bring all the spare undergarments you can." I squeeze her hand before turning to the Inn, in shock and numb that my worst fears are coming true right before my eyes.

I picture killing the imperial fae in many gruesome ways, but it doesn't subdue my anger or fear. The panic still charges my veins and has my heart galloping within my chest. There are no thoughts in my brain as my legs move automatically, taking me back to the Inn. Whispers break out as terrified, suspicious faces look back at me, their eyes full of pity.

I can take the fear, the sadness. But the pity—that hurts the most.

The Inn is empty and the kitchen is silent as I make my way upstairs to mindlessly stuff clothes into my ragged canvas travel sack.

I've done this song and dance before, so it's nothing to shove my few belongings together. My hand stills as I reach for the books on my nightstand. They're too heavy.

There will be more books. Staying alive matters more than keeping your books.

I repeat the words a few times, forcing myself to believe them. Lastly, I grab my father's dagger and stuff it into my waistband. The silver braided hilt molds to my hand, the metal so cold against my hot palm that I swear I see steam. Even freezing to the touch, the weight of the dagger grounds me.

I haven't used it in years—but the blade will be wet soon enough.

I ditch my dirty, wet clothes and toss them into a pile in the corner, putting on a clean pair of work pants, two long-sleeved shirts, my leather coat, and my heaviest winter cloak. The dark gray fabric is heavy on my shoulders but the thickly woven wool instantly warms me. The ends of the cloak are worn and torn in some places.

Putting it on again brings mixed feelings that I simply don't have time for. It will keep me warm and alive, and that's all that matters.

I stuff my remaining spare outfit into my bag and head down the stairs, not looking back for a single moment.

Taran is loose and waiting for me in the stable walkway. He nudges me, picking up that something is wrong. He presses his soft nose into my cheek, and I almost break as the emotions explode within me, but I suck in a tight breath and shove it all back down behind the thick iron walls deep inside me.

I can't break.

I apologize for having to hurry him, but he just leans into me as we walk through the half-ruined town. The rain has stopped, but mud still splatters Taran's hooves with each step. Dyana holds a small bag, but most of her belongings went up in flames with the Birdcage. When we decided to stay in Twyn Fells, I had instructed her to keep a spare bag with her keepsakes hidden in the stables, just in case.

I motion to Taran, bending so that my knee can be used as a step stool for her to mount him. She awkwardly steps on my thigh and grabs my shoulder, and I push upwards, lifting her onto Taran just behind the saddle. She adjusts, getting her balance on the thick saddle pads. I had put two on, knowing it will help absorb the shock for both Taran and the two of us. I clip each of our bags to the saddle, one on each side to distribute the weight before Dyana helps me up into the saddle. If Taran wasn't the largest horse in the entire barn, this trip would be difficult. But thankfully, he's a breed that can safely carry this much weight. That doesn't do much to assuage my guilt at the difficult journey ahead. As much as I'm happy he'll be with me, I also hate the future I'm subjecting him to.

I rub his neck, and a wave of comfort and affection followed by firm acceptance wraps around me as my magyk reads Taran's emotions. My emotions bubble and a single line of tears drips down my cheek. This is his choice, one I would never force upon him, and Taran chose me.

The soldiers watch this all, and as soon as we're ready, they mount their own horses, surrounding us from all sides and ushering us through the town arch. Neither of us says a word as Taran walks us through town. We pass the edge of the town vicinity as Dyana's arms tighten around my waist, and I nod mutely. This is the goodbye we always knew was possible but have tried so desperately to prevent. Dyana's tears wet my cloak as she leans her head against my back as we leave Twyn Fells, saying goodbye to the place we've grown to call home.

CHAPTER 3
DYANA

"Get a fucking move on, human scum!"

My legs tremble as I squat down and relieve myself despite the fae soldier shouting at me a few feet away. Amalia stands in front of me, arms crossed, and doing her best to glare away any onlookers. I bury my embarrassment and do what I do best—smile and pretend. That's how we operate—I keep things lighthearted while Amalia stares menacingly in the background. The fae soldier shouts again and Amalia stiffens as I clean myself up with a spare cloth.

"Would you like us to die from infection?" Amalia asks in a sardonic, rude voice. "Because that happens when humans don't relieve themselves fully often enough. Not that I'd expect you to know fuck all about a woman's anatomy." That last sentence is muttered low enough so the fae wouldn't hear. Saying that might actually push them too far, not that I disagree.

"I don't give a fuck if you're half dead. The High Council needs human candidates. They never stipulated the... condition they needed to arrive in." The other soldiers laugh in agreement. Amalia just stares, unwavering beneath her dark brow. She sighs and clicks her tongue, calling Taran who drinks at a small mountain stream. He raises his head, black snout dripping with water, and makes his way over quickly. All the while, Amalia just stares. A few of the fae have to look away, but she just cocks her head at the ones remaining.

I clear my throat and grasp Ama on the shoulder, signaling her little standoff can end. "Could use some of that berry porridge right about now," I mutter, wrapping one arm around her waist as we settle on Taran's wide back. "I can't believe she's really gone." I didn't mean to admit that but it jumps out anyways. She's quiet as we mount up, her pale, freckled face is withdrawn.

"I wish I could forget it," she finally whispers as I settle in behind her.

I lean my forehead into her back and squeeze her arm before whispering into her gray wool cloak, "That porridge does sound good though." She snorts and I feel a slight ease in her tension. Amalia clicks her tongue, urging Taran into a slow trot as the fae soldiers continue on. Despite the icy wind coming off the snowy mountain tops of the Ulster Wald constantly hitting my face, I'm lulled into a half-sleep by Taran's rhythmic gait. I wake when we slow down and start through the Pass of Brón Mór, a rocky cliff trail along the steep mountainside.

It's another night before we make it out of the Pass. We make camp, using the dense forest next to the cliffs for cover. Taran sleeps on the ground next to us, and I'll never admit this aloud but snuggling with a horse is great when the alternative is dried leaves. Despite the freezing temperatures and the barn smell, Taran's thick white and gray fur and intense body heat keep us warm. Amalia uses her big gray cloak like a blanket, and we use the rest of our spare, clean clothes to wrap around ourselves like we used to when I was little. It works surprisingly well, despite the mocking insults from the soldiers who watch it all from the comfort of their shared, covered tent.

The next day we emerge into the southern part of the Ulster Wald. My stomach growls with hunger, and I grab an oat ball from the saddle bag, handing one to Ama as well. They taste like sawdust, but it's better than nothing. I've had to survive off worse.

A tail smacks me in the face, and I look to see Taran staring at me from the corner of his eye. I snort and hand him an oat ball too, which he gobbles down with exuberance, munching on it happily as we start winding through the easier forest path. The ground is covered in mud from the melting snow—the hat that I have on does little to protect my ears from the painfully frozen air coming off the mountaintops.

My eyes start to close as I tuck my head into the nook on Ama's shoulder and nod off, knowing she's got things under control. I've offered multiple times to take the reins and let her sleep, but she always refuses. She might pretend otherwise, but her entire body has been as tense as a rock this entire trip. Understandably so, but she's barely slept, and the dark circles under her eyes show it. There would be no convincing her, but guilt still manages to weigh on my heart as I fall into a light sleep.

Year 482 PBM

"RUN, DYANA!" My foster mother screamed my name. I've tripped and am lying on the wet forest floor, quickly dampening my knit dress and tights.

Everything was fine when the carriage suddenly overturned and fae mercenaries swarmed us, grabbing Mrs. Arkos. She sobs painfully as Mr. Arkos watches and begs them to stop. He's on his knees in front of a particularly scary-looking raider with black hair and eyes a little lighter than my own. He must be from the Westlands too. I don't know anything about my real parents, but my foster parents are really nice. I like them.

The mercenary laughs and says something rude that I don't understand before pulling out his dagger. Mr. Arkos empties all of his pockets, begging for mercy. But Mrs. Arkos is quieter now, her amber eyes firm. When the mercenary grabs her again, she fights him—hard.

"DYANA, RUN!" She screams, "RUN!"

She surprises me by producing a small knife and stabbing the mercenary. She clearly doesn't know how to use it and just knicks his side, but it's enough. The fae blurs—they move so fast I can't even see it. Then Mrs. Arkos's throat starts bleeding as she falls over, choking.

Everything goes quiet.

I think they're shouting. Mr. Arkos seems to be screaming but I hear nothing. Just white noise as I watch the blood fall from her dying body. She chokes up more blood before her eyes go pale and her hands still. Then everything recoils back and I remember what she said to me. I don't even watch as they kill Mr. Arkos. There's no time to be sad. I stumble up to standing and turn, running into the Ulster Wald.

I hear brief shouts behind me so I run further into the forest, moving as fast as I can.

"She'll die out there soon enough. Leave it." A stern voice says before the sound fades into the distance. I keep going until the only noise I can hear are my own thoughts shouting at me.

Run.

Run, Dyana, Run!

The only thing in my thoughts is her voice and the sound of her dying screams followed by the silence and thump of her body hitting the ground. Over and over again, until minutes become hours and hours become days. I run until there is nothing left except a steady stream of tears trailing my frozen cheeks. When I spy a large, dry empty log, I jog over and collapse, passing out.

The next day, I do the same, that voice repeating in my head. My stomach hurts so bad I can't breathe and my legs feel like jelly but the adrenaline continues, pushing me. I keep thinking I hear something behind me, as if they're following. I don't have any idea how long I've been running, but the exhaustion is coming in hard. The light is fading and I don't see a good log to stop at. Even walking is hard and I stumble, almost falling. As the sun sets, my legs finally give out and I crawl into a ball near the base of a large spruce tree, unable to find the energy to find shelter. Rain starts to fall and I curl closer to the base of the tree, but it's no use. I'm quickly soaked and shivering as my limbs freeze, growing cold and numb. My mind fades into dreams of blood.

"Get up," I'm shaking so hard I can't focus, but the small voice says it again, "Get up!" She shakes me but I'm so numb I barely feel it. I can barely open my eyes but I pry them open. A girl a few years older than me stands in front of me, at least, I think it's a girl—not that it matters. The figure is dressed in various leathers and furs, topped with a dark gray cape; all meant to blend in with the forest. Her hair is a mess, a gray so dark it's almost black...but it's the cold, pale blue eyes staring back at me that make me whimper and push away.

"No, I'm..." the girl sighs and rubs a dirty hand across her face—a skinny, calloused, dirty hand. "I'm not going to hurt you, but if you stay out here in the wet cold, you're going to die." I say nothing. She sighs again, "Fine, I tried. You can stay out here and go hypothermic, freezing to death, or you can follow me and get dry by the fire. Your answer matters to me very little, so decide quickly." Despite her cold eyes, as she stands next to me, I can't help but notice the heat wafting off her. She nods and walks away, thinking I chose death over her company. I don't trust her, but...I'm so cold.

I'm scared, I don't know if I should follow her but...the howl of a Dyre Wolf nearby makes me jump and I remember that there are many things in the Ulster Wald that go bump in the night.

I scramble up, body aching and stiff, and hurry to follow her, limping along We walk for several minutes and duck through a thick wall of branches and leaves, and at first glance, there seems to be a large, fallen tree log but the image wavers, allowing us to walk right through it. My skin tingles.

Magyk.

This is magyk.

I'm so tired, I can't muster any excitement—or fear. We emerge at a large open cavern wholly hidden from any wandering eyes. The girl walks over to a large roaring fire and I stumble over to it, crying out as the heat starts to thaw my freezing limbs. The girl says nothing, she just sits on a log and watches before handing me a canteen of warm water.

"Drink, the warmth will help." I chug the canteen down and sigh happily. She then hands me something that looks like jerky and a bowl of soup. I have no idea what's in it, but I'm too tired and hungry to care. I scarf it all down quickly.

The girl watches, leaning against the wall of the cave, her arms wrapped around her knees, tucking them towards her. Leaves rustle behind us as something else enters the cave and I jump to my feet about to scream when the girl snaps at me.

"Quiet. This is a friend." I watch with wide eyes as a black Dyre Wolf the size of a pony walks in with several others behind it. Huge paws and sharp nails tap on the ground as they walk over and sniff me. To my shock, a few tails wag, and one even licks my chin. "Yes, and no," the girl says, and I realize she's not talking to me, and she's not talking to herself.

"You—you can talk to them? The wolves?" I ask, shocked and excited. She ignores me as she motions the Dyre wolves over to her. One stays at my feet, watching me with bright green eyes. I tremble with fear, but it's so lovely to be warm that I just try my best to ignore them or imagine them as huge dogs and not terrifying monsters.

The girl is quiet for a few moments and then nods her head slowly, "Not them—him. I can talk to him."

"Cool," I gasp tiredly. She just blinks.

"What's your name, child?" the girl asks, passing the refilled canteen back to me, I chug more warm water. "Yes, I know we will need more water, Virgyl." I hear her

mutter at the black wolf, who sneezes as if to say, "Told you so." I'd forgotten her question for a moment, distracted by the beasts.

"I'm Dyana. Dyana Arkos. Well, that's not my real last name. My real mom died giving birth to me, so I don't know my real last name. Mrs. and Mr. Arkos adopted me from the orphanage and said they would foster me until I turned 18," I finish. I think I said too much, but it's too late to take it back.

The girl smiles softly at my rambling and then blinks, the smile falling. A confused look enters her pale blue eyes. They're hypnotizing—and kind of scary. So pale they're almost gray. But sometimes, when she blinks, I swear they glow.

"I'm not a child, you know. I'm seven years old. That's a grown-up."

"You're seven? And you're...running away? Or are you lost?" My mouth goes dry as I realize...I don't know.

"Both. Mercenaries saw Mrs. Arkos praying. She prays to Morrigyn every day. She never asked me to pray too, but some fae saw her..." The girl stiffens and takes a deep breath before standing and walking around the fire toward me.

She hands me some too-large clothes and I quickly change, realizing I'm still soaking wet. I sigh happily as I finally get dry, and the girl motions for me to sit back down so she can wrap my hair in a cloth, helping to soak up any extra water.

She's so prepared. The cave is giant, and she's built rooms into it somehow. I can see the corner of a bedroom in the back, which looks mainly like a pile of furs and blankets on the ground, but still.

The girl sits back down across from me but this time on the floor. She curls up next to the black wolf, which rests its head on her lap. The girl looks down at the wolf, sighing. "You can stay here until you have a plan, but you'll need to help forage."

Another rustling bush has me turning, and I gasp as I watch a large white Dyre Wolf pad in, three small wolf puppies trotting in behind her.

"They're so fluffy!" The big ones are scary, but the babies are just so cute. I bend down, and one of the babies immediately bounds over, jumping into my lap. I giggle as it licks me, causing the towel to fall off my head, my damp hair hitting my back.

The Dyre Wolf puppy then begins playing with the strands, chewing on them with naughty growls.

The mother wolf watches from a safe distance, her blue eyes constantly on me, watching me just as the wolves do. Not in a threatening way, more like they aren't quite sure what to do with me. Eventually, the puppy falls asleep, and I start to do the same. I'm mostly asleep when a pair of warm arms suddenly pick me up and deposit me on something warm and soft.

"What's your name?" I whisper at the retreating figure as the wolf named Virgyl drops several puppies next to me. They immediately curl up against me and fall asleep.

The girl doesn't answer, and I've almost fallen back asleep, until finally, from across the cave, she responds in a numb voice.

"My name is Amalia Roth."

CHAPTER 4
AMALIA

NOW:

Taran's hooves squelch in the mud as we walk through the forest. The suns were low in the sky towards the West, so we'd stay in the woods for another night. The saddlebags are stuffed with mushrooms and edible herbs I'd been picking each time we stopped, and a few more oat balls and apples. Dyana and I have been in many situations where food was scarce, so our stomachs can handle only eating once a day.

I blink hard, my eyes dry and tired. My adrenaline has been high since that day in the square; a frantic, nervous feeling that I can't shake. I'd told Dyana to sleep since there was no way I was relaxing around the fae soldiers. Their eyes are always on us. They have been watching us the entire journey. The dagger I keep tucked into my right boot is the main thing keeping us safe during the nights—as well as Taran standing guard.

The adrenaline and fear of the day slowly wash away, leaving exhaustion and anxiety in its wake.

The next day arrives, and after a night of fitful rest plagued with nightmares, the exhaustion that arrives is heavier. I can feel it in my bones and with every breath. But I can't falter, not now. There is no time for falling apart, so I force my emotions away, force the sorrow, fear, and anxiety into that place deep within me.

I steel myself; my will is *iron.*

Five days of hard riding and my legs feel like they might fall off. I'm also trying very hard not to throat punch most of the fae soldiers who'd taken to barking at us when we'd dismount. I'm attempting to practice a little self-control.

We emerge from the dense forest and down into the valley North of Eahmond. It feels weird to be out of the forest after five days of close quarters. We're too out in the open, and the sky is far too wide and unending to feel safe. Not after seeing a Dragon.

Poor Taran needs to be groomed so badly. I brought a small travel brush but the mud is too caked on; I need real stable supplies to properly care for him. But he hasn't faltered, even though I know he's tired. I move my reins to one hand and weave the other through his thick black mane, palm warming as I send him my love and gratitude. Warmth and happiness echo back.

Dyana knows about my gift, but she's sworn to secrecy and knows I don't use it often. Unfortunately, I can't always turn it off, but it comes in handy with horses. It's why I've always been so good with animals and tended to look for a job that dealt with them.

I can't speak to animals directly. Instead, it's more of an empathetic transfer. How I've always pictured it is I share my emotions with them, showing them how I feel rather than just using words. They can feel what's in my soul and my heart, which helps them understand, and then I can read their feelings back. It gives me a leg up on most humans and fae, but it's not a gift I advertise or ever mention. All anybody knows is that I have a way with animals, and that's exactly how it's going to stay. Dyana knows, and she's the only one who ever will.

It's not illegal to have magyk, but it's well known throughout the Kingdom that any rare magyks meant attention of the wrong kind—the attention of the *fae*—and that's the last thing I want. Dyana will take my secret to the grave, because she knows the ramifications of my magyk.

The flow of warm emotions is interrupted, and Taran lets out a light huff at the feel of the pure terror that flows through my veins at the thought of anything happening to Dyana. He tries to reassure me, sending me comforting feelings, but horses are prey animals, and unless I want him darting off or spooking and throwing us off, I need to calm my thoughts.

"What do you think is going to happen, Ama?" Dy whispers into my ear, squeezing me tightly. She's trying to be brave, but I know how terrified she is—I am just as scared, and every moment is a battle to suppress it.

"I don't know, little bird, but I wish I did." My voice is so quiet it can't even be considered a whisper. I rarely call Dyana that anymore, only for special occasions.

She talked so much as a child that I once told her she reminded me of a chirping baby bird. The nickname came about afterward, but since she's twenty and five, I stopped calling her that, not wanting to embarrass her. I wrap my arm around hers, squeezing, "Whatever it is, we face it together. I'll keep you safe Dy, I promise." A tiny piece of my heart shatters with the knowledge that I might fail. As the hours fade and we pass Eahmond, getting closer and closer to the outskirts of the city, my anxiety rises. I always have a plan. That's what I do. I'm the one with the plan—but there's nothing. My thoughts won't stay still long enough to think things through logically. Instead, it's an endless cycle of, *What if? What if? What if?*

With every second, we grow closer to Castael Laryn, and so does the realization that we might actually die.

I refuse that future too.

At midday, we reach the top of a large cliff overlook. The soldiers around us stop, most of them dismounting to go and piss. We learned quickly that they paid no mind to any sense of decorum or manners, whipping out their cocks at any point in time. I don't trust a single one of those pointy-eared fucks. My eyes narrow in a glare as I take them all in before Taran steps up to the edge, letting us take in the view.

Down a thick cliff overlooking the valley north of the Abhaynn Gheal River sits the city of Castael Laryn. The castle, which most call the Black Citadel, is at the southeast end, surrounded by a huge moat. Even now, I can see its gargantuan black towers blotting out the sky.

The fae decided on this location for their capital due to the convenient location on the river, and its centralized location. It allowed their armada to quickly make its way through the giant continent, especially with the magyk that made it possible to travel upstream. The Abhaynn Gheal divides our country into four regions: the Northlands, the Southlands, the Westlands, which starts a few miles south of the end of the Ulster Wald, and the coastal Eastlands. The North was the largest of all four due to the sheer size of the Ulster Wald, but we were also the poorest and least populated due to the harsh weather conditions.

The fae ruled through fear, not respect. Although they wanted both, they ensured the citizens of the Ur Daoine stayed in line through any means possible. Still, in the past few hundred years, it had become increasingly violent; public executions for anyone who stepped out of line, curfews for humans. The wealth discrepancy was particularly obvious as we looked down on Castael Laryn.

"Have you ever seen a city this large, Ama?" Dyana says, at a loss for words.

"Only in stories and drawings, never with my own eyes."

Dyana is quiet for a moment. "This is real, isn't it? This is all really happening. I keep thinking maybe I'll wake up and it'll have just been a dream, but this is real."

"It's real," I reply, reaching behind me to squeeze her hand. "Right into the belly of the beast, but we'll do what we always do: we figure it out. No matter what, we always figure it out. Okay?" I try to comfort her, but even I doubt my words.

"I don't even know how to fight, Ama. How in the nine hells are we going to make it out?" Dyana's voice is frantic.

"You can't think like that, Dy." I say, but inwardly I echo the sentiment.

She sighs, "Ama, you've been trying to teach me how to throw a punch for the past eighteen years, and I still can't even do that right. I can dance, but fighting has never come easily to me. What are we going to do?"

I squeeze her hand again. I need Dyana to be brave, even if we're both faking it the entire time.

"This is just another performance," I gesture to the fae around us with my eyes.

She exhales hard. "Right. Just a performance. I'm good at that."

"You're great at that, I even recall a riveting performance of Julie the Dragon Rider, complete with a wig made out of straw," I retort.

"Shh! You know that's a secret." She pokes me playfully on my shoulder.

The fae interrupts us as they return to their mounts. "Break time is over." I glare at him and imagine stabbing him with the dagger I always keep hidden on my person. This fae is now at the top of the mental list I've been of all the people I will eventually kill. The list is rather long already, but Gods they were making it longer by the day. They were vile, rude, and pretentious to boot. The fae soldier hacks up a wad of black mucus and spits it on my shoe.

Don't kill him. Don't do it, Amalia.

~~Gods, I want to kill him.~~

I send Taran a feeling, and he gets a few steps forward of the fae soldier's horse before bucking lightly. Dyana squeaks since I didn't warn her first, but I hear a large hoof connecting with hard armor as the fae soldier is thrown to the ground.

"Oh, sir, are you alright?" I ask in a childlike, innocent voice. "Bad, Taran!" I pretend to scold Taran, who snorts, enjoying this as well. "He never bucks. I'm so sorry. It looks so muddy down there." Dyana has to turn her face away to keep from laughing as I shake the mucus from my foot and try not to gag. Taran sneezes as I feel his amusement brush against my mind.

"Father save me. I can't wait until the Gauntlet starts. I want to watch as your throat gets cut in round one, and your life bleeds out of you." he says coldly before they all turn, heading down the cliffside path.

Not before I cut yours. Enjoying the thought, I click on Taran, and we follow the group and go down the road that leads to Castael Laryn.

CHAPTER 5
DYANA

The steep, rocky road winds down the cliff overlook as we approach the capital city. I've never seen it, only heard stories about the behemoth, the black stone keep they call the Black Citadel, with towers so tall they pierce the clouds, climbing towards the realm of the Gods.

Are the stories right?

There's a large gust behind us and the sound of large wings flapping. Taran panics momentarily before Ama calms him with whispered words and a calm hand. Just as I look up to see what it is, the sky goes dark, as if something is blocking the sun...something large. Terror floods my body and my lungs empty as I look up and see the scaled belly of a large, dark blue Dragon flying overhead. Taran squeals as the Dragon's tail slaps down dangerously close to us, the spikes nearly knocking us over. Ama calms him so that we're not thrown from his back.

Pure, undiluted fear makes my heart feel as if it's about to burst. The same thing happened in Twyn Fells ten days ago. Dragonfear, they called it. Dragons are made of magyk. It's a natural reaction they cause in any who might be their prey—it makes us easier to catch. I thought it was just a story, something else to make us afraid and powerless, but no, Dragonfear is very, very real. I'm left with goosebumps and nervous sweat trailing down my back, and my hands tremble as everything within me says **RUN, RUN, RUN, RUN.**

A being covered in armor rides atop the Dragon as the Dragon moves further into the distance, circling Castael Laryn. Ama pushes Taran to continue moving, and we pick back up, my arms tight around her waist. She doesn't mention my trembling, thankfully. The fae soldiers don't even react, they just laugh, and some mumble about how much they hate Dragons. I half want to look to the sky again, not for another Dragon but as if the Gods might smite them for saying such a thing.

I don't look because I'm scared there will be no response. How do they choose which fae gets to ride the Dragons? As the Dragon flies towards the capital and turns to the east, the figure on its back gets clearer. A fae mounted in what looks like some sort of harness seated in between the spikes of the Dragon's back. This one only has two legs, whereas Bloodwyng had four, but the blue Dragon has larger wings that are tipped with claws. It circles, slowing its speed before descending into the city; to the Dragon Pit.

Seeing the Dragon reminds me of the dread I've felt ever since that day in the square. Ama will work herself to the bone trying to get us out of this, but I know the truth. Our fates were sealed the moment that fae landed in our town.

We made a promise to each other many years ago to keep each other alive and protect each other from harm; even if that harm was ourselves. Grief is a constant bedfellow for those of us who have lost someone. I like to keep busy and distracted, but Ama...she isolates. I've seen her go weeks without speaking a single word. Amalia and I promised to hold each other steady when the world became a raging current, and we sealed that promise in blood. We bear the small matching scars to prove it.

I rub the raised, bumpy line without thinking. Something about the imperfection of it is grounding. It reminds me I'm not alone. Even when it feels like all hope is lost.

THE BLACK CITADEL

CHAPTER 6
AMALIA

To call the Black Citadel a castle is a gross inaccuracy. The sprawling acropolis is surrounded by a giant moat and contains more peaks and terraces than anyone could ever count. The hundreds of thousands of glass windows, parapets, and towers are taller than anything I've ever seen. Every stone, every windowpane, every piece of metal are all made of up shades of black and gray. No, the Black Citadel isn't a castle; it's a damn fortress.

We've just ridden underneath a large arch in the wall surrounding the city when a wave of odor hits us.

"Gods, the smell..." Dyana retches, covering her nose. I don't say anything, but my eyes are watering taking in the scent of urine, feces, and sweaty bodies. The city's outer edge was the slums—the poorest denizens crammed into tiny homes there. Hence the smell. Our noses will adjust in time, but it takes all of my self-control to not cover my mouth. I wouldn't give the fae that honor. Not as I watch them sneer, spit, and shout at the humans and lesser fae they passed. Not as I saw the fear on the resident's faces, the whites of their eyes showing. My anger is quickly becoming my shield.

How could the fae let their citizens live like this? Especially in Ur Daoine? How could they enjoy putting terror into the people they ruled? There's no honor in that. No respect. No one looked up to the imperial fae. It's just fear, and a lot of envy of their lifestyle and the privileges they are afforded. That's why many humans actually looked forward to the Gauntlet. For the chance to win a life they otherwise would never get the chance to live. In this dark and dreary life, 100,000 gold marks made a difference for generations.

When you go hungry long enough, the potential prize of endless food is too tantalizing to resist.

I'm lost in thought as we make our way through the city. Castael Laryn is bustling with fae, demis, and other magyka—but there are a few humans. We make our way through the winding streets, and Taran's hooves sink into the mud with each step as we finally pass the poor side of town, and I see more humans. Everyone watches our mini procession, but it's the guilty resignation in their eyes that weighs on me. There's no other choice. If you're a human born in Ur Daoine, you're raised knowing whether you lived or died was inconsequential to those in power.

As we get closer to Black Citadel, the houses and rows of stores become nicer and bigger. The streets are cleaner, and everything is quieter as fae and demis walk about next to small carts and stands selling fancy sweets and fancy patisseries of freshly baked bread. It's idyllic—and off putting. We pass a temple of Sol Constantus, where there's a line out the door of those wishing to pay their regards.

The stares of pity become stares of hate. Dyana clutches my waist tighter, and I urge Taran into an extended walk as he increases his speed. The guards in front of us suddenly veer to the left, walking along the moat's edge that guards the Black Citadel. We walk on for about 10 more minutes before we come to an enormous domed building, half of which has an open roof.

The Dragon Pit. Home to the Gauntlet training quarters, the Fray champions, and all of the Dragons in the godsdamn Kingdom. The Arena, where the fights occur, sits at the top. The actual Dragon Pit is far underground. Nobody knows how many levels down it really goes, but that's where the Dragons are kept.

I'm tense as a rock, muscles clenched and jaw grinding as we come to a halt in the middle of a small square gathering area next to what looks to be the Citadel and Dragon Pit's stables. It's housed on the North side, away from the city—and away from prying eyes. The fae guards and the stable denizens all turn to look at us; most with red, grotesque glowing eyes. Dyana gets down and I quickly follow, my legs screaming at me with every single movement after so many days in the saddle.

"I've heard horse meat is a rare delicacy, so get your fat beast taken care of before I call for the butcher and turn it into my dinner," one of our guards growls before walking away, dismounting and handing his horse off to some poor fae lackey. I see red at his words, but Dyana grabs my arm.

"I'm fine. Let's go," I murmur, but Dyana's not convinced. Despite that, she follows beside me as I lead an exhausted Taran into the barn, but the fae don't go anywhere.

"You're meeting the rest of the… contestants, down there in half an hour," the guard says. I ignore him and he clears his throat then hacks up a disgusting wad of spit, making my stomach turn. We disappear into the stables quickly, and both let out a breath as we get out of sight and lead Taran into an empty stall.

"So gross, so, so gross," Dyana says as I look around for grooming tools to take care of Taran. "Uh, so I need to pee…" She looks around. The soldiers look back at us with their beady red eyes. The fae look a lot like humans but are taller, stronger, and with heightened senses and longer life spans. Oh, and the ears, but many types of magyka have pointed ears of some kind anyway. Imperial fae, on the other hand, look otherworldly. Not in any particular way, but there's something about them that was just *more*.

Except one.

Achan Drayven, the High Councilor of Ur Daoine. With hands that are black at the fingertips, as if he dipped his hand in ash-soaked paint, and multiple thick black horns sticking up from his long black hair. His eyes are like dark red rubies—stunning and terrifying at the same time. But the black veins trailing his face and the black veil over his eyes is something you never forget.

"Go behind Taran in the corner, into the pile of wood shavings. I do it all the time at the barn."

"Okay, but the way you say that so casually is something we will be discussing later, Amalia," Dyana says, chastising me as she shoves her way behind Taran to the far end of the stall.

"Wah, wah! Stop being a child and go pee. I'll stand in front of you so they can't see," I announce.

"If you weren't such an ass, maybe you'd have more friends!" Dyana calls, but based on the sound, she's heeding my advice. I snort and my eyes roll back into my head so hard I worry for a moment they might be damaged.

"You're my friend, ass and all." Dyana emerges and shakes her head, but her small smile lightens my heart ever so slightly. I wink, which makes her scoff and grumble a bit about how she doesn't want to ride a horse again for a while.

"Alright, I'll come to visit as soon as I can. Get some rest, you deserve it." I whisper the words into Taran's soft muzzle and he just nudges me lightly, nuzzling my face. I hand him the carrot I found in the feed room and his fuzzy gray ears immediately perk up at the sight of it as he gently takes the treat from my hand and crunches away happily. While I rub his neck, a wave of gratitude and love is sent my way, through the path in our minds. Tears threaten to form in my eyes at the amount of effort I know it took him to do that. His endless love and devotion always warms my dark, shriveled heart during the moments we're together.

Finished up, we hurry into the entrance of the Dragon Pit near the stable. A hole in the wall like a door should be there but it's not, leads into a claustrophobic spiral staircase made of stone. The ceiling is high but only torches light us—there are no windows as we descend down into the earth. I steel myself as my heart starts to race, sweat gathering in my palm. The knowledge of how many thousands of pounds of stone are on top of our heads with absolutely nothing to keep us from getting crushed was a thought to save for later, and I can't afford to lose the little food currently in my stomach.

I don't like small spaces, but as I do with the rest of my emotions, I shove my fear behind those iron gates in my mind. I can't afford to have a panic attack right now, but my palms and pits are coated in sweat.

The end of the staircase suddenly opens up to a stone hallway lined with trophies and Dragon bones. We walk side by side towards the end of the hallway and then into a large open area. That fucking feeling happens, the one when you realize every person in a room turns to look at you—*I hate it*. But Dyana just smiles lightly and waves. Some of them scoff and look away, but others watch as we join the outskirts of the crowd. Around 30 humans stand aimlessly, some in small groups, some by themselves. Most look to be around our age, but there are some that look like they could be our parents.

Well, *Dyana's* parents.

The North is the least influential territory out of the four Ur Daoine regions, with the Southlands and the Eastlands being the most powerful. A few Westland candidates lean on the wall, similar to Dyana in coloring, with their dark brown hair so deep it's almost black, and various shades of brown eyes, from amber to obsidian.

Everyone is dressed in some kind of uniform already, making us stand out even more in our muddy, dirty, and probably incredibly smelly travel clothes. My hair looks like I just came out of a troll pit whereas Dyana pulled hers back in a braid, like I taught her.

This must be what that guard meant about us getting here a bit late. We seem to be the last candidates to arrive. Most of the other candidates look a bit shell-shocked and nervous, but some joke and laugh. We join the edge of the crowd, hoping to blend in as much as possible.

"What're we waiting for?" Dyana mumbles to me.

The same question is in my own thoughts. "I don't know, " I reply quietly, "but I don't like it—"

I pause, interrupted by two big doors open across the room from us, and the breath leaves my body. The chaotic bundle of thoughts bouncing around in my brain comes to a perfect halt as the tallest, most wildly beautiful male I've ever seen walks through the door.

The crowd quiets. The male just looks at us with assessing golden eyes that seem to glow as if lit from behind, underneath dark brows and chin-length wavy black hair. The male is in old fighting leathers that look like they might burst at the seams simply from the amount of muscle straining against them. His biceps are roughly the size of my head. The male moves, beginning to circle us. No sooner than it took for the thought to go through my head and the male is suddenly in front of me, his eyes boring into mine.

I think, for a moment, time ceases to exist and we simply are. Everything stops. It's just the mystery male with the gold eyes. I start to lean forward but catch myself, snapping out of whatever daze that was. What am I doing? I can't look away from those eyes—pure, molten gold that glows like a freshly lit forge. The male straightens, becoming even taller. I don't even come to his shoulders. He crosses his arms, staring at me in what I now recognize as a blatant challenge and act of dominance. There's no other reaction; he simply waits for me to submit.

If he wants a simpering, wet towel of a girl, he'll be sorely mistaken.

Maintaining eye contact, I cross my arms and match his pose, openly challenging him. Some sort of low, vibrating noise rings through the room and I realize it's coming from him. He's...growling.

The male is so clearly inhuman that it's not a shock.

We stare at each other, unblinking, and someone coughs nearby awkwardly. It seems to jolt the male, who looks away finally and continues on his perusal of the rest of the candidates. Which, to most magyka, means I won the challenge, and I've won dominance. A shiver of wicked delight runs through me.

The male continues his perusal of the rest of the candidates. He's definitely not fae, nor any type of magyka with pointed ears. His are soft and round at the ends, like mine.

All of this to say, everything about what just happened wasn't actually all that shocking.

Not really.

What has my stomach in knots and my heart on the floor is the baby red Dragon curled around his neck.

CHAPTER 7
AMALIA

The little creature squeaks and yawns, burrowing into the male's hair as its red tail curls happily. Several people in the crowd gasp in awe.

I always imagined Dragons as large, fearsome creatures like the green Dragon in Twyn Fells. But this is just a baby. Innocent, still pure, and blissfully ignorant of the horrors of the world around them. Its scales are still soft and flexible, and where one day there will be spikes lining its head and down its spine, there are soft nubs.

Everyone's gasping and completely beside themselves at the Dragon. Dyana shakes my hand lightly, as I realize I've been standing there, staring intently. I can't take my eyes off it.

How are you supposed to act casually in the presence of a Dragon? The baby Dragon opens its eyes as it moves around to get comfortable. Brilliant emerald eyes look right at me, and it's like a lifetime passes as I fall into the Dragon's gaze.

Something rubs against my magyk lightly, sending goosebumps across my body. I fight the gasp threatening to make its way out of my throat. But I stay still and attempt to be calm. The smell of ozone bruises against my senses as the Dragon's mind curls up against mine, inquisitive and warm. I usually have to be touching an animal to forge a mental connection.

"Friend?"

I blink rapidly as shock threatens to make me shake. The pain of my grief could send a grown male to his knees. For so long, I've forced myself not to care. But it's a knife to the chest, as the Dragon's voice repeats again in my head. My magyk is bursting against its cage, excited and energized by the Dragon's presence.

Numbness is an empty, lonely place. Everything is stunted, including joy. And a small piece of me desperately wants to hold it, care for it forever, and protect it with all of my might.

That's the thing about numbness. At least you don't have to worry about getting hurt or betrayed.

"Friend?" the Dragon squeaks again, its voice like a layered bell. I could listen to the sound all day and shed tears of joy over and over again. But I cannot.

So I try to shut the connection to the Dragon off, grief slicing into me at the loss, but it's difficult, and my magyk strains. The Dragon might be a baby, but they're beings of pure magyk, and even a baby could pull a mental punch. I grimace and try to fight the bond. I finally slam it out, and the effort rocks me back a step as I release a harsh breath.

Dyana looks at me inquisitively from the side of my eyes, unsure about my odd reaction. But she quickly looks to the front, where the male begins speaking.

His face isn't slender or graceful. He's not beautiful in the traditional, perfect sense, but there's something about him that is *more.*

My stupid fucking heart is all in knots over a male: *pathetic.*

Don't get me wrong, I've enjoyed plenty of lovers from time to time, and not just men. But the brief flirtations and tussles in bed were a means to an end. They solved a temporary problem.

The male surveys us all—a predator surveying his prey—and I knew that even if we all tried to take him on, he might still win. Then the male gently flips the baby Dragon so that it's cradled in his arms, on its back.

It's too much. My thighs threaten to clench at the thought of those big hands on me as my skin begins to heat...

Get it together, Amalia, fucking hell.

"For better or worse, you're here to compete in the Gauntlet." Some moments really feel like the Gods are sending me a giant "fuck you" as they conspire on how to make my life as difficult as possible. As the male speaks with a voice like pure sex and power, I consider climbing to the heavens to deploy my retribution for this torture.

"Over the next five weeks, your body is going to go through hell." The man doesn't even have to shout, we all hear him clearly. He commands the room without even trying.

"Well that's encouraging," Dyana mutters, and I snort lightly.

"If I put all of you into the Gauntlet now, none of you would make it through round one, and I'd get to watch as your bodies are fed to the Dragons. Isn't that right, little one?" He looks down at the Dragon in his arms, and it licks its lips in response. "It's my job to prepare you to turn your sorry souls into worthwhile soldiers who will put on a damn good show. My name is Os, Gauntlet head trainer and your worst fucking nightmare." He pauses, looking around the room, meeting each of our eyes. "Look at you. What a godsdamn disappointment. For the next five weeks, your ass is mine. I say jump, you say how high. You don't breathe without me knowing about it."

Maybe it's my imagination, but I swear to God those gold eyes land on mine and linger just a second longer than the rest. His gaze is like a bolt of lightning hitting my chest, making my heart race. I don't react outwardly, but inside I'm a maelstrom of feeling. He quickly moves on, going over the rest of the room.

"I'm going to break every single one of you down and build you from scratch until there's nothing left of your past selves. All of you will walk into the Arena, but only one will walk out of here a warrior. If you're worthless enough to get disqualified, you'll be the laughing stock of the Kingdom." Goosebumps cover my body at his words, followed by anger. "Make no mistake, candidates, the Gauntlet is a game. It's a source of entertainment. That means the fae will get what they want no matter what, and they want a good show. So we're gonna give them one. You'll have to learn to fight like a fae, and you'll hate me for that. But after you break, we're going to build you back up and make you stronger than you ever thought you could become. You'll have to—if you want any chance of winning by slaying a full-grown Dragon."

Os stops and pets the tiny Dragon settling in around his shoulders like a happy cat. "You might see this and think it's harmless. And you'd be right—they're pretty harmless when they're this age. But imagine a 15,000-pound animal that can breathe fire so hot it melts iron and would turn you to pure ash. A full-grown Dragon's fangs are about the size of some of your forearms. You'll barely stand a chance anyway, but right now? You wouldn't last more than 5 seconds against a full-grown Dragon. You'd just be a tasty snack. Human meat is a delicacy to Dragons, you know."

Os pauses briefly, "So, today you're going to get set up in your dorms, and we start at sunrise tomorrow morning. You'll be given a map of the Arena in your room, and every morning we will meet by the stables. You're to be there precisely at sunrise; if you're late, you'll be doing double the workouts. From there, we will warm up, and then you'll work on strength and weapons training. We won't get to the Dragons until week 3 because you're just not strong enough. The High Council doesn't want things to be too easy." He turns and leaves the room but continues to talk. We all scramble to catch up. His long legs mean he travels almost twice the distance.

He's clearly some sort of upper magyka. The fae aren't much nicer to the magyka of Ur Daoine. They get to live fancier lives, but are still completely controlled. No stepping out of line. And each year, dozens of female magyka from the east and the Infinium sands disappear and are never heard from or seen again. Families despaired, never to find answers—just empty beds.

"You each get a room with your town partner. I don't care if you change rooms, I'm not your fucking daddy, so don't act like children and I won't have to beat you into a pulp. But step out of line or act up and you'll be on Dragonstall duty for a month. Killing is reserved for the Gauntlet." Os notes this casually, turning and walking back out the doors. He stops and hands the Dragon to a similarly dressed male waiting outside the doors.

"*Friend?*" The baby Dragon's voice suddenly sounds in my head. The young creature barrels through my mental blocks again. It's high pitched and androgynous; the voice is young and hesitant but full of joy so pure I have to close my eyes and take a second.

"*Yes, friend.*" That's all I can give it because words are difficult right now, even unspoken ones. Touching a Dragon's magyk is like touching the sun. It envelops you instantly. I can feel it sinking into my body and soon I feel anxious as my energy builds. But I just ignore, ignore, ignore; or at least attempt to. But the Dragon is so happy at my response that I nearly fall to my knees as another wave of magyk hits me. I must have taken a breath oddly because Dyana glances at me from the corner of her eye.

I would love to meet it and bond with it. I want to so desperately it hurts. But I can't. For so many reasons, it's not possible—will *never* be possible.

In return, I feel a bit of sadness and confusion, and I carefully send love back so that the sweet creature knows it's not its fault. It feels happy at that, but the sour taste of sadness still lingers on my tongue as the mental link dissolves and the Dragon is carried away. My eyes unwillingly follow it, before we continue after Os through multiple corridors. We reach a...gathering room, I suppose. With a few tables and ratty, threadbare couches that seriously look like you might catch a disease just from coming into contact with it. There is no art on the walls, just pure stone and torches. But there are 15 doors, the towns named on each.

"Find the door with your town name on it. That's your suite and your home for the next five weeks..." he pauses, "the mess hall is through that archway. You'll get meals here twice daily. I won't beat around the bush; it's no fine dining. But if you're going to become soldiers, you need to eat. A lot. So skipping a meal will mean I put you on Dragon shit duty, and let me tell you, that's a lot of shit." he says, and I'm left with that lovely image. Dyana looks horrified at the idea, particularly after how bad the smell in the slums were. So, no missing meals then.

"At mealtimes, eat until you are properly full. You need the calories." I realize then he says this because we're all clearly underfed and underweight. Embarrassment starts to rise in me, but I beat it down because it's not our fault that prices increase while wages decrease. We're all in the same boat. How dare he blame us for something that is the fault of the very people he willingly works for?

Is our reality sad? Yes. Many days I went to bed hungry, hoping I would never wake up. But I work hard, I never miss a day, I always say "yes" when extra help is needed, and I always do the jobs nobody else wants to do. Some worthless male will not make me ashamed of my reality, and I certainly would not be made to feel like a pity case. My spine strengthens, and I stand tall, staring at Os with a stubbornness only achievable through sheer will and a touch of insanity. Nobody, not even some fae-loving magyka, will shame me for the way I'm forced to live.

After a few moments, he just clicks his tongue and continues on. It must have only been a few seconds but gods, it felt like ages. Why does he keep looking at me? Is he looking at everyone?

You don't care, Amalia. Stop godsdamned caring!

"Get settled, get some food, and get some sleep. That's an order, not a request." With that, he turns and walks out the door, and a quiet feeling in my head wishes he wasn't. But as soon as he's out of sight, the conversation picks up as everyone goes and finds their town names on the doors. Dyana and I walk around until we find the door that says Twyn Fells, and then follow that to another hallway with our town name on it. Inside, a small sitting area greets us next to two tiny twin beds with blankets that have seen better days. A door labeled "bathroom" leads into a small room with two tiny tubs, a sink, and a hole in the ground to use as a toilet.

I see the fae kept the plumbing to themselves; how magnanimous. Dyana and I plop down on our beds, dropping our meager belongings on the stools at the foot of each mattress.

We spend some time just laying in silence, taking in the past few days, past few moments, hell, everything that happened in the past five days. There hasn't been a true moment of peace since that day in the town center, and the sudden weight of the silence is suffocating. I want to relax, but the quiet gives my thoughts space to soar, and suddenly I'm so worried about what will happen next that I can barely breathe.

"The trainer is...intense." Dyana finally says. I exhale quietly and try to focus on her words as we stare at the ceiling.

"I don't think I'd pick such a polite word, but yeah. He's going to be a problem." Hopefully, she can't hear the trembling in my voice. Thinking of Os definitely helps cause I'm immediately pissed off. The audacity of males really makes me want to kill something sometimes.

"Or maybe you just want to sleep with him," Dyana states casually. I jerk up to a sitting position as my jaw drops and I look at Dyana, who lies there perfectly content.

"Where did I go wrong? How did I let you turn out like this?"

Her eyes roll and she scoffs. "Yeah well, your celibacy plan was lame from the start. But come on, Amalia, don't play the prude. It was you who taught me the birds and the bees. Go ahead and say it: you want to fuck the trainer!" I cringe at her language, fully aware that she gets it from me and that I'm a terrible hypocrite.

"That celibacy plan worked much better after I beat Davys Grenard to a pulp after his hand,"—I use air quotes—"slipped and just happened to touch your breasts."

Dyana cringes. "Okay fair. But that was the past, let's get back to the present. The trainer. Wanna tell me what that whole staring thing was about? I've never seen such uncomfortably long eye contact in my life."

"No clue. He's not even that attractive anyway." I know my mistake the moment I say it. I went too hard on the defensive. Dyana sits up quickly.

"Wait, wait. I'm sorry, what was that? Amalia Roth, you dirty liar! You know that male is far more than just a bit attractive. Hell, I'd fuck him, and I very much prefer vaginas." I just look at her, brow raised. "Someone has a crush on the trainer. How the tables have finally turned! Did you get all hot and bothered when he started talking about breaking us?" I blush at that, unable to hide it, and my hands fly up to slap my cheeks to cover it.

"I always knew you were into some weird stuff. You like challenging people. For example, take me," she flops back and crosses her legs primly, "I was a challenge because you had to take care of another person. Although I helped." I raise both brows this time. "No, no, don't even act like I didn't! You were an unhinged feral woodland creature. My knowledge of the outside world was key in preparing you for life in public. But you still had to take care of me, and we're the opposite. You love being quiet and hiding away with your animals. I like talking and dancing."

Dyana gestures to herself, "Social," and then gestures to me, "Unsocial." As per usual, Dyana talks me right to the edge of my patience.

"Fine. Fine! Os is attractive, and the eye contact thing was hot. But it doesn't matter for one huge reason: we have to figure out how to survive the next five weeks and then the Gauntlet. That is damn plenty to focus on, and you know it. There's no time for little crushes and frivolity."

Dyana coughs, "Boring," and I shove her and slap a pillow at her face, making her laugh before I go back to planning.

"I'm being serious. We have to train, and we have to train hard. If we want any chance of getting out of this, it's going to be because we're winning. I've thought it over for the past ten days and there's no other way out. We have to win, Dy. That's the only option."

She rolls her eyes at me and sarcastically retorts, "Yeah, fine," but I see the grave look in her eyes afterward. Because she knows I'm right. But we've always dealt with hard things by distracting ourselves with humor. She's just nervous and trying to ignore it. I don't blame her; I'm doing the same.

"Who knows, maybe he meant he'd break me and my bed. And I don't think there's enough room for both of us in this tiny thing."

Dyana chuckles in return. Her bright smile is amused, "It's my room too, so just don't do it on my bed, please. Put your undies on the door or something to warn me first, too."

It's my turn to roll my eyes.

CHAPTER 8
AMALIA

Dinner was a blur of some stew with mystery meat, but it was warm and did the job. After countless days of rationing stale oat balls, warm, semi-fresh food is a luxury. I'm in no spot to complain.

I prefer not to eat meat, but that's not always an option, so I just shove my emotions behind my iron walls and pretend it's not real. Nobody questions what it is; nobody socializes either, everyone still exhausted from their respective journeys and the stress of the entire situation. Based on the whispers and side conversations we've heard, everyone has arrived over the past two days, so we weren't that far behind.

Dyana and I eat in complete silence. It's the first time in a while I've seen her thrown off, and it ignites a fury inside of me.

That day in the square plays over and over on repeat through my thoughts and in my dreams.

The Gauntlet hasn't even started, and I've already failed. I promised to always protect Dyana, and here she is. Decidedly not safe.

After dinner, we return to our rooms. The other candidates avoid us. I've never been the type of person people just approach.

Dyana is the sun, and I, the storm.

People stay far away from me, but her? She enters a room and everyone wants to be her friend.

We get changed into threadbare sleep shirts and crawl into bed. Despite the uncomfortable mattress and the instant ache it sends to my left hip—another reminder of a meeting in the Ulster Wald gone sour—it's comfier than the ground. After many years of repetition, I always woke up in time to be at the stables just before sunrise, making me our official alarm clock. Still, that did nothing to help my anxiety.

Dyana blows out the candle on our shared nightstand, and soon she's lightly snorting, the noise echoing throughout our new abode.

I'm not asleep, though. The exhaustion has me worn down to the bone, but my brain won't shut off, and I can barely unclench my muscles.

The thoughts just keep running behind my eyes faster and faster.

How do we get out of this?

Can I get us out of this? Is that even possible?

I should have stayed in the forest.

We should have escaped to the forest.

I've killed us both already.

Oh gods, I'm going to kill us both.

I can't lose her too.

Please don't take her from me too.

I toss and turn all night, restless and unsettled as the fear takes over. Morning comes, and Dyana blinks sleepily as I anxiously putter around the room.

"This sucks," she mumbles, her voice coated in sleep.

"No time for a pity party today. Get to it." I throw Dyana's clothes, pelting her in the face. She makes an indignant squeak and mumbles about sadistic tendencies before she begins to get dressed, shivering in the cold morning air.

"It was so much easier waking up early when there were cute wolf puppies," Dyana grumbles. I snort. It wasn't much, but I miss it so much that sometimes it hurts.

It's surprisingly cold in the Pit. But that's what happens when you're so much farther away from the suns. "Excited to see what mystery meat they have for us today?" My sarcasm could cut through a tree. We're both dressed in similar worn black fighting leathers that have seen better days. They're certainly worn in, that's for sure. It made the fabric nice and soft but nothing fit right. My pants were slightly too long, so I had to tuck them into my black boots. They are also a little bit big, but I only have thick northern wool socks with me, and luckily they fill out most of the empty space. It's not perfect, but it'll do.

Dyana looks gorgeous as per usual, but her pants are too short, and the top is a little too snug, hugging her slender figure tightly.

We flood into the quiet hallway, seeing only a few other candidates, and we all make our way to the stables. Os isn't there yet, so we must be a bit early. I take a moment to say hi to Taran who is already up and eating his hay breakfast. His squishy nose wiggles with happiness as he almost mows me down for the carrot I brought him. It was a bit soft and wonky from the journey after I found the patch of wild carrots in the Southern Ulster Wald one morning. I saved it as a special "thank you" for carrying us for the long journey. Taran's soft lips gently grab the carrot, and he munches away happily before returning to his hay. I take a moment to rest against his back, listening to his deep, thumping heartbeat.

Drowsy happiness and love brush against me, and I send the same right back. I whisper my fears into his fur, and he stands steady, allowing me to try to calm my heartbeat. It's been galloping in my chest ever since last night, but as I listen to Taran's beating heart, my breathing begins to slow and my focus comes back—for the moment at least.

"Thank you, old friend," I mumble as he nudges me with his head, rubbing his forehead against me and asking for scratches. "I don't know when I'll be back to see you next, but I hope it's soon."

I hate this.

The chatter outside grows, and I give Taran a final kiss on his fuzzy cheek. When I turn to head out of the stall I realize Dyana has been watching the entire time. She's seated on top of some bales of hay, half asleep.

"Spying on me?" I smirk as I poke her in the side.

"Rude," she huffs. "It's relaxing being in here. But mostly I just like watching you with the animals. You're so talented, and you don't even know it." I send her an icy glare, and she just rolls her eyes.

"Animals just trust me, that's all." My words are hollow, the fear of who might overhear already giving me anxiety. Dyana knows better than to speak about that in public. "Let's go see what sort of hell is in store for us today." The two suns are beginning to crest on the horizon, the sky lightening in glorious shades of pink, orange, and white.

"Alright, candidates, gather round," a voice shouts, booming across the meeting grounds. Os emerges from a doorway, and—oh my Gods. He's shirtless. A giant scar bisects his right pec, the skin pale against his deep sepia complexion. Dozens of scars travel down his torso, but it's the black glyph tattoos covering it up that surprise me.

Gods, how many abs can someone have? I spare a glance over at Dyana, who smirks at me knowingly. I glare back at her immediately and shake off my shock, although my mouth waters slightly as I take him in, particularly how his tight-fighting leathers hug his rather generous backside. His legs are like tree trunks encased in those pants—I shake my head and cut it out.

"We're going to run around the perimeter of the city twice. We will begin this way every morning, and in two weeks, we will increase again. If you don't complete the course, you'll have to run an extra lap tomorrow. So whatever you do, even if you stop, keep going." He looks up suddenly and his nostrils flare lightly, like a wolf scenting prey. A huge shadow covers the sky and a gust of wind bursts over us, knocking most of the humans down. A giant Dragon flies overhead, its belly covered in green scales.

The Dragon from Twyn Fells. Bloodwyng.

Fury, resentment, and pity war equally within me at the sight.

"Now just imagine that is chasing you. Imagine how fast you'd need to run. Anytime you're thinking of giving up, I want that image nailed so hard into your fucking heads that it's the only thing you see when you close your eyes each night. Got it?" Os's voice booms once again, and I pry my eyes off the disappearing Dragon to see that his eyes are again on me.

"Let's get going." He turns and immediately sets out at a steady jog, and everyone scrambles to get up and jog after him. I wait for Dyana to dust herself off, and then we set off slowly, bringing up the rear. What the other candidates don't realize is right now speed is less important than stamina. None of us are used to running this much, so lasting through two laps is more important than how fast you can complete it. At least for now while our bodies adjust.

I had told Dyana this last night as we were falling asleep, so she and I set out at a very sedate, slow jog. We're well behind the others, but we keep pace to follow the path and know where to go. The smell from the slums briefly assaults our noses as we run to the edge of the city, ducking through an alcove and turning so that we're running along the outer city wall.

Halfway through the first lap around the city, we're both breathing hard and coated in sweat. My sides are in stitches, and I feel like throwing up. Dyana does, and we stop while she empties her stomach of all its contents. I rub her back lightly, and we quickly pick things back up.

At the end of lap one, I throw up too, stomach heaving and clenching outside of my control. I'm in okay shape from working at the stables, but I have no endurance and lack the muscle tone of someone with a regular diet. Running is making that perfectly clear.

Dyana holds my hair back, as some of it has escaped the loose braid. Everything hurts, and every breath feels like it stabs my lungs.

But we keep going. Keep running, keep pushing through the pain. On the second lap, we pass multiple candidates who have collapsed on the ground, similarly heaving up their guts and groaning in pain.

Dyana glances my way, but I shake my head. We can't afford to help anyone. She glares at me pointedly, and I remember once that she was someone I couldn't afford to help. But I did help her, even though I didn't have to.

We slowly jog forward and come upon a young woman on her hands and knees, panting heavily. Dyana rams into me, and I let out a painful, loud sigh, begrudgingly stopping. A shock of shoulder-length curly red hair contrasts against lightly tanned olive skin absolutely covered in pink and brown freckles. Gray-green eyes meet mine as I crouch next to the young woman and gently tap her shoulder.

"Get up. You have to finish the lap," I try to say this softly, but I'm breathing so hard it sounds breathy and wheezy. "Come on, we're almost done."

The woman just shakes her head. "I'm not sure I can," she chokes out. "Each step feels like a damn knife is stabbing me in my sides," Her voice is beautiful and lightly accented, marking her Eastland heritage. But I can hear her exhaustion. Dyana crouches on her other side.

"You're from the Eastlands, right?" Dyana asks in between panting.

The woman nods. She looks to be in her mid-twenties, around Dyana's age. But looks can be deceiving.

"What happened to your teammate?"

The woman laughs around painful pants. "He left in the middle of the night. Or tried to, I suppose. This was all too much for him. I didn't see what happened, but I doubt he made it far." We're all silent for a moment at her words. "He was a gooseberry farmer, with a wife and three kids. His daughter tried to volunteer for him after his name was called, but they wouldn't let her."

Nobody makes it out of the Gauntlet alive. And that was still rare. You could only be let out of the Gauntlet alive if you were rendered completely unconscious for the remainder of the round.

A few Gauntlet's past, fae attendants came to haul out what they thought was just another dead body from a fallen candidate during the semi-finals, but it turned out the human had just passed out. The fae discovered this when the so-called dead body gutted a few of them. Naturally, that restoked some... lingering anger and resentment, shall we say, about the Great War and the humans who fought against the fae.

Having to be indentured to the High Council for the rest of your miserable life was a worse fate still.

The red-headed girl coughs, and I share a quick glance with Dyana, her deep mahogany eyes pleading.

"Alright, come on. You can do this." We're all coated in sweat as we get the woman standing, her wild red curly hair sticking to her forehead and red cheeks.

"What's your name?" Dyana asks, her hair damp with sweat. We all look worse for the wear currently.

"Mirielle, and thank you," the woman says gently, her breathing slowly calming. She's taller than me—shocker, most people are. But where Dyana is slender, Mirielle is generously curved and soft.

Mirielle's warm gray-green eyes meet my own, her gaze kind and honest. I'm taken aback at the trust I see in them. I found myself another misfit loner to take under my wing. I sigh to myself at the knowledge that somehow, even though I have enough trust issues to fill the moat lining the Black Citadel, I can't say no to Dyana.

It's a big enough task to keep myself alive in the Gauntlet, but I had to keep Dyana alive too. I'm not going to get attached to this Mirielle person—who very well might die in the preliminary round. If Dyana were smart, she would do the same. But based on the enamored twinkle in her eyes, I'd say it's likely too late for any forgetting. I just hope she knows what she's doing.

"What part of the Eastlands are you from?" Dyana asks Mirielle as we take a second.

"I'm from Sud Azyl. It's right on the Southeastern Coast."

"Gods I'd kill for some sunshine and warm water. I've always wanted to swim in the Midheym Sea. Is the water really so clear you can see fish and mermaids?"

Mirielle smiles and even I'm taken aback by her raw beauty, "It is."

Dyana gasps in amazement. "I've never even been swimming. Ama doesn't know how, so she couldn't teach me," Dyana pauses, looking over to where I'm glaring daggers at her. "What? There's nothing wrong with not knowing how to swim."

My grumbled response makes Dyana roll her eyes.

Mirielle laughs pleasantly. "I could spend every day at the beach. Every morning I used to wake up and go swimming while the suns rose in the distance." Mirielle pauses, her eyes going dark. "The beaches are closed now. They're only to be used for the Ur Daoine military armada and the Dragonguard."

Dyana blinks in surprise but I'm not shocked. It was only a matter of time before the fae tightened their leashes.

Mirielle speaks about her home as if she'll never see it again, and I feel for her. I do. But as I stand, Mirielle just became another bump in the road on the way to our finish line—and that's a problem. One I'll save for a later time.

"So, Mirielle, what was your life like before all of this?" Dyana's questions are innocent enough, but I know better. She's flirting. She *likes* the red-headed stranger.

"Breaktime's over. Let's get this shit finished," I pant, pushing into a slow jog despite my protesting legs, and the stitch in my side making me unable to take a full breath.

This is a lot harder than it used to be. The weight of age is heavy on my shoulders. But my will is iron. I push through the pain even when I can't feel my legs anymore, running on numb legs and feet.

We're halfway done with the second lap when Dyana stumbles. I wrap my arm through hers and start dragging her along. Dyana lets out an odd squeak and that's when I notice Mirielle on her other side, an arm around her waist, dangerously close to her ass.

If I wasn't breathing so hard it felt as if my lungs might implode, I'd scoff. But I'm fairly sure doing that might kill me right now, so instead, I turn my attention back to Dyana.

"Come on, I know you can do better than this." It's so hard to speak but I try and force the words out anyway, coughing in between. "You can dance for hours, Dyana Arkos. You can run the rest of this miserable lap and show that asshole trainer what strength looks like."

"You can do better than this," she mocks in between panting.

"Brat," I chide her, but she laughs, which turns into coughing in between as we finish the brutal final quarter of our second lap. By the time we get there, multiple people are sprawled on the ground, and I'm in so much pain that I stop moving, I'll never get up again. Dyana's arms wrap around her abdomen as she winces in pain, and next to her, Mirielle is bent over, spitting blood on the ground from breathing so hard.

Not Os, though. Instead, he's just standing there. Sweaty but not winded at all. He looks as if he was out for a godsdamned leisurely stroll—yet another reason to despise him.

"That's so not fair," Dyana mumbles. "Are we that out of shape?"

"Yes, but he's also that in shape," Mirielle says dryly with a raised brow.

As if he heard us, Os turns and walks up to us with a hard look in his golden gaze, "Go get breakfast. You'll want to skip it because your stomach hurts like a bitch, but you need it. If you throw up, you won't get more food, so don't waste it even if you eat slowly. Someone will retrieve you at zero nine hundred and bring you to the training rooms for strength training."

Several groans echo in response to the news, but Os continues to look at the other candidates milling about in various states of misery. The three of us slowly limp our way to the door, passing Os on the way down. I glance over at him again, realizing he's waiting for the rest of the candidates, even the ones who had to stop and rest. He could just leave them there, but he stands vigil, waiting for them to be finished at whatever pace that may be.

Strange male.

I can't think much more of it because soon I'm piled into the packed staircase as we all stumble down to the mess hall, everyone limping and moving slowly—the smell of so many sweaty bodies packed together infiltrates my nose, and my stomach threatens to turn again. I quickly switch to mouth-breathing; a trick I picked up from all those years working in the stables amongst the manure and sweaty animals.

Turns out "breakfast" is just bland, flavorless porridge that looks like white sludge and hard-boiled eggs. It looks as disgusting as it sounds, but we all tentatively eat, stomachs feeling worse for the wear. Everyone looks nauseous for the first few minutes, but as our stomachs settle, the hunger kicks in. I still have to force myself to finish the bowl and shove the dry egg down my throat, but it's the biggest meal I've had in a while, and I needed it.

A short alle selle demis dressed similarly to Os walks in the room, and we all turn. Dyana, Mirielle, and I snagged a small table in the far corner so we could have our backs to the wall; a rare blessing.

The demis has beautiful umber skin and obsidian eyes, and they're dressed similarly to Os. Likely a Southlander.

"I'm Lyn, one of the trainers here. Follow me. And no, I don't care if you're not finished. If you're a slow eater, that's on you."

Ah, so they're all mean.

We quickly hustle to the bussing station and drop our bowls before jogging out behind Lyn.

"Gods, no, no more running, please," Dyana groans.

"I'm gonna puke," Mirielle whispers and I look over in horror to see her swallow down the vomit threatening to escape.

Lyn takes us up one level so we're just underneath the arena. The stairs make me feel nauseous, but we make it in one piece. Lyn then takes us to another large training room with weights and weapons against the walls. It's a huge empty space with a dirt floor, probably meant to mimic the Arena.

Os has us line up, then takes us through a grueling series of pushups, sit-ups, and weighted movements until everyone is on hands and knees or sprawled prone on the ground. There would be no admitting this out loud, but my body is in agony. Dyana, Mirielle, and I all shakily make our way over to the water stand.

"My ass is so sore I don't think I can ever sit down again. It better look so damn perky after all of this or I'm gonna be really mad," Dyana says dryly.

"I genuinely can't feel my right leg." Mirielle responds, glaring at the trainer responsible for all of our current misery. "He is evil! Pure evil."

I cough to cover up my snicker and go to add to the conversation but words fail me. That moment of hesitation when you realize you don't actually fit in is a humbling one. It's not that I don't fit in; rather, I can't just...be normal and ignore our impending doom like Mirielle and Dyana can, apparently. So instead, Dyana and Mirielle bond over a mutual dislike of the trainer.

After a good 10-15 minute break, we all sit on the ground. Os returns, this time followed by a big group of strong and similarly dressed people, including Lyn. There must be about 15 in total, one for each town.

"Trainees, meet your trainers. Each town is assigned a dedicated trainer. They will teach you how to use various weapons and hone your fighting skills. You'll learn how to use most of the weapons you see on the walls here," he says, gesturing around with his left arm, "but most importantly, you'll learn how to fight Dragons. Every trainer here has slayed multiple full-grown Dragons, so listen close and pay attention. You're to do what they say, no questions asked. And if you do question it, getting on Dragon shit duty will sound idyllic compared to what I'll do to you. Got it?"

That wasn't ominous or anything. Dyana and Mirielle glance my way, and we all look equally shaken and nervous. I try to be strong for them, but in some moments it's hard. I'm just as scared, even if it's for different reasons.

"In three weeks, we will go to the Fray, and you'll get your first taste of Dragon fighting. When I call out your town name, you will go with your trainer and begin today's session."

He begins to call out various town names. Mirielle ends up with Lyn, and everyone stares, jealous that she gets the undivided attention of a single trainer. We're the last town to be called and we get paired with a tall woman with a nasty scar all down the left side of her face, narrowly missing her eye. It does nothing but enhance her beauty. Her chin-length black hair is so dark, it's almost blue. Dark black eyes meet my gaze as she surveys Dyana and me, arms crossed and unblinking, before she sighs, annoyed.

"We've got a lot of work on our hands." She turns and walks away; no name or anything. No sort of introduction. She just leaves, expecting us to follow like obedient little sycophants. Dyana looks at me, confused. I sigh and motion with a tilt of my head that we should follow.

My patience is hanging on by a godsdamn thread.

CHAPTER 9
DYANA

"Damn, that *wretched* woman." I curse. Every step is agonizing, every muscle and bone in my body aching. Ireyna, our trainer—whose name I managed to pry out of her—is a fucking *sadist*.

Mirielle caught up with us after training, but as we walk back from the extra lap around Castael Laryn the trainers made us run, we're all quiet—and aching. I want to say something to her. To sound interesting and worldly, but my brain is silent. I'm in too much agony to think of a witty way to flirt with her. Amalia is limping decidedly less than I am, but then again, I often forget how strong you have to be from working with horses day in and day out the past few years.

"All of the trainers need to go back to whatever hell they escaped from." I blink with surprise at Mirielle's words before I break out in laughter. Mirielle smiles, and butterflies explode in my belly.

"*Oof—*" I smack right into Ama, having been too engrossed in Mirielle to realize she'd stopped. "Why did you stop? We're turning left to go back to the Dragon Pit."

Ama looks at me like I told her the sky is pink. "We have to go to that Welcome Ball tomorrow, remember? Os told us to head to the Black Citadel when we finished with training for the day."

"I did not forget," I deny. Mirielle smiles but Ama just rolls her eyes at my blatant lie. Instead of going down to get food, we ascend the winding stone staircase, the only light from the torches every few meters. When we emerge into the fresh air, we continue straight, crossing the courtyard and walking toward the Black Citadel. The frozen air is painful against my exposed skin, but I'm so glad to be in the fresh air that it's easy to ignore.

As we make our way up the road, the Black Citadel begins to emerge. A hulking, sharp building of black stone and metal. There's no color in sight, down to the bark of the trees lining the pathway. The quiet is unsettling as we get closer to the Citadel, and suddenly I'm opening my big, rambly mouth.

"Is Sud Azyl a big town?" *Oh my Gods, why are you being so weird right now?*

"It's small," Mirielle says with a smile, not at all thrown off by my question. Her messy red hair is in a simple ponytail, making her gray eyes stand out even further. Depending on the light, they sometimes look light green, but I will never admit that I've paid enough attention to notice something like that. She would think I'm such a freak.

"Small? Sud Azyl is not small. It's the biggest port city south of Larsyn Bay," Amalia scoffs. I blink—how does she know that? Amalia continues quickly, "My father used to read me histories of Ur Daoine when we were on the road. I had trouble relaxing my thoughts in the evenings, and it helped calm me down. He and my mother took turns, but she liked listening to him." Ama stops and takes a long breath, exhaling hard and shaking off the memory. She doesn't talk about them much. I'm surprised she would say so much in front of Mirielle. But the latter doesn't seem fazed.

She accepts it, nodding. "I suppose you're right. When you live in one place your entire life, even bigger towns can feel very small. It's nowhere near the size of Castael Laryn, but it's more spread out."

Ama nods. "That's a good point."

I throw in another question before I can think better of it, "How long did you live there?"

"My whole life," Mirielle's eyes darken and we all pause, feeling the weight of everything going on.

It's heavy. This burden we have no choice in carrying.

"Is your family still there?" I ask softly, and Mirielle nods lightly, her eyes sad.

"My father is. He suffered a fall a few years ago, so he's very fragile and I spend most of my time caring for him. My mother left us when I was young."

"I'm sorry you feel the pain of loss, too. You're in familiar company, Mirielle." Not quite an olive branch, but for Amalia, that was probably as much as she could offer. It took her over a year to fully trust me. I trusted her immediately, but she gave her trust away in small doses—understandably. When you deal with a certain amount of pain or trauma, it leaves scars. Not visible ones, invisible scars underneath your skin and across your bones, marking you as grief's prisoner for the rest of your days.

"Most people in our village...they've all lost people. Mothers, fathers, sons, daughters, wives, husbands..." I fade off, and we all turn to look up at the Black Citadel now towering over us, reaching high into the sky.

"We know very well who to thank for that," Amalia hisses, and I swear the fog shivers in return.

"Mother save us. How are we supposed to mingle with them?" Mirielle mumbles.

Amalia scoffs again, "Don't worry, they won't talk to you. They will talk about you. Humans and lesser magyka aren't worth their time. In their eyes, we're little more than animals, while they're Gods." Amalia tries to sound unemotional, but I can hear the trembling in her voice. "We'll be paraded around like prized pigs waiting for slaughter."

I snap to face her and shake my head lightly. Her mouth goes flat as she closes her eyes and breathes, frustrated. We're all silent momentarily as the gravel crunches beneath our boots.

"Thank you, both," Mirielle says softly. "I know I said it that first day, but I'm glad I'm not alone for whatever happens next."

My thoughts go a bit haywire at the adorable smile she sends me. I took one look at her this morning, with her gorgeous curves and her tight-fitting uniform, and just about lost my mind.

"We should stick together, the three of us." Mirielle's confidence and genuine nature put me off balance. Everyone always has other motivations behind their words and actions, but she seems so honest.

"I agree," I say quickly. Ama covers her snort of laughter with a cough. But she nods anyway.

"Not to be a downer, but we do need to address the, uh, Dragon in the room so to speak…" I break off and it goes quiet as we continue to walk toward the Black Citadel. I shoot Mirielle a glance, wondering what she's about to say.

Mirielle looks at me, "Are we going to have to kill each other?"

I nearly trip and fall on my face at the question, shocked that she asked it so casually.

Amalia just looks at Mirielle for a moment as we all pause. She shrugs, "Possibly. But that won't matter as much until the latter rounds when it narrows down. Unless you piss someone off. At any given time, we must assume the other candidates want to kill us."

"Amalia!" I gasp. She just told Mirielle that yeah, she might kill her. What is wrong with this woman?

"No, it's alright; I know all about the Gauntlet. My great-grandmother died in it," Mirielle says.

"Wait? I thought they didn't pick legacies."

"Oh, you can get picked a second time, even if you win. It happened to someone in the ninth Gauntlet. But I heard all the stories. Not even the Gauntlet winner emerges unscathed. It's just not possible."

"But it is possible to have two winners. It's rare but possible."

"Possible, not probable," Mirielle corrects, her voice surprisingly cool. Not towards Amalia, but towards the fae who put us all in the place of having to go through conversations like this, where we decide if we're going to murder one another.

We approach the moat's edge, near the bridge crossing onto the Black Citadel grounds. The water beneath the moat is so dark it's nearly black. Bubbles of noxious, rotten honeysuckle pop and fizz, creating a wall of disgusting smells. Something big swims beneath the surface, just a large shadow, but it's enough to stop me.

"Yeah, making a run for it sounds like a good plan." I gulp in fear as my heart begins to pound in my ears. Ama arches a brow at me, but Mirielle's big eyes are wide with worry. I huff and say under my breath, "I'm kidding."

But I see that large shadow beneath the dark surface of the moat water and can't help the few steps back I take.

A warm hand on my upper arm catches my attention. Mirielle smiles gently, "It's just a kelpie. They're pretty harmless. Come on," she tugs lightly on my sleeve. Despite my fear, butterflies explode in my stomach at her touch.

Amalia goes first, striding confidently across the bridge. She does pause in the middle as the Kelpie breaches the surface. A warbled squeak falls from my mouth as I catch a glimpse of the monster. Sharp fangs protrude from a black, slimy snout. The kelpie whinnies and the sound is like a scream. I'm the only one to cover my ears. But Mirielle does wince slightly. Amalia's eyes just harden as she squints, cocking her head slightly. The Kelpie splashes and I catch sight of its tail, which is long and made of some sort of seagrass. It kicks its back hooves, the ends lightly finned, and that's when I notice the chain around its ankles.

The Kelpie is stuck here.

"In a few years, there will be no magykal creatures in the wild. This Kelpie is likely one of the last of his kind," Mirielle says with melancholy. "Come on," her hand drops from my arm to wrap around my own cold hand. With her help, I walk over the remainder of the bridge, but I realize Ama isn't beside us.

I look back and she still stands in the middle of the bridge, right at the edge, overlooking the water. The Kelpie has disappeared back to its murky prison, but Ama watches as if she can still see him.

She eventually turns and walks towards me, but the anger in her gaze, even after knowing her for eighteen years, makes me shiver.

Amalia approaches us, jaw tightly clenched. "We stick together for training. I'm not willing to make any sure promises now, but we have five weeks left of this. For now, we're allies."

"Okay," Mirielle says with a nod. I nod too.

"Dyana," Amalia says as we approach the Black Citadel gardens, "why don't you room with Mirielle so that she's not alone? We would only be a few doors away from each other. Plus, I could use a night off from your snoring." I glance up at the sky, wondering when the Gods will answer my prayers and smite me to save me from the eternal embarrassment of nosey older sisters.

"I'm going to kill you," I hiss under my breath. Amalia just arches a brow in that annoying way of hers.

"Are you sure? I'll be fine," Mirielle tries to protest. Amalia just holds a dirt-smudged hand up, stopping her.

"You're alone the rest of the time. Consider this an alliance trial run." Mirielle looks suspicious and goes to protest, insisting she's perfectly capable on her own—and she is. I watched her in training yesterday and today, and despite her lack of running endurance, she was an incredibly fast sprinter and very graceful with her punches. Her delicately curved neck and generous, soft curves are so beautiful; whenever my eyes close, all I see is the color red.

But, does she want to be friends? Or does she want something more? Nothing she's said or done so far makes it clear either way. I don't know her well enough to be able to decipher when she's flirting versus merely offering polite female friendship.

"I'd really like that, actually, if Dyana wants to." Those gray eyes watch me calmly, but I swear there's a wicked twinkle in them. Clearly the stress is giving me hallucinations.

"Of course," I say, trying to sound calm and completely normal. "The last few days reminded me just how badly Amalia grinds her teeth. It sounds like a beaver gnawing on a damn tree in the middle of the room! Some quiet will be much appreciated."

Amalia glares at me and rolls her eyes, but I just smile tartly.

"I do not sound like a beaver..." she grumbles to herself.

"Mhm, tell yourself that." Fae guards mill about in armor, shooting us glares and whispering.

"Careful, ladies, wander about for too long and you might get snatched up by wandering hands." A fae yells at us, and a few others chuckle. They begin to walk closer, trying to close our exits.

"Can you direct us to the lower east wing? We're candidates and we need to find our rooms." Mirielle steps forward, and all eyes move to her. They take in her generous breasts and the curve of her hips with hungry eyes. But her polite, unassuming words lull them briefly.

"Fine. If you fall behind or get lost, it's not on me what happens next."

"Move." The fae who offered to show us the way shoves through the remaining fae who stand, staring and pushing past us coldly, glaring the whole time. Mirielle looks at us, panicked. Amalia looks at the remaining soldiers milling about before she nods, turning to follow the other fae.

One fae is better than twenty. I can't see it, but I'm sure Amalia has her dagger hidden somewhere on her.

We walk quickly to catch up, wincing as our sore muscles scream in protest. The feeling of wrongness in the air, which began at the moat, only intensifies as we travel deeper into the castle. We must be in the servants' wing because all we see are more fae soldiers and both demis and human workers dressed in housekeeping and serving garb, which was a startling uniform made of black, floor-length robes. No color anywhere; not on the walls, the floors, or the clothes of those who live and work here.

It's as if all of the joy has been sucked out of the world and we've entered some alternate realm. The sound of dozens of footsteps echoes against the shiny stone floor. They've sanded the stone so finely that it resembles a kind of marble or crystal finish. But the way it was making the sound echo was downright unsettling.

After a few minutes we make it to our wing, and the fae soldier sneers, spitting on Amalia before wiping his now bloody drool-covered lips with a laugh. I gag at the bloody spitwad now coating her pants.

"I'll remember that." Her words are stated calmly, but she says them like a curse, and for a moment, I swear I feel the earth shake and rumble in response. The fae blinks, then scoffs.

"Watch your mouth, puggō, or I'll shut it for you." The fae walks away, leaving us in the hallway. None of the other candidates show their faces, but perhaps all haven't arrived yet. We quickly find the doors with Sud Azyl and Twyn Fells listed on the front, and Ama squeezes my shoulder as she nods to where her door is.

"If anything is up, wake me. You know I won't be sleeping anyway."

"Try to sleep. Who knows when we will ever have beds this nice ever again." Ama just sighs, annoyed at how right I am.

Mirielle opens the door, and we step into the room. It's decorated similarly to the rest of the castle, all dark shiny stone and black metals. The fabrics are all black or dark gray, and the wooden chairs are even a rare type of black oak.

Mirielle sighs and sits on a nearby bench in the small conjoined sitting area. The rooms looked small from the open doorway, but the bed was larger than any I'd ever slept in and was stacked high with fluffy black and gray blankets. Porridge waits for us on the coffee table and we quickly scarf it down. Once all of the food is gone, I'm struck with insecurity, not knowing what to do or say next.

"I'm beat. I'm going to get in bed. We should keep the fire going since it's pretty chilly, and that way we can see in the dark. Like a little night lantern to keep the Gray Wytch away."

"You know that story?" Mirielle nods, smiling. "Heard a traveler from the North tell it. People from all over Ur Daoine come to Sud Azul, so I got to hear all sorts of tales if I hung around in the right places long enough."

"Sounds like an exciting place to be."

Mirielle shrugs, "To me, it's home."

Home.

"I wish I knew what that felt like."

"You don't consider Twyn Fells home?" Mirielle asks.

"No, it's just where we landed, and Amalia and I both found work quickly. Twyn Fells is where I live, but it's not home."

"I hope you get the chance to experience home someday, Dyana." There is no pity in her voice, just genuine hope. My stomach turns upside down as she stares at me and I want to say more.

But I don't. *Can't.*

Flustered, I stand up. "Any hope of that happening means we have to train as hard as possible. And make it past tomorrow night without Ama deciding to kill someone." I don't laugh but Mirielle does, before she pauses and notes the serious look on my face.

"Wait, what? Amalia is going to kill someone tomorrow?"

"Uh...you know what, don't worry about it. I'm sure it'll be fine," I clear my throat awkwardly and Mirielle looks taken aback. I've said too much already. I falter, unsure what to do, and then nod at Mirielle, but that turns into something like a bow, and suddenly it's gotten really weird and Mirielle is just looking at me, perplexed.

"Okay, see you in the morning, goodnight!" I say the words so quickly it blurs into one. I turn, hightailing it to the room.

After a few minutes of self-berating about the most horrendous flirting job I've ever done, likely buggering it all up, I crawl into the blissfully comfortable bed.

The door stays cracked and it's so quiet that the rustling sound of Mirielle's bare skin sliding under the sheets across the sitting room is the only other sound besides my own breath, as I try to fall asleep, knowing what awaits me in my dreams—red hair, and gray-green eyes.

CHAPTER 10
AMALIA

My head hits the gravel floor, rocks scraping up my hands, knees, and forehead. I swallow the loud groan that wants to be released from my throat at the burning pain on my palms and bare skin. But since we were apparently privy to the Black Citadel's team of healers, nobody cares if we got injured. If I had a gold coin for every time Ireyna kicked me to the floor in fight training in the past 48 hours alone, I'd be a wealthy woman.

"Have you forgotten everything I told you yesterday? Pay attention!" Ireyna's deep voice booms. This woman is a fucking menace. We're outside in the cold on the Citadel grounds. The gravel grinds into my knees as I force myself to my feet.

Dyana clears her throat, but I minutely shake my head. We've known each other for so long that it's easy for us to understand what each other is saying even when no words are spoken. But if Dyana spoke up on my behalf right now, she'd only get worse treatment from Ireyna.

"I'm so sorry, Ireyna, I didn't hear that. Could you speak up a little?" I say with faux emotion as I smile and wipe my dirty, bloody palms against my pants. The pain is sharp, but I grind my teeth harder as I brush off. Ireyna scoffs, but her eyes are blazing with anger. I drown out the pain and assume the ready stance for the coming collision, legs shoulder width apart, weight down in my feet, core strong, hips slightly closed.

Father taught me the basics when I was young. I have skill and strength, sure, but technique? None.

I exhale hard and wince with pain. Shit, bruised ribs. That's a problem. But it doesn't matter; the only way I will yield for this crazy bitch is if I'm unconscious.

"Pathetic. You have no talent and no skill. How are you supposed to succeed out there, candidate?"

I spit and a wad of blood hits the dirt floor, "I'd rather be a worthless nobody than a bully."

Ireyna thinks she's trying to force me to submit, but my respect is not given, it is earned, so I just sink into my stance, and breathe.

"Again!" That's all the warning Ireyna gives me before she's a blur of movement and standing in front of me within a blink, jabbing and punching at my sides. I block her jabs, but my ribs protest and it makes me slow as pain clouds my concentration. I block a right-side punch to my kidney, and she fakes me out and head-butts me hard. I saw it coming and could have moved faster, avoiding it, but instead I let it happen.

The lesson to be learned is not for the loser.

Stars burst behind my vision, and my eyes water with the pain from my forehead. I stumble back one step but stop, adjusting my weight again. A large bump is forming, but Irenya doesn't waste any time. I've barely rebalanced when she's there in front of me yet again, doing some jump kick towards my cheek that has me bending backward to avoid, but her boot still comes within inches of my cheekbone. I lean forward, I push into a series of punches and kicks, but I can't raise my arms much and my aim is sloppy. Ireyna rails a punch to one side of my head and a kick to the other. I fall to one knee as the pain makes my vision fuzzy. With a shout, I charge, knowing it's all I have left. I run straight at her, using my body weight as a battering ram and knocking her to the ground. She doesn't expect the scrappy move. It's zero grace, all function. But it works. I grab her hair and slam her head against the ground twice, gaining the upper hand for a moment, but she twists out of my grip until I'm straddling her chest, and she swings her palms up, slapping my ears. I scream, falling to the dirt floor as my equilibrium disappears.

Burst eardrum. I lose sense of where the ground is, and my stomach clenches painfully as nausea takes over. I try to stand but fall again, losing my balance, and end up back on my hands and knees. Dyana paces in the background biting her nails down until they bleed, a bad habit she picked up when she was 12.

"Pathetic," Ireyna sneers as I pant, blood trailing from my right ear.

Ireyna gets up, walks over to me, and bends down until we're eye to eye. "You are going to die here, worthless little puggō. Say your prayers while you still can; Limbo awaits." Oh good, a Sol Constantus zealot. They worship the national religion implemented by the fae. It's not officially illegal to openly pray to any other deity, but it usually doesn't end well. Most in Ur Daoine believe in a polytheistic divinity. The fae pay no mind, though, instead putting up temples to Sol Constantus in all the cities around the country. Except for Twyn Fells, funny enough. We only had a small monument and no temple.

"Ah, using religion as an excuse for violence, how shocking. Tell me, does Sol Constantus approve of you beating and abusing innocent humans who were ripped from their homes and brought here against their will? I thought he was a loving, forgiving type of God. The Father of us all, you claim. What would he think of his creations behaving like this? Or do I have that wro—" Ireyna's palm connects with my face as she slaps me so hard I bite my tongue, blood pooling in my mouth. I spit the blood back out on her face and laugh at the horror in her eyes, causing her to charge, tackling me to the ground, sending gravel shooting into my eyes. The hard ground scrapes up my hands and arms as the wind gets knocked out of me. I frantically try to open my eyes, but everything is blurry. I can tell just from the air of superiority in the movement that Ireyna walks over and bends down next to me with what I'm sure is a mocking smile all over her face. I lean back and try to avoid the touch, but it doesn't work, and my eyes water as she grabs me by the hair.

"It's said that anyone with hair this color is a wytch. Either way, humanity still taints your soul. Purgatory is where you and your kind belong, wytch."

I snort, eyes watering further as they sting with the movement and my blinking, "You know, I wish I was a wytch so I could shut you up already." I groan, pushing up to stand, forcing her to back up slightly. "You're so talkative, and I need a break from your noisy presence." Out of the corner of my eye, now that my eyesight is starting to come back a bit more, I see Dyana's jaw drop.

Not from what I said, but from the fist that immediately bashes straight into my face. Pain explodes and my vision goes black.

There's just darkness, but I feel flashes of pain, and hear screaming. Then it's quiet.

Someone jolts me, and I hear pained moaning,

I think that's me.

"Enjoy hell for me, wytch," Ireyna says. I don't see anything, but I hear her voice in this half-detached place. Something hits my face again, and there's a huge crunch as hot blood floods. Pain explodes in my head as I lose consciousness and plummet to the ground, falling further into the darkness as it envelops me, and welcomes me into blissful, quiet nothingness.

I've been waiting.

"You took it too far, Ireyna," a voice growls. A male; he sounds angry, but it's hazy. "You know better than to let some snide comment shatter your control!" The male shouts.

"Since when do you care? Are you getting soft for a little puggō? You know better, Os! They're doomed for Limbo."

"Cut that sacrilegious bullshit, Rey. Why did you let her get under your skin so much? Why her?"

"Shouldn't I be asking you that since you're here?"

"Answer the question." The voice lowers, furious.

There's a sigh, "She reminds me of that stupid story of the gray wytch. I look at her and I see my childhood nightmares, gray hair and all."

"Your past doesn't mean you get to nearly kill one of the candidates, Ireyna, Gods above!" The male curses, "Our job here is to train them and get them ready, not take them out of the game before it even takes place!" The voice roars again and something shatters. "Hurt her or any of them again and you're out." The male voice says, but I don't care anymore.

Not yet.

Give me peace, if only for a moment more. In response, the darkness wraps its arms around me yet again and yanks me back into the blissful void.

The pain pulls me up from the depths, returning me to consciousness. My face hurts and my eyes might as well be held shut with heavy weights, but a soft, gentle hand is holding mine.

I'd know that hand even if all of my senses disappeared. The sound of soft, familiar crying yanks me from the corners of my mind and into the present. It takes all of my energy but I slowly blink my eyes open, lips pressed together as I turn my head and look down at Dyana, who sits on the floor, holding my hand. I squeeze it and she gasps, looking up.

"Seems like you need a chair." My voice is raspy, and my jaw hurts with each word that comes out of my mouth, but it's just an ache. I sit up slowly, and Dyana stands, ready to keep me stable. I run a hand over my face, feeling no scar or injury. "Huh."

"The High Council's healers. The Archmage even stopped by, something you'll be glad to have missed; he was so creepy. It took 3 healers to reconstruct your face," Dyana pauses and I wait for the incoming explosion. It takes a few seconds and then Dyana starts to pace. "I watched as she broke your fucking face, Amalia!" Dyana steps back, shouting. "That's unacceptable. If our roles were reversed, you would rip me a new asshole over this."

"There's no need to shout—"

"No, you don't get to do that. You're not going to belittle how godsdamned traumatic it was seeing you get nearly beaten to death. And you just expected me to stand there, silent. I thought you were going to die, Amalia!"

I wince as I stretch my jaw from side to side lightly, feeling only some light scarring. I sigh, pulling Dyana to sit next to me. She resists for a moment before finally acquiescing. I say nothing because my words would just be an excuse. I'm not mad; I understand her anger.

"You're right," I say gently. It's hard to admit but I force myself. "I was scared, and then Ireyna spouted her Sol Constantus bullshit and I got angry."

"Angry enough to lose?" Dyana asks, but she's less shocked. I see understanding settling into her soul from behind her warm brown eyes.

"Angry enough to do many things; losing is merely one of them," I mutter.

Dyana sighs, "I'll go tell the healers you're up, but I'm fucking mad at you, okay?" She goes to leave.

"And Ireyna?" I ask, poking her slightly. Curious about how she'll respond.

Dyana scoffs, "I'm plenty mad at her too, don't worry. But no, Ama, I'm mad at you. Because you could have fought back and you didn't. I saw you, you held back!" She accuses, eyes fiery and hurt. "You promised you would protect me, that we would get through this together, but how can you do any of that if you're so willing to martyr yourself? Do you think you're just expendable? Do you think I could—" she breaks off, choked with emotion. I hold my breath, feeling ashamed. Dyana swallows against the sadness and fear, but tears quietly fall as she meets my gaze. "Do you know what it would do to me if you died, Ama? You're all I have too, you know. And that means you need to protect my best friend instead of acting stupid to prove a point and get Ireyna in trouble."

I blink, "I have no idea what you're talking about."

I look at her innocently, but she just raises her brows, not buying it. "I'm sure you don't."

I shrug. "The point, I think, was proven. Although perhaps that was just a dream."

"Okay well, I do need to go tell the healer you're up. That's the only reason they allowed me to stay. And then I can break you out of here."

I try to smile, but it's painful, and I wince.

"More pain meds it is, I see." Dyana nods, a stubborn look in her gaze as I lay back, and she leaves the room. I'm shoving my thin bed sheet off the second she's out and trying to stand up. This is, of course, an immediate regret when everything suddenly doubles, and my vision goes a bit wonky.

Lovely. They healed my jaw and nose but not my concussion.

I groan with anger and lay back down as my vision comes back. That stupid ball tomorrow is going to be exciting.

I take deep breaths, trying to relax while Dyana grabs the healer.

There is no sound at all—nothing besides my breathing. No obvious change in the room, yet the air changes and all of the hair on my arms stands on end.

I'm being watched. My heart quickens as I open my eyes and glance to the door.

It's a punch to the heart when my eyes meet ones of pure gold as I temporarily forget how to breathe.

Os leans against the doorframe, arms crossed. We just stare at each other, and after a few moments, he tilts his head. What a strange male. I must have hit my head fucking hard because I blink, and one moment Os is a normal, albeit very unfriendly male, and the next, he's a glowing supernova encased in bright fire. I blink, and it's gone.

Gods, this concussion is terrible.

"You're lucky, waking up before the Welcome ball. If you missed it, they would have killed you," he says plainly.

"Such kind hosts, your friends." The male's right eye twitches lightly, and he pushes off from the door. Instantly, he stands at my bedside, arms no longer crossed but leaning against the headboard, looming over me.

I jump despite all efforts not to.

Gods, he's fast.

But Os just ignores my comment, tilting his head again, eyes assessing as he watches me with curiosity, "It took three fae healers to fix your face. They had to break some of your other bones and part of your left femur, using it to mold a new jaw. Then they had to regrow that bone too, which is why you now have a little purple scar on your left thigh."

I meet his gaze, refusing to show any emotion as he continues. He nods to my jaw, "They spent an hour alone just attaching your new jaw. It was hanging off your face when you came in."

"They did a shit job. It still hurts," I say coldly.

"It will. All magyk has limits, and they healed you the best they could. What you're left with is unable to be healed further. But the swelling will go down in a few days."

"You speak from experience."

"Yes." That's it, no other explanation, just one word.

The Gods have indeed cursed me.

Os slowly turns his head and looks at the door, blinking before his eyes are back on me. "Your teammate is surprisingly strong. I thought she was going to try and wrestle me to the ground when I went to carry you to the healers."

He sounds genuinely befuddled at the idea of Dyana thinking even for a moment that she had a chance at taking him down. I can only imagine the righteous fury in my sister at the idea of some stranger carting my unconscious body away. Heads would have been rolling if our roles were reversed. When you have lost as much as we had, you hold on fiercely to what's left. I smirk at the thought of Dyana shocking everyone with her righteous fury. But Dyana lived with her heart on her sleeve and loved fiercely. I would expect nothing less.

"All you magyka think humans are so weak when in reality, you're just jealous that they feel more, what with the short life span."

"Finished preaching, then?" He's not mad, he just watches me in that eerie way.

What are you?

"Not preaching, just the truth. You think Dyana and I are weak. I just don't like bigoted magyka who think they're better than everyone else." I force my fear, frustration, and stress into anger, like usual. It's easy to do. There's so much to be mad about when all humans have adjusted to constantly being looked down upon and treated no better than the shit beneath their boots.

"You're angry." He cocks his head again, leaning down a bit more. I try not to react again, but I get a whiff of his scent; a smoky, burnt vanilla mixed with leather and musk. His magyk brushes against me soon after, and I recoil. But he doesn't move, which pisses me off even further, the audacity of him.

"Yes, of course I'm angry!" I hiss the words as I scooch away from him. "Fae and the other races treat humans like vermin. As if we're dirty. Well, you know what, we are because you and your fucking overlords don't allow enough food to be traded, so we're all starving. Yes, I'm angry, and you will never understand that."

His face suddenly changes, and I freeze. His pupils are slanted.

"You've made up your mind about me quickly." he says, his voice deeper, richer, smokier. I hear it in my bones and underneath my skin. "But you're right. Most magyka and fae here think of humans as animals, so you'd be wise to watch that pretty mouth of yours and be careful not to talk like that when wandering ears could be listening. Say any of that to one of the fae, and your head will be added to the pile of skulls decorating the Arena while they watch as the Dragons feast on your scrawny flesh."

He says none of this with anger, just grim certainty. His eyes, though. The eyes of a predator watch me. But that voice—that voice is so familiar. Distant, disjointed memories flood my mind.

Os...yelled at Ireyna for hurting me earlier. Why did he do that?

"Yes, I'll keep my mouth shut so you can train us to die for them. What a great plan," I snap back, not meaning to sound quite so poisonous. But my heart races in his presence, my temperature rising as my panic grows.

Why am I acting so weird? I slap myself across the face—the male steps back, blinking rapidly, surprised.

"Had a little itch in my jaw," I say pleasantly with a casual shrug. He watches warily, but there is no fear in his golden gaze—that's new.

Maybe he'll leave me alone if he thinks I'm a bit off my rocker instead of just trying to cover that for some star-cursed reason, I have no self-control around him! I'm usually more under control than this since I've spent almost two decades trying to be forgotten. But my head is already jumbled since Ireyna sent me for quite the tumble, and he smells so good but is a total ass.

I look up and notice that his eyes are fixated on my mouth, not with curiosity but with hunger.

At the realization, all thought, logic, and sanity leave my body.

"Tell me something, Amalia Roth," A slight accent sounds on a few of his words as he takes the few steps between us, standing next to me at the end of the bed. Those gold eyes travel down my body, and I realize I am clutching the bed sheet—and I'm dressed in some thin, flimsy white nightgown.

Os takes his damn time enjoying the view. Hearing him say my name is like a drug, and I close my eyes for a moment, fighting my growing lust. I hate my body for its reaction to this male. But Os crouches down, leaning his hands on the bed until we're almost nose to nose, and he's hovering over me. His face is scarred, but it's subtle. Hard to see from far away. His scent is heady, and as he invades my senses further, I become more detached from reality. I'm jolted back to the real world, however, when he opens his mouth and says, "Tell me why you planned to lose."

Shit.

Os has been paying much closer attention than I was aware of, and now I have a new problem to deal with. As much of the truth as I can give, then. To make it easy.

"I lost on purpose because Ireyna is a racist bitch, and I didn't want her to retaliate if I fought for real. She seemed to be waiting for an excuse to hurt me."

Mostly true.

"You weren't trying, though, even after the first major injury," Os says, nodding to my ears. They've been cleaned, and my hearing feels fine, but that explains some of the aching. I'd forgotten.

"You're right. I'm more out of shape than I let on, and it was hard to think through the pain."

That is also true, but that's enough looking at me under a microscope. Let's turn this around.

"I was unaware you were monitoring my fight that closely. Perhaps you just like seeing women get beat up?" I say as if puzzled.

Let's see what your buttons are, Os.

"Don't; it won't work."

"What do you mean?" I ask innocently.

"This little game. You're trying to push my buttons to elicit a response. But I'll warn you; it won't work." He growls, flashing his teeth, although, for a moment, they look like brutal fangs.

He leans forward until his face is just a breath away from my shoulder, and he inhales my scent. Is he...*smelling* me? Gods, I must smell horrible. But fuck if it's not making me tremble with need.

"If you bite me, little liar, you'll find I bite back." Os smiles and my skin gets a bit tingly as heat floods my core. My body is screaming to push him and find out more, but my mind is kicking me.

~~There's enough to worry about; I don't have time for lust.~~ **Ignore it. Ignore it. Ignore it.**

Os leans back and the distance between us allows the air back into my lungs. I silently inhale a deep breath and center myself; or try to.

"Be careful, Amalia Roth. I'll destroy you and leave nothing left. How terrible it would be to deprive the fae of another glorious death." Os says flatly.

"I apologize." You could cut my sarcasm with a knife. I'm unable to do more than say the words. Os continues to look at me quizzically, but I can't meet his gaze again, so I look away and trace my jaw again.

I don't even feel him move but his fingers caress my jaw, feeling the previously broken bone.

I'm frozen, unsure what to do, and terrified this moment will end. He rubs his thumb over my bottom lip.

Oh, Gods.

The plain hunger in his gaze ruins me, and I go to lean into his hand but he pulls away quickly, standing up with a muttered, "Interesting," before leaving the room.

Excuse me, what the *actual* fuck?

The moment is broken when Dyana approaches with an unknown, thin looking fae. The umber-skinned fae with white hair is dressed in the customary garb of a healer: white loose pants, and a matching white loose tunic, topped with a dark gray robe. Why anyone in the medical profession would choose a primarily white outfit was beyond me. But the fae's eyes are a bright, grotesque red.

"Miss Roth, good to see you're awake. Bless Constantyn, we were able to heal you. You're an integral part of the Gauntlet, after all. My name is Landys, I'm the Archmage's assistant."

Lovely.

They walk over to me, and it takes everything in me not to flinch when their cold, clammy hands check over my face. They smell like something floral, but my nose isn't quite working. Lilies, maybe. But it's heavy and oppressive in the air, and I start to cough.

"You mean my death needs to be entertaining." I roll my eyes, crossing my arms.

"Silence, heretic." Landys snaps, and Dyana has to look away to keep from laughing.

If they only knew.

Landys drones on about how I should go pray my sins away but I ignore them and they finally shake their head in anger, and the healer heads off. But those red eyes stay with me, making me feel violated somehow.

"Are you okay?" Dyana asks, worried as I get dressed in a spare healer's outfit they had set out for me. Another all-white outfit; the sacrificial lamb ready for slaughter.

"It aches, but it's nothing I can't handle. I'm okay, I promise." We slowly walk through the lower Citadel as Dyana leads me back to our rooms.

"Please don't do that again," Dyana whispers as we approach the door to her and Mirielle's suite. "I should come with you, stay with you tonight. You shouldn't be alone after that."

"Dyana, I'm fine. And I'm sorry, truly. I just…"

"I know," she says softly, grabbing my hand and squeezing it briefly.

"I'm sorry."

"I know that too," She squeezes again before dropping it. "But I really should stay with you tonight."

"After the ball, then. But go and get ready with Mirielle. I want to take a long bath—in silence," I say.

Dyana rolls her eyes but nods reluctantly, turning to head into her room. She pauses, looking back as she opens the door. We look at each other, each rubbing the small, identical scar on our palms.

"I won't leave you," she says.

A soft smile appears on my face, unbidden. "I know, Dy," I say quietly. I nod, turning and heading a few doors down but she calls softly, "Love you, Ama."

I glance over my shoulder and call back, "And I, you," before disappearing into my own room.

Another lie.

Always so many lies.

My panic from earlier returns as the bald, clinical color of the room closes in on me. Dyana told me we have five hours before we need to be ready for the ball, so I fall back on the fluffy bed and let the anxiety rush out in silent sobs, my chest tight and my lungs straining. I cry until there's nothing left but a slight tremor, rhythmically running through my body. My jaw protests painfully as I silently scream. Exhaustion comes over me as I fall into a restless sleep and ignore the charred handprint marring the pillow beside me.

CHAPTER 11
AMALIA

The bath was so luxurious I fell asleep in the tub, even after my nap. It's the most rest I've had in years. I'm fully awake now as I stand in front of the small closet in a thin towel, hair dripping and cold down my back, looking at the so-called outfit that the fae decided to give me for this evening.

"You have got to be kidding me!" I hiss, slamming the closet door and peek my head into the hallway. A few guards are lingering about, and I wave one of them down, "There's clearly been some mistake, I was given the wrong dress for the ball. I require a new one," I say, but they snort and ignore me. My heart races at the thought of being so on display. For so long, I've hidden under hoods, scarves, and baggy clothes.

They want to make us feel out of our depth.

I attempt to tame my hair once it finally dries, but my arms are tired and my patience thin, so I leave it unstyled. The smoke-gray strands hit my lower back, wavy and thick from being so thoroughly cleaned for the first time in many years.

One look in the mirror after wrestling my way into this pathetic excuse for a dress, I begin haphazardly smudging a bit of kohl around my eyes. It makes my already pale gaze look silver.

The silky gray dress is paper thin and looks almost metallic in a particular light, like liquid steel. I don't do any other makeup, already tired of playing dress up as I take in my appearance. But the top of the dress is so thin it's partially sheer, leaving my breasts on display. My hard nipples are fully evident as the fabric clings to every curve and valley of my body.

The dress—if you could even call it that —appears to have a full skirt, but with every step, a thigh-high slit on both legs becomes visible. Combined with an extremely low-cut back, I feel completely and utterly naked. No bit of me is truly hidden, not even with the few strips of dark fabric.

The black metal shoulder piece I clasp on was set out with the dress. It covers my shoulders with a black-looking chainmail, falling around my shoulders in an armor-like manner.

Earrings were also on the bed, and I cuffed them around my ears, noticing that they had fake little points at the top, so sharp the second one bites into my thumb. I suck the blood off and scoff as I see myself in the mirror. It looks like I have metal fae ears.

Nope. I rip them off before I can even complete the thought. *Not happening.* I attempt to yank the armor off, suddenly feeling claustrophobic as the person looking back at me in the mirror turns increasingly into a stranger.

Except for my eyes. My father's eyes stare back at me. I stop tugging at the armor and reach forward, raising my hand to trace around the reflection of my eyes in the mirror. Every time I see myself, I see everything I've ever lost.

I miss you so much. I don't know how to do this without you.

The words stay tucked away safely in my mind as I harden myself and slide my feet into the simple black sandals left for me. A knock interrupts me, and a soldier enters before I even respond. I spin, hissing at him in outrage. Before he can react, I have my dagger unsheathed from where I'd hidden it against my waist and am pointing it right at him, "Do you barge into everyone's rooms? What if I had been naked?"

"Put your pathetic steak knife away, human, or I'll throw your sorry ass in the dungeons," the soldier sneers, his bright red eyes alarming and creepy. "Are you under the impression you're a guest here? How sad. Now, you have one minute to finish whatever you're doing."

He does this whole speech with his helmet still on, which feels strange. The headpieces all curve in a way to mimic Dragon horns, and combined with their creepily glowing eyes, sharp features, and fangs, it's a grotesque image. The less time I had to spend with the fae, the better.

Dyana waits in the hallway, gorgeous in a royal blue gown. My heart bursts with pride—and fear.

She sees me and gasps, her eyes wide "Ama, I—oh *wow.*"

"Stunned to silence? I never thought I'd see the day," I chide her, unable to help the smirk that grows on my face. Dyana rolls her eyes, ever the frustrated younger sibling in our friendship.

"Well, what do you expect when the only thing you've worn in the past eighteen years are work pants and worn sweaters?" Dyana scoffs.

"You've seen me naked, plenty," I glance down with a grimace, "Not much different than I am now."

Dyana is resplendent in a simple, bright blue gown with a metal under bust, lifting her small breasts. The color is regal against her tawny complexion. I'm a ghost compared to her.

"No Ama, you look...." Dyana breaks off, "Well, gorgeous, but honestly, kind of terrifying."

Great. The last thing I want or need is more attention.

"Where's Mirielle? I thought you would get ready together."

"I decided to get ready on my own. I was...Gods Ama, she makes me nervous! She's so beautiful and I just, I don't get nervous, not like this. But she's so calm and confident; it's intimidating, okay? She intimidates me and it's driving me nuts!"

The door behind Dyana opens, and Mirielle steps out in a sage green long-sleeve gown with a deep slit in the front and billowing sleeves. The fabric sparkles with each step she takes. Dyana squeaks, attempting to cover it with a cough, but her eyes are wide as she takes Mirielle in. Her generous breasts are almost falling out but she looks stunning. She managed to tame her frizzy curls into an artful updo, emphasizing her graceful neck. A metal belt cinches the look. Dyana is frozen, jaw on the floor, as Mirielle joins us.

"Oh my Gods, Ama you look—"

"Basically naked?" I interrupt cynically.

"I was going to say incredible." Mirielle pauses and looks at Dyana, "You both look incredible, wow." I have to look away at the heat in both of their gazes, feeling like I'm intruding on a private moment.

I think it's safe to say the attraction is mutual.

"You too," Dyana says huskily before clearing her throat, "But we need to get going." We're to meet one floor down near the bottom of the stairs. A few other doors open, and more similarly dressed candidates come out. People of all ages, all colors, and all human. Some look as young as eighteen, whereas others could well be grandparents.

If you were over eighteen and most or partly human, you were automatically on a list of possible Gauntlet candidates and there's nothing to be done about it. We follow the crowd of tentative humans down some stairs, the chains of my shoulder pieces clinking with each step.

Everyone is dressed in their fae-chosen finery, and then I see a few people wearing fake, metal-pointed earpieces, and I'm unable to hide my disgust. When we reach the bottom of the stairs, a bald, finely dressed fae addresses us. They are neither feminine nor masculine but a perfect blend of both and neither, dressed in long silver robes.

"Hello candidates, I am Tolys, and I will be your host for The Gauntlet." The fae's glowing red eyes—there were a lot of fae here with red eyes—were eerie as they assess us, unblinking. They clasp their hands and continue on. "I will announce you town by town, and you'll enter with your partner. You will then be presented to the High Council and the entire court so they can get a good look at you." The fae pauses, smiling pleasantly, "Speak to no one. Do nothing except stand there silently and when the presentation is over, you may watch the dancing but at no point in time will you participate in the actual ball by any means. You now belong to the High Council. You are not guests. If a fae asks you anything, you answer. If they ask you to do something for them, you must accept." The fae stops and flashes a creepy smile, "Do enjoy the evening. It's all for you, after all."

"Great," Dyana mutters.

"Stick together," I say firmly. "When the presentation is over, we get out of there." Both Dyana and Mirielle nod as their faces tense, nerves rising.

We're called one by one into the waiting ballroom as a soldier opens two large doors while Tolys shouts their name and town before the doors shut once again. Naturally, Twyn Fells goes last as the northernmost village. Dyana and I wait as the room empties, and Mirielle leaves with a tight exhale when Sud Azyl is called, hands shaking at having to descend alone. Dyana reaches over and squeezes her hand before she goes, a gesture not lost on me.

"Last one's up," Tolys calls. That's us. We walk up towards the door and I'm suddenly angry that there was no place to hide my dagger with this dress when I'm arms reach from the greatest evil this world has ever seen. But there's no other choice and no chance to think on it further as the fae soldier opens the door, leering at us as we walk into the darkly lit, palatial room.

"Twyn Fells!" A voice like Tolys's, but magykly enhanced echoes through the large ballroom as we look down upon the crowd of fae, their red glowing eyes all pointed at us with bored amusement.

"Dyana Arkos." Shit, Dyana has to go first. I squeeze her hand as she swallows and descends the stairs. The crowd of finely but modestly dressed fae watch, whispering to themselves. Dyana makes her way down the walkway, head high and shoulders back, through the parted crowd before kneeling at the base of a large dais—three ornate black chairs on either side of an even more giant carved, black stone throne.

The High Council.

Every thought leaves my brain, and all of the blood leaves my body. I almost look down to see if my heart has dropped out of my chest but I can't move or take my eyes off the male in the largest black chair, which I now realize is a throne. A throne in which sits the male from nearly every one of my nightmares.

The High Councilor, also known as Achan Drayven, although I call him by another name; *murderer.*

I knew he might be here. It's why I haven't been sleeping. My imagination holds no weight to the reality of stepping into the same room as him. His magyk is so potent I almost vomit, the taste of rotten apples makes me gag, but I swallow it down as my heart races.

"Amalia Roth!" Tolys calls. The shock quickly morphs to rage as I stare at Achan Drayven and begin to descend the stairs. Dyana now waits with the crowd of other candidates lined up below the dais, directly underneath the High Council. I refuse to cower as I descend the staircase, but the feeling of hundreds of eyes on me is so violating. My anger is my only armor as my vision tunnels.

He killed them. He killed my parents.

I don't feel my feet, but they bring me closer and closer. The High Councilor watches, bored, his black horns arching behind him. I knew he was alive, but I haven't seen him since that day. Anger quickly turns into panic as the fear from that day rejoins my present.

He killed my parents.

Their dying screams echo in my ears as I walk forward, and when I kneel, I feel the ash of their bodies underneath my hands instead of the cold stone floor. I don't breathe. Don't move. Don't speak. Don't think. All I can hear is my racing heart as I look up and into my enemy's eyes. I'm back in that tiny house as the walls shake around me.

He killed my parents.

The High Councilor looks at me with no familiarity, dismissing me with a bored flick of his hands, unaware of who sits before him. Every muscle in my body aches as I tremble with a long-forgotten rage.

He killed my parents. You killed my parents, and someday I'm going to cut off your godsdamn head for it.

Out of the corner of my eye, I notice Dyana watching me, pleading with her eyes. As I stand, my eyes meet the High Councilors briefly. I robotically join her, forcing myself to look away. The weight of his magyk makes me dizzy as I stand—the concussion from earlier doesn't help. I grind my teeth, the events from earlier completely out of my mind, and it sends shooting pain through my jaw and into my face. The pain grounds me as I watch with calm, wicked fury as he opens his mouth and begins to speak.

"Welcome to Castael Laryn—" That horrible, hissing voice is worse than I remembered.

"You can't escape me." I flash back and forth between the past and the present.

"—and welcome to the 25th Gauntlet!"

"I will always find you." The memories assault me.

"Every Gauntlet we remember the brave fae souls who lost their lives in the Uprising—"

"There's nowhere to run."

"—and remember the misguided ways of the vicious, evil humans who thought themselves higher than the mighty fae.

"You belong to me, little girl."

"All of you undoubtedly will die, except for the lucky human left standing!" One of the other high councilors whispers, and the High Councilor rolls his eyes, "Or two of you, should someone get disqualified." He says the word as if it's poison in his mouth, puckering his lips in distaste. "Let me make this perfectly clear now; should any of you think of using disqualification as a way to take the easy way out, don't. If any of you are found to be faking injuries at any point in time, the punishments will be severe." The crowd snickers as our group shuffles awkwardly. The High Councilor continues on, "This Gauntlet is the hardest one we've ever had. I think many of you," he looks to the crowd of sycophantic fae, "will be pleasantly surprised with what we have in store." I continue to flip between past and present as my vision tunnels, and my skin begins to flush with heat and fury as my heart races faster. With each blink, I can see him covered in my mother's blood, and I look down at my palms, expecting to see her blood there too. But there's nothing.

My nightmares turned into reality.

"But after hearing whispers of so many humans kidnapping innocent demis all around the country, I've decided perhaps we've been too generous, too gentle. After taking solace and conferring with our Lord, Constantyn, He sent a vision, showing me the path forward. The prize for this Gauntlet is hereby decreased to 50,000 gold marks. I don't like to be mean,"—the other High Councilors all look sad, as if this was a difficult decision for them—"but I will not feed this nasty, sinful rumor mill further. Perhaps if the humans and magyka decide to behave by the next Gauntlet, we will reconsider. But it seems you need to be reminded of your place again." The crowd laughs as Achan sits down. I'm seething as my chest flushes and my skin begins to heat. It's never enough. We fall on their swords when they tell us to jump, but it isn't enough. They will forever crave more money, more power, and more fear.

Fucking monsters.

Claiming humans are kidnapping people, blaming their wrongdoings on us. I don't need to look around the room to see the vapid, ignorant glint in their otherwise empty eyes. No matter what he says, his people believe him. To them, he *is* a God.

I look around at the crowd, and molten gold eyes meet mine—Os. He's in fine black armor over pristine black fighting leathers, his shoulder-length hair pulled back, making his eyes even sharper. He looks dangerous, but he just stares at me, unblinking.

For a moment, I'm pulled out of the darkness of my mind. There's just us as I lose myself in those eyes. But he blinks, and the spell is broken as sound rushes back in. I look away, frustrated at myself for looking like a moon-eyed young fool.

The look in his eyes, though; it's hungry.

I continue my perusal of the crowd as another Councilor, a tall female starts talking, going through some weird spiel about the generosity of the fae, going on about the usual Sol Constantus bullshit. My eyes go behind the Council to the few imperial fae lingering. A tall fae leans against the back wall, clad in a simple but finely made black outfit. His silver-white hair is typical for fae but cut unusually short. Only long enough to run your fingers through. Tattoos crawl up his neck, decorating his jaw—another surprise.

I've never seen a tattooed fae. That was a practice of the old world, not commonly done anymore. When I look at the fae's face, his eyes meet mine, and he winks, before snapping back to listen to the High Councilor.

Heterochromia. He has different colored eyes: one a deep amber, the other light green shot through with streaks of bronze.

How strange, indeed. My heart races again, but this time for a different reason. My cheeks flush with embarrassment at being caught staring, so I look away and return my attention to the Councilor speaking.

"Now, this is a momentous occasion, so let us celebrate!" The Councilor lifts both hands in the air just slightly, signaling something. Magyk brushes against me softly, and I gasp, muscles tightening as power bursts through my body each time the magyk touches me.

Dragon magyk.

Four fae attendants walk in dressed in long white robes, each of them carrying small, wiggling bundles. Scaled, wiggling bundles.

Each fae attendant holds a juvenile Dragon, about 30 pounds or so, meaning they're about a year old.

Dyana gasps next to me and grabs my hand. I can't even squeeze it back. Because why are they here?

Why are baby Dragons here? They're so small, their squeaks so confused and scared as they flap their tiny wings. Each sound reaches into my chest and clasps my heart tightly. Nothing else matters except the four little minds reaching out and touching my own. Their magyk makes me want to cry; it's like touching raw starlight. They shine like beacons in my mind, their innocence glowing and untainted by the cruelties of this world.

"Friend!" A sweet, small voice chimes in my head, causing me to freeze and ice to fill my veins.

"Friend! Friend!" More voices chirp in my head as they instinctively latch onto me with their magyk. My tongue is heavy in my mouth as my brain wrestles between fear and a delirious need to protect them. It was making my stomach turn to acid as my heart races faster and faster.

Why are there baby Dragons here?

The Dragons keep squeaking as they're brought up to the High Council. My breath starts coming hard as my eyes dart quickly. Out of the corner of my eye, I see a flash of gold eyes and look, but Os is gone.

"Why here?"

"I don't know, sweet one." My magyk thrashes against my control, trying to bond.

A beautiful, wiggling red baby Dragon is handed to Councilor that had been speaking—Councilor Varas grabs the Dragon by its leg, dangling it in the air.

"Hurts. Help me, friend." A desperate voice cries in my head.

Oh my Gods. It's the Dragon from the day we arrived. That's why the voice sounded familiar.

My panic unleashes some of my magyk against my will. It latches onto the baby Dragon and bonds with it, fully meshing its emotions with mine.

"You're not alone. I'm here." I whisper the words to it but also to myself. But I don't know what to do. I can only watch, nauseous, as the Councilor shakes the Dragon. My feet step forward without thinking, but Dyana yanks me back.

"Ama, don't," Dyana whispers, but she has to tighten her hold on my trembling arms. The Dragon's magyk merges with mine, frantically seeking refuge and help.

Councilor Varas pulls out a knife.

No. No, please.

"The fae rule because we rule the Dragons. Humans would do best not to forget that." The other attendants holding the remaining baby Dragons step forward in unison, withdrawing their daggers.

This isn't real.

"It's okay, it's going to be okay." I whisper frantically to the baby Dragon, but it's pointless.

This—this can't be real. Yet it doesn't stop.

"A treat, in honor of the endless generosity of the High Council. Let the blood of the Gauntlet freely spill."

"Scared—" the Dragon's thought doesn't finish. Councilor Varas raises the red Dragon, slides the dagger through its neck, and beheads it. All the thoughts in my head go still, and my legs threaten to give out. Then there's a shriek, and another, as the remaining attendants hold up the other three baby Dragons and repeat the action. I stumble backward, smacking into Dyana as my neck explodes and pain floods my body. Some of the candidates begin crying and shrieking outwardly, but nothing else exists except the Dragons in front of me. Their pain is my pain, and I feel their pure, precious magyk get sucked from the land of the living, leaving only an empty void in their wake. My hands crawl up my neck subconsciously, expecting to see blood from a cut.

But there's nothing.

Blood hits my face, and I look up only to see the Councilor pulling the Dragon apart with her bare hands, laughing as if she's playing an amusing game before tossing pieces into the crowd. Candidates begin to throw up at the sight based on the gagging and moaning in the background. But the court of the Black Citadel screams and shouts in excitement, laughing at our horror as they scramble on top of each other for a bite of young Dragon meat.

"What's wrong, little humans? Don't like the taste of Dragon?" Another of the Councilors laughs, an older male with blue-black hair.

It's all in the background. Candidates start moving and running out of the room, panicking. The fae laugh and throw trash at them.

"Oh Gods, Oh Gods, Oh Gods," Dyana chants, panicked, somewhere close behind me. But I can't move, speak, think, or do anything but stare at the red Dragon's head sitting at Councilor Varas's feet.

Someone claps their hands and the music starts up loudly. Fae shout and dance, their faces covered in blood, laughing all the while at our horrified reactions.

But I can't look away.

It was just a baby.

Blood sprays everywhere as the Dragons' heads are tossed around. Some fae poke at them with forks and knives, popping eyeballs and cutting them up just to see what happens. The doors to the ballroom open and a fae chef comes in followed by some attendants rolling a large cart filled with more wiggling small bodies.

Nightmares are no longer limited to my dreams; it's here. On cue, my eyes flick to High Councilor Achan Drayven, and my knees give out as I watch him bite into a whole roasted newborn baby Dragon, not even the size of a puppy, skewered on a stick.

They did this.

They killed them.

My hands shake so hard as I pant heavily, my skin heating as my anger turns my veins into molten lava. The feeling of the baby Dragon's pain repeats repeatedly as a scream builds in me.

It's only been a few moments since this all began, but the world moves slowly as I turn to the side and meet Dyana's eyes. What she sees in my eyes terrifies her, and she begins looking around the room frantically.

"There. Ama, the doors are over there. Let's go!" She proceeds to grab hold of my shoulders and shove me around the edge of the ballroom, Mirielle following close behind. Nobody notices; everyone is too horrified by what's happening. The fae are getting drunk on wine and blood, laughing into their goblets of wine. Some dance, some have gotten so high off the blood they've started fucking in the dark corners. Some decided not to save it for the dark corners.

But my vision tunnels until all I can see is the baby red Dragon and the explosion of emotion building inside me. I can't breathe. Everything goes sharp, and my mind blurs as my panic becomes a physical thing that settles in over my body; pure, undiluted horror at what I just saw takes over as sob tears from my throat. I'm crying so hard I can't breathe, and it's just me gasping for breath.

A strong arm so hot it almost burns suddenly wraps around my waist.

"Calm yourself." A rich, smokey voice shoves into my brain with a force that has me cringing.

"Get your hands off her!" Dyana hisses.

"Go back to your room and lock the doors," I say, my voice ragged as if I'd been screaming.

"What? Ama—" she protests but I turn, not even present inside of my own body as the fury grows bigger and bigger.

"Dyana!" I snarl, becoming more unraveled by the moment. Dyana blinks and steps back. I haven't used that voice with her in a long time. I try and take a breath, but my chest is too tight. Through clenched teeth, I say, "Go, Dy. Please," I turn, not waiting to find out if she actually decides to listen to me, and break into a run, not stopping until I'm outdoors, gasping in the cold air. There's no sound, but I know Os is still behind me judging from the scent of sweet smoke filling my nostrils. I walk fast, aimlessly, looking for the most hidden part of the garden where I can lose my shit without anyone seeing.

"Leave me alone," my voice is venomous and ragged as I try to get Os to let me break down in peace.

"No."

My breathing starts to come fast as the past few minutes replay in my head.

"Breathe." Os orders in my head, and even despite my protesting mind, my body responds, and my lungs expand as I suck in a deep breath. It's painful and tastes hot and bloody, the iron tang of the ballroom gone but still stuck in my nose. He continues to drag me, and I fight him every bit of the way, wiggling this way and

that. Not even in an attempt to hurt him, just to run and run and leave here and escape.

"Again." he repeats, wrapping his arms around me, his large hand rubbing my back. Silent sobs still wreck my body as every muscle clenches at the soul-deep pain within me. I would push off the affection, but I can't even move.

"Calm yourself, Amalia."

How the hell is he able to communicate with me like this? If he hears my stray thoughts, he doesn't say.

"Breathe, damnit!" that rough voice says again in my head.

"Get out of my fucking head." Is all I'm able to say in return but my body does as he commands, as I try to shove him out but my adrenaline is so high that I can barely concentrate. I just keep seeing flashes of the ballroom. Something drips lightly into my eye and I reach up to touch it.

Dark red and smoking slightly. Dragonblood. From the baby Dragon—

Oh gods. I fall to the ground and empty my stomach.

Os follows closely behind, eyes hard.

"Leave me alone," I groan, wiping hot bile from my mouth as the tears begin to fall in earnest again.

"No." His simple, unexplained answer and unaffected tone set my fury aflame.

"I said, leave me the fuck alone!"

"And I said no. You're a flight risk."

"Oh, get off your godsdamn high horse. We're all flight risks, you overgrown herring," I push to standing and shove his chest, "Now leave!"

"You don't want me to see you upset." The tall asshole just cocks his head, gold eyes curious. "That's why you're getting angry. You're embarrassed?"

I gasp, "Are you reading my emotions?"

"Yes."

"Ever heard of the concept of privacy?" I hiss the words, but he just stands there, arms crossed. The panic gets worse as the smell of the blood on my face gets more potent.

"I need, I need to get this off."

"What are you talking about?

"Get it off. Get the blood off. I need—I need to get it off. Get it the FUCK OFF." I'm screaming and tearing at my dress, suddenly unable to breathe, let alone exist a second longer covered in the blood of such innocent, incredible creatures.

"Calm yourself."

"Get it off, get it off, **GET IT OFF!"** A reedy whine falls from my lips as the smell intensifies and my panic bubbles over.

"You have to calm down."

"Can't." My skin heats up more, and I look around, frantic. A fountain sits in the middle of the garden, so I sprint over and jump in.

"What the fuck are you doing?" Os snarls as I wash the blood from my face. The water is freezing, icy in some places. My stressed panting covers the sound of the water hissing as it hits my hot arms.

"Gods save me from idiotic females," Os grumbles and I'm yanked out of the fountain as he tosses me over his shoulder.

"If you don't put me down, I swear to Gods I will rip out your godsdamn throat, you hulking bear!"

"Stop talking and be quiet," he orders, so I punch him hard against the back. The asshole doesn't even have the decency to pretend to grunt. Does he even notice I'm punching him? There's a sharp noise, followed by a burn of warmth. I go quiet.

"Did you just slap my ass?" I snarl. He responds by doing it again and I begin making plans to kill him in his sleep.

"Be quiet. Or you'll get us both in trouble if any soldiers catch us. You think they need any more excuses or reasons to beat any of us bloody?" He doesn't take me back to the castle. Instead, we go back to the Dragon Pit.

I throw in some more punches and make sure to hold on with my nails when he turns. He doesn't stop, just growls and shakes me a bit, jostling my aching face as we walk down the stairs to the living quarters in the Pit. But Os stops only two floors down, not three.

"Wrong turn?"

"I don't trust you to be alone right now, little liar."

"Good luck with that." My body goes still, every muscle tensing against his hard shoulder in full rigor mortis. I can't see where we're going, but he opens a door and the smokey sweet scent I've come to know as his multiplies.

"Put me down," my voice is empty and ragged. He stops suddenly and lifts me down. I slap his hands away, "And if you value your life, you'll never call me that again." The darkness in my voice could suck the life from a tree. Os observes me silently.

"What is this?" I gesture around stiffly.

"My quarters."

"Okay, well I'm going back to my rooms," I turn, pushing past him to leave but he just catches my arm.

"Not looking like that, you aren't," his eyes heat as they lower.

"What are you talking about? If I'm caught in your rooms, it'll be both of our heads," I hiss at him.

Looking like this? What does he mean? I glance down. *Oh.*

I guess when fae fabric gets wet, it turns sheer. It would have been nice to know that before I went and jumped a godsdamn fountain.

CHAPTER 12
DYANA

Mirielle and I are silent as we quickly follow the path back to her room.

I'm so worried about Ama.

What just happened was horrible. But the raw pain and searing anger I saw in her gaze... it's been a long time since I last saw her like that. When it comes to animals Amalia doesn't have the best record of self-control and the farther I get from her, the more I realize that separating is a monumentally bad idea. Mirielle quickly opens her door before locking it behind us.

"No need, we're not staying."

"But she said for us to stay here?" Mirielle asks carefully.

"We need to go get her. I don't trust Os."

"Okay. Then we go get her," Mirielle nods and starts to get changed. I do the same. We both meet in the bathroom, washing the blood splatter from our arms.

"They really eat them. I heard whispers but thought it was just talk." My voice is hollow as the past few minutes flash behind my eyes. "They were babies, Mirielle. I eat meat but Gods, that was so cruel."

"Yes, it was. And unfortunately, it's very real." Mirielle sighs, pulling her red hair back before pausing and gently reaching a delicate hand to wipe the tears from my cheek. Our eyes meet, hers are full of sadness. But no surprise.

"You knew they...eat baby Dragons? Why didn't you say anything?" I ask.

Mirielle sighs and looks down guiltily, her hand dropping to her side and flexing nervously. "I didn't know how to bring it up, honestly. Even saying it aloud sounds wrong. And I know about it, because I saw them do it when I was just a child," she confesses quietly. "A delegation from the High Council once visited Sud Azyl. That night, they brought a few juvenile Dragons with them for the...feast. I've had nightmares about it ever since."

Mirielle must read the question on my face because she continues, "I didn't eat it, Dyana. I wasn't invited to, and I would have said no if I was. I swear." She grips my arms and begs me to believe her.

I do, surprisingly. There's something so trustworthy about her, and the commotion of the evening has my emotions in such a jumble, her steady calm has saved me.

"Okay. Okay. So the fae eat Dragons. Fuck." My mind races. "I don't understand how so many people don't know about this?"

"Fear, I think. Only fae are given the meat. Mix that with the Dragonfear and it will ensure you stay silent. But a lot of people do know, actually. You've been in the North too long, Dyana."

"I thought...well, I don't know what I thought but it wasn't this." I admit numbly, looking down and at the blood splattered all over my dress.

"Come on," Mirielle grabs my hand, her skin soft and warm. She squeezes it gently, offering a lifeline just as I start to drown in shock. "Let's get out of here and get changed so we can go find her. I need to make sure she's okay." Before I can overthink it, I lace our fingers together, squeezing her hand lightly back, not to mention the butterflies currently having a party in my stomach.

Mirielle and I quietly tip-toe down various hallways and hide behind statues when fae guards make their rounds, patrolling in their ostentatious black metal armor. We run down a small pitch-black hallway, but when voices sound from ahead, and the telltale clang of fae armor sounds, we quickly duck into a shadowed alcove.

I try to stay calm, but my breath hitches as we push farther into the shadows, causing my back to press into her generous chest. Her hands land on my waist as she pulls me closer, and I fight a moan. Even in the dark, I can feel her chest move up and down with each silent inhale and exhale. I subconsciously match my breath to hers.

The fae approach, but I don't even know what they're saying because just as they pass us, Mirielle's thumbs start drawing slow, torturous circles on the inside of my hip bones. My head falls back until our cheeks almost touch as I go limp in her arms.

Despite the darkness cloaking us, I can feel her gaze.

"How come we don't get meat that young?" The fae's conversation comes into focus and I'm jolted back into the present.

"It's not fair, I'll tell you that," another one answers.

"For once, I'd like to have some Dragon that isn't old and grizzled. Not enough fat on their bones."

"Both of you shut it or it'll be your heads the Dragons are eating next."

The three guards continue their grotesque conversation as they disappear down the hallway. Mirielle doesn't drop her hands, but I'm scared she'll reject me if I make a move.

"Let's go," I whisper. My heart stutters as we step from the shadows and into a panel of moonlight—the silver of the two moons streak against her wild red curls and clear gray eyes. Mirielle looks at me with disarming honesty. I let loose a rocky sigh as we hurry out of the castle and finally make it outside. Already I miss the feel of her hands on my skin and her soft scent in the air.

CHAPTER 13
AMALIA

My heart races as I stand before Os completely exposed in my wet dress. When I jumped in the fountain, the only thing on my mind was cooling off my impending meltdown. There was too much at stake to risk losing control of my emotions like that, so I saw the water and jumped. But the result it would have on my dress was lost on me at that moment.

I'm minutely aware of Os watching me, his golden eyes hungry. My mind is still in a haze as I take in his room.

It's much nicer than our dormitory but similarly made. No windows, but the large stone room has high ceilings, making it seem larger than it is. A small sitting area with worn leather chairs is next to a large fireplace, which is carved into the wall. There must be some sort of ventilation system in the upper levels. The heat makes me shiver as I'm suddenly hyper aware of how cold the wet fabric is, causing my nipples to harden into stiff peaks.

I'm particularly jealous of his extremely large bed, decorated in shades of gray with cloudlike pillows and a white, thick knit blanket at the bottom. Despite the fireplace, small warm yellow orbs decorate the high, arched ceilings, making it look like fireflies twinkling in the air; demis magyk at work or an Elemental magyka like a Nymph.

"Sit down; you're wearing a hole in my rug," Os orders, sounding annoyed as he disappears into a closet.

I glance under my waterlogged sandals to see a thick white rug covering the stone floor. It's heavenly to pry them off and sink my cold feet into the soft fabric. The sensation is grounding. For a moment, I consider never leaving the soft rug. Luxurious fabrics like this are a privilege, available to few.

Os's bronzed skin glimmers in the warm firelight as he emerges from the closet. He changed into dark cotton pants and an unbuttoned shirt.

Unbuttoned and showing every single carved muscle. To my surprise, Os is covered in scars. Some faint, some more recent, but they only enhance his raw, untamed beauty.

He tosses me a shirt, and it hits me in the face.

So, not a demis. He doesn't strike me as a magyka, though. But certainly not fae, due to the number of scars. A shifter was my initial thought based on his movements and enhanced strength. My eyes fly up to his, and I see he's been watching me the entire time.

There's a wickedly pleased look on his face. "Take all the time you need."

"I was just thinking of all the places I still want to punch you."

"That was your version of a punch? How pathetically weak. I could barely feel it," he says the words dryly, but based on the way—the hungry way—he's looking at me, this isn't harassment. Os is playing. I was unaware the male even knew the meaning of the word fun. For shifters, playing could mean anything from flirting, friendship, or familiar bonds, so I ignore the way my body buzzes at the feel of his gaze.

"Turn around. I need to change," I motion with my finger for him to look away, but the male just leans back and quirks a brow.

"I forgot humans are such prudes," he grumbles, but his eyes don't move. I don't respond—I merely raise a brow in return and stare. Os sighs and looks up with a low growl.

I look down, and gods—the fabric clings like a second skin. My curls, damp for various reasons, are visible at the apex of my thighs despite all of my efforts otherwise. Os has officially seen it all.

But he expects me to be a normal, human prude, and I remember the challenge in his eyes the first time we met. So I meet his gaze as I reach to peel off the dress, but the sleeves are stuck on the shoulder piece. With a grunt, I shift and work on unclasping it. I manage to get the shoulder piece undone, but my hands are all wet, and I've started to tremble with the cold. This isn't happening. I manage to get part of it off, but while I'm working on the other side, it gets stuck in my tangled, wet hair. I'm trapped, and it's pulling as my gray strands get even more caught. A pathetic whimper falls from my lips as the chain tugs on my hair.

"Need some assistance?" Os murmurs and I look to find him leaning back in his chair, watching me closely.

"Typical male," I mutter before wincing again. A heavy sigh falls from my mouth and resignation kicks in, "Actually yes, I do. I think I'm stuck." My dress is half hanging off, but considering that it's not covering anything, there's nothing much to be done. Even thin and soaked, the dress becomes my only shield between me and the utterly gorgeous male in front of me.

Os lifts me at my waist, carrying me over to the fire, where he ceremoniously places me. I don't have time to process when he's at my back, inspecting the situation.

"Don't move. You'll make it worse." he orders, voice low. But he doesn't start at the shoulder pieces. His hands land at the base of my spine as he traces slowly up my back. I gasp at the heat from his fingers, so hot it almost burns, but it's a different kind of burn; a heat of need.

My hips want to sway backward, but I lock my legs in place. *Don't give in to this.*

For a male his size and temper, it's surprising how deftly and gently he untangles my hair. Soon the shoulder pieces are free, and he tosses them to the ground. My neck piece is caught in my hair, too, and he quickly moves on from that, stepping even closer, so close I can feel the heat from his chest on my bare back. I remind myself to breathe because I hold my breath at every brush of his fingers. My legs are completely jelly, but I fight with everything I have not to give in. I won't throw myself at any male; they can throw themselves at me and I *might* consider it.

Might.

He goes to lift the neck piece off fully, but it's still tangled. "Fucking imperial fae designs..." he mutters, frustrated at the intricate item. I go to respond, but Os rips the aforementioned fabric in two with a snarl that couldn't possibly come from a human. His large hands don't even strain with the action. Os leans forward, pressing against me as he lifts the necklace off before tossing it on the floor with the other offending items. I expect him to step away. But he starts running his hands through my hair, clearing the knots and tangles.

"So unusual. Like liquid smoke." he murmurs to himself as he works on the right earring.

I snort humorlessly, "That's a new one. I'll add that to the list alongside 'ugly' and 'scary'."

Shit. Why did I say that? My control around this male is terrible, something I will be very disappointed in myself about another time.

"Humans fear what they don't understand." The words warm me again, my skin suddenly heating back up but in a different way. It's been so long since someone touched me. My eyes close as he continues to brush my hair, massaging my neck and scalp. A soft moan falls from my lips as I lean back into him. No force here or in any other world could get me to leave right now.

"Your scent is very strange."

I glare at him from over my shoulder, "Just what every woman wants to hear." The adrenaline is finally leaving my body, leaving me feeling a bit drunk and weakening my control.

My emotions are slipping—

—the good *and* the bad.

Os takes in another slow inhale; his lips almost pressed against my skin. His exhale makes me shiver. Every part of my body feels hotter than the fire behind us. "Humans usually have a very particular scent."

"And you, Amalia Roth, you don't smell like a human," he bursts into my mind, and I try to shove him out to no avail. *"You smell like home."*

I blink, stunned. "I smell like home?" I repeat slowly, surely I heard him wrong or misunderstood.

Os looks at me, completely unaffected. "Your scent reminds me of home."

"Right..." I clear my throat, unsure how to respond. "Thanks."

Os is silent as he continues the untangling. For once, I'm not too fond of the silence. Usually, I enjoy it but right now it's suffocating. "I don't know why I would smell like that since I'm not from here. I've never left the North until now. So it must be from being near so many fae tonight." I rationalize.

"Perhaps." Os steps forward, so I shift away, bumping into the wall next to the fireplace. The heat from the fire is blazing. Os skims my ear with his lips as he whispers, "But there is much you don't know, little liar."

I whip around to face him. *Self control. Self control, Amalia.* I shove aside my lust and yank forward my anger at being called a liar again.

I hate that word. Mostly because it's true and there are days when I hate myself for it, too.

Os blocks me in fully as he leans his forearm against the stone wall behind me, putting one of his large legs directly between mine. He grabs my chin, pulling until I look up at him, my face held in his large palm. I expect something; I don't know what, but just something. Instead, he just stares. His eyes are such a brilliant gold they're almost glowing. He leans down, so close I expect him to kiss me. His lips brush against mine so lightly I can't be sure they touched, or if I imagined it all. The teasing works as I begin to burn with need.

I lean forward to kiss him, but Os pulls back with a satisfied look, "Get changed before you catch a cold."

When I blink, he's leaning back in his chair again, watching me with hunger.

That *asshole.*

You want to play? Okay, let's play. My eyes flare with stubborn anger as I smirk, and his head tilts, sensing that something has changed. I stand there and slowly push the sleeves of my dress down one by one. I tease the edge of the fabric and slowly expose my breasts in full, nipples pink and at attention. The arms of the chair creak loudly as Os grips the arms hard. His eyes give him away, as does the tongue that darts out of his mouth. I continue pushing the dress down, taking my time. I roll it past my hips and down my legs until there's nothing between my skin and his eyes. I slowly step out of the damp fabric, reaching down to pick it up. Too fast for him to follow, I ball up the wet dress and throw it at his face, hard. It makes a wet slapping sound that knocks him back slightly.

"Oh, what *terrible* human aim I have," I comment airily before walking over in nothing but my bare skin and bending over in front of him to grab the shirt in the chair next to his. "So sorry," I whisper, and Os growls so loud I feel it in my chest. But my face remains nonchalant as I throw the shirt over my head, a sigh leaving me at the feeling of the warm, dry fabric. Then I look down.

The shirt is nearly as sheer as the dress. It covers more, but lucky me, it's still sheer.

"Did you pick this on purpose?" I demand, angry again.

Os turns and walks to the side table in the small sitting area, pouring himself a glass of wine from a jug. He takes a sip before turning back around and facing me, as he repeats my own words with a smirk. "So sorry."

"Fuck you," I snarl.

"Ah, there she is," Os says, his face stony. "That's the real you, not this fake, fearful, rule-abiding mask you put on." Goosebumps break out along my arms at his words—at his *knowing*. Os continues devouring me with his gaze and licks his lips, and I swear I feel his mouth on my core as he does it. I clench my thighs together tightly as his nostrils flare.

"I have no idea what you're talking about," I reply cooly, unwilling to give him an inch. "It's you who needs to do some answering. Why did you get me out of there? Me losing my shit doesn't mean anything to you. My life is inconsequential. So why do something about it? And on that note, how can you speak to me mentally?" I demand, needing to change this conversation fast. He just calmly observes me. Nothing shakes him.

He's silent for so long that I nearly start pacing. Finally, he nods in agreement. "I'll answer some of your questions, little liar," he pauses. My hand is already raised, ready to slap him for calling me a liar again, when he continues, "I'll answer your questions if you tell me why an Arkaydian pretending to be human is competing in the Gauntlet."

CHAPTER 14
AMALIA

His words hit me like an arrow through the heart. Everything comes to a screeching halt, and I freeze. My heart begins to thunder in my chest; I fight every instinct screaming, **MOVE, RUN, LEAVE, DANGER,** and instead force myself to sit casually back in the chair, resting my forearms on the arms. Tap, tap, tap. I can't help but nervously tap my finger against the wood.

"I have no idea what you're talking about," I say coldly. "But I do know that suggesting an Arkaydian still lives, let alone in Ur Daoine, is treason." I raise my brow. I need to get the topic changed fast. Externally I'm cool and calm, but inside, my heart races.

"It is indeed treason," he agrees, completely unaffected by my attempts to steer the conversation away from this. "But I felt you, Amalia Roth. I felt you die with them."

I run my tongue along my teeth, ignoring the fear quickening my heart. Gold eyes burn a hole into mine that stare clear, strong, and so pointed you couldn't help but tremble in their gaze.

"You're delusional. You felt nothing; you only saw someone shocked and disgusted at a heinous act," I say, cooly, admitting to nothing. Before he can respond, I continue, "A heinous act that you are a bystander to, by the way. That red Dragon they brought out was the one you were holding just a few days ago. Yet when they emerged with it, what did you do? Ah," I snap my fingers, "that's right. You did nothing. So let's not point fingers just because I have feelings."

Os's jaw goes tight and he closes his eyes, taking a deep breath, leaving me wondering if I pushed too hard.

He finally opens his eyes. "I'm not going to turn you in, Amalia. I realize you think I support the fae but let me be perfectly clear. I do not support the fae in any way, shape, or form, and you're right; what happened tonight was horrific and a perversion of nature. I curse the Gods every night for not unleashing the full weight of their fury upon the High Council's heads for their actions against Dragons."

I watch him for a moment, unsure, "So you say."

"What I said is true; all of it. I'm not going to turn you in," he says with a sigh, "but, little liar, you need training or you're going to get yourself, and your friends, killed. You're throwing around animus bonds without any thought to the consequences." I examine my nails and focus on keeping my heartrate even, not wanting to give him a leg to stand on.

"Ah, I knew there was a catch. Trust with a caveat, right? You'll only keep this secret if I submit to your demands. It's comforting, how predictable you are. As if you really expect me to trust you."

He says, somehow in complete control of the situation, even though I'm now standing over him as he sits in the leather chair. "I'm no friend of the High Council and no friend to the fae, be they Imperial or lesser." He bares his teeth at the word 'friend'.

Os's eyes go dark, and he scoffs. *"Get one thing into your pretty little head, I am not fae."* he snarls in my mind, and I cringe despite my attempt at control. *"Best you learn that now because I'm the only one who can teach you about your magyk."*

"Then why do you want to teach me illegal magyk, and how the hell do you know how to do it in the first place?"

"A few types of beings in Ur Daoine have the gift of empathy."

"I'm not an empath, I can only work magyk with animals."

"That's because you weren't taught correctly," he says, and it's like a knife to the heart—because he's right. My parents died when I was young; I've taught myself most things in life. I don't share this thought with him though.

"Let's get back to you though. How are you empathetic? Are you a shifter or something?" Please, anything to get this conversation away from me and my past. Os stands up, towering over me by over a foot. He stalks into my space, and I back away, but Os just follows—the hunter and the hunted.

My heart pounds and my blood quickens. I no longer feel tired, just present and confused and angry and intrigued. He continues to stalk me across the room until I'm leaning against the wall next to the fireplace, the heat searing into my skin. He crowds me in more.

"It's considered extremely rude to ask a shifter about their genus. I've seen people get beheaded for it."

"How exciting. Answer the question."

"No, I don't think so," Os tilts his head, and my cheeks flush with anger.

"You know what I am. How is that fair?" I protest.

"How about we make a deal?" he rumbles, "I promise to keep your secret if you promise to keep my... lack of certain allegiances to yourself. Deal?" he says, tongue licking out lightly and tasting me. It's a bolt of lightning to my senses. I gasp silently, back arching out of my control.

"Fine. But let's just agree that it's clear you're clearly upper magyka. I won't pry more than that, but that much I do know." I say, glaring at him, challenging him to try and refute my statement. He glares back.

"Fine. I'm upper magyka, but I am not fae. That is all I can give you."

I nod, pleased at least with that slight admission—but I will find out more. The endlessly curious side of my brain is alight with the possibility of solving the mystery in front of me. But that can be later—I reluctantly let it go for now and go quiet, unable to think of anything else.

Os reaches up and plays with my flat, stringy hair, wrapping the charcoal strands around his large fingers.

"Is this a part of the deal?" I ask plainly. I'm too old and too damn tired for word games. Os steps forward and shoves one of his legs between mine, pressing against my throbbing clit and making me gasp. Fuck, I want to rock against him and ease the building ache. I'm no virginal young flower. But my lovers have been few and far between, particularly since Dyana and I moved to Twyn Fells.

"Is what part of the deal, little liar?" he responds.

Fuck, I want him so much it's killing me. But I don't know him, and that seed of distrust is still present. I am so wet it is beginning to drip down my leg, and his nostrils flare, scenting me.

Oh gods, he smells my arousal. I close my eyes and take a few deep breaths, trying to center myself while accidentally rubbing myself against him. A moan almost slips out, and I clamp my lips shut tightly, causing him to press his hand into my jaw harder, pursuing my lips confidently yet gently until my mouth opens just slightly.

Then he does something that almost knocks me off my feet.

He leans back and *smiles*. A hungry, vicious smile, and I see two small fangs on either side of his mouth. He's magnetic already, but when he smiles? He's devastation and ruin.

"You know..." he licks his lips, looking at me like his next meal, "I feel like we can kill two birds with one stone. Let me show you just how much you can trust me. Let me take care of that needy cunt, Amalia."

I think I'm having a heart attack.

"Do you permit?" he hisses the word, brushing a kiss on my cheek. His lips are soft and pillowy, his scruffy, short beard tickling my face. Os kisses my cheek again, lips lingering, before trailing down to my jaw, tipping my head back.

Oh gods, oh gods, oh gods.

"When I taste you, it won't be the Gods you cry out for, little liar," he purrs. I didn't even mean to share the thought with him but I'm past the point of self-control. Every bit of my body is on *fire*.

"Do you permit?" he asks, his voice low and rough in my head. I pant, shivering with need. I feel a pull toward him that I can't deny. But I still barely know him. He feels that doubt and leans away.

"I—"

BANG, BANG, BANG. I'm about to respond when someone knocks on the door so hard it rattles.

"Ama, are you there? Hello?" Dyana whisper-yells, frantic.

"Ama?" another voice calls. Shit, Mirielle is with her too.

"Godsdamnit." Os growls, leaning forward, forehead leaning into mine as his lips brush mine again in a kiss so light and gentle that it warms me more than the fire next to me. His lips taste of fae wine, and before I can even react or process what the fuck is happening, he leans forward and pulls my bottom lip into his mouth, sucking on me like I'm some nectar-covered fruit. A moan falls from my lips before I can help it, and then it's over before it even begins, but the taste of him still lingers. My eyes close as I inhale and process the loss of his presence, my heart racing.

"Ms. Arkos, Ms. Zenyth, what a surprise," Os says sardonically as he opens the door, but Dyana shoves her way in, Dark hair loose and falling against her back. Mirielle follows close behind, her curly red hair pulled back in a bun. The latter looks distinctly uncomfortable to be in Os' room.

"You do realize the risks of all of you being here. How do you know you weren't followed?" He snaps before taking a breath, trying to get his breathing under control. "Although I can't say I'm entirely surprised. You three do stick to each other like lichens."

"Did you just call us parasites?" I ask, aghast.

"Yes, I did." he says matter of factly. I go to yell at him but Dyana interrupts.

"I may be human, but I'm not an idiot. I made sure I wasn't followed."

"She's right," Mirielle agrees, standing next to Dyana, both having changed into their training clothes. "We went out a side entrance and weren't followed. I assure you."

That's interesting.

"Wait, wait, wait." Dyana looks at me, interested. "Where are your clothes, Ama?" She gestures to the oversized shirt. "Where is your dress? And why is your hair all wet?" Dyana pauses, eyes going wide before she smirks. "Oh, I see. Come on, Mirielle; we can talk with them in the morning. I think we interrupted something." Dyana winks at me, over theatrical, so everyone notices.

Gods, kill me now.

"Shut. Up." I hiss. She just smiles and winks, obviously at me. Gods help me from pestering little sisters. She goes to say something else, and I quickly walk over and put my palm over her mouth.

"Os knows, Dy." She goes still under my hand, eyes wide before she focuses on Os with fury. "He figured out I'm Arkaydian."

"Holy shit." Mirielle gasps and looks at me with wide eyes. "You're Arkaydian?"

Well, that's just fucking great. The number of people who know about me just doubled.

I look at Dyana. All of the blood has rushed out of her face as she looks at me with panicked eyes. I exhale and try to rein in my anger.

It's not her fault. Don't take it out on her. I remind myself. If Os can hear, he doesn't say.

I look down at my hands. "Yes," I reply carefully.

Dyana stares Os down like she's trying to kill him with her eyes.

"I'm not going to tell anyone, Dyana Arkos—" Os pauses as Dyana glares harder, but I remove my hand, and she crosses her arms, untrusting.

"—*If* Amalia agrees to train her magyk with me so that she doesn't almost get you all killed again," Os finishes.

I scoff. Of course there's an *if*. There always is.

Dyana's face turns red, "You're blackmailing her? You asshole!"

I turn to Os, eyebrow raised, "She's not wrong—and I did *not* almost get you all killed."

Os stares at me, his eyes cold, "Did you feel the babies die, yes or no?"

Mirielle and Dyana blink, looking at me in shock.

I grind my teeth and admit the words around tight, angry lips, "I felt everything." My voice croaks, hoarse with grief and fury.

"Gods, Ama!" Dyana gasps, "You can't torture yourself like that."

"They were alone, Dyana!" I snap. "I couldn't let them die alone!" Dyana looks guilty, and Mirielle glances down at the floor uncomfortably. "I don't seek out danger, but I also can't just ignore everything in front of me. It's just too much to ask of me, Dy. I can do it all except that. If I can't save them, the least I can do is cushion their fear and pain. I accept that burden and the weight it carries, and I don't need anyone to help me with it."

Os speaks up, "This is why you need to train. You had no control over your magyk back there, did you? You couldn't help but bond them."

I grind my teeth, glaring at him, "Yes." I bite out.

Dyana sighs, "Shit."

Os shrugs, "I won't tell anyone if you decide not to train with me, but I won't need to. You will out yourself before the Gauntlet even starts."

I stare at the wall, refusing to look at him.

"This is awkward," Dyana breathes. "Is he right, Ama?

"I don't know," I admit.

Dyana turns and looks at Os again as she crosses her arms. "Nothing is happening until you prove we can trust you. So, prove it."

"I have no desire to see Amalia dead, and my loyalties are my own." he replies coldly.

"But what's in it for you?" I ask, meeting Os's gaze.

"I seek knowledge. There's much about Arkaydians I don't understand, and this could be the last opportunity I have to gain more knowledge about them, as it's likely you're the last living one."

It's a silly answer, yet, I understand. When we first entered the room, I noticed a few built-in stone shelves next to his bed were loaded with books in different languages; he must be a reader, like me.

"And you have no other choice," he adds finally.

He's not wrong. Dyana looks at me with a question in her eyes. I take a deep breath and run through things quickly, considering every possible way this could go wrong. After a few moments, I open my eyes and face Os.

"Okay. I'll train with you, but only if you give us extra fighting lessons and help us win the Gauntlet."

"I can't guarantee you'll win," he responds as if I'm an idiot.

"I'm aware. But we're going to train harder than anyone else here, and you're going to help us do it."

Os sighs, realizing what he's getting into.

"We are?" Dyana asks, but we ignore her.

"Fine. Three times a week, I'll give you all extra fighting lessons, but Amalia, you're here every day afterward. We have a little over four weeks to do this."

"Gods, my legs are going to fall right off," Mirielle mutters.

"How are you going to make sure nobody gets suspicious? Isn't it weird that you'll just be suddenly training us privately?" I ask, considering the blowback.

"I'm in charge here. They do as I say, and I say you three are such shit fighters you need extra instruction just to ensure you make it to the opening ceremony alive."

Great.

"Amalia, you'll train with me daily and learn to control your magyk, because if you lose control in the Gauntlet, you'll lose. Not because a Dragon eats you or another candidate kills you, but because the High Council will slit your throat before you can take your next breath. And your friend?" He looks over at Dyana, an eyebrow raised. "You, Ms. Arkos; you will be interrogated and tortured, your skin will be peeled from your body, and your nails pulled off, and when you're just about to break, you'll tell them every single thing you know about Amalia. And then when they're done with you, they'll kill you and feed your corpse to the Dragons." He says it so casually, but each word shoots icy fear into my veins, and my chest tightens as the horrible images he just described fly through my head.

He's right. He's right, and I *fucking hate it*. I *hate* this place.

"Fine," I say gratingly, ready for this conversation to be over.

"So what's the name of our alliance? The fearsome four?" Dyana asks, poking at Os. Mirielle is just stunned and quiet next to her.

I'm not sure I fully trust Mirielle, but I have no choice now. Her gray eyes meet my own, and she nods, kindness entering her gaze.

"This plan better work, Os," I say while Dyana considers more ways to annoy Os and make him even grumpier than he already is.

"It will." Os's smokey voice purrs through my head.

I hope he's right—our lives depend on it.

"I TELL YOU THIS.
I WANT IT ALL TO HURT."

— Dante Alighieri, 1265–1321.
The Divine Comedy: Inferno

SCAN FOR THE PT. 2
READING PLAYLIST

PART TWO:

THE FORGOTTEN

CHAPTER 15

"Get back in your fucking stall!" The fae handler pokes me with his forked prodding poles; the sharp points dig into my hard scales as they scream so hard I flinch. Pain flares across my pelt.

The ache in my body is never-ending. Every move sends aching pains through my bones and joints. The pain is a constant—there's no reprieve.

Every morning when I wake up, I wish for release. But centuries of desperate prayers have gone unanswered. No matter how much I ask for relief from this wretched world, Great Livyathin does not answer.

The chains wrapping around my ankles clank loudly while they rub my scales raw as I limp into the tiny metal box the pointed ones call my "stall".

This is no stall, no home—this is a prison and we're all waiting to die.

The pointed one pokes me again, and I yelp in pain as, this time, the prongs slide in between two scale plates, puncturing my skin. They know exactly where to make it hurt. Blood wells, the heat intermingling with the stinging pain of the open wound. Yet another scar to join the hundreds that slash and decorate my body.

I would growl at him and fight back harder, but I'm so tired.

"God, I can't wait until someone kills that one. Fucking meat bag." I hear the pointed one snarl and spit the words. His hot, noxious breath hits my nostrils, and I grimace. The fae have always smelled wrong, but some were nauseating. The two attendants unlock my metal muzzle. My scales are permanently damaged from the hundreds of hours spent wearing that torture device. My throat is dry and painful, and I desperately drink down water in the trough at the far corner of my stall. Threadbare straw coats the scratched, freezing stone floor. A small window with bars sits at the front of the stall and on either side of the walls, but it is so difficult trying to maneuver in this tiny space I rarely used it.

In the early days, I spoke to my neighbors. Dragons who were once my friends, my family.

They're all dead now. The stalls used to be stacked, the cavern packed tightly with Dragons. It is so much quieter now. Only a few dozen of us left, which is why my tormentors have been taking us to their dark, twisted labs, experimenting on us. I'm not even sure what has been done to me. So often, I wake up, and there's a new scar. But the testing makes me nauseous, so despite my large bulk, shivers constantly wrack my thin body.

"Hopefully the bitch is put in the Gauntlet this year," his companion laughs viciously.

"Good. I've been craving a nice Dragon roast," my handler replies.

The metal door is slammed shut behind me, closing me into my barely lit jail. It is so cramped, more so for older Dragons like me. I can't fully stretch my wings and have to crouch down; otherwise, I hit my head on the ceiling.

This is my prison, and I will die here, wasting away with four metal walls as my only companions.

I huff sadly, the collar at my neck spelled to prevent my fire from getting hot enough to use, but smoke still trails into the air. I watch for a few moments, making shapes in the smoke the way my mother taught me. I try to remember her, but the details are foggy. Her knowledge is mine, as it is for all female Dragons. We inherit the memories of our foremothers. But after centuries of searching for something, some way to get us out, I stopped looking for answers; for there are none.

I painfully curl into a corner, my tail wrapped around me for warmth. My left arm reaches out, popping and cracking as I gather some straw to rest my head on. It's uncomfortable but better than just the floor.

The noise a few stalls down alerts me, one of my stallmates is being taken for their daily appointment.

The fae is unable to hear them; few beings other than a Dragon can. My kin cry, singing a mournful song in our lilting, bell-like language; a song of death.

Every day I break a little more.

No, breaking is too tame of a word—it's a shattering of self and soul. If the fae don't kill me soon, I will do it myself. Better die by my own claw than at the hands of pure evil.

I don't even remember how long I've been here. These days, any chance I get, I escape to my dreams, where wide open blue skies await, and I can sail through the clouds with the wind on my face. I've forgotten what it tastes like, the fresh air, the clouds. But as I wait for the day my death finally releases me to fly with my brothers and sisters, I pretend.

CHAPTER 16
AMALIA

Oof.

The breath is knocked out of my lungs as I hit the hard ground for what has to be the hundredth time today. Loose dirt flies up my nose and into my mouth.

"Try harder," Os barks from the side of the training room.

"You don't have to be such an ass about it," Dyana hisses. Os ignores her.

"She's fine, and more importantly, she's still holding back," he says, looking at me pointedly. I let him know exactly what I think of that and flip him off.

"You know," I groan as I push to standing, "I know this might be shocking to hear, but I don't enjoy this."

"And I don't care," he says plainly.

"Yeah, we can tell," Dyana mutters and I fight a snicker.

"We go again," I call to Os, wiping my face on the bloody fabric of my hand wraps. In the background, Dyana shakes her head and mutters about my idiotic tendency to go overboard and hurt myself. Os just walks forward and crosses his arms. Dyana and I tried fighting each other in training, but Dy just kept laughing and couldn't take it seriously.

Os also separated our training time, with Dyana and Mirielle going first against him, and me last. He's been sparring nonstop for the entire day, and yet the male has barely broken a sweat.

"Take me down," he orders, cocking his head and assessing me with a brief squint, "unless you're too weak and tired, then we can stop for the day."

Damnit. I snarl internally and externally, anger immediately stoked and blood heating. I slowly circle him, keeping him always in my sight. I fake him out and go to punch him, which he blocks, and I immediately hammer his side with another punch. He doesn't even grunt, and I spin away.

"Is that what you call trying hard?" he scoffs. "You not only have to kill all of the other candidates, but you also have to kill a Dragon and survive an entire Gauntlet. Stop fucking around!" He punches my head, making my ears ring and my jaw ache. I bite my tongue accidentally, and hot, metallic blood floods my mouth.

"Oh, you're gonna get it now." I hear Dyana say from the side of the room.

"Yeah, this doesn't bode well." Mirielle agrees, both of them covered in dirt and bruises. I turn my attention back to the asshole magyka in front of me.

"You're holding back, too," I say with a bloody smile and spit at his feet.

"If I didn't hold back, you would be dead," he says matter of factly.

"Let's find out, shall we?" I challenge, rich anger boiling my blood and shredding my control.

I dart forward and fake left, kicking his legs out from under him when I lurch to the right. Os goes down hard but the world turns upside down as he grabs my shoulders and yanks me down with him. I land hard on my back with a gasp and Os rolls himself on top of me. I buck and try to shove him off, but he's as heavy as a damn boulder and doesn't move in the slightest, so I try another method, headbutting him and smashing my skull into his nose, shattering it and making myself see stars.

"Hard-headed asshole," I groan. Even in my head, he feels like heat and smoke.

"Pay attention," is all he says back, grabbing his nose and cracking it into place with a loud crunch. Fuck me, that sounded painful. He shakes it off so easily.

An idea strikes me out of nowhere.

"Again," I say, rising to a sparring position. Os nods and blurs, appearing in front of me. But as he goes to punch me, I go completely limp. He catches me on an instinct I'm banking on, and I'm left pulled tight against his chest. As I open my eyes and look up at him, I arch my back lightly, rubbing against him. His pupils dilate, and I swear those molten gold eyes glow for a moment. His dark brown hair falls into my face as some strands escape the tie holding it back.

I meet his gaze with a wicked smile and he tenses as I arch into him again. Something grows hard against my leg, something large. While he's distracted, I maneuver my legs into the right position to heave his bulk to the side, rolling us so I'm straddling him. A fact which he doesn't look too disappointed about, based on the smug glint in his gold eyes. But he doesn't hold back; he just grinds into me slowly before launching a brutal punch to my sternum that sends me flying. The breath leaves my lungs as I hit the ground hard and groan.

"I hate you," I snarl, and he smirks.

"Stop holding back, Amalia. Stop letting your fear rule you!"

I get up and spit out some blood—must have bit my tongue when I hit the ground.

"I am not afraid!" I hiss back as I lower my shoulders and sink my weight into my core and legs, sprinting at him with a roar. He just steps aside, but I already knew he was going to do that, so I just shift my arms and grab his left one, yanking it backward until it's bent uncomfortably and he's on the ground. I don't even give him a warning; I just pull, popping the shoulder out of the socket. But I'll never admit aloud how difficult it was to even lift one of his huge arms.

"I am not *afraid.*" Spit falls from my mouth with every word. But a tiny part of me screams *liar, liar, liar.* I've been afraid for so long I don't know how else to exist. Os just *hmms* as he stands casually with only a minor grimace, and his arm makes some alarming cracking and popping noises as we all watch, eyes wide, as his shoulder pops back into place.

"Okay, that's just too weird," Dyana admits, "and we need to get to training with Ireyna on time. No need to give her extra reasons to beat our asses, so I'll leave you two to..." Dyana waves her hands towards us, "I don't know, whatever this weird brand of foreplay is. But please try not to break my best friend too hard." She winks in my direction.

"Dyana!" I hiss, but she just turns and walks away, the little shit. My cheeks are on fire as I get up.

In most situations, we refer to each other just as best friends. If the situation was serious, we would revert to our truer relationship as adopted sisters. There was nothing official, nor did we share a last name, but the scar on our palms marks us as family. Whatever we call each other, that fact never changed. And sometimes she was just a little shit.

Os had already decided it would be the least suspicious if Dyana and Mirielle continued training with the others as well, so we only separated from the others a few times a week, lessening the amount of questions. Dyana and Mirielle would now go back to sparring with Ireyna , leaving Os and I to head to his rooms for magyk training.

"You have the shielding skills of a child," Os says, disgusted with my attempt at keeping him from my mind.

"And you're an asshole. Are we finished reciting facts now?" I ask, frustrated at my lack of progress. It's humbling to be reminded how much I don't know, and that humble feeling quickly turns to grief.

We're seated in front of the fire on the floor, facing each other. Runes in an ancient language I don't recognize are drawn onto the floor with chalk, forming a circle around us.

"I didn't even have to try to get into your mind, Amalia. It was out there for anyone to get a hold of. But more importantly, you felt the Dragon die because you automatically opened yourself to it and created a bond. You should be able to resist that urge. What are you, twenty-something? How is it you don't even know how to shield properly?"

I sniff, "Thank you for the reminder of my stark inadequacies. Some of us aren't privileged enough to have a teacher at all. Some of us were supposed to have teachers, but then the fae murdered them. So how about instead of commenting on how terrible my magyk skills are, you actually help me so that I don't have to go through a godsdamn conversation like this again!"

Os gazes at me with a strange look on his face. Respect, maybe. But there isn't a drop of pity, and for that, I am thankful. The last thing I want right now is someone's pity.

"Let's start at the beginning, then," Os nods, quickly moving on. I exhale and try to listen. "Many beings in our world can harness a power called magyk, with the exception of humans. For some, their magyk manifests as the ability to change shapes, and some get mastery over elemental powers."

"Okay, I appreciate it, but I know this part already."

"Shh." Os bops me on the nose like a naughty cat. I sputter for a moment, unable to believe he just did that. He continues, "All magyk is either active or passive, never both. But Arkaydians are one of the only species ever known to have the ability to use both passive and active magyk at once. They—and you—are essentially magyk reservoirs. Because you're constantly burning magyk off passively, you must store massive amounts to support the active use."

As he continues, I wrap my arms around my legs and rest my chin on my knees.

"The only other known species with this quality are elves, Dragons, and imperial fae. Tell me, do you know why there are both fae and imperial fae?"

"I know the imperial fae have greater power and are always royals."

"That's true, but you're also wrong. Imperial fae use magyk they shouldn't. Somehow, whether from the Dragons they consume or through more sinister methods, imperial fae possess both types of magyk as well. But fae do not."

I ponder his words, suspicion growing in my mind. "But they're the same species?"

"Yes, they are. Sometime later, we can discuss the how and why, but the important thing to note is that this particular instance of magyk is unnatural. The imperial fae possessing both types of magyk is a perversion of nature. And you are the very opposite."

I blink, surprised.

"Arkaydians are in sync with nature. Your powers feed life and magyk back into the world, and your empathy means you have no ego."

"My sister would disagree with you on that," I mutter. A ghost of a smile appears on Os' face, shocking me.

"What do you think your powers are?" His question catches me off guard and I blink, thinking. I still don't trust him, so this would need to be handled delicately. I can't zone out daydreaming about his stupidly handsome face.

"I can nudge animals."

"Nudge? Elaborate."

"I can push my will onto them. Or, my feelings, I guess. When I open up that...path, an animal can feel my emotions, and I theirs."

"You're an empath."

I frown, brow scrunching. "No, it's more like telepathy."

"I'm not asking you, I'm telling you. This is your passive power, which is extremely rare. Telepathy is a skill, it's simply contact. You're an empath because you go a step further into actual energy transfers. But you don't even have to try when you're bonded with another mind. It's not just animals either; you can do it with people, you just haven't realized yet. Animals are easier to connect with, and their minds are simpler, which is probably why you learned to do it so young. Now you get to learn the rest."

I nod and let out a long breath. I didn't know that. There's so much I never learned, and Virgyl could only fill in so many gaps.

"Ok. Well, I have the animal part down."

"First, you block me from your mind." I roll my eyes at that smokey voice. Even though he sits across from me, the touch of his mind on mine feels as intimate as a kiss. It sears my nerve endings and sends tingling down my arms.

"From what I know, it's different for all Arkaydians. Even though many magyka and demis have some degree of mental powers, your magyk is much different. But you're essentially going to barricade your mind. When I learned how to do this, I would always imagine a thick metal wall lining my mind. No one can come in without my permission. I can reach out and speak into your mind, but you can't enter mine."

"Show off."

"Try imagining a stone wall, and you build it up block by block. Or two doors locked together and bound from opening. Thicken and curl them around your mind," Os says.

And then, in my mind, Os begins to sing.

My eyes pop open, and my jaw drops as a gorgeous voice fills my thoughts.

"Pay attention," he snaps. I close my eyes again but, woah. The words are in a language I don't understand, but I can feel the sadness in the song.

I shake off the haunting sounds bouncing inside my head and concentrate on those two iron doors locked deep inside me.

These are not the walls he was talking about; I wonder if he notices them.

But I'm alone; the singing is far away now. I smooth the dents and scratches out before ascending to the top of my dark, starless abyss of a mind. I sink my consciousness into feeling the edges of the space. It's all liquid, but I keep going until I feel the edge, where my mind ends. I flood the space with smoke until a thick fog encircles everything. I continue, layering and layering until it changes, solidifying and turning to dense metal. I close the last tiny hole in the wall, and the music stops.

The silence is deafening. I pry open my dry eyes to find Os watching me, arms resting on his knees.

"Good." Os nods. "Now, do it again."

"Again? Gods, give me a moment. My eyes are so damn dry."

"Well, you were out for a few hours."

"Excuse me?" I turn, confused.

"You were in there for a few hours, Amalia. Time moves differently in the mental sphere. Still, you were rather slow. I did it in half an hour my first time."

Gods, I want to punch him. He rolls to the side, propping his head up on one arm as he gazes at me, the firelight dancing against his skin, making his eyes look like molten gold ore.

I uncross my legs and wince at the stiffness and feeling of blood rushing back into place. Tingles break out across my body, and I lightly tap my feet against the floor, adjusting to the feel.

"Well, it sure didn't feel like hours," I mutter, going to stand, swaying.

A blur heads towards me as he catches me, my legs giving out.

"Gods. Don't let me be in there so long next time," I say grumpily.

"Why are you cranky?"

"Well, apparently it's been hours, and I'm hungry." My mood continues to sour, and frustration simmers.

"Ah—" He blurs, suddenly standing over me and bending down as he hoists me in his arms. I let out a very undignified screech as he tosses me up and carries me to the living area, setting me down in a soft brown chair, surprisingly gentle with his touch. Os squeezes the hand curled around my waist before letting me go, cold fingers brushing the skin above my waistband. Shocks roll through my body—the cold is so nice against my hot skin. My mouth falls open lightly, but he lets me go before I can do much more, and I immediately miss the touch.

I chide myself. Clearly, food is needed. I dig into the large platter on the coffee table, full of fruits, meats, and nuts.

"You eat like a feral boar," Os says, shocked. I grab an almond and ping it at him, catching him in the eye.

He snarls as it hits him.

I flash him a saccharine smile, "There's nothing wrong with a healthy appetite."

He still looks sexy even while glaring at me, "I never said there was anything wrong with it. I would simply prefer the food goes in your mouth, rather than my face."

We fall silent as he grabs a book and sits next to me, reading while I finish eating.

Os huffs. "Well done. For the past few minutes, I've been trying to speak to you mentally, but was unable to form a bond." he says with a hint of a smile, his golden eyes luminous.

My heart thumps hard at that peek of a smile from him, and I ignore it dutifully.

"I want to speak to you, how do I open up just that channel?" I ask.

"Good question. You essentially program your wall or whatever you're using to our unique signatures. There should be some sort of tinge—maybe a scent or even a taste—unique to that person. Every being has this. You're going to infuse your wall with whatever this unique element is, creating a pathway through it." He looks down at all of the food still left. "Take a few minutes, get something to drink, use the restroom, and then let's try again, and this time, infuse your wall with both of our signatures."

"We're doing all of this again?" I mutter weakly.

"Oh yes," Os says before popping a strawberry into his mouth. I turn and walk away, but the image of his full lips pursed around a strawberry with the juice dripping down his face will be seared into my retinas for the rest of my life.

CHAPTER 17
DYANA

"Ow!" I gasp as Mirielle's wooden practice sword slams into my back, causing pain to bolt up my spine.

"Shit, sorry," Mirielle says under her breath. We agreed that we would take this seriously, but what Ireyna doesn't know won't kill her—*unfortunately.*

"Pay attention to your surroundings. Listen for the movement in the air and the crunch of dirt under their footsteps." Ireyna orders from the sideline as Mirielle and I pause our sparring. We're both panting hard and sweaty, hair plastered against our foreheads.

"How are you so good at this?" I ask between heavy breaths.

Mirielle just shrugs, "We all have things we excel at where others don't. I've got two left feet when it comes to dancing." I chuckle, imagining her tripping all over herself. She continues, "Plus, we've only been doing this for what, a little over a week?"

"Alright, that's true. It just comes so naturally to you and Amalia," I say, trying to hide my resentment of their inherent skills.

Mirielle looks thoughtful, "Think of it like a dance. The sword," she motions to the wooden practice sword, "or whichever weapon you like best, is your tool. But the movements are all a dance between two people."

I blink. I hadn't thought of that before.

"Enough chit-chat, let's go!" Ireyna barks from the sidelines and Mirielle and I both roll our eyes.

"When we get out of this, I'll teach you how to dance," I whisper, and our eyes meet for a moment. When her gray-green eyes meet mine, so wide and honest, it feels like she can see right through my walls. We assume ready positions on the opposite sides of our small sparring circle.

Today I'm practicing defensive moves while Mirielle is working on offense. We switch back and forth daily, and since Ama has private training with Os—something Ireyna is none too happy about based on the permanent sneer on her face—I get to partner with Mirielle. Her own trainer moved to help some of the other candidates who needed additional training.

Honestly, they don't care much for the rules here. As long as we save our lives for the Gauntlet so that the High Council can get entertainment from our gloriously violent deaths, they don't care what we do.

Luckily for us, Os has the final say. But that doesn't mean the other trainers are happy about it, and Ireyna is taking her frustration out on the two of us. We're not using real swords yet but blisters already coat my palms. The pain is constant, not something new. So I've been doing what I do best—ignoring it.

"Begin," Ireyna calls. I take a deep breath and watch as Mirielle stalks forward, eyes sharp and wooden sword raised. I analyze her movements and circle to the right, walking backward to keep her in my line of sight. She sprints forward with a yell before raising her sword and bringing it down toward my side. I sidestep further into the center of the circle and avoid it, but Mirielle quickly recovers and walks back towards me again, going to repeat the move but on my other side. I sidestep again, but she fakes me out, tripping me with her extended foot.

I go ass-first into the hard dirt, sending a bolt of pain up my tailbone. Mirielle raises her sword with both hands as she approaches me. I try to scramble up just as she goes to bring it down on my shoulder—the kill shot in this instance. Dirt and rocks dig into my palms, but I quickly push to standing, breathing heavily now. I finally bring my sword up and meet Mirielle's next blow, my arm vibrating with the force.

She smiles as her gray eyes meet mine, both of us with red cheeks and sweat dripping down our foreheads.

Despite the depressing reason we're here, I'll admit—I'm having fun sparring with Mirielle. I've never been a fighter, and I know I'm still not the best at it. I might never be. But Gods, getting sweaty with Mirielle and playing is actually exciting. Every time I successfully laid a kill shot on her or managed to defend myself is like a shot of pure adrenaline. But the constant close contact drives me insane, and the sweat from our hot bodies makes her citrusy scent even stronger. It's taking all of my self control not to kiss her—and more.

But I'm still not sure she likes me in that way. After that moment in the alcove, the dreaded night of the ball, nothing has happened.

We parry back and forth a few times before I switch and go on the attack. This time when she tries to bring her sword down on my right oblique, I block and take her moment of pause to kick her in the chest, sending her flying down to the dirt. I'm above her before she can get up, bringing my sword down on her chest.

"Dead," I say, panting.

Mirielle laughs, "Yes! That was perfect, Dy!"

Mirielle landed hard on her back, so I reach my hand out and help her up. We're almost nose to nose when she finally makes it to standing, we're both panting and smiling, but then the rush of noise from the other candidates finishing their own bouts for the day rolls in—we're not alone.

I dim my smile slightly and take a small step back. Did I imagine the hurt in Mirielle's eyes? Or was that real? I fight my rising guilt and need to explain myself. But my thoughts are interrupted by Ireyna.

"Congratulations, you almost did well." The tall, black-haired woman sneers at us. Her almond eyes are sharp and fierce. "We go again tomorrow," she looks down her nose at us with a sniff, "if you don't progress faster, you're going to die on round one." With that, she walks away, and we limp along, depositing our wooden swords into a large bucket by the door with the rest of the weary candidates.

"So helpful," I mutter.

"That's a kind way of putting it." Mirielle laughs. "Ireyna is awful—and every muscle in my entire body hurts. Don't listen to her though, you're doing great." She chuckles again with a cough.

"Same. I think my body is going to permanently be in pain now. I'm too sore. There is no coming back from it. This is just our life now."

"Ugh."

"So, how did you and Amalia meet, exactly?" Mirielle and I are in her room, sitting on one of the beds. Mirielle sits on the floor atop a pillow from her non-existent partner's bed while I lounge against the pillows. The room itself is identical to mine and Ama's, so much so it was a little jarring at first. Since Ama will be in magyk training for the rest of the day until dinner, we have an hour or so to just rest.

"It's a long story," I answer, not sure I'm ready to delve into my past that much.

"I would say something about having plenty of time, but I guess that's not entirely true, is it?" Mirielle says softly. She's mending some holes in her uniforms with a small sewing kit she brought with her. All of the candidates were only given four sets of clothes. It seems like a lot, but the air is cold and damp down here so nothing dries quickly. We all do our laundry with a small bar of soap in the tiny bathroom, but everything takes a few days to dry.

I wish I could say I knew how to sew, but beside her uniforms are my finished ones. Mirielle insisted on doing mine too, despite lots of loud, frantic protests that she shouldn't. She smiled softly, grabbed my uniform, and sat atop a pillow on the floor, her head next to mine.

I'm lying back in bed, reading one of the two books I brought. Old, worn books that Amalia stole for me when I was still a young girl. I had others in my room at the Birdcage, but these were my first books, the most special. So I kept them in my emergency bag, just in case the worst happened. After reading an exciting chapter about a mermaid luring sailors to their deaths with her haunting voice, I put down my book. This book is what made me fall in love with the idea of the ocean. I've never seen it, only lakes and rivers. But the way it's described in the book is so beautiful.

Mirielle hums lightly as the firelight from the melting candles strewn across the room flickers, drawing shadows against her face. Her deft, nimble fingers work quickly, handling the needle easily as she patches the holes we scraped into our uniforms.

"You're really good at that." *Oh my Gods, Dyana, what kind of comment is that? Shut up!* I clear my throat awkwardly, "Sewing, I mean. Ama can do some but when I tried, I just kept poking myself with the needle." I laugh nervously.

Mirielle glances to the side with a smile. "Confession? The pads of my fingers are pretty numb from poking myself too many times when I was younger. It happens now too. I think that's part of why fighting comes naturally; my hands are calloused and hardened from all of the years of needlework." Mirielle pauses and holds up her hand. In the candlelight, I can see the callouses and marks. But it's so light and subtle, that I wouldn't notice otherwise. Before I can contemplate what a bad idea this is, I grab her hand and feel the callouses. Mirielle gasps lightly and I pretend the sound doesn't light my body on fire. The calluses are still soft. I didn't even notice when she held my hand before.

"Sounds painful, I'm sorry, Mir." She stiffens, blinking, and I panic. "Oh, uh—sorry. I should have asked before calling you that."

Mirielle smiles, clasping her hand around mine, "Don't apologize. My mother used to call me that. I haven't heard it in a long time, is all." Mirielle's eyes go distant as she disappears in memory for a moment.

"Still, I'm sorry it brings up bad memories."

"Stop apologizing!" Mirielle laughs, "It's not bad, just distant. Somedays it feels like yesterday that I lost her, but as time goes on, it gets...less painful. It makes me miss her, but it also reminds me of her." She looks down at her other hand, contemplating. "The memories wash away with the passing of the tides. The smell of my mother's hair, the sound of her voice. I remember a voice, but...the specifics are fading." She pauses and meets my gaze. "I'm thankful for the reminder."

"Sounds like you two were really close." There's no jealousy in my voice, and I'm happy for her, truly. But Amalia and Mirielle both had such wonderful families. Have clear memories of them. I went to three different families before I was adopted by Mr. and Mrs. Arkos. I was only with them for a year before they were killed. Still, they were pleasant, kind people. But it just felt like living with relatives, not parents.

The parent-child relationship is something I will never experience. I want to understand how Mirielle feels, but all I can do is listen.

"My mother is the one who taught me how to sew. I didn't like it much at first, but I always did it with her, so it became a source of comfort once she was gone." Mirielle bites her lip and lets go of my hand as she moves on to the next pair of pants, finishing her patch with a tight knot and biting the thread.

"How old were you when...?" I let my words fade out as I pretend to get back into my book.

"I was seventeen. She was sick for a long time—the plague." Mirielle pauses briefly. "My family petitioned the High Council for the antidote. It's given out in a lottery system, and there's never enough each time for everyone. They need people to stay sick, otherwise, there would be no demand. We lost the lottery every time. After three rounds, it was too late. No medicine would help." Mirielle sighs, "So she left us. I held her hand as she went into the Mother's embrace. I often wonder if she took a part of me with her. I haven't felt complete since."

It was the story for so many in Ur Daoine these days. A century ago, a great plague swept across the kingdom. The High Council quickly came up with an antidote, but apparently the ingredients are quite rare, so there's a limited supply.

"I'm so sorry," I whisper.

"It's not your fault, but thank you nonetheless." She nods and smiles. I know she's only one year older than me, but Mirielle carries herself with the confidence and wisdom of someone much older.

We fall silent as we each disappear into our own worlds in the hour we have left until dinner. But I can't help the thoughts that run through my head on a loop.

The High Council has taken everything from us.

Amalia's parents. My foster parents. Mirielle's mother.

Everyone, every single person I've ever met in Ur Daoine has lost someone due to the High Council's selfish cruelty.

Yet here we all are, despite all that they've done to us. Here we all are, waiting to die.

CHAPTER 18
AMALIA

It took another three lessons, but I've finally got mental blocks down. After a whole week of training, not just my body but my rarely used magyk, I'm dead to the world. Yesterday, Os practically had to carry me back to the dorms after our lesson. Dyana freaked out and pestered me with questions when I showed up with him half-holding me up, but I was so exhausted I fell right into a dark, dreamless sleep and stayed that way, completely missing out on the one day off a week we get.

I had planned to ride Taran, but my body and mind gave out. The next evening I woke up in the dark, disoriented and unsure of what day or time it was. Despite Os's warning about eating, skipping dinner and falling back asleep was too tempting, so that's exactly what I did.

Despite my lengthy sleep, today's run was equally brutal. Working with magyk is mentally exhausting, and when combined with my already tired body, I could pass for a corpse. Which is fitting, I suppose, since I'm drowning in the weight of my guilt and grief for not being able to see Taran.

I love animals, but what makes me deserve their love in return? I'm not a good person—something which Dyana absolutely hates hearing. But she doesn't know the whole truth. She knows most of it...but not everything.

My gray hair is tangled in a messy, half-undone braid from sleep, so I quickly rebraid it. Winter is finally hitting Castael Laryn, so I wrap my black scarf around my head, protecting my ears from the cold wind.

My braid smacks painfully against my back as we complete our morning run. I'm lagging behind Dyana and Mirielle today, still groggy from sleep. We're the last to finish, all breathing heavily. My side aches with splints as I bend over at the waist, my hands on my thighs as I catch my breath.

Because of the private training before my one-on-one magyk lessons with Os, I see Dyana less and less, and she's spending more time with Mirielle in return.

Deep down inside me, past my iron walls, a tiny, lonely part of me is jealous of their growing connection. Not because I feel romantic with Dyana in any way, shape, or form, I have and always will see her as a sister and friend—and I also had to remind myself that Dyana doesn't have to have just one friend. Just because I only have one friend doesn't mean she has to do the same. My inability to make friends is due to my prickly demeanor and permanently angry face...among other things.

I sigh into my breakfast. Os announced that tomorrow our run will be longer. Endurance is a struggle for all of us since we're still building muscle, so we will also start getting a second, later lunch.

I'm still not sure that another lunch makes up for the increasing misery of these runs.

Our meals aren't anything special, just porridge and occasionally some mystery meat and vegetables. I force myself not to imagine where said mystery meat comes from. We're all burning energy like crazy with how hard we were all working out.

Dyana and Mirielle join two of my training sessions with Os each week, and the other two were just me. We do extra strength training and then sparring. On the days they join, I spar last, which means I get a brief break to sit down and catch my breath after our strength training.

We're officially into our second full week here, and I'm getting anxious. We have three more weeks of training, but it starts so soon.

Of the two days off we'd had so far, I slept the entire day, missing meal times. Dyana kindly snuck a bowl out for me each time, leaving it on the nightstand in case I woke.

Training has become a blur, and time has become a figment of my imagination, yet the weight of the upcoming Gauntlet is breaking me. Ever since seeing Achan, my night terrors have returned, each night waking up screaming as Dyana looks around worried. She's exhausted, too, which causes me endless guilt, but we are all in the same boat. Mirielle hasn't fared any better. She's gaining muscle too, her curves more prominent, but her body is covered in bruises, and she groans as she stands up next to me.

"Gods, I would kill for a bath," Dyana bemoans.

"Seriously, even my tits are sore. That shouldn't be possible!" Mirielle agrees.

"Yeah, I'm sore in places I never thought could even get sore," I add.

"Oh?" Dyana raises an eyebrow at me, and we both get up, joining Mirielle with equal groans of pain. "Does Os make you sore there?" she says cheekily. I swat her with my napkin, making her giggle.

"Gods, I wish," I say honestly, and they crack up in return.

"Ama, you should make a move!" Mirielle whispers conspiratorially.

"Oh, come on, not you too." I groan, making them laugh again.

"Mirielle is right, Ama, and you know it. He's so hot! He's got that whole grumpy and scary yet sexy thing going on. And if we're about to die, you might as well go down freshly fucked." Dyana nods. Mirielle looks a little shell-shocked at the mention of sex, and then her cheeks flush as she quickly shoots Dyana a glance.

Interesting.

I sigh, "Morrigyn, save me from annoying little sisters."

Dyana just cackles. "You know I'm right," she sings.

"First off, he's our trainer, which makes him off limits—if I was even interested, I mean." Dyana rolls her eyes and I smack her arm. She just sticks her tongue out at me. I clear my throat, continuing, "Second, he works for the fae."

Dyana blinks, "Nope, try again; we know he's just as much of a prisoner here as we are. Is he still an asshole? Yes. But if you're into him, do you have a legitimate reason not to trust him, or are you just being stubborn?"

"I am NOT into him." My words end up muffled as Dyana uses her height against me and smacks her hand on my face, shutting me up. I slap it away, making her giggle.

"I don't even like men, but I know that man is fine as hell. I've also seen you two sparring. The sexual tension between you two is thick enough to cut with one of those dull-ass wooden practice swords." Mirielle snickers in the background but covers it with a cough when I turn and glare at her.

"Sorry, Amalia," she says guiltily, "but Dyana's right."

I sigh, and Dyana continues, "Not all fae are evil. Are most of them horrible? Yes. But that doesn't mean they all are, and we know for certain that Os is not fae. I'm not his biggest fan, but he said he hates them; he's made that clear, and I'm inclined to believe him. I saw the hate in his eyes, which means you did too." I sigh again, frustrated.

I know that, but everything is already so complicated. Yet even as the words pass through my thoughts, an ember inside me burns for him. Needs him, desperately.

I'm just scared of what will happen if that ember catches fire; if I *ignite.*

After another week of training, my mind and body are exhausted. Os has moved on to helping me use my Arkaydian magyk in a more offensive manner, but it's a struggle, so he gave me a few days off.

Tomorrow is our next official day of rest and I can't wait to spend it with Taran.

"What are you going to do tomorrow?" Mirielle asks as we eat our dinner.

"Sleep all day again?" Dyana adds. I kick her underneath the table and she snickers.

I shovel tonight's porridge into my face and lean back in my chair, digesting. "I'm going to spend it with Taran, I miss him and being at the barn so much."

"At least you got to say hi to him yesterday," Dyana says. She and Mirielle came with me after strength training yesterday to see him at the stables near the Dragon Pit. He'd nickered for a whole thirty seconds upon seeing me, and then kept searching my pockets for a spare carrot. To my surprise, Mirielle had saved him a carrot. He kept nuzzling up to her after she fed it to him.

Mirielle is clearly comfortable around horses. Taran kept sending love down our bond as I itched his belly and behind his ears. I had noticed a pulled muscle on his right shoulder, so I also sent him some relaxing thoughts as I massaged it out.

I tried to do it subtly, but couldn't help my smile when Taran yawned, releasing his built up tension once I was finished.

I caught Mirielle giving me a prolonged, odd glance when we made our way back to the Dragon Pit, but I'm sure that was just from the dirt all over me thanks to Taran.

"What about you?" I come back to the present and finally ask the question back to Mirielle.

She shrugs, "I'm not sure, I was thinking about going into town and exploring."

Dyana looks excited at the prospect but I shake my head, "I don't think that's a good idea." Dyana's smile sinks, "It's dangerous out there. Plus you heard what the fae said; we're not guests here. Everyone in the city is going to come watch us die, remember? They want us dead and they enjoy the Gauntlet. Those aren't people to feel safe around."

Dyana nods and Mirielle does too, though they both look let down.

"I'm sorry, it's just not safe."

"You're going out, though," Dyana says, her warm mahogany eyes meeting my own.

"Yeah, outside of the city. I don't want to spend any more time here than I already have to," I mutter.

Dyana drops it, but I can see her disappointment. I want her to be happy, but I also want her alive. It's becoming impossible to have both.

CHAPTER 19
MIRIELLE

"Are you certain?" the male under the hood asks me.

"I've seen and heard enough. She tried to hide it, but yesterday in the barn made it perfectly clear. She's an Arkaydian. You've known me for five decades. You know when I'm lying. If I wasn't certain, I wouldn't have even risked a meeting in the first place," I snap at him, frustrated at the guilt beginning to eat away at me. "Gods, holding back is hard."

"I know the feeling," the hooded male replies. "If you're certain, I'll push for a meeting."

"Wait, really?" I gasp. He's usually much more reserved with decisions like this. Something is speeding up his plans.

"Yes. But I can't stress enough how closely you need to monitor this situation. Nothing happens outside of your notice. And above all—"

I interrupt him, annoyed at another reminder, "Don't get caught, yes I know."

The male catches my wrist, squeezing tightly. I hiss at him as my small fangs descend, but he ignores me as his eyes glare into mine from the black shadows of his hood.

"Don't test me, Mir, not right now." His eyes are dark and abnormally cold. Guilt rises within me.

"Bad night?" I whisper.

He sighs, "When is it not?" Pity sits heavy in my heart at the abuse he's endured for centuries. "This might be the only opportunity we ever get."

"I knew what I was signing up for, Wraith. I will not let this fall into the High Council's hands." The male's grip softens, and I place my hand over his.

"It's more than our own lives on the line if we fail," he reminds me.

"What happens if we succeed?" I rush out, afraid to feel hope.

The tall male sighs. "Let us first focus on what's in front of us. That's the priority."

I nod; he's right. "What of the trainer? We need him on our side and he's not exactly the easiest immortal to deal with."

The male sighs again. "Send up your prayers to whatever God you believe in that he doesn't kill me when I talk to him. The last time we spoke was decades ago, and it didn't exactly end well."

Great, that's just great.

"You handle him; I'll handle them. Her teammate is part of the package; they don't go anywhere without each other. And I think she's already leaning toward us. I've dropped some hints and can feel her hatred towards the High Council."

"Fine. Do it."

I nod, taking a deep breath. My thoughts immediately go to Dyana and my cheeks heat.

He raises a brow, smelling my emotions, "You like the teammate."

Shit. Rebels aren't supposed to get attached, particularly with our marks.

"So?" I challenge. He told me many years ago to never back down when I feel passionate about something, despite being his subordinate.

"Mir," he says softly, "it's the Gauntlet. There isn't much hope for any of them."

"But what if this actually works? What if this works and we survive?" He goes still at my words.

"Let's worry about that when we get there. For now, we tell them the truth. If what you say is true, then we need the Arkaydian to succeed.

"When?"

"Soon, I will send a message when it's time." With that, he disappears back into the shadows.

The truth...which truth do you mean, old friend?

The truth...which truth do you mean, old friend?

CHAPTER 20
AMALIA

Exhaustion finally caught up with me. I woke up in the exact same position I fell asleep in.

I'm surprised my legs are still working after so much running. Training with Os is even more horrible; I had to take a break at one point because of the pounding headache behind my eyes. The constant magyk work is draining after a lifetime of actively trying to subdue it.

It's been five days since we started working on the active side of my powers, and it's a struggle. We've spent hours practicing daily, but unlike my passive powers, this is much harder to grasp.

Working with a person's mind is so different from working with an animal. Os has explained it to me repeatedly. I understand the concept, but it's just not happening. I feel so frustrated. Still, I try because there's no other choice.

My mood, however, has grown more sour with each passing moment. Os, the godsdamn sadist, hasn't just increased our morning jog; he also increased the difficulty of my strength training and has moved on to swordsmanship. Dyana said everyone has moved on to weapons, but it didn't make me feel better.

Our day off couldn't have come sooner. I struggled to pry myself out of bed this morning and it felt like weights were on my eyelids, but the thought of seeing Taran pushed me.

As I approach the barn, a happy neigh calls out as a warm, apple-scented magyk wraps around my soul.

"Hey buddy," I say, voice low and happy as I greet my second closest friend and confidant. Taran's white and gray snout is like velvet as he smooshes his nose against my cheek. Soon, he moves to nibbling my hair as I scratch his thick, furry neck.

Grooming is how horses say, "I love you." But I happen to be able to feel his love, too.

Taran steps into me, leaning his huge, fuzzy bulk against my chest as he wiggles his soft lips in my hair. As I give him scratches in return, the heat of his fur warms my freezing cold hands. It's getting colder in Ur Daoine. Nearly as cold as Twyn Fells, but without the harsh wind coming down off the mountaintops.

Taran uses his head to push me into his chest so we're hugging. I feel for his mind behind my wall: happiness, love, and trust, so much trust it makes me tear up as I turn and press a soft kiss to his cheek, stroking his neck lightly.

Sometimes it feels like animals are the only ones who see me. Seeing behind my armor and my iron walls. I send Taran gratitude and love as I send a rare thank you to the Morrigyn—or whoever is listening, for sending him to me, before I get started grooming and tacking him up.

We make it out of the city without being seen since the two suns are only just beginning to peek over the horizon, painting the sky in a wash of pink and orange.

Taran's hoofbeats clop against the stone and dirt road. Various chickens and roosters run about, squawking to announce the beginning of a new day. Cats chase the chickens, some with celebratory feathers sticking out of their mouths.

I feel all of them, their little minds like small bursts of light in my mind. But the walls are still up, and no bonds are formed. I can feel their emotions, but I'm not tied to them this time. As much as I don't want to admit it; my training is working. My magyk is getting stronger—and easier to use.

Already, I can feel the tension easing out of my body. It feels so good to be back in the saddle. The rhythmic clomping of Taran's hooves is oddly comforting. As Taran walks through the city gates and past the wall boxing off the city, I click softly and squeeze my calves, and we transition into a smooth trot.

When Taran makes it closer to the Annag, a dense forest around the city's southwestern edge that spans across the Abhaynn Gheal, I give him the reins and let him stretch his legs as we break into a fast canter.

Breathe.

Big, gulping, cleansing breaths relax my chest as I drift into the hypnotic roll of Taran's cloudlike rocking. That lingering seed of fear is still in the back of my mind.

Breathe.

Taran may be on the large side, but he's surprisingly fast in small bursts. He lets out a happy neigh and tosses his head, racing against the wind as we gallop so fast that I wonder if his hooves are even touching the ground. My eyes water from the wind as my hair gets blown out of the braid, but for this moment, however brief, the weight of life is lighter. My arms fall to my side as I drop the reins. Taran slows into a rocking canter as we trace the outskirts of the forest.

Breathe.

A thundering noise behind us makes Taran tense, and my eyes snap open. I look back, gray hair flowing in the wind and partially distorting my vision.

A male on horseback follows us. Based on his dress he's not an imperial fae. He wears worn riding clothes like me: a casual cotton shirt and leather pants tucked into boots.

But holy Gods, his horse makes Taran look small. The male and his massive black horse race towards us. I look forward and push Taran harder, not wanting him to catch us.

I've done nothing wrong. It's not illegal to take my horse out riding. There's no reason to be worried about someone else out on a morning ride. But the thoughts do nothing to calm my racing heart and the feeling of being chased.

I dislike this feeling. I am the hunter, not the hunted.

The suns have risen higher in the sky, breaking through the clouds, and for a moment, the horse's black coat appears to shimmer, almost shot through with metallic red, and the outline of a horn appears on its forehead. It's gone with my next blink, but I saw it long enough to know the truth. Well, that and the fact that its teeth are sharpened into fangs.

The male is riding an Oryx, a legendary, vicious breed of warhorse with a mouth full of sharp teeth and a poisonous horn. There's a red sheen to its dark eyes that's visible as they close in on us.

I urge Taran faster but the Oryx and its rider stay right on our tail. The Oryx shrieks, I flinch, the abnormally shrill sound hurting my ears. The male laughs and shouts, urging the Oryx even faster. It shrieks again and complies. Taran jolts to the side a bit, caught off guard by the noises. I grab the reins and send him calming thoughts, pushing him back into a gallop.

"Come on, we can beat him," I whisper to Taran, pushing more magyk into him. He gallops faster than any horse his size should be able to. Taran quickly overtakes the Oryx, and it lets out another shriek. Much to my surprise, Taran neighs back.

The icy wind slamming into my face has turned my face numb, but I don't even feel the cold; I just feel Taran's joy and the hot burn of my magyk at work.

We race down the forest's edge so fast that I wonder for a moment if I really am flying. Mud flies as Taran's hooves hit the ground heavily. The forest narrows as we approach the Abhaynn Gheal.

The male slows, suddenly falling behind, which is when I see it. One of the older trees in the Annag has fallen on the path. Rot covers the thick trunk, completely blocking the path.

I glance back and see the male looking at me with concern as if I don't see the log. A long-buried kernel of something from a happier time bursts out of me. I laugh, turning forward as Taran's ears perk up at the sound of my rare joy. It's a risk, but after all of the magyk practice recently, I put my trust in my friend, sending Taran more magyk along with a specific image and the feeling of a question.

He neighs happily in response and races right at the log. The male behind me shouts, but I ignore it.

The reins go fully slack as I stand up in my stirrups and lean forward, just as Taran takes a giant leap.

For a moment, time ceases. It's just Taran and I soaring through the air with the world at our feet. Taran's happiness flows into me steadily like the strongest drug. I want to stay here and never leave. It's light and joy, and so, so brief.

Everything comes rushing back as Taran lands, jolting me back into reality. My sadness is infinite, as is my resentment at those imperial fae bastards. He neighs again, bucking a few times as I laugh some more. I can feel how proud he is of himself and how much fun he's having getting to run. We slow as I drop his reins and let Taran walk to the river's shore for a drink.

There's a shriek behind us before something explodes, sending shards of wood everywhere. The male and his Oryx appear out of the dust storm.

Gods, I knew Oryx were dangerous, but nothing like that. A sly smile sits on the male's handsome face.

"I'm surprised a horse that size could make the jump," he laughs, dazzling me with brilliant white teeth and a hint of fangs. Taran just sends him a glare, pinning his ears and baring his teeth.

He's not human, then.

"How the hell do you have an Oryx?" I ask, ignoring his jest about Taran, although he's already on my wrong side for calling my horse fat.

I see a flash of his horn again and sharp fangs, but Taran smacks the Oryx with his tail before nibbling lightly on its black, shiny mane.

Of *course,* Taran loves the Oryx. Yes, it's a gorgeous, fantastic creature of myth, but it could also eat him.

But yep, there they go, maneuvering closer so they can itch each other's necks, which brings me right alongside Mr. Mysterious. I finally look up and almost fall right off the side of the saddle as I meet mismatched eyes. The left is bright green and the right is rich amber.

"What can I say? I am a male of many talents and unsavory contacts. But I found Aanad in the meat trade after her mother was slaughtered. She was dying, only a few days old, and on her way to slaughter, so I bought her and nursed her back to health. She's been by my side ever since, the spoiled little brat." Aanad flicks him in the face with her tail, and he grabs his eye, glaring at her.

"Well deserved spoiling, it sounds like," I murmur as Aanad the Oryx raises her head from Taran's neck, softly sniffing my palm. I'm proud my hand doesn't shake, but she just smooshes her nose against my hand; I'll never admit this to Taran, but her nose is the best thing I've ever felt. "You're beautiful," I whisper, scratching her velvet cheek. I don't want to tempt fate and rub her forehead, but I'm transfixed as the horn wavers in and out of existence.

"Oh good, just what she needs. A bigger ego." The male smiles, and I return it.

Wait, I'm smiling? What the fuck? I blink, my smile falling, but the shock of the feeling of happiness is jarring. There aren't many people who understand my love of horses. Dyana never joined me for rides. She doesn't mind riding, but it's not her idea of fun. It's nice to talk to someone about this. There's something honest about horses.

The male in front of me takes off his hat, running a hand through his silvery white hair as he stretches his arms, showing a peek of intricate black tattoos decorating his neck and trailing up behind his head like shadowy tendrils.

"Why were you following me? I ask, voice flat. The male blinks, smirking.

"She thinks I followed her. Did you hear that, Aanad?" The male leans forward and pats the Oryx on its thick, muscular neck before looking at me. "I do this ride every morning. Or at least, I try to. Timing doesn't always work out. So I believe you are following me and joining in on my ride." I glare.

"Be that as it may, you started the race, and what were those results again? Oh, that's right, you lost. How did I forget?" I poke, but the male just smiles. "We need to be getting back," I nod at him, clicking my tongue and urging Taran forward.

The Oryx quickly catches up as the male comes up beside us. "May I escort you back to the gates?" the male asks. We take the long way, walking around the log this time.

"Ah yes," I respond dryly, "surely I'm too weak to make it back myself, being human and all."

"I never assumed you were human." There's a smile on his face, but my muscles freeze as I process his words.

"And I never offered that information. Now if you'll excuse me," I grit out the stupid, polite words Dyana spent so many years drilling into me, despite the fact that I want to tell Taran to kick the male in the head. But that might risk harming Aanad, which means it's out of the question. The male puts his hat back on and gathers his reins.

"You're right, that was rude of me. I'm sorry," the male says with a sigh of regret. I turn, surprised. I can't remember the last time someone genuinely apologized to me other than Dyana.

"Yes, it was," I pause, hesitating, but I force the words out, "but I...appreciate the apology." I nod goodbye and push Taran into a trot then a canter as we race back to the city, the unknown fae male just behind us.

He could catch up. I know Aanad can go faster. But the mystery male with the mismatched eyes is...polite. He gives me space despite having the faster mount, respecting my desire to leave his company.

Strange. Definitely not a fae.

As I get closer, I look back, and Aanad and the rider are gone, no sign of them anywhere. As if they were never there to begin with.

CHAPTER 21
DYANA

"So, what are you going to do today?" Mirielle's lilting voice rings like a bell throughout the room. She stands in my doorway, wringing her hands lightly. But her gray eyes have a warm glint, and she fights a smile.

Is she nervous? Oh, Gods, why is she nervous?

"I was planning to read more. Ama's out riding her horse, but I might try and see if she wants to play some cards later if you want to join. I might have stolen them from The Birdcage. They're worn, but it'll work." Mirielle nods, looking around the small room. "What about you?"

"Well, that's actually why I'm here. Would you like to go into town with me? I thought we could go get some food from the street carts." I'm so stunned I think I might pass out.

"Um—" *Great start, Dyana.* "Yes! Yes, of course. But are we allowed there? I thought it wasn't good for humans to be in the upper areas of the city."

"It isn't, but I've heard the lower areas are just fine." she says with confidence.

"I don't know..." I bite my lip, and Mirielle's pupils go wide as she follows the movement. My skin heats as my heart starts to race. "Amalia said we shouldn't go out in public."

"C'mon, it'll be fine. We're fighters now, aren't we? Plus, only the court has seen us. Nobody else knows who we are."

"I don't know, Mir. It depends..." I say, but already I feel my hesitation collapsing as I focus on her gray eyes and the spattering of brown freckles across her cheeks and nose.

She blinks again, "Depends on what?"

"Well, it depends on how hungry you are because I may have snuck in some gold marks I've saved up, and I'm really fucking tired of porridge. Let's go get some real food."

Mirielle cracks a smile as relief coats her gaze.

"Wear traveling clothes so you blend in," Mirielle says, grabbing the doorknob, "Meet you in the hall in ten?"

Ama is going to kill me.

"Good Gods, that's so good!" Mirielle bites down on the caramel apple I bought her. I moan happily as I bite down on my own. Tart apple juice explodes in my mouth, mixing with the buttery sweet caramel. Completely worth the sticky hands afterward. Mirielle grabs us each a cup of mulled wine next. The smell from the cart is heavenly, and we each hold our cups tightly, relishing the warmth. The aroma of clove, cinnamon, and orange is intoxicating. It's early winter, so it's still absolutely freezing, but luckily the snow hasn't started yet. I grab us a bowl of simmered mushrooms and a couple of sweet rolls.

"Here, I thought the food in Sud Azyl was exciting." Mirielle takes a bite of the mushrooms, moaning at the flavor.

The sight of her pink tongue darting out to lick her lips...I desperately want to lean into her. Gods above, control yourself. Ugh, my conscience sounds like Amalia. I wonder what that says about how sane I am?

"Yeah, but the Eastlands are warm most of the year, right? You don't need mulled wine, or many of these foods 'cause they're kinda meant for cold weather, right?"

"True. But Gods, it's so good." She laughs and takes another sip. "Maybe the cold isn't so bad if this is the food you get to eat in exchange."

"Oh, just wait for the snow. I only like it for a few days and then I'm done, but it's so pretty. Everything gets covered in a thick layer of white. But when it's that cold, it's hard to be outdoors. It's pretty for a few days, and then it can be...isolating."

"It sounds like a lot of your life has been pretty isolated," Mirielle says softly. I glance at her, surprised. There's a sad smile on my face, but not for the reasons she thinks.

"Life in the North is hard. It's a tough place to have a life."

Mirielle wraps her arm around mine, and we walk arm in arm as we take in the smells of freshly baked bread and rich spices. The market is surprisingly large, and we finally emerge after an hour, having stopped at a few more stands to get some fish, tomato stew, and sweet roasted chestnuts for dessert.

After weeks of bland porridge, this is paradise.

We turn, making our way back to the Dragon Pit leisurely. Mirielle shocks me by grabbing my hand and pulling me along. A nervous giggle falls from my lips, unsure of what she's planning. She pulls me towards an alley, and images of her shoving me against the wall and ravishing me start flashing in my mind—until Mirielle comes to a halt when four males emerge from the darkness, surrounding us.

"What do we have here? Two pretty birdies so far from their nest," the shorter male leers at us, his teeth black and rotten. Mirielle and I take a step back as they close in. "Very pretty."

"We don't have any money, so let us go," Mirielle states calmly, her hand tight around my arm.

"Leave us alone; we're not causing trouble," I hiss firmly, tugging Mirielle to my side. "And that's rude." Mirielle closes her eyes, sighing, but I don't regret it.

"Little birdie has a mouth on her." The men all laugh as the one speaking continues to stare at us with beady brown eyes. He reaches into his pocket and draws out a rusty, curved dagger that looks wicked sharp.

"I'm going to clip your wings, pretty bird." One of the males lunges forward, grabbing me, while the other goes for Mirielle.

"Let go!" I shout and slam my head back into the male holding me. He howls in pain but doesn't let me go. Instead, the males continue to hold us as we struggle.

"There's my pretty bird." The male's rotten breath hits me like a wave as he breathes heavily.

"Fuck this," I've barely processed Mirielle's muttered, oddly annoyed words before she's free of the second tall male's arms and spinning into a brutal kick to the male's jugular. He gurgles, hands to his throat, as he drops to his knees. Another male shouts, charging her. I watch with wide eyes and go to shout her name, but my jaw falls to the floor as I watch Mirielle become a blur of movement.

What the hell?

She kicks the male in the ribs hard enough that something cracks, loudly. He falls to his knees, screaming in pain, but Mirielle just flattens her hand, bringing the edge down hard on his neck quickly—he falls unconscious with a thump on the ground. The male holding me finally lets go with a muttered curse and charges her.

"Behind you!" I shout as I turn to the shorter of the males who now stalks towards me.

"Come birdie, let Syvan sort your friend out." Those rotten black teeth and that insane look in his beady black eyes make me want to vomit.

I knee him in the crotch and he groans, going to his knees. I turn and try to run away, but he grabs my ankles, tripping me. My jaw hits the ground hard, and I bite my tongue, hot blood flooding my mouth with a tang of iron. I spit it out quickly, but my tongue still aches.

The male drags me towards him against the ground as he shakes off the injury.

"Bad, bad birdie."

I try to jerk my head back to hit him in the skull, but he's prepared and throws me over his shoulder as he stands. I shriek, kicking and punching with all my might, but his grip is firm.

I punch him in the back and kick my legs, but out of nowhere, I'm falling and hitting the ground again, this time on my back. Stars flood my eyes as I lose my vision from the impact. As it starts to return, I see Mirielle wiping off a small dagger she must have hidden on her, as she stands over the male's unconscious body.

"Dyana? Are you ok?" Her voice is concerned as she quickly rushes over and helps me up, her hands cupping my cheeks as she looks me over, checking for injuries.

"You mean besides the fact that the last two weeks of training have failed, and I'm absolutely going to die a horrible death in the Gauntlet? Yeah, besides that, I'm fine." I clear my throat.

"Are you sure?" Mirielle turns my face to the side, checking my cheek. Her hands are covered in blood, but she's calm while I'm trembling from the adrenaline. Really calm.

"Why are you pretending to be a human, Mirielle?" I ask plainly. I'm done with the word games.

Mirielle blinks, going still. "What do you mean?"

"Uh." I look around, eyes wide. "What else could I possibly mean? You just took down four males who, based on the slightly pointed ears, weren't all human themselves—and you're fast. Like, Os fast."

Mirielle winces, looking to the sky. "Dammit. This isn't how any of this was supposed to go," she mutters to herself.

"I'm not mad," I start, and her eyes flash to mine, "Well, not about that. I'm mad that you've been holding back for the past two, almost three weeks." I talk over her. "You've been holding back when we spar, Mirielle. What the hell!" She looks down guiltily. "How am I supposed to get better when you're not even giving me a fair shot?"

Mirielle sighs, running her hand through her hair, "You're right. I'm not human, and I have been holding back, and that's not fair to you. I'm sorry, Dyana."

I snort, leaning forward to put my hand on her arm. "Don't apologize. I get why you wouldn't say anything. Trust me." *Little did she know.* "But all my life, people have always held back with me. You saw, I still can barely fight someone, and I have to fight for my life in a few weeks. You holding back isn't going to help me get better. So, since this is clearly a cover, don't blow it, but please don't hold back anymore. I won't break."

"Dyana, this cannot get out. If the High Council finds out I'm demis, they'll kill me. Please don't say anything."

I smirk, "I'm good with secrets. Don't worry. I won't say anything—"

"—Not even to Amalia."

I blink. A war starts within me. I don't hide anything from Amalia, but it's not my secret to keep. Damnit.

"Fine, but she needs to know eventually. Trust me, she'll be ok with it."

"Thank you," Mirielle sighs warily.

"But what are you doing here, then? You shouldn't have even been able to be nominated."

"They think I'm human. I've pretended to be one for a long time.

"Wait—how old are you?"

Mirielle winces, "Three centuries, give or take a few years?" She says it like a question as she waits for me to explode.

"Wow," is all I'm able to say. She waits as if I'll cringe or dislike her for being so much older than me. But as I usually do when I'm nervous and my heart is racing, I open my stupid mouth, "Well, I've always been attracted to older women." I go still, in shock that I actually said those words. I clear my throat awkwardly, "We better be getting back—"

Mirielle cuts me off, pressing her lips against mine. My hands immediately grasp her soft hair as I arch against her gorgeous, curved body. I want to run my hands over every curve, every scar and freckle. I want to memorize every feature until it's all I see when I close my eyes at night.

I'm trembling with need as waves of pleasure hit me as she pries open my lips gently and winds her tongue expertly with mine. I moan again, unable to stop. Nothing else exists but her lips. She pulls away, leaving me a panting, discombobulated mess.

"I like you, Dyana."

"Oh," I know my pupils are blown out because I can't look away from her flushed, pink lips.

She chuckles, and my core goes molten in response, "Do you like me too?" I grab her thick coat and yank her towards me as an answer.

"Of course, I like you, idiot. Now shut up and kiss me again." I press my lips to hers. She giggles happily, her warm, soft lips devouring mine. The tips of her fingers trace the edges of my breasts, and suddenly I'm shivering, but not from the cold. Her fingers trail underneath my coat lightly, just coasting over the swells of my chest. But right when she's just about to brush against my hard nipples, she pulls away with a knowing, wicked smile.

"It's time for us to get back, right? Don't want to make Amalia mad," Mirielle winks and turns, heading back to the Dragon Pit.

I jog to catch up, but my legs are wobbly, "I'm gonna kick your ass for that tomorrow."

Mirielle hums, "Is that what they're calling it these days?"

This female is going to be the death of me.

CHAPTER 22

The chains chafe against the raw scales around my ankles as they clank against the ground, dragging behind me with every agonizing step.

Drag, clank.

Drag, clank.

Drag, clank.

Drag, clank.

My pace is slow; each step takes all of the energy I still possess in my haggard, thin body as I fight against the weight of the heavy chains. Four fae surround me, two carrying my lead and two with their giant magyk prongs to ensure I behave.

Long ago, I would have been offended that just four fae could subdue and control me. The dangerous Dragons have around 20 of the pointed ones around them at all times. But the fae know I won't fight back. Not anymore. What's the point? There is no escaping this place. Fighting back only makes things worse. Hope left me many years ago. I've seen too much pain, too much evil, too much *death*.

In the early days, I killed many fae. All of the Dragons did. But then, they starved us, ripped off our scales, and burned us. They *burned* us. Used our own flame against us so that we would welcome, we would beg, for their magyk chains.

"You hear this one is slated for the Fray this time?" the one carrying my leash asks their friend as he trails behind me with his prong, ready to slice into me again at any sign of my resistance. I long to use my spiked tail to crush him into the floor like the little shit worms they all are, but the last time I tried that, I was shut in the tiny metal box for days without food or light, and starved for a week. By the time they gave me food, I couldn't lift my own body. I considered ending it all there and using one of the few talons I have left to slice open my main arteries. Just end it all and be done with it, but I couldn't.

I'm too weak, even for that.

I'm ready for this wretched life to be over. I can't even look at my own tail, sick of seeing my worn and destroyed scales. The broken, jagged spikes. Once, I was a glorious crimson red, but the color has long since seeped from my scales.

Glory is simply a memory, freedom a figment of my imagination. My brothers and sisters long dead, friends slaughtered and consumed for their power. My existence is now to serve at the fae's mercy.

"Yeah, maybe we'll finally get a real show with this one. Although she used to be more feisty. But at least she'll make good bait for The Bastard." The other fae laugh as my heart sinks.

Relief. Sad, final relief was close at hand, although already I dread having to face Abeloth. The Bastard, they call him. A Dragon I was friends with a long, long time ago. The war broke Abeloth and he eventually sided with the fae, committing a crime he would never be forgiven for, even though the fae butchered his entire family. Now, he's one of their most prized fighters. In the past, I would have longed for the opportunity to rip his throat out. He was an embarrassment to my entire kind. But there's no point.

Drag, clank.

Drag, clank.

The fae shoves me back into my pen, and I go willingly, turning so they can take off my muzzle.

"That's a good bitch," they reply, turning the key to let my huge metal trap fall to the floor as I turn and quickly drink what little water we do get, before devouring the plate of old, rancid meat deemed not good enough for the fae. My stomach clenches in pain but I ignore the horrible taste, eating every bite as they shut the thick metal door to my stall, and the walls begin to close around me.

Instead of dreaming of a clear blue sky and sailing amongst the clouds tonight, I dream of an inky black abyss swallowing me whole, forever erasing my pain.

CHAPTER 23
AMALIA

My thighs are *wrecked.* Tomorrow is going to be hell, but it's worth it. I actually had fun today—or as much fun as someone can have in a place like this.

Rides with Taran always make me feel like I can finally breathe again after weeks of suffocation.

We're back at the stables now. As I untack and feed Taran, my mind wanders to the strange fae male and his Oryx. I don't trust any fae, but he didn't seem like a normal fae.

I look at the corner of freshly filled straw and plop down on it as Taran happily munches on his hay between giant gulps of water, making an absolute mess. Exhaustion takes over as the sounds of the stable and the faraway noise of the city fade away until there's only Taran's quiet, rhythmic munching as I fall into a light sleep.

At one point, the ground moves, and I'm awoken as Taran flops down next to me, causing a minor earthquake. He places his giant, fuzzy head against my side and lets out a happy sigh. I press a soft kiss into his forehead, sending him love down our bond. I lightly rub his cheek, and we doze off together, enjoying a small moment of peace.

"Well, isn't this sweet?" A poisonous voice interrupts my dreamless sleep. Before I fully open my eyes, a hand yanks my braid, dragging me out of the stall. Out of the corner of my eye, I see Taran shove to stand, snapping at the fae. The one dragging me turns and punches him in the face.

My magyk explodes into Taran as I take his pain from him. I don't even think about it before it's already done. My forehead aches but Taran's gratitude makes it worthwhile. I try to send him images of staying away from the fae, hoping he understands.

The fae turns and continues dragging me through the barn. I could scream, but I know it won't do anything. So as much as I want to yell and shout, I stay silent. The small rocks in the dirt dig into my palms and knees, sending bolts of sharp pain through me. I crane my neck, trying to slap and kick the male dragging me through the dirt, but he doesn't let go, and I can't get the proper leverage.

The other fae soldiers watch as I'm dumped at the feet of someone wearing fine leather boots. I cough from the dust that gets into my nose and brush the dirt from my eyes.

"Fuck you too," I mutter, pushing myself up, but the fae who dragged me steps in and slaps me on the back of the head, knocking me back down. My skull hits the ground hard, and I hear an angry whinny in the distance before a loud banging sound as Taran begins kicking the wall of his stall, trying to break out and get to me.

"Don't. Stay there, stay safe. Please." I send the thought, hoping he understands. The banging stops, but I feel his outrage.

"Sir," the fae male starts, "I found this human trash asleep in the stables. Clearly, she's a vagrant." My eyes are so watery from the specks of dust flying into them that everything is a little blurry, but I turn and look up as I move to stand again. A hand reaches out and grabs mine. I look up automatically and—

Him. Every thought leaves my brain as I take in those mismatched eyes.

One green. One brown.

The fae from earlier stands in front of me, dressed this time in the fine, dark clothing of the imperial fae.

"Hello, horse girl." His eyes twinkle with mirth, a knowing smirk on his face. "What's your name, human?"

He was gorgeous in his riding gear, but now he's devastating. He's changed into immaculate black leather pants and a leather high-necked vest with a gray tunic beneath, partly covering his arms. But he'd shoved up the buttoned wrists of his shirt, showing his tattooed forearms. His hand flies out and the male clasps my chin, pulling me towards him until he can whisper, "I asked you a question, horse girl."

"Who's asking?" I ask, my voice bored, but inside, I burn with anger. He's imperial fae. I don't care if he seemed nice this morning, I really don't.

He's one of them, even if his coloring is different.

The imperial fae pulls back until our faces are only inches apart. His eyes are cold in a ruthless sort of way. It's the look of someone who has killed and who won't hesitate to kill again.

With a jolt of clarity, I recognize it. "You were at the Welcome Ball—*watching* me."

"Was I?" the male teases, a playful glint in his eyes.

The fae who dragged me clears his throat and announces loudly, "You are in the presence of Crown Prince Nyall Drayven, General of the 3rd Army and Heir to the High Council Seat. You will show respect to his Highness, lest you lose your head, bitch."

The godsdamned Crown Prince. You've got to be joking.

"I apologize, Your Highness." Based on the twitch in his eye, my mocking tone isn't lost on him. "I was unaware that visiting my horse is a crime in Castael Laryn."

"It's not, but being a vagrant is." His voice is an arrogant, confident drawl befitting his pompous station, but so different from this morning. "So tell me, what are you doing here, and why shouldn't I throw your ass in jail?" His eyes sparkle; he's enjoying this. I push myself up again but remain kneeling after a glare from the soldiers surrounding us.

"I'm competing in the Gauntlet, and this is my day off. I'm not a damned vagrant," I bite out from between clenched teeth.

The fae who shoved me steps forward again, and I turn, angling my body to receive his attack and go on the defense.

"Enough," the Prince says, his voice hard.

The fae soldier releases my hair and steps back with a bow. "Sire, I'm—" Nyall barely raises his hand, barely moves, but ropes of bright white light burst into existence around his fingers. The fae shuts up, head bowed in complete dismissal, and the Prince's magyk dissipates.

"A candidate? From which town?"

"Twyn Fells, Your Highness," I reply, equally cold.

"I see. And your name, candidate?"

I glare, "Amalia Roth, Your Highness."

"Amalia Roth." He says my name slowly, rolling each letter off the tip of his tongue. "What an interesting name—"

A loud voice booms throughout the square. "My son! What are you doing with that human wretch?"

Nyall Drayven's eyes stay locked on mine, but a flare of pure, undiluted fury blazes behind the Crown Prince's gaze. It's gone again before I can think much more of it. The subject of the Prince's magyk is nothing compared to the wave of fury rising within me at the male who approaches us.

Achan Drayven. The High Councilor of Ur Daoine. Right in front of me.

My hands itch to grab my dagger hidden in my boot, but the look in Prince Nyall's gaze makes me hesitate. A warning lies within his mismatched gaze, and he minutely shakes his head.

I drop to the ground quickly, knees slamming into the dirt and gravel, but my fury and panic numb the pain as my heartbeat rushes in my ears. Despite the freezing cold air, sweat forms at my hairline, and my neck gets hot.

I don't need to look up to know what the High Councilor looks like. It's seared into my nightmares. Long, straight, inky black hair surrounding great, branch-like black horns jutting from his head. He's the only imperial fae to have horns in this manner—it looks like his son didn't pick up the trait, either. He walks slowly, smiling wickedly at Nyall..

"ALL HAIL HIGH COUNCILOR ACHAN DRAYVEN!" one of the soldiers shouts as they call and repeat.

"HAIL. HAIL. HAIL." Three times in unison they slap their chests with their right hand like war drums. All citizens in the vicinity fall to their knees, foreheads to the ground as the High Councilor slowly walks past, not even sparing them a glimpse.

Wait. *Drayven.*

The Crown Prince is the High Councilor's son.

This is Achan Drayven's *son.* His *heir.*

My stomach turns, and my breakfast threatens to make a very swift appearance as I connect the dots.

Fear and the galloping of my heart have rendered me completely frozen, unable to do anything except kneel in the sand before my parents' murderer like a damn idiot. But my mind races alongside my heart, and I've already thought of the dozens of ways this could go wrong in a heartbeat and what that would mean. My chest is so tight it's painful to breathe as I begin to pray that so many years of effort aren't about to go to waste.

Please, don't recognize me.

I beg the Morrigyn for luck. Beg for guidance, but as per usual, she doesn't answer.

On the outside, I don't move or make a sound.

On the inside, my screams tear down the realms.

"I was just learning who this human was that my soldiers found napping with the animals, Father. It's one of the Gauntlet candidates," Nyall says, sighing, his voice bored. High Councilor Achan hums.

"Sleeping in the stables? Humans are dirty creatures. I've always told you so." Achan responds.

"Right as always, High Councilor," Nyall says, but his tone hints at mocking. Just enough to make me blink. Achan doesn't notice.

"High Councilor Drayven, is there a problem with my candidate?" Os's voice isn't loud, but even over the crowd, I hear him clearly. The Crown Prince watches

Os with a dark glint in his mismatched eyes. Os glares right back, flashing a hint of fang. Nyall Drayven just smiles in return, showing off his own set of fangs.

Idiotic males.

High Councilor Achan steps closer to me and I sneak a glance. His eyes glow a dark ruby red against skin so pale, you can see his black veins. He has no whites of his eyes, just black outside of burning red irises and black veins streaking out to his face.

To look upon High Councilor Achan Drayven is to feel pure, unadulterated terror, not all that different from Dragonfear. Which now makes sense.

He consumed Dragons, perverting their magyk for himself. My hands tremble with the effort it's taking to stay calm. To not use the dagger hidden at my waistband and tear his eyes out of his godsdamn skull.

There's a gentle nudge against my mind, and I tense as Os's sweet, smokey scent suddenly tingles my nose. I let him in quickly, struggling to open my mind and close it without alerting the imperial fae or reacting.

"Don't say a single fucking word, Amalia." he snarls, and for a moment, I'm taken aback at the raw fury in his voice. Just nod and agree.

"I don't need your help, shifter."

"You're so fucking stubborn. Do as I say if you want to escape this alive, Amalia. Don't lose control."

"I hate you," I reply coldly, but it's a farce. I know he's right.

"Ah, Ostia. Tell me, why is one of your little candidates outside their quarters, sleeping with the animals? Are you so weak you can't even control a group of pitiful humans?" Achan asks, mockingly.

Os must be short for Ostia. Interesting.

"Don't." I forgot he was listening.

"Who's the liar now?"

His only reply is a low growl that vibrates the inside of my skull.

"Of course, High Councilor. This one has been a bit troublesome, but I will personally oversee her punishment. Double laps tomorrow followed by stable duty." he says casually, and I wait in the tense silence that follows.

"Yes, that will teach her to stay in line. But," the High Councilor tsks, "humans are stubborn creatures. They need to be reminded of the order of things occasionally." I don't have to look to know the High Councilor is smiling.

Nyall sighs loudly, "But look at her, Father. She's so tiny and weak. No meat on her bones. The Dragonfear will be worse torture than any whip could imbue. She's going to die in the first round anyways." Nyall adds while picking off a piece of invisible lint.

What was he up to?

"Don't interrupt me, boy," The sky grows dark as thunder rolls, and a harsh wind picks up, making my eyes water. But I keep my face downturned, the picture of piety.

"You, soldier," from the corner of my eye, I watch as he points at the one who threw me to the ground and dragged me out here, his black-tipped hands ending in grossly long black nails. "Remind the candidate of her place, will you?"

The fae laughs, approaching me slowly, glowing red eyes set upon me. He grabs my braid and yanks me close, "I'm going to enjoy this, human scum."

I don't grab him back, but I do turn to whisper in his ear, "And I'm going to enjoy slitting your throat because if you ever touch my horse again, I'll fucking kill you."

That's all the warning I get before he blurs and a fist slams into my face. Stars burst behind my eyes, and the pain explodes as the metallic tang of hot blood fills my mouth. There's a voice in my head, but I can't hear anything. The pain is too much.

Unconsciousness takes me, and I drift away into a black ocean with a starless sky.

CHAPTER 24
AMALIA

Year 420 PBM

"Give it up, Jhon," the fae yells. I'm hidden underneath the kitchen cupboard, but I can still hear them speaking from the thin walls. The violent wind from earlier has calmed. Puff wiggles into my neck, rubbing his head against me in a calming manner. Usually when he does this, his whiskers and tiny toes are ticklish, but there's no laughter now. With each press of his tiny black nose, he sends bursts of love tinged with overwhelming terror.

"Go home, Drayven. The girl is dead. We slit her throat and dropped her body in Midheym Sea, Achan. You lost." Father mocks.

"You're lying," Achan responds, his voice so cold with rage that Puff and I both shiver, freezing.

"It's true," Mother replies in a hollow voice. "I'm the one who killed her."

They're...saying they killed me?

"LIES!" Achan shouts, and a gust of wind makes the house shake again. I cover my mouth in an attempt not to scream. Puff burrows into my shirt, curling against my neck as he shivers in fear. "I can hear her fluttering heartbeat hiding in that fetid shack behind you."

Oh no.

Father put a ward on me to muffle the sound of my heartbeat...but we didn't ward Puff.

The man hears Puff's racing heart and thinks it's me.

"You're a paranoid lunatic," Father says.

"How about I burn the house to the ground, then? Let's find out which one of us is right, Jhonathan."

There's a loud noise and some scuffling. "I knew you were a liar," Achan croons, using magyk to project his voice inside the house. "Come out, little girl. There's nowhere to run."

"It won't fix your problems, Drayven. She isn't your solution. It will never be enough for you, the power. You are not a God, so stop trying to become one!"

There's a deep, sickening laugh in response. "And where is that Goddess of yours? Where is the Morrigyn?" Father doesn't respond and the fae laughs harder. "Yes, that's what I thought. The Gods abandoned you, Jhonathan. They abandoned you and I am your salvation. You should be on your knees, begging for mercy. But you never were one for politics, Skadus. This is your last chance. Hand over the girl, let us be done with this."

"Never." Mother replies.

"Sentimental Arkaydians," the fae male mutters.

My shaking increases, and I can hear Puff's heart race even faster. I clutch him tightly, curling my head down against my chest. My tears dampen his silky fur.

"Please, Achan. Don't do this," my mother begs.

Achan ignores her and projects his voice so that his whispers echo throughout the cabin. "Come out, Arkaydian."

"She doesn't belong to you, Drayven, and she never will." Father doesn't shout, but I hear his voice clearly. There's another noise then: panicked whispers and swords being drawn.

"I love you, my darling," Mama's voice suddenly whispers across my mind. Her warm scent surrounds me.

"I love you too, Mama," I say back immediately.

"You and your mother are the best things to ever happen to me. Never forget that little spark. Remember what we taught you if something happens to us. Repeat it back to me now." My father commands.

"Go north. Hunt and fish like you taught me. I'm an orphan from Eahmond, and my parents died in a traveling accident. Find an orphanage that will adopt me." *I repeat the words Father has told me so many times.*

"And what will you not do under any circumstances?"

"Use my powers or reveal my identity. No matter what happens."

"What family name will you use?"

"Roth."

"Good. Whatever you do, don't deviate. Stick with the plan. I love you so much, little spark. I wish we had more time—" *he breaks off, voice choking. I can feel his warm, big hug around me and the love he sends my way, although it's tinged with fear.*

"What do you mean?" *I go to ask him, but the connection is severed. I look around, desperately trying to see outside without making any noise. I crawl on my hands and knees as Puff squeaks in my ear. Stuff I can't see cuts my hands, and I wince but keep going. I need to see my parents.*

The cabin begins to rumble, and the floor wobbles. A tiny hole of light opens from a can falling over, and I hurry over despite the tremors. It only just allows me to see what's happening.

My parents stand, facing away from the cabin, hands clasped. They turn to one another, and my father wipes a tear from Mother's face. Magyk flies towards them, hitting a ward. Father told me about those. Red magyk hits an invisible barrier, but I can see holes getting burned into it as Father winces.

"What the fuck do you think you're doing?" *The fae named Achan snarls,* "Stop them!"

Mother sobs, closing her eyes as Father flashes a glance right at me.

"I love you, my darling daughter."

"Always," *Mum's choked voice joins in as Father raises a bloody hand to grasp my mum's face. The moment they touch, everything explodes.*

The light blows through the entire forest, but the house is unaffected. I slap a hand over my mouth to keep my scream silent as I shut my eyes against the burning light.

Minutes, days, years; it seems to go on forever, yet it all happens instantly. There's a loud POP, and darkness floods in as everything goes silent. I open my eyes and lean back towards my seeing hole.

No amount of training stops the gasp that falls from my mouth. A scream builds in my throat as I watch their singed bodies, covered in black burnt skin, hands still clasped, as they fall to the forest floor and explode into a cloud of ash.

The scream does leave my mouth when I spy the fae male with his big black horns emerging from the shadows, injured but very alive, and walking towards the cabin.

NOW:

"Wake up, A gahrá," Os's smokey voice echoes around me.

He appears in front of me, where I sit in an all-black room, lying on my back and looking up at a starless sky.

"I'm not sure I want to," I admit honestly. I know this isn't real, just a figment of my imagination, so there's no reason to pretend.

"Why not?"

"Life is painful. This is easy."

"You're healed now, Amalia," Os says carefully.

"I'm not worried about that. I'm not worried about anything at all, actually." Os is silent as he watches me before slowly lying on the floor beside me. "In here, I'm not plagued with fear. Here, I'm...free." I turn my head to the side to look at him, unafraid of this made-up dream version. "That's how I know this isn't real."

Os is thoughtful as he responds, "These lives we've lived...I wouldn't wish that on anyone." Os turns his head to the side slowly, gold eyes glowing like the sun. He looks more relaxed, and his light scruff is perfectly unbothered. Peace suits him.

"It suits you too, little liar," Os's voice interrupts. Wow, even in my imagination, he can read my thoughts. How strange.

"I don't like that name," I tell him.

"Then I won't use it. But is it wrong, Amalia?"

I ignore that question, sighing aloud.

"I do need you to wake up, though. Your little friend is quite persistent and won't stop talking. It's very annoying, and I can't get her to stop."

I snort, "Dyana *is* very persistent. I taught her well."

"I'd say she's surpassed you."

I smile, and Os blinks, rolling to his side.

"Do that again." The order rolls through me, and I roll my eyes, but the smile stays on my face. We say nothing for a few moments, just watching each other. It's easy to get lost in his eyes.

"This is real?" I ask quietly.

"Yes. It's called dreamweavyng. But this place is only as real as you make it, and it will never be as vibrant as the real world. Which is why you need to wake up. Your friends need you, Amalia."

I look at the endless starless ceiling above me and sigh, "You're much nicer here, you know. I wouldn't hate you so much if you did more than just lecture me and growl menacingly."

Os gets up, squatting down next to me to give me his hand as he helps me up. But instead of letting me go when I get to my feet, he pulls me into his arms so that my chest is pressed against his.

"I can be very nice, Amalia," Os cups my jaw, tilting my head up towards him, "but I think you like it when I'm mean, too. If you want me to be nice, all you have to do is ask."

I'm stunned into silence, but he just leans in and brushes his lips across my cheek, his hot breath searing my skin.

"Now, *wake up.*" Os suddenly pulls his arm back and slams the palm of his hand right into my sternum. It feels like claws rip into my soul, bodily shoving me out of my comfortable, secluded abyss and flinging me back into myself.

CHAPTER 25
AMALIA

"Shush me one more time, Ms. Arkos and I will lock you out," I hear Os say.

"You can try! Pull the stick out of your ass and sit down, Os. You've been pacing for hours. Is it so hard to let someone read in peace? Plus, she needs her rest," Dyana hisses.

"You were most certainly not reading in peace. You gasp every 3 seconds and regularly talk back to the characters! It's annoying!"

"Blah, blah, blah," Dyana mimics him and I hear Os's long-suffering sigh.

I'm on my back in what feels like a bed. A fireplace crackles softly in the background, the sweet, smokey scent telling me exactly where I am and whose bed I'm on.

My teeth ache and my jaw feels sore, but it's minor. I carefully open my mouth and move my jaw left and right, testing it. My teeth feel really slippery, and as I run my tongue over the tops, I find some spots that were previously chipped.

They grew my teeth back.

I suppose it's a good thing that all we have to eat here is porridge. The idea of biting down on something hard makes my stomach turn.

"I'm not trying to rush you, but for the love of the Gods, open your eyes before I throw your friend out on her ass for being an annoying pest!" Os growls in my head, his annoyance clear.

"Do it, and I'll knock your lights out, trainer." The threat is so cold I can feel Os hesitate. Back in the real world, I let out a long sigh and move my arms to try and push myself. Dyana gasps and rushes over just as the dizziness hits. I wince, fighting it.

"Ama, oh my Gods, you're awake." She helps me into a sitting position. The pain in my jaw is beginning to settle further, dulling down to a bit of stiffness. "Are you okay? What the fuck happened? Last I saw, you were sneaking out at the ass crack of dawn to go to the stables, and next, that rude lumbering OAF of a male is carrying you in, frantic and shouting as you bleed to death. What the fuck!" She's talking so fast that she begins tripping over her own words, and suddenly I realize I'm feeling her emotions as if they're my own.

That's new. I didn't even try, and I'm in her head. Adrenaline rushes through her as her fear becomes overwhelming. Her dark hair is frizzy and tangled, a sign she has been running her hands through it nervously—something she hasn't done since she was a child.

"I'm okay, Dy, it's okay," I whisper in her mind, and Dyana's mouth falls open.

"Ama you... you're in my head. What the fuck?"

"Language."

"WHERE DO YOU THINK I LEARNED IT FROM?"

I wince as her shouts rattle the inside of my skull, *"Quieter, please."*

"You almost died, so I'm going to say 'fuck' however much I want, thank you very much. Now, how are you in my head? Can you do this with everyone? What the hell happened out there?"

I sigh and answer aloud, "Those are questions for a later time."

Dyana takes a deep breath, "The mind-speak thing, yes. The fact that you almost died? No, we're talking about that right now, asshole," she whisper-yells at me.

"I was just taking a nap with Taran after our ride. I have no idea why that wouldn't be allowed but apparently it's not." Dyana nods, motioning for me to continue. "One of the fae soldiers caught me napping, and I guess he thought I was homeless, so he dragged me to the Crown Prince," I say his name pointedly, the anger about his true identity resurfacing, "and then as my luck would have it, his father showed up. Who, in case you didn't know, is High Councilor Achan Drayven."

Dyana eyes go wide in horror. "He has a child? A son?!"

I nod, and she wraps her arms around herself. "Then Os came out and declared that my punishment—although I'm still not even sure what the hell I did wrong—would be double laps in the morning and a day of stable duty. Which is oddly nice," I mutter the last part to her under my breath.

Os calls from across the room, without ever raising his voice, "Not the horse stables."

Then it hits me. "Oh shit."

"Mind your language," Dyana mocks, mimicking my voice. I poke her, glaring. "But what do you mean? What other stables are there?"

"The...Dragon stables," I whisper.

"Dragon stables?" Dyana screeches, her rich brown eyes aghast.

"Guess so."

"Oh my Gods, oh my Gods, you're going to get eaten alive!" I see the exact moment Dyana's mind starts to go wild as the fear overtakes her.

I put my hand on hers, "I'm not going to get eaten alive, Dy."

"I think there's a pretty high chance you fucking will, Amalia! How are you being so calm about this?" Her breathing comes faster.

"Dy, breathe. You know me. You know I can do this."

Dyana continues to look unconvinced, but I feel her worry ease minutely.

"The High Councilor didn't think that Os's punishment was sufficient, so he had the guard that found me leave an extra little present for shits and giggles after spewing his Sol Constantus nonsense about how the fae are better than everyone."

Dyana cringes but is furious. "Gods, Ama. I'm so sorry I wasn't there."

"I'm glad you weren't there. You don't need to apologize, Dy. I'm the one who is sorry. I told you I would stay out of trouble, and now this."

"It's not your fault either, Ama. You didn't do anything wrong. I'm just glad you're okay." Her dark eyes are warm and grateful as she takes me in, alive and well. But I can see the stress on her face and feel it bubbling within her.

I hate this.

"We only have three weeks left of training. What the fuck is the High Councilor thinking injuring candidates so badly?" Dyana asks in bewilderment.

"This is nothing new. They wouldn't give two shits if you died," Os says plainly as he walks back into the room. He must feel my stare because his gold eyes turn to meet mine. "The Gauntlet has always been about two things: to make a profit and to make a point."

"A profit and a point?" Dyana asks.

Os nods, face pensive. "They charge an arm and a leg for the opportunity to watch you be torn to pieces. If they could get away with it, they'd have one every year. I won't be surprised if they push for it to be more often, actually. But that's because it allows them to make their point. That humans are no better than animals, and fae are superior."

"But you work for them," Dyana blurts. "You're complicit in their crimes!"

Os sneers and yanks his shirt off, baring his deep, bronzed, muscular chest. Before I start to drool, he turns and shows us his tattooed left side. Os gestures towards the black glyphs that form shapes resembling flames trailing up his side and back.

"Do you think I'm here willingly?" he snarls and the tattoo glistens for a small moment.

Gods. That means...

"That's a compulsion, isn't it?" I say in shock.

His gold eyes bore into mine, and he nods, "Very good."

"I thought a compulsion was just a spell, not a tattoo," Dyana says, confused.

"It's supposed to be a spell, but the imperial fae have far more magyk than anyone realizes. They brought in mages from the South who taught them how to enchant physical things, like metals and inks. I'm as much of a prisoner as you are. Your job is to die. My job is to ensure you put up a good fight."

"So that tattoo...forces you to be here?" she questions.

"In very basic terms, yes." Not once does he look away or break eye contact with me.

He is trapped here—and very likely trapped in this form, too. We're all silent for a moment.

"I should find Mirielle. Are you okay getting back to the room on your own, Ama?" Dyana asks and I nod, distracted by my thoughts. I stand up and wince at the soreness in my muscles.

"Of course. I'll follow shortly, okay?"

Dyana nods and wraps me in her arms, "Please stop getting almost killed."

I sigh into her hair, taking in her sweet, floral scent.

"I'm trying."

"I know," she replies, pulling back and running her hand across my cheek. She gives me a knowing look and turns, leaving Os's room. The door shuts with a thud, and then it's just the two of us.

Os says nothing. He just pads over, barefoot—Gods, even his feet are attractive. That's just unfair.

Whether he hears my lewd thoughts or not, I'm unsure. He just nods for me to follow, and I walk behind him into the bathroom.

I'm stunned at what I find. The floor is made of raw stone, and there's a natural waterfall shower next to a large tin copper tub. A large white marble counter with a sink is on one wall, to the left of a closed-off relief area for the chamber pot. It's bigger than my whole room at home. Not quite as nice as the bathrooms in the Black Citadel, but compared to the buckets we've been using, it's downright luxurious.

I nearly jump out of my skin, gasping as Os grabs me by the waist and gently lifts me onto the counter near his sink. He's so tall that even now, he's taller than me. But being this close is overwhelming. His sweet, smokey scent is everywhere. With each inhale, all I can smell is him.

Os steps forward, causing me to widen my thighs, which I'm now realizing are bare. All I'm wearing is one of Os's long shirts.

"Who dressed me?"

"Dyana did. There was a lot of blood," Os mutters, stepping close until we're almost chest to chest. He opens a jar of some balm, and the smell of sweet herbs and dried wood drifts through the air.

"It was...upsetting. Seeing you injured."

My heart stops.

He...didn't like seeing me injured? I want to ask more. I remember our conversation in my mind...at least, I think I do. But what if it really was just a dream? Maybe I made up that nice version in my head and my sanity really is hanging on by a thread—it wouldn't be the first time.

The walls between dreams and reality are getting thinner by the day. Os scoops some of the balm onto his fingers. With his other hand, he reaches up and gently grasps my cheek. It's sore to the touch and I wince. He pauses, turning my face to the side.

"How bad is the pain?"

"I've felt worse."

Os is quiet for a moment, "You don't need to be strong all the time, Amalia."

On instinct, I grind my teeth in frustration at his knowing words. But sharp pain bursts into my jaw and I have to swallow a groan. Os just lifts a brow.

"Fine, it hurts, but it's just when I grind my teeth."

Os nods, leans forward, and rubs the balm along my jaw, tracing what must be the scar. His large fingers are surprisingly gentle as he massages the balm in, the scent relaxing my tensed muscles.

My eyes drift closed as I lean into his touch. He presses forward more, allowing me to rest the top of my head on his shoulder. He opens the neck of the shirt I have on just enough to massage the balm down my neck and onto my shoulders.

The herbs in it are numbing, and soon the ache in my jaw is gone. I go limp in Os's arms, my full body weight against him as my eyes close in pure bliss.

No one has ever taken care of me like this. Dyana is so much younger than me that I always took care of her, not the other way around. My throat clogs with emotion and I force the tears away, trying to stay in the present instead of in the ghosts of my past.

"I did the best I could, but...there's some light scarring. There was too much damage. But, if you apply this balm daily, it will help with the pain and soften the scar tissue, which will lighten it." His voice holds no pity, and for that, I'm grateful.

"Have a lot of experience with scars?" My voice is scratchy and low from the massage.

He finishes and closes the jar, wiping his hands and I immediately miss the heat of his touch.

"I have too much experience with it," Os responds finally. We look at each other for a moment, his gold eyes glowing hotter than the two suns.

"Can I see it?" I ask. Os hesitates, but I stay firm. He nods, grabbing a small hand mirror from some drawer to his right and handing it to me.

With a tight breath and little thought, I raise it.

My eyes are almost gray; the color seeped out of them with my exhaustion, matching the dark purple circles underneath my bottom lashes.

I look like shit. I look tired. But that's not what holds my attention. It's the pink and red scar that bisects half of my jaw, all the way from my right jaw joint, down to beneath my chin. It feathers out, almost like the branches of a tree. With the tip of my fingers, I trace the lines. They're raised and angry, but the wound is completely closed.

I glance at Os, who has moved to lean against the wall, arms crossed as he watches me. He's still shirtless and his loose pants hang low, showing off the v of his lower abdomen and a light trailing of hair.

"Thank you," I whisper, and hold the mirror out to him, finished with it. He moves off the wall, grabbing the mirror and setting it next to me on the counter before boxing me in with his arms.

Logic disappears. I take in his chest, raising my hand to trace one of his biggest scars. It's right over his heart, and despite being covered partially by tattoos, the skin is still rough and raised. Someone tried to stab him in the heart. At my touch, he exhales hard and his eyes fall shut.

I wonder when the last time was that someone took care of him.

Os is still under my fingers, his skin is blazing hot. I'm surprised he's not steaming. But he doesn't do anything, doesn't react at all.

My hand falls, and I gently push off the counter, using my arm strength to lower myself to the ground. We stare into each other's eyes for another moment before I nod.

"I should be going, then."

Os just watches me, his eyes curious.

I walk past him and pull on a pair of leggings I spy on the floor. They're far too big for me, but it'll do for getting me back to my rooms. Os says nothing about me taking his clothes. He just leans against the wall near his bathroom, watching me as I putter about.

I shove my feet into my still bloodstained boots, cringing at the smell. I'll wipe them down later. After I lace them, I head for the door, pausing before I open it.

I glance over my shoulder, meeting his gaze once more, "We all have scars here, and the invisible ones are far worse."

I turn to open the door and suddenly Os's hand is on my arm, searing my skin. I gasp, but he just leans in and brushes his lips against my ear, "Goodnight, Amalia."

I meet his gaze, those golden eyes missing nothing.

"Goodnight, Os."

CHAPTER 26
DYANA

I walk back to my room in a daze. My legs move but I can't feel it. I can't feel anything. All I can see and smell and taste is blood. Amalia's blood—and her jaw hanging off her face.

That's all I see, over and over again. My clothes are stained with it, although it's hard to tell with the dark colors. I feel it though. I feel the streaks of blood on my stomach and arms. The hot metallic smell is still in my nose. Os burnt Amalia's clothes and the dozens of towels he used as he healed her. But I've been in bloody clothes for hours, and with each passing second, my panic increases.

I don't even notice that I've passed Mirielle, nor do I hear anything she says. I'm aware of her coming up next to me, but I just walk faster. I have to get to my room. I have to get these off, or I'm going to explode.

"Dyana, wait!" Mirielle calls, but it's like she's far away. I don't stop, not until I'm barreling into my room.

My hands shake so hard I can't even get my shirt off.

"Hey, what—" Mirielle pauses, trailing off as she sniffs and realizes I'm covered in blood. She grabs my hands, noticing they're covered in red streaks. "Dyana, what happened?" She drops my hands and cups my cheeks, eyes blazing with concern. A raging tempest ready to unleash a storm. "Whose blood is this Dyana?" I open my mouth but can't form words. "Dyana, answer me! Is this your blood? Are you hurt?"

I continue to shake, so she wraps me in her arms. Her comforting touch makes me shatter as the tears start to fall.

"Come here, it's okay now. Let's get you into some clean clothes, love." Mirielle murmurs, her voice gentle. She leads me into the small bathroom. I numbly follow, silently sobbing, arms wrapped around my waist as if I need to be held together.

One of the tiny bathtubs is full of cold, dirty water.

Mirielle glances at me before kneeling and putting her hand in the water.

My vision is blurry from the tears, but I watch as the water turns clear and steam starts wafting off the top.

"Y-you," I try to say, crying too hard to talk.

"I can't do much, just slight temperature adjustments and I can make any water clean." She smiles again and stands, walking over to me. Mirielle takes my arm and gently guides me to the small tub before stripping my clothes off.

There is nothing romantic about this moment, and yet it's the most intimate moment I've ever experienced. She pulls my soaked top off and pushes down my pants. I stand naked, coated in blood as she takes my arm and guides me into the tub. I'm tall, so it's a very tight squeeze and I have to pull my knees up all the way to my chest. Mirielle disappears for a moment, leaving her sweet citrus scent in the air.

I cry harder, head on my knees, my eyes closed to the world.

Mirielle reappears with a small bar of soap and an empty cup that she stole from the mess hall one day.

She kneels behind me and begins to clean the blood off. She dunks the cup in the water and wets my hair before soaping up her hand and scrubbing my scalp. Her movements are slow and careful as if I'm some treasure.

"They—Gods, Miri. They b-beat Amalia. Her face, oh Gods, h-her jaw was hanging off her face." I sob again, barely able to get the words out. "If it wasn't for Os, she would have bled to death. She almost died. I saw the panic in Os's eyes. I saw exactly how close of a call this was. She can't die. She's all I have. I-I don't want to be alone again."

I cry harder then, unable to talk. Mirielle rinses my hair and finishes cleaning my stomach and arms. When she's done, she grabs a clean towel and has me stand before wrapping me up and guiding me back into the room.

She sits me on the end of the bed and begins drying me off, making sure there's not a single drop of blood left.

When she's done, she sits beside me and gathers me in her arms again. Her red curls tickle my face.

"Is she...is she okay, Dy?" she whispers.

"Sh-she's okay," I stutter, gasping for breath around my sobs. "She—" my voice hiccups, "she will have pain in her jaw for the rest of her life. But he mended bone and muscle. I-it was the worst thing I've ever seen in m-my life. I could hear it. I had to cover my damn ears at one point. It was so fast compared to the fae healers."

"You're okay, Dyana. Amalia is okay. Os healed her. It's okay." Mirielle sinks to the floor with me, wrapping herself around my back like a shield. I clutch her arm as she just rubs my back lightly, arms tight around me. "You are safe. Here and now, you are safe. Be here, Dyana. Stay here." She whispers over and over again, her hand rubbing my back and caressing my hair.

I cry until my eyes are swollen and stinging, but Mirielle never lets go, never stops holding me, as if she's aware her grasp is the only thing holding me together. The tears finally slow and my breathing calms. I lean into Mirielle, practically sitting on her in nothing more than a towel.

"Os is something more, then." Mirielle remarks.

I pause, "I think so."

"Is he someone we should be worried about?" She asks the question calmly, but I hear the threat in her question.

"As much as I dislike him, he saved her life. He's an ass, but he's not so bad. I can tell that he cares." Mirielle just 'hmms' in return.

I pull back, pushing my still damp hair off my face, and wince at Mirielle's damp shirt.

"Yeah." I sigh, and then look to where her white tunic is now stained with my tears. "Gods, sorry I—"

"No apologizing," She cups my face with her soft hand and for a moment I wonder if she might lean in and kiss me. But the door opens, making me shriek.

"It's just me," Ama says, her voice still a bit hoarse. We quickly scramble to stand. "You ready for dinner?"

Ama pauses, cocking her head as she takes in my state of undress.

"Are you wearing a towel to dinner, Dyana?" she asks in that all-knowing older sister voice.

I glare, "No, I was just getting dressed."

She raises a brow but lets it go. We both get changed. The silence is awkward. I finish getting dressed first since Amalia is moving slowly. If you pay attention to her, you can see the small winces and pauses, which tells me she's in a good amount of pain. But outside of that, she's acting like normal—even if her eyes are leached of color. The scar on her jaw is startling. All things considered, it's minor. But it's still angry and red, standing out against her fair skin and brown freckles. She was intimidating before, but now...she's terrifying.

Considering what she went through, we just stand there, unmoving and hollow. How can she act so casual right now? When a few hours ago, she almost died?

"Never thought I'd be glad for porridge," Ama mutters. "Let's go."

She heads out the door, and Mirielle and I share a glance.

CHAPTER 27
AMALIA

I slowly limp to Os's room after training. Every step sends shooting pain up my legs and through my sides.

This morning's double run was miserable, but I stayed on my feet the whole time. The moment we stopped, I passed out and embarrassingly woke up to Os standing above me. Then I threw up all over his shoes—and myself. A bucket of water and a change of clothes later, and here we are.

Strength training after the laps was even worse. When we left breakfast, and everyone went to stand up, for a moment I thought I might have to crawl out on my hands and knees. Dyana had to haul me up to my feet.

In their infinite gratitude, the training team announced that the High Council was increasing our food intake to help bulk up our muscles, so we now get a second, late lunch. They want warriors—not scrawny little humans.

After our second lunch, seamstresses from the Citadel showed up demanding our measurements. It was a struggle to get through it without punching someone in the face as they pinched and poked at me.

The Gauntlet is close enough that they've begun building our fighting leathers and armor. The fae, in overtaxing the rest of the Kingdom and charging an ungodly amount for tickets to the Fray, are sitting upon a mass amount of wealth. Hence the extravagant outfits. Anything for their entertainment, right?

"You're late," Os calls as I push open the door to his room, arms shaking.

"Fuck off, I can barely walk," I snark as I slowly limp to the sitting area next to our practice area. Os walks out of the bathroom and gives me a pointed look.

"I'll take you down to the Pits and show you where you'll be working. You'll clean stables for four hours, and then you'll be able to come back for dinner. There will be a shift switch of the soldiers on duty, which is how you can tell you're done." He pauses, "But first," his eyes rake over me, and I catch fire, "you need to bind your hair and wrap it. Trust me when I say you don't want to draw any attention. It's also for the smell."

"Great," I mutter.

He holds up a dark brown scarf and motions for me to turn. Confused, I face the constantly crackling fireplace as he stands behind me.

When Os runs his hands through my hair, I gasp. He begins easily weaving my hair into a simple three-strand braid.

My Father used to braid my hair when I was young. My mother taught him how to do hers, and he loved getting to teach me as she watched, proud and desperately in love.

It's heartbreak and need as I flash between past and present. I hate it; I hope he never stops.

"How did you learn how to braid?" My voice was raspy as if I'd spent hours crying.

He's silent for a moment, weaving and tightening the braid. His fingers brush against the nape of my neck. Goosebumps break out all over my skin as my temperature heats, heart racing at his gentle touch and the feel of his warm hands on me. Os ties a thin piece of leather around the end of the braid, securing it. He lays it gently down my back.

"My sister taught me." Os continues wrapping the scarf around my gray strands, tucking the braid in and looping and weaving until it comfortably covers the majority of my hair, although some shorter strands in the front peek out slightly.

"She taught you well." My voice is scratchy.

She taught you well? Gods, I'm bad at this. I berate myself as Os wraps the scarf around my neck, large, scarred hands brushing against my skin lightly as I suppress a shiver. The scarf smells like him and it's erasing my ability to think properly. Looking down, I see that he's given me a way to cover my mouth by pulling the excess scarf up, in case I need to filter out some of the scent.

"Are you reading my mind?" I glare.

"You were practically shouting."

"Great," I huff.

He goes to say something but closes his mouth, deciding otherwise. "Let's go. The sooner you start, the sooner you'll be done."

It's a struggle not to feel a bit disappointed. I don't know exactly what I want him to say. But that dream is seared into my memories, making me question more and more if it really happened.

Long before it was the Dragon Pit, the large cavern far underneath the Arena used to be a temple dedicated to Morrigyn, Goddess of War and Wisdom. The natural sweeping cave system had freshwater streams and giant stalagmites, making it a visual wonder. People traveled for days just to see it for a brief moment. It was the gem of Arkaydia. Morrigyn was not the only God worshiped in Arkaydia, but Morrigyn was the most widely observed Goddess. So the humans worked with the magyka and the Dragons to painstakingly craft a giant, stone statue of Her in Her honor. It was a shock that the Dragons offered to help, considering they pray to the Dragon God, Livyathin—or so I've read.

It took decades, but once it was complete, all beings and creatures flocked to pay tribute and give thanks to Morrigyn. For all life comes from the Mother.

That safety was soon ripped away when the fae appeared through a portal in the middle of our world.

The change was immediate, according to the histories. The moment the fae arrived, the magyk of Arkaydia began to dim.

Then came the pillaging and the burning—yet the Morrigyn didn't save anyone. Thousands died, but sadly, the majority saw that the fae had powers beyond their wildest dreams. The fae were there, and the Morrigyn wasn't. So they bowed down, welcoming the Cult of Sol Constantus.

What was once a place of glory and worship is now a pit of misery.

I pant, my side aching as we finish our descent down the longest, darkest set of stairs I've ever seen. I'm not even sure how long we've been walking down.

"Most people trip on the stairs," he comments, but I don't respond because there's light below. We're there.

Os stops as the stairs end. The ground is uneven and the air is damp and hot. The tang of sulfur is heavy in the air. I'm already sweating.

My mouth drops open as I take in the sight before me as we step into the light of the Dragon Pit.

The caves are enormous. The space is huge. Far above us, holes connecting to other cave systems line the ceiling. Then I see it. Dragons wearing what looks like a bastardized horse halter made of metal crawl in and out of the caves far above us. They fly through the air with large gusts, threatening to blow me over. Their melodic screeches leave me simultaneously terrified and in awe. The Dragons are all different colors. Most are covered in intricate, harsh-looking black armor. The Dragonguard is made up of the few Dragons that were able to be tamed. Now, they're the High Council's ever-constant threat.

I only see seven Dragons, but there are dozens of caves.

"How many are there?" I ask.

Better to do this here, he says. I go still, not at the sound of his voice in my head but the way his magyk is brushing against mine. Usually it's just a faint brush against my senses, but this time it feels like it's surrounding me, encasing mine and weaving through it like wildfire.

Sweet smoke is on the tip of my tongue as my anxiety lessens.

It's not gone, but it's calmer. Slower. My heartbeat settles as a balance washes over me.

Fine, I respond, giving him no sign of my confusion at what's happening in our minds.

The Dragonguard is made up of 12 different Dragons, all born to the High Councilor's breeding program. he says, and I'm taken aback at the raw fury in his voice.

I'd heard whispers, but was hoping it was a lie.

Os's face is stone and fury as he shakes his head. *"They sedate the Dragons with magyk and...collect the sample from the males, and then impregnate the fertile females. One Dragon can often produce a clutch of multiple eggs. When they get too many, the hatchlings are killed and eaten."* His jaw clenches so hard I'm surprised his teeth don't shatter.

Another piece of my sanity withers away as the pieces fall into place and I grasp the reality of life for a Dragon. Fingers suddenly brush against my own. It's brief, so brief, but Os clasps my hand and squeezes.

My eyes jerk to his. His golden gaze burns with resentment and grief—so much grief I'm almost knocked back a step.

The fact that I know my own grief is mirrored back keeps me steady.

"What about the Dragonguard? They're just loose in here?" I clear my throat, trying to swallow down my fear. Dragons can smell it.

Os looks up, a curious expression on his face. One of...regret, I think.

"Their halters contain a shock system that prevents them from coming down here," he says calmly. *"You don't need to worry. It's best to ignore them."*

We head for one of the many rows of giant metal stalls. It would seem impossible that anyone was able to build such a thing, but based on the slight sheen of the metal, this was the work of some high, complicated magyks and the fae are not known for being able to work that type of magyk. Someone helped them build these. Someone...powerful.

An invisible wave hits me, the scent of animal droppings and hot, tangy blood assaulting my senses and making my eyes water. I force myself not to gag. I pull the scarf higher over my mouth.

It's a fucking prison.

I'm nauseous as I catch glances of Dragons through tiny, meager barred windows as we walk past.

Thought and logic leave me as I glimpse their scarred, bony bodies. They're so skinny. The huge beasts are stuffed into these boxes as they look out to me, their glowing eyes wide in terror. I see some tremble at the sight of us, panting in fear, and it's an effort to keep my legs working.

I want to fall to the ground and cry. My hands tremble so hard it hurts.

"It's not a prison," Os says. *"It's death."* I feel his own heart breaking at this, his grief like a giant tidal wave washing over to me, making my chest tighten to the point of pain.

Is this how he feels all the time?

"How?" I ask, not specifying what I want to know, but Os understands.

Once a month, the Arena hosts the Fray, where knights and soldiers can fight each other, and the winners are allowed to fight a Dragon. All of the Dragons in here? They're waiting for their fight—and their death. Whether through the Fray or the Gauntlet, death awaits them.

"This is...hell." One of them, at least. But I don't include that last part.

Os glances at me, *"Yes. It is."*

I look around, continuing to follow him and passing various fae attendants on the way. Each stall has a window with black iron bars, small, maybe as tall as me. Some I don't see anything in, but I gasp and trip when bright yellow eyes fill another, pupils following me. I hear thumps and screeches against the metal inside, but they get nowhere, unable to do anything but scratch. Every single Dragon I see is nearly starved to death. There are scars, open sores, broken scales and jagged teeth.

The stench of rotting flesh is so strong I can barely breathe.

One Dragon throws itself against the stalls over and over. Os clenches his teeth so hard I actually hear one shatter. As we pass the trembling metal doors of the stall, listening to the Dragon cry out in frantic pain as it tries to kill itself, I have to pause and run around a corner to empty my stomach. The noise is too much to handle.

"Are they ever allowed to fly?" I ask, but I fear I already know the answer.

"No, they're taken on walks but that's it. It's been centuries since they last saw the sky." Again, that grief hits me, and inside, I scream.

No God would allow this to happen to their world. Would sit by and watch, unhelpful in the face of such atrocities. The Gods are gone and all that's left is chaos and despair.

I glance to the side, seeing two fae attendants with sneering faces poking into one of the stable windows with what look like metal prongs, laughing. A screech of pain hits me as I see blood spurt out the window, the prod breaking skin. I do throw up then but swallow it back down, grimacing at the rancid taste, almost choking. Os glances back at me in alarm.

"I don't know if I can do this. I don't think I can do this," I whisper to him.

"You can do this. It's only a few hours. Don't look around; don't do anything other than look at your task. Tune it out," he orders with complete confidence. "The stalls you'll be cleaning are empty. You'll get in, get your wheelbarrow, scoop the shit out, and then move to the next."

I take a deep breath, steadying myself and my racing heart.

Fine. Let's get this over with.

"When the handlers come back, just ignore them. Move on to your next stall and get the job done. They won't bother you if you keep your head down. No talking back, no being a brave fool. Get in and get out." I nod with his words, and our eyes meet. He gazes at me with a resolute and firm look on his face.

My heart clenches when I see pieces of stone line the ground—the shattered statue of Morrigyn. Forever broken and in plain sight, as if the fae wanted to remind us that our God abandoned us.

"Follow close and say little." Os orders, and I just nod. Following behind him dutifully and refusing to look around. My hands are shaking and my eyes are wide, but I just stare at his large back which is currently covered in one of those black tunics he always wears.

"What stall is the candidate assigned to?" he asks, stopping. I run into his back but try to silence my oof. That sweet smokey scent at once overtakes the smell of shit and blood, and I have a moment of peace from it before I realize he's speaking to someone.

"Row 30," the unknown attendant says, chuckling. "*All* of it."

Os stiffens at this but says nothing; he just nods.

"Good luck, little human. You're going to need it," the fae says. We continue on, and I force my eyes not to widen in alarm as I catch the pale white fae with black hair and grotesque red eyes.

When the fae smirks at me, I see deformed, too-long fangs and shiver. It licks its lips while it looks at me before laughing again and continuing on. The attendants wear red uniforms, the long robes ultimately protecting them with hoods pulled up around their heads. I wonder briefly if the color is because they get blood on them regularly.

"Row 30 is for the oldest Dragons. This means they're probably tired and worn down. But the older a Dragon is, the more powerful they are. If any of them are brought back to their stall when they're finished walking, move on to the next empty stable immediately. Keep yourself as far away from them as possible. They might be old, but they are completely feral and more dangerous than your wildest imagination."

"Lovely," I mutter, as the situation seems to get worse and worse with each passing moment.

We come to a row at the far end of the cavern finally, and Os gestures to a cubby with a wheelbarrow and pick.

"Bring the wheelbarrow back here when it's full, and dump it down the shoot in the back," He points, and I see that there's a hole in the floor that opens up if you press a button with your foot.

"Close the chute when you're done and repeat. That's it." He hands me some gloves, and we just stare at each other, two rocks in a stormy sea.

"It will be okay. Keep your head down, get this done, and get out. I will meet you in my rooms. If I came down to get you, it would look suspicious." I'm not surprised. I close my eyes for a moment and use the breathing techniques he has been teaching me.

In through the nose, out through the mouth. My emotions simmer and calm slightly as I shove them deep inside my iron walls, locking the door tightly behind them.

"Good. Keep doing that," he nods. We stare into each other's eyes for a few more moments, and I want to say something but I am frozen, unable to do so. *"Stay*

safe. Stay in control. I'll see you when you're done, Amalia." He nods again and then leaves with a slight huff as if frustrated.

I watch him depart, following the sight of his back for a few moments. I notice the other fae attendants and quickly avert my eyes, putting on the gloves Os handed me, grabbing the wheelbarrow and rake. It's heavy and bangs against my ankles, threatening to make me hiss, but I just keep my mouth shut and my eyes to the ground as I head for the first open stall.

Get in.

Get done.

Get out.

I let out a deep breath and prepare for the wave of putrid feces that hits me, telling myself this is just another day at the barn, scooping horse shit.

It's just... really, really big horse shit.

I'm on my second stall, zoning the fuck out as my arms ache with the repetitive scoop, turn, dump motion. My shirt clings to my damp, sweaty skin, and my leggings are absolutely fucking ruined, shit and dirt smeared everywhere. I don't think I will ever be able to get these clean again. They need to make some magykal pants or something for anyone working down here, stars above.

I'm not sure exactly how long I've been down here, but I guess it's been a few hours, so I likely have one or two stalls left. I roll the wheelbarrow out of the cleaned-out metal box that some Dragon calls home. I ignore all the claw marks on the wall, refusing to look and acknowledge how big the talons would have to be to make such scratches on such an undamageable surface.

So I don't look, refusing to let my mind think about it for even a moment. This is just a really, really big horse stall. I've been daydreaming these past few hours or however long it's been, thinking of one of my favorite books. A woman with powerful magyk disguises herself as a man to become a Knight, but she falls in love with her commanding officer—the King, and they start an illicit affair. Besides her talking cat, he is the only one who knows her secret. I've read it dozens of times, but it's still heart-pounding, regardless of the fact that I know the ending. She was everything I wanted to be. I fell in love with her a bit, I think.

I continue to zone out and daydream about my books as I shove the wheelbarrow up, dumping the Dragon dung with a groan.

Gods, that was so fucking heavy.

I start the process over again, returning with the much lighter and now empty wheelbarrow and going to the next stall. This had twice as many scratches.

Nope. It's not there. Focus on the dung. The lovely, lovely dung. I remind myself, keeping my head down. The scarf around my head is soaked with sweat, but I keep it pulled up over my face anyway. I've seen a few attendants walk by but no Dragons, and so far, surprisingly, I've been left alone. With the scarf, all they see is someone cleaning stalls. The rolling, layered screeches from the Dragonguard above became hypnotizing rather than overstimulating.

Each call was slightly different and sounded like multiple notes made up into one tune. It was a sound so clearly otherworldly that you couldn't help but pay attention.

It's beautiful. Almost like they're singing a song that we are just too mortal to understand.

Time passes, and I zone out again. I'm almost finished with the stall; just the front right corner is left. I let out a huff and rub my arm along my forehead. I'm so sweaty, it's dripping into my eyes.

I hear a distant thumping and the sound of chains dragging on the ground, followed by the low murmur that has to be some fae attendants talking. But the dragging and thumping was new.

Drag, clink.

Drag, clink.

Drag, clink.

The sound gets louder and louder. And I haphazardly finish my corner, hurrying out. It's a struggle not to let the wheelbarrow tip over, but as I turn to go to the chute to empty this thing again before I start the next stall, I see something turn the corner.

A giant scaled, crimson snout with slanted nostrils as big as me. And it keeps coming. Keeps emerging into the walkway. Getting bigger and bigger until it fully emerges.

I understand the huge stalls now.

The crimson Dragon towers over us. But it's so skinny, and it looks so weak. The giant muzzle around its head, a gross, painful-looking metal device, gives it just enough room to open its mouth a few inches, but not enough to fully bite anyone.

Gods.

I dart into an empty stall to stay out of the way, out of sight and reach. But I can't tear my eyes away from the beast as it fully comes around the corner. It limps slightly, and I notice the thick metal chains as wide as my arm wrapping around each of its scaled legs. The Dragon's red scales are covered with scars. Two attendants with prods follow behind and poke it when it walks too slowly. The Dragon's tail flicks and they poke again, making it wince. I want to go over there and slam this rake down on their stupid fucking heads. I want to do that so bad.

But I can't—and it kills me. Kills yet another broken piece of myself, leaving me in tatters.

Some day, another piece will break, and there will be nothing left to hold me together.

The Dragon has a few missing fangs and some that are just broken in half, but the few that are whole are taller than my body and wicked sharp. There must be a spell that absorbs the shockwaves of its movement because it's giant, and yet the ground does not shake. It's far bigger than Bloodwyng, the Dragon that destroyed our town. This Dragon's wings have holes in the delicate webbing, and one looks like it was broken and healed slightly out of place.

Despite that all, it's beautiful. It's so beautiful I want to burn this world to the ground for doing this to such beauty.

A thin black chain clasps around the red Dragon's neck. As soon as I concentrate on it, sending my magyk to investigate, I bounce off a thick ward, and the taste of rotten, sour apples hits my tongue. More high magyk that the fae should not be capable of. There's something else, too. I smack my lips, silently. Trying to place what it is.

As the Dragon passes the stall, I can't help the tremors that shake my hands as my heart races from the adrenaline of seeing a giant claw as big as my body land on the floor just before me. I keep my head down, scarf covering my nose, and shadows cloaking my frame. The Dragon never sees me, but I look up slightly after its head passes.

The Dragon's belly is made up of more delicate, smaller scales compared to the large plates covering its back. A Dragon's belly is its most vulnerable area. Where this Dragon's scales should shine, there are just scars and wounds, some barely closed.

I watch as the fae attendants in their stupid red capes poke and prod it with a long, sharp prong. It growls but continues walking, not even trying to use its tail to take them out.

The Dragon is herded into its stall, where I hear another high-pitched shriek of pain and the clank of metal. The fae attendants laugh, talking to themselves.

"Gods, I can't wait for Friday. Do you think it'll win?" One of them asks the other.

"No fucking way, look at her. She's ancient and crippled. Who knows if she can even fly anymore." He chuckles with pleasure. "I wonder if she'll squeal when the Bastard rips her throat out." I gag, silently covering my mouth with my hand as I take a deep breath. The Bastard must be another Dragon. Gods, she's in the Fray.

This Dragon is going to die.

"I can't wait to find out," the other responds. "Although at this point, she is so skinny and worthless, the meat on her bones is probably rotten." My knees go weak, and I almost stumble as I realize they're talking about eating the crimson Dragon and what else they'll do with her dead body afterward.

Horror fills me, and my hands go cold at the knowledge that the creature I just saw will be slaughtered and consumed in three days. The attendants pass by me, and I mark them, memorizing all of their features, furious. How could they treat such a beautiful, mythical, majestic creature like a Dragon this way?

A large door is shut, closing it in, and the fae walk back the other way, passing by the stall I'm in. They don't notice me. The shadows conceal my body, and I stay perfectly silent. As soon as they get around the corner, I take a deep breath and quickly wheel the wheelbarrow back to the chute. I don't look in the window, I keep my eyes to the ground. I make it to the chute and push the wheelbarrow up again until all of the dung slides out. Once I lower it back down, I robotically move to the next empty stall, which happens to be one past the crimson Dragon. I tentatively push the wheelbarrow along, passing the first stall I cleaned, and then walking past the one the Dragon went into. I'm almost past it when something comes over me. I don't know how to describe it, but it's almost as if the Fates reach down and turn my head to the side. Because the next moment has me looking into the stall window. But I see…nothing. No guards, no distant talking. A bell tolls lightly in the distance, signaling the end of shift, and I hear the shrieks of some of the Dragons harmonizing along with it. It's layered and so sad. Tears fall from my eyes at the pain and longing in their voices.

My mind goes blank and suddenly my legs are moving. I leave the wheelbarrow behind me as I take another step, and another, until I'm standing right in front of the giant window.

I take another step until I silently press against those bars, trying to get a closer look.

At first, there's nothing. Just darkness.

"Dragon?" I whisper, taking a closer look.

This is a bad idea; why am I doing this? Just as I'm about to head back to the wheelbarrow, smoke wafts up from the ground. I cough as it hits my face, but then, emerging from the dark, whirls of smoke, comes a snout.

A crimson, scarred snout and glowing orange and yellow eyes.

I don't move, but every drop of blood in my body and every thought in my head becomes perfectly still, in absolute opposition to my racing heart as the Dragon moves with a groan, shoving its body up towards the window, positioning so it's staring right at me.

Oh shit.

CHAPTER 28

Tiny blue eyes stare at me. They remind me of an Ice Dragon's scales; frozen and cold.

The girl is scared. She looks human, but her scent is strange. Bitter and sweet. I can't put my claw on her scent, but it's old. Very old.

And very powerful.

Who are you, little rabbit?

She's still here despite her fear and heart racing like a racing bunny rabbit.

The girl takes a deep breath. "Are you okay, Dragon?"

The girl is...concerned? How strange.

I test the girl, bare my muzzle, showing off my fangs. She's barely the size of one of them, but the little rabbit doesn't move. She's terrified, but still, she doesn't move. Instead, she closes her eyes and takes a deep breath. Her heartbeat slows. I cock my head, curious.

I press closer and huff out another large cloud of smoke that hits her in the face, making her scarf fall and uncovering her mouth. I see dark gray strands that escape from where her hair is tucked in.

Has the world changed so much since I last roamed the skies? It had been so long. It's been so long since I freely roamed the lands, I have no grasp of what is common and what is not.

The little human looks young from far away, but my eyes can see the sunspots on her skin, the freckles decorating her face, and the lines of someone who isn't necessarily old, but who has experienced much grief in what life they've lived.

The human takes a breath and turns to leave, but pauses. Those tiny round blue eyes meet mine again, and they look...sad.

Not in color, shape or size. But in...grief.

I huff out another breath, smoke trailing and making shapes through the bars. She just looks at me.

"I'm not sure if you understand me, Dragon. But I'm.." the rabbit pauses, collecting herself. "I'm so sorry. You deserve so much more than this. I'm sorry. I'm so, so, sorry," she repeats the apology repeatedly as tears fall from her eyes, and she squats down, covering her face as she cries silently for a moment.

This little girl is sad for me. So sad, her eyes now leak.

It's been centuries, lifetimes, since I saw any being react this way in the face of Dragonfear.

Perhaps it's the knowledge that my life is finally at an end that motivates my actions. But I reach out, wrapping the rabbit gently in my magyk. Humans usually have no mental barriers, so I reach out to her mind and connect with her.

The girl jolts, trying to block me. But no walls can keep a Dragon out if they really want in. Our magyk is much stronger, just as Livyathin intended.

She turns back, looking at me, before approaching the bars once again. We're nose to nose, as we sit, breathing each other's air. When I exhale, her hair billows in the hot wind. But she doesn't wince.

Not once.

I'm in her mind, in her thoughts, but I say nothing. Testing her, seeing what she'll do.

I blink in shock, inhaling as her magyk brushes mine. Not human at all.

In the old days, I would never deign to let anyone, let alone a human, into my mind. It was considered the most intimate act to communicate this way with any being other than a Dragon. But times have changed, and I am old.

"Hello, little rabbit." I capture her magyk within mine, locking her into place. Her eyes go wide, and her mouth opens, and I feel her pure shock at being chosen to hear the voice of a Dragon for the first time in more than five hundred years.

CHAPTER 29
AMALIA

"Hello, little rabbit," A female voice made up of multiple tones and octaves, as if dozens of voices are harmonizing at once, blasts into my mind with the force of a newborn star. I stare in awe, eyes wide, and I look around again to make sure we're still alone. The dragon is speaking to me.

Holy shit.

"Hello," I whisper back in shock, unable to think of anything better to say.

"What do you want?" the Dragon demands, and I wince, my head pounding at her loud voice. My hands begin trembling as my heart races faster than a galloping horse.

"I-I just wanted to say I'm sorry."

Gods, what a stupid answer. But I'm floundering, out of my depth in the face of this creature of legend.

"Yes, you said that already." She doesn't sound old, but I can feel the weight of her magyk as if the entire world was spread across my shoulders. This Dragon is old, and very powerful. I start to get warm and a little lightheaded, but once again, I pause, taking a deep breath and forcing my heart to calm the same way I would with a nervous horse.

"What is your name, rabbit?" she asks.

I force my terrified mind to form words, *"My name is Amalia. Amalia Roth."* I'm unsure why this is even happening and what the fuck I'm doing, but there is something about this Dragon I feel intensely pulled to.

"Run along then, Amalia Roth. This is no place for you." The Dragon huffs smoke at me and goes to turn away from the small window.

I stiffen at the sudden hurt her words caused. Not because of her but because of what they remind me of.

The truth.

"There is no place for me anywhere, Dragon."

The Dragon pauses, facing me with her glowing, fiery gaze. *"There is nothing you or any two-legged being can do. No power exists that can stop the fae. Those who might have had a chance are long dead, exactly like we're soon to be,"* she responds. The pain and exhaustion in her voice breaks my heart, leaving even less of my sanity and will behind. *"But I thank you for your heart, young one. Now, my body aches, and my soul is tired. Leave me, Amalia. Leave me to my fate in this wretched place. It's the only thing that can be done."* The Dragon turns, curling into the corner. I step closer to the bars to watch her skinny body curl upon itself as she uses her tail for a pillow on the almost bare, somewhat straw-covered hard floor.

"You're in the next Fray, aren't you?" I ask.

"Yes. Soon, I will be rid of this tiresome existence. The age of the Dragon ended a long time ago." My eyes fill with tears at her hopeless words, yet I understand. If I were her, I would feel the same.

"Some days, I wish to be rid of my own existence. The fae pollute everything they touch, eventually killing it," I admit.

"You've lost someone to them?" she asks, curious, as she adjusts her head to face me.

I'm afraid of this life, this situation, everything; but in this moment, I'm not afraid of this Dragon.

"My parents. I lost my parents."

"No siblings?" the Dragon asks, curious.

I hesitate. *"Sort of. A...family took me in and raised me as their own, but they were shunned. It was a lonely life. For all intents and purposes, I've always been alone. I have a sister now, but not by blood. We're each other's only family now. But sometimes..."* I pause, *"sometimes I miss them so much, even all of these years later, that I think I might actually die. Sometimes, I think I should have died with them."*

"I am sorry you know what it's like to lose a family, too. I've watched mine get tortured and killed for centuries. There is no beating them, young one. The end result

will always be the same. Best to have as little of their attention on us as possible, with what time we have left, and to get as far from here as possible."

My eyebrows raise. She doesn't realize I'm a candidate. But the bell chimes again, signaling the start of the next shift and the guards that would soon return.

"Go." the Dragon orders.

I pause, aware of the weight of this moment. *"Thank you for the honor of speaking with you, great one. I don't normally pray, but I will pray to the Fates and Great Livyathin in your name."*

"You know of Great Livyathin?" she asks. The fae banned any Draconian book or text.

"I have never seen the texts, but my parents told me stories of the Dragon God as large as the sky itself. They explained everything about this world, including the religions of all species." I take a breath, and the Dragon says nothing, just closes her eyes, and I assume the conversation has ended. I turn to leave, but not before taking one last glance at her.

A fallen God.

"May Livyathin be with you, great one." I bow subtly, acknowledging the ways of old where all the species who walked on two legs lived in deference to the great Dragons. I start to walk away but pause when she says one last thing.

"My full name would be incomprehensible to you. But you may call me Kydis."

"Kydis." I exhale hard, struggling to keep myself together when my grief threatens to tear me right in two. *"Goodbye, Kydis."* I whisper as I take one last glance and walk away, knowing if I ever come down here again, her stall will sit empty.

A feeling sparks in me, then. Something new. A tiny kernel deep inside me that latches on and waits, biding its time.

I let it.

I hurry up the stairs from the Dragon Pit in a daze and go directly to Os's room. I don't know why, but it feels important.

Except…if I tell him about Kydis, he'll ask more questions. Questions which I am not sure I want to answer. Fuck. I stop, unsure.

Os healed me, sure. But he can heal anyone.

How do I know I can trust him with something as precious as this?

At the word trust, I stiffen.

No, I cannot trust him, I can't trust anyone except for Dyana. I made a promise that I intend to keep. Having decided not to tell Os about my Dragon encounter, I spin around, ready to head back to the dorms.

"Oof!" I slam into a rock-hard body and it makes my jaw ache instantly. It's like running into a giant boulder—the person doesn't even move, and instead, I bounce off and start to fall to the floor. There's a blur and my descent stops, leaving me hanging only a few inches from the ground. The person pulls me to standing and I look up to multi-colored eyes.

One of green and one of amber.

The immensely pleased Crown Prince Nyall Drayven holds me in his arms with far too much comfort.

"Thank you, Lord Drayven." I grit out the words as I glare at him and push away. "What a pleasant surprise to see you in the Dragon Pit." I yank my arms and he lets me go, watching me with amusement.

"Amalia Roth," he rasps. "Pleasant, indeed. Be careful where you're going, Amalia Roth. Run into the wrong fae, and you'll lose your head." He smiles, flashing his pointed canines.

"Hmm. Losing my head or speaking to a Drayven," I lift both hands, pretending to weigh the options. My left-hand drops. "I think I prefer option one."

The Prince laughs, his eyes sparkling. Gods, he's attractive.

"You're a feisty one, aren't you?"

"Anything is better than being a Drayven."

He flashes a sad smile and *hmms* under his breath. I glance around, aware of how loudly we were speaking in this echoing hallway. If I'm seen with him, it actually will be my head.

"I've dismissed the guards, don't worry," Nyall says, seeing my concern.

"What privilege you have, Prince," I reply icily. He pauses, and another ghost of a smile twitches on his mouth before he approaches me, leaning in.

"That privilege isn't my status, Amalia," he pauses, his face inching closer to mine until we're breathing the same air. "It's power," he says. "See, they know that their magyk is no match for mine. They're afraid of me, they all are—my Father included. I'm the wild card, and that makes me the most dangerous one in the room."

I take a step back, wary. "Pretty speech. But from where I stand, you're still a prince. You haven't felt the pangs of hunger for days on end, nor the fear of wondering if you can even survive until the next day because you can't afford wood for a fire...that, Prince, is a privilege. To deny the power of your status would be hypocritical." Nyall just looks at me and cocks his head. "What are you doing?"

He doesn't respond, silently watching me. I squirm, uncomfortable and unable to stay still under the weight of his gaze. Nyall reaches up, and I freeze, not daring to breathe as he caresses my cheek and curls a piece of my gray hair around his finger, tugging lightly. I'm frozen, unable to breathe as he leans in, the scent of honeysuckle and musk assaulting my senses.

Prince Nyall leans in more and pauses, blinking at the realization that my dagger is pressed against his throat.

"Slow reaction, Prince. Aren't Fae supposed to have heightened senses? It seems yours are a bit dull."

Nyall's eyes twinkle with mirth. "You've got quite the bite, horse girl. Threatening to kill the Crown Prince *is* treason, you know." He makes no moves to remove my dagger.

Do it. He's Achan Drayven's son.

His father killed your parents. Get your revenge.

He took your family, now you take his.

My thoughts race, but I don't move. Because the Prince doesn't either. Not out of fear, instead, he's...calm.

"Go on, do it. Stab me. Kill the heir to the High Council seat. I think you'll be surprised at what happens next."

He pushes forward, and my dagger nicks him, drawing blood. I watch as it drips down his inked skin in a stream of crimson. Then I see it—a hint of black weaving through the red.

Red and black blood. Nyall Drayven is not a pure-blood fae.

He has their sharp angles and predatory grace, but that ruthless charm and sinful arrogance were unique, and imperial fae bleed silver. The Prince with Midnight Blood is something else entirely.

"Touch me again," I say, voice icy, "and it'll be the last thing you ever do."

He looks at me, calm and thoughtful and wholly unconcerned about his imminent murder at my hands. "So different from the woman I met in the Annag."

"That was before I knew the truth," I snap, dropping my dagger and taking a big step back. "You're just another evil Drayven bastard." I pull the dagger back and tuck it down into my boot.

"If I were to tell anyone about this conversation, you would be executed and your body tossed to the Dragons of the Pit," Nyall says casually, nonplussed.

"You won't. You could, sure. But after executing me, your Father would then turn to you. The fae don't look kindly upon one of their own, let alone an imperial fae, who was bested by an insignificant human woman. I wonder if you'd be exiled, or if they'd just kill you too."

"I am the heir to the High Council seat." He says the title, but there's no emotion behind it.

"That means nothing to a species that holds pride above all else. Do you really think you're irreplaceable?"

He smiles and reaches up, tugging on another curl.

"Do I need to get my dagger out again?" I ask with a violent smile. But the Crown Prince's mismatched eyes go distant, and a rush of thick, powerful magyk brushes against me. His magyk coats my tongue, and the taste of honeysuckle gets even stronger.

The Prince's magyk stops, and he looks down at me. "I will give you a piece of advice. Never assume that a familial bond equals loyalty."

"Am I supposed to believe you're not loyal to the High Council?"

"Believe whatever you want, Amalia Roth. I have a feeling nobody tells you what to do or what to feel. But look past the obvious. Perhaps you'll find something unexpected." He moves so fast I don't even see it, but suddenly, my dagger is in his hands, and he's cut off a few strands of my hair, sliding them into his pocket. I launch on him, but he just steps out of the way and calmly hands me back my dagger. I grab it and go to kick him, but he just avoids it again.

Gods, he's fast.

"Goodbye, Amalia Roth. I'll see you again soon, I'm sure." He winks and turns, walking away, but his voice still whispers in my ear. "A gilded cage is still a cage. Do not mistake a golden prison for a paradise."

Once he turns the corner, I silently follow, going slowly and adjusting the way I step to remove any trace of noise. As I trace his steps, the scent of cedar and violet assaults me, mixing with the honeysuckle taste on my tongue. His scent and his magyk combined.

I stop, however, when I peek around the corner. And I watch as Nyall Drayven, half-breed fae and Prince of Ur Daoine, son of the High Councilor, knocks on Os's door. The angle is wrong and I can't see Os's face, but when the door swings open, Os replies, voice low and smokey, before ushering the Crown Prince in.

I've seen all I need to, though.

I'm suddenly very relieved I didn't tell Os about this evening. I'm not telling him anything until I know where his loyalties lie, and from where I see it, those loyalties are not looking great.

CHAPTER 30
AMALIA

Year 417 PBM

"Father, why can't we stay here?"

Father crouches down, his warm brown eyes shot through with sparkling silver. He gathers me in a big hug, cradling the back of my head as he kisses my cheek.

"I like it here. I saw some bunny rabbits this morning! They were so cute and fluffy that I even got one to come up and sniff me! I used my magyk, just like Mother taught me."

"I have the smartest daughter in all the worlds!" he shouts, lifting me in the air. I shriek happily, giggling as he throws me into the air. The wind brushes my white curls, and I pretend I'm flying through the clouds with hundreds of Dragons. When I fall, he always catches me.

After a few moments, he sets me down, and our laughter quiets. Father has been quiet a lot lately.

"I know, spark. I wish we could stay too. But we can't. We must keep moving."

"But why? I'm not bad. I'm not even special. Why can't we just stay?" The tears start falling as I complain. "I want to have people friends, not just animal friends. I want a home, Father. Please."

"Oh, my sweet girl." Father wraps me in his arms, squeezing tightly, as if he alone can protect me from the world. "You have the biggest heart of anyone I've ever known, and I love that about you." Father pauses, "We never knew you'd be so special, you know. Never guessed it in our wildest dreams." He lets go of me and cradles my face, putting both big hands around my cheeks. "You are a dream come true, do you understand me? This is not your fault. Never think that. But it's our job to keep you safe, spark."

"But why do the bad people want me?"

Father sighs, running his hands through his white and silver hair.

"Ama darling, you need to get packed up." Mother comes in, and looks at us, a sad smile forming on her face. "What's this? Cuddles without me? The betrayal!" Despite being sad, Mother always manages to make me smile.

"Ama was asking why we have to move so often. Maybe you can help me explain."

"Oh, darling," Mother slides behind me and wraps her arms around us both from behind, resting her head against mine. Her warm scent of neroli and sandalwood is always so comforting. "Many years ago, I met a dashing Prince from a faraway land."

I gasp, "Like in my stories?"

"Yes, sweetheart, just like your stories."

"Did you and the Prince fall in love?"

She smiles wistfully as my Father lovingly caresses her cheek.

"We did, little spark."

"You're a Prince?" I gasp again.

Father smiles, "Not exactly, but close enough. When I met your Mother, I gave up my...authority and left my people. They wouldn't let us be together, but love is a rare and powerful creature, spark. I love you and your Mother more than there are stars in the sky. I would choose you both over power and wealth every single time."

I bite my lip, "But...you left your family?"

"I did, but soon after, most were killed by the fae. Some are still safe, but I'll never see them again."

My eyes tear up as I look at the sadness on my Father's face.

"Why did they kill them?"

"Because the Prince was very special," Mother says, hugging me tightly.

"Like me?"

"Like you, but also not. You're extra special. It's why our people were enemies."

I furrow my brows, confused, "What do you mean?"

"It wasn't always this way. Back when Ur Daoine was a place called Arkaydia, Magyk was a thing of wonder. But when the fae arrived, they soon realized that the people of Arkaydia had far more Magyk than they imagined. So, they did what they did best—gossip and stoke the flames of paranoia."

"Pare-uh-nee-uh?" I ask, sounding the word out.

"Very close, little spark." Father chuckles. "It means fear and worry for no reason." I nod, concentrating. "After whispering and worming their way into the ears of the Kingdom, Magyk began to be feared. So, the bloodlines separated, cutting themselves off to protect their existence. But the fae did something else. They told everyone that the Prince's bloodline was too powerful to exist."

"Oh no," I whisper, worried for no reason.

"So they could no longer sire children."

I nod, but I'm not really sure what he means. "And then you had me!"

Father chuckles again, deep and raspy. "Not quite yet. You see, little spark, I couldn't have a child for all I knew."

"But…"

"Amalia." He's using that tone. "It's rude to interrupt someone."

Shame fills me. "Sorry."

Father squeezes me, letting me know it's ok.

"The fae ensured my bloodline would end because our power posed too much of a threat, much like what happened to your Mother's people. But the fae, as they usually do, underestimated our power. Their plan didn't work, so imagine our surprise when we learned your Mother was pregnant. It turns out the fae did have something to fear—the combination of our Magyk is greater than any imperial fae or Elf. It's why they're after us now, little spark. They want your Magyk."

"Do…do they want to kill me?"

A breaking noise like a sob bursts from my Mother's throat.

"No little spark, they don't want to kill you," Father rasps, his eyes dark with regret. "They don't want to kill you; they want to use you."

NOW:

After a long night of gruesome nightmares, you would think I'd be lagging. And I am; I'm exhausted. But the only thing I see when I close my eyes is Kydis looking back at me. The only thing I hear in the silence are the screams and moans of Dragons slowly withering away in metal cages. The only thing I smell when I try to take a deep breath is their hot blood mixed with rotten eggs in the humid pit.

That's all there is.

I woke up this morning, and that ember burning deep inside me had grown into a steadily burning fire. As the seconds, minutes, and hours passed, my anger grew more and more.

Fury pushed me during our morning run, like hands at my back, forcing me to go faster and faster. I passed multiple of the stronger, fitter candidates, many of whom were male, ignoring their shocked murmurs as I left them in the dust. The Southland was the most wealthy human state of the Kingdom, so the Southlanders all had healthy, muscular figures. They had a leg up on the North—never going hungry.

A group of Southland males sneered and cursed as I passed them.

I was not the first to finish, but I was pretty damn close. And not everyone seemed all that happy about it.

"I thought she would be an easy kill," a male candidate murmurs as we walk to the mess hall. The fae orbs lining the ceiling adjusted, making it look like sunlight was brightening the hall. But with the exception of the Arena, the Dragon Pit was underground.

"She's been having extra sessions with the Head Trainer. Maybe they thought she was so bad, she wouldn't even make it to round one." One of the candidates, an androgynous bald person around my age, snickers, and a few others elbow them in agreement.

"Maybe Os is just fucking her," a snide girl around Dyana's age adds. My eyes narrow as my fury rises, but I ignore it, knowing this was inevitable at some point, but already my skin crawls as I feel everyone's gaze on me, following me, judging me.

I think everyone was so tired these first few weeks, we had all kept to ourselves. Sure, there were some groups, like the Southland males, but it seemed that most candidates stuck with their town partner and no one else. Except Mirielle.

"Whore," someone whispers loudly. My head cocks to the side, processing.

"Cheater," someone else whispers louder.

"She's trying to fuck her way into the finals," another says, and my head snaps to the side. Trying to find whoever dared say that.

Someone saw me and Os. But the training isn't a secret—just the magyk part.

Another laughs, "I thought he was with that scary-looking demis Ireyna. I saw her trying to dry hump him as she cleaned his throat with her tongue once."

"I'd fuck the gray-haired girl, but only if there was a pillowcase over her face. Those blue eyes are fucking creepy, man."

"I heard she sleeps in the stables with the horses. She probably neighs like a horse or something when she comes too. Can you imagine? 'Oh, yes that's it, neighhh'." The group breaks out in laughter behind me, clearly aware I can hear their every word.

You've been here before. You've been through worse. Suck it up. Ignore them. Do you want to win? Well, they sure as fuck are worried about you now, I berate myself.

When it's my turn to fill my bowl with the pale and lumpy porridge, Dyana and Mirielle limp in from the run. Both have red cheeks from the cold, but there is a twinkle in my best friend's eye that gives me a rare moment of pure, undiluted joy. She deserves to be happy, more than anyone. That kind of happiness wasn't in the cards for me.

I find us a small, empty table and we all sit down, each of us quiet as we scarf our food down.

"So, how was it? Did you see a full-size Dragon?" Mirielle asks around a spoonful of porridge, unable to wait any longer. We'd all been too tired to talk before running the circuit, but Dyana already knows. I'm thankful she didn't tell Mirielle yet, and I meet her green eyes. We smile at each other for a moment—she understands that trust isn't my specialty.

"I did. A few of them, actually." I look down and try to play it casual. I hadn't gone into all of the details on what happened with Dyana, just that I saw Dragons. I didn't want to scare or worry her, so I had only given her the barebones and kept the details to myself. It felt…strange, keeping secrets from her. I suppose it joined the others. Dyana knew almost everything about me—almost.

"One walked right past me. I've never seen something so big. It was unbelievable."

Dyana smiles. Mirielle looks astonished.

"Gods," Mirielle says, and Dyana laughs around her spoonful.

Something else flashes in her eyes. It's fast, so fast I'm not sure if I just imagined it. But it was…regret.

That thought gets stored away for later. Now isn't the time, but I won't forget what I saw.

"I'd piss myself. Or just faint, and I'm woman enough to admit that as the Goddess' honest truth," Dyana announces. Mirielle snickers, a fond look in her eyes.

Oh shit.

Mirielle is in love with Dyana. I don't know if Dyana loves her back or wants anything more than sex and companionship, but that look in Mirielle's eyes?

It was love.

Dyana doesn't notice my lack of laughter as she continues to chat about a book she wants to read. A few minutes later, a group of Southland candidates walk by, and I hear a myriad of hushed insults slung my way under their breath.

"Desperate slut." *Boring.*

"You're gonna die, freak." *Uncreative.*

"Horse-lover." *Next.*

"Have fun being Dragon dinner." *That one's new.*

"Lesbos scum." *What?*

That insult wasn't at me. I look at the Southland candidates who sneer openly at Mirielle and Dyana, who are sitting close enough for it to be clear there is something between them.

Something in me snaps.

I'm tired of being judged—of the whispers and the sneers. I'm even more tired of being a coward and doing nothing about it. But I can deal with it. I can suck it up and bite my tongue. What I won't deal with is anyone attacking my family. It might draw attention my way, but after yesterday and all that I witnessed, who...no, what I met? No, after so many years of staying silent, always hiding, never acting out, never drawing attention, I'm fucking done.

"Say that again." I shoot the male who said the rude word a look as Dyana's jaw falls to the floor and Mirielle chokes on her porridge, spraying it across the table.

"Ama! What are you doing?" Dyana hisses. I shush her with a wave of my hand.

The Southlander looks at me in horrified confusion and I smirk, "I said, 'say that again'. Don't be a cunt, muttering it under your breath like a scared little puppy. If you're going to insult someone, you ought to do it properly. So say it again to my fucking face."

His umber eyes glare at me as a few people around the mess hall chuckle. His black hair is tightly shaved against his head, but he has a full, long black beard. White tattoos in the ancient language of the N'yrenya tribe swirl down each arm, glowing against their deep mahogany skin. The white ink comes from a special type of clay that's found only in the Infinium Sands, and when mixed correctly, it almost appears to glow.

"I'm going to enjoy slitting your throat soon. You and your little lesbo friends." He says the word with a smile and makes a slitting motion across his own throat. Behind him, his motley crew laughs along at the joke, impressed by his behavior. The male looks at me and spits on the floor, shaking his head and turning to leave.

Dyana jolts and that's when I look to see that one of them spit on her shoes.

Well. Anonymity was nice while it lasted.

"With your pathetically sad sword skills? You fight like a girl, Reymand." I remembered his name only a moment before.

The Southlander—Reymand —pauses, turning. Males are always most triggered when you insult their skillset. Virgyl taught me that when I once suggested he was a lazy hunter. I lost my hearing for two whole weeks from his bark and learned males are rather sensitive.

"You little bitch," Reymand sneers. "What, Os didn't fuck you right last night or something? I'm surprised he can even get it up for a dirty animal like you." He oinks and moos, mimicking farm animals and everyone laughs along with his squealing. I ignore the jeers and look unimpressed.

"You sound a little obsessed, Reymand. Are you stalking me, Southlander? How pathetic." I turn forward to Dyana, and she turns her wide eyes into a casual look. Mirielle lets out an anxious laugh at that and slaps her hand over her mouth, chuckling behind it. I turn to look back at him, but a flash in the corner of my eye is all the warning I get before he's suddenly behind me, hand gripping my hair and slamming my head into the table. Stars burst behind my eyes as pain shoots into my face. Dyana and Mirielle jump to their feet and Reymand steps back, having made his point. I just smile innocently, but my voice is wicked.

"Oh my, you're jealous, aren't you? Jealous that I'm getting fucked and you're not." I spit the lie out, hoping it's as indestructible as iron.

Reymand steps towards me again, but despite my quickly swelling face and bleeding nose, I'm still faster. I let those iron walls inside of me open and breathe in as a burst of magyk floods my veins. I stand faster than he can see, and flash to his side, avoiding the punch he was throwing my way. His fist hits the air, throwing him off balance. Before he can recover, I grab him by the shoulders, turning him towards me, and knee him in the balls, making him groan and whine in pain as he clasps his crotch with both hands.

"Talk about my family like that again—no, call any woman that word again, and it won't be my knee in your crotch. It will be my knife."

Reymand moans in pain, writhing on the floor. I put one foot on his chest, pressing him down.

"Do you understand?" I whisper. "Say it, or I'll cut off your fingers."

"Amalia!" I hear Dyana in the background but I ignore her.

My rage is a wild, untamable thing. It's a wave that once formed, cannot be stopped. It will destroy everything in its path.

"SAY IT!" I shout, getting in his face and pressing on his chest harder.

"Fine! Fine! I'll never call another woman a Lesbos—I mean, that word. Now please, let me go," he begs and that's when I let up. He curls into a ball on the ground of the Mess Hall, moaning in pain as tears fall from his eyes.

My heart begins to slow and I force back my rage. Dyana looks at me with concern. Mirielle's eyes are wide with shock. I look around the rest of the room and see everyone else whispering about me, looking at me warily.

I sniff, aware that everyone is staring. I lost control again. But ever since seeing the Dragon Pit...I'm so angry.

With a dirty sleeve, I wipe the blood off my face. My jaw hurts so bad from the table slam, but the problem is my broken nose. I'm going to have a permanent lump on it at this point.

The pain in my jaw is making my ears ring, so I don't notice it, not at first, but the room goes silent. I feel it—the change in the air. A heavy, nervous energy that could only mean a predator was now in our midst. A hand suddenly lands on my shoulder and I know who it is in an instant. I'd recognize that searing heat anywhere. I let Os turn me, facing him as blood continues to fall from my nose. I let my hand drop, and it begins dripping down my neck and onto the floor.

We say nothing, but his mind caresses mine as he inspects my face. His eyes burn with anger; the gold so intense it's like staring into the heart of one of the suns. He helps me up, hand dwarfing mine. The heat of our skin makes me feel breathless. But I yank my hand back, and his eyes narrow quizzically.

"Are you alright?" he asks. He could ask me this in my head, but he's making a point. The fury behind his eyes makes my skin tingle. The veins on his arms and on his neck bulge, and his nostrils lightly flare as he inhales.

He's enraged.

"I'm fine, thank you, Head Trainer," I state coldly, my fury bleeding into my tone. I swear I see a tiny bit of hurt flash in his eyes, but this is business. We are nothing to each other, really. We are acquaintances and nothing more. Attraction doesn't change that.

Os nods and turns to walk over to the candidate, groaning on the floor. The candidates huddled around him run off, abandoning their friends to save themselves.

I watch in silence as Os kicks Reymand, which rolls him over. The candidate groans again. Os kneels down, accessing him. He darts forward quickly, grabs his nose and cranks it to the side.

Crunch.

"You broke my thucking nothe!" he shouts.

Blood spurts all over the candidate's face as he screams and tries to shove Os away. Os barely even notices. It's like a fly trying to kick a horse. Gods, I'm not sure even the fae were that strong. What the hell was he?

He looks down at the cowering candidate, who is now crying out, begging him to stop.

"Dragon stable duty for the next two days, Mr. Cyrus."

"But the Thray!" Reymand moans. Os shrugs.

"Don't care. You'll clean during the Fray, which I'm sure you were hoping to see. Everyone else will get to enjoy it." Os motions to the rest of the room casually. "Don't worry," Os slaps Reymand hard on the chest, making the male moan again, "there will be more chances to learn about Dragons. When we have our first Dragon lesson, you should go first. Doesn't that sound nice?"

Reymand trembles in fear. Os nods, standing up. "Make sure to be careful down there. It would be such a shame if you were to get eaten, wouldn't it? But you know, the Dragons get pretty hungry." There's a low rumble, like approaching thunder in the distance, and I swear the air turns electric. Os looks around slowly, meeting the gaze of everyone in the room for a few seconds.

"Everyone else here is smart enough to know not to touch her. Not to touch any woman here." He growls slightly, voice lowering, and I shiver. "Leave the killing for the Gauntlet, and if I see any one of you fighting outside of training, again, I'll rip out your fucking throats and go about my day without a second thought. Got it?" It's said so casually it takes me a moment to fully understand the threat.

"Oh, and Mr. Cyrus?" Os has everyone mesmerized. "I've never had any problems getting hard. But if you comment on my sex life again, I'll rip your dick off and feed it to the Dragons while you watch." With that, he turns and walks out leisurely. I realize my jaw is on the floor and snap it up, quickly looking at Dyana.

"Roth. Training, now." Os says, not yelling, but he magnifies his voice using magyk to be heard across the entire room.

"Somebody's in trouble," someone whispers.

"I would not want to be on his angry side," someone else says.

"He's going to kill her," another murmurs.

Not if I kill him first.

Dyana and Mirielle hurry over to me, concerned.

"That was so fucking hot, oh my Gods!" she whispers to me, waving her hands in quiet excitement, and I snort, cupping my aching nose. It's bruised, I don't feel any broken bones, but I am going to have a hell of a black eye.

"Shame about the nose though," I mutter. Dyana and Mirielle snicker.

"How's your jaw?" Dyana asks.

I grunt and she winces, "That bad?"

"I'll stop at our room and get that damn balm Os gave me. He's an asshole, but that stuff works."

Dyana bites her lip, hesitating, "Please be careful with him. I don't want you to get hurt."

I blink, realizing she means more than what she's saying aloud. We all ignore Reymand moaning and complaining on the floor as his friends try to pick him up, and head to complete the rest of our training day. Dyana catches my gaze and looks at me purposefully.

"ASK HIM TO HEAL YOUR NOSE." I wince as the words are shouted into my mind.

"Gods above, you don't need to shout."

"SORRY! Sorry. Is this better?"

I glare at her.

"Ask Os to heal your nose. If he healed your jaw, he can help with the pain."

"Fine." I sigh. *"Also...Os knows the Crown Prince. They're friendly enough to spend time alone. I saw them meeting on my way back from the Dragon Pit."*

"WAIT WHAT? WHY THE FUCK DIDN'T YOU TELL ME? THAT WHEN YOU GOT BACK? OS ACTUALLY IS WORKING WITH THE FAE? THAT LIAR!"

"Oh my Gods, stop yelling! I can hear you just fine. I don't know what it means, but until I get answers, I'm not fucking trusting him, healing skills or not."

"Ask him about it. Be upfront. Our lives are at stake here, and Os asked us to trust him. So, confront him about it. If we're to trust him, he can't keep something like that a secret. But, like, after you get him to heal your nose, just in case he changes his mind."

"Fine," I say aloud, putting a finger in my ear to try and rub out the tinnitus ringing after Dyana's ungodly noise level, and we go our separate ways. I look back and see Mirielle bump lightly against Dyana and they laugh. But there is something shadowed and guilty in Dyana's face. It's been there all day, but back in those woods, so many years ago, I promised her I would never invade her mind without permission.

Despite my nagging anxiety telling me to figure out what was bothering her, I left her alone.

She will tell me when she is ready. At least she has Mirielle. Her gray eyes sparkle with joy when Dyana speaks. Mirielle is an otherworldly beauty, but the warmth and calm confidence that radiated from her is mesmerizing.

I'm happy for her. I just hope she knows what she's doing because Mirielle Zenyth is very much in love with my best friend.

Which is a problem, since I have to kill her.

I jog to my room and grab the balm before catching up to Os outside of his room. He enters through the large wooden doors and I follow, panting lightly. But luckily all of the running has helped, because I'm not too winded.

"Aren't we training?"

"Not today," he says. I'm so confused; we always train.

Os stands in the center of the room as his door latches shut. At that noise, Os explodes, blurring to the sitting area and tossing the chairs against the wall, shattering them completely.

"He put his fucking hands on you. He touched you!"

"Reymand? I egged him on. He said something rude to Dyana and I snapped."

"He hurt you. Your jaw is barely healed. It hurts, doesn't it? I bet you can barely talk, you idiot. What were you thinking, pushing him into a fight?"

"He did, but I was fine. Clearly, since I bested him in one move. I'm not your property, Os, you don't have the right to say who can touch me and who can't." I don't mean to yell, but it comes out as a shout. Os roars again, and the sound is like a shot of pure fear.

"I'm not saying you're my fucking property, Amalia. But I can still defend you."

"I don't need anyone to defend me."

"Bullshit. You DO need someone to defend you because you're still holding back!" Os roars again and punches the wall, panting and furious, almost like he—

Oh. *Oh.*

I try not to react but my shock still must be evident. Os stops, going quiet, chest rising as he pants silently.

I slowly cross the room, sitting on the loveseat which is the only remaining piece of furniture after Os's tantrum. Os walks towards the fireplace staring into it, arms crossed.

This is his secret to tell me. Everything about him makes sense now, and I look at those scars much differently.

"I'm not holding back, Os. I'm being careful; there's a difference."

"Bullshit," he says, looking at me. *"That is total bullshit Amalia."*

"Bullshit?" I blink, suddenly furious again, "You wanna know what's bullshit? The fact that you're friends with Crown Prince Nyall Drayven. You lied to us. You said you're not any friend to the fae, yet imagine my surprise to see you greeting him like an old friend last night."

"You were there?" His eyes narrow.

"I came back to your room after stable duty yesterday. We ran into each other and when he left, I decided to follow him because I don't trust a word he says. I watched him saunter his pompous ass right into your room, Os. What the hell?"

Os blinks, "Did you try to kill the Crown Prince, Amalia?"

I pause, "I don't know what you mean."

Os looks at me flatly, "You can't just stab the Crown Prince of Ur Daoine. I was wondering why his shirt was bloody. The fucker claimed it was a bloody nose and as per usual, it seems he was lying."

"Oh, calm down," I respond, "I barely even broke the skin. And he cut off a piece of my damn hair, so I'd say he's lucky I didn't knock his brains out."

"He took. A piece. Of your *hair*?" The last word is roared so loudly my bones vibrate. "I'll fucking kill him."

I blink and Os blurs and he's sitting next to me, his legs pressed against mine. His scent surrounds me as he turns me so I face away from him. He quickly unbraids my hair. I can't keep track of where his hands are. He runs his hands through my hair as I sputter, confused. He immediately finds the place where the Prince cut off some length, and at the sight, he snarls, blurring to throw a piece of pottery at the wall.

"You and the Prince aren't friends then?" I ask carefully.

"I would rather stick my head in a wasp nest than be friends with that prick," Os snarls.

Alright then.

"Why was he in here, then?" I ask.

Os pauses at my question, hesitating. "Interestingly enough...he wasn't here to talk to me. He was here because he wants to talk to you."

My heart skips a beat, "I'm sorry; what did you just say?"

"The Prince would like to meet with you."

"He came here to talk to you, to ask for a meeting with me?" I ask, stunned.

Os sighs again, "Yes."

"But...why did he come to you and not just find me himself?"

Os just raises a brow at me, "Well, I am in charge here."

"Right. But I ran into him in the hallway. He could have just talked to me then." Os turns and walks to the sitting area of his room before taking a seat. He clenches his jaw in frustration before letting out another breath.

"Nyall...would like your help. Our help, actually. He wants to talk to me, too."

I blink. Then laugh—hard. "You've got to be joking," I giggle, "You expect me to believe that Crown Prince Nyall Drayven, son of the High Councilor, came here to ask you for what? Permission to ask for my help?" The sarcasm in my voice could cut glass. I laugh harder, "What world is the Prince living in that he thinks I would ever help him? I would rather die than help a Drayven."

Os just grunts, "I agree."

"What did you say to him?" I sit down in the chair across from him, crossing my arms.

"I told him he's a spoiled little prick, and I wish I had torn out his throat when I had the chance."

"So, you know each other."

Os's gold eyes jerk to my face. "Unfortunately. Speaking of, how do you know him, little spark?" His gold eyes are cunning as he looks at me. I sigh and lean back, crossing my arms.

"If you must know, it was when I went out for a ride. I didn't know who he was at the time."

"Hmm." He grunts.

"Not friends then, I take it?"

"Decidedly not. I would rather rip out my claws."

"Why do you hate him so much?"

Os sniffs. "I don't want to talk about it."

"Okay, so you told him no then."

His jaw clenches again as he gazes at the fireplace. Os falls silent and looks at me, something surprisingly vulnerable in his gaze.

"I told him I would speak to you first and support whatever you decided." I blink as surprise and shock fill me.

"Why?" The question isn't angry, just genuine curiosity. Why would this powerful male want to defer to me for something this important? It wasn't self-doubt. Just doubt of his motivations. Os gets up and walks over to my chair before surprising the hell out of me again and kneeling in front of me. Of course, he's so tall that it looks kind of silly, but my heart thumps faster nonetheless.

"Because the whole thing was," Os pauses, looking for the right word, "odd. I think Nyall was serious. He seemed worried and frantic. And he knows how I feel about his father. I've never been quiet about my dislike. If he came here, it means his father doesn't know about it. Whatever this is, it's not the High Council. And that makes me curious."

"Curious?" I ask.

Os meets my gaze, "Something felt different. I'm not sure what."

"Okay, well, my answer is obviously no."

Os nods, "I'll pass it on through the right channels."

I furrow my brow. "Why so much hate for him?"

Os pauses, "I could smell you on him. I almost killed him on the spot. That's why I pulled him into the room. I wanted to ensure no one would witness as I flayed his skin from his flesh.

"Okay, that's extreme," I state calmly. Os ignores it.

"You were that mad because he smelled like me?" I ask, and Os just shifts uncomfortably. "Look, I'm trying here. I'm trying to trust you. I believe you about Nyall; I can see how much you dislike him. It's hard, but...I'm trying. Okay? Now, I think if you shared, it might help. So why did that make you so mad, Os? Why do you want to flay someone for smelling like me?

Os sighs, looking at the crackling fire. *"You know I'm a shifter."*

I nod as he traces his hands along my legs, making goosebumps break out across my body. He takes another breath before resting his arms on my legs and placing his chin on his hands. Then, his pupils change fully, turning from round into serpentine diamonds. His gold irises expand, taking up his entire eye. The change is terrifying yet hypnotizing.

"I will always be mad when someone hurts you, A gahrá, because according to my beast, we're familiars."

CHAPTER 31
AMALIA

No, that can't be true. Especially if he is...no.

My heart starts racing, and my breath comes in short bursts as my chest tightens. I stand and walk to the middle of the room. The chair squeaks as Os stands, going to follow me. He approaches tentatively, worried about my reaction.

"I can feel your panic, A gahrá. Please just list—"

"Tell the Prince I'll meet with him. But I promise nothing." I can't even look at him. Can't bear to look at the hurt in his eyes—and I can't bear for him to see the sorrow in mine. I turn and head out of his room.

"Amalia, please." His thoughts slide into my head.

I shove him out, and he grunts in pain.

No wonder he can get into my head so easily.

My breath comes faster and faster as I jog out of the Dragon Pit. My feet are a blur as I break into a run and race up the steps in the narrow hallway leading to the upstairs world.

The fresh air doesn't help. I feel like I'm going to explode.

My breath fogs the chilly air, but I don't feel the cold. I don't feel anything except grief so deep it's a physical pain.

I'm without a coat, but I run into the stables. Taran immediately nickers, but he goes still as my nerves slam into him.

He neighs and instantly comes over, rubbing his soft black nose on my hand, concerned. I don't even bother tacking him. I grab onto his thick mane and leap onto his back, with no bridle or saddle. We've been partners long enough that he knows exactly what I need and want.

I have to get out of here. The walls of the Dragon Pit and Castael Laryn and this whole fucking place are closing in, and I can't breathe.

"Fast, Taran. Get me outside of the city. I need to be alone."

"Amalia, please. It's not safe for you to go out alone." Os shoves his way back into my mind, and I push him back out. But my Magyk welcomes him, making it hard to resist.

I ignore Os, though, and race out of the stables on Taran's back as he breaks into a fast trot. I don't know if Os ever leaves my head, but his magyk fades, and his protests go quiet.

We emerge into the busy city and Taran quickly leads me through the crowded streets, people clambering out of the way. Taran barrels through them, heading straight for the city walls. Complaints and yells follow as people get upset, but I don't care.

There is nothing inside me but sorrow.

The second we leave the city walls, Taran breaks into a rolling canter.

"Into the forest, out of sight," I send him a picture of what I want. He complies with a neigh, tossing his head as he speeds up even more.

We gallop away from the city walls until they become tiny and distant. Taran doesn't slow as he dives into the Annag, avoiding branches and trees with nimble grace. I let him go for a few minutes until we're deep within the forest, away from prying eyes. Taran feels my emotions and slows to a walk. I slide off his back and stumble over to a small creek, tripping on rocks and logs but I don't care. I step right in the freezing water and fall to my knees. My shoes and pants flood with icy cold water that burns my hot skin.

Still, I don't feel it. The cold is nothing compared to the storm within my heart.

I cup the freezing cold water and toss it on my face, repeating the action three times until I'm gasping, cold down to the bone. My breath comes in loud pants now as I rock back and forth, the river water soaking my thin pants.

I don't care about the cold.

I care that I found my familiar and they're not here.

They were supposed to be here. They...my parents were supposed to help me find him. We always talked about it, about how we hoped one day I would find my familiar. They were supposed to be here and they're not...and I hate them for that.

It wasn't supposed to happen like this.

Why the fuck is it happening like this?

Why did they have to die? Why couldn't I have died with them so I wouldn't have to live this shattered life?

I should have died with them.

I start to shiver but welcome it; it numbs my shattering heart. I hear Taran behind me as he walks into the water, hooves splashing. He grips my shirt with his teeth and yanks me up to standing, dragging me back into the forest.

A noise sounds in the forest, something broken and full of grief.

It takes a minute to realize the sound is...me.

The dam inside me breaks, and I fall again to my knees, but this time onto soft leaves as sobs finally burst from my chest.

I can't remember the last time I let myself cry.

"It's not supposed to be like this. It wasn't supposed to be like this. WHY DID YOU DO THIS TO ME?" I shout at the Gods that abandoned us—that abandoned me. I curse Morrigyn for leaving me to this cruel fate. I repeat it over and over and crawl into a ball as the tears continue to fall. I hear a groan behind me as Taran kneels, lying down behind me, nuzzling me with his velvet soft muzzle.

A familiar bond is sacred for Arkaydians. It's only possible for those with Arkaydian ancestry. Mother said it was a gift from the Gods to enhance our power. She claimed Arkaydians were the only ones who could create a familiar bond because of our close relationship with nature. In every familiar bond, there is always an Arkaydian. But the familiar can be any magyka, any creature with magyk that ties into the world around them. It's always about magyk.

Familiars can boost each other's magyk and they can heal each other. The bond gives thems the ability to share power in extreme measures. It's a completely symbiotic relationship, and according to Mother, it's meant to mimic nature.

But they're gone. My parents are gone and I feel like I'm drowning, unable to stay afloat. Constantly struggling to get air. I'm supposed to be a rock, firm and unmoving within the roaring sea. Instead, I'm adrift, with nothing to hold me steady.

A soft nose nudges the side of my face as Taran gently gets my attention. I sit up and turn around, wrapping my arms around his neck and leaning into his soft mane.

"They were supposed to be here for this, Taran." The words spill out of me with a pained sob. "They were supposed to help me find my familiar. How am I supposed to do this without them? How am I supposed to do any of this when they're dead?"

The tears come again, but Taran surprises me by making a low, sad, nickering noise before nudging me off his neck and laying his head in my lap so we're forehead to forehead.

I cry in earnest, then. Quietly and painfully soaking Taran's thick fur with my sorrow. But Taran doesn't move. He just presses his head into me as I wrap my arms around his large head and soak his forehead with my tears. Then he begins licking my cheek with his smooth, rubbery tongue.

It takes a moment to realize he's...cleaning up my tears. And when I do realize it, it just makes me cry harder.

I don't know how long we sit there, but the sky turns red and pink as the two suns sink lower on the horizon. The light filters through the trees and coats us in streaks of warm orange light. My tears have slowed, but I feel empty inside. My magyk is elated, but my heart is broken.

"I miss them so much sometimes it feels like I can't even breathe. I know I have Dyana, but...sometimes I still feel so alone. How am I supposed to go on when they're gone, Taran?" I whisper into his fur as he lifts his head.

He looks at me, his warm brown eyes thoughtful as he huffs. His eyes narrow in concentration as he presses his soft nose against my cheek again.

What I don't expect is the magyk that washes over me.

I gasp, eyes wide as I look at him in shock.

He's never done this.

The magyk is loving and warm. It's protection and peace as his magyk twines with mine, dancing inside me.

It steadies me. I feel stronger, like maybe I can face this. But I'm still so afraid.

He pulls back and pushes to stand, careful not to step on me. He shakes the dust off his fur before he bends down, bowing as he lowers his front legs, making it easy for me to get on his back.

His magyk twinkles with happiness as I slide onto his wide back and burrow my hands in his thick fur. The smell of apples, barnwood, and sweet hay floods my nose as his magyk wraps me in safety.

"Fam—lee. Tahr-an fam—lee." A quiet male voice, tentative and gentle, sounds in my head.

Oh my Gods.

"Taran, how...?" I can't even finish the sentence. Taran can speak. He can talk to me, really talk.

"Lo-love," he replies. *"I talk be-caus I love."*

A sob bursts from my chest again as I lean down and wrap my arms around Taran as he bends his neck towards my right foot, nuzzling me lovingly as I listen to his voice for the first time.

"Yes, Taran, you are my family. I am yours, and you are mine. I will always love you." He nickers happily, and I feel him echo the sentiment.

His love is my lifeline. The pure acceptance I feel from him makes me feel less alone.

Maybe I'm not always the rock. Perhaps I'm the ocean, uncontrollable and wild, and the ones I love are the rocks, tethering me to shore.

"Ama not allonee. Never allonee."

The tears flow harder, both sad and happy, as I hug Taran tighter. *"You're right, I'm not alone. I just...I never expected this. Never dared hope. Ever since they died, it's just been about staying alive. It still is. But now... it's all gotten so complicated, Taran. There's so much on the line, and I'm so afraid. If I fail, if I can't do this, then everyone dies. I can't...I can't lose anyone else, Taran. Sometimes, I'm so scared that I can't even breathe."*

"Ama bray-v. Ama strong. Ama kind."

Despite it all, despite the sorrow, I laugh, surprising myself. It's a sad, hollow sound, but it's something. *"I'm trying, Taran. I'm trying to be brave. But it's so hard. I'm...I'm so tired."*

My tears dry against the deep red of the setting suns and we make our way back to the Dragon Pit. Taran walks slowly, understanding that I'm in no hurry to get back. The rhythmic clomping of his hooves matches the beat of my heart, forcing it to slow, forcing air back into my lungs.

"Ama friend. Ama fam-lee."

"Taran friend. Taran family. Always." I repeat back to him as I begin the process of shoving my emotions, my grief, and all of the broken pieces of me down behind my iron walls. It never goes away; I just hide it, ignoring it and pretending it doesn't exist.

I was too tired and emotionally drained to explain anything to Dyana when I got back to our dorm last night. She took one look at my tear-stained, puffy face and instantly started fretting over me like a worried mother hen. Dyana shoved the furniture around our room and pushed our two beds together before tucking me in. We slept facing each other, hands clasped, like we did when she was little.

She didn't ask for details, nor did she apologize or pity me. Dyana knew better. Instead, she did what she's always done: quietly accept my pain. Whatever it was that was upsetting me, she would be there by my side. Not pushing for more, not asking questions, or demanding answers and explanations. She simply existed with me, reminding me that I'm not alone.

I woke this morning tired but lighter, with the scent of Taran's magyk still surrounding me. We've never communicated from this far away, but I send Taran a wave of love, wondering if he'll feel it.

He does. He also tells me he's hungry by sending me images of wheelbarrows full of fat, juicy carrots and ripe apples, which makes me smile.

I can do this. I have to do this.

The morning run was grueling, and strength training was awkward as hell. Os acted like nothing had happened. But there are a few moments when I catch him looking at me, his eyes wary.

We're just leaving the Mess Hall after quietly having our breakfast, which is where we all normally part ways, with Dyana and Mirielle continuing on to sparring with Ireyna and the other candidates, and me going to meet with Os for magyk lessons. But I grab both of them by the backs of their shirts and shove them into an alcove. Dyana makes a very undignified squeak and Mirielle turns quickly, alarmed, hand raised and ready to slap me. But she stops when she sees me, confused.

I blink, "Were you going to hit me?"

Mirielle sniffs, "Maybe."

I raise a brow. Interesting.

"Uh, Ama, is everything ok?" Dyana asks, concerned and confused as to what I'm up to. I look around, waiting until the rest of the candidates pass us.

"Gods, she's finally lost her mind. I knew this would happen someday," Dyana mutters to Mirielle.

I look around the ledge, ensuring there is no one near, and take a deep breath.

"Nyall Drayven wants to meet with me," I admit. Mirielle jerks, her gray eyes going wide. Dyana's jaw drops.

"Um I'm sorry, you mean Crown Prince Nyall Drayven? THAT Nyall Drayven?" Dyana's voice reaches extreme volumes and very high pitches when she's upset.

"Yes."

"Son of the High Councilor."

"Yes."

"Heir to the High Council of Ur Daoine."

"Uh-huh."

"The same one who watched his father try and bash your skull in?"

"Yep."

"The same High Councilor and father who killed your godsdamn parents? And had my foster family killed? And didn't save Mirielle's mom?"

I sigh wearily, "Yeah."

Dyana opens her mouth again and I can feel the shout building in her chest as her anger builds. Mirielle slaps her hand over Dyana's mouth,

"No yelling." Mirielle chuckles, but it feels forced. Her face during this whole thing has been tense and worried. Dyana grumbles behind her hand and pulls it away.

"He wants my help. That's all I know. He asked Os to ask me, for some stupid reason."

Dyana scoffs, "And what did Os say?"

I hesitate, "Well, Os deferred to me, actually. The Crown Prince would like to meet with him too."

Mirielle's green eyes are sharp, "When?"

"I'm waiting to find out, but probably in the next few days," I respond.

Dyana raises her hand, "Uh hold on. What do you mean you're 'waiting to find out'?"

I sigh, "I told Os to pass on to the Prince that I will meet with him."

Dyana squawks, "Absolutely not! What the fuck, Ama? You're the last person who needs to be meeting with the imperial fae!"

I glare. She's dangerously close to saying far too much with prying ears around.

Dyana blinks, realizing her mistake. "I mean, you hate them. You're planning on killing the Prince, right?" Mirielle chokes and Dyana pats her back. "Right? Tell me that's your plan."

I roll my eyes, "No, I'm going to hear him out," I pause, "and if I don't like what he has to say then yes, I will kill him."

Mirielle's eyes are wide and alarmed. "Y-you can't just kill the Crown Prince, Amalia. The High Council will find out and then you'll be next."

I shrug, "Don't care."

Mirielle covers her face with her left hand, clearly frustrated. Dyana glances at her, confused.

"I mean I don't want you to get killed, Ama, so maybe you shouldn't kill him?" I raise a brow. "Yeah, I know he comes from a shitty family, but Mirielle's right and I need your stupid ass to stay alive."

I glare at Dyana again but she doesn't budge. Her mahogany eyes are firm as we communicate without words or magyk, just as friends turned sisters who know each other far too well.

Her eyes say, "I support you killing him but it's not worth the risk."

Which is really annoying because she's probably right.

"I will," I clear my throat, not wanting to say the words, "consider not killing the Prince. But I can't make any promises."

Dyana stands up straighter, her chin raised, "Then we're coming with you."

Mirielle looks at her, unsure. Dyana just reaches over and squeezes her hand.

Mirielle clears her throat, "Right. Yes. We'll come with you." But her words are scared. She's nervous about meeting the Prince, which is a logical response—if I let them come with me.

"Absolutely not, you're staying behind. Both of you."

Mirielle looks at Dyana and straightens to her full height, looking down at me, "We're going with you whether you like it or not."

Dyana nods, "And then when you get all murdery, we can make sure you don't commit treason."

Ugh.

"If you come with me, I cannot guarantee your safety. Or Dyana's for that matter!" I whisper but it's just a quiet shout. "I'm trying to keep you both alive! Does that count for nothing?"

Dyana's green eyes soften, and she leans forward, grabbing my hand. "We're coming, Ama. You can't keep us safe forever. In just two weeks, we'll be fighting against Dragons and Gods know what else. Let us help you for once."

I take a step back as my heart clenches at the thought of anything happening to the woman in front of me—women, actually. Somehow, despite all of my efforts against it, Mirielle has become a friend.

Dyana smiles softly, "You've protected me long enough, Ama. Give me the courtesy of letting me protect you in return."

I clench my jaw. "Can I think about it?"

"Nope."

I grind my teeth in frustration. Dyana has always been stubborn as a mule.

"Fine. I will tell you as soon as I know when and where it will be."

"Swear it," Dyana demands, eyes fierce. A smirk forms on my lips. I taught her well.

"I swear."

Mirielle watches this all with sharp, calculative eyes. But as she looks at me, I sense no ill will or anger. Just her usual warmth and acceptance. However, there's a mix of grief and worry mixed in. Likely just about the Gauntlet in general.

Can't blame her for that one.

CHAPTER 32
AMALIA

"Think of your active power like a web you can throw."

"Like a spider web?" I ask in disbelief. Os sighs in exasperation, forever tired of my purposefully obtuse questions.

"You know what, sure, call it a spider web. Just give your power a shape. It needs to be something that feels organic to cast out of you, that can exist separately from you."

Something that can exist separately from me...

"A Dragon." Something in Os's gold gaze shutters, and he takes a long blink, processing my words. "Interesting choice," he grinds out. "Alright, send that shape out and find our minds. Before, we've come to you, but you need to be able to go to others. Find the lights."

I'm not sure what he means, but I fall into the meditation we've practiced and try it.

Inhale through the nose, exhale through the mouth.

Inhale through the nose, exhale through the mouth.

I repeat this for a minute and tune out my surroundings. I cast my Dragon out to fly into the black abyss and study it. It's made of white light that sprinkles off as it flies. But it doesn't burn me.

Instead, the flames are cold. I expand my range a little further, and a bright, brilliant golden light comes up in my mind's eye. I reach over and grab onto it, imagining my Dragon sinking its talons in.

"Good," Os says, letting me in.

"So whenever you've spoken to me in my mind, you find my...light like this?"

"Yes. Now try that again, but this time I will block you, and I want you to force your way in. Don't ask nicely."

I withdraw and come back to myself and try it again. And fail, and fail some more still. But finally, when I use my magyk to sharpen my Dragon's talons and imagine them piercing through, I break in.

"Again," he demands.

We try a few more times until I can more easily get in, but I'm still sweaty and exhausted.

"One more time and then we're done. But now use your magyk and when you push in, push OUT towards me with it."

"Okay," I huff and take a breath. That spark deep inside me flares slightly, but I don't let it expand much. I gather the magyk locked behind my iron walls and infuse my Dragon with more of it until it shines like a light behind my eyes.

I take a deep breath and gather the burning force of my magyk and shove it at that golden light, piercing his shield like an arrow.

I hear a big thump and open my eyes to see that Os is almost on the other side of the room. But he flashes me a wicked smile, his teeth sharpened into fangs, "Very good. It seems you have some bite after all."

Heat flushes through me at his words but I ignore it as my stomach suddenly grumbles, loudly. Os gets up and his teeth go back to normal, but his gold eyes still twinkle with a purely male satisfaction.

"Less power next time, but good." He nods. A knock at the door makes me jump, and I instantly go on edge.

"Peace, A gahrá. It's just the servants bringing food." A new heat flows through me at that; hot fury at the thought of anyone believing in indentured servitude. It's cruel and inhumane.

Os pads barefoot over to the door and opens it, retrieving a massive tray of fresh fruit, meat, and cheese.

"Eat. You need it. Magyk burns twice the energy as regular exercise. The more you use it, the more fuel you need to put in your body." He throws a fur blanket down onto the floor, carrying the tray with a single hand, and sets it down in front of me. I grab some cheese and crackers and quickly shove it in my mouth. Os just grabs some unknown sort of cured meat and starts eating as well. I get water from the table beside me and take a few swallows. The quiet is...tense between us. I wipe some water off my upper lip and swallow nervously.

"When did you know?" My voice is hoarse with emotion. "The...familiar thing. When did you realize?"

Os chews slowly, gold eyes strangely soft as he looks at me, the firelight playing off his bronzed, scarred skin.

He exhales, "My beast knew the moment I got your scent. But I...didn't want to believe it. It wasn't until the day outside the stables that I knew for sure."

"You mean when you healed me."

"Yes," he hesitates, looking at me. "Except I don't actually have healing magyk." I blink, confused. "My kind can only heal our own kin," he continues. "It's not considered a power, it is simply part of our nature. The only exception is if we manage to form a familiar bond. Then, and only then, can we heal someone outside of our own species. I saw you hurt and my magyk reacted, well, quite strongly. That's when I realized it wanted to heal you. My beast, it demanded that I heal you even if it drained me of every drop of power I possess."

"Oh," I say finally.

Os nods as I process. We eat in silence for a few minutes.

"You—" Os looks down, and I'm amazed to say I think he might be nervous too, "you don't have to accept the familiar bond, Amalia." He pauses and takes a breath. "I will never force you to accept it. I can't, actually. An Arkaydian is the only one who can complete the bond, so you don't need to worry, please."

I nod a little and chew on my bottom lip. "What happens if I reject it?" I ask, and Os goes pale, closing his eyes as he composes himself.

He opens his eyes and looks at me, "Nothing will happen. You can reject it if that's what you want. But it means I'll never find another familiar. Arkaydians can form unlimited familiar bonds."

I go still. "Interesting."

Os shifts his glance away for a moment., "Yes. But for me, there will only ever be one chance."

Gods. "So this is your only chance to bond?"

He nods "Yes. For us...there is only one."

I gulp, "How long do I have until I need to... um, decide?"

"There is no time limit, A gahrá. I've lived for centuries. I've seen Kingdoms rise and fall. I've seen peace and I've been to war." His eyes go distant as I process just how old he actually is, but that gold gaze snaps back to me. "None of that comes even close to how I feel about you. You're in my soul, Amalia. I would wait a lifetime and then some if that's what you need."

I blink back the emotion that threatens to flood my eyes. "And what happens if I accept? My—" I pause, trying not to cry. "My parents told me some of it, but it was so long ago that it's a little blurry."

Os smiles sadly. "If you accept, we would be bound together for the rest of our lives. You would gain my lifespan, as well as some of my power. I could heal you from great distances, and you me—and when you die, I will die with you."

My heart seizes and I go to shake my head no.

"I am not afraid of death, A gahrá," he says softly. "But you are safe. If I die, you will continue on. There is a reason Arkaydians were revered. Their magyk is unlike anything else in the world. You would, however, feel my death."

"Feel it?"

Os hesitates briefly before responding "Yes."

I sigh, leaning back against the cold floor and looking at the wood and stone ceiling.

"What else?"

Os leans back too. We're in the same position that we were in my dreams a few days ago.

"Both of our magyks would get a boost. Our...life forces would merge into one, and with that, we would both have access to each other's magyk, should the other will it."

"You could use my power, you mean?"

Os nods.

So the worst-case scenario then. Great.

I hesitate, "If I make it out of here alive... I'll think about it."

"You're not going to die." Os growls, kneeling next to me, gold eyes so furious they're practically ablaze. The room heats several degrees and I begin sweating, but not from fear.

"You don't know that," I say sadly. He goes to interrupt me, but I place my hand on top of his, and he goes still. "Even if you wish it to be false, we both know there's a high chance that I will die in the Arena, Os. That's the reality of the Gauntlet, and no power or magyk can change it now."

Os puts my hand between both of his, cradling it like a treasure. "You're right, but I'm going to do everything in my power to ensure that you win."

We stay like that for a few minutes. The feel of the cold stone mixed with the heat of his hands and the blazing fire is oddly soothing.

I sigh, tired but feeling better after some food. Os lets go of my hand and helps me up. We stand there, staring into each other's eyes for a moment.

I go to say something, but he stops me, putting his hand on my cheek. It's scorching hot and I want to melt into him, but I don't.

"You don't need to say it. I know." He moves his hand, placing it over my heart. It jumps at his touch.

Still, I need to say it. "Yesterday...it wasn't about you. Someday I'll be ready to talk about it, but not now. I just...I need you to know it wasn't about you, and I'm sorry for running."

Os just smiles softly, "I know, A gahrá. I am in your soul. Just...know that you never have to run from me."

I nod, biting my lip. "You would really wait for me?" The words are barely a whisper but both the man and the beast stare back at me.

"I would wait an eternity for you, little spark."

"If only we had that much time," I choke out the words around the emotion clogging my throat. Os just brushes his thumb under my eye, catching the stray tear.

"We will, I swear it."

"Thank you, for—" My emotions choke me.

"I understand, Amalia. I see you and accept you for all that you are. You don't need to explain yourself to me. You never need to explain."

My eyes fall closed as his words batter me, causing all sorts of emotions to rise. All I can do is nod. He leans down until we're forehead to forehead.

"I see you, A gahrá." His sweet smokey scent floods my senses as Os presses a soft kiss to my forehead, his warmth grounding me. *"I see you for all that you are and all that you aren't. I see your heart and all of your broken pieces. I accept you just as you are."*

The emotions are too much and I step back, overwhelmed, heart racing for reasons I can't even begin to understand as my skin begins to heat. Unable to say anything else, I step out of his embrace and nod, retreating to the door.

"Nyall wants to meet after the Fray tomorrow."

I clench my jaw as I open the door and glance back at Os, those gold eyes ever knowing. "I'm bringing Dyana and Mirielle." I expect him to fight it, but he smirks.

"Good, that will throw the little fucker off."

"Goodnight, Os." I close the door with a click.

"Goodnight, A gahrá."

CHAPTER 33
MIRIELLE

"This isn't going to work," I say, pacing before him. My nerves have been frayed ever since Amalia told us about the meeting. A bad feeling has weighed on me for the past few days, a nervous anticipation mixed with clouds of regret. When Amalia pulled us to the side this morning, I took one look at her pale eyes and knew that was it. Knew that was going to be the moment that changed everything. Then she started speaking, and my heart ceased beating.

"Still, she agreed. You know that was the hardest part," the male replies calmly.

I whirl, "Yeah, it was. She agreed to the *meeting*. That doesn't mean she will agree to help us, and if she says no, where does that leave us?

"Peace, Mir." He wraps me in his arms, towering over me. He rubs my back lightly, and I sigh, pressing my forehead into his chest before pulling back. He smiles at me, "This will work. Trust me, alright? You've trusted me for the past century and a half, so trust me for a little longer. This isn't over yet. I know this will work. It has to."

I nod, biting my nails absentmindedly. Whirling, I pace over to his sitting area and plop down on one of the outlandishly comfortable and expensive chairs. My head falls into my hands as reality sinks in further.

"She's going to hate me, Nyall. They both will," I say, voice hollow as I look at the Prince who somehow has become my closest friend. I sigh, "It hurts. I didn't know it would hurt so much." I look at him, "You know I've never cared about being liked, but I don't want them to hate me."

He walks over to sit in the chair beside me, the fabric squishing under his weight. "Maybe not. We need to tell them the truth, Mir. All of it. Then, and only then, do we stand a chance."

"Fuck!" I scream into my hands. "Why did I have to fall for the goddamn target, Nyall? How could I be so stupid?"

Nyall's hand lands on my shoulder, and I pry myself out of my den of hands and hair. "Love isn't stupid, Mir. It never is. It's the most worthwhile, powerful thing in existence. Don't you see? That's why the High Council is so evil, why the fae have fallen so far into the darkness. It is because the only thing they love is power. Nothing else."

I bite my lip, "I know that. I know all of this. But...I wish that doing the right thing wouldn't hurt the one I—" I stop, looking away.

"I'm sorry. I realize that's not enough, but I'm sorry," he says simply. There isn't much else to say but that. I agreed to this possibility when I joined the rebellion in the first place.

"Yeah. It...it felt so nice, having friends. Real friends, you know?"

Nyall smiles, "Wow, now I'm not a real friend? The pain! The heartbreak!"

I snort, but it feels forced, "You're my leader, you pompous asshole. But you're also family, so at this point, you're obligated to be my friend. I'm talking about friends where there's no obligation to work, nothing but sticking together because we simply enjoy each other's company." Nyall looks away, and my heart clenches as I realize the effect of my words.

"Nyall, I—" He holds up a hand, stopping me.

"Don't apologize, it's quite alright. Just because I've never had the privilege of a 'real friend' as you call it, doesn't mean you should feel guilty for finding that. Like you said, we're family. I want you to be happy," he pauses, "but I also want you to have a future, Mir. And that means this all has to work because otherwise, there's no future for us except pain and death."

I look down at my hands, blistered and calloused from weapons training, before looking back at Nyall, who stares at me with mismatched eyes. "Then we make this work."

Nyall clenches his hands, "No matter the consequences."

"No matter the consequences," I reply, then clear my throat.

CHAPTER 34
KYDIS

It's quiet at this time of night. Just the constant dripping of water down the cavern walls. Most of the other Dragons are fast asleep, simply too exhausted to stay conscious. Far above us, the caves where the tamed live are equally quiet.

Vile, treacherous beings—but they don't know any better. Most were born never knowing freedom or the joys of soaring through the clouds with the hot suns warming their scales, no destination in sight.

Then again, I barely remember the feeling. Every century, the memories get increasingly distant, a blurry image rather than a clear picture.

I adjust, curling into an uncomfortable ball as I tuck my tail under my head, trying to get comfortable. I don't know why I even try, knowing it won't work. The evil ones have dragged me to the lab every single day for the past week. My body is sore and I ache all over due to their cruel experiments.

I wish I could say I fought them, but I'm past that. There's no point but to lay there as they strap me down with chains, poke me with their instruments, rip my scales, and torture me.

Soon, I will be reunited with my kin in the afterworld, flying through the clouds alongside Great Livyathin.

A few stalls away from me, a Dragon begins crying.

Soon, we will all be free from the confines of this cruel, cruel life. Soon, this will finally be over.

CHAPTER 35
AMALIA

"I feel like I'm finally starting to get it!" Dyana says to Mirielle after our training with Os. We all swapped, sparring with each other and doing sprints in between.

"Yeah, you should've seen her, Amalia. Dyana managed to beat both of her bout partners. I swear, even Ireyna looked impressed." Dyana blushes hard. Seeing her flustered is so amusing; she's always been the confident, forward one out of the two of us. But Mirielle has her acting all shy and giggly. I don't know Mirielle well enough to fully trust her. I'm not about to trust someone we might have to fight, but I'm happy Dyana is happy.

Happiness is in short enough supply these days, so I keep my mouth shut and keep my worries to myself.

The Fray is tonight, and I've felt on edge since waking up. The pit in the bottom of my stomach has gotten heavier as the day has gone on.

Os has been harder than usual the past few days in our training. My body is covered in bruises and marks from his punches and jabs. My body aches with every step from all the times he's whacked me with various weaponry. We had moved to more advanced sword work as well as spears.

"The key to fighting a Dragon is to have a weapon big enough that it will actually do damage. Small daggers aren't going to pierce their thick hide. Long swords, maybe some short swords— depending on how sharp they are—and staffs are going to be your best bet for piercing through their scales and getting to their flesh." When he told me that this afternoon, I tried to not show my revulsion at the idea of killing an animal. He grabbed my chin, yanking my face towards his with a growl.

"No. None of that. You don't hesitate for a single second. Burn that empathy to ash, Roth. The second you step into the Arena, everyone and everything is your enemy." I cursed and tried to escape his grip, but he held firm.

"I'm aware, but I will never be okay with any of this."

He growled but let go, shaking his head as if trying to shake off the anger. "It doesn't matter. In there, the fae will do everything possible to ensure you lose. Forget everything you ever thought was true. The moment you step onto that sand, nothing but staying alive matters. Nothing."

I considered telling him about my encounter in the Pits.

About Kydis.

But something in me still felt the need to keep that to myself. Something is holding me back. Too many times in my life, I've found my trust completely broken.

Os's magyk brushed against my mind as his rich voice sounded in my head, *"Do not mistake my words for not caring, Amalia. The only thing that matters now is staying alive long enough to win and get you as far from here as possible."*

The moment plays over and over again in my head as we finish eating dinner. At that moment, Ireyna walks in, interrupting my thoughts about the past few days. Her short black hair is pulled sleek against her head, making her look just as harsh as she behaved. She wears black fighting leathers with fine silver armor and thick black boots.

"Candidates, tonight you get your first lesson in Dragon Fighting. You've trained and expanded your knowledge, honed your bodies, but you don't know jack shit about how to actually beat a Dragon." She pauses to survey us with dark onyx eyes lined with kohl.

"Tonight, we will attend the Dragon Fight. Pay attention. Because in just a few weeks, two of you will be the ones out there facing them down. Look for weaknesses, and don't fuck around. Understood?"

Several in the mess hall whoop in excitement. Others look sick to their stomachs. I'm in the latter category.

My foot slips briefly, and Mirielle shoves her hand on my back behind me to right me, keeping me from falling as we climb another massive set of stairs. That's what my life is now: endless, never-ending stairs.

We're all out of breath when we finally emerge into a long, wide hallway. I'm shocked to see a few windows, having gotten used to being fully underground most of the time.

Thump. Thump.

Thump. Thump.

Far in the distance, loud drums sound. As Ireyna walks down the hallway with us nervously in tow, the drums get louder and louder. Fae soldiers wait at two enormous wooden doors, and they open it upon noticing us. That's when the drums get even louder. So does the screaming as we walk into the audience section of the massive open stadium.

The Arena.

There must be tens of thousands of people crammed in here. Every seat is filled as fae, magyka, and demis scream and shout. The noise and crowd is an assault to my senses. It's so loud that I can barely hear Ireyna shout.

"Follow me." She leads us down a walkway to a private section right up front, where a few rows of empty seats await.

We follow her as she walks down shallow stairs to a section of empty seating near the floor. The floor of the Arena is just meters away from us and must be at least 300 meters long and 200 meters wide. Fae soldiers are stationed at every entrance and along the rows of seats. For the rich, there are private boxes separated from the rest of the masses. But the entire stadium is packed full. The top of the Arena is open, the overcast winter sky bringing in much-needed light and fresh air.

This is it then? A small peek at their old lives, at what they used to have?

The thought both crushes and consumes me.

The energy of the Arena is electric, and the hair on my arms stands on end. Most drink mead out of large metal goblets, and I spy some wealthy imperial fae with tables of food in front of them. The ground of the Arena looks to be covered in sand, but there are dark stains all throughout where blood has spilled already this evening, as well as marks in the sand where bodies were pulled out. My hands are freezing cold, but my cheeks grow hot as I think of the fact that in just two weeks, we're going to be in there.

Everyone talks excitedly amongst themselves, but the three of us are quiet. Dyana's pupils are wide as she flexes her hands carefully, and Mirielle stares at the Arena sands with fierce resentment. That rock in my stomach grows, and I tap my foot to try and work off some of my nervous energy. Dyana's hand lands on my bouncing knee as she looks at me in understanding.

She's never given me a hard time for my love of animals. I hunted when I had to to keep us alive, but she held my hair back when I vomited afterward. After a few days, I grew numb to it. I ate meat but didn't let myself think of where it came from. It was a necessity, not a choice. But the thought of seeing animals killed for fun makes me sick. Seeing an animal killed in any way makes me so angry I could tear the stars from the sky.

My mind kept turning to the crimson Dragon. Those gray eyes that truly saw me, that stripped me of my founding flesh all the way down to the bone. The dozens of scars, both old and new, marring her gorgeous red hide. The hopelessness I felt in her heart was so familiar. It's kills me because I know what it's like to wish for death. To feel such misery and despair, death seems easier than one more day of life.

The drums beat faster until they stop in unison.

Ireyna sniffs and hisses back at us in the pause of silence that follows as the stadium goes quiet, "Pay attention, and don't make a fool out of yourselves."

Helpful as ever.

I didn't get a minute of sleep all last night, unable to stop thinking of Kydis. When I close my eyes, it's her glowing ones I see. When I stop listening to the world, I hear her voice...and I'm supposed to just sit here and watch her die.

A voice booms across the entire area, magnified by magyk.

"Citizens of Ur Daoine! Welcome to the FRAY!" Screams erupt in response, deafening me and making my ears ring, while I pretend not to notice Dyana grabbing Mirielle's hand.

"Have you had fun yet?" The crowd screams in agreement again, more than answering the voice's question. "I thought so. Well, folks, we have a real treat for you tonight. The High Council has blessed us with a real show," the announcer chuckles. "Feast your eyes upon our Reigning Champion with over 100 bouts won, the Executioner, the Blade of Death, the Bringer of Blood. Citizens of Ur Daoine, may I present to you...THE BEAST!" The voice shouts, and the screams double as a large being in head-to-toe black armor walks out from a tunnel just a few meters away from us.

The fighter emerges into the Arena, and I get a good look at them. They're wearing a simple black sleeveless leather vest with silver arm guards and black fighting leathers for pants tucked into black boots. A silver helmet covers their head, completely obscuring them. Whoever they are, they're huge. The figure must be over two meters tall.

The fighter walks across the sand until they're opposite of us, facing away, as they stab their sword in the sand and kneel, going down on one knee. I look up and see a large private booth directly above them, but it's blocked by a one-way mirror. The crowd quiets as the mirror dissipates and the High Council appears.

My jaw clenches as I take in High Councilor Achan and the rest of the imperial fae, his red eyes and beatific smile as creepy as ever. Achan is dressed in all red today, bringing out the perverse glow in his eyes. He smiles, waving at the crowd. But I don't see a smile. I see a snake waiting to pounce.

The rest of the High Council waves from their giant marble thrones, three on each side of Achan. It's clear who's in charge. The rest of the High Council is scary, but Achan is even more so.

A High Councilor dressed in a long white dress with a plunging neckline, showing off pale skin and black veins, smiled at the crowd. Unlike most of the fae who wore their hair long, this High Councilor has a completely shaved head, just a hint of black fuzz against their shiny scalp. They have painted their lips the same shade of red as their eyes—a startling and strangely attractive combination. That must be High Councilor Nerasha. Another imperial fae with skin as dark as glorious night sat next to Nerasha; their hair is pure white. A fae smiles at something Nerasha says, so I continue checking out the rest of the room, which is when I lock my gaze with an eye of amber and an eye of green.

Nyall Drayven, in all of his audacity, catches me looking and smirks. He's dressed more casually than the rest of the imperial fae, an outfit similar to fighting leathers, only much nicer and in various shades of gray and silver.

"TONIGHT, the Beast faces off against the Blue Demon! Will this be another Kill Count on the champion's list? Or is this the night we say goodbye to the Beast!"

The crowd boos and hollers, their hatred of Dragons clear.

Achan stands, lifting his hand. A wave of power washes over the stadium as stone begins to move, vibrating the entire stadium. The fighter kneels as a large groaning sound bursts from the walls, and the Arena starts to lower.

The seats vibrate as I lean forward and watch as the arena floor lowers 20 meters down.

They're putting space between us and the Dragons. The sound of large chains suddenly clanks, and the stone wall parts, revealing a massive dark cavern. The fighter turns, facing the cavern, as they pick up their sword and twirl it with languid ease. An ease that feels familiar.

"Uh, Mirielle, do you know who that fighter is?" I ask over the noise of the crowd. Mirielle shakes her head, unsure. But a noise emits from the cave, causing the entire crowd to go silent as a massive, light blue snout emerges from the dark.

Piercing yellow eyes appear through a cloud of thick black smoke. The Dragon steps into the light of the Arena with a giant, taloned claw. It's not quite as big as Kydis, and it looks a bit younger. But each step vibrates the stone underneath my seat.

Fae attendants wearing the Cult of Sol Constantus robes emerge, carrying giant metal chains that control the Dragon, holding it in place.

The crowd gasps, and I hear some candidates behind me throw up and cry out in fear. A few stand and go to flee, but Ireyna is there, shoving them by their collars back onto the stone benches.

The metal muzzle the Dragon wears drops to the ground, and fangs bigger than my entire leg flare as the Dragon growls. The attendants jab it with an electrical prod, making it screech in pain. The light blue Dragon shakes its head in pain as it tenses, eyes furious.

One of its horns is broken off at the base, the edge sharp and broken. The other curves up with a wicked point at the end. Thick spikes line down its spine all the way to its barbed tail that drags on the ground as it tries to stalk closer to the Beast. Some fangs are broken, like Kydis had, but it only adds to its menace.

"Oh my Gods, oh my Gods," Dyana whispers as she reaches over and grabs my hand. Mirielle puts her arm around my friend from her other side as they both fight the Dragonfear. Dyana shivers, and I push some calming emotion onto her, siphoning out her fear.

She takes a shaky breath and nods at me out of the corners of her green eyes.

"That's what we have to beat in order to win?" she asks quietly. I look at her and nod, and a blanket of hopelessness covers us all.

"RELEASE THE DRAGON!" The announcer shouts, and the crowd quiets slightly as they stand. The chains are dropped, and the attendants try to run away, but the Dragon lunges to the side, biting one of them in half and cutting off their screams. Some laugh, and some boo as we all watch the first drops of blood hit the ground. The Dragon shakes its head as it chews the rest of the fae. Intestines and half-chewed organs fly into the air, hitting the crowd. Dyana covers her mouth as she gags, watching a piece of the fae's foot land before us, bone sticking out of torn, bleeding muscle.

I hear Dyana gag again. Mirielle rubs her back lightly and whispers that she should look away. I hate that she has to see this, but the Gauntlet will be even worse.

I kick the piece of flesh away, getting blood on my boots. But they've seen worse. Mirielle doesn't look away, I notice. I don't either. But my heart races as I watch the fighter take this all from the ground.

The rest of the attendants scramble behind the quickly closing doors, and the Dragon head butts the door just as it shuts, cracking and denting the stone. Fae magyk quickly floods the gaps with a red glow, fixing the stone.

The Dragon tilts its head and stretches its jaw, slowly turning around and setting its bright yellow eyes on its next target. The Dragon flexes its claws, sharp talons dragging in the sand as it takes in the fighter.

How is the Beast supposed to kill a Dragon with one sword?

The blue Dragon flares its nostrils and tastes the air, a forked tongue flicking out from between its giant, broken fangs, the edges sharp and painful.

Its yellow eyes size up the fighter, letting out a layered screech—a predator sighting its prey. The Blue Demon growls and the scent of urine in the air tells me a few candidates lost control of their bowels at the sight and sound of a hunting Dragon.

I can't say I blame them. But it only increases my nausea. Fear for the fighter jolts through me, and my heart races, feeling like it might explode out of my chest and fly away with each *thump, thump, thump.*

The Dragon prowls forward, tail swinging back and forth as the sharp spikes hit the ground roughly. It flexes its giant wings, showing holes where the flesh has been torn. Dark, tattered blue wings tipped in sharp spikes, the membranous, thin skin between the wing joints are almost translucent. Everything about this creature is meant to be dangerous, but it's in a rough state. A glint flashes on its neck as it gets closer, and I notice another of those thin chains wrapping around its scales.

I flare my magyk towards it and jerk back as the taste of rotten, sour apples floods my mouth.

More higher magyk the fae have no business playing around with.

I examine the warding around it and flinch at the recoil as the magyk slaps me. I can't remove it.

The Dragon charges with a roar that almost shatters my eardrums. The audience gasps and screams in anticipation. The Dragon flaps its wings once, not jumping in the air but instead using them to propel it forward faster and more forcefully. The gust of wind it creates hits us, and sand gets in my eyes, making them burn. The other candidates cry out, and I go to throw my arm over Dyana's eyes, but I'm surprised to see Mirielle already doing that.

I shoot to my feet as I watch the Dragon use its powerful back legs to jump, going to pounce on top of the fighter, mouth open, ready to bite.

I exhale painfully, and I see Dyana grab Mirielle's hand out of the corner of my eye. The Dragon hisses in frustration, capturing my attention, and roars out a massive wave of smoke, briefly blinding the fighter. The Dragon takes advantage of the moment and swings its tail at the back of the fighter's legs, but he just flips in the air, landing on all fours. The Dragon whips its tail around, trying to thump it directly on the Beast. But he just rolls out of the way again. The Dragon charges, and the fighter darts under it, sword quickly severing all of its ankle tendons. Blood spurts as the Dragon roars in pain and fury. The blood sizzles in the sand, and the hot iron smell floods the air, making Dyana gag again.

The Dragon's pupils shrink as the pain makes it feral. It lashes out with its tail again, catching the fighter on the shoulder. He doesn't make a sound as he's tossed into the air, landing in a crouch. Bright red blood starts to drip out of his shoulder armor and trail down his arm, dripping off his fingers.

The blood rushes from my body as I look at the fighter. The Dragon's sharp claws had ripped the fighter's black vest right off. It falls to the sand as I take in the black tattoos and scars that decorate the fighter's chest.

"Come on, kill the damn beast already, Os!" Ireyna shouts.

The fighter is Os.

The Beast is Os.

A strangled sound falls from my mouth as the crowd begins to hurtle cups and food at the Dragon and Os, distracting them. The Dragon shirks and snaps in fury.

I don't breathe as I watch Os charge the Dragon with a shout. My heart falls from my chest as the Dragon charges back, wings flaring as it flaps them for increased velocity.

This time, the Dragon goes low and opens its mouth, preventing Os from going underneath it again. Blood flows down each talon from its wounds, and the smell permeates the air. I can feel the heat from it.

My heart leaps, and I gasp as it gets within meters of Os, and we all stand up. I stop breathing and grab Dyana's arm just as he leaps into the air, over the Dragon's head. The Blue Demon tries to follow him, head bending backward, and comes within inches of biting his leg. But Os lands on its back and grabs onto one of the sharp spikes. The Dragon writhes and shrieks, trying to shake him off. But Os just walks forward, step by step, holding on tightly to the rows of spikes and horns that line its spine as he snarls back. Raising his sword with a mighty yell, he plunges it into the Dragon's neck, in between two spikes.

The cry of pain it makes causes another piece of my broken, shriveled heart to disappear, crushed into dust and ash. The sound is pain and relief and sorrow. It's every emotion all at once, but the relief in the sound is enough to kill me. Tears start falling, unbidden.

Os yanks the sword out and leaps to the ground as the Dragon crashes to the sand with a giant **thump** that vibrates the entire Arena. But the Dragon fights, still. Snapping at the air and clawing at Os. So he turns and calmly walks towards the writhing Dragon, avoiding the claws and spiked tail that thrashes back and forth. With a calm resignation, Os slices his sword across the Dragon's throat. Dark red blood spurts out of the Dragon's wound, coating his armor as it gushes into puddles on the sand. It coughs, crimson spraying everywhere as it drowns in its own blood.

It lets out a final gurgled screech as the light in the Dragon's yellow eyes goes dim, extinguished forever as it dies before us.

Os kneels as the blood from his shoulder drips down his sword and onto the already blood-soaked sand. He puts his hand on the Dragon's cooling snout as he leans forward and whispers something to the large beast. The crowd goes wild with thunderous applause as they chant his name.

"BEAST! BEAST! BEAST!"

I'm silent as my ears ring from the noise and my heart and head thunder with righteous emotion. The other candidates jump to their feet and cheer.

All I can do is stare, either at the dead Dragon or Os. I feel everything all together at once, and it leaves me frozen. My skin starts to heat, and I clench my jaw tightly as I fight the rising tide of magyk inside me. My back is ramrod straight as I watch Os pull off his helmet and look right at me.

That fucking *liar*. The fury allows me to dampen that ember deep inside me, forcing it into submission as I glare back, furious he didn't warn me about this.

"You want to be my godsdamn familiar? How about not lying to me first?" I rip into his mind with so much force I watch him take a step back as I hiss at him before slamming the doors shut on my way out, locking him out of my mind. It doesn't work. He forces his way back into my mind as his smokey magyk fills my nose.

"Firstly, you never asked, and I thought you knew, and second, what about any of this makes you think for one godsdamn second that this makes me proud, Amalia? That I wanted you to have to see this? That I fucking enjoyed that?"

I swallow against the rising anger within me, but it's the pure, agonizing pain that makes his voice tremble that really does me in. The panic comes quickly. Something about Os's admission makes me even more terrified of what is going to happen next.

It's the feeling of losing all hope and the realization of what this all is going to mean.

Inhale through the nose, exhale through the mouth.

Inhale through the nose, exhale through the mouth.

"Control, Amalia." Os's voice storms into my head, no longer amused but stern and almost...concerned.

"I'm fine." I snap back.

"Ensure it stays that way," he snarls. Fuck, I'm so glad he didn't die, but I also want to stab him in his annoying face. But the breathing helped. The panic isn't gone, but it's tamed...for now.

"HE'S DONE IT AGAIN! BEHOLD, THE BEAST! UR DAOINE'S CHAMPION!" The announcer shouts, and the crowd goes wild again. Some throw flowers at him, and I see a few pieces of lacy lingerie. He tucks his helmet under his arm and bows to the imperial fae before striding out.

Not a single wave to the crowd. And they eat that shit up. Females shriek his name, desperate for a moment of his attention. But he ignores it all and walks out a smaller set of doors, leaving the Arena empty.

The one-way mirror blocking the view of the High Council's private box goes transparent momentarily, and the crowd goes silent, bowing.

"Bow," Ireyna hisses at us, and I realize most everyone already has their heads down in subservience. I hurry and bow, although my jaw is clenched so tight, I'm surprised I don't shatter a tooth.

High Councilor Achan stands up from his throne, where he is seated next to the six other High Councilors.

"You're still nervous," Os says, and I see him walking down towards us, arm bandaged already.

What the fuck is he that makes him so fast? I only knew of fae having the ability of that much speed.

Dragons are scary creatures. It's both truth and a total lie. Ireyna runs over to Os, throwing her arms around him. Now, it's my turn to snarl, but I swallow it along with the jealousy burning in my gut.

He laughs at something she says, and it's a wound to the chest as I realize I've never seen that. But I shouldn't feel this way. I shouldn't want to see him laugh or smile. I shouldn't want anything because what is the damn point if I'm going to die in a few weeks.

My heart apparently has other plans in mind, but I shove down the pain and shut my mind off as I turn away, chest tight.

Our section must have some sort of ward over it that blurs our appearance slightly because nobody in the nearby crowd reacts to Os's presence among us.

I force my gaze forward with another clench of my jaw, but the pit in my stomach grows at the sight of them together. Maybe Reymand *was* right. Maybe they're a couple. But then, what the fuck did that mean for me after the other night? My fists clench as my mind races.

Inhale through the nose, exhale through the mouth.

Inhale through the nose, exhale through the mouth.

I ignore the crowd and watch that fuck Achan as he panders to the adoring crowd.

"My, what a fight that was!" The announcer laughs, and the crowd laughs with him, hypnotized. "But the evening is far from over. In honor of the upcoming Gauntlet in just two weeks, the High Councilor himself, the highest unto Constantus, has put together something extra special." The crowd goes wild. "A special fight to mark the 20th ever Gauntlet games." He pauses with a wicked smile, "The two Dragons you're about to meet are some of the oldest in Ur Daoine. Fighters in the Great War," the crowd boos loudly, going on for a good few seconds, "both slaughtered so many innocent fae!"

"DEATH! DEATH! DEATH! DEATH!" The crowd chants, ready to see the slaughter.

"May I present to you—the murderer of High Councilor Fionn, the Doom of Elysium, **THE CRIMSON QUEEN!**" Those great silver doors open, and my heart falls out of my chest as Kydis's scarred face appears through the smoke.

CHAPTER 36
KYDIS

The metal muzzle falls to the ground with a large thunk as one of the evil ones unlocks it. I shake my head and lick my lips as I stretch my stiff jaw, the joints clicking in pain. The attendants freak out at the mere thought of me opening my mouth at all and poke me with their special prods, electrocuting me between my scales. I groan and twitch as I try to fight the pain that washes over me. They tug on my chains as the large metal doors start to open.

They mentioned my many titles—none of them which came from me. The fae love to paint Dragons as the problem, as murderers. But all of my three hearts are heavy at the memories of death and destruction. At the kin I've lost and the race I've watched go from thriving to almost gone from existence.

And with war, comes death. It was the way of the world. But it didn't make it any easier. I wanted to say I didn't revel in death, but right now, the thought of snapping the heads off some of these fae traitors would make me very happy.

I banish the thought because there was no hope of ever getting real revenge. I would never escape them, so I won't waste my energy imagining a better life.

My two other hearts sink in defeat as they announce the names of my opponent.

"And her opponent! The Destroyer of Ny'Anthrys, Scourge of Livyathin, he's eaten multiple handlers and is so feral, he's had to be moved over 50 times. Behold, **THE BASTARD!"**

Long ago, I knew him as Abeloth. Memories of the War assault me. Abeloth and I fought alongside each other, as did so many of my kin. I've fought in many wars, of course, but that was the war to end all wars. Finally, we could achieve the peace we'd have centuries before. Or it was supposed to be.

Abeloth went mad as we began to lose. The fae sent in imperial assassins to our nesting grounds, and my old friend returned home to the slain body of his mate, and their eggs crushed, the hatchlings inside perished. It broke something fundamental in him. As it did so many of us.

I watched my own mate die. We were part of a special contingent that allowed Elves and Mages to ride us. All of us who agreed to it understood the risks.

The pain of losing my mate never lessened. Sometimes, I dream of her white, glimmering scales and the delicate taper of her horns, with her bright green eyes. She was the most beautiful thing I've ever seen. Still is. But she was also the bravest Dragon I've ever known. When the leader of the Magyka needed a mount, she volunteered.

It ended in her falling to her doom.

I'll be with you soon, my love. I pray to Great Livyathin that this might finally be the day I'm released from my pain and suffering.

The doors open and I'm tugged forward into the light.

The light blinds me, and I growl as I flinch and adjust as they continue to pull forward. My molten blood freezes at the sound of a vicious shriek—Abeloth. I blink and look across the arena at my old friend. His green eyes are wide and manic as they dart around. He snaps at the pointy keepers as they electrocute him and force him forward. His scales used to be a brilliant copper, but he almost looks muddy brown now. He has more scars than I do, but he's one of the few Dragons left alive who is bigger than me. He loved to poke fun at me when we were younger about how small I am compared to him.

I had caught up quite a bit, but I'm still the slightest bit smaller. He limps, and I notice he's missing one of his legs.

"Hello, old friend," I trill to him. Very few beings are able to hear the pitch of a Dragon's voice. It's beyond most two-legged's capability. Only those with a touch of beast inside them and some imperial fae could hear it.

"DEATH. ESCAPE. DEATH. FIRE!" His responses are scattered and manic, and one of my hearts drops. He's in the afterlife now.

"I'm sorry, Abeloth. May Livyathin guide us to the afterlife and may we fly with our kin once more."

He just screeches and continues repeating, *"DEATH, ESCAPE, FIRE, DEATH, PAIN, LOST!"* over and over again, so I sever our connection. We're tugged out of the walls and the chains are removed. The painful, embedded chains around each of our necks stay on.

It's to be death by tooth and claw then. So be it.

I ignore the jeers and cups tossed at me as I await my fate and begin my death knell.

CHAPTER 37
AMALIA

I can't do this.

I can't sit here and watch these two Gods tear each other apart for money and entertainment. They were enslaved, starved, and tortured, and then expected to fucking perform. The Dragons don't deserve this punishment for the simple crime of existing.

I look at Kydis and see every scar on her crimson body. I see the resignation in her sad yellow and orange eyes, and something inside of me breaks beyond all recognition. I've been broken many times, but this is different.

Something feral inside me is loosened and let free as my heart thuds in my chest. My nails dig into my palms, puncturing them.

Os knows something is wrong. I can feel him nudging my mind and can feel the weight of his golden gaze upon my own.

I face him slowly, each movement painful and forced, as my eyes meet his.

Whatever he sees in my face makes him freeze. He blinks, taking in my panic. But I don't wait to see how he reacts.

He's not what my attention is on now.

I look at Dyana, her green eyes concerned as she meets my own. We promised each other many years ago that no matter what happened or our idiotic choices, we'd be there supporting one another every step of the way.

Dyana isn't even sure what I am thinking, but she knows me better than anyone. She knows that I need to do this, whatever it is. Instead of panicking, she simply reaches over and grabs my hand, squeezing. I nod gratefully and squeeze her hand back.

No one notices the small drips of blood coloring the ground.

The entire stadium gets to its feet, and I go with them, pushing to stand at the ledge, leaning against the metal rail. I hear some pushing and shoving as Dyana and Mirielle join me, along with some other candidates.

I'm not breathing as I watch the feral brownish Dragon roar and charge, galloping across the sand on its three limbs. My heart stops and I watch as Kydis bows her head in resignation, refusing to fight back.

No.

I refuse this fate. Without looking, I dip one finger in the stream of blood and begin tracing a symbol on my other palm.

"Move. Do something!" the crowd screams, but it's no use. Kydis doesn't listen to them.

I don't scream. I don't make a sound as I trace the six-pointed star, just as Father taught me.

Kydis doesn't move a muscle as the brown Dragon lowers its head and rams into her horns first. Kydis lets out a scream and I realize I'm screaming along with her. She falls to the sand with a deep thump as the brown Dragon crows victoriously. Kydis tries to stand up, but blood flows from the gouges in her side. She pants in pain but doesn't attack. She just stands there, taking it.

I don't accept this. I will not.

I seal the star, each of its six points even with the other, before annointing it with a symbol in the center. A single word in my Father's language.

That ember deep inside me flares and I gather all of my power as the brown Dragon roars, extending its torn wings and leaping into the air with a flap, jumping on top of Kydis and knocking her to the ground with a huge thump. The brown Dragon snaps its jaws and Kydis rolls to the side, barely avoiding it. But the brown Dragon grabs her tail, biting down hard and making her shriek in pain.

The noise robs me of my breath as my skin heats and everything tunnels.

"FIGHT BACK! FIGHT BACK!" Dyana shouts next to me, but it's drowned out by the screams and shouts of the hundred thousand other beings in the stadium. Os bangs at the wall of my mind, wanting in, but I ignore him.

The brown Dragon grips Kydis by her tail, blood streaming from his mouth as she cries out, and swings her into the air, flinging her into a wall with a crunch.

She crumbles to the ground, panting and groaning.

No.

"Get up," I whisper. Somehow, I know she hears me.

I finish drawing the symbol and feel my magyk erupt.

I frantically cast my mind out and shove into Kydis's, making her flinch.

HEAL! I command, and my magyk rushes into her with the force of a bolt of lightning. Kydis jolts. But the symbol has been cast; there's no stopping it now.

"Hello, Amalia Roth," she says weakly. *"Get out of my head. Let me die in peace."*

I unleash a snarl at her that sounds more Dragon than human as the brown Dragon stalks toward her, ready to make the final kill.

"You deserve to live, Kydis." I pant into her mind as I yank on my magyk and let that riotous ember flare inside of me.

"Maybe so, but my time is through. The age of the Dragons is ending."

"Then the age of the Dragons shall rise again." My words are a whisper and a threat and a promise. I say them aloud and repeat them in her head. I feel Os's gaze on me and I hesitate long enough for him to weasel into my head.

"Amalia, your magyk! Reel it in—" I cut him off. I can feel him go still as he reads my soul as if it was his own. He sees my intentions and motivations and shock floods him.

"A gahrá, please." His mental voice chokes off with surprising emotion.

"You can't stop me." I throw my wall back up and kick him out of my mind, and with a deep breath, push my magyk through Kydis' body and let it burn.

I cannot heal, not really. But with animals, I can fuel their own magyk so they can heal themselves.

She screams in pain, which makes the crowd cheer. They don't realize the pain is from me as her magyk knits her wounds together. I push more magyk into her, more than I ever have before. My vision goes blurry and my ears begin to ring.

Something happens then. Kydis jolts again and I feel as her well of magyk latches on, pulling more and more from me to heal her wounds.

Then she stops bleeding and the flow of my magyk meets a hard wall.

I gasp, grabbing onto the rail and smearing the glyph on my palm. But nothing more is needed as Kydis continues healing herself beneath the brown Dragon trying to kill her.

"You're an Arkaydian, and something else, too," Kydis says in awe.

"Yes." My voice is rough from the magyk use.

I don't have much left but with all of the anger and fury I possess, I launch what's remaining of my magyk into the mind of the brown Dragon. My legs give out at the act and Dyana grabs hold of my shoulders, wrapping her arm around me as if she's comforting me through sadness instead of weakness due to magyk use.

I stab into the brown Dragon's mind, and he roars in pain as my vision goes black.

"DEATH. DEATH. DEATH!" the Dragon shouts over and over again in his mind. His thoughts are completely shattered. Using the one last pathetic ember of power left inside of me, I mentally deliver a hard slap to the brown Dragon, making him stagger and flinch as he stumbles and shakes his head, confused.

The crowd goes quiet, waiting to see what happens. I sit down, panting heavily, and throw one last thought at Kydis.

"You deserve to live, Kydis. So get up and show these assholes exactly why Dragons are gods—and they are not."

The brown Dragon shakes its head and tries to focus, roaring as it gets ready to charge.

I do something then that I've only done once before, a long, long time ago. Hastily I scribble another symbol on the top of my hand, using my drying blood to paint it.

I seal the symbol with my thumbprint this time and instantly a ward forms around me. One that means no one can sense my magyk. It's one of the most draining glyphs to use, and I've only ever been able to hold it for 30 seconds at most. It does, however, give me the ability to still connect to animals with my mind.

With only the brown Dragon and Kydis listening, I remove every ward, wall, and barrier around my mind and bare myself body and soul to them. My magyk roars in happiness at being let free. Kydis stills and the brown Dragon falters.

"It's you," she says, a new tone to her voice—fierce and hopeful. *"The last Arkaydian. You're alive."*

My magyk leaps happily. The brown Dragon shakes it off as my ward drops and I lock my magyk back down. It takes a few moments and so much concentration I think I might pass out, but they're back.

"I am alive—and I will not watch you die, Kydis," I respond.

"For all that you've given, and all that you still have to give; for you, Amalia Ruth, I will fight one last time," Kydis responds, and my magyk cools, going dormant as exhaustion settles over me. I quickly wipe my hands on my pants, obscuring the blood.

The brown Dragon charges, and still, Kydis doesn't move. I hold my breath and watch as he goes to lower his head and ram her again, but just before he can, she rolls up onto her back legs and leaps into the air, making a complete vertical ascent, only once she's well above him do her wings flare out with a boom. Kydis ascends a little more, and the brown Dragon goes to join her, but just as he flaps his wings and jumps into the air, she dive-bombs him with a screech. She opens her mouth and crashes down on him, taking his neck between her teeth and crunching down hard. The brown Dragon chokes and writhes, scratching her, but it's unable to get free as she clenches even harder. Blood gushes from between the crushed scales, coating her mouth, and with a shake, she completely separates the brown Dragon's head from its body, flinging it across the arena with a mighty roar.

Blood sprays some of the crowd, and they go nuts, licking every drop. Kydis lets out another roar, this one even louder than the next. The crowd screams and shouts, the amount of Dragonfear in the air stronger than anything I've ever felt.

It's a roar of victory and pain and grief and fury. Unlike anything I've ever heard before. The roar goes on for what feels like hours, but then finally, Kydis stops, breathing hard as everything goes silent.

Gods. *God,* actually.

Kydis's orange and yellow eyes are hard as she stands and flares her red wings with a mighty roar. This was the Dragon of Legend who almost won us the war. The Prefect of the Golden Legion is a legendary unit made up of the strongest, most battle-experienced, terrifying Dragons.

"THE CRIMSON QUEEN IS YOUR VICTOR!" the announcer screams, and the crowd goes wild again. A net falls from the ceiling, covering her. She writhes and struggles, snapping at the net as the wall opens with a creak. Attendants run out and put Kydis' chains back on as she struggles.

One attendant is knocked to the ground and she stomps on him quickly, crushing him with a squelch. I want to glance away but force myself to watch and pay witness. The fae have enslaved and tortured her kind. I will not look away from the vengeance she sought.

The fire in her gaze makes my blood rush, and my own ember flares in return. I'm smiling now, wickedly so, and I watch as she takes out three more attendants until the High Councilor finally has to shout, "GET THAT DAMN BEAST UNDER CONTROL!"

Twenty attendants run out, all scrambling to get Kydis under control. They finally get chains over her neck and pull her to the sand while they quickly work to attach her muzzle. She bites one attendant in half, intestines and organs falling to the floor as she spits out the flesh. They latch the muzzle on so she cannot roar, but the quiet growl she emits shakes me to the core.

Make them pay, Kydis.

Make them *pay.*

CHAPTER 38
KYDIS

My mind races as plans come together in my head. I send a prayer to Great Livyathin for strength and courage.

The image of my mate appears in my mind, her beautiful white claws outstretched, waiting for me on the other side. But today is not the day we will be reunited. It won't be long yet, but today is not that day.

Not yet, my love. I'm still needed. We will be together soon, but not just yet.

I would be back in the arms of my mate one day soon—but not today.

This time, when I'm thrown back into my stifling metal cage of a prison, I look my handlers in their disgusting little red eyes and memorize them as they remove the silver muzzle around my snout.

I mark you, fae. You and all your kind. If there is to be an end of all things, you will end with us. For the prophesied has been born again.

They cannot hear me, of course. But others can. My kin. Confused and anxious whispers start to build, but with a single thought, I silence them.

"The Right Hand of the Morrigyn is here, and with her power, we will escape, burning this festering kingdom to the ground on our way out." Using my newly refueled magyk, I cast my song throughout the entire cavern. The fae just blink back, not understanding me.

I stare at them and smash my tail against the door, denting it. *"I mark you for death and the darkest pits of hell. The Morrigyn is calling—your time is near. The Gods have not forgotten us, and neither will you. But you will remember what it is to fear."*

Softly, it starts, like from a distance or far below. A thumping. But it grows as more and more pick up the call. Drums in the deep as if Great Livyathin himself was emerging. An ancient, long-forgotten rallying call. One not heard in many centuries, not since the Great War when Dragons last roamed free. A song not heard since the days when we lived in peace upon the shores of Elysium.

Tails slap down, over and over, the sound amplified and echoing. I join them, calling out with one last message. At my shouted words, the drumming increases. I can feel the change in the air. The energy rolling through me makes me ignore my tail injury as my blood turns molten.

Hope. It's the sound of hope. Something I thought no longer possible. Yet I hear it in the cries of my brothers and my sisters, my kin both old and young. I feel it in the thumping of their hearts as they match the beating of my own. Separated and broken, but we are not alone. We are Dragon—we are the burning, righteous flame. And with the Right Hand of the Morrigyn, the last Arkaydian, we will have our freedom at last.

The thumps and booms of our tails slapping the stone floor grow until dust falls from the ceiling. The fae begin to panic and frantically thrust their electrical prods through the small window of my cell, stabbing into me. I scream in pain but turn, biting the poles in half instead of cowering. A few hard cracks tell me that I broke some teeth on it, but it's worth it to see their scared little faces and the whites of their beady red eyes as they scream and run away.

The slapping goes silent as I yank out the prongs, tossing them to the ground as my blood drips down my scales. Magyk brushes against mine.

"We're with you, my lady."

"About fucking time—"

"Death to the fae!"

But the call that repeats over and over again is the same.

"The Queen calls!"

"We fight with the Queen!"

"For the Queen!"

The last stand of the Dragons begins now.

"You did thirst
for blood,
and with blood
I fill you."

— Dante Alighieri, 1265-1321.
The Divine Comedy: Inferno

scan for the pt. 3
reading playlist

PART THREE:

THE FAITHLESS

CHAPTER 39
DYANA

I walked into the Fray tonight hopeful that we might figure some way out of this. My naive, idiotic brain was convinced that maybe, just maybe, we could win the Gauntlet and make it out of this alive.

There is no hope after what I just saw. Not after hearing the sound of Dragons shrieking in pain as they tear each other to pieces.

We're going to die in there.

My hands shake, cold with my adrenaline against my cotton training uniform, as we follow Ireyna back to the dorms.

Everyone is quiet and tense as reality sets in. Amalia practically stomps with every step, her pupils blown out as if she's somewhere else. She keeps taking a second to steady herself as if she might fall over.

I don't know what Amalia did in there, but I pray to the Mother it went unnoticed. I've trusted Amalia with my life many times, and she's never let me down, but there's so much working against us already. We don't need the consequences that attention will bring. I might seem like the impulsive one, but really, Amalia always has been. She's just quieter, harsher, and meaner. When she snaps, devastation follows.

Whatever it was, whatever happened, Amalia must have deemed it worth the risk, and I'll stand by her side no matter where the road takes us. But that doesn't stop the fear from making my heartbeat thud in my ears with every step I take.

There is no hope for any of us. Not with a Dragon standing in the way of victory.

The warring emotions in the air make me restless and on edge. I keep sneaking peeks at Ama out of the corner of my eye, and I can tell Mirielle is concerned as well. My best friend has a frenzied, raw look to her that makes fear bubble up inside of me.

I've only ever seen that look on her face one other time.

Year 487 PBM

"Shit. We have to run." Amalia shoves me into the rain as we abandon our things in the cave. She tosses a small bowl of water we had filled from the brook nearby on top of the fire, dousing it with a vicious hiss. Amalia pauses for a moment, looking out into the forest, and for just a second, her eyes glow like winter ice.

Then the howls start. Echoing through the trees all around us.

Virgyl and the others—she must have warned them.

When Amalia's wards tripped, I was frozen at the thought of running into the males who killed my foster parents. But I come back to myself as Amalia grabs various knives she has hidden around the cave before pushing me into the rain.

Mud splashes with every step as I try not to slip on the slickground. My too-big boots make running hard, but I try, even as Amalia tugs me forward. Thumps and yells echo behind us as they catch sight of our fleeing figures as we head deep into the forest.

"Fuck, how did they find us?" Amalia growls, so much like Virgyl I half expect her to have fangs instead of teeth. "Quick, Dyana, we have to keep them away from the cave. No one can know it exists." Amalia shouts over the pouring rain and roaring thunder. Lightning strikes a tree nearby with an explosion so loud that I can't help but scream. A loud groan echoes through the forest as it crashes to the ground, causing Amalia to skid to a halt, and I run straight into her back. The tree hits the wet ground with a huge thump, and splinters fly. Amalia quickly turns around and blocks me from the debris.

"You need to hide Dyana," Amalia takes me and helps me down into a hollow log near the base of a large tree, and she quickly arranges a bush to cover the entrance. "Whatever you do, stay hidden."

I nod, shivering. Amalia's gaunt face is haunted as she takes a breath and runs off, hiding. The log doesn't do much to protect against the rain. I shiver harder as it soaks me to the bone.

"Well, well, hello, pretty." A sinister male voice sounds above me before a hand darts into the bush and yanks me out, hurting my neck with whiplash. I scream as the male grabs me, and I hear similar shouts as I see Amalia being thrown to her knees as she fights tooth and nail against the two males holding her.

"It's our lucky day, boys. I heard talk of a Wytch hiding out in the woods. Turns out, for once, the talk was right. The High Council pays a pretty penny for rare magyk users." The four males chuckle.

Amalia escapes their grasp, using the slick mud from the rain to slide away. She pushes to her knees and takes a few steps back until she's standing in front of the trees, eyes unfeeling and cold as the rain makes her gray hair look black. Streaks of mud cover her skin as she watches the males like a predator assessing its prey.

The group of males step closer as if to trap her, but Amalia doesn't move an inch. One of them laughs nervously, thrown off by her odd behavior.

"You shouldn't be here," she says calmly, eyes flat. Howls echo from the woods behind her, making the men look around nervously, some holding up bows and arrows, others lifting their swords. Amalia looks at their weapons, at the sharp edges of their blades. While it stirs terror within me, she is unmoved.

"That won't help you," she says flatly.

The males look at each other, confused. The one clearly in charge snarls and steps forward, "You're coming with us, girl. Run, and we'll have a little fun first. Behave and," the male pauses, "nah, never mind. We'll have a little fun first anyways." The male cups his crotch, and I shiver in fear.

"You shouldn't be here," Amalia repeats the words again, and the males laugh. But then her eyes start to glow again as another pair of glowing eyes appear behind her. A giant Dyre Wolf silently pads out of the dark forest, his fur as black as the night sky. Virgyl joins Amalia, and soon dozens of eyes glow in the dark, surrounding the men.

"You should have let me stay lost," Amalia's voice is as dark as Virgyl's growl.

"Do you think you and your dogs can do anything to stop us?" The male in charge laughs, but the others tremble in fear. The male at the front lifts his hands as hot, orange flames spring to life in his palms.

"Close your eyes, Dyana."

I look at Amalia, confused, as I realize her words were not spoken aloud. Her mouth never moved and yet I hear her in my head. I look back at Amalia, who continues to look at the males as Virgyl bares his huge fangs. "Close your eyes. Please." *Her voice is a desperate plea in my head. I bite my lip, trying to ignore the male holding me.*

"Okay...I trust you." *I take a deep breath and shut my eyes, squeezing my lids tightly and bracing for the worst.*

Even though I have no idea what the worst might be.

"You should have let me stay lost," Amalia says, but her voice echoes through the forest, amplified. "Because now I have to kill you."

A male laughs, but the sound is cuts off. I squeeze my eyes shut harder.

"What the fuck is that? What is she doing?" The males begin to shout and I hear screaming, followed by footsteps and the sound of loud gushing.

"Stop that. Stop!"

"Oh fuck, run! RUN!" The voices quickly turn into screams as the hands that hold me disappear suddenly, and the air heats. But I keep my eyes shut. Even as the smell of burnt flesh fills the air.

I keep my eyes shut, only opening when two soft, small hands press into my cheeks.

When I open my eyes, Amalia kneels in front of me as Virgyl, mouth wet with a dark substance, pads over to lick my cheek. Amalia grabs me tightly and strokes my damp hair as the rain continues to fall.

"You're okay, it's okay. I won't let anyone hurt you," she whispers the words over and over as Virgyl and the rest of the pack keep watch.

I ignore the piles of ash on the ground and on our skin, turning the rain black.

"We have to leave. If they know where we are they might come back," I whisper. "I don't want them to hurt the wolves, Ama."

Amalia takes a deep breath, trembling. "I know. We cannot risk the pack…so tomorrow, we leave. We find a new home, one where no one will ever recognize us. But we do it together."

Virgyl tosses his head back and lets out a howl that makes my ears bleed. I cover them, in pain as Amalia silently cries bloody tears into my damp hair, mourning the loss of the only family she's ever known.

NOW:

Mirielle's hand on my arm snaps me out of the memory, but the smell of the piles of burnt bodies is something I'll never forget.

That was the only time she ever spoke in my mind, up until a few weeks ago.

That night changed everything.

The look in Amalia's eyes that day is the same look I saw tonight, and fuck, it terrifies the hell out of me.

Os leads the group with Ireyna, and I'm a few people behind as we finally emerge from the long stairwell descent and into the lit hallway. She and Os chat the entire time as we follow dutifully, breaking from a single file into groups with those we know so everyone can talk about the Fray.

Os and Ireyna knew each other, but I never realized they were this friendly. And after Reymand's comments the other day, my mind couldn't help but whirl a bit.

"Ama?" I whisper. She glances my way, her cold blue eyes wild.

"Hm?"

I nod towards Os and Ireyna. I see her jaw clench as she takes them in. She likes him way more than she will ever admit.

"He's not mine." She says, but a ghost of sadness echoes in her voice.

"Do you want him to be?" She blinks and sighs.

"Perhaps." Her voice whispers into my head.

"Then do something about it."

"It's the Gauntlet, Dy. What is supposed to happen? There is no happily ever after for us." She says, her voice flat.

"I don't know, Ama. But you can't just give up living because you're afraid of what's around the corner. Stop living your life so afraid!" Mirelle's eyes are wide as I finally stop.

Ama just looks at me, eyes furious, but only for a few seconds before it turns into hurt, as she turns and continues walking in front of us.

"Shit. Shit!" I whisper, kicking myself.

Mirelle grabs my hand, lacing our fingers.

"It'll be okay," she says softly. "Just talk to her." She doesn't realize that I can talk to her even though she's not next to me. I don't know if she's still listening, but I try, anyway.

CHAPTER 40
AMALIA

Ireyna looks at Os suggestively, leaning up to whisper in his ear, and I briefly contemplate how much trouble I would get in should I remove her head from her shoulders. Os's eyes meet mine, his golden gaze furious.

"We are talking about what happened tonight. Particularly the part when you knew how to lock me out." Os snarls in my head as he looks back at Ireyna with a smile. As if I don't even exist. But...isn't that what I wanted? I mean, want?

"Looks like you're a little busy right now." I smile and continue walking. *"Do enjoy your evening."*

I shove him back out of my mind with a growl, iron doors slamming so hard that for a moment, I can actually feel his simmering fury in the air. I keep walking as Dyana and Mirielle follow behind, but a large hand grasps my arm.

"We have business to attend to." Os's voice is cold as his gold eyes gaze down upon me.

Oh he's mad. He's really mad.

Mirielle and Dyana pause, the former's eyes going wide as they both remember our meeting.

I never forgot about Nyall Drayven.

"Another time then?" Ireyna sidles up to Os's side, leaning into him suggestively. Os just nods and I bite down the fury that rushes through me.

I ignore it and pretend it's not there, that a tiny bit of my heart isn't on the floor getting squished under leather boots. We have to wait for Ireyna and the rest of the candidates to leave before following Os to his rooms. Ireyna hangs out for a while, shooting us dirty looks and asking Os multiple times if he's sure he can't grab a drink with her. I've planned at least five ways to kill her when we finally escape. No one speaks as Os starts for his room, the three of us in tow. Dyana's earlier comments are burned into my thoughts.

I've lost so much already, I can't lose her too. There's so much to be afraid of. But she's not wrong, and that's the part that hurts most.

Os opens the large doors to his bedroom, and we find Nyall Drayven already seated in one of the chairs by a roaring fire, sipping on a glass of honey wine. Those mismatched eyes slowly look our way as a slight smirk plays on a face bathed in warm firelight.

"Drayven." Os's voice is a near growl. "Breaking and entering, now? Is being an arrogant, rich prick not enough for you?"

Nyall nods, lifting his glass of wine in a toast. "Congratulations on another victory, old friend."

Os walks over and casually smacks the glass out of Nyall Drayven's hands. It shatters, breaking into a hundred tiny shards.

The Prince just laughs.

"We are not friends," Os snarls, getting in his face.

Nyall just winks at me, and Dyana's jaw drops to the floor.

"Get on with it. I'm tired and your presence is unwelcome." Os snarls as he stands in front of the fire, basking in glowing flames as he crosses his arms and stares at Nyall Drayven. I swear it surges higher in response to him.

I take the seat closest to him and Nyall, putting Mirielle and Dyana as far from him as possible.

"Why, Os, surely you've told your friends here how many centuries we've known each other? Or did you forget to mention the part you played in trying to overthrow the High Council the first time around?"

Os looks furious as he starts toward Nyall, but I raise my hand, stopping him. Os doesn't hesitate, doesn't miss a single beat. A single, silent command from me, and he stops, completely backing down.

I stare, shocked for a moment before I blink, shrugging it off and assuming a calm, unbothered facade. "You're pissing him off on purpose."

The Prince just smiles.

"You know what, Os is right. Your presence is unwanted, so how about I make this easy, I don't trust a single word out of your mouth anyways, half-breed. I know you're trying to shock me into trusting you, but it's not going to work so cut the act."

"Ah, the horse girl has some bite, then."

The play on words makes me grind my teeth. But the flirting in his voice tones down as he leans back, eyes accessing.

"Get on with it, Drayven." Os sneers.

Nyall sighs and his face goes hard, all emotion gone. It's startling to see. Nyall bows his head, turning to face me. "I need each of you to give a Blood Oath. What is spoken here must not be repeated."

"What the fuck?" Dyana's voice is high-pitched as she reacts to the outlandish ask.

"You're out of your damn mind if you think we're taking a blood oath with you, fae. Over my dead, godsdamn body." Os is shouting now.

"Then you all will die."

We go quiet.

I glare at him, unsure, "And helping you somehow means we'll survive?"

"No." Nyall Drayven shakes his head. "I mean you have to take a Blood Oath to even have this conversation with me because I am under a ward that prevents it. If I try to tell you the truth, the magyk will kill me before I finish speaking."

"Explain," Os thunders, his voice furious. Nyall's face is drawn and serious, the shadows on the angular planes of his cheeks making him look pensive and dramatic.

"As much as you can, at least." Mirielle says, surprising me.

Nyall clicks his tongue and begins, "I can say this much. The world is dying. You've all seen it, felt it. This is just the beginning. It will get worse. The forests will die, the Midheym sea will eventually dry up. Horrible storms will destroy the land before plunging us into a winter so cold, no one will survive. There will be nothing left."

"How do you know this?" I ask, heart racing. I don't want to believe him but...I feel it. I feel the truth in words. I've seen the way the forests have grown quiet and still. I've seen the trees begin to die and rot.

Something is wrong with Ur Daoine.

"I can't say anything further because I'm warded from telling anyone who isn't related to me by blood. My father thought he was being smart, but he didn't realize that if someone drinks my blood, the ward considers them family. Hence the need for the Blood Oath."

"Fine," I snarl, Os and Dyana's heads snap towards me, their eyes shocked. I lift a finger and point it at the Crown Prince, "But only if that blood oath protects us, too. You will swear to never tell a soul about our meeting or anything discussed in this room. The blood oath will ensure you uphold that promise, or it will kill you."

I turn to Dyana, "That's what he hasn't said. A blood oath is binding and if any of the oath takers break it, the blood will multiply and drown you alive. Death from drowning in your own blood. It's a horrible way to go and not to be taken lightly, so this only works if the Prince is bound to the same rules."

Nyall raises a brow, a small smile on his face, "Smart girl."

Dyana sputters next to me for a moment but then pauses and takes a deep breath.

"Okay. Okay. If he promises too, I'll take the blood oath."

"As will I," Mirielle pipes in, clasping Dyana's hand tightly.

I look over to Os, who glares at the Crown Prince. "I follow your decision, A gahrá."

I blink, shocked at the trust in his voice.

I face the Crown Prince, everything in my body screaming at me not to do this.

Yet I do it anyway. "Fine."

Nyall nods, withdrawing a sharp dagger. The hilt is braided black steel inlaid with rubies that shine in the firelight. The blade is rather large for a dagger, but the edge is wicked sharp. Nyall slices it across the meat of his palm and lets it drip into an empty wine glass. Using the unwounded hand, Nyall flicks his finger, and ropes of white magyk seal up the wound with a wet sound. Nyall tosses the dagger at Os, who catches it without glancing.

"The spell requires three drops of your blood. All of you."

Os slashes his palm open with rough abandon, causing Dyana and Mirielle to wince. Os walks over to the glass, letting his blood drip into the chalice. It burns and sizzles as it falls, once, twice, three times.

Hmm.

Os then grabs the chalice with another glare at Nyall—who just watches this all with amusement—and walks over to me, going down on one knee in front of my chair.

The sight of him kneeling at my feet is enough to blank my mind of all thought and worry. Os gently grabs my hand, looks me in the eyes, and drags a sharp, black claw across my palm, slicing open my skin. I didn't even see his nail shift. His magyk brushes against mine, and I realize he's taking the pain of the cut from me because I feel nothing. Not a single second of pain.

Is that the familiar bond? Or just him?

He brings my hand over the glass, letting three drops join the rest, but he never takes his gaze off me.

Suddenly, his eyes begin glowing and the air turns electric. The hair on my arms stands on end. My palm heats, and I watch in awe as the wound heals, sealing together easily. But some blood remains, and with a glint in his eye, Os brings my palm to his mouth and licks me clean.

I'm not sure I even move or react, but inside, I'm exploding as desire heats me, and the feel of his mouth and light stubble against my sensitive skin is enough to make me burst into flames. I exhale hard as he finishes licking my palm clean, aware we're being watched.

Each swipe of his tongue sends an electric shock through my body as if he was licking the bundle of nerves at the apex of my thighs. While his eyes are serious, the heated twinkle in his gaze tells me he knows exactly what he's doing to me.

"I am with you," he says in my head.

I shudder and fight the shattered sound that threatens to emerge from my lips at his words.

"I'm still mad at you," I say, breathless even in my mind.

"You're mad? I'm mad. You're in so much trouble for earlier." He sends another shock through my body, this time with his magyk, and it goes straight to my throbbing core. I gasp, my legs turning to jelly.

"How interesting," Nyall notes, amused. The sound of his voice snaps me back into the moment and I blink. Os stands and hands the chalice to Dyana and Mirielle before moving to stand behind me, one hand on my shoulder.

His lips are strained with my blood and the sight makes me feel unhinged.

"Just sit there and shut up until we're done, Prince," I manage, my voice raspy with lust.

"Touchy," Nyall says, unbothered. Os stares at Nyall in a way that tells me he's plotting a gruesome death should Nyall become too annoying.

I watch as Mirielle helps Dyana slice her palm open before tearing a piece of fabric off her tunic and wrapping it around the cut.

My friend will be left with yet another scar. But she stands straight, her brown eyes strong and brave as she does the same to Mirielle, slicing her hand open and letting it drip into the wine glass.

Mirielle looks uncomfortable though, something akin to fear in her gray eyes that keep darting towards Nyall.

She quickly passes the chalice back to us and rips another piece of fabric off, pressing it to her own wound.

"Take a sip and repeat after me."

Os shoves the chalice at the Prince, "You first, Drayven."

Nyall rolls his eyes but brings the glass to his lips and takes a small sip, "Blood spilled, blood bound. I vow to not tell another soul what is said upon this hour."

I blink at how simple the spell is. But it's to the point. He passes the chalice back to Os, and the air grows heavy with magyk as Os repeats the phrase.

"Blood spilled, blood bound. I vow to not tell another soul what is said upon this hour."

When it's my turn, Os brings the chalice to my lips. His eyes are on mine as he tips the glass, bringing the blood to my mouth.

The blood is hot and spicy. I taste Os immediately, like a smokey whiskey burning my throat. Dyana is there too, her sweet honey and floral lavender coating my tongue.

Mirielle's taste follows a bright and crisp salty citrus.

My eyes shoot to Nyall, who watches with a satisfied smirk. A burst of honeysuckle nectar hits my tongue as I take a final sip. A flood of magyk washes into me, and I distantly wonder if this happened to Os and Nyall too as I shiver in pleasure.

Os passes the cup to my friends, and they each take a sip, repeating the words. A sharp snap of magyk echoes through the room and we all jolt as the blood oath settles into place. A glowing silver string connects us all for a brief moment and then it's gone.

"Why are we here, Prince?" My words echo into the space as the male's smile drops. He leans back, crossing one leg over the other as he stretches his right arm over the arm of the chair and rubs his mouth with his left.

"I want you to join the rebellion and help me overthrow the High Council." We all blink as Nyall leans forward, looking me dead in the eyes. "Help me kill my father, Amalia Roth."

CHAPTER 41
DYANA

There's a beat of silence as we all take in what the Crown Prince just asked.

Then something happens that shocks me to the core—Amalia laughs. And she continues laughing for what seems like ages but I know it is only a few seconds.

"You," Amalia tries and chuckles again, "you want me to help you kill the High Councilor? That's fucking rich." She shakes her head and the laughter dies. Amalia sits back in her chair as she looks at Nyall Drayven with disgust, "I've spent just about every single year of my life thinking about killing that bastard. My whole life, I've dreamed of it. Planned it out in detail."

Mirielle turns to look at Amalia, eyes wide. If Os is surprised, he doesn't react.

"Help me do it, Amalia," Nyall says.

Amalia snorts again, "Idiotic male. You're the one that doesn't understand. I've already tried to kill your Father and guess what?" Nyall blinks, shocked. Ama just smirks, her eyes raging, "It didn't work. Whatever it is you think you've found? It won't work."

The Prince exhales and leans back in his chair, "I'm a Siphon."

Amalia freezes, blinking as she processes this news, "How interesting. Tell me, Prince—is siphoning a fae magyk?"

I can't help but interrupt, "I'm sorry, I'm confused. What's a Siphon?"

Nyall looks at me briefly and I shiver under the weight of his mismatched eyes. "Siphoning isn't a fae magyk, which is why I'm one of the only beings in Ur Daoine who can do it."

"One of?" Amalia asks, sitting forward, her eyes sharp and alarmed. "There are more?"

"Stop!" I start, "Explain what the hell you're talking about. Enough of this damn code."

A few things happen, then. Nyall grinds his teeth, Os growls so loudly it shakes the lounge Mirielle and I are sitting on, Amalia sighs, and Mirielle ...well, she looks away.

"The illustrious Crown Prince is only half-fae," Amalia says.

"Yeah, that part I got," I mutter.

"But he hasn't told you about the other half. Shall you tell them, Prince? Or shall I?" She taunts the Prince.

Nyall shrugs. "Fine."

Amalia turns to me, "He's a godsdamned Elf."

"Half-elf, actually," Nyall says, but we ignore him.

"Wait, what? I thought the Elves died a thousand years ago? How is that possible? And how do you even know this? Why does it feel as if I'm the only one learning this information?"

Everyone looks away, but Amalia keeps her eyes locked with mine. Regret shows in them.

"You knew this, and you chose not to tell me?" I turn to Mirielle, who bites her lip nervously, "Either of you?"

"Don't worry, Ms. Arkos. I'm quite sure they didn't tell you because this is a hard truth to accept."

"Right, and this big truth is so awful because..?"

Mirielle looks at me, quirking her brow. "You were never told stories of the Elves? About the ancient, magykal land that disappeared into the depths of the ocean?"

I shake my head and look towards Ama again.

"Why didn't you tell me these stories?"

Ama looks away, and her cheeks heat lightly. She clears her throat and clicks her tongue, "I never knew much. My parents told me a few stories but what I know, I read about."

I nod, trying not to feel hurt but failing miserably. "Okay, so tell me the stories then. What's so bad about the Elves?"

Nyall crosses his legs, "I'll tell you, but be warned, it's not a pretty story. No one likes talking about the Elves. My Mother was an elf, the last living female. Because of her, my powers actually exceeded those of the High Councilor. Or, they used to. It's why he's always hated me and what pushed him to start consuming the Dragons. He...he wasn't always this bad." Os snorts and Nyall grimaces, "Okay, he's always been terrible. But the weight of his evil increased tenfold after he decided to start consuming the flesh of the Dragons."

"Um, the story?" I say, noticing he's getting off track.

"Right," the Prince says, adjusting in the chair and getting more comfortable. "Two thousand years ago, the world was different. Magyk was richer, stronger. But far to the South on the other side of the world, a society thrived. We don't know the name of the land, only the name of the people. Elves. Beings so magykal they rivaled the power of the Dragons. It only took a few instances for the rest of the world to learn about them and even less for everyone to view them as Gods.

"The thing about power is it's never enough. You get some, and now all you want is more. And so the Elves became greedy. Over the course of eight hundred years, the Elves studied. Dedicated themselves to the weavings of the universe, of life itself. But the Elves looked too far and took too much. You see, the Elves wanted to become true Gods. Beings with the ability to travel to different planes, different worlds, and different times. But most importantly, they tried to control life. And that, dear Dyana, is a power only meant for true Gods to wield. Humans, Magyka, Fae; we're not meant to have that kind of power. To wield it is to break the world. And that's what the Elves did. They harnessed life and death, which today we call Dark Magyk, and they destroyed themselves because of it."

I listen to Nyall with a pit in my stomach, not liking where this is going.

"It's been said it was on a normal day just like this that there was a sudden crack that echoed throughout their continent. Seconds later, the land began to rumble and break, turning to dust as it slowly, torturously crashed into the ocean. A century later, Arkaydia rose to power. But as the years went on, the Elves were forgotten, only to be mentioned as a cautionary tale for what happens to immortals and mortals who get too greedy and forget their place." Nyall pauses, "But here I am. As you can now guess, a very small group of Elves survived. The Elves were smart with some things, but not with common sense things like bringing enough women with them to ensure their ability to reproduce and keep their species alive. My Mother *was* the last living female Elf."

"Wait." I speak up, clearing my throat, "So the Elves aren't a problem then, right?" Everyone looks at me. "I mean, if there are no more female Elves, the lines will eventually die off. It will take time since fae are long-lived, but they'll all die, right?"

Nyall hesitates. Everyone is quiet in that particular way that says 'we know something.'

I'm getting really tired of being kept in the dark.

"My Father made a deal with the surviving Elves. They would teach the High Council Dark Magyk and the fae would spearhead their new project of gaining God-level Dark Magyk, in exchange for one thing. The Elves hesitated, so Achan put the final pieces of his plan in place. He offered all the women the Elves could ever want. They would be diluted Elves, sure, but Elves would continue on and their species would be saved. IF they gifted him the last pure-blooded female Elf. My Mother."

"You..." I gasp, realizing what he means. "You were the experiment. Combining powerful Magyka breeds to create something new. Something stronger."

Nyall sips his drink and tips it at me, "Good job. That was the goal. It was the final test. His last chance at success before he killed my mom. They'd become pregnant dozens of times, but the child never survived more than a few minutes after birth. Except me. You can imagine his disappointment when Achan realized he actually did succeed, but that it would never work, because I've always hated him. I'd rather be tortured for a thousand years than do what he wants, and he knows it. I played the part for a few years, but then the Great War happened and I knew what he was planning. And now here we are. I'm the shame of the Kingdom and an ever-present thorn in his side. He plays the magnanimous Father figure in public, but in private, he can't even look at me." Nyall unbuttons his shirt a little and even I blush at seeing his tattooed, muscular chest. Nyall turns to the right, showing off his neck. "You might not be able to read this, but this one here on my neck?" He points to a large set of glyphs across his neck and throat, "This is where he branded me. All because I didn't want to pray to his sniveling God."

Woah. I exhale. "Okay. And...and you said you're a Siphon? Is that...the successful part?"

Nyall nods. "Yes. However, when I became aware of his intentions, I started to hide the extent of my power. Achan knows I have magyk, but he thinks his test failed."

"But he's seen you weave," Amalia responds.

I frown, "Weave?"

Nyall leans back in his chair, crossing his legs, "My magyk is different. I've always seen it as weaving." He holds up a large tattooed hand, the veins black, crawling up to black painted nails. He whirls his fingers and ropes of white light crawl around his hand and arm, going under his shirt and up to his neck.

It's beautiful.

"The first time I siphoned, I was eight. Father beat a servant to death in front of me, a kind woman who often cared for me since he never bothered to. Nena." Nyall smiles fondly, "When he killed Nena, I snapped. I didn't even know the spell for the weaving but my hands were suddenly moving, weaving the most complex spell Achan had ever seen outside of the Archmage, or himself. But Achan knew I wasn't taught this spell. It was in my blood, my soul. That made me stronger, and it made me a threat to his power. So he sent me to apprentice with the healers. I studied with them for a few centuries before leaving. He thought that I'd be under his control, thanks to the watchful, prying eyes of the Elves. He didn't realize I'd quickly learn all they could teach me and then start building my own weavings. Ones that can drain the life force from a person without a second thought"—Os growls and the room grows hotter. Amalia looks furious, but Nyall continues—"and one that can fill something with new life, too. I can transfer the life from one being to another. That's what a Siphon is."

"You're insane, Drayven. You know that kind of magyk comes with a price! I knew you got into Dark Magyk, but to tamper with the forces of life and death is to curse the Gods. Are we not cursed enough already?" Os snarls before beginning to pace behind us. "Mother save us; you're an insane bastard. You also conveniently left out how using Dark Magyk is killing you."

Amalia jerks, shocked.

Nyall just shrugs before continuing, "When my Father began consuming the flesh of Dragons five centuries ago, everything changed. He's gained a lot of their power, and it's wildly unpredictable, but as you have probably noticed, it's also breaking him mentally. And Os is right. There is a high likelihood a weaving of this magnitude will kill me, but that's a risk I willingly take. If it stops my Father, it's worth it."

Amalia sits back in her chair, leaning on Os's hand as her eyes go distant, "Power always comes at a price."

"Yes, it does," Nyall replies, his voice almost...sad. "I learned that the hard way. The Archmage only *seems* meek. In private he is..." Nyall breaks off.

"He?" I ask, confused. "I thought the Archmage was Ains Selle."

Nyall smiles. "It's a valid question. Many think the same, but the Archmage is Alle Selle. He uses both 'he' and 'they' pronouns."

That makes sense.

This is not what I expected of the Prince. The arrogance? Yes. But there is a conscience in Nyall Drayven's eyes that is rather unexpected. I still don't trust him but he doesn't seem like one of the fae, let alone an imperial fae.

"So are you...a, um, God then?" I ask, still a little confused.

Nyall shrugs, "Not really, no. I can use their power but I'm not omnipresent or able to manipulate time. The Gods don't exist. They're simply stories people told to make the world around them into something digestible. Gods make the world make sense."

Amalia *hmphs.* It seems we agree on something, then.

I blink, shocked. "You don't believe in the Gods?"

Nyall clicks his tongue, "When my Mother was being beaten in front of me, I prayed to the Gods. I asked the Mother, hell, even that made-up piece of shit Constantus. I prayed to any God I could name. Yet my Mother continued to bleed out. The Gods did nothing. I watched as Dragons were slaughtered, their babies stolen from them and eaten, and still the Gods did nothing. I watched as the Magyk drained from the land. I feel it withering away every single day. And the Gods do *nothing*. Which means there's only one truth, the simplest one. The Gods didn't do anything because they don't exist. Or if they did, they were like us. Immortals—or mortals—with rare Magyk. That's it. No more and no less. People love to tell stories, and the truth can be spun in many different ways."

I...I guess I agree. And yet, I know the Gods are real. They have to be. Otherwise, what's the point?

"What does a half-elf want our help for, then? You seem to have the plan all set. Clearly you want to Siphon your Father. I still don't see why I'm needed. You said it yourself, you're more powerful than him. So do it. Kill him and be done with it." Amalia's eyes are hard and calculating as she watches Nyall.

"First, it's not just you I need." Nyall's haunting eyes glance at Os, "I require your assistance too, Beast."

Os bares his teeth at Nyall and spits out a language I don't recognize. Each letter is steeped in magyk that hits me in waves, making me dizzy. Mirielle grabs me when I sway, almost falling off the lounge. The heat of her hand through my top yanks me back to reality. I turn and meet her clear, gray-green eyes. They soften immediately as we share a brief glance, and she squeezes my arm before letting go.

I want to tell her to never let me go, but I stay quiet.

"In order to make this work, I'm going to need the Mother of all distractions. It's not just the High Council that is the problem, it's the godsdamn Archmage. He's an extremely powerful magyk user and will need to be taken out in order for this to work. I've studied him for centuries. I know his weaknesses. We need to take out Achan before the Archmage is alerted. Plus, siphoning will only work if Achan is already wounded, and unfortunately, the prep work needed for a spell of that level will keep me occupied." Nyall is quiet for a moment, "Which means someone else needs to distract and disarm Achan, hold off the Archmage if he appears, and fight off the soldiers since everyone from the Black Citadel will be in the Arena for the Gauntlet."

"No," Amalia says flatly. I inhale sharply as the Prince's eyes go dark.

"Look me in my eyes and tell me you don't want to get revenge for your parents, Arkaydian," he says.

Shit!

My jaw drops, and my eyes bug out of my head as Nyall casually references Amalia's heritage. I glance at Mirielle, who looks back and forth between them, biting her lips nervously.

Amalia just hums lightly as her eyes begin to glow. Besides that, nothing changes, but there's an electric weight to the air like the silence just before a storm comes crashing down. The shadows in the room seem to expand, getting even darker, and the fire sparks violently. It's only for a few seconds, but we are all tense.

Amalia and Os look so similar with that glow in their gazes. I never noticed it before, but the cold, hungry look in their eyes is the same, and I know if Nyall acts out, this is going to become a bloodbath.

Amalia pulls her dagger from her sleeve, twisting it expertly as she drawls, "I almost succeeded, you know. I'd reckon I was the closest. Many have tried to kill your Father, my own Father included. But the night of my parents' murder, I could feel his death within my grasp. You want to know why I won't help you, Prince?" Her voice gets darker as she glares beneath her brow at him, eyes cold and fierce. "Because I hit him with enough power to level the Ulster Wald itself and it barely made a difference. I watched your Father emerge from a magyk blast that should have turned him to dust, but he was merely a little scraped up. Whatever he's done to himself—and I'm sure there's more than polluting himself with Dragon magyk—whatever he's done in his fucked up labs, has changed him. Made him something more. I tried to finish the job my parents started, but it was all for nothing."

The room is dead silent as Nyall sits back, processing.

"I know this must be difficult for you to understand, Prince, so let me be plain. Your plan isn't going to work. Not even your Elven magyk will take the High Councilor down. Whatever he's been doing to himself, he's too far gone. Siphoning will only weaken him. The only thing that stands a chance at killing him is Hellfyre, but no wielders are left alive after your Father's Cleansing." Amalia stands and motions towards me, "So I thank you, Prince. Believe me when I say, I would love to kill your Father, but we're already at death's doorstep. I don't need you to shove us through the door and quicken our demise with a foolhardy plan that will only make things worse."

I go to stand, but the hand on my arm suddenly squeezes, pulling me back.

"Just.. hear him out, please." The voice is broken, cracking with emotion.

It takes me a moment to realize it's Mirielle. Everything slows and my heart skips a beat. I turn as if in slow motion as Mirielle's eyes go wide and pleading as she stands.

No.

Os begins to growl as Amalia's eyes burn with the promise of death as she slowly turns to look at Mirielle.

"You know, I almost believed you. I didn't even want to stop that first day but Dyana convinced me." Ama leans forward, her face a mask of death, "I should have left you in the dirt, you lying bitch. You're his little spy, aren't you? That's how he knows all about me. You told him everything you learned like a whipped little puppy running home to its master. How adorable."

The reality of what's happening sets in and my hands begin to shake.

I stare down to the floor, every moment with Mirielle playing on repeat in my mind. The shared looks, the stolen touches. Was any of it real? Was it all a lie?

"Yes, I'm sorry, I couldn't tell you. You have to believe me, please—"

Amalia cuts Mirielle off, "Too bad. I don't believe you. You know, I knew there was something off about you and it all makes so much sense now. Tell me, Prince, was it a coincidence, our meeting? Or did you two plot where I was most likely to be that morning?"

"How much of it was a lie, Mirielle?" My voice snaps out like a whip, and Mirielle jerks back as if struck. My accusation echoes through the space. "Is there anything real about you, or was I just another one of your fucking targets?

Mirielle wrings her hands nervously, begging me with her eyes to believe her, but my heart is frozen as numbness takes over.

"Every moment with you was real, I swear."

"As if I would believe anything that comes out of your mouth. I can't believe you're a godsdamn spy. I'm such an idiot. I thought you—" I can't say it. I can't say that I thought she cared.

"Dyana, please." Mirielle stands and I take another step back. She closes her eyes as a tear falls.

"Not like there was anything to begin with, but we're done." I stand next to Os, walking on numb feet across the sitting area. Os surprisingly shifts to stand slightly in front of me in a protective gesture that almost breaks me. But I zone out and try to keep my composure despite feeling like my heart is shattering into a thousand tiny pieces. It's my own fault, really. I should never have trusted her, and I know Amalia would agree. She'd never tell me that, but it's easy to understand now why she doesn't give her trust out often.

I should never have given mine to Mirielle.

"You know what? No," Mirielle says. "I'm not going to sit here and let you turn me into the bad guy because we're actually on the same side and here for the same fucking reason. We're here because the High Council has stolen from us. Every single one of us. They've taken our happiness, our lives, our families, and yet, we do nothing. The Gauntlet is for them! They enjoy seeing us suffer, seeing us tortured. Hell, the crowd cheers at our deaths. The bloodier the better, right? That's how little we mean to them. To the fae, we're no more than the worms in the mud beneath their boots," Mirielle pauses, now standing up and breathing heavily. "Yes, I am a rebel. Yes, I was going to sneak away from training the first day, which is why I stopped. Yes, I told Nyall some of the things I learned. But nothing else was a lie, and everything I did lie about is because I'm trying to make sure no Gauntlet is ever hosted again. The High Council has to be stopped, Amalia! I don't have an ulterior motive other than to survive long enough to do that, and guess what? That's all you want too. We're on the same side here. My story, everything I told you, it's all true. I'm here to help Nyall and to save our Kingdom. I will not let Ur Daoine become the next horror story told to children thousands of years from now. I will not let anyone else be killed for their selfish whims."

Amalia scoffs but Mirielle crosses the room and gets in her face. Os growls but Mirielle ignores it. "Listen to me! Maybe you've forgotten, hidden all the way in the North, how bad things have gotten in the rest of the Kingdom, but I didn't have the luxury, Amalia. Not as I watched my Mother slowly waste away over the course of a decade, knowing there was a cure but not being able to do anything about it. Not as I watched my Father get down on his godsdamn hands and knees to BEG that monster for a cure. Do you know what the High Councilor did? He laughed and mocked my Father, forcing him to grovel for his evening entertainment. My Father was forced to service them, Amalia, and I was forced to watch. Do you know what that's like? Watching your Father be assaulted all evening long? Do you know what it's like when even after all of that, the High Councilor looked him dead in the face and told him he'd changed his mind, there would be no cure given after all?" Mirielle raises a finger and points it at Amalia, making me tense. "You are not the only ones who have lost and suffered. We all have suffered. That's the point. That's why I'm finally doing something about it so that this all can just fucking stop. It has to stop." Mirielle pauses, taking a breath. "Please, help us stop this."

Amalia's voice is still stern as she watches Mirielle, "This all is assuming we believe anything you say."

"You should, it's true," Nyall adds. "And she's right. Each of us has lost something, isn't that right, Os?" The latter just growls, eyes bright.

But I'm not looking at Nyall. I'm looking at Mirielle. My sadness shifted into righteous anger. "You told him our secrets. How could you?"

"I already knew, Mirielle merely confirmed." Nyall says, looking from me to Amalia, "I knew what you were the moment I watched you feel those baby Dragons die. I saw the pain in your face and that's when I realized exactly what you were. By the way," he pauses, "I really was out riding that morning. But when you magyked your horse jump much higher than it should have been able to, my earlier suspicions were confirmed."

Mirielle's gray gaze eventually falls to the floor. Amalia is quiet, but Os's growling still fills the room.

"They let my mother die, Dyana." Mirielle whispers as she sits down next to Nyall in a casual way that tells me they've known each other a long time. Her voice cracks, gray eyes flooding with pain as she looks at me, "After two centuries, enough is enough. Somebody has to say enough. Please believe me."

Amalia just blinks at the passionate speech, unamused and unmoved, but I go cold.

"So you lied about being human then, too?" Amalia asks, scoffing. "I wonder what other lies you're hiding, rat?"

Mirielle's eyes blaze with fury for a moment and then it passes, replaced with an empty sadness. "I never lied because you never asked, Amalia. But yes, I'm not human. My parents were both demis. Mom was half demis, a Syren. It's common in the Eastlands to have at least one parent with demis heritage and water magyk."

Ama glances over at me and I wince.

"I feel your guilt. You knew this?" Her raspy voice appears in the back of my mind.

"Um, yes." I hesitate. *"I thought it was her secret to tell. I didn't know... well, I thought we could trust her.".*

Amalia's eyes go sad for a moment at the pain in my voice.

She glances at Nyall. "What I still don't understand here is why you chose me to help and not some other candidate?"

"I saw how you watched the Dragons tonight. You're bonded to one of them, aren't you?"

"Uh, what is he talking about, Ama?" I don't have a clue if she's listening or not, but I ask anyway.

Os makes a choking noise.

I feel her hesitate, and I pretend it doesn't hurt.

"I was going to tell you..." she says, breaking off.

"I do not control the Dragons," Amalia spits the word, disgusted at the thought. "Nobody controls a Dragon, not truly. But I can...influence them. I don't take away their own will; I just shift it. It's harder with the older Dragons. Their minds are much stronger."

Nyall quirks a brow, "Are you bonded with the Crimson Queen, Amalia?"

"I'm sorry, the Crimson Queen? Y-you're asking if she bonded with the Crimson Queen? The literal man-eating giant Dragon we just saw not two hours ago?" My voice rises in pitch as my thoughts race.

Then I look at Amalia. No one else would know her tells, but I can see the twitch of her cheek.

She's embarrassed. In that moment, I realize I have two choices: I can act like a normal person and be horrified that she somehow got close enough to a Dragon to bond with it, or I can back her up.

I look at her and see the hesitation in her eyes. Not regret, not shame. The uncertainty that I might judge her for this decision.

I step away from Os's side before raising my hand to point a finger at the Crown Prince of Ur Daoine "First off, I don't like the tone you're using when you talk to her, and that means I don't like you. You will speak to her with respect, or I swear to all that is good and holy I will scream so loud it shatters your fragile little fae eardrums and your evil daddy comes running, so don't test me. I might not have magyk, but I do have a great set of pipes and 24 years of pent-up anger that I am eager to use." I pause to take a breath, "Second, so what if Amalia bonded with a Dragon? You don't have any say in her decisions. You haven't earned the right," I look him dead in the eyes, "and at this rate, you *never* will."

A warm feeling enters my body as I feel Amalia's magyk, and her voice enters my mind.

"Dy, it's okay. You don't need to protect me right now."

"Family protects each other. You're my family, Ama. I'll always be with you—even if I am also a little pissed off at you but we'll deal with that later." I feel the depths of her love. Things she often has trouble putting into words.

"Kydis is... my friend."

I look down at Amalia, surprised. My friend by chance and sister by choice sits in her chair, back straight and chin high, refusing to be judged or shamed by anyone.

Mirielle's jaw drops and Nyall looks disgustingly pleased with himself, making me want to punch him in his smug little face. Os just watches, unsurprised and unmoved. But he does move his hand to Amalia's shoulder, and I see her pupils dilate briefly in response.

"Kydis?" Nyall asks, voice gentle.

Amalia nods, "Yes, that's her name. The one she gave to me, at least."

"She...told you this? She spoke to you?" Nyall asks in disbelief, nearly choking when Amalia nods.

Oh, my Gods. My eyes go wide in shock despite all that I already know. Amalia spoke to a Dragon.

Nyall takes a big breath, eyes wide. "We have some magyk users, myself included, who have some mental powers, but all these centuries later and every single one of them but the Dragonguard has refused all attempts to communicate. You're the first person to talk to any of the wild Dragons since...before the Great War, Amalia." Nyall laughs in disbelief. "Holy shit." He takes a moment to gather himself before leaning forward. "I need to meet your Dragon friend. She might not talk to me but with you there, it will work."

"Why do you deserve that honor? Why should Kydis give you the time of day?"

Nyall blinks, considering the question, "I've tried to speak to the Crimson Queen for centuries, but she never said a word."

Amalia watches him warily, "That doesn't answer my question. Why do you deserve the honor of speaking to a being as great as her?"

Nyall just looks at me with clear, unwavering eyes, "Achan Drayven's death would be beneficial for many parties, horse girl. The Queen included."

We're all silent in the wake of his words. Os looks over at Nyall, cocking his head oddly as his pupils change to slants. "We need time to think on it and will give you your answer in a week's time."

Nyall nods. "I need to know by the opening event at the very latest. We will need at least a week to plan, and any later than that would mean there's not enough time." Os nods back as Nyall goes to leave.

Without even looking, Os calls to Nyall, voice casual, "And if you so much as think of telling anyone about any of this, Drayven, I'll tear out your spine and use your bones as toothpicks before your little Blood Oath can even react."

I blink, eyes wide at the threat.

The Prince rolls his eyes "I forgot how dramatic you always are. I'm magykly bound to not say anything, you oaf. Besides, it's not in my best interest to share your secret. I'm the one asking for your help here, remember?"

"I'll think about it," Amalia says, standing and signaling an end to the conversation.

Nyall winks at her. "Don't think too long, horse girl."

Amalia sneers, "Don't hold your breath, Prince."

"Dyana, wait, please!"

Amalia and I fast walk out of there, and Mirielle jogs to catch up.

"I need to handle this." My voice is dark, and Ama nods, but not before sending a thought into my mind.

"Call if you need me. I know I don't need to say it but, Dy, just... be careful with her. We cannot trust her."

"Agreed."

"I'll see you in the room." She squeezes my hand and emotion clogs my eyes. No matter what happens, we will always have each other's backs. After those months in the woods and everything we went through, the promises we mad e...there is never any doubt in my mind that she will be there for me. We were forever and then some. Her soul was made of the same material as my own. Ama continues down the hall, and I turn with a tight breath as Mirielle catches up. Her gray eyes are luminous and pleading as she goes to grab my hands. I yank them out of her reach, and she awkwardly pulls back.

"Dyana, please. I'm so sorry. I wanted to tell you; I was planning on telling you."

"You know, when you told me about your...history, I thought you trusted me. You broke that trust."

"I know. I will do everything in my power to prove to you that you can trust me."

"It would be a wasted effort. There's nothing you can do. You lied about who you were, Mirielle. There's no going back from that. I'll forever be wondering what was real and what was fake. Not that there was much there to begin with," I snort, but my heart aches for her, and my hand is cold without her touch.

Mirielle is quiet but nods. "I will earn your trust back, Dyana Arkos, I swear it."

"Don't bother," I turn to walk away, but her hand on my arm stops me. I go to look at her, but she's shoving me back against the wall of the hallway. I wriggle and go to shout, but she silences me with her mouth. It's so quick I'm blinking when she steps away. But she just looks at me, eyes vulnerable.

"I will bother, you idiot, because I'm falling in love with you."

My mouth falls open as I look at her, eyes wide. "You...what?"

Mirielle shrugs, a nervous smile on her face. "I tried to make it obvious but...I was scared I'd push you away. Even if you will not have me, for whatever time we have left, I am yours. I love you, Dyana." She steps closer, raising her hand as if to caress my cheek. I lean back against the wall and away from her touch, and her gray eyes darken with sadness as her hand stills, falling to her side.

"We should get back to the dorms then." Mirielle clears her throat. "May I walk with you?"

"Fine," I mumble, dazed at everything that's happened in the past few minutes and more confused than ever before. "But I don't really want to talk." Mirielle nods, and we walk silently back to the dorms.

The candles are burnt down low, casting shadows against our figures as we reach a crossroads in the hallway.

"Goodnight, Dyana," Mirielle whispers. She opens her mouth again like she wants to say something else. I almost want her to apologize again, to say those words again. Part of me doesn't want her to say anything at all. My heart is in a hundred directions, and I'm not sure what to do.

"Night." I scurry back towards our rooms and shut the door quickly when I get there. I knock my head against the door and slide down onto the floor.

Arms wrap around me from behind. "I'm so sorry." She helps me up and into my bed and positions us so my head is on a pillow in her lap. Ama leans over to our tiny nightstand and grabs a brush, running it through my hair as I cry myself to sleep.

Amalia doesn't try to fix my problems. She doesn't provide a magical solution.

But she's there. She's always there.

CHAPTER 42
MIRIELLE

I was right.

They hate me.

Every time I see that hurt look in Dyana's eyes and the betrayed look in Amalia's, I get nauseous. Not so much because I care what Amalia thinks, but I don't hate her. To know that she hates me...I didn't think I would care so much. About any of this.

As we stand before Os and the other trainers, I have to keep stopping myself from looking to where Amalia and Dyana stand—far away from me.

Alone again.

I've been telling myself this is how it was supposed to be from the beginning. No emotional ties, just me on my own. But the hurt is hard to ignore.

"Listen up!" Everyone quiets at Os's shout. "Now that you've been to the Fray, it's time to begin learning how to kill a Dragon."

My stomach drops as a juvenile Dragon the size of a horse suddenly appears at the far side of our training arena, the wooden doors squeaking open. It's muzzled and chained, led by two fae attendants who openly sneer at us. The Dragon is a deep green with yellow and gold spikes. It's beautiful.

I hate that we have to kill it.

The Dragon is brought up to Os, who takes over the chains and holds them with one hand. The fae attendants step back, and Os drops them. The candidates collectively jump back, but Os merely takes the muzzle off the Dragon.

The fae attendants hiss at him in another language, but he waves them off.

"This is your opponent today. One of the Dragonguard trainees. He is much smaller and more docile than the Dragons you will meet in the Arena."

Then Os begins looking the Dragon over, the latter of which stands there, staring at us as if slightly confused...and a little scared.

Os gives the Dragon a command, and it sits up on its hind legs since this one has four legs. According to Os, Dragons have four legs and normal wings, or two legs and clawed, sharp wings. This one has the former.

We learn that Dragon scales are weakest under their bellies, around their ankles, and behind their horns.

Then it's time to practice. Os has us line up a single file as we each wait our turn to avoid the Dragon's flames.

The smell of burnt hair and charcoal assaults me as the line moves forward, and I get closer to being the next one up.

The majority of the candidates will need a healer. So far, only two other candidates have been able to avoid the flames, but they still were left with singed hair and burnt-off eyebrows.

"ZENYTH!" Os shouts.

"You don't have to shout," I whisper quietly. Os is Magyka; that much is clear, so I know he can hear me even though the humans can't.

"I don't care," he says back. "Now you run."

That's all the warning I get before he says something to the Dragon, and it turns to face me.

I have no weapons and nothing to hide behind. Just my speed as I sprint across the sandy floor of the training room.

There's a scream behind me as heat suddenly explodes at my back. I dive to the right, feeling the heat more to my right.

The fire misses me by a few inches, nearly singeing my training shirt. I huff, blowing a red curl out of my face as I get up and continue my weaving run. By the time we're done I'm out of breath, but the Dragon never got me. The other candidates look at me in fear—and some with anger.

They hadn't realized the threat hiding behind my friendly act. Now that the Gauntlet is almost here, I'm done hesitating.

I join the rest of the finished candidates to the side, all of whom glare at me, and watch as everyone else goes through the same song and dance.

Dyana doesn't get burned, but the left side of her hair is a bit singed. Amalia comes out completely unscathed, which doesn't surprise me. The green Dragon is beginning to get restless, and its eyes are tired. But still, it follows Os's commands to the letter. When we finish, Os carefully puts the muzzle back on before the fae attendants come and lead the Dragon out.

The Dragon cowers at the sight of the fae, its little body trembling, pupils blown out.

Please, Mother, let Nyall be right about this. Let Amalia see the right path forward so we can free the world from the cruelty of the fae.

I finish my prayer and watch as Amalia smooths Dyana's hair, ever the protective older sister. I knew she'd be the real problem. She clearly has significant sway over Dyana's decision.

We lock eyes, and she glares, her eyes nearly silver beneath her dark brow.

Sometimes, she gets this look. A quiet, silent type of fury that burns harder than a blazing wildfire. Not much scares me anymore, but that does. She does.

I've bared my secrets.

Which is why it pisses me off to know she's still hiding hers. What I don't understand is why I have a horrible feeling that whatever she's hiding is worse than anything I ever could have imagined.

CHAPTER 43
AMALIA

"I want to show you something," Os says.

I'm panting from a particularly brutal magyk lesson, trying to connect to animals all throughout town at the same time. Connecting to multiple minds at once is putting a strain on my magyk. It's never been used this much before and I'm exhausted.

Os tosses me a cold sandwich and I don't even question what's in it. I'm sure he's guessed by now that I don't like animal meat, but we don't get the privilege of being choosy.

It's any food or none, and if I don't eat, I'll pass out from the magyk work.

"What now?" I mumble around bits of the cold sandwich. It's bland but the bread is fresh and there's some sort of fresh vegetable in there, so I just concentrate on those flavors and the feeling of my stomach getting full.

"You can eat on the way," is all he says before he walks towards the door. I sigh, pushing up on my feet from where we had been sitting on the floor. My legs are jelly as I follow behind. I try to eat the sandwich slowly, not wanting to make myself sick, but it's soon gone. I burp loudly, and in front of me, Os sighs.

I roll my eyes and imagine stabbing him.

"Save the stabbing for the Gauntlet, Amalia."

Now it's my turn to sigh.

We then settle into a comfortable silence as I continue to follow him. When we end up at another training room, I come to a stop.

"Gods, you're a sadistic asshole, you know that, right?"

Os turns to look at me and his gold eyes burn with wicked fire. "I told you, I want to show you something. It just so happens to involve a little sparring, too."

"You know, good. Cause this makes me want to kick your ass all the way into the Midheym Sea."

Os raises a brow, "It would be easier to do that with the proper sword."

Huh?

I crinkle my nose, confused, but he just motions for me to follow him to the other side of the room where it looks like some weapons are being displayed. I drag my feet, following behind him. It's easier to ignore his tight ass in those leather pants when I want to smash his skull into the damn sand!

"I'm terrified," he says flatly.

"It's rude to eavesdrop," I say sweetly. He just ignores me.

Then he grabs something metallic. It clangs against the table but he's so damn wide I can't see what it is. He turns before I can lean around him. I jump back, startled.

"You're being stranger than normal," I note.

He huffs, and his magyk brushes against my mind, "I...have kept these for a long time. I found them a long time ago. The other candidates are picking weapons today, although some brought their own. I thought you could use them."

"What do you—" I choke on my words as he pulls off the black fabric, unveiling the twin swords underneath.

"Oh my Gods, what the fuck are you doing!" I hiss, grabbing the fabric and tossing it over the swords. "You have to hide those. I can't use them, are you mad?" I pant, looking around to make sure we're not being watched.

Os snorts, "No one is here, Amalia."

"You don't know that."

"Actually I do," he raises a brow, "because this is my personal training room."

I blink. "You…have your own training room?" I glance around, the room is maybe a quarter the size of the rooms the candidates have been training in. It's not huge but still, rooms and a private training area? Lucky bastard.

"Yes. We're alone, I promise."

Well then. "I still can't use those. I can't."

"Yes you can." He pulls off the fabric once again and tosses both swords in the air. I gasp and frantically catch them.

"I'm going to stab you in the eye, you cannot throw the Swords of Morrigyn, Os!"

"Feeling a little pious, A gahrá?" he mocks.

I sneer, "These are Arkaydian relics, you ass. It has nothing to do with religion. These have to be a thousand years old, maybe more. They need to be hidden and kept safe, not used in a damn sparring lesson."

"They're yours, A gahrá."

I blink. "No."

Os just looks at me, "They're your birthright. You're the last living Arkaydian and according to the scrolls, Neiman and Macha were created by Morrigyn Herself and gifted to the leaders of Arkaydia to protect all the beings of its great lands."

I stand there, stunned, as I look at the two swords. Silver and onyx wind around each other, dotted with carved moons and stars. The silver of the hilt makes way to a blade of black titanium, an ore only found deep, deep underground in the Eastern Ulster Wald.

The fae have tried to mine for it since they arrived, but the land was barren.

Their presence in our world killed the black titanium, turning it to ash. They kept at it for a few centuries before abandoning the mines, realizing it was hopeless.

Black titanium was extinct; there was no more to be found.

The blade looks like silver, but it's pure black instead of a bright, brilliant gray.

I expected the metal to be cold to the touch, but the hilts of the twin swords are warm. Almost like they're alive.

"H-how do you have them, Os? How is this possible?" I look up at him in shock.

"I found them in the Dragon Pit on my third day here, after the High Council captured me at the end of the Great War."

"But—"

Os stops me, a hand on my arm. "It doesn't matter how I found them. Use them in The Gauntlet."

I stare, "That's a horrible idea. The High Council will notice the Black Titanium and then I'll be dead."

Os looks around, "Nyall was right, you know. He's a right prick, but he was right. We used to know each other."

I nearly drop the swords, "Uh, okay? What does this have to do with anything?"

"If you would shut up for a second and let me finish, I'll tell you," he says, pointedly. I just glare and roll my eyes. "After I was...captured, things were rough, as you can imagine. One evening, I snuck out of my cage and went to get the baby dragons. I didn't have much of a plan other than to rescue as many eggs as possible and get them out of here. But I was caught." My heart stops. "Then some stuck up fae shows up claiming to be the Crown Prince of a new Kingdom named Ur Daoine, what the High Council had come to call this land. He stopped them from beating me to death."

"What?"

Os nods, "I've never seen someone lie like that before. Out of nowhere, he came up with an elaborate story about how I was hand selected by the High Council themselves to protect the eggs because Dragon hatchlings won't actually hatch unless they can feel the presence of another dragon near."

I blink. "Is that true?"

Os huffs, "Shockingly, yes. How he found out about it, I have no idea. But it worked."

"And the... babies?" I ask, scared.

Os looks at me sadly, "There was no way for me to get them out safely. It...took a lot of convincing from him to realize that, but it was true. I would have gotten them all killed. So instead, I waited with them, moving into their hatching area. Years later, they finally realized that the hatchling area is close enough to the dragon stables to be considered a 'close distance' and I was moved back to a regular stall. I put up a hell of a fight, which is when they threw me in the Arena. It was meant to be an execution but I beat everyone they put against me."

"Gods."

"Hm. Now, centuries later, and here comes the Prince asking for a favor."

"There's more to the story than that," I whisper, seeing the emotion behind his eyes.

He clenches his jaw but nods lightly, "Be that as it may, I told Nyall I would pass on his message in exchange for a favor. Regardless of your decision, I would help him...if he wove me a glamor."

I blink, "A glamor? Those are outlawed."

Os smirks, "Not for royals. Now say the word 'Hydan'."

"Hydan," I say aloud and the blades flash, turning a bright silver color. The hilts begin to move under my hands as the carvings turn into a plain, braided metal. "Holy shit."

"Now say 'Treuwaz'."

"Treuwaz," I repeat, and the glamor releases. "Huh."

Os nods, pleased. "You will use these in the Gauntlet. Black Titanium is the sharpest metal in the world. This will give you an edge over the others," he pauses, swallowing, "and make it easier to pierce through dragon scales."

We look at each other then, hating this reality.

My sorrow soon turns to anger, and I see that fury mirrored in Os.

"Okay," I breathe. "I'll use them...thank you, Os."

Os nods, accepting my thanks. "Then let's practice."

"Let's practice," I agree, and suddenly I'm not so tired anymore.

CHAPTER 44
AMALIA

"Amalia, stop holding back!" Mirielle shouts.

It's been a week. A whole week since I learned what a little traitor Mirielle is.

I've thought of at least a dozen different ways of killing her.

Some quick.

Some...not so quick.

Seeing Dyana cry herself to sleep almost every night since it happened makes me want to hurt someone.

But despite that, despite knowing she's demis, I've become so accustomed to holding myself back, to acting human, that it's hard to let the curtains of mortality fall.

"Remember you asked for it," is all I say as I swing both of my short swords and take up a ready position.

We get in our starting positions, parallel to each other across our sparring circle, both of us with arms raised and swords up. I swing mine a few more times, making a figure eight in the air. Mirielle blinks at the fancy sword movement.

Our knees are bent with our feet shoulder-width apart. The blades of our swords are dulled since they're for practicing, but a hit still bruises like hell, as my battered body can attest to.

Ireyna gives the signal to start, and Mirielle shifts to my left. I go to the right as we slowly circle each other. Her gray eyes are hard and fierce as she observes me, watching for any moment of weakness.

I've always thought that fighting isn't all that different from dealing with animals. It's all about reading body language and asserting your dominance over the other person. So I wait and let Mirielle make her first move, making her think she's in control. With a yell, Mirielle raises her sword and leaps towards me. She brings it down right towards my chest, but I spin out of the way, easily sidestepping the movement.

"Is that really the best you can do, Zenyth?" I mock. As much as I don't want to admit it, all of my drills with Os have helped. I'm used to dodging a dangerous giant of a male instead of Mirielle. But her movements are more graceful and precise. Os is all brute strength.

Mirielle lunges again, shoving her sword forward as if to stab me in the side. I twirl out of the way again, and she huffs in frustration. Her leg swings out as she tries to kick mine out from under me, but I just spin and slap my palm into her solar plexus, hooking my leg around her moving one, and use her momentum to flip her to the ground. She hits the hard dirt with a grunt, and I step back. She stands up painfully but gets back in position. I blink in surprise at the sharp look on her face.

She lunges again, trying to fake me out by darting right, but I see her intentions and bend backward to duck underneath her before raising my sword and bringing it down flat on her back, knocking her down face first.

"Oof," she lets out a pained breath when she hits the ground again, and I quickly put one foot down on her back and hold my sword to her neck.

"Checkmate," I rasp, moving my foot and sword, kneeling down to give her a hand up despite my heart screaming at me not to give her a single drop of kindness.

"Again." Her ordinarily soft voice is hard—and mad. I blink, surprised. Mirielle gets up and dusts herself off, hands red and scratched from catching herself.

"Fine. Water first," I announce, walking over to the side of the room to get a drink of water. It's not clear and not at all clean like the crisp mountain water we had in the North, thanks to the Ulster Wald. This is city water.

Which we unfortunately have to drink in order to survive. Mirielle follows, and we gulp down the dirty water in silence, turning to watch Dyana's fight. She's going up against Reymand, and he's currently winning.

I don't think about it before I start to go over there, ready to beat him to a crisp, but Mirielle grabs my arm, stopping me.

"Don't go over there. You know she'll be pissed if you interfere in front of everyone," she says plainly.

"Tell me what to do again and see what happens," I respond casually, yet the evident threat is still in my voice.

I know Dyana's self-conscious about holding her own, and all this week, I've caught her doing extra pull-ups or push-ups in our room to burn off her anxiety. She's been channeling all of her rage into training, and it's paying off. Her shoulders are more defined, and her abdomen is becoming shredded with lean muscle. I, on the other hand, was getting stretch marks from where my muscles were growing. I'm still soft, but there's hard muscle now too, thanks to a regular diet. My ribs and hip bones don't stick out as much as they used to.

But sometimes I look at Dyana, and all I see is that scared, muddy little girl lost in the woods again, hypothermic and on the brink of death—and the thought of her getting hurt again makes me want to explode.

I turn back, nodding to Mirielle, who takes her place across the small sparring circle from me. I crack my neck as Mirielle stretches her shoulders before we raise our respective weapons.

"Attack!" Ireyna calls, signaling the start.

Mirielle shocks me and blurs to my side, flipping her sword in the air and using the blunt end to jab me in the head. I bend backward, but it still hits my temple, and pain blossoms.

I turn, ramming my knee into her shin, making her stumble, but she recovers quickly. I have to increase my speed even more to avoid her. Mirielle swings her sword expertly, but my thoughts are moving too fast to fully process. I walk backward, each step a delicate dance as I meet every swing. She yells and suddenly spins low, one leg shooting to trip me. I fall but throw my hand out, yanking her down with me. We both hit the sand, and the air leaves my lungs as I get the wind knocked out of me. Panic floods as I struggle to breathe. Forcing myself to calm down, I wait a few seconds then push to standing, forcing a slow, deep breath into my lungs. Mirielle rises at the same time, but I'm slightly faster. I raise my sword, bringing it down to her side. She grunts and drops her own sword to the sand, jumping to her feet and charging me with a roar.

I bare my teeth in a wicked smile as she tackles me. I twist us midair, so this time she's the one who lands her back.

I have to be fast. I roll her to her front, and she whips her head back, her skull crashing into my nose. Blood floods my mouth as hot liquid streams from my nostrils and pain bursts through my face, but I ignore it. I straddle Mirielle's back, pinning her arms to the small of her back with one arm. The tip of my dagger is pressed against Mirielle's throat. She freezes as I press the tip against her just enough to slightly break the skin.

"Yield," I say, spitting out a wad of blood from where it's dripping down the back of my throat and into my mouth.

She coughs, "Fine. I yield."

I roll off her and spit more blood onto the sand, wiping my face with my sleeve. My jaw is aching again, but I'm getting used to it. The pain isn't as bad as it was. Os was right about that balm, too.

Mirielle stands, the look in her eyes is strange. Frustrated, ashamed, and wary. There's fear that wasn't there before. "Are you afraid of me, rebel?"

Mirielle scoffs, "You wish. I'm over two hundred years old, Amalia. I was going all out, but you barely even broke a sweat."

I shrug, tired of this conversation.

She watches me warily, "You're always holding back, aren't you?"

I need to distract her. Quickly.

A yell from across the training ground answers my wish. Our attention snaps to the right, watching as Dyana tackles her opponent and kicks his legs out from underneath him before she swings her sword at his head. She's switched to offensive maneuvers.

Dyana battles a Northerner from a village a few days south of ours—Pfern was his name, I think. His mousy, short brown hair is soaked in sweat. Pfern rolls, and the sword just hits the dirt, sand flying everywhere. He jumps up and parries, sword hitting hers as she pivots, going on the defense. He's fast and cornering her, and I feel my heart race.

It's just practice. It's fine—or at least that's what I tell myself. But Pfern suddenly jumps up and lands a vicious kick to the center of Dyana's chest, sending her fly-ing. I flinch as her body thuds to the floor. She cries out in pain, and I immediately go to punch Pfern into the next realm, but Mirielle grabs my arm, stopping me, hands shaking as she battles a rage of her own.

Pfern walks over and puts the tip of his sword at her chest. But not before bending down and whispering something that makes her eyes go wide, her mouth dropping open. She screams suddenly and uses her arms to knock the sword away, and she leaps on top of him, knocking him to the ground as she punches him in the face repeatedly.

Mirielle's eyes go wide, but I can't help the bloodthirsty smile on my face as I watch my best friend finally let her anger free for the first time in her life. Ever since I met that tiny, rain-trodden girl whose dark eyes were wide with fear, I've been waiting for the day when that fear turned to burning rage.

Today is that day.

Pfern wraps his leg around her hip and flips her, pressing his forearm into her neck to make her choke. He leans forward and bites down on something before ripping back with a quick jerk. Blood flows, and Dyana screams as I watch Pfern spit out a part of her ear.

My vision goes red, and I prepare for blood, but Mirielle beats me to it. He looks up at her as she stalks toward him, a storming tempest.

He says something, but Mirielle ignores him, kneels down, and presses her hands to Dyana's bloody face. Dyana shivers and fights tears as she tries to sit up, cupping her bloody ear. Mirielle helps her before stripping off her tunic, leaving her in just a breast band. She wads the cotton shirt against her ear gently, and Dyana groans in pain.

I'm next to Dyana a few seconds later, wrapping an arm around her waist as she leans into me.

Out of the corner of my eye, I notice Mirielle turning and watching as Pfern stands up. Before he can take a single step, Mirielle grabs my sword and races toward him. Someone shouts, and Pfern turns around but not fast enough.

We all watch as Mirie unleashes herself. The other candidates quickly move out of the way as Pfern frantically tries to meet her blows. But she's faster—and better. There's a calm expertise in her movement that only comes from many years of practice.

Mirielle brings her sword down right on the seam of his elbow, causing the entire arm to go numb and drop his sword. But she doesn't stop. She swings the dull edge of the blade into his oblique muscles, making him groan in pain. Mirielle follows it with a knee in the crotch, and he falls to the ground, moaning.

She blurs, landing a brutal kick to his chin, and I see teeth fly as blood pours from his mouth. He falls to the sand, groaning in pain, but Mirielle just walks over and reaches down, grabbing him by the hair and dragging him through the sand. He struggles once, and she pauses to stop and kick him in the kidney. The training room goes silent as Mirielle drags him all the way to our feet, leaving a trail of blood in her wake. She finally lets him go, and he hits the ground with a hard thump. Pfern tries to get up, but Mirielle just walks around him and presses a foot into his back before grabbing his hair again and pulling his head back so he can look up at Dyana's bloody face.

"Apologize," she demands calmly.

"Fuck you!" Pfern spits.

"Wrong answer," she says before smashing his head into the ground twice before yanking it back up. "Apologize," she demands again.

He mumbles something, so she shakes him roughly, adjusting her foot on his back, making him groan. "Are you so weak that you've lost the ability to speak? Say. It. Louder!" she yells.

"I'm sorry, okay? I'm sorry! Let me go!" He screams as Mirielle kicks him in the side again, making him moan in pain. Before he can react, Mirielle jerks down, her teeth suddenly sharper and slightly pointed. She bites down hard on the soft flesh of his ear before yanking her head back and ripping off the flesh with a wet tearing sound. Pfern screams, and she spits the now detached piece of ear right at him. Mirielle leans down slowly towards the sobbing man, and whispers not-so-quietly into his bleeding ear.

"I heard what you said. What you promised to do. So enjoy the next few days, Pfern. They'll be your last." Mirielle smiles, shoving him to the floor.

A few candidates check on him, but for the most part, everyone leaves him to moan and bleed onto the training room floor.

Mirielle walks over to us as Ireyna yells that training is done for the day. I glance to the side of the room and notice Os, who watches the proceedings with boredom. We haven't talked about anything other than training since our meeting with Nyall, and I hate the awkward feeling in the pit of my stomach.

I shrug it off as we all walk to the healer's rooms and watch as Dyana flinches and itches her arm as they seal the wound. There's a small scar left, but other than that, her ear will recover.

"I've heard that women love scars, Dy," I say, trying to placate her. I glance sideways at Mirielle, who gazes at Dyana with such want and regret it makes my cheeks heat, but she quickly clears her throat and looks away.

"Gods, I would sacrifice my left leg for some wine right about now," Dyana says as we scoop our bland porridge. This time, it looked like some fowl had been mixed in along with peas and carrots. Lovely.

"They may be evil demons who crawled out of the deepest parts of the Hell, but the fae know how to make good liquor." I blink, surprised at Mirielle's words.

"You've had fae wine?" Dyana asks tentatively. We all take a breath, remembering the current situation.

"Yes. There's a large vineyard just west of Sud Azyl, so we get a discount on it for working the fields and helping with the harvest every year. The town has to divide up the few bottles up for grabs, so I've only ever had a few cups of it." There must be more to the story there, but Dyana turns the conversation back to something more positive.

"What does it taste like?" Dyana asks quietly.

"For me, it tastes like sparkling lemons and sea air. Not fishy, mind you. But just...bright. Every sip made me feel as if I was standing right on the beach. It was incredible."

Dyana smiles briefly before she realizes her actions, the smile dropping.

I'm furious at Mirielle for putting her in this situation. But I want Dyana to be happy.

Mirielle sits with us, and we let her, but we're all quiet during our afternoon meal. It was still disgusting four weeks later, but I've gotten good at ignoring it. Once your belly goes empty enough times, you learn to suffer in silence and eat the food given to you, regardless of if it was enjoyable or not.

"Thank you for..." Dyana breaks off, her voice going quiet. "Just, thanks." I pretend not to notice as Mirielle blushes.

"Always." Words whispered and hope rekindled. Although there are some wounds that can never be healed.

"I still don't trust you," Dyana mumbles.

Mirielle nods sadly. "Then I'll prove myself to you. Both of you. I swear it, Dyana."

Dyana chews on her lip as I think on her words.

"Fine." Dyana's head snaps to the side, looking at me with surprise. "But no more lies, and if you hurt her again, the Dragons won't be what kills you; I will."

CHAPTER 45
KYDIS

"Are you sure, my Queen?"

"Is it as you said?" My kin continue to badger me with questions as I walk through the plan with them yet again. *"Is the girl really the last Arkaydian?"*

"Yes. It's true." I answer honestly each time. *"I felt her power myself."*

"But, my Lady, how are we going to escape?" Voices overlap.

"Yes, what's the plan? You've spent the past five centuries doing nothing! How are we supposed to believe you now?"

"Shut up, Rymer. You suckled your Mother's teats for nearly three decades!"

"Bite me, Carmys. You don't even remember how to fly!"

"SILENCE." A loud voice suddenly bellows, shushing the rest. *"Let our Lady speak."*

The others quiet down, whispering his name not in awe but in *terror.*

Vesimyr. The Executioner of Elysium.

"Dragon Killer," they whisper. *"Kinslayer!"*

The last time I saw him, I was but a hatchling. He was magnificent, with scales in all shades of silver and gray and huge white horns curving up from his brow. That was before the fae murdered his family. He went on a rampage like no Dragon had seen before. Burning towns to the ground, sending ships to the black, empty depths. Every Dragon in the world knew of Vesimyr. I had no idea he was in here. A few stalls were recently moved around as more Dragons die and their cages turn into burial grounds.

I thought Vesimyr died in the Great War. Just as our frontline forces were about to hit the High Council, like a meteor falling from the stars, Vesimyr appeared, diving from the clouds and decimating the fae's first line of defense. He didn't stop. For days on end he attacked them, trying to buy Elysium time to show up. Then he was gone, shot down with six giant arrows built specifically to kill Dragons.

He's been here with us this entire time. How did I not know?

And why is he defending my rule? Vesimyr was never a fan of the monarchy. Yet now he speaks on my behalf, using his fear for good.

"I have a plan. We need to strike a deal with The Beast." Voices erupt in dismay and anger as tails slap walls as my words echo through caverns.

"Explain, Lady." Vesimyr's voice is ancient, and for a Dragon, that's saying something.

"The Beastkyn lives? We should have killed him when we had the chance!"

"Abomination!"

"We can't trust him," they whisper, their song one of fury and distrust.

"Quiet. The Lady has not yet finished." Vesimyr doesn't roar, but his song is the loudest, strumming with an undertone of power that makes me shiver.

"The Arkaydian is not whole."

"Another half-breed?" someone sneers.

"SILENCE!" Vesimyr bellows and the entire cave shakes, but the whispers go quiet.

"The Arkaydian is a half-breed, my Lady?" Vesimyr inquires further. Not in challenge but in curiosity. Predicting the questions my kin will ask.

"Yes. She's powerful; I can feel it, but we need her Beast. I smelled the familiar bond on them. It's not completed yet, but even then, merely the presence of a familiar bond will increase both of their powers. With the girl and her Beast, it will be enough."

I hope.

"Will the Beast agree?" Vesimyr asks.

"He has to. We have no other choice."

"Are you so sure she will help us though? The reason the Arkaydians went extinct is because they sided with us during the Great War. Does she know we're responsible for the end of her people?"

I sigh, *"I don't know how much she knows, but I felt her heart. I believe she will help."*

Another of my kin shouts, and Vesimyr growls, quieting them.

"I read her soul. She's...she bonded our younglings before they—" I break off, too emotional to continue. But I am a Queen, even if I have no throne. With a deep breath, I steel myself and continue, *"Before the two legs stole our hatchlings. Before they were taken from us and sent to Great Livyathin."*

"They really bonded with her?"

"Yes. She took the pain from them so they didn't suffer, even though it caused her great suffering. She didn't hesitate to put her life on the line to save theirs." I pause. *"When I looked into her eyes, I saw something."*

"What did you see, maia Reina?" I inhale sharply at the title. No one has called me that in an age. I take a deep breath, and my ember flares as smoke trails out of my slanted nostrils. I curl up, trying to get comfortable, and whisper the words that have echoed in my head since the moment I met young Amalia.

"I saw pain. Deep, neverending pain. The girl has lost much. I felt it. But I also saw an unending, unyielding trust. Somehow, even terrified, she willingly placed her life in my hands. I felt her accept whatever fate I wished her to befall. That's why I know this will work. This is our chance."

"If you believe it's worth the risk, then it's worth the risk. Arrange a meeting with the girl and her Beast, and we'll convince them to help us."

After hundreds of years, I'd learned nothing in this life is a guarantee. But in this small moment, curled up in this cramped, damned metal box, I did something dangerous. As I drift into the realm of dreams, for a brief moment, I let myself hope.

"We are with you, maia Reina."

"We will see the skies once again before our time is through."

CHAPTER 46
AMALIA

The Gauntlet is broken into three stages: the culling, the semi-finals, and the finals. Because each round depends on how many candidates survive, there can be multiple rounds for each stage.

We fight until there's just one left.

Only five can enter the semi-finals, and only two can enter the finals. This means if too many candidates are left in any one round, we have to start killing each other.

In Gauntlets past, the most significant loss of life was in round one. But there is no limit to how many rounds the remaining candidates have to go through. It all depends on how many are left alive. That's why there's so much training beforehand. The more of a fight we put up, the slower we die, which means more rounds and more money in the High Council's pocket.

The Gauntlet usually lasts two to three weeks, depending on the candidates' strength.

Thanks to a freak occurrence a century ago, the High Council was forced to change the rules for the finals. As long as they were from the same town, two candidates could win and split the prize.

It all sounds simple, of course. The fae thought themselves extremely smart, but their goals are simple.

Blood. Death. Money. Fear.

That's it. That's all they want—and it's why someday, somehow, I'm going to kill them all.

After weeks of grueling training and honing our bodies into weapons, it's finally time to put our skills to the test—or die trying.

Dyana, Mirielle, and I are at one of the uncomfortable mess hall tables, discussing our new uniforms for the Gauntlet. Despite our falling out, Mirielle continued to sit with us, although there were a lot of awkward silences.

I still don't trust her but I can play nice. She might not admit it, but Dyana wants me to. I can see it. Still, one wrong move, and Mirielle is Dragon food.

However, the topic of our new fighting leathers and armor means a momentary ceasefire on any untoward feelings. The moment we step into the Arena, whatever happened beforehand doesn't matter, and that reality is hitting us all.

Yesterday, the candidates were given outfits resembling what the Pit Fighters wore: snug-fitting black or brown fighting leathers, thick shin-high boots, and varying fine silver armor. The High Council—and all fae, really—love a good show. That means we have to get dressed up like preening peacocks, including "signatures" to make our looks more individual. What they didn't include when we were told all of this is that the unique additions to each of our outfits are so the fae and anyone watching the Gauntlet can bet on us.

They bet on our lives. On who will die first and who will last the longest, and the High Council naturally takes a generous cut. I grabbed a black scarf to pull over my lower face as well, but hidden beneath a pile of fabric was a piece of red fabric as dark as Dragon's blood. I grabbed that, too.

Seeing myself in the mirror, dressed like a warrior in one of the stories Father told me as a child, my pale eyes burning with fear and fury—it was too much. I felt like both my most authentic self, and a complete and utter stranger.

Every time I see myself, see my Father's eyes and my Mother's freckles, it's a reminder of all I've lost.

Sometimes I hate them for that.

I've been on edge ever since the fitting. This nervous, jittery feeling keeps washing over me and is keeping my chest tight. The quiet doesn't help. In the moments of silence, all I can hear is my own heart thudding in my ears.

Thump, thump.

Thump, thump.

Thump, thump.

While Dyana and Mirielle chat in front of me, beneath the table I pick at my nails until they bleed, needing something to push my nervous energy into. Dyana glances in my direction, squinting at how my hands are out of sight. She sighs sadly, and I have to look away, unable to take her pity. She knows my tells.

"I need to get to training. I'll see you later," I mutter before walking out. Mirielle just nods at me and continues to talk to Dyana.

Telling a Drayven my secrets is something I'll never forgive Mirielle for. But that's my choice; Dyana has to make hers, and I had to respect that. Even if it irked me. She was her own person, and if she wanted to give Mirielle another chance, then so be it.

Out of the corner of my eye, I watch as their fingers accidentally brush. Dyana jerks her hand away, looking at Mirielle with wide, unsure eyes. Mirielle tries to hide a smile, but there's hurt in her eyes as she clears her throat and focuses on walking with a bit more distance between them.

I make my way to Os's room and let my mind wander, but it just grows my anxiety. By the time I get there, my chest is so tight that it physically hurts.

My jaw aches too. I keep forgetting that I shouldn't grind my teeth, but the stress is too much. By the time I reach Os's door, my skin has begun to heat, and sweat starts dripping down my back as my breath comes faster and faster.

Everything becomes a bit blurry as I stumble in, hands shaking.

The room is empty, nothing but the roaring fireplace crackling to the side. But there's another sound—the sound of water rushing. Os must be bathing. When he was patching me up after the day with the stable incident, I noticed a water spout thing that I think is called a shower. This allows him to bathe standing up. To say I'm jealous is an understatement. Cold baths in the cramped, tiny buckets work, but it's not enjoyable. My eyes fall on the sitting area, and I consider my options.

I could sit by the fire and wait. I should.

I *should* do that.

But all I can see when I close my eyes is Dyana dying in the Gauntlet right in front of me, and no matter how I try, I'm not fast enough to save her. Before I can think otherwise, I'm walking over to his bed. I unlace my boots, wincing at the blisters and sores that stick to my dirty socks.

The stone is cold underneath my bare feet, and I breathe a slight sigh of relief.

But my chest still hurts, and my heart is still racing.

There's another noise in the bathroom, a low vibration that I feel inside my skull.

I don't know what I'm doing, but suddenly, I'm walking over to the bathroom, inching closer to the open door. Before I can second guess my decision, I peek into the room and lose my ability to breathe.

Os is not a male—he is a God. It's the only explanation that makes sense as I watch water pour down his tightly muscled body, his deep umber skin covered in scars and tattoos that only add to his feral sexuality. His dark brown hair is nearly black as he runs his hands through it with soap. My mouth drops open, and a slight sound leaves me as I take in his firm, muscular ass. Os runs his hands through his hair again, rinsing out the rest of the soap, and I gulp as the movement allows me to see what's between his legs.

A *God,* indeed.

I look up and see him watching me, watching him, his gold eyes sparkling.

I freeze. Os tilts his head for a moment as I stare at him, and he nods, turning again so he faces me fully as he continues to wash his body. I take him in again, eyes slowly roving over his body as he rubs himself with soap, and when I return to his face once more, his eyes don't sparkle—they burn.

Then I begin to burn, too.

Fuck.

With one last look at him, I turn away quickly and shake my hands, trying to cool off, but his scent in the air is making my heart quicken, this time not from fear but from something else: need.

Maybe it's the stress, maybe it's just Os, but my panic from earlier returns with a vengeance.

I can't get enough breath into my lungs, and my skin grows hotter still, making me dizzy and turning my mouth bone dry. Despite knowing what a horrible idea this is, I sit down on Os's bed, falling back against the cool sheets as I close my eyes and try to calm my racing heart.

His scent is all over the sheets, both helping my panic and increasing my need. I groan, rolling over to my front and burying my head in the covers. The darkness wraps me up like a blanket.

"Comfortable?" a low voice asks, and I feel movement on the bed.

I grunt in return, not wanting to lift my head and leave my dark realm of safety.

"I wasn't aware it was naptime," he notes.

So much for a moment of peace. I lift my head and look over at him, "I'm not sleeping, I'm—" I choke, cut off at the sight in front of me.

Gods above, he's dressed in nothing except for a small towel wrapped around his hips, and water droplets trail a line down his hard chest. He leans against the pillows next to me, watching my every movement. My mouth waters as I follow that droplet that continues down his chest and past his towel, and I quickly look away, shutting my eyes at the instant heat that rushes through me.

Gods. I'm in his bed, and he's naked.

"It is my bed, you know. I can do whatever I want in it. But I rather like the sight of you in it, A gahrá." I have to close my eyes because his words make my blood rush. "I'd like it even better if you were naked too." I inhale sharply and press my face into his sheets again, needing the steady dark so that I don't implode.

Os doesn't touch me; he just lays next to me. But I can feel the heat wafting off his skin, and his scent of sweet smoke and male intensifies.

"If you're not sleeping, what are you doing then?" he wonders, looking at the ceiling. I glance over at him and sigh, flipping to my back and abandoning any hope at finding calm.

Then I see what he's looking at. I've never noticed them before, but above his bed and all around his room, strange patterns are etched into the ceiling.

And they're...familiar. "Are those..." I search for the word Virgyl taught me, "constellations?"

Os smiles softly, "Yes. When I was young, I loved looking up at the night sky. This is the only piece of home I have left."

This time my heart clenches but because I understand all too well what he means.

So I try to be brave. "I'm not sleeping, I'm trying to calm down." Os doesn't respond, doesn't judge. He gives me space to explain, so I continue, "Ever since my parents died...there are times when I get so stressed, so afraid, that I can't even breathe. Sometimes I'll pass out and sleep for days on end afterward." I admit. The quiet crackle of the fireplace is all I hear outside of our breathing. "As I've gotten older and my magyk has matured, when I, um, panic or get really nervous, my...control tends to slip. Which does nothing but make me even more terrified of losing control." I let out a hard breath, "I've been trying to calm down all fucking day, but it's not helping."

I press my hands over my eyes, craving that darkness again.

"And watching me in the shower made it worse?" He asks in a way that's simply curious, not judgmental.

Nonetheless, my hands fall to the side, and I shoot him a glare and mutter, "It certainly didn't help."

He huffs a rare laugh, and I feel rather than see his smile.

I don't explain that seeing him in the shower made me lose my control in a different way. Or that seeing him smile, hearing him laugh, makes me want to burn this world to the ground just so he'll do it again.

"That's becoming less and less believable every time you say it, A gahrá." He pauses, turning his head to look at me. I roll to my side and rest my chin on my hand as we stare at each other for a moment.

"I know," I admit.

"Why are you nervous?"

"The Gauntlet. I know... I mean, I have known it would happen. That this is all real. But Gods, I'm just—" my voice breaks. "I'm fucking terrified. I can't...I can't lose anyone else, Os. Dyana is all I have. Losing her will destroy me, and I'm scared. I'm supposed to be brave. I'm supposed to save us, and yet I'm so fucking scared I can't even breathe." There's a blur as Os suddenly sits behind me, gently taking me in his arms and pulling me so I'm lying against his chest. He wraps his large arms around me, tucking me against him.

He doesn't give me placating words, because we both know my fear is legitimate. We might die.

"When I met Dyana, I was a hollow shell of grief and anger. She doesn't know this, but I...I didn't really want to live anymore, Os. I felt so alone and suddenly, this scared child appeared, just as lost and abandoned as I was. She thinks I'm the one who saved her but that's a lie. She's the one who saved me and I. Can't. Lose. Her." The sobs come in full force now, and Os just holds me, running his hands down my arms and nuzzling my hair. He doesn't solve my problems with fancy words, but he holds space for me. He sees me, and lets me exist in all of my broken, tear-stained glory without judgment or censure.

Then, his chest begins to vibrate. It's low and deep, almost like the purr of a cat, but not. The sound travels through me, vibrating my bones and soothing my heart.

"I don't know how I'm going to keep us all alive, and I...I don't think I can kill a Dragon. Every night when I go to sleep, I see those baby Dragons. I watch as they're slaughtered over and over again and I can't do it. I can't kill one." My breath comes faster and I gasp for air as my chest tightens to the point of acute pain. I sit up and bend over so my head is resting on my raised knees but Os stops me, turning me so I'm curled up on his lap. He pulls me in tight and lays his hand over my heart.

"Breathe, A gahrá," something brushes against my magyk quickly. A type of compulsion, perhaps? But my body responds to his command.

"Good. Slower." My lungs follow his command as he brings me back from the brink. *"It will be ok, A gahrá."*

"But you don't know that. Nothing is certain anymore."

He nods, "You're right, I don't know that. But look at me, Amalia." He gently tilts my chin, so I look into his burning gaze, "What I do know is that I'm going to do everything in my power to ensure you make it out the other side. I also know you, Amalia—whether you like it or not. I know your power and your tenacity. You are righteous fury and you're going to fight like the gates of hell itself are at your back because you have the biggest heart of anyone I've ever known, and there's nothing you won't do to protect the ones you love. So unleash that righteous fury on them, little spark. Make them fear."

My tears fall harder at his words.

I know he's right, and yet I wish I had as much confidence in myself as he has in me. But it's true; I will fight until my dying breath to protect Dyana. I will save her, even if it breaks me.

"I won't let you break, A gahrá. And even if you do, I will put you back together again. Whole or shattered, I'm yours. You will not be alone again. And you forget, Dyana has been trained by the Black Citadel's champions. You might not like her, but Ireyna is the best fighter, second to myself. I think Dyana will surprise you—sometimes all we need is the proper motivation. Plus, you have a huge asset with Mirielle, even if she can't be trusted. Use her feelings for Dyana, Amalia. Leverage them to keep Dyana alive."

He has a point.

"Do you mean that? All of it?" I ask, nervously.

He looks back at me with a sad smile, "Every word. We are familiars, Amalia. Regardless if you choose to complete the bond, a familiar is for life. I would give my life to save yours without hesitation."

My heart sputters to a halt at the idea of losing him too.

"Don't. Don't you fucking dare."

Os just smirks again, "You wouldn't be able to stop me, little spark. You've protected everyone else around you for your entire life, haven't you? But who is there to protect you, Amalia? You deserve to be saved, too."

I scoff, pulling out of his arms and scooting away. "I don't think so. I'm not this good person you make me out to be, Os. I've done horrible things."

Os turns me so we're kneeling on the bed, facing each other.

"That's where you're wrong. I do know you, little spark. I've been waiting over a thousand years for you, and I would wait a thousand more. My soul knows yours, and your soul knows mine. You just have to listen."

Little spark...

"Wait...that nickname," I say as the echo of a memory sits just beyond my grasp. "How do you know that nickname?"

He hesitates at my question, "For the past few years, I've had strange dreams—dreams of someone else. A little girl with hair as white as snow and eyes as cold as ice. I never knew what it meant until I healed you, and the dreams became clear. I've been dreaming of you, Amalia. For many years. I was yours, long before we even met."

I do what I do best and retreat into my mind as confusion and fear overwhelm me. He's seen my past, seen my parents. Seen things about me that no one else has ever seen or known before.

On one hand, there's such relief that I want to cry again. Ever since they died, I've been so alone. So much of what happened, only I know. When you can't share a memory, it begins to fade. Os makes the memories feel real again.

Relief and horror and confusion and fear. It's overwhelming. I'm thinking so much at once.

There's a gentle press against my mind and the smell of smoke as Os asks permission to enter my head. We're silent for a moment, just existing as our magyks intertwine.

"I never wanted it to be like this. I never wanted to become this." I admit. "All the secrets. All the lies. All the death, depression, and loneliness. Sometimes, I wish I had just died alongside my parents instead of going through this alone."

I feel Os wrap his arms around me in the real world, and I curl into his chest. We're silent for several minutes as my heart starts to calm.

"You will never be alone again. I swear it," he promises.

I'm silent, and I know he feels my doubt. But my heart relaxes, easing as my chest pain loosens. Maybe, just maybe, he was right.

"I feel your doubt. I want to give you something. Os is a piece of my last name. My real name, my true name cannot be translated into modern language, but there is a nickname my sister used to call me, and I would like you to use it too."

I'm standing on the edge of a cliff, waiting for him to continue. Names have power. I never considered that Os wasn't his real name.

"My name is Remus," he says aloud. "When we're around others, you may call me Os, but when it's just us, I want my true name on your lips, Amalia." I inhale a sharp breath as the vulnerability in his voice pierces me.

"Remus." I whisper the word aloud and his eyes close. When they open, the heat in his gold gaze overwhelms me as he cups my cheek.

"I see you, Amalia Roth. I see you for all that you are. You do not need to hide or temper yourself around me. I accept every part of you."

A small noise emerges from my mouth, somewhere between a sob and a laugh.

"Aren't you with Ireyna? It's fine if you are. I saw you two earlier—"

It's a lightning strike to the chest as he lets out a booming laugh.

It's like the sun peeking out behind the clouds, seeing him laugh. Seeing that smile.

Then that low vibration becomes louder. And that noise seems to have a rather visceral effect on my body as I become very aware that only a towel and my clothing separate us.

"Are you jealous, my spark?"

His. His spark.

He changed the nickname. Just enough where it doesn't hurt.

"I would never be jealous," I snort, affronted at the idea.

Os...I mean Remus, just grabs my palm and brings it to his face gently, nuzzling and pressing soft kisses to my palm. Tasting me. Scenting me.

His eyes meet mine, his golden gaze burning a hole through my soul, *"I am not with Ireyna. A few centuries ago we had a night of fun, but I have no interest in her."*

I surreptitiously ignore the relief at his words.

"When that little fuck dared to touch you, I wanted to rip his face off and eat his heart. But you need no man to defend you. I see your inner fire, feel it burn against my skin. I love when you're unleashed. Stop holding back and pretending to be something other than exactly what you are. A predator. I want the real you, Amalia Roth. Unleash yourself. Show me what it is you hide."

Those words wouldn't turn me on if I were a better woman, but Remus is right.

And I am not the better woman.

I yank my hand back from him and slap it over my mouth, cutting off any reply I had, and he just looks back at me with a tiny smirk, gold eyes full of mirth.

"What does A gahrá mean, Remus?" I whisper after a moment.

Remus closes his eyes and that vibrating purr grows louder, so loud I'm surprised dust doesn't fall from the ceiling. "Say it again."

"What does A gahrá mean, Remus?"

He gently sets my hand on the bed, yanking me close so that I straddle him, his thick length rock hard against my throbbing core. He undoes my braid in a blur of movement, causing him to grind against me, and a moan falls from my lips. Once my hair is loose, he runs a hand through it before fisting it and forcing my head to look up at him as I gasp. Remus leans forward, lips barely pressed to the corner of my mouth, but I'm unable to move.

I'm at his mercy.

Against my mouth, he whispers the answer. "In my language, A gahrá means 'My Beloved'."

CHAPTER 47
AMALIA

My beloved.

All this time, that's what he's been calling me. My heart falls from my chest, right into the hands of the male in front of me.

This giant, scarred male who didn't balk even in the face of a Dragon. Who didn't blink or shy away in the face of my panic, my anger, my past. This male whose golden eyes seemed to pierce the layers of my very soul. This male who saw me. Who laughs with me.

Who *smiles* for me.

The warmth that floods me is something I haven't felt in many years. It's a kind of happiness I thought I'd never experience again.

I realize I'm staring at him, silent and gobsmacked. I panic and take a page from Dyana's book, "So you've been flirting with me for weeks, huh?"

Remus chuckles, pressing his forehead into mine as our magyks intertwine, brushing against all of my senses and sending goosebumps across my arms. I know he's been reading my emotions and has felt my shock.

But he just sits there, accepting me fully, for all that I am.

"You care." I whisper softly. I smother that voice in the back of my head, bashing against my skull, reminding me that I might die in a few days.

But...I want this moment. With him.

"I care, A gahrá." he says, "I care very much."

Os cradles my face, his large hands cupping my cheeks as his thumbs brush the silent tears dripping from my eyes. I didn't even realize I was crying.

"I will never lie to you, A gahrá. I fought this in the beginning. I've spent so many years thinking there was no hope. That I would spend the remainder of my days watching as everything I loved was destroyed right before my eyes, leaving me to die alone. And then there you were, covered in dirt and smelling like a horse stable. But I took one look at your eyes, and my beast knew. Even if the male in me was in denial." His eyes twinkle with emotion. "Right before my very eyes, my salvation."

I shake my head, "I'm no savior."

Remus just watches me, "You're mine."

"Even if we don't complete the bond?" I can't help the disbelief in my voice.

Remus smiles softly, "Yes, A gahrá, even if we don't complete the bond. Is it so hard to believe that I will accept however much of yourself you're willing to give?"

A small noise escapes my mouth as the dam inside of me breaks and I surge forward, kissing him with reckless abandon, my hands burying themselves in his still-damp hair.

I pour everything I have into Remus. I give him my jealousy, my fury at seeing him touch another woman. I give him the bone-deep terror that keeps me up at night, wondering if I'll actually be able to do this. I give him my want, my soul-deep need to be loved, to have companionship and company. I give him everything. Every piece of me that I hide away from the world, even from myself. I'm still clothed but I might as well be naked as I strip away my walls and let Remus see me.

Remus growls against my mouth, "I'm not holding back anymore, A gahrá. Damn the rules and damn the High Council. You are mine and I am yours, and nothing will keep me from you. Nothing." He grabs me by the waist with a vicious snarl, tossing me back onto the bed before crawling up my body, and pushing his thick thigh between my legs, pressing against where I ache the most.

I arch against him as he kisses me again, sucking down the moans that fall from my lips as he rubs his thigh against me harder.

"What about training?" I gasp against his lips.

Gods, why am I asking about training right now? Shut up, brain!

"You've earned a day off," Remus says, pulling back. I follow him, leaning forward until he places a large hand against my chest, pushing me back against the covers.

I'm starving, and he's the meal.

"Is this what you had in mind for my day off?" I smirk as I grind against him.

His eyes shut and when they open again, the hunger I see makes my thighs quiver. *"A gahrá, when I take you, the only thought in your head will be 'more, more, more'."*

He leans down to kiss me again, and those embers deep inside of me flare. Our weeks of training kick in as I wrap my legs around him and flip us quickly. He laughs as he hits the mattress.

My turn.

I crawl up him slowly, straddling him so his length is seated right against my core. The towel falls off as I grind against him, and he growls, eyes wild.

I lean down and kiss his jaw and neck. "More," I whisper.

Remus freezes as I make my way over to his mouth, grinding against him further. I press another kiss onto his hot lips, pulling his lower lip into mine and biting lightly. I let it pop out of my mouth with a smile before repeating, "More."

He shudders, "Godsdamnit, spark. As much as I want this, I also know you still have doubts. I feel them."

I pull back, embarrassed. "But—"

He interrupts me, "We have time, A gahrá. Even if it doesn't feel like it. I will make us time, okay?"

That foreign warm feeling floods me again. He knows me.

"Oh, but my my spark, there's plenty we can do in the meantime, and I want to hear you *roar,*" he reaches forward and yanks open my tunic, ripping the fabric with ease.

He snarls at the breast band, muttering something about how their creation should be considered a crime. He pulls a hand back and I watch as one nail transforms, lengthening into a long, curved black talon. He slices through the band before slowly tracing a line from my collarbone down to my navel with that sharp tip. I gasp, unable to help my reaction.

At the exact same moment, Remus brushes his magyk against me right on top of my core. Then his magyk flicks against my clit, over and over. I moan as the burning intensifies. At the same time as the flick of his magyk, he drags that sharp talon across my right breast, slicing right over my nipple. The pain makes me shriek but it turns into a gasp as he quickly latches on, sucking my nipple into his mouth as my blood spills down his throat.

I explode. Screaming his name as my magyk and body erupt. But he never stops. He continues sucking and kneading, all the while the sound of his beast purring vibrates my bones. Reality begins to disintegrate until there's only *Remus, Remus, Remus.*

Then he switches sides, slicing my left nipple and drinking more of my blood. I'm writhing in ecstasy, with no thought in my head.

Remus growls against my breast, releasing my nipple with a wet *pop*, "I need to taste you."

There's a blur and he's suddenly standing, yanking me down the mattress. I let out a rather undignified squeak as he yanks my legs up and rolls down my leggings, bearing me completely.

Sure, I could take time to worry about the overgrown hair between my legs, but Remus looks at me like a male starved. There is nothing in this moment that could make me stop him. I let my knees fall open, completely baring my core as his purring grows louder. I let him gaze at every inch of me and revel in the hungry look on his face.

"Everything that you are and that you aren't; you are perfect, Amalia Roth. You are perfect and you are mine."

Remus blurs then the next thing I know his mouth is between my legs as he his mouth is between my legs and he spreads open my lips with his fingers. He runs his nose up me, burying himself in my moisture. I squirm, panting.

"Gods, I've wanted to taste you for weeks," he mutters, trailing a finger through my curls, getting them damp with my lust. He looks up at me and his tongue spears into me and *ohmyfuckinggods* it's enlarged—and forked.

He shifted his *tongue.*

"You fucking bastard," I curse him with a loud moan as he fucks me with his tongue, and I climb the mountain of ecstasy yet again.

"Ride my face, Amalia. Unleash yourself," he says, words muffled by my lips.

So I do. I unleash myself and reach down to grip his hair and hold him tightly against me, riding his face with wanton abandon as he fucks me with his tongue.

I am destroyed and remade again by this male between my legs as he consumes me, body and soul.

Remus lets out a loud groan as I jump off that cliff edge, plummeting into ecstasy, screaming his name.

But he doesn't stop. Instead, my moans encourage him. He reaches up and uses his thumb to flick against my tight bud in unison with the plunging of his forked tongue.

That's all it takes and I explode again, falling to pieces at the pleased sounds he makes...it's too much. But Remus still doesn't stop, instead adding in his fingers while sucking on my throbbing bud. He stretches me slowly as he pumps his finger in and out and I moan his name.

"Come on, Spark. Give me everything," he demands, adding a third finger and stretching me in a way that's both painful and divine. A hoarse cry falls from my lips as I scream his name and fall across the edge yet again. His mouth replaces his fingers as he sucks down every drop of my pleasure.

Remus sits up, a pleased look on his face as wipes his wet mouth with his hand, before licking his fingers clean. His tongue is still forked, and his pupils are now thin slants, golden eyes glowing with a ferocity I've never seen. It's terrifying and intimidating and perfect.

This is *Remus.* Feral, aggressive, undone.

The pale scars and dark tattoos covering his chest flex as he reaches a hand into his hair, brushing it back before crawling over to me. He pulls me into his arms. I'm limp, panting, and covered in sweat.

But I'm not finished yet.

I push off him with shaky arms, leaning back and up onto my knees. He watches me with hunger and I firmly grab his hard length, squeezing just enough to draw a violent snarl from his lips.

I lean forward, pressing a kiss to a scar bisecting his right pec muscle, "More, Remus. Give me more."

His mouth drops open lightly, showing a hint of fang at my touch, and he hisses, all of his nails extending into black talons. "If you touch me like that, A gahrá, this will all be over soon, and I'm nowhere near done with you."

But I don't let go and soon he's pumping into my hand, tortured moans falling from his lips as he clutches me tightly. I smirk and use my other hand to pull his throbbing sack and he loses it, snarling so loud I'm surprised dust doesn't fall from the ceiling as he pushes me onto my back.

Maintaining eye contact, I smirk again and lean back, baring my neck to him in a gesture of submission. Remus goes completely still before a noise leaves his throat like a multilayered growl. A noise I have heard before...but he moves too fast for me to fully process the thought and my mind empties of all sense completely. He's a blur and I'm in his arms, my hand still clasped around his hard length, as he stares at my neck.

Many shifters consume blood during mating. It's quite common amongst many magyka. But to bare your neck to your partner...it was the ultimate sign of trust. And something I knew would be his undoing.

Remus clasps my face in both of his hands and presses a trembling kiss to my lips, "I am not worthy of you, Amalia Roth. But until the end of my days, I will ever try to be." He takes one hand and traces it up my neck, pausing to rub a circle around my fluttering pulse. "I will not break the trust you've given me." He releases me, "If it's too much, say stop." And then he dives in, not with a bite like I was expecting, but with a kiss so soft I gasp, wrapping my legs around his waist until his length rubs against me, putting my will to the test.

Remus just sucks the thin skin of my neck into his mouth before letting go, not biting down.

I writhe at his teasing. "I didn't peg you as the type to play with their food," I hiss, pushing his buttons.

Remus chuckles, the sound vibrating against my skin.

"My impatient little spark," Wicked delight weighs on his words, and suddenly he bites down hard, causing a jolt of pain to sear through me. But it's gone as if it never happened and in its place is a rich wave of tingling, hot lust.

"Oh my Gods. Remus—" I whine aloud, unable to form intelligent words as my mind unravels. I can't control my hips as I begin rubbing myself against him, unable to stop moving. Remus moans against my neck as he continues sucking down my blood, pausing to lap me up wantonly.

"It's not enough, I need —"

Remus pulls back, his mouth and chin coated in my blood. *"Tell me, A gahrá. What do you need?"*

Remus moves so fast I can't track it but now he's laying at my side instead of on top of me and my legs are spread as he squeezes my aching clit, making my hips jolt. Then he turns me, yanking me so my back is to his chest, and one of my legs is pulled open, wrapping around his hips. He pulls open my inner lips, teasing me and feeling my wetness.

"Oh Gods, I can't—" I moan, urging him to move or do something to ease the neverending ache building inside of me.

"Yes you can, A gahrá. Come for me again, give me more." Then he *moves,* vibrating his fingers moving so fast I can't help the scream that falls from my lips as stars burst behind my eyes. Just as I'm about to detonate, he slows and I cry out.

"You...you fucking bastard," I pant.

"Say please, A gahrá," he purrs, humming against my neck as his tongue flicks against my skin.

"Never," I gasp. Then he twists his fingers and my entire body jerks. "Pl-please," I moan, "Make me come, Remus or I swear to Gods I will tear down the fucking WALLS."

"I thought you'd never ask, A gahrá." And then he's plunging into me, adding a fourth finger and stretching to the point that it almost hurts.

Almost.

I scream, not a care in the world for who could hear, as my back bows and my vision goes black.

I am the ruiner and the ruined as I cease to exist and simply float, no thought in my head but the ecstasy rolling through me. I come over and over again, soaking his sheets and his hand as Remus wrings me dry of every ounce of pleasure I possess.

"Remus," I slur, my voice scratchy and nearly gone.

Remus pulls back from my neck finally, and my head lolls to the side as I watch him bite down on his own tongue, drawing blood, before he leans back down and proceeds to lick the wounds clean. Seeing my blood coat his face and chest has me feeling a little unhinged. I reach up and run my hand through it, tracing patterns down his neck. His lips are still coated with my blood and I lean up and lick him clean, the taste of hot iron in my mouth.

He yanks me into another deep kiss. I'm unsure how long we lay there, tangled, bloody, and covered in pleasure. Time ceases to exist as I lose track of where I begin and he ends.

I expect him to continue, to want more or seek his own release, but Remus just pulls back and turns us slightly so I'm tucked into his chest. He wraps his arms around me so that my head rests on one of his large biceps—which is shockingly comfortable—and presses his hands against my chest, right over my heart. I slide my hands around his and hold him tightly.

"Get a little rest, my spark. I know you're not sleeping well lately," Remus says, pressing a kiss into my hair. He scoops me up and tucks me under his soft sheets.

I can't even form words so I just mumble nonsense, nodding as he joins me, tucking me into his side.

"I'm sorry, Remus—" I start, but my words are slurred.

"No. You have nothing to be sorry about."

I sigh even though that tinge of embarrassment and guilt are still present.

"I will keep you safe, A gahrá. I promise."

Body and mind finally exhausted and relaxed, I fall asleep in Remus's arms, sweaty, sticky, and wholly wrung out. There are no nightmares this time. Maybe because I finally have a beast of my own to scare them away.

CHAPTER 48
DYANA

Seeing Amalia do the walk of shame this morning was one of the top five funniest moments of my entire life. Her hair was a disaster, and I'm fairly sure I saw some streaks of dried blood.

Magyka are into some weird shit, but whatever makes her happy, makes me happy. I naturally made some lewd jokes until she slapped me with the end of her rolled-up tunic, catching me on the ass. I cackled as she muttered about how she should have stayed in the forest with the wolves.

That was only an hour ago, but this morning feels like a different lifetime as we stand in the tunnel to the Arena. Even from down here, the screaming of the distant crowd and the deep, thumping of drum beats reach us, making dust fall from the ceiling.

Ama walks at my side at the back of the group since we were lined up in order of distance from the Kingdom. It seems we're always last.

There's a sharp focus and righteous determination behind her icy gaze today. Whatever she and Os got up to last night helped. The thought of naked, tangled bodies has me craning my neck to try and get a glance at Mirielle. Despite the heartache she caused. Despite the fact that I still don't trust her. But...I don't want her to die.

Every step brings us closer to the Arena. Our armor jingles, echoing in the tunnel. We're all dressed in our new outfits. Each of our looks vary slightly, but we all wear dark fighting leathers and silver armor with iron and silver weapons. Some candidates wear long sleeves, and some are in sleeveless vests. But all are topped with various pieces of armor. No one wore a full suit, but we all were decked out in Castael Laryn's finest.

Tomorrow is the first round of the Gauntlet. Today, we're presented to the crowd so that the lovely people of Castael Laryn can decide how to place their bets. Because that's all we are: entertainment and coin.

Our group stops before the sand, as the trainers are called. Os goes out first, then Ireyna and the five others. One by one, the names of each town are called until there's only a few left before our turn. The roar from the crowd is deafening now. More dust falls from the tunnel's ceiling as the roaring crowd thumps their feet in tune with the drums.

In my peripheral vision, Ama flexes her hands. She takes a few deep breaths and closes her eyes. My own heart races and my own palms get clammy with sweat. I go to wipe them on my pants, but they shake so hard it's difficult to aim right. My short sword is at my back and my ax is at my waist. I chose the two most simple weapons. Aim and chop works well for me. There's not too much finesse. Various other daggers are strapped to my body.

Two plain swords are strapped to Amalia's back, the blades wicked sharp. Watching her wield two blades at once is mesmerizing.

The crowd roars again as the line in front of us gets shorter, and we step closer to the light.

I pinch myself on my thigh until it hurts, something I always do when I'm anxious.

This is real. You are alive. You are real.

I repeat the words over and over in my head as I continue pinching my leg. Ama's never said anything, but she's seen glimpses of the scars.

Suddenly, a roar bursts from the Arena. A roar that could only come from a Dragon.

Pure fear shoots into my heart as every muscle in my body clenches. I go into fight or flight mode, and it takes every ounce of effort in me not to flee. A whimper falls from my lips, and Ama grabs my hand. The instant her skin meets mine, the fear abates and I can finally breathe.

"They have a Dragon out there right now?" My voice is high-pitched and anxious. "Why would they have a Dragon when the fighting doesn't even start until tomorrow?

Ama shrugs, cocking her head as she listens, "Not sure. Sounds like a juvenile."

I blink, "You can tell the Dragon's age?"

Ama just continues looking out into the Arena. Was she reading its magyk?

She nods slowly, thinking, "I guess so. Not down to the year, but I can…feel if they're young or old." She smacks her lips, as if tasting the magyk.

We've known each other for over eighteen years, and still, she always surprises me.

"Don't they kill the young ones though?" The question is uncomfortable to ask. The next town is called, leaving only one in front of us, and we take a few steps forward, even closer to the light of the Arena.

Ama spits in the sand, furious. "It seems they keep some."

I just nod, lightheaded all of the sudden, "Great. That's just great. Are you hot? I'm hot. It's so hot all of the sudden." I ramble, voice getting higher and higher as my panic rises.

Ama grabs my arm, "Breathe. I've got you. Walk on the far side of me. Closest to the wall. We're going to stay as far away from the Dragon as possible, okay?" I nod, trying not to faint or throw up, or possibly both at the same time.

Amalia squeezes my arm again, "No matter what happens, we stay together."

I nod, forcing breath into my lungs, "Always."

That scar on my palm heats up as I repeat the same words I did that night in the forest. The night we actually became sisters. "We are family, and family sticks together."

A ghost of a smile appears on her lips as Twyn Fells is finally called, and we step into the light. I lose my vision briefly as we walk into the sandy Arena. The glare from the sky above sears my retinas. I've gotten so used to the dark of the Dragon Pits that the bright light takes a few moments to adjust to.

The crowd continues to roar, but it's magnified in the large space of the Arena. I blink rapidly, trying to clear my vision as we walk towards the line of the rest of the candidates, but my ears ring from the loud noise, and the world tilts a bit.

I shake my head hard, trying to snap out of it. A green Dragon the size of Taran is growling and snapping at everyone in the vicinity. Two small horns jut up from either side of its head. Spiky spinal plates line all the way from the horns down its tail. Sharp black talons the size of my damned foot tip its four clawed feet. Short, thick legs pace back and forth as it tugs on the leash wrapped around its neck. The thick metal chain is held by multiple fae attendants with electric prods.

The Dragon wears no muzzle, though.

The other candidates are arranged in pairs in two columns, each town standing together. I see Reymand, the one who Os threw across the Mess Hall after Amalia defended me, and Mirielle is a few before him. She looks back, her red hair wild. Her green eyes go wide as she sees me.

I just stare.

I should nod—or maybe wave I guess—or do something, but I'm frozen.

Two quick booms sound, and the crowd goes quiet.

"WELCOME ALL TO THE GAUNTLET!" I jump at the loud voice over the speakers. The crowd shoots to their feet in applause.

I feel jittery, like I can't stay still. My stomach rolls, and my breakfast threatens to make an appearance. High above us, the High Council's private viewing chamber goes transparent. The High Council waves as High Councilor Achan stands. What did the other High Councilors even do? They rarely speak. Achan seems to always be the one doing anything.

"Welcome, candidates," The High Councilor magykly projects his dark voice through the Arena. Amalia stiffens as we both notice Nyall Drayven, the Crown Prince of Ur Daoine and head of the Rebellion, standing at the back of the room.

He's dressed in all black. *Shocker*.

"My friends," The High Councilor gestures to the crowd. "It's an honor to host the 20th Gauntlet!" The crowd goes wild as he roars. "As you know, 500 years ago, humans led a rebellion to overthrow our right to rule this land."

The crowd boos, and I roll my eyes.

"The humans thought they could overthrow us. They poisoned the ears of many with their vicious lies. For Sol Constantus himself blessed our rule, and anyone who denies it are HEATHENS, meant only for the darkest pits of the Abyss. To defy Sol Constantus is to damn your soul and go against your country." More boos follow, and trinkets and food are being pelted down on us. A rotten tomato hits me in the head. A carrot pings off Ama's forearm. But we don't move. We just stand there and take it because there's no other choice.

"We transformed this weak, damned country into a mighty Empire blessed by the Father himself. Now Ur Daoine is the most powerful country in the world!" The crowd erupts in applause and approving shouts. "We hold the Gauntlet to remember the brave fae who died in the war. Their sacrifice will not be in vain and their lives will never be forgotten. One candidate will win, because we are anything if not fair and honorable." The crowd cheers, completely buying the venomous lies he spouts.

"Humans!" Achan lifts a shriveled black hand, the claws black and overgrown, and gestures down towards us. "Almost all of you will die. One town, or one candidate will not." The arena *boos* the mention of two winners. Achan grimaces and gestures at the crowd to quiet down. "I know, your pain is my own. As you know, due to the incident during the last Gauntlet, humans can't be trusted. But rest assured, the deaths we are about to see will be glorious and you shall receive your reparation well though!" The crowd bursts into applause. Achan turns back to us as another High Councilor, a woman, stands up and speaks.

"Candidates. Here are the rules. If you collapse and are unconscious for more than 60 seconds, your spot will be forfeit and you will be disqualified. Any human who is disqualified will automatically enter compulsory service into the Ur Daoine Armed Forces. Only one of you will walk free, and only one of you will win." The cheers escalate as I hear someone else vomit in front of me. My hands shake uncontrollably as the smell of urine permeates the air.

"With that, it is my honor as the High Councilor of Ur Daoine to announce the 20th Gauntlet is now open!" She shouts the last word, and the crowd goes wild.

Some candidates look around nervously, others pull their weapons from their sheaths and lift them to the air with victorious shouts, trying to win the crowd. I continue to stare at the Dragon.

"BEGIN!" The announcer shouts and the leash on the Dragon magically drops to the ground as the attendants run into the opening in the rapidly closing wall. The entrance on our side closes and the ground moves as we descend rapidly. The Dragon roars as we all look around.

We come to a hard stop and I have to grab onto Amalia's arm to stay standing. A magyk line appears in the sand on the other side of the stadium.

"Your only goal is to make it past the black line," the announcer says. "Good luck." The crowd chuckles and cheers.

Fuck.

The Dragon screeches and lunges forward, shocking everyone into action. A few run and bang on the closed doors on the wall, others run towards the black line. Explosions set off as they step on small lumps in the sand. Candidates scream and limbs fly. The smell of burning flesh assaults my senses as Amalia grabs my arm, pulling me forward.

"Follow my steps, Dy!" Amalia shouts and I keep my eyes down as I run behind her, only watching where she steps so that I can mimic it. We weave in and out of the sand as the crowd screams. A wall of fire erupts in front of us and Amalia skids to a halt, making a hard right, I don't turn fast enough and get part of my eyebrow singed off.

We make it all the way around the fire when the Dragon shrieks and flies toward us.

Amalia shoves me to the ground as we duck, barely avoiding its sharp talons.

"Run, we have to get to the line before it comes back."

It's about 70 meters away and we launch into a sprint. Some of the other candidates are already past the line, and I notice Pfern is unfortunately one of them. Reymand and the other Southlanders all made it but all look rattled and many hold shrapnel injuries or are covered in burns.

The Dragon careens to the left, narrowly avoiding us and instead barreling right into some other Northerners who were running behind us. I hear someone shouting and look up to see Mirielle screaming at us and pointing. I hear the flapping of wings and realize the Dragon is trying to get airborne. Its snout is covered in—oh god—blood and patches of human tissue.

"RUN, AMA." I scream, realizing this might actually be it. We sprint with all our might to the black line. 10 meters. 8 meters.

5 meters.

3 meters.

I crash into Ama as we both leap past the black line. There's a gust of wind behind me and a sharp snap just as we get airborne. Something sharp bites into my shoe, pulling it off with a few scrapes against my foot. Pain flares in my ribs as I land on the hard sand with a groan. A deafening roar sounds behind me as something crashes against a wall.

I turn and my heart stops as I watch the green Dragon throw itself against an invisible wall that darkens with each hit. A ward tied to the black line. Amalia rolls to her feet and walks to the barrier.

"Ama!" I hiss her name as I quickly stand up. I reach forward and grab her hand as she goes to raise it. She glances at me as if in a trance. Her pupils are dilated and it's almost as if she's not there.

"What the fuck are you doing?" I yank her from the barrier and hope nobody pays too much attention.

CHAPTER 49
AMALIA

The green Dragon rams the top of its head into the ward again. Dark lightning bolts of magyk flash each time, but it holds steady. The Dragon roars in frustration, ignoring the final candidates that run past the finish.

Distantly, I'm aware of Dyana frantically hissing at me.

But I'm far away, inside the Dragon's mind.

There's something wrong with this Dragon. Something strange.

It's mind feels...poisoned. The taste of rotten apples grows stronger in my mouth as I try to connect with it. But its magyk is...painful.

Its pupils are fully dilated and it looks around, frantic.

I wince against the painful magyk and push past it. Outwardly the Dragon simply continues to blast the ward protecting us.

But it's hard not to fall to the ground and cradle my head at the frantic screaming going on inside of it.

"HURT HUNT KILL"

"NEED KILL NEED TO KILL"

"H-help,"

"HUNT HUNT KILL"

"Som-someone h-elp."

"KILL KILL KILL"

I do fall to my knees then, vomiting in the sand, panting. I want to scream and bang against the warding until my vocal cords are shredded and bleeding.

"NEED HUNT NEED KILL"

"S-scared"

"HUNT KILL KILL"

I try to calm it but it's no use, so I pull out of the Dragon's mind.

Its screams repeat over and over in my head, though.

I know what this is—and I'm going to fucking kill them for it.

Achan begins to talk as I push to standing, turning away from the Dragon and walking to wait next to Dyana.

But I'm not there.

My body moved but my thoughts are elsewhere, only on the Dragon. My magyk surges, searching for the poison, ready to burn it out.

"Pull back, Amalia. It's too much magyk. Pull back now or they'll notice," Remus's low, angry voice bursts into my head. I snarl back, unable to speak. *"Please!"*

"FINE!" I scream, yanking my magyk away from the Dragon and shoving it behind those iron doors deep inside me.

But the fury doesn't abate— and neither do my thoughts.

"Congratulations!" Achan says, "Twenty-five of you survived the first round of the Gauntlet. We went easy on you this time, but rest assured, the next round will be quite a bit harder." Achan waves and panders to the crowd before the announcer reads off the towns that lost a candidate.

"What the hell was that, A gahrá?" Remus snarls, and those slanted, gold eyes flash in my mind's eye in return.

"Did you know?" I snarl.

Remus sighs, *"I wish I didn't."*

"They're under a fucking compulsion, Remus. The fae took away their gods-damn will and you didn't think to tell me?"

"I thought you knew. I'm sorry, A gahrá."

But I'm already past it, *"Nyall said he was one of a few Elves that survived. If they're using compulsions on the Dragons, they have more than just a few Elves here."* He's silent for a moment.

"I know," Remus isn't surprised. *"The Elves have...labs. Places they take the Dragons, where they work the darkest of their magyks."*

I connect the dots at his words. *"They...they're experimenting on the Dragons?"*

"Yes, they are."

Suddenly Nyall Drayven's voice, wicked as midnight, rolls into our heads, *"I did tell you I wasn't the only Elf here. Did you not wonder what the others were here for? This is so much more complex than you realize, horse girl."* I imagine punching him in the face. *"Now, as fun as this little lovers spat is, you owe me an answer. I'll come to the Beast's rooms tomorrow. I cannot afford to wait any longer."*

Remus starts off on him immediately, doing what I can only guess is cursing him out in some ancient language from the sounds of it. But Nyall doesn't reply, instead his magyk brushes against mine before he turns and leaves, the taste of honeysuckle lingering in my mouth.

My mind races. This changes things—and yet it doesn't.

If the Elves have restarted their experiments on dark magyk, Nyall was right. Our world will die.

And the fact that they have enough power to experiment on Dragons means it's already too late. They're too far gone to be stopped.

We exit the Arena, walking on numb legs. The moment we step out of the light, Dyana slaps my arm.

"Ama, what the Mother loving fuck was that?"

But I've stopped, watching as fae Attendants come and wrap the Dragon in chain nets. The Dragon just pants and sits, calmly letting itself be chained up. It doesn't even thrash. My stomach turns at the sight, at the complete perversion of nature happening here. The predator is sitting for the prey.

"You were supposed to play it cool. The entire godsdamn stadium just watched you touch a WARD, Amalia!" I ignore her complaining.

"Did you know, too?" I ask, and Dyana looks confused, but my eyes are on Mirielle. The guilt I see in them tells me everything I need to know.

"Ok now wait a second. We just fought for our damn lives. Who knows what about what, Amalia?" Dyana exclaims.

Mirielle ignores Dyana, nodding at me sadly. "Yeah. I knew."

One second I'm still walking up the corridor and the next, I have Mirielle against the wall, my hand around her throat. Dyana shouts, trying to pry my hand off her.

"You should have told me!" I hiss, spit hitting her face.

Mirielle scoffs, "I can't read minds, Amalia. I thought you knew."

I bare my teeth at Mirielle, furious. "Well, I didn't. Apparently everyone but me knew, and no one thought to tell me before expecting me to go in there and slaughter a Dragon. Your pal Nyall left quite a bit out of his pretty little story, didn't he? When did the Elves and the fae begin experimenting on the Dragons with Dark Magyk, Mirielle? When did that fucking start and why did that go unmentioned?"

Dyana blinks, "But wait—what? Aren't compulsions illegal?"

I sneer and drop Mirielle, letting her go, "Not if you're the High Council. What happened to no more lies, Mirielle? Do you know what the Elves would do if—" I stop, unable to even finish the thought.

"Arkos, Roth, Zenyth! Round One is over, save it for tomorrow." Ireyna yells. I leave her behind, walking in front and wrapping my arm through Dyana's to keep her away from Mirielle.

We all walk in silence back to the dorms.

We have two days until Round Two, which we thought was Round One. But I can't even talk as I yank off my dirty armor, leaving it in a pile on the floor, and dunk my head in the bucket of water in our bathroom. The second my head is submerged I let out the scream that's been building in my chest for hours.

Water goes up my nose but I don't care. I surface, gasping in a large breath before dunking back under and screaming again.

Cool, soft hands land at my back, rubbing lightly.

I lift my head, gasping and pushing my wet braid out of my face. Dyana sits behind me, pity in her eyes.

We say nothing as she begins unbraiding my hair, combing it with her fingers. I rub my hand against my face, wiping off the water.

"I hate this," I whisper.

Dyana nods, "Me too."

I want to say more...but even Dyana doesn't know everything.

That remains the only words said between us as she grabs me a small, threadbare towel and we each climb into our beds.

She falls asleep quickly, but I stare at the ceiling all night. The cries of the tortured Dragon are still loud in my ears.

"Can't sleep?" Remus whispers in my mind.

"No," I admit.

"Me neither," he responds, his voice sad.

"Tell me a story," I say suddenly. I pause, wondering if that's odd.

"A story? Let me see..." he pauses, going silent.

Say something, I want to scream.

But I don't.

Just as the thought runs through my head, he speaks up, *"There was once a Dragon as big as one of the Suns. He was made of pure light, and his scales shone like crystals. There weren't many Dragons at this time; only four. And the Dragon got lonely, so one day he left his cave in the sky and decided to visit the land below. There he met the most beautiful Dragoness he'd ever seen..."* Remus's voice fades as sleep finally takes me. But even in my dreams, he continues telling me the story of the ancient Dragon lovers and their cave in the sky.

CHAPTER 50
AMALIA

I kick Remus's door in and see Nyall in one of the chairs by the fire. Judging from the look in Remus's gold eyes, I clearly interrupted another lecture.

"Oh good, I thought you might have gotten lost." Nyall nods, and Remus responds in that ancient language again. Mirielle shouts back to the males. I blink, eyes narrowing. She knows the ancient fae language?

"Another secret, Mirielle?" I hiss. Everyone in the room goes still and Dyana makes a choking noise.

It takes a moment to realize I just spoke in everyone's minds at once, and I barely even tried.

Nyall clicks his tongue, and Remus stiffens, although his eyes look rather pleased.

"Amalia didn't know about the compulsions...or exactly how much the Elves were helping the High Council." Mirielle says, and I catch the resentment in her tone. "And I did not invite you into my head, Amalia, so get the hell out."

"Lie to me again, and I'll kill you," I say simply, pushing my voice into everyone's heads. Dyana whimpers as the shadows in the room grow darker, making Mirielle go pale.

Remus ignores it all and walks over to me as Nyall and Mirielle begin to talk in that ancient, lilting tongue.

"Are you ok?" His smokey voice is low and quiet, not wanting to push.

"I'm fine...Thank you, for—"

"You don't ever need to thank me, A gahrá." He understands the words that go unsaid, and a knowing, sad glint enters his eyes.

"I didn't know they would start the Gauntlet yesterday, my spark. They usually let the trainers know but yesterday was unplanned."

I lean into his hands lightly, *"It's not your fault, Remus."*

For a moment, it's just us. Dyana sits by herself by the fire, looking a bit lost, while Mirielle paces, arguing with the Prince in another language.

"It's not your fault, Os." Dyana surprises me. Her dark brown hair is braided back, her voice is hollow and scratchy. She looks at us with hurt in her gaze but acceptance.

I smile softly, grateful. "She's right. Their goal was to surprise us, and it worked. We need to expect the unexpected."

Prince Nyall butts in, "Perhaps I can be of assistance."

I don't even turn to look at him, "No."

"No?" he asks, raising a brow.

"No. I would rather die in the Arena than work with an Elf."

"You were aware I was a half-elf before today. Why does the knowledge that there are more Elves in Castael Laryn make such a difference?"

I blink, "Why does it make such a difference?" Out of the corner of my eye, Dyana flinches. "Oh, I don't know Nyall. Why would pure-blood Elves make a difference? How about the fact that they know how to break the walls between worlds and literally jump through time? Or maybe it's the fact that they use Dark Magyk? Or could it be the fact that they've restarted their experiments, this time using Dragons to help them achieve their goals. That all makes a pretty big difference, Prince. You'd have to be a godsdamn idiot not to see that." Mirielle winces at that. "I'm not going near Dark Magyk, and you all would be smart to do the same. There is no way for your plan to work. It was already impossible, but if they're packed with Elven magyk, you're completely fucked. Not to mention I can taste the Dark Magyk on you, that fucking honeysuckle."

I seethe as Remus shifts to my side to glare down at the Prince. No questions asked and Remus is on my side with this.

I ignore the way my heart skips a beat at his immediate backing. Remus's tongue flicks the air, long and forked. He shifted it again. Dyana's eyes go wide and Mirielle takes a step back.

A deep, rumbling sound fills the room. Vases and artwork shake against the wall as dirt falls from the ceiling stone.

Remus bares a mouth full of fangs but Nyall just rolls his eyes.

"You want the truth? Fine. The Elves are a bunch of power-hungry cunts. Most of them, at least. My mother had no choice when Achan raped and impregnated her. She was born into slavery and sold to the highest bidder when Achan decided he wanted to begin experimenting with progeny. She wasn't with him by choice. Not long after I was born, Achan said he wanted to have another. My mother drove a knife into her heart and killed herself to ensure that didn't happen. One half-breed was already too many." He pauses, "You're right. The minute they started experimenting on the Dragons, the second they started working those compulsions, I knew we were heading in the direction of the Elven homeland. The Dark Magyk they're weaving is poison, and it's fucking strong."

"And yet, you practice Dark Magyk," I point out. Remus is still growling but he's quieted some.

Nyall just watches us, blinking. "Correct."

"Explain yourself." Remus snarls, making the stones rumble again. Prince Nyall just shrugs.

"Oh my Gods, he's trying to reverse it, you dense idiot! He's learning from them so that he can fucking reverse it." Mirielle shouts, her patience having snapped. "You sit here and question and preach, but if you took a second to actually listen, you'd realize that he's trying to reverse the damage their magyk is doing to the land! He's trying to restore Arkaydia to its prior glory, and you'd know that if you just shut the hell up and listened."

There's a beat of silence as I stare at Mirielle.

"Mirielle?" I ask sweetly.

She shrugs, sighing, "Gods, what now? Did you find some other reason to hate me?"

A dark smile grows on my face, "Hm. Not yet, but the day's still young." I pause, "Call Remus an idiot or speak to him like that again, and I'll slit your throat in your sleep."

Dyana's jaw hits the floor. Nyall just smiles as Mirielle's eyes go wide. I spare a glance at Remus and roll my eyes at the look of wicked pride on his face.

"That possessive enough for you, Beast?" I send the thought his way.

Wry amusement greets me. *"So you're allowed to be mean to me, but no one else is?"*

I sniff, *"I'm mean to you when you actually deserve it."*

Remus's rich, smokey laughter is all I get in response. But the sound—Gods, the sound. Such joy. For a moment, my soul is lighter.

Mirielle huffs impatiently, "Just hear him out. We all hate the Elves and the fae. We all dislike Dark Magyk. Nyall just has to be a martyr about it."

Her word choice makes me pause. "Explain."

Nyall gestures for us to take a seat.

I shake my head, "I'm fine right where I am."

"So prickly." The words whisper into my head and I go still. Remus doesn't react which tells me Nyall is only in my mind. I focus for a moment and dissociate, gathering a large portion of my magyk into me. I let my iron walls burst open for just a second; long enough to shove him out of my mind so hard he's thrown out of his chair, slamming face first into the marble floor.

Dyana sends me a thumbs-up as she tries hard not to laugh. But the Prince isn't mad. He just chuckles and gets up, dusting himself off.

"Get in my head without permission again, Prince," I walk over and lean over him, "and I'll kill you."

Nyall's eyes glitter with wicked mirth. "Is that a promise, horse girl?"

Dyana sighs, "Mother save me."

"Mirielle is correct," Nyall says, standing up and brushing himself off. "I've been using and studying Dark Magyk so that I can drain the High Council and take all of their stolen rotten magic, purify it, and funnel it back into the Earth. Give back everything they ever stole."

Dyana just blinks, confused. "Wait, so Dark Magyk is different from your magyk?"

Nyall nods patiently, "Most Siphons can only handle a small amount of magyk at once, actually. I'm using Dark Magyk to expand my passive magyk as well. Even if I do a direct siphon, it could burn me out to hold that much magyk at once."

He makes it sound so simple. I push him for more. "How sure are you that will work? Have you tried weaving it yet?"

The Prince just smiles. "Oh, it works. Ask your beast here. Tell me, Os, how are those wards feeling? A little looser the past few days, maybe?" Remus goes still.

"Yeah, Father hasn't noticed yet but two Elves and three imperial fae went missing recently. His head is too far up his own ass for him to notice, let alone care. But you noticed when I took their power and put it back in the land, didn't you? You felt their hold on you weaken."

Remus cocks his head, eyes narrowing as he mutters, "I'd been wondering about that."

I press into his mind, *"What does he mean?"*

"I can't leave the city grounds and can't transform. I haven't been able to access my proper form in five centuries. But two days ago, I noticed the noose was a little bit...looser. What you saw me do with my nails and tongue is normally impossible."

I pause. *"So it works then. His plan works."*

Remus brushes his magyk against mine as his low voice growls in my mind, *"My wardings have also loosened a bit since meeting you, A gahrá. It could be the familiar bond, not the Prince."*

Hmm.

I hesitate, *"What if there's a chance I could...remove them fully? Your wards, I mean. Without any need for Dark Magyk."*

Remus turns to look at me, a curious glint in his eyes.

"I would say we could discuss that more later, spark."

My eyes meet his. The trust I see brings a sea of emotion, but I keep it hidden beneath my stony facade.

"Dark Magyk still corrupts its users." I turn, watching Nyall for a reaction. He just nods and begins rolling up his shirt sleeves, showing off heavily tattooed forearms. But woven amongst the tattoos are veins of pure black.

Like Achan's.

"I'm paying the price. I'd wager I've sacrificed...a decade or two of life so far." Nyall's mismatched gaze meets mine. The Prince is indeed paying the price.

What I really want to ask is why? Why are you doing this?

Instead, I settle for, "What's in it for you?"

Nyall just watches me, his eyes sad. "That's a simple question, Amalia Roth. I'm doing this for a better world. Even if it kills me, I refuse to sit back and watch as the High Council destroys the world. I can't look out at my people and see another sea of terrified, bloodsick faces—or hear another moment of their Sol Constantus bullshit and how we're all doomed for hell unless we pray to some God who, funnily enough, only talks to the High Councilor."

The words sit in the air, and I look around the room to realize that each of us, one way or another, have been wronged by this world. By the fae, the Elves, all of it.

We've all lost someone or something because of them.

But I can't. The risk is too high with everything else we're worrying about. I sigh, having arrived at my answer the minute I met him.

"After the Gauntlet...if we win? Maybe. But I'm sorry, Prince. My answer is still no. Surviving the Gauntlet is all that matters right now. I won't increase our chance of dying—it's high enough already."

Mirielle explodes. "When this world shatters apart, will you wish you'd done more, Amalia Roth? Will you look back at this moment with guilt?"

"I know that right now, the only thing I can focus on is surviving to the next fucking day." My voice is shaky but strong as I stand. "That's it. That's the line in the sand. I can't think about what will happen next week because I'm too busy worrying about dying tomorrow. "

Nyall stands, too. He doesn't get mad, although I see a sad acceptance in his eyes.

"I know, and I'm sorry. This is all horrible timing and I understand your answer. There's...there's no good move here. We all risk so much. But, life is a risk here. I'm sorry I couldn't change your mind, but I understand. Your secrets will be safe with me, Amalia Roth." He sighs, looking at me with remorseful eyes. "Best of luck. For what it's worth, I truly hope you don't die."

He leaves and Mirielle follows. Dyana mumbles something about meeting me back in our room, and she leaves too.

But Mirielle's words repeat over and over in my head.

Will I look back and wish I had done more?

CHAPTER 51
AMALIA

"Aren't you supposed to be the responsible one?" I ask, trying to keep up with Remus. But after the meeting we just had, my humor is forced.

"I felt that you were still awake. Come on, keep up." He turns then, disappearing down a dark corridor.

I can't decide whether to kiss him or punch him in his stupidly handsome face. Perhaps both.

We go on for quite some time and descend down near the Dragon Pit. I can feel the moisture dampening the air, which is now heavy and hot with the smell of sulfur and dung. Sweat beads at my hairline, dripping down to my jaw and dampening my shirt.

But we don't go into the main cavern like last time. Instead, I follow Remus's large figure quietly to a smaller hallway, which leads into what kind of looks like a large, open stall with lots of straw and shavings on the ground. Shavings that are moving...

Oh! I gasp, unable to help myself as small baby Dragons emerge from the shavings with sweet cooing sounds and squeaks.

Paying no attention to Remus, I kneel, coming eye to eye with a white baby Dragon sitting back on its hind legs and looking up at me. It trills some sort of greeting, cocking its head at me with wide blue eyes. It shuffles forward, crawling on unsure legs until it slowly lays its head in my lap.

I look over to see Remus sitting down in the shavings next to me. Two baby Dragons, one blue and one red, fight for a spot in his lap, and one ends up slapping its tail across his face. Os sighs, but his eyes twinkle with mirth. I can't help the giggle that escapes me at the sight.

A soft, scaled warm nose bumps my hand and I look to see the white baby Dragon asking for attention.

"Hello, little one." I whisper, gently prodding it with my magyk.

The Dragon trills happily before using its small but very sharp talons to crawl into my lap. I wince at the scratches but don't react. The baby Dragon settles into my lap, pressing its head into me. Its horns are so soft still, almost rubbery. I run my hand across its hide, surprised at how soft its scales feel. I lean down and press a kiss to its head, and it nuzzles me happily.

The baby Dragon's magyk smells sweet, like honey and warm milk, reminding me of Mrs. Hunton's morning porridge. Other baby Dragons emerge sleepily from the piles of shavings, all cooing and trilling as they suddenly surround us. Most just lay back down, snuggling up against the warmth of our legs.

"They're normally more rambunctious than this, but it's their bedtime so I thought it might be a good time to visit." Remus just looks at me, something like regret in his eyes as he scratches the belly of the blue Dragon with one hand and plays with the little red Dragon crawling around his shoulders with his other hand. "Dragons are very complicated creatures. Many people once prayed to them as Gods. Some thought they were Gods. Maybe they are. But what everyone always gets wrong is their nature. Dragons are actually shy, peaceful creatures. Many live solitary lives in the comfort of their cave. They only hunt for food, never for sport, and most prefer animal meat to human or any two-legged creature. It's been said some Dragons only eat plants, preferring to live off the land rather than other living creatures."

Remus smiles as the red Dragon uses his hair like a blanket as it gets settled behind his neck, curling up like a little cat. "When the Dragons were free, it was rare to hear of any incident where they harmed an innocent."

I run my hands across the small body curled up in my lap as I listen, entranced by his storytelling. It's about the size of a Dyre Wolf puppy, it just has scales instead of fur. The Dragon's bright blue eyes blink up at me sleepily, trusting and kind.

I feel an innocent, wobbly nudge against my mind, so fresh and new in this world of complex magyks. The being in my lap doesn't understand the pain that rolls through me, but it senses something off, and instinctively it leans in into me, pressing a tiny talon against my stomach lightly, holding on as if to keep me centered.

I lean down and press a soft kiss to its scaled face, risking fang and claw.

"I'm so sorry." I whisper. Over and over again until tears fall freely. *"I'm so sorry I can't save you. I wish so badly I could save all of you."* My heart breaks.

I feel more than hear Remus's realization. "This was a bad idea, I'm sorry. I didn't mean to upset you. I thought you'd like to see the babies…"

"No, Remus. I'm…I'm so glad you brought me." I choke out, trying to reign in my emotions. "Truly. I just—" I pause, on the edge of yet another cliff.

"I get it. I bond with them too." I jerk my head to the side, meeting Remus's golden eyes.

"What do you mean? You…which ones do you bond with?" I ask, so caught off guard.

Remus just nods sadly, *"All of them, little spark. I bond with all of them."*

"You—wait, what? You form a magyk bond with every baby Dragon? All of them?" I fall short as my voice fades out. I sit in silence, staring at this man I once took for a complete and utter fae-worshiping asshole.

"The older ones won't tolerate any bond, but the younger ones don't know better. Before they hatch, their magyk begins looking for older Dragons to form a connection with. It's in their blood," he pauses. *"These bonds are different than a familiar bond, as you know. I cannot heal them, but I can feel their pain and shield them from it."*

"But, what about the ones you fight? Do you feel it?" I ask, scared for the answer.

He just nods again, his golden eyes dark.

"Most of the time, yes." He says aloud.

My heart is frozen in horror. "Remus you…you've felt all of them die? How are you still sane?" Grief fills me, and I watch as the strong, ferocious male in front of me begins to cry. Golden tears like liquid metal drip from Remus's eyes as he looks around at the baby Dragons in the stall with such fondness that it steals the breath from my lungs.

"I'm not sane, *A gahrá.* No one is in this place. But I have hundreds of years of practice pretending to be fine. After a while…you go numb. Until the quiet moments, at least. Then I feel it all." Remus pauses before continuing, "You ask often why I'm in a bad mood, or why I was mean. It...gets hard. Feeling it all and not being able to do anything about it. Somedays I wonder if I even have a soul left at all, because a piece of me dies alongside every single one of them. And I let it happen. Because there's absolutely nothing I can do about it but damnit, I refuse to let these little ones be alone in a world already full of so much pain and loneliness. Even if it's for a brief period—they deserve some semblance of a family. They're completely innocent, just caught in the High Council's web of cruelty. If I can give them any bit of peace and love before their time is up, I will. Even if it means I lose another piece of myself in the process."

The torture in his voice kills me. That's what it is. This place. It's a prison, and we're all in some way being tortured to death.

I gently pick up the Dragon in my lap and cradle it against my shoulder. It tucks itself into my hair as it sleepily trills at me. I caress its head and scoot over to Remus, sitting down next to him as I use my other hand to pick up two of the Dragons who were sleeping in between us, and place them on my lap. They curl together with a few sleepy squeaks, clearly hatchmates with identical dark green coloring.

Without words, I lean my head against his shoulder, cuddling up to the red Dragon in his hair. The Dragon licks my nose, sending me happy, sleepy feelings of contentment.

For a while, we just sit in silence and listen to the baby Dragons breathe as they all get comfortable and go back to sleep. I feel Remus's anxiety as he awaits my response, and his eyes betray the fear of my possible rejection. But he doesn't push me.

I take a deep breath and begin. Not with everything, but with some.

"I was five years old the first time I killed someone."

His mind caresses mine and hovers around me as comfort. He just waits, ready to hear whatever I'm willing to share.

"I didn't even know what I was doing. I bonded with every animal in sight in those days, much like I still do, I suppose. I've never been able to stop it. It used to drive my parents nuts. But they wanted me to learn my magyk, so despite the danger, they always encouraged me to practice when I wouldn't be seen. But one day, a man came around, looking for my Father. I don't even know what he wanted, but all of the

sudden, the man started shouting. Threatening to turn Father in for his magyk. We were near the horse stable, and when the male went to shove my father, I snapped. I burst into the mind of every animal nearby and yanked them all to me. Bears came running, and birds dove from the sky, all converging on this unsuspecting male in moments. I watched his skull get crushed under our pack horse's hooves. I watched as his body was beaten to a pulp and torn to shreds until there was nothing but hair and a pile of blood left. But the worst part about it all was I felt no remorse. Just fear and anger. But I never once regretted it. I still see that image in my dreams, even all these years later."

A part of me is ready for Remus to realize what a monster I am and finally walk away. But he just laces his fingers with mine.

"You protected your family, A gahrá. Don't ever be ashamed of protecting the ones you love."

I continue, unable to stop the torrent of words now that I've started. "Ever since then, I've always gravitated towards animals more than humans. They are inherently more trustworthy. I know they will protect me. And so I promised that day to protect them too. It's people who are the corrupt ones."

"I agree." Remus reaches his free hand over and turns my head towards him, gently pulling my chin until my eyes meet his. "I see you, A gahrá." He releases my chin and places his hand over my heart.

I place my free hand over his, and his slow heartbeat thumps under my palm. "I see you too, Remus Ostia."

"Time for some sleep," Remus says knowingly.

I raise a brow at him. "You're the one that kept me up late, you know."

He just smiles softly. "Was it worth it?"

I get up and go to one of the small nests in the straw and deposit my little sleeping friends. I kiss the baby Dragons, breathing in the sweet scent of their pure, innocent magyk once more, whispering words so quiet, not even Remus with his supernatural hearing, could pick up. I give it my secrets and hand over my heart. It knocks against my mind again, and I keep my walls sealed. But using the powers of my mother, I push all of my love toward it, and it coos happily before curling up with its brothers and sisters to go back to sleep.

Looking back at Remus, I slowly grasp his hand, marveling at how much bigger it is than my own. I trace the scars on his calloused palm.

Looking up at him from beneath my lashes, I admit, "It was worth it."

Just as we leave, a voice bursts into my head with the power of a hundred suns, causing my vision to go black as stars explode behind my eyes.

"Amalia Roth. I need your help." The weight of her magyk crushes me. Distantly, I know Remus is saying something to me, but I can't hear him. I can't even verbalize, but I feel him push into my mind.

"Kydis?" I whisper. *"How are you able to speak to me from so far away?"*

"I am Dragon, and you healed more than just my body, little Arkaydian. Distance is no consequence for my power, even for one as old and weary as I. But it matters not. I need your help, young one. If you genuinely want to do something about our enslavement, if you meant what you said, come to my cell in five minutes at the changing of the guards. Bring your beast, too. Our chat is overdue,"

Just like that, her magyk is gone and I can breathe again as I gasp for air. I'm in Remus's arms.

"Did you—" I gasp, trying to catch my breath but my heart is racing so fast I feel like I might burst into a million pieces.

Remus's pupils have turned into diamonds and his tongue is forked as he growls low, "I heard."

"We have to go, Remus." He just looks back at me, assesing. He could say no, he could protest and bring up all of the reasons why this is a bad idea, but he takes a deep breath, his eyes shuttering for a moment.

When they open, dark, cold resolve burns within them.

"Fine. Let's go." For a moment, his gold eyes are full of remorse, but it's gone before I can process it. We race through the halls, careful to remain unseen before descending that dark staircase as we dive deep into the earth.

The cavern is quiet. No sound of boots walking across the damp stone floor, no guards lingering at each row of the stables. None of the Dragonguard within the ceiling cave system are to be seen. They must be asleep in their caves.

We silently weave in and out of the stall rows. Remus grabs me and yanks me back on one of them when a guard almost sees us.

My heartbeat races while his is a thudding drum inside my head.

Row after row, and finally we get to the end. To the biggest block of cells. After making sure no guard is to be seen, we sneak past giant metal stable doors until we get to the one I remember.

Thanks to all of this damn jogging we've been doing, I'm only breathing a little hard. Remus, that ass, isn't breathing hard at all. But we stop at Kydis's stall and approach the bars tentatively.

For a moment, there's nothing.

Just the sound of our shaky breathing.

Then, through the darkness, two eyes, glowing as if lit from behind, two embers in the deep. A crimson snout taller than my entire body, with fangs the size of my body emerges out of the shadows. Her scales are worn and scarred, but not as bad as it was before. Her coloring has come back, turning into a rich, deep crimson. But her eyes—there's a determination there. A rage where there was once only resignation.

I look upon a very different being than the one I last met. Even now as Kydis comes further into the light, nearing the bars of the window, the Dragonfear sets my heart racing.

This is the Crimson Queen. This is a *Goddess*.

Kydis huffs, blowing smoke in our faces, but it doesn't burn my eyes. Instead, I feel welcome in its soft embrace.

"Thank you for coming, young one." Kydis easily enters our minds, her ancient voice almost bringing me to my knees. Goosebumps break out across my body as my body fights the fear that is racing through my blood. She turns her gaze to look at Remus, and I notice he stands back a little, head down in submission.

Somehow, I know that she's speaking to both of us as she bares her fangs in a terrifying Dragon grin.

"Hello, Beastkyn. It's been a long time."

CHAPTER 52
KYDIS

The Beastkyn raises his eyes, and I see centuries of resentment, anger, and guilt burning him alive.

"You requested my presence. Why am I here?" It's difficult not to shudder at the Beastkyn's voice. So like the voice of my kin and yet, not. His magyk is different. Advanced from ours, in so many ways.

"A long time ago, my Mother tried to banish you from Elysium," I say, and beyond them I hear the whispers of my gossiping kyn.

The Beastkyn grinds his teeth, *"Yes. She did. It was clear I was not welcome."*

"You chose to get rid of your Drayke form, the form Livyathin himself gifted us at the beginning of time. To many, that's the greatest sin a Dragon could ever make."

The Beast stays quiet, his eyes closed in acceptance of whatever punishment I want to dole out.

A voice like poisonous midnight booms, *"You will address our Queen with respect, Beastkyn."* The girl jumps at Vesimyr's voice as he joins our mental connection, bumping his head against his stall a few doors down. For a moment, the cave shakes. It's brief, but I felt the movement.

Livyathin's thorny claws, has Vesimyr grown larger?

I watch as the girl takes a deep breath, swallowing down the Dragonfear that is causing her tiny heart to race. Behind her, the Beastkyn looks at the ground. Remus Ostia might walk free, but he's a prisoner just the same.

"Apologies, highness. My manners are...rusty."

The girl coughs, covering a laugh.

I huff impatiently. *"I care not for pithy apologies at this hour. My mother was wrong."* The Beastkyn's golden eyes land on me and I feel the weight of his gaze, the force of his magyk, and fight a shiver of fear. *"Let me say that again, Beast, for I will only say it once more. My Mother, and all of Elysium was wrong to shun you. What we saw as a sin was actually the greatest gift Livyathin gifted us—we just didn't know it yet."* I blow out another cloud of smoke. I nudge my snout against the bars, getting their attention. *"Beastkyn, my kind has wronged yours many times over, and for that, I am sorry. On behalf of the Empire of Elysium, I offer my apology."* I pause and connect with all the minds in the cave. *"Let all who hear me know that the Beastkyn, known as Remus Ostia, is a friend of the Dragons."*

The Beastkyn's chin hits his chest, his shoulders twitching as his emotions shatter. I feel his profound shock and his trembling awe. *"Thank you, my Queen. I am... thank you. I am in your debt."*

"Yes, you are," I respond, watching as the girl blinks. It's been ages since any Dragon has been chosen by Livyathin to complete a familiar bond. The God's claws are at work here.

"You have done much for our kind, already, and for that I thank you. Thank you for protecting our hatchlings when we cannot. I can read in your memories how you shield them. We are forever in your debt, but first..." I reach a talon through the bars as I adjust, body cramping, *"First, I claim your debt, Remus Ostia. We need your help. Both of you."*

The girl's jaw drops but I watch her eyes go hard.

She's in, but it was never her I was worried about.

I look at the Beast. *"I have a plan to get us out of here. We've been working on it for centuries. But it is dependent on a very particular type of magyk."* I pause, taking a breath. *"The only way to break the warding that keeps us in here, that traps us in these metal boxes, is to combine Arkaydian magyk with Dragon magyk."*

The girl's head snaps to the side, looking at the Beast. He gazes at her with clear adoration—and hesitation.

Vesimyr's deep voice pipes up, *"The chances of you two meeting are so slim that this must be woven by Livyathin himself. You can free us. You can get us out of here. Use your familiar bond to amplify my magyk. Infuse your Arkaydian Magyk with mine, and we can escape."*

The Beast hesitates, looking at me with regret, *"I mean no disrespect, your highness, but I'm warded. And even if they were to be dropped, it would be some time before I'm back to my full strength. My magyk is not what it once was. I will help however you need, highness, but I don't know how much help that actually will be."*

I turn my gaze to the girl, who bites her lip raw. I can smell her blood.

I know what she's capable of.

"Remus," the girl starts, *"I think I can remove it. It's gonna hurt like hell but we've been through worse. If..."* she pauses, taking a deep breath, *"if you trust me, let me at least try. When the warding is gone, I'll hit you with a big dose of magyk and charge you up the way I did with Kydis. Then I can charge up, um..."*

"Vesimyr," the Dragon booms. *"My name is Vesimyr, child."* The girl blanches but shakes it off.

"The Executioner," someone whispers and I hiss, ordering them silently to be quiet. If the girl hears the whisper, she doesn't show it.

"Right, Vesimyr, I think...I can use Os as a conduit. Once his warding is gone, I can push my magyk through him, into you."

Remus hesitates.

"Well, boy? Are you going to be a stubborn old mule just like your sire and grandsire were? Or do you trust your familiar?" Vesimyr booms. I huff another cloud of smoke.

"Peace, Vesimyr. Go gentle on the two-legged ones. They may be brave, but they are still fragile."

Vesimyr grumbles but quiets down.

There is no hesitation in the Beastkyn as he answers, *"I trust Amalia with my life."*

At this, the girl is frozen, eyes wide. She leaves us for a moment and I feel her mind drift, but I gently pull her back.

"Now is not the time to hide, young one. Feel your feelings once you're tucked away, safe. We don't have much time left, and there is more to discuss. I can feel this scares you, but we all must face our fears one day."

The girl nods, swallowing, *"Okay,"* she breathes. *"I'll try to remove his warding."*

"Good," Vesimyr snorts in agreement with my words. I feel his guilt at what comes next as I try to ignore my own.

"Amalia Roth, it is neither your responsibility nor your duty to get involved in this. You should know, the amount of magyk this requires might very well kill you."

There is no surprise on the girl's face. *"I do not fear my own death, Dragon. I fear living in a world where the ones I love are dead."*

My eyes close at her pain. Every Dragon goes silent, understanding that feeling far too well.

"Please help us get out of here," someone whispers into our connection.

"I don't want to die in here," another admits.

"Please save us," another begs.

A Dragon, begging. Oh, how far we've fallen.

"Help our people see the skies once again, Amalia Roth, even if it's simply to say goodbye," Vesimyr says in a quieter, gentle voice.

I nod, straining and extending a claw to her. With a trembling hand, she places it upon my talon. Her hand is so tiny. Tears stream from the girls' eyes. But she just meets my gaze, and something in that moment connects us. I feel the touch of Livyathin's mighty claws at work as I watch Amalia Roth's eyes begin to glow as her sorrow turns to fury.

"There are already so many chances to die, what's one more?" Amalia's eyes flash, and I swear the cave begins to darken. *"I will see your people freed, Kydis. I swear it—even if it kills me."*

The Beastkyn has to turn away, pacing. His true self, possessive as all Dragons are, is fighting tooth and claw against the thought of anything happening to his familiar. But he walks up to the girl, cradling her small face in his small hands.

"Are you sure, A gahrá? You said you didn't want to help Nyall."

The girl shakes her head, *"This isn't about Nyall. This is different. I can't just...I can't do nothing, Remus. Not anymore. I'm tired of only being afraid. I'm tired of hiding in the shadows. I won't help Nyall, but I will help the Dragons. I have to."*

The Beastkyn smiles sadly, but it doesn't reach his eyes. *"I'm with you, A gahrá. For a better world."*

The girl looks over to me, *"For the forgotten and the voiceless."*

Vesimyr snarls, *"It's time to show those fae bastards what fear really looks like."*

I hum, connecting to all of my kin, *"The Arkaydian and her Beast will help us. We will escape here, I swear it."*

"We are not forgotten, we are feared!" Vesimyr booms.

In the quiet depths of midnight, a new sound rises, filling the cavern row by row and stall by stall as my kin repeat our words.

"We are not forgotten, we are feared."

"We are not forgotten, we are feared."

"We are not forgotten, we are feared."

In their layered voices comes something else that's new. A feeling I thought long lost within me: *hope.*

"Now, Amalia Roth." I clear my throat, using a claw to pull her closer until we're nose to nose. She places her hands on my snout, trying not to trip, and ends up a meter away from my fangs. *"First, you're going to take a message to the Elven Prince. I believe I have something he needs."*

CHAPTER 53
MIRIELLE

The task for the second round seemed simple. But when it comes to the fae, nothing is ever what it seems.

Make it to the other side of the Arena alive. That's the only goal, exactly like round one. Except this time, when we arrived in the Arena, it was empty. No Dragon waiting for us, thank the Gods. But that means whatever it is we have to go up against is hiding, which doesn't bode well.

The deep pounding of the Arena drums vibrates my breastbone underneath layers of leather and armor. Chainmail clinks with every step we take as we take our place on the Arena sands. It took many years to learn, but I take the adrenaline rushing through my system and use it to focus my eyesight and senses further. I sink all my weight into my legs and tighten my muscles one by one as I let go of my emotions.

The crowd is packed and rambunctious, screaming at us and hurling more rotten food. Various insults are slung at us.

I tune it all out. I can't let it get to me.

Dyana and Amalia stand a few rows behind me, similarly dressed. Dyana's dark brown hair is pulled into a simple ponytail, accenting the unique neckpiece she chose. It's lined with shades of silver and black and encircles her neck in a royal ornamentation. Despite the fact that I've looked at her approximately a hundred times so far today, she hasn't looked at me.

Not once.

Every time I see her hesitate, a piece of my heart crumbles. It's worse because I understand why she's hurt. I get it.

I knew when I joined. I knew there would be sacrifices. But Gods, I didn't know I would meet her. I didn't know there would be anything I cared not to lose.

Amalia stands next to Dyana, her dark gray hair braided and covered by a black scarf she's pulled over the bottom half of her face.

There's a righteous fury burning in her eyes, and it scares me.

I can't explain it, but something about her has always felt too wild. As if she were more animal than human. More like Os, even. Though they bickered constantly, the two were so similar in their mannerisms and their extremely short patience.

I'm well aware I'm not Amalia's favorite person right now. Honestly, I couldn't care less. We need her help, but beyond that, she can dislike me all she wants. I care about Dyana's feelings, not hers because Amalia is not my favorite person either. Not after she turned down Nyall. I know everyone has to make their own choices in life, but I can't respect anyone willing to just sit back and let this kingdom turn to ash.

I don't blame Dyana for going along with whatever Amalia says. Amalia is essentially her older sister and the only mother figure she's ever had. I understand it. But a small part of me wants to scream at her to think for her godsdamn self for once.

Her fear is going to cost her everything she loves. I just wish she'd understand that.

The Arena is empty except for a long line in the sand on the far side of the stadium.

Nyall sent me a message this morning. He's heard whispers that this round was going to cut a lot of candidates. The High Council was unhappy with how few died in the first round.

Sick bastards.

I scan the sand, looking for anything off. There are a few very subtle piles. I'm not sure anyone else would even be able to notice with their human eyesight.

But *I* notice.

I run through a few scenarios quickly in my head, options flashing before my eyes, before I land on what I hope to the Fates is the one that will work.

The announcer comes on and drones on for a bit about glory and honor before giving thanks to Sol Constantus.

How anyone believes that a male created life is beyond me. I've always prayed to the Mother and Lir, God of the Tides. Like the shifting tides, Lir was neither male nor female. They are everything and nothing. And yet many in Ur Daoine believe wholeheartedly that Constantyn Himself sent the High Council to save us.

It's easy to convince the desperate and hungry. Give them food and they'll follow you for life. Give them purpose, and they'll give you everything.

I know better.

Constantyn is no God. Or if he is, he's not ours. But still, the Mother, Lir, Livyathin; all of the other Gods who once occupied our world are silent.

They do nothing as the High Council destroys our world in the name of the usurper God.

The crowd roars, cheering as the announcer finishes his prayer. Then, they begin chatting, demanding a bloodbath.

The private box for the High Council stays opaque this time.

Good. Achan Drayven was fucking creepy to look at. Without warning, the announcer begins to count down, and we all quickly unsheathe our various weapons.

Some candidates carry axes—like Dyana—and some carry swords. One wields a bow and arrow. Another wields a sword curved into a near circle.

Amalia is the only one to wield two long swords. They're plain, but if I look at them long enough they seem...wrong, somehow.

I shake it off, unsheathing my staff and extending it to its full length.

I am the only one to wield a staff.

Forsaken.

Gifted to me by my Mother on the day of my birth, I've trained with Forsaken since the moment I knew how to walk. Having to use dull practice swords these past few weeks has been maddening.

It's smooth under my hand despite the intricate carvings of waves and sea Dragons covering it from tip to end.

I spare another quick glance back. Dyana has her short sword in one hand and her ax in the other. As a dancer, I expected her to pick something graceful, like a bow or a curved sword. When she chose the ax, I almost fell over.

Amalia unsheathes her swords with a loud metallic twang, twirling them expertly, warming her muscles up.

The soft wood of Forsaken grounds me as I grasp it and roll through a quick figure eight working. With the right amount of pressure, it splits in two and turns into two, double-edged blades. I bear many scars on my hands and arms from years of perfecting the back and forth.

Now, it's second nature. Today, Forsaken gets to be unleashed.

"FIVE!" The announcer shouts, continuing the countdown.

"FOUR!"

I can't mindspeak like Amalia, but I can shout really loud.

"Amalia!" I shout in my head, picturing the feel of her magyk.

"What?" she hisses, invading my head with a burst of magyk that leaves the taste of burnt lavender in my mouth. I don't have to look to know she's glaring a hole into the back of my head.

"There are traps in the sand. Dozens of them."

"THREE!"

She curses. *"I don't see any."*

"Not human, remember?"

"TWO!"

"Follow me or it will kill you."

She curses again, *"Godsdamnit, fine!"*

"ONE!"

A metallic taste fills my mouth, and the sharp scent of lightning fills the air right as a large gong sound goes off, and the announcer shouts, **"BEGIN."**

Everyone next to me jumps forward, but I wait and Amalia and Dyana run up behind me.

"Kill anyone who tries to attack us. I'll ward off any attacks from the North and West, you look for East and South." Amalia orders. Dyana just nods, eyes wide.

There's no other choice.

"No hesitation. If you don't kill them, they kill you. Don't think about it, just do it." Amalia says, cutting off the connection between us.

I empty my mind of any other thought and run ahead, carefully navigating the subtle mounds of sand, Amalia and Dyana right on my tail.

Shouting erupts from in front of us as Reymand and the Southlanders attack the other candidates.

One of those piles turns to a jet of steam so hot it makes my eyes water even from this much of a distance. The candidate who stepped on the pile is instantly incinerated, their ashes quickly scattering on the wind. There isn't even any blood.

Gods.

The scent of singed hair and crispy skin fills my nostrils and I fight the urge to vomit. A strangled noise leaves Dyana but we don't stop running, weaving in and out of the invisible piles of sand that mark a trap. More jets of steam explode across the Arena sands as candidates step on the wrong spot. The sounds of the dying fill my ears when out of nowhere, a giant Archidna explodes out a pile just ahead of us, making me jerk to a halt. Amalia and Dyana hit my back, making me take a step, but I hold them back.

"MOVE!" I scream as the Archidna scuttles forward, its eight legs propelling it far faster than you would ever think it could move. It grabs candidates with its pincers, bringing them up to its sharp, fanged mouth and chewing on them whole. Blood trails down its black mouth and it screams, a deafening, high-pitched sound that shatters my eardrums. I can feel the hot blood dripping down my neck from my ears.

Noise goes faint, as if I'm underwater. But I run forward, using the Archidna's eating as a distraction to get by. When I look back, Dyana and Amalia sprint behind me. Just as I'm about to turn forward, Dyana trips, falling directly under the Archidna's stomach.

Amalia doesn't even have time to react, but I've already turned around and am running to help. Dyana rolls out from under the Archidna as it stabs its sharp feet into the sand repeatedly.

With a scream, I spin my staff above my head and run underneath it, cutting four of its legs off with a single movement. The Archidna shrieks, black blood spraying my face.

"Get out, go!" I shove Dyana to her feet and move her forward. The Archidna shrieks and works harder to get me. I separate Forsaken and spin both pieces in quick circles, creating moving saws. I mow through its legs as I dance between them and try to get out from under it. It falls, only one leg left, and in one single move, I attach the two sides of Forsaken and thrust it directly into its eye.

It's dead before I run away, back to where Dyana and Amalia are panting and waiting. They let me retake the lead, but I stumble as my vision doubles. I look down and see a blurry, small cut on my arm.

Archidna venom. Damnit.

I stop, but Dyana doesn't stop fast enough, and she careens past me. My heart falls out of my chest, and everything slows as I watch the sand pile she just stepped on explode into a jet of hot steam. I'm fast as I fight against time itself to move faster, quicker, to get to her. I grab her arm and yank her back but it's not fast enough. Her other arm is caught in the jetfire as a scream that falls from her lips will haunt me until my dying days. She screams bloody murder as I pull her to safety, the skin on her forearm bubbling and charred.

Oh Gods. Dyana screams again, and her legs give out, but Amaila wraps her arm around her waist and forces her forward.

"Come on, come on, we just have to get across the line and then we will get you to a healer. Don't you fucking give up, Dy. Don't you dare. We've been through worse, remember?" Amaila's frustrated motivations help and Dyana keeps running even as she sobs in pain. "Remember when Virgyl accidentally trampled you when we were playing chase, and you broke your nose? I had to crack it back into place, and you punched me. I was so proud—and in a fuck ton of pain."

Dyana tries to laugh, but it just comes out as more sobs, "This hurts so much worse than that."

"I know it does. I know. We're almost there, though, we're almost to the finish line and then we will get you to the healers. Look at me, Dy!"

Dyana sobs, her tearstained gaze meeting Amalia's terrified one.

"Suck it up. Push it down. Put the pain away Dyana. We have to run—I need you to run, okay? Run, Dyana!"

Other candidates try to pass us, and I hear a whoop as the crowd goes wild. I whirl, my curls hitting me in the face.

Fuck. Reymand and four of his cronies passed the finish line.

We have to hurry. I weave around the piles, but a wall of fire bursts out of another pit right in front of me. Amalia grabs my collar and yanks me back, my face still tingling from the heat.

There go my eyebrows.

Just before we get to the finish line, a group of four candidates come up on our right side, ramming us off course. Not Reymand, but that asshole Pfern and a few Eastlanders.

Instead of running towards the finish line, the group attacks us with a cry. Dyana's knocked to the ground, screaming in pain as the sand mixes with her raw skin.

Amalia shouts, charging one of the Eastlanders with a vicious scream.

"Amalia! Get Dyana past the finish line! I'll hold them off." I shout, coming to a stop.

"Don't be a fucking martyr, Mirielle!" she yells back.

I scoff, using my staff to meet the thrust of Pfern's sword, blow for blow. "Just do it!"

Amalia snarls and uses the pommel of her blade to punch the Eastland candidate in the side of the head, just above the ear. He falls over with a cry. She doesn't hesitate, grabbing Dyana off the ground, the latter of which passes out. Amalia grunts as she hoists Dyana over her shoulder.

"GO!" I scream as Pfern attacks, kicking sand into the air to blind the other Eastland candidate and stop him from going after them. Amalia races towards the finish line and I breathe a sigh of relief the moment she gets Dyana to safety.

With renewed focus now that I know Dyana will make it, I turn my attention to the three attackers and shut my feelings down.

One is getting up from the sand, shaking their head as they try to shake off the pain from Amalia's blow.

Pfern just stalks towards me, an ax in each hand. The Eastland candidate I kicked sand at is still frantically rubbing at his eyes, but will soon be a problem.

Emotion goes away and intense focus replaces it. After all, they all still think I'm human.

But the image of Dyana's skin charring and falling off and the sound of her pained screams, the knowledge that neither they nor Os will help us in dismantling this whole fucking system? It was too much.

I'm done playing it safe.

With a battle cry that could wake the dead, I split Forsaken and charge, meeting their blows at twice their speed. Pfern swings his axes with abandon but he's no match for me.

We dance the death waltz, and they can't keep up. The Eastland candidate finally clears his eyes and runs over to join Pfern. He swings his longsword down upon my shoulder, but I've already swung low, narrowly avoiding it just before I take Forsaken and rip into his guts.

For a second, there's nothing, then blood explodes as his intestines fall out, and he screams, struggling to hold himself together as his organs fall to the ground in a pool of blood and misery.

I don't wait to watch him bleed out; I'm already parrying blows from the other two.

The Eastland woman slashes her sword towards my face, and I lean back, but Pfern swings an ax at me simultaneously. A sharp warmth followed by a sting. There was no choice. It was decapitation or a cut to the face.

Before they can recover, I spin, bringing both halves of the hard middle of my staff up and slap them on her ears. She screams and falls to her knees, unable to see or hear.

Pfern roars behind me, ready to plunge the sword into my back; I swing Forsaken's two halves and shove them backward, stabbing him on either side of his chest.

I yank them out, and blood drips quickly down his armor from the giant gashes I left behind.

They will die if their wounds aren't treated, but none are dead...yet.

I call that self-control. For it takes infinite amounts of it to reel myself back and turn away as I begin walking towards the finish line.

Some people just aren't very appreciative of the gifts they've been given. The Eastland woman screams and throws herself at my back.

I hear Amalia and Dyana shout, but there's no need.

Just as she's almost on me, I duck, using her forward momentum to flip her forward and spin her so she lands on her back.

She never even noticed when I sliced her femoral artery. Blood shoots out in a jet stream, coating my face and clothes.

There's a noise behind me and I turn, but not quickly enough as pain explodes all along my arm.

Pfern stabs me in my upper arm with a small dagger, making me scream. I spit in his face and yank out the blade as hot blood flows down my arm, dripping down my fingers and onto the sand.

"I was going to let you live, you little shit," I sneer at him, and he just laughs. So I take both halves of Forsaken and shove the sharp tips into his skull, piercing both of his eyes as he and I roar in unison. "But you know what, you don't deserve it. Give my regards to hell, Pfern."

He falls to the ground, body twitching as his brain dies.

I look at the other candidates who wait past the finish line. They all watch me, eyes wide in disgust. Some sob openly. Dyana is half-conscious in Amalia's arms.

The crowd goes wild as I walk calmly past the finish line. The other candidates move to get as far away from me as possible. But Amalia just watches, her keen eyes missing nothing. She cocks her head so slightly I'm sure she doesn't even realize she does it. But she looks at me with something that surprisingly seems a little like respect.

Whispers reach my ears, even over the roar of the crowd.

The other candidates are worried. And I just made myself someone to beat. Nyall is going to tear me a new one for this, but he can kiss my ass.

I hurry over to Dyana and grab her clammy palm as she groans in pain.

"It's done, Dy. We made it past this round." I risk a kiss to her palm as she moans in pain again. It kills me to see her like this.

"Well done, candidates!" The announcer screams as I join Amalia and Dyana, the latter of which looks like she might pass out at any moment.

"Wasn't that quite the show?" they ask the crowd and the audience screams, deafening me. The High Council's booth becomes visible suddenly and Achan steps forward. Nyall is there, his marbled eyes simmering with fury. Nobody else would notice but I've known him for long enough to see through his words.

"Looks like the Dragonguard gets a special treat tonight!" High Councilor Achan shouts, pointing at all of the mutilated, half-burned dead bodies.

The crowd screams again, and a prickling sensation brushes against my skin. Twenty-five of us went into today's round; only twelve remain.

"The third round will begin on the full moon. Are you ready?" The crowd screams various affirmative answers. "Candidates, you have survived this round," Achan turns his gaze down to us. "In two days, more of you will lose. But for one, you're that much closer to freedom!" He raises his arms as if he just made some amazing speech, and not spouted more doom.

Blood drips into my mouth. I would wipe it off, but my armor and hands are just as coated. We made it through round two by the skin of our teeth.

"Come on, we need to get you to a healer." I go to lift Dyana up, but Amalia catches her before I can help.

"I've got things handled just fine, thanks," she glares, but I just shove her off, ignoring her.

"I just saved your fucking life, Roth. I'm coming with you whether you like it or not. I'm not here for *you.*"

Amalia glares at me again and hisses at me slightly, but together, we carry Dyana to the healers as fast as we can.

It takes the healers hours to repair Dyana's arm. The Archmage himself even showed up and lent a hand, although the second I heard he was on his way, Amalia and I made ourselves scarce, waiting around the corner instead of in the healing room.

Still, I watch as she goes stiff as a board when the Archmage and his retinue pass by. Even from far away, the Archmage is terrifying.

Unlike Achan, the Archmage is perfect. So perfect, it's immediately off-putting. The symmetry to his face seems unreal. His hair is such a pure, perfect shade of silver that it can't possibly exist in nature.

He's beautiful and completely alien. It was impossible to tell his age, as he looks neither old nor young. But the magyk that follows in his wake burns, leaving me dizzy for at least half an hour. Amalia doesn't fare any better. She has to sit on the floor, head against her knees, after how dizzy the magyk made her.

If the Archmage is a full-blood elf, and they have more Elves here, then maybe Amalia's right. I've never felt this magyk before.

It's been hours, but the Archmage finally leaves as we overhear that Dyana's arm is as healed as it's going to get. I feel Amalia ready to charge in there but I hold up a hand, forcing her to wait until the Archmage passes us again. The dizziness returns and we take a moment to steady ourselves.

"Gods, that's awful," Amalia mutters.

I snort, "That's Elves for you."

"Their magyk is so...heavy."

I just hum, knowing what she means. We walk back into the healing room since the coast is clear but Amalia pauses, looking my way for a moment.

"Thank you. For what you did today." She sighs, wiping her face with a blood-stained, dirty hand, "I still don't trust you though."

I just watch her as she inspects some invisible piece of lint on her pants.

"When I care about something, I protect it. I love her, Amalia. Regardless of her feelings for me, I will always protect her."

She meets my gaze finally and nods, perhaps finally seeing that I actually do care about Dyana. Amalia continues into the room and I follow, saying nothing.

We greet a sleepy Dyana, whose arm looks much better, even covered in a web of light brown and pink scars.

For a moment, she looks happy to see me.

But there's that moment again. That *pause.*

It takes all of my strength not to fall to the floor and sob as she turns away to look at Amalia, her face breaking into the widest, brightest smile I've seen in many days. It's the smile of seeing a loved one, of seeing family.

We reunite, but I feel like an outsider, prying on a private moment between family. Despite the fact that I just put my life on the line for the woman I love.

A woman who doesn't love me in return.

This, I think, is the worst wound of all.

CHAPTER 54
DYANA

"You've got to be kidding me," I groan, staring at the Arena filled with rivers of boiling hot lava. "How the hell do they have lava?"

Amalia clicks her tongue, answering in my mind instead of out loud, *"They have lava because they have Elves. Elemental conjuring is one of the most advanced types of magyk there is. Only a few Dragons can create lava. The Dark Magyk this must have taken..."*

"CANDIDATES!" the announcer screams. **"WELCOME TO ROUND THREE!"**

The crowd goes wild, screaming and cheering.

Then the lava moves.

Amalia rolls back as if something hit her in the chest. My jaw drops. Several others gasp.

"Th-they..." I stutter.

Amalia stops me, *"They chained Dragons in the fucking lava. They're...torturing them."*

She stops, cocking her head like she's hearing something in the distance. Ah, Os must be in her head again. Her eyes glaze over in a particular way whenever they speak in each other's minds. She snarls, kicking the Arena sand.

Guess that talk didn't go so well.

"How the hell do we get through this?" I ask.

Amalia glares at the High Council's private box. The announcer speaks up, "Candidates, today's round is simple. Make it across the lava and you move to the next round. But beware, the lava BITES!" The crowd laughs and cheers.

"BEGIN!"

We all jump. There was no countdown this time. Fuck!

"Follow me!" Ama shouts. She unsheathes both of her swords and I take off after her. Footsteps sound next to me and I see Mirielle approach.

"We have to jump!" Amalia shouts, Mirielle nods and we approach the first river of lava. There are small rocks in the middle, but as we get closer, something bubbles underneath the magma. A tail emerges, half burned but still spikey and dangerous.

Then the head appears and the Dragon snaps at us, causing drops of lava to splatter the ground. We avoid getting burnt narrowly as Ama veers right, finding a different set of rocks.

But there's a Dragon there too.

"Ama..." I whisper in my head.

"No!" she screams. *"No. I'll...distract them. You two cross. Then you distract and I cross. Got it? Easy."*

I exhale hard. Mirielle however speaks up, *"I know you don't want to, but we have to kill them. They're positioned near each rock crossing, Amalia. The only way to get across is by killing at least one."*

Amalia snarls again, *"You will ONLY kill a Dragon if it's the last fucking resort. Do you understand me?"* She gets in Mirielle's face, shoving the taller woman. *"We only hurt the Dragons as a last godsdamn resort. We're trying my way first."*

Mirielle scoffs, but nods. Frustrated, Ama cracks her neck and takes off, unsheathing both of her swords a few meters away. She gets closer to the river of lava, but farther away from the rock crossing. Then her eyes glaze over again as her pupils dilate.

There's a huge bubble and an angry surge as the Dragon screeches, lunging at her. The chains hold it back but it has enough length to land nearly on top of her.

"GO!" Mirielle shouts at me and I jump, realizing I need to move. We race across the rock path, avoiding the bursts of hot steam and splattered lava.

When we get across, Mirielle unsheathes her large staff, splitting it in half.

"Our turn," she says, smiling a little. I unhook my ax, gripping it with both hands.

"What's your pla—"

"HEY! DRAGON! COME OVER HERE, YOU USELESS SHIT WORM!" Mirielle screams, stomping on the ground in front of her. The Dragon pauses its attack on Amalia, whipping its burnt head around.

Oh Gods. One of its eyes has burst, and the socket is full of burnt, oozing skin. Half of its scales are peeling away from its body. One talon is shriveled up, the claws permanently bent inward.

The Dragon screams and I scream too as it jumps at us, flapping useless stubs that used to be its wings. Just as it lands, Mirielle shoves me out of the way and we hit the sand hard, rolling.

"MOVE!" Amalia screams, running past us as she crosses the rock path. She yanks me up as Mirielle uses her core to flip to standing, following behind as we abandon the first Dragon and try to cross the next river.

We repeat the same song and dance for the second river, but when we approach the third, we're all drained. The last Dragon was bigger than the first one, and that isn't a trend that bodes well.

The screams of other candidates sound behind us at the second river.

I watch as a few fall in and are melted alive.

I also see a few get eaten by the Dragons. The sound of those fangs cracking human bone and the squelch of organs being punctured will haunt me until the day I die—which very well might be today.

We approach the third river, only two candidates behind us, when things change.

A woman from the Westlands lunges at Amalia, knocking her to the ground. I go to attack when a male runs at me. Mirielle jumps in between us, parrying his blows. Which is when I notice the giant Dragon emerging from the third river.

Whatever color it used to be, it's now burnt to a black crisp. Both eyes are gone and its tongue is cut off. Fae symbols are painted on its extremely large fangs. I step forward as Mirielle bumps me. That single step in the sand gets the attention of the Dragon. It roars and we all freeze.

"Gods."

"Fucking kill it!" the male screams, running headfirst towards it. Then he begins to run away when the Dragon moves much faster than a dying creature should be able to. It jumps and a wave of lava explodes at the male. He's not fast enough, the lava melts his feet with perfect timing for the Dragon to bite his head off, swallowing it whole.

The Westland female hurls, hyperventilating.

"This one will be harder to distract," Amalia says in our heads. I can tell it's with resentment that she asks, *"Mirielle, help me distract it. Dy, you and the other woman get across. If she tries anything, push her in."*

My heart stops. *"Push her in?"* I ask weakly.

"GO!" she screams and I grab the woman's arm as Mirielle and Ama run towards the Dragon. Then they start sprinting, veering sharply to the left. The Dragon follows the sound of their footsteps, tracking them. It lunges and they both speed up, narrowly avoiding it.

That's when I remember I have to move.

"Let's go!" I scream at the Westlands woman, dragging her along as we race across the final rock path. Just as we're halfway across, the Dragon goes still. Cocking its head as it turns back towards us, scenting our fear, hearing our panting breath.

Amalia and Mirielle begin screaming and pelting it with rocks, but it doesn't stop. It continues towards us, waves of lava billowing out with every push through that burning magma.

"Run!" I shove the Westlands woman in front of me, pushing her as we approach the end. The line where the other candidates await is so close. Just two more rocks. We jump, the distance between the rock steps becoming wider and wider. At the last one, the Westlands woman pauses, turning to me. She goes to push me but loses her balance.

I try to catch her but I'm not fast enough. I watch as the Dragon snaps up her screaming form.

Something hits me, and I realize it's an arm. The Dragon's head is inches away from my face when it jerks, sending me flying. I hit a large rock step and land on my knees, almost tumbling into the lava.

I stop, panting heavily. The hot air burns my arms, irritating the new scar tissue. I hiss and jump up as the Dragon screams.

The sound is like knives to my eardrums.

It's mad. Probably because Mirielle just cut its tail off based on the shriveled organ she now waves around, drawing it back to her.

Amalia just stands there, watching it.

Mirielle shouts at her but I can't make it out.

I have to move. I jump the remaining rock steps and make it across, falling to my knees at the finish line.

Turning, I watch in horror as the Dragon leaps at Amalia—and she doesn't move.

"AMA, NO!" I scream in her head.

With a scream rivaling the Dragon itself, Amalia takes a step to the side, just as the Dragon lands, she slices its throat, her two blades coated in steaming blood. She screams again, and I swear for a moment, the ground trembles.

She and Mirielle walk—not run, but walk—slowly with fury in their eyes.

Which is when another, smaller Dragon jumps out of the lava and tackles Mirielle, sending her flying.

Her leg hits the lava and I stop breathing, but Ama is a blur, catching Mirielle's arms just in time to pull her up and out. I have no fucking clue how she did it but Ama grabs Mirielle and hauls her over her shoulder, carrying her over the final rock step. The small Dragon leaps again and Amalia just raises a single sword and shoves it back, stabbing it in the throat. The Dragon falls back into the lava, dead.

The crowd goes wild. But Mirielle's leg is—

Gods. It's destroyed.

Despite everything that's happened, seeing her like this makes me want to scream. I kneel down, looking over her.

"It's okay, it's going to be okay. We'll get you to the healers," I say frantically. There's no answer. "Gods, we have to get her to the healer, or she will die."

"She will be okay," Ama whispers in my head. *"She might lose her leg, but she'll be okay. She's demis."*

Mother, please help this damn announcer to finish talking. Mirielle has to be okay.

Please be okay.

CHAPTER 55
AMALIA

"Come on, Mirielle. We're almost there." We pant heavily, hauling an unconscious Mirielle between us as we try to make it to the healers.

My ankle throbs. I didn't even feel when I twisted it, but each step we get closer to the Healers is increasingly miserable.

Dyana's scarred arm is fine, miraculously, but she took a brutal hit to her right kneecap. In the moment, I doubt she even noticed. Adrenaline does that. Non-life-threatening injuries get put to the side. But she's starting to limp a little.

My chest plate is barely hanging on, and a sharp edge digs into my collarbone painfully. Mirielle moans, passing out again as she becomes dead weight in our arms. The lava burned away most of the skin on her lower leg, revealing raw muscle.

A healer drags Mirielle from our arms as we stumble into the doorway. They shove a wooden stick between her teeth as they begin to poke and prod at her leg. Even with the muffling, her screams are deafening.

"Can't they work faster?" Dyana begs, her hands trembling as she watches Mirielle writhe in pain.

One of the healers snaps at us, "Sit. Your knee is in no shape to be walking."

Dyana grumbles but sits, dirt and blood smeared all over her face. A healer starts fussing over her, looking at that knee. I pause and glance around the room. Every other remaining candidate is here. We all sport rough injuries.

I send my magyk to Dyana, connecting with her easily.

"She'll heal fast."

She sighs, and I feel the fear in her voice. *"Right. I just... Gods, her leg."*

"I know. But look at what the healers did for your arm. They will help her, and soon, she won't be in pain."

What else is there to say? I can't make the healers move faster. Dyana just closes her eyes as she limps over to a chair closer to Mirielle, despite the healer yelling at her to sit down. Dyana plops down in the chair and the healer follows, checking over her knee again. She winces but just grits through the pain.

I suppose today is a good day since the Archmage has yet to make an appearance.

"You're in pain," Remus says, his voice rolling through my mind.

I sigh, although inwardly, I relax at the sound of his voice, *"I'm fine. It's just sore."*

"None of that, little liar," he replies, and I growl at the nickname. I feel him smile. *"You are in pain. I can feel it. Let me heal it for you."*

Heat flashes through my body at the thought. I glance around. Dyana's already almost done with the healers, her eyes only on Mirielle, who has been transferred to a bed.

"Dy, are you good here? Re—" I pause, realizing he might not want his true name shared. *"Os wants to look at my ankle. If you want me to wait, I will."*

"You know you'll have to walk to get there, right? Why not just fix it here?" Dyana is nothing if not horribly observant.

"Maybe I want to see him." That's the best I can come up with.

Despite it all, Dyana pokes fun at me. *"Knew you'd admit it eventually."*

"Gods." I sigh, but I know she's forcing it. We both are.

"I love you too. Now get out of here. I'm staying with Mirielle until she wakes up."

I grit through the pain as I slowly make my way to Remus. His mind brushes against mine as our magyk connects, and the pain eases. The throbbing in my ankle cools and it's a relief to take a step without a twinge of pain running up my entire leg.

"Since when can you heal me from a distance?" I ask.

He's quiet for a moment, "I think you and Nyall are both right. Whatever he did to the land, whatever magyk he fed it...my warding is getting weaker by the day." I quicken my pace as Remus enters my thoughts again. "It's also you, my spark. Your magyk, it's getting stronger."

He's right. I haven't been able to use my magyk this often, well...ever.

"It's also us, Amalia. The more you...accept me, the stronger our magyk will become."

"Letting you drink my blood and making me come started the familiar bond?" I ask.

Remus laughs, *"The bond isn't there. Don't worry, A gahrá. Think of familiar magyk as...symbiotic. Like a mushroom and a tree. Our magyk is meant to be used together. The closer we get, the stronger it will become."*

"Just, not as strong as it could become," I mutter.

He huffs, *"Yes. And if we stopped spending time together, the...effects would fade, over time."*

My heart skips a beat.

I ignore it, starting to climb the steps to the floor below us where Remus's quarters are.

"You hesitated a second too long with that right parry today. And you were distracted. Where was your focus?"

I roll my eyes, *"'I'm so glad you're alive, Amalia. You did such a good job staying alive, Amalia'."*

Remus smiles at my mocking, *"Do you need me to tell you I'm impressed, A gahrá? I always am. But the rounds are only going to get harder from here. My goal is to get you out of there alive, which means you need to listen instead of getting irritated when I point out your mistakes. You can't afford to miss anything."*

I sigh, annoyed, but he's right. He knows it and I know it.

"Would it make you feel better to know that watching you fight always makes me hard? That whole time, all I could think about was you riding me, covered in my blood. I didn't give a fuck about anything else; just you. There is only you."

I stumble and almost faceplant into the stone steps. He just chuckles as I right myself, pressing a hand over my racing heart. The image of our naked bodies tangled together invades my mind and my legs nearly give out. It's a struggle to force myself to continue up the rest of the stairs. I quickly walk the rest of the way to his room, needing nothing more than to see his face.

"Come here, my spark—let me heal you." His voice is low and dark. I know the frustration comes out of fear of getting hurt.

Then he does something with his magyk that makes it feel as if his tongue swipes right between my legs and I stumble, catching myself on the wall. His low, smokey chuckle makes my skin tingle.

"You play dirty, Ostia," I say, trying to sound firm but it comes out as a moan.

Remus chuckles, *"Hurry up, and I'll show you just how dirty I can play...if you can get your legs to work."*

I flick him with my mind and picture giving him my middle finger, but he just laughs.

Then, that vibrating purr begins spreading through my chest, straight down to my core.

Despite all of the death and horror happening around me, Remus has somehow managed to bring a bit of lightness to my heart. The feeling fills a part of me that's long since been empty and hollow.

Not much makes me feel hope anymore.

But as he greets me, gold eyes warm as a soft smile appears on his scarred face, I think maybe this is what hope feels like. It's fleeting and brief, but for a single moment, it's there. That maybe we can win, and maybe there is something between us. The next moment, Remus is in front, gently picking me up and carrying me to his bed. He sets me down so softly my heart clenches.

Remus carefully peels off my boots and socks, cupping my ankle and healing me with reverent hands, I realize this isn't hope.

I think, perhaps, this is *love.*

We have one day in between bouts, so I woke up with plans to head to the barn and take Taran out for a ride. Spend some time grooming him and maybe bring my book out to read a bit. Just as long as I don't fall asleep, since that's not allowed.

Dyana is spending the day with Mirielle, shockingly. She blushed like wild when she told me, but I withheld any snide remarks about being careful. She already knows my thoughts on the matter. They're not exactly back together and not everything is forgiven, but with Mirielle saving her life multiple times? Yeah, anyone with a heart would be swayed by that.

I hate that I still don't trust her fully. I know I should—she saved my best friend's life. But I'm still suspicious.

I round the corner to the barn after making the long climb up to the surface. The sky is gloomy and gray as I emerge into the wide-open courtyard. The fresh air assaults my senses, and for the first time in many days, I feel like I can actually breathe.

But there's...*hmm.*

I pause and sniff, looking around. There's a strange feeling in the air. A strange smell. But I can't place it. Various fae and demis mill about, with the noise of the city in the distance. Nothing new there. Nothing abnormal. But there's a sense of wrongness about the day, a pit in the bottom of my stomach that gets heavier by the second.

Something is wrong, but I can't tell what.

I approach the barn, ready for that familiar nicker.

But it never comes.

That pit in my stomach gets heavier as my heart begins thudding in my ears. I take careful steps, approaching the window of his stall.

There's no gray and black head leaning out to say hello.

Something is wrong. My chest tightens painfully as fear floods me, and my hands begin to shake. On trembling legs, I step into the barn.

"A gahrá, what's wrong? I feel your fear." Remus asks.

I can't respond. I step into the barn, peeking into his stall.

His empty stall.

Where is my horse?

Where is my friend?

My body is slower than my mind—I'm already thinking of dozens of reasons why he wouldn't be in here. Maybe someone else took him out for a ride.

Yes, that's it. He'll be back.

They'll bring him back.

But something tells me to keep walking.

Some inner voice makes my legs move as I slowly move through the barn, passing other horses along the way.

But none of them are Taran.

"Taran, where are you?" I whisper into the darkness of my mind, searching for his spark. A dim, green light appears in the distance. It's weak and barely noticeable, but I pull as much magyk as I can and stretch.

"Taran? Where are you?" I ask, trying not to sound frantic.

But there is no response. I reach out, brushing my magyk against his dim spark.

I fall flat on my ass, landing on my tailbone. But that pain is nothing compared to the pain I feel inside Taran's mind.

"H-hel-p. Hel-p me."

Gods, no. Please no.

My entire body breaks out in a red flush as my skin begins to heat. But I ignore my magyk.

"I'm coming. Where are you, Taran? Gods, tell me where you are!"

But he says nothing else.

I take another step and another, pushing myself to move faster but shaking with fear.

"It's okay, Taran. It's going to be okay. I'm coming. I will find you, I swear." I repeat the panicked words over and over, feeding him magyk, trying to dull whatever is causing the pain.

It doesn't help—he's just a maelstrom of panic and pain.

Then, a sound.

No.

No!

NO. NO. NO. NO. NO!

I know that sound.

I know it. I've heard it before, in my dreams.

I can't feel my legs as I make it to the end of the barn, listening...as something is butchered.

Some sort of broken sound falls from my lips as I turn to look into the final stall.

Everything stops.

No thought exists in my head.

No air in my lungs.

My heart does not race, my blood stands still as I fall to the ground, knees hitting a puddle of sticky, dark red blood. Taran's blood.

There, strung upside down from hooks in his stomach and neck, hooves tied together, is Taran.

There, holding a sharp knife, stands the fae skinning him, separating skin and fur from muscle.

The bald fae puts a sharp knife down as he slices off Taran's tail at the bone, making more red blood gush down to the ground, covering Taran in splotches of crimson.

The fae laughs as Taran writhes.

Taran is—

Gods, no.

Taran's still alive.

I'm not a good person.

I never have been. For a while, I wondered if the Mother would forgive me for what I've done.

For all the lives I've taken.

But the Gods are gone. The Mother isn't here; I am.

Distantly I'm aware someone is screaming.

It takes a moment to realize that person is me.

Taran's voice plays over and over in my head as I roar so loud I wonder if for a moment I could tear the heavens from the sky.

I'm on top of the fae who was skinning him. I don't know how I got here.

The only thing I know is he has to die.

In the back of my mind, I hear Remus screaming, but nothing under the two suns will stop me now.

Several other fae hands grab me, trying to pry me off, but I continue screaming before biting off one of their fingers like a carrot. It rips clean off with a hard crunch as blood and flesh fill my mouth. More screams now as hands pull my legs. I slam the back of my head into them, cracking their nose with my hard skull and managing to get free.

I do not escape or run away. Instead, I crawl back to the fae who was slicing Taran to pieces, straddling him. He writhes where I've already cut him, bleeding from multiple wounds.

There is no sound, nothing in my mind, as I bring my hands up, cupping his head and slamming it back into the ground. His arms slap me but I just step on one, breaking his elbow. Then the other, I snap backward until the humerus bone breaks through his skin.

I lean down, screaming in his face as I reach up, pressing my thumbs into his eyes. There's a wet pop as the soft tissue collapses under my pressure, but I continue, pushing until I punch both thumbs into his skull.

His body twitches before going still as he bleeds out. And still, I scream.

More hands grab me, and I lash out, hitting and scratching and biting anyone that comes near me.

But I feel nothing—just a hollow void deep inside that wants to swallow me whole.

What more can the fae take from me?

How much is enough?

How much do I have to give?

Arms pull me back as guards swarm. I don't even notice, I just hit anything I come in contact with. A noise breaks through the ringing in my ears.

A single noise. So small, I barely notice it.

But Taran is still alive. In slow motion, I turn, wiggling free of the guards before crawling over to him. Hands pull me away but I reach with all of my might, trying to touch Taran. I kick out, and the hands let go. I scramble up, using the dagger in my boots to slice the rope attached to the hooks. He hits the ground hard, but with my magyk, I take the pain.

I clasp his bloody face with equally bloody hands, bits of flesh and skin stuck under my nails face in mine.

"I love you, friend. I love you so much. Thank you for giving me something to look forward to everyday. Thank you for protecting me. Thank you," I sputter, sobbing inside and out.

When his brown eyes meet mine, I break, crying out. *"F-fri-friennd. All-ways."* he says, gasping for breath, so, so weak. I cry out again, unable to take it.

"Rest now, Friend. I'm here. I'll always be here," I whisper between sobs, gently taking my magyk and brushing it against him, sending him love and joy and sorrow, as I snuff his light out forever. "Always."

His heart stops beating, and I sit back, no sound but the ringing in my ears as I tilt my head back and scream.

A sharp hit to the temple sends everything to black. I welcome the dark pool of my mind with open arms, and all the while, those iron walls deep within me begin to melt.

I don't want to wake up.

I'm aware enough that I know I'm in some kind of dungeon, based on the dark, moldy smell and the dampness to the air. Or it could be the sound and smell of unwashed prisoners moaning.

I hope they leave me here.

What's the point of saving everyone if I have to watch everything I love die before my very eyes?

I pinch myself, the blood now dry on my hands. The pain does nothing, so I simply curl into a tighter ball, tucking myself into the corner of the dark holding cell.

There is no sound, no distant footsteps. One second, there's no one there; the next, Crown Prince Nyall Drayven seems to step from the shadows, appearing a few meters away, just behind the bars.

"You can stop pretending to be asleep. I know you're awake." Prince Nyall Drayven's voice is a sensual whisper in my mind.

"Go away, Nyall." There is no fight behind my words and his eyes grow concerned.

"You're damn lucky I intercepted the soldier who was on his way to tell my Father about this. Still, we must be quick."

"Leave me here. Let me die." I croak.

I feel the Prince's worry, *"You're coming with me whether you like it or not, horse girl."*

I'm up before he can take a single breath, my hands around his throat, through the bars of the stall. He doesn't move but I tighten my grip.

"Don't. Ever. Call me that again," I say, spit hitting his face. I'm panting and frantic. Suddenly feeling claustrophobic in the dank dungeon.

I drop my hands and push away from him but he grabs my arm, stopping me.

The Prince is dressed in all black, almost invisible. His amber eye, the darker one, looks split through with silver as it glows in the light. Then a ring around his green eye appears, glowing as well.

He's terrifying and beautiful. And in this moment, I don't care. He could be a five-headed monster with tentacles and I wouldn't care.

There is nothing in my heart left to care.

There is only pain.

"What happened?" Nyall bends down and wipes my face gently, catching my tears with his thumb. *"Amalia, what the fuck happened? The guards were talking about some girl who snapped and attacked everyone."*

I can't say the words, so instead, I spear my magyk at his mind, shattering his wards. He steps back, flinching, but I'm already shoving the memory into his head.

I can't tell him what happened, but I can show him.

"Oh, Amalia..." I sob silently as I watch horror overtake him. *I'm so sorry, sweetheart. I'm so, so fucking sorry.*

Nyall makes a movement with his hand before stepping right through the bars as if they were invisible, but there's no time to process that as he wraps his arms around me, ignoring the fact that I'm covered in blood,vomit, and Gods knows what else.

"He loved you, Amalia. Know that. I've watched hate towards animals, and I've watched animals hate. Taran trusted you—a gift of which few people ever are lucky enough to receive." The tears fall openly but I stay silent as the numb void inside me grows larger still.

"Go away, Nyall," I say, but there's no force behind the words.

Nyall pulls back and I blink, startled. His green eye is shot through with glowing white and silver magyk, and his amber one is gleaming like freshly polished bronze. But he just scoops me up, easily carrying me with one arm around my waist, which unfortunately leaves my front tightly pressed to him. The crown prince then makes a motion with his free hand, weaving magyk that begins to appear in his palm.

"I'm not leaving you, Amalia." The gentle tone almost breaks me. His hands land on my waist as he leans down, murmuring into my ear, "Hold your breath, sweetheart."

That's all the warning I get before the world blurs, and my stomach turns upside down. His spell shifted us right out of the Black Citadel dungeons and into the gardens outside the fortress.

My legs crumble as dizziness overtakes me but Nyall just hauls me forward as we disappear into the labyrinth of gray flowers.

"Why are you doing this, Nyall?" I ask again as he puts his arm around my waist. Everything hurts but I welcome the pain. It sharpens me.

He shrugs, *"Maybe I'm not the monster you want me to be, Amalia. Do I need a reason?"*

"The fae love to deceive," I cough.

Nyall sighs, "Gods, you're maddening." He reaches up, running a hand through his pale blonde hair. "Fine, Amalia. You win. I am doing this because every fucking time I look at you, I see the pain in your eyes, and it breaks me because it..." He takes a deep breath, "because it reminds me so much of my own pain. I know what it is to feel alone, Amalia. I know what it is to wonder if there's any point in going forward at all."

I look away, uncomfortable at how much he sees.

We come to a stop as he hauls me around a corner quickly, hiding in the shadow. "Who knows? Maybe all of this is for nothing, and no difference will be made. Maybe we're not meant to make it out of this and our time is simply through. But I'm sick of looking into the faces of my people and seeing their misery. I don't care if this kills me, Amalia. But if it gives anyone even the smallest chance of happiness, of hope for the future, then the pain is worth it."

He holds up his black veined hand. "If my death is what it takes to get there, then I welcome it. In that, we are alike."

I know it's cruel to say but I can't help it when my mouth opens, "It's a fool's plan, Prince."

Prince Nyall just shrugs. "I don't care. The only thing I care about is stopping them. Can you honestly say you're content to just sit back and watch the world burn, Amalia? Where is the line in the sand? Where is it? Because I don't see one. There is no line to the fae. And that's the fucking problem here. There is nothing they won't do to achieve their goal."

I shake him off, walking on my own despite my aching body, but his words replay in my head on a loop. I'm halfway past the barn before I realize what I'm doing and come to a stop. Nyall looks around, worried we'll be seen. But I can't take my eyes off the barn.

Where is the line in the sand?

When will it be enough?

How much must I continue to sacrifice until there's no one left? Not even me.

"Come on, we need to go before we're seen," Nyall says, placing his ring-covered hand on my lower back. It's so gentle I almost break all over again, but he just guides me to a different, hidden stairway, and we make our way to Remus's room.

"He's the bravest male I've ever known. Os, I mean," Nyall says, hesitant. *"He's a damn grouch and old as dirt...but he's a good male."*

"I never asked your opinion," I reply coldly. Nyall just smiles, before barging right into Remus's room.

Nyall is yanked away from me as Remus throws him across the room.

Remus punches Nyall, giving the Prince a nosebleed. The blood reminds me of Taran. A pained noise falls from my lips. One second, Remus has Nyall in a chokehold. The next, both are at my side.

Remus grabs my face between his hands, cradling my cheeks gently. "A gahrá, tell me you're okay. Did he hurt you?"

"Did you not see?" I ask, my voice scratchy and low.

Remus shakes his head, *"You...blocked me. Don't do that again, A gahrá. Not when you're in pain."*

Whatever he sees on my face makes him go still.

"Amalia, talk to me. What happened? Why were you in such pain?" he murmurs, cupping my face.

"Oh my Gods, Ama, are you okay? Where have you been? You didn't show up for dinner and I got so worried!" Dyana opens the door from the bathroom to see me standing there. She almost knocks me over as she wraps me in a tight hug.

"You smell awful. You look awful too." Dyana pulls back, curling her nose. But she sees what's behind my eyes and goes still, just as Remus had.

"He's gone," I say numbly.

"What?" Dyana asks, taken aback. "Who is gone, Ama?"

"Taran is gone," Remus answers for me. I feel him in my memories, sifting through what happened. I open myself to him, allowing him to see.

Dyana's hand flies up to cover her mouth, "Oh, Gods."

"They skinned him alive. Tortured him..." My voice is detached as I replay the events but it's muffled as Dyana wraps her arms around me again. I almost shatter completely but push her back gently.

I can't take the comfort.

I don't need comfort.

I need pain.

I need it to *hurt*.

At that moment, Mirielle enters, "Dyana, I haven't seen her anywhere—oh good, you're back." Mirielle pauses, laughing nervously, "Why does everyone look like someone died?"

Remus growls, but I cut him off as I turn and face the empty side of the room, unable to see the look on their faces as Dyana explains what happened.

Everyone is silent for a while as the scene in the barn replays in my head.

"It's enough," I say finally.

I meet Mirielle's confused gaze. A few moments later and her eyes soften, surprise filling them along with a horrible, sad understanding. She nods.

"It's enough," I repeat. I turn, facing Nyall. "I will help you, Prince. On one condition." Everyone goes still as I turn and face them, numbness and rage burning equally bright inside my heart.

"A gahrá, are you sure?"

"Yes."

Nyall looks at me, oddly serious. "What's your condition, Roth?"

"Your father's life is mine. It will be my swords he falls upon, my eyes he sees when he takes his last breath. He is mine."

Everyone goes quiet. Dyana's hands fly up to cover her mouth.

"Ama, you...you really want to help them?" Dyana asks tentatively. I just hold up a hand.

"It's enough, Dyana. I've had enough."

Nyall glares at me, "You forget yourself, Arkaydian. Achan's life is mine to take." I blink, fury rising, but Nyall surprises me when he continues. "But, I'm always willing to share. When the time comes, we will be the ones to finish it. If that works for you—"

"Done." I say. He nods, unsurprised.

"If Amalia is in," Remus grumbles, "then I am as well. But test me, Prince, and I'll clean my teeth with your bones."

Nyall just smiles, daring Remus to challenge him. Gods, those two are a bad combination. "On that note, welcome to the Rebellion. Now let's go over the plan..."

Oh, shit.

"I wasn't done. I need one more favor."

Nyall pauses and looks back at me, sighing. "Your beast looks far too nervous for this to be anything good."

"Listen, you want our help, this is what we need. We're putting our lives on the line for you, Prince. The least you could do is listen."

Nyall nods, grunting.

"If we're gonna help you with this, there's something I need your help with in return."

"Naturally," Nyall replies dryly. "What is it?"

"I recognize that you must have some long set plan in place," I start. "But that plan will have to change, because we're going to free the Dragons." Dyana, Mirielle, and Nyall all turn to look at me, eyes wide. "All of them."

Dyana blinks, "I'm sorry, what?"

Mirielle just watches, eyes wide. "And when is this happening?"

More blinking, but Nyall just watches me with sudden curiosity.

"The final bout. I believe you mentioned something about a distraction, Prince. Well, there's your distraction. I'll make sure the High Council's attention is on me and buy you the time you need if you help us break the warding on the Dragon stalls, allowing them to escape."

"Oh my Gods, you're insane!" Mirielle says. I ignore her. Dyana gazes at me, eyes wide. But she's not surprised. Just processing.

"That's...certainly a distraction," Nyall says, but I see his thoughts racing as he recalculates, adjusting his plan as we speak. "How are we supposedly doing this?" he asks, rubbing his temple like he's already regretting this.

I sit in one of the chairs by the fire, wincing at the pain. Without a word, Remus follows and stands at my back, bringing a hot hand to my shoulder. Magyk washes over me as my wounds bind together, fading into bruises.

I glance at him. *"Your magyk is getting stronger."*

He nods subtly.

I exhale hard and turn to look at Nyall, "I bring a message, Princeling. From the Crimson Queen."

Everything about the Prince goes from relaxed to still in a single second as everyone except Remus explodes, shouting questions at me all at once.

I hold up a hand and it goes quiet. "She said the answer you're looking for lies with Lazarus. No clue what it means, but I'm assuming you do."

Nyall stands, pacing in front of the fire, "Is that all?"

I shrug, "I told you everything she said. But she did say if you agree, she'll tell you more." Nyall rubs his jaw and thinks. I can see his thoughts moving quickly behind his eyes.

"Well, I guess we're saving all of the Dragons in a week." He laughs in disbelief, eyes wide.

Mirielle balks, "Nyall, you can't be serious!"

Dyana glares at her.

I cluck my tongue in disappointment. "Who's the coward now?"

Her light eyes flare in anger as her cheeks flush. Dyana looks pissed at me for saying anything, but I regret nothing.

"You're damn right I'm serious. It's the perfect distraction. Everyone in the entire city will be packed into the Arena, and all of their eyes will be on the Gauntlet."

"It's suicide. Now you'll only help if we pull off something impossible?" Mirielle sputters.

"Look around, Mirielle. This has always been a suicide mission. You wanted to be a hero. You wanted to make a difference. Well, here it is. Here's your chance. Suck it up and be the hero."

Remus blinks, and lust fills his gaze as he watches me with admiration. Nyall huffs a light laugh too. Dyana just looks at me with wide eyes.

"Fine, but if this was a foolhardy plan before, it's even more impossible now. But yeah, fine. Let's go free the freaking Dragons," Mirielle says, her tone one of disbelief and frustration.

Dyana is the first one to speak up, but even though we're surrounded by new allies, she speaks only to me.

"If we do this, there's no going back."

I know that look. I know what she means even though she doesn't say it.

I just nod,. "I know."

Her dark brown eyes mist as the tears begin to fall. "You've...you've thought about this? You really want to do this?"

"I have." I pause and inhale, her calming scent is all around me. "I need to do this. I've sat in the shadows long enough, Dy. I accept the consequences of this choice." Dyana inhales sharply and emotion fills her eyes.

She blinks tears away but nods, trusting me.

"But, Dy? Look at me." I walk over and go to grab her arms but realize I'd smear blood all over her, so I keep my arms at my sides. "You don't have to help us. I told you, I'll always keep you safe. I won't be mad if you don't want to be involved. The choice is your own."

"Of course, I'm helping, you idiot. Can't let you go off on your own now, can I? Who would break up all of the fights you 'accidentally' start when you 'look at someone the wrong way'?" She sniffles, pulling away from me with laughter in her eyes.

"I will guard her, Amalia. Nothing will get past me." Mirielle suddenly stands next to us, her gray eyes fierce. I wait for Dyana to protest but she nods lightly, eyes fraught.

"Fine. Now can somebody just freaking tell me how in the actual four hells we're going to same all of the Dragons?" Dyana forces her voice to sound brave, but I can feel the fear emanating from her.

There are many good reasons to be afraid of what we're about to do.

Time to make a plan. And pray to the Gods it works.

"I HAVE COME TO LEAD YOU
TO THE OTHER SHORE;
INTO ETERNAL DARKNESS;
INTO FIRE AND INTO ICE."

— DANTE ALIGHIERI, 1265-1321.
THE DIVINE COMEDY: INFERNO

SCAN FOR THE PT. 4
READING PLAYLIST

PART FOUR:

THE FEARED

CHAPTER 56
DYANA

Something changed when Amalia found Taran that day.

When she...snapped.

Her eyes are cold now, sapped of all life and color. Sometimes, I catch her staring at our dorm room ceiling in a daze.

She hasn't spoken since that night. Not out loud, at least. Even in our minds, she's unusually silent.

That feeling I used to get around the Dyre Wolves, that feeling of being on edge, as if one wrong move would result in violence—or death. That's the feeling I've had around Amalia since she arrived back from the Black Citadel dungeons covered in dried blood and dirt.

Mirielle is different, too. For once, she's the one on edge and anxious, while Amalia is now filled with ruthless surety.

We're all unraveling at the seams.

Amalia went to Os's room tonight. She's been spending more time with him.

I'm happy for her, but I'm scared of who she's becoming.

"Dyana? You here?" Mirielle's soft voice calls from the doorway. She slowly walks into the room as I shake my head and stand.

"Yeah."

"Are you alright?" she asks.

It's a stupid question. None of us are alright.

"Fine," I bite out.

Her brow quirks, and she steps into the room, her bright citrus scent immediately surrounding me.

"Liar," she murmurs, "your scent changed, and I can hear your heart racing.

My cheeks flush, "That's cheating."

She huffs a laugh, but her eyes are hollow. "I suppose you're right."

Mirielle takes a few more steps and sits at the end of my bed, motioning for me to join her. I click my tongue in acquiescence and sit, the bed dipping under my weight.

"Nothing is alright though, is it?" My voice wavers. "Not really. I've heard the plans. But no one is saying how high the likelihood is of this all going completely, horribly wrong. And in the Gauntlet, something going wrong means you die, Mirielle. If anything goes wrong, we will all die."

I expect Mirielle to disagree, but she just tilts her head back, watching the pale stone ceiling for a moment.

Finally, she sighs. "You're right. There is no way we're all getting out of this alive."

I blink, taken aback. "You...you agree?"

Mirielle hums lightly, "Yes, I do." She turns to look at me, her green-gray eyes full of emotion. "I've lived a long time, Dyana. Long enough to understand and accept reality."

My thoughts spiral as the realization hits me. "You were never planning on surviving...were you?"

Mirielle looks at me, her eyes sad. "No, I wasn't."

Everything slows down as I process her words.

She never planned to live. She came here...planning to die.

"But," she continues, and I jump as her hand clasps mine, warm and soft. "That was before I met you, Dyana."

My chest tightens to a painful level as the walls close in. I look up at the ceiling; it's easier than looking at the pain in her face.

"For what it's worth," I say, my voice wobbly, "I don't want you to die."

Mirielle squeezes my hand tightly, "I don't want you to die, either."

She meets my gaze, and I see tears fall on her own cheeks.

"If the Mother truly decides my time is through, I'm glad I got the chance to know you, Dyana Arkos. You might think me a liar and a spy, but know this—not one second of my feelings for you has been anything but the truth. You didn't even notice, but I saw you on the first day before we met."

"You did?" I ask, surprised.

She just chuckles. "I did. Your cheeks were smeared with dirt, and your hair looked like a bird's nest." My jaw drops. "But your beautiful brown eyes burned with life. Passionate, joyous life, even despite our horrible situation. You are a light in this dark and awful world; you are a light, my light, and my heart is yours."

We sit there, hands clasped, looking into each other's eyes. My heart is being pulled in every different direction, and there is no clear path forward. But Mirielle just waits, watching me with understanding and regret. The candlelight in the room flickers against her pale skin, turning her red hair alight. Despite her wild appearance, a calm certainty sits within her.

Before I can second guess why it's a bad idea, I scoot over, close enough I can lean my head on her shoulder.

Mirielle shudders, letting out a ragged breath as she wraps one arm around my shoulders, tucking me in next to her.

"I'm still mad," I whisper.

Mirielle is quiet for a moment, "I know."

Be brave, Dyana.

Be brave and live.

I take a deep breath, "Well then, since we're all about to die, you might as well kiss me because I—"

Mirielle's lips cut me off, pressing gently against mine. I'm surrounded by her scent as her hair tickles my cheek. She cups my cheeks with her gentle hands, pressing soft kisses to my jawline.

But I need more, so I drag her back to my face and she laughs.

Then she takes my lower lip between her own and sucks.

Clothes quickly disappear as we fall into each other. I will spend the rest of the evening memorizing Mirielle with my hands and lips. Memorizing her taste. The soft skin of her thighs. The stretch marks that decorate her hips and tummy.

She's so beautiful.

I use my hands and my tongue to worship her, and then only after she's quivering and covered in sweat do I finally stop.

But demis' endurance is apparently better than humans because she shocks me by blurring, flipping me beneath her and pulling my legs so I'm up on all fours, head pressed into the bedsheet, ass in the air right in front of her face.

She spreads my lips open and traces her tongue all the way from my slit to the puckered skin between my cheeks.

"Mirielle," I gasp. But that quickly becomes a deep moan as she buries her face between my legs.

She does not eat; she devours.

I take a bit of my own advice and ignore the doubt and anger within me, shutting off my worries as I lose myself to her touch.

"WELCOME, LADIES AND GENTLEMEN, TO THE GAUNTLET SEMI-FINALS!"

The announcer's voice deafens me as we wait for our cue in the Arena tunnels. Ireyna is at the front, Os at her side. It's so strange to see him as a trainer, now that I know all that I know. It's even stranger to see him play nice with Ireyna considering what a raging bitch she is.

"Listen up!" Os shouts. We all jerk to attention as he turns, facing us. "The semi-finals is different. Only eight of you remain, and only two can move forward."

My knees turn to jelly as the others gasp.

Amalia and Mirielle, however, are silent.

"I want you to look at the person standing next to you. Then at the person behind or in front of you," Ireyna says. We all glance around at each other. "Good. Now get ready to kill them."

My heart drops, nausea flooding my mouth with spit.

"No lines, no races. Your only objective is to survive—and to eliminate the competition." Os's voice is hard as he addresses us.

I ball my hands into tight fists to hide how badly I'm shaking. The announcer echoes in the background, telling the crowd something similar. They roar, cheering in excitement, demanding blood.

"Everything that's happened before this? Leave it here. When you walk onto the Arena sand, the only person you care about is you."

My gaze snaps to Amalia, whose face is hard as stone, her eyes burning with fury.

I hate this.

I know we've planned, but sweat still coats my palms as my heart begins to race.

Os nods, "Good luck."

Nobody speaks.

We all just stand there, all equally terrified and angry. Our towns start to get called. Despite the fact that Amalia and I are always last in line, things go quickly since only eight candidates remain.

Last night and this morning we went over the plan.

Over, and over, and over again.

First, we take Mirielle out, faking her death with one of Prince Nyall's spells—a detail which, even after literal hours of explanation, I'm still a little murky about.

Once Mirielle is disqualified, she will join Nyall and Os as Amalia and I advance to the finals, where we'll be the distraction. While we keep the High Council's eyes fixed upon us, then Os and Mirielle will lay the spell to open the Dragon's stalls as Nyall begins weaving the spell he referred to as a Lazarus configuration. Apparently, it's some super dangerous spell that could kill him, but it's what will drain the magyk from the High Council.

While Nyall prepares that, we'll distract the High Council until the spell is ready. At his signal, we'll set off the spell to open the Dragon stalls at the same time that Nyall drops the configuration. Guards will swarm but Os is going to haul ass back up here. After that, it's about ensuring the Prince's spell is fully completed. We'll cover for him as he finishes siphoning, and then, in theory, the High Council will die and the Dragons will escape. Nyall then takes over as temporary head of the Kingdom while they reform Ur Daoine back into a democracy.

In *theory*.

The reality is none of us have thought about what happens next.

The chances of this going well were zero to nil and Gods, my heart is racing. I'd already thrown up my breakfast this morning, right after Ama braided my hair. I took one look at her in her stained, battle-worn armor and broke down.

There can be no breaking down, now. I try and slow my heart but it's futile.

"TWYN FELLS!" the announcer booms. Our town is called, and we both take a deep breath in. Amalia raises the scarf over her face, leaving only her burning eyes visible. I let out a shaky breath and our eyes meet for a single moment.

One moment. One look.

We say everything that needs to be said, yet no words are exchanged.

"I am with you, Dy. Always." Amalia's whispered words send me back in time as we emerge onto the Arena sands.

"Always," I whisper back, hoping she can't hear the terror in my shaky voice.

Year 482 PBM

"You talk weird," I say, shivering. The fire is warming my bones, albeit slowly.

The girl made me strip naked, hanging my wet clothes a safe distance from the fire so they could dry. She draped me in various furs and deposited me next to the fire so I could get warm.

We went foraging earlier. Amalia showed me how to know which berries are poisonous and which can be eaten. The rich, sweet and sour flavor of the red berries was so satisfying. I'm surprisingly full from it. But the rain started to fall, just as we were heading back to the cave.

Like me, Amalia is nude. She wears nothing except for fur blankets draped around her body.

I ignore the scars.

Amalia looks at me again, her head cocked as she processes what I've said. She sniffs, hesitating, "It's...been a long time since I've had to..." she pauses, searching for the word, "socialize."

"How long?" I glance around at the large cave.

Her eyes narrow, "A long time."

"But you're only a few years older than me," I say, wrinkling my nose.

"More than a few," Amalia mutters. The large black Dyre Wolf at her side sneezes, but I get the feeling he's laughing. I lean forward, checking her face, but there is no sign of age upon her.

"How old are you?" I ask.

She shrugs, "Old enough."

"Then why are you out here, all alone?"

She blinks again, looking down at the wolf at her side. "Because it's the better option."

"Why?" I've wanted to ask her that for a while now. Amalia pauses, looking away. Virgyl licks her palm, bringing her back.

Sometimes I'll look at her and it's like she's somewhere else. Her eyes get all hazy and she'll sit in silence for hours, as if her mind is elsewhere.

Amalia struggles to form the words, "I...never considered it hiding. I survived. That's all there is. Survival. But I suppose you're right. I am hiding."

I scooch over, burying my hands into Virgyl's thick fur. The large Dyre Wolf licks my head and pushes his cold nose against my cheek, making me giggle.

Amalia stays quiet.

"Why do you hide?" I risk another question. She just bites her lips.

Amalia hesitates again, "I hide because I made a promise to someone I loved very much."

I blink, scrunching my forehead. "You promised to...stay hidden?

Amalia nods, "Yes."

I sniff, "Why?"

Amalia snorts, "You ask many questions, child."

"I'm not a baby, or a child!" I retort.

Amalia sighs, "You are to me."

I roll my eyes, "Fine. But why are you hiding? Why are you here all alone?"

There are some woofs in the distance as the rest of the pack gets comfortable, settling in various spots around the cave.

It's tiny, but a small smile appears on Amalia's face, "I'm not alone. Not truly."

I bite my lip, "You're the only person here, though. Nobody lives in the Ulster Wald. No one. Except you. Why?"

The cave is silent as Amalia grinds her teeth. She sighs again, getting down on the floor and curling up next to me, her head draped on Virgyl, using him as a furry pillow. Amalia tucks me into her arms, and I almost squeak in surprise. But the feeling of comfort and safety grows. Between the warmth of the fire and the peace filling me, I begin to fall asleep.

"I hide because out there...it's dangerous, Dyana. I hide because I do not wish to become someone else's weapon."

"A weapon?" I mumble. But she just shushes me.

"Go to sleep, Dyana."

I make a sleepy noise as the darkness crawls in. But I have enough energy left to get a few more words out, "You're not alone anymore."

In the background of my dreams, I'm distantly aware of the sound of someone crying.

NOW:

The crowd's roar deafens my thoughts as I look over, meeting Ama's gaze. She watches the High Council with intense focus, unwavering.

As we take our place on the Arena sands, the announcer gives some stupid speech about how lucky we all are to be here, how lucky the candidates are to be able to give their lives to the kingdom, blah blah blah.

I hopped lightly from foot to foot as the nervous energy runs through me. Amalia glares, motioning for me to stop, but I can't.

"CANDIDATES, THE LAST TWO OF YOU LEFT ALIVE WILL CON-TINUE ON TO THE FINALS!"

I inhale sharply, and he begins to countdown. I quickly reach back with a shaking hand, unsheath my short sword, and grab the ax secured to my right hip.

"FIVE!"

"FOUR!"

"THREE!"

"TWO!"

"ONE. BEGIN!" The doors open on the far walls of the arena and a wall of smoke rushes out.

Followed by not one, not two, but three Dragons.

No handlers, no presentation, nothing.

Just three Dragons, each the size of five horses, charging straight towards us with high-pitched roars.

One is gray and looks like it's covered in spikes, and another is bright yellow with pinkish wings. A blue Dragon follows them, with white whiskers dotting its face. But all of them are missing the gold chain around most of the Dragons' necks which means—

"FIRE!" someone shouts as Ama tackles me to the ground just in time to avoid being burned alive by a stream of fire from the gray Dragon. It jumps into the air, hovering above us. Guards poke at it from above, ensuring it doesn't go too high. The yellow Dragon gallops towards us. Screams echo as the first candidate loses their life.

A Northland candidate, a tall, bearded male, and two Southlanders charge the yellow Dragon, as the Eastlander goes for the blue.

"Shit, we need to kill the gray!" Mirielle shouts as she slides in the sand next to us, avoiding another shot of fire.

"No!" Amalia yells back.

Mirielle just shoots her a glare, "There's no other choice. It's us or them. Now, MOVE!"

Amalia makes a frustrated, broken noise.

"Give me a boost," Ama looks over to Mirielle and nods.

"What?" Mirielle's eyes are wide.

Ama glares, "Just fucking do it!"

Mirielle growls and suddenly, they both veer to the left, going toward the gray Dragon.

Oh shit. Oh shit!

Mirielle drops down on one knee, her hands in a basket, and my jaw hits the floor as I watch Amalia run full speed, using Mirielle's hands as a step stool as the latter uses her demis strength to catapult Amalia into the air, and straight at the gray Dragon.

"This isn't the plan!" I scream.

But nobody listens. They only watch in sick glee as Amalia roars, raising her swords, bringing them down on the Dragon's back in sync with her landing, severing its spinal cord. The Dragon screams in pain, and Amalia screams along with it, the grief and rage in her voice is so immense it becomes a tangible being. As the Dragon collapses to the ground, Amalia slides down it's wings, landing in the sands easily. Tears stream from her face, but her eyes are fury.

The crowd goes wild and I can hear the gasps. There is no mistaking her lack of humanity now. Both Mirielle and Amalia just exposed themselves. But there's no time to worry as the gray Dragon falls to the ground, and Amalia slides down, landing easily in the sand, her blade still dripping hot Dragon blood.

We spin at the sound of another Dragon's roar. The yellow Dragon charges right at us, having mowed through the Eastlander candidate. Gods, there are torn bodies everywhere. Only two other candidates remain. Amalia yanks my collar as we break into a run, sprinting from the approaching Dragon

"Mirielle, do it now," Amalia shouts, looking over her shoulder behind her.

Wait, what? They stop running and turn on me,

I shout, "Ama what are you doing? We should be RUNNING!"

Ama looks up, her eyes apologetic as Mirielle becomes a blur, coming up behind me

"Forgive me," she whispers in my ear before everything goes black as she slams her staff into the side of my head.

There's only one thought in my head as I lose consciousness.

Amalia *lied*.

CHAPTER 57
MIRIELLE

She will never forgive me for this.

Dyana hates that she's the only actual human out of our silly rag-tag group. She hasn't said anything, but she doesn't have to.

I know she hates feeling like the weak one.

I've seen it in her eyes. Never jealousy or resentment, just frustration.

Taking this choice away from her will be the final straw, and it's taking every ounce of strength in me to not shatter completely at the fact that I'll never feel her lips against mine again.

Amalia approached me a few days ago and told me her plan, but I had long been considering it.

Dyana must live.

She's the youngest here; she's human.

And a long time ago, magyka and Dragons promised to protect them. It was their duty. We are all Morrigyn's children, mortal or not.

We must protect those weaker than us. It's the right thing to do. It's why the Gauntlet is so perverse. My ancestors were in disbelief when the High Council announced that humans would be the ones paying the price.

Dyana cannot see it, but being human isn't a weakness. She shines brighter than any of us because of her humanity. We all see it. And I now realize that she's the glue holding us together. We're all worn down, but she pushes us forward. Makes us try harder by reminding us of the passion and innocence of a fully lived life.

We've all talked about the risks here. But what I never told Dyana is that the biggest risk will be in the Final bout. Amalia figured it out first, which means Os or Nyall told her. Although I suspect she already knew as much.

Our distraction will make or break this plan, but it also involves the most risk.

When we enter the Arena for the finals...we won't be walking out.

Dyana's hate is worth her life.

Every fiber of my being wants to pick her up and get the Hell out of here. But we need her to stay unconscious for the remainder of the round.

She has to be disqualified.

It's the safest way forward—for her, at least.

Amalia shouts, just as the yellow Dragon jumps into the air and pounces on us. It opens its yellow mouth, getting ready to fire. I jump left as Amalia jumps right, each of us going to one side of the Dragon. I separate Forsaken again and slam both ends down through the Dragon's tail with a yell. It screeches in pain, and Amalia runs underneath it, her swords cutting its main arteries.

It begins to bleed to death, writhing around as hot blood drips down onto the Arena sand, steam rising as it sizzles on contact. Amalia, face covered in tears and eyes burning with a rage unlike anything I've ever seen, simply unleashes another furious scream as she stabs one of her swords into its heart, killing it instantly. As the life fades from the Dragon's eyes, Amalia slams her bloody swords into the sand, falls to her knees, and screams—the sound so full of rage and sorrow that my eyes instantly fill with tears.

It's palpable, and for a moment, her pain is a physical thing stabbing into me. The entire stadium erupts in cheers, but her scream is louder. Suddenly, she stops, breathing heavily as she pushes to stand. Amalia turns around, panting, face and scarf covered in blood.

But her eyes.

Mother save us.

Amalia's eyes burn with the promise of death.

There are only two Northlanders left. Both of them look worn down and tired, a bit unhinged. We're all covered in blood and soot from the streams of flame, but every Dragon lies dead. Our final enemy is on two legs, not four.

"You take the left, I'll take the right," I growl, striding forward.

"Try to keep up, rebel."

We twist and turn, dropping into a dance of blood and death as we meticulously disarm and take down the two remaining candidates easily. Too easily.

The Arena goes quiet. The only sound is our deep panting before the crowd erupts in rabid screams, making my ears ring.

The circus animals nailed their performance. Fucking bloodthirsty pricks.

Amalia and I pant heavily, sliding each other a weighted glance. Her face is still the picture of rage and fury. I fight my instinct to take a step back. My demis side is thrashing in terror.

It's not Dragonfear, but it's damn close. Close enough that I know she's lying to every single one of us about her heritage. But that's for later. We have bigger problems.

"CITIZENS OF UR DAOINE! YOUR GAUNTLET FINALISTS!" The crowd erupts in cheers again. Pieces of bread and food are tossed at us like we're their prized little piggies.

Nyall doesn't believe all fae are evil. And I know that he's not bad, which inherently makes him right. But looking out at this sea of hundreds of thousands of fae, magyka, and demis makes me think that maybe Amalia was right after all.

Is there any humanity left to save? Or are we already damned? Perhaps we're all dead, and this is Hell. It certainly feels like Hell most days.

The crowd continues to cheer as Amalia steps closer, nodding to me, "Well, the easy part's done with."

I snort, "Yeah. On a scale from 1 to 10, how fucked are we?"

"How about an eleven?" she says dryly.

"Yeah, that sounds about right."

It's so subtle I barely catch it, but Amalia's eyes go to Dyana's still prone figure. I can't believe she's still out. I'm officially worried I hit her too hard.

"She's been out too long; she should have woken up a bit by now," I mutter.

"I'm keeping her asleep," Amalia says casually.

I blink, "Right. And you...you just know how to do that?"

Holy shit, how can she do that?

Amalia just meets my gaze, "I know many things, Mirielle Zenyth. You'd do well to remember that."

Mother save us.

"She's going to hate both of us, Mirielle," Amalia murmurs.

I nod, "Yeah. Yeah, she is."

"But you're wrong. My betrayal is worse than yours. You take her and tell her it was my idea."

I blink. "What?"

She shushes with a hiss, "Just do it." I protest, but we're interrupted by the announcer again.

"CANDIDATES! PRESENT YOURSELVES TO THE HIGH COUNCIL."

We both sigh and walk over to be directly beneath the High Council's private booth. The warding that keeps the High Council hidden goes transparent as Achan Drayven in all his sickening disgrace, appears. The other High Councilors sit at his side. Nyall is at the back, stony and unreactive as per usual. His public face is on. So different from the kind, passionate male I've come to know. The High Councilor stands, his dark horns looking bigger and uglier by the day.

I wonder how long it's going to take Amalia to find out the truth about Achan and the other High Councilors.

She thinks she knows the whole truth, but I'm certain she doesn't.

"Amalia Roth from Twyn Fells and Mirielle Zenyth from Sud Azul. Congratulations! In two days, you will face one of our fiercest dragons." The crowd goes wild as Achan pauses, sending them another grotesque smile,." In two days, one of you could win 50,000 gold marks and your freedom. Unless you both die, of course."

"Are you sure we can't kill him yet?" Amalia grumbles under her breath, her hands flexing with anticipation. I hold back a laugh.

"Tonight, you will join us for a special dinner to commemorate the occasion and celebrate how far you've come, for in two days, your death awaits." Achan smiles darkly before the High Council's booth goes dark.

I blink, "What the hell?"

"Was that planned?" Amalia whispers angrily.

I shake my head, "No. No it definitely wasn't. I don't know what this is about."

"Shit." Amalia echoes the sentiment in my head. This just got a *lot* more complicated—and deadly.

"Keep her asleep until the crowd dies down," I say to Amalia once we've exited the arena but wait in the tunnel entrance. There's no point in hiding from the other candidates since they're all dead, but we do need to wait until the crowd dies down. We're both silent as we wait, but while I lean against a wall, Amalia just paces.

"They're almost gone." Amalia just nods in response, but I'm filled with uncertainty. "Amalia, what are we going to do?"

She pauses, glancing at me, "Do you mean about tonight?"

"Yeah."

Amalia *hmphs*, "The rebel, coming to *me* for guidance. Why, Mirielle, I thought you hated me."

I have the sudden desire to punch her in the throat. But...I don't honestly think I can take her—and that's terrifying.

"Don't worry, Roth. I still hate you. But due to actions of our own planning, we're partners in this. So regardless of if you give a shit about me or not, we're going to have to reply to each other. And *you* would do well to remember that even if you're the better fighter, I've been on this earth longer than you. I know things you don't, and I know that kills you, but suck it up. We need each other and there's no way around it."

Amalia clenches her jaw and continues pacing as she fumes. I go back to leaning against the wall and cross my arms, my metal arm guards clanking at the movement.

"I'm not sure how long I can be around Achan before I snap." I blink at Amalia's sudden admission. She doesn't look at me, but...shit, if she's struggling enough that she's telling *me* about it, that means it's serious.

"Ok. So we don't stay long. We need our rest, anyways. They will buy that because it's the truth."

"Right." Amalia nods, her voice shaky.

"I get it, Amalia," I say, trying to be kind.

She laughs but it's cold and hollow. "No, you don't. But you're going to."

The words unsettle me as the arena goes quiet, finally empty. We run back into the bloody sands as human servants dressed in aprons file into the arena with buckets and wheelbarrows, picking up body parts as they go. Luckily they ignore us as we grab Dyana and carry her out quickly.

As soon as we get into the tunnel Dyana wriggles her hand.

"I just let go. Remember what I said, Zenyth. This is all my doing," Amalia says quietly, ever the martyr. But what I can't figure out is *why* she's so willing to take the fall.

By the time Dyana opens her eyes, we're almost back to the dorms.

The halls are empty and it's weirdly quiet.

"You lied," Dyana croaks, "You fucking lied. Both of you."

Amalia responds calmly, "Keeping you safe is my priority, Dyana. I swore I'd keep you safe, and now you will be.

"Screw you and your godsdamn promises! You said you'd keep me safe, not take my choices away from me. This was not your call to make, Amalia!" Dyana shoves us off her as she staggers. She whirls towards me, "And you. I was actually starting to forgive you, despite many, many reasons why I shouldn't. How could you do this? How could you take this choice away from me, Mirielle? Why?"

I go to respond but fall silent as words fail me.

She's right and we all know it.

Amalia interrupts the silence, "I'm sorry, Dyana, I really am. But I will never apologize about keeping you safe, and there is no way you would have accepted this idea if we let you in on it."

"But why, Ama? Why would you do this?" Dyana's voice cracks and she begins trembling as tears start to fall. I hear Amalia's inhale and watch as she tenses. If I didn't know her, I'd say she was afraid.

But I don't think it's fear; I think she's in *pain.*

"Because I don't want to live in a world without you in it, Dya. You think that you owe me for taking care of you for so many years, but *you* are the reason I'm even alive, you damn idiot. *You* are the only reason I haven't given up." Amalia pauses, voice thick with emotion. I feel my tears rise again as I watch them, the hurt on both of their faces, the vulnerability in this moment. Yet again, I'm an intruder in their little family. "You are the sister I always needed, and the friend I always dreamed of having. You gave me purpose, Dyana Arkos. I got us into this, so please, let me get you out of it."

Dyana looks away, tears streaming. "You." Her voice is hard as she turns back to us. "You said *you.* Not *us.* You're not planning on surviving, are you?"

Gods.

Amalia just smiles at her sadly, "I'm planning on surviving, Dya. But we did the math. Whoever enters the Final bout, likely will never walk out—and I refuse that fate for you." Amalia pauses and steps forward, grabbing Dyana's hands gently. "You once told me to live, and you were right. But Dyana," Amalia reaches forward and tucks Dyana's bloody hair behind her dirty ear, "*you* deserve to live, too."

Amalia steps back as Dyana starts to cry in earnest.

"I still deserved a choice in all of this. I know you love me, I know you're so much more experienced and older, but Ama, I am my own person, and my opinions matter. I deserved a choice and you stole that from me."

Amalia nods, stepping back to stand next to me. "I know," her voice is hoarse. "But we don't have time for this. Hate me all you wish but Mirielle and I have to go meet the High Council."

Dyana blinks, "Wait, what? Right now?"

"Yes," I say. Dyana goes between glaring at us and blinking as she tries to process everything rapidly.

Finally, she sniffs, holding her head high."Good luck, then. Try not to die, but I guess that's what you want, isn't it?"

"Dyana wait—" I say, Amalia just shakes her head as Dyana turns and walks to their dorm slamming the door shut on her way in.

"Don't bother. We deserve this. We knew what would happen, and we still chose this. Accept it. She knows we don't have time for this, she will keep to the plan, and if any of us manage to survive, it'll be dealt with then. It's us who have to worry, now."

Somehow, I feel that Amalia's words are more for herself than they are for me.

I head back to my own dorm and the quiet is suffocating.

A fancy dress is on the bed waiting for me. A dark green that plays off my red hair. The water in the tiny bucket the Fae considers to be a "suitable tub" is cold, but I squeeze myself into it anyway, using a damp cloth to wipe my skin off and rinsing my hair until there's no more blood.

There's no time to do anything but braid my damp hair into a coronet around my head, otherwise the dress would get soaking wet. I don't particularly want my last night alive to be spent shivering and soggy.

I don't even bother checking the tiny mirror after shoving my curved body into the snug dress. It's skin-tight and made of silk that feels heavenly against my roughed-up skin.

I hate that it feels so *nice*.

Sliding my feet into some pair of sandals left for me, I head out the door. No point in doing rouge or eye kohl. No point in trying. The Fae definitely aren't worth it.

Just as I close my door, I hear another open and Amalia walks out—

Oh, Mother save us.

There stands Amalia, her gray hair down and wavy from her braid, in a white long-sleeve gown with a neckline so plunging it goes to her navel, and absolutely *covered* in blood.

I try to form words but I'm honestly so shocked I just stand there, gaping like an idiot.

"You didn't wash your hair, then." *Gods, why did I just say that?*

Amalia just smirks, her eyes still burning with icy rage.

"If we're the sacrificial pigs, we might as well dress like it."

Dyana steps out behind her, looking pale and a bit queasy at the sticky blood in Amalia's hair. Even worse, she apparently didn't bathe because blood and dirt streak every inch of her skin.

Dyana doesn't spare me a single glance. It's stupid—to want to feel pretty at a time like this. To want her to notice after everything that's happened.

I just thought...well, I don't know what I thought. I'm not sure about anything anymore. I thought I knew what I signed up for when I joined the rebellion and volunteered for the Gauntlet.

How childish of me.

Dyana doesn't even say goodbye before disappearing back into her room. Amalia just starts walking, her long dress trailing along the stones behind her. I catch up and we ascend out of the Dragon Pit in silence. Os meets us in the stable yard.

I don't even like men, but the look in his eyes when he sees her is enough to make me flush with heat. Os may be scarred, but damn, the man—or whatever he is—is damn gorgeous. But he only has eyes for Amalia, it seems.

"Are you joining us, beast?" Amalia asks, her voice husky.

Mother, why do you curse me so?

Os's eyes heat briefly before he shuts down and turns into the emotionless trainer we've all come to know and hate.

"As head trainer I'll be attending as your chaperone. In case you," Os pauses, looking Amalia up and down, "misbehave."

I swear the air just got twenty degrees hotter.

"No promises," Amalia says with a dark smile.

I snort at the idea that *she'll* behave. She's the one I'm worried about!

Os smiles and my jaw drops. "The plan is the same. But the acting starts now. From this moment forward, you're rivals. Even in private, assume there are eyes on you. None of this camaraderie. We only have to do this for a day, but it has to be believable."

The plan, as we decided, is to play it that the finalists hate each other. For the distraction to work, we're going to have to fight each other and put on a damn good show while doing it. But in order for it to work, we have to convince the High Council our dislike of each other is genuine.

I turn to Amalia, "That won't be difficult."

She just looks at me, eyes cold, "The feeling is mutual, rebel."

The three of us start off towards the Black Citadel. Os, like us, is dressed in Fae finery, but that lucky son of a Kraken gets to wear comfortable *pants,* unlike us.

"How long is this dinner?" I ask as our heels crack on the gravel walkway.

"Hopefully not long. I'm going to say you need to leave and get sleep. It's already late. It's a legitimate excuse. Nyall will be there which should help." Os glances at Amalia.

There's something they're not saying, and it definitely involves Nyall. My hackles rise in parallel with my fury. I've never felt protective over anyone outside of my family, but Nyall Drayven is someone I consider to be family. If Amalia and Os hurt Nyall, there will be hell to pay.

"No stabbing, no acting out. Hold back one more night." Os continues listing what we can and cannot do in a neverending lecture about how we have to behave.

"Fine," I mutter, annoyed that he won't shut up.

"Both of you," he growls, looking at Amalia.

She shrugs, causing Os to let out a long-suffering sigh.

"The only goal tonight is to survive. None of our other plans matter if tonight goes wrong." Right, no pressure. My heart races as we cross the moat to the Black Citadel, the dark water bubbling menacingly. I swear I see something large underneath the surface. A big shadow of some kind, and there's a slight ripple.

I break into a fast walk, with Os and Amalia in tow, as we make it across the moat and approach the dark fortress that is the Black Citadel. For a moment, we all take a breath, silent and anxious. Amalia clenches her hands into tight fists, her face hard, and walks towards the castle. Os follows, leaving me standing there. My legs are moving before my brain makes the conscious decision to follow.

Into the belly of the beast, then.

CHAPTER 58
AMALIA

Dressed in white, headed right into the villain's lair.

How fucking *ironic.*

Dyana said nothing as I got dressed. She just stared, watching as I freed my hair from the constraints of my sticky braid. Dried blood covers me from head to toe. It even dripped down my body underneath my clothes and armor.

The screams of the Dragons I've slaughtered ring in my ears as I walk into the Black Citadel.

I thought I understood the meaning of pain.

Plunging a sword into an innocent Dragon fighting against its will and watching as the life faded from its beautiful eyes...that's a new kind of pain.

The Gauntlet was always going to require a sacrifice. That sacrifice would break everything I promised my parents before they died.

"Stay safe. Stay hidden. Never let the High Council or the fae discover who you are," Father whispers. *"Repeat it to me."*

I sigh, "Yes, Daddy. Stay safe, stay hidden, and never let the High Council and fae learn who I am."

"Good girl."

Words repeated every single night as he tucked me in for bed, after he and my mother read me a story.

We were always preparing for the worst-case scenario.

In two days, my promise will be broken.

But first, for this plan to work, we have to survive tonight.

And so I enter the villain's lair, not as the damsel or the hero, but as the judge, the jury, and the executioner.

The Prince waits for us on the Black Citadel steps, a large sword casually at his back. Nyall is dressed in a long, sleeveless black jacket with silver buckles atop a fine black long-sleeve shirt and matching pants. Rings decorate his fingers, and his black tattoos peek out of his collar, rising up his neck to line the right side of his jaw.

Nyall looks at my outfit and smiles, his mismatched eyes alight with wicked amusement. "Father is going to be furious."

There's a small braid underneath my hair. I reach back and grab the dagger hidden within the woven strands, twirling the blade between my bloody fingers. "Stare at the dark long enough, Prince, and you'll find the dark staring back." I toss the dagger and catch it, hiding it back in my braid faster than the human eye could track.

Prince Nyall flashes me a wicked smile, "Do try not to kill anyone. I need you alive."

"I make no promises," I bare my teeth, "Now let's eat. I'm ravenous."

"As am I. I'm starved for your blood and the sweet honey between your legs. I miss the taste of you," Os purrs in my head. *"When we're done here, you're going to sit on my face so I can feast on you and that perfect pussy of yours. I do love dessert."*

My legs turn to jelly and moisture floods between my legs. I shoot Remus a heated look, winking at him as we're let in through the large stone and marble doors of the Citadel entrance. Nyall slows, walking next to me. He smirks, mismatched eyes twinkling with wicked mirth.

"Dessert is my favorite meal of the day too," Nyall drawls in my mind, the scent of his honeysuckle and amber magyk making my blood rush. I almost trip but he grabs my arm, chuckling darkly, and when I'm steady he lets go, walking in front of me.

My racing heart can't decide whether to be horny or terrified.

Perhaps both.

Bulging, dead eyes watch me. The roasted ram is facing my seat as demis and human servants artfully carve slices of cooked meat off its skewered body.

It's the horns of the ram that concern me.

They're huge, with the base as big as my fist, and curled up at the end. Which means this is a northern ram.

And northern rams reside in only one region of Ur Daoine. A specific region with a specific climate. The Ulster Wald.

He knows, he knows, he knows, he knows.

No, stop. He only knows I'm from the North. There's fish here, too. He doesn't know.

He knows, he knows something, oh Gods he knows something.

He's just trying to appear thoughtful. It's all an act.

Liar, liar, he knows something, he knows.

My thoughts race as my paranoia increases. I fight it with all my might, ignoring the ram as much as possible. The large black marble table was covered in an ostentatious tableau of food featuring various rare animals and fancy vegetables.

It would be suspicious not to eat, so I just pick some plain-looking vegetables. Their flavor bursts in my mouth, a mix of warm spices and herbs. But it turns to ash in my stomach.

I cannot eat—or enjoy food—at the table of my parents' murderer.

I can only pretend.

The sound of each slice and carve of the juicy, roast meat had me flashing back to Taran. I have to close my eyes for a moment, trying to center myself as my skin starts to heat and my heart begins racing.

Taran.

My friend.

For a moment, I feel my magyk growing. My foot tap, tap, taps anxiously as I flex my fingers, trying to keep my shit together while I try and shove all of my emotions and magyk back behind those iron walls inside of me.

My iron walls have begun disintegrating.

"Two demis, weak and diluted, as our finalists. I must say, I didn't see this coming. I will have to speak to my General. We mustn't have more of you skulking about unnoticed," Achan Drayven says, and the other High Councilors nod and mutter their various agreements.

He thinks I'm a demis—perfect.

"Demis are so watered down these days, there's practically no fae left in them," Nyall says blandly, taking a sip out of his ostentatious metal and gemstone goblet. The picture of an arrogant, asshole royal.

"That's what happens when you lay with a human, boy. They suck away all of the power and magyk, leaving a boring husk. Tell me," Achan turns to us, and I hold my breath, "was that the best you could do out there? Is that all the pitiful magyk you have?"

The High Councilors laugh, snickering.

Next to me, Mirielle stares a hole into her plate as she eats her food in small bites, methodically. Nyall leans back in his chair, sipping from his wine goblet casually.

"What say you, candidates?" One of the other High Councilors asks; a male with flat white hair split down the middle, hanging down to his ears. It's a strange haircut when paired with his round, glowing red eyes.

"You are correct, your Grace. That is the extent of our powers. We can jump, and are a little faster than humans, but that's all. For all intents and purposes, we are just worthless humans." Mirielle's is the picture of piety and reverence as she bows her head in respect.

Achan and the other High Councilors at the far end of the table look my way and I nod in agreement.

The less I open my mouth here, the better.

"It's exactly situations like this that prove why we were needed here. Our work in Ur Daoine isn't done. These pitiful creatures need our guidance," Achan looks to Nyall, who just nods, ever the obedient son. The other High Councilors nod again in agreement as they take sips of the wine that I suspect isn't really wine. "Magyka, deciding to dilute their genes with human blood. It's disgusting. Your ancestors are exactly why so few outside of the fae possess much of any magyk at all."

The High Councilors discuss how stupid it would be to breed with a magykless human, but I just tune it out and push the roasted vegetables around my plate. Remus nudges my leg with his foot, and I glance at him from beneath my brow. His eyes are calm despite the storm of a situation we're in.

Attendants take away our plates, clearing the table and making way for dessert.

"Miss Roth, is it? Your choice of attire is rather interesting. Ruining the nice outfit, we were kind enough to provide you."

I take a shallow breath and respond. "To be in the Gauntlet is an honor, your Grace. We get to compete in your honor, so I wear the blood of my enemies in your honor, highness." I force out every word, and it nearly kills me. The High Councilors just nod, and Achan sniffs.

"Your hair...it's a most unusual color. Were you born in Twyn Fells, girl?

~~Fuck, fuck, fuck, FUCK.~~ *Do not react. Stay calm. It's fine.*

~~HE KNOWS, HE KNOWS, HE KNOWS.~~ *Calm. Be calm.*

I force myself to feel nothing.

"I believe it to be a side effect of the human dilution in my blood, your grace."

"Hm," he considers my words, nodding. "Yes, you're likely right."

A bald, androgynous Councilor leans forward, "You know, I knew someone long ago who had hair the color of steel. Yours is much more mousy and lifeless, of course, but perhaps he's your distant ancestor."

My eyelashes twitch as I reach one hand down my side to unsheath the dagger I hid on my upper thigh.

"Patience, my spark. Now is not the time," Remus cautions, suddenly in my mind.

"Boring," I mutter.

"I enjoy this side of you, A gahrá." I roll my eyes at him with my magyk, reluctantly sliding my dagger back in its sheath as the High Councilor looks at his peer.

"You dare suggest a thing?" Achan asks, indignant. The room darkens, and the taste of sour apples fills my mouth.

The Councilor stutters. "Not seriously, your Grace. It was merely a jest. This little demis is a nobody. Clearly!" For a few seconds, nobody moves, but then the servants reappear, carrying dessert. Some type of toffee pudding, by the looks of it.

Gods, I love toffee pudding. I had it once at an inn. Dyana was shocked I'd never tried it, so we splurged and got one to share. It was the best thing I've ever tasted. But I won't be tempted.

Achan Drayven doesn't deserve to witness my joy. But my mouth waters as a servant sets the bowl down in front of me, the sweet smells of warm caramel and butterscotch in the air.

"If Councilor Aydis was right, we would have known long ago. Clearly, Miss Roth is a nobody. Everyone thinks she's a freak, so I hear. Isn't that right, son?" Achan looks at Nyall, and there's some sort of leashed violence in his glowing red eyes.

I turn slowly and meet Nyall Drayven's mismatched gaze. He looks me over, goosebumps pebbling across my skin. Remus is tense, back ramrod straight as he glares openly at the Prince.

Nyall just shrugs nonchalantly, "Yes. The Dragonguard who went to Twyn Fells says she's the town outcast. But then again, Twyn Fells is filled with outcasts. Only a freak would live in a place so cold and isolated."

I'm going to strangle him.

"If you can beat me to it," Os growls in my head.

"Quite right, son. You might be a worthless bastard, but at least you got some of my intelligence." I blink, and Mirielle's jaw drops as the High Councilor so casually insults his own son, bastard or not. Achan has seemed polite towards Nyall, but as I think back on all of the stories Nyall's told us, perhaps that's just another facade.

"Let us talk of better things!" Achan continues, "The Gauntlet Finals are in two days, so I had this special dessert made just for you, my finalists. It's a momentous occasion, and the Father is very pleased with the sacrifices made in His name."

Sacrifices?

Is he joking?

I can't ask this, so I just imagine stabbing him with one of the knives they used to skin the ram.

"Well, what are you waiting for?" Achan barks, "Dig in!"

Everyone begins to eat as the delicious scent hits us. Mirielle moans happily, unable to help herself as she takes a bite. Nyall passes, instead asking for more wine in his already thrice-refilled goblet.

I begrudgingly grab my spoon. I can't say no now that he's ordered us all to eat. I take a small bite and bring the spoon to my mouth, wrapping my lips around the warm caramel bread. The pudding is just hitting my tongue when the High Councilor turns and looks at Remus, who still hasn't taken a bite.

"You, in particular, will enjoy this dessert, Os."

Mirielle and I pause, realizing Remus hasn't moved.

A low vibrating sound echoes around the room. Remus is...growling.

"Remus? What's wrong?" I whisper. But there's no response. I swallow my bite, confused, when my magyk suddenly bubbles, and my stomach clenches in searing pain. Mirielle moans, grabbing her own stomach and twitching slightly.

Something is wrong.

I pant through the pain and glance down at the toffee pudding when it hits me.

No. Gods, no. Please, no.

"You see, Miss Roth, it took us many years to tame this one," the High Councilor nods to Remus, "He was practically a feral animal when we found him. Fell in with the wrong sort during the war. So, we decided to have him killed. But color our surprise when he killed over a dozen of our strongest Dragons. His own kin—well, of a sort. He's like you, actually. A freak amongst his kind. Instead of killing him, we decided the best punishment was indentured servitude. So here we are; he's teaching you to kill the very beings that raised him. The very beings you now consume."

~~No. Please no. Oh my Gods. Please tell me~~ *I didn't just eat a Dragon.*

~~This isn't real. This isn't real.~~ *This is real. I just ate Dragon meat.*

~~I WILL KILL THEM FOR THIS~~. *Stay calm.*

The pain in my stomach increases and saliva suddenly floods my mouth as my skin flushes.

I stumble out of my chair, falling to my knees just as my stomach rejects every bit of food I've just consumed. The High Councilors just laugh as Mirielle does the same, hurling into a spare bowl.

"Dragon eggs are perfect for baking, you know. And their dried bones make lovely flour when ground up."

~~KILL THEM ALL. KILL THEM ALL.~~ *Save it. Make them regret this.*

I retch again, unable to get the taste out of my mouth. Achan Drayven nods at Remus.

"Eat it, Remus," Achan says, leaning back in his large metal chair. "Eat the meat of your people. I command you." Threads of red magyk curl around Achan's hand and shoot into Remus. He trembles beside me as the compulsion takes over.

I moan in pain again and my stomach clenches painfully as my magyk rejects the Dragonmagyk currently trying to assimilate with me.

I try to push into Remus's mind, but he's locked down so tight I can't get to him. My legs are shaky as I force myself to stand, sliding back into my chair and panting from the pain. I move my foot over to touch his leg, and he exhales hard, wincing as blood begins to stream from his eyes, ears, and nose.

My heart is racing as I watch, helpless.

"Are you going to disobey me, beast?" Nobody says a word. "I COMMAND YOU, EAT THE DRAGON FLESH!" Achan clenches his fist and Remus groans as the warding tattooed on his body starts to burn.

~~*DO SOMETHING. DON'T JUST SIT AND WATCH.*~~

Remus groans against the magyk and lifts his spoon, bringing the food to his mouth. He struggles against Achan's hold but can't resist.

~~*Fuck you*~~ *Morrigyn, how could you allow this to happen?*

Remus's hand is shaking as he brings the spoon closer to his mouth. The pudding made with Dragonflesh only inches from his mouth when I make my decision. The Gods aren't here and it's on me to pick which path to take.

~~*DO SOMETHING. HELP YOUR FAMILIAR.*~~ **I refuse this fate.**

"High Councilor," I say neutrally, ever the picture of pathetic, simpering humanity, "perhaps you could clear up a local folktale the humans in the North have. You are the most knowledgeable of the imperial fae. If anyone knows the truth, it's you." I smile, and I'm sure my eyes are manic.

The High Councilor pauses and Remus stops, spoon still close to his mouth, but its progression momentarily halted.

"Make it quick, girl. I am tired of your presence," Achan growls. "Humans always have so many questions."

I nod, and Nyall Drayven sneaks a glance at me, eyes curious.

"Of course, Sire. I was just wondering if you ever heard the legend of the Gray Wytch? It's a local story told to children in the North to scare them into behaving. Teachers and parents would tell their children of an evil Wytch who would come to town in the middle of the night, slinking in with the fog. Then she would snatch them right from their beds if they misbehaved. It's said she would take the children back to her den deep within the forest and let them be devoured by her rabid Dyre Wolves. The wolves would save the heart for her. Apparently that was her favorite part to eat. The Wytch has long since disappeared, but it's said she still patrols the Ulster Wald, and if you are quiet enough, you might hear her screams amongst the howls at night."

Prince Nyall glances at me again, eyes calculating. He's smart; I'll give him that.

The High Councilor sniffs, "It's been years since I heard that tale. There was never any Wytch—that's a made-up term humans came up with to feel like they could use magyk if they tried hard enough. It's a silly human legend and nothing more."

The other councilors nod, but I see a few anxious gulps.

I smile again, "I'm glad to hear, your Grace. I knew you could shed light on the subject. I'm so relieved to hear she's not real."

Nyall Drayven sighs, "Father, I think it's prudent that the candidates retire. They're so weak; if they don't get enough sleep, their performance will be fucking pitiful."

The High Councilor sniffs and releases the warding magyk on Remus, whose spoon falls, clattering as it hits his plate.

"Fine. Everyone out." All of us, the other High Councilors included, stand and bow, quickly exiting.

Human servants enter through the marble doors just before we leave the room. They're naked with a large chain connecting their two ankles, unable to escape even if they tried. The sound of robes hitting the floor behind us makes me want to vomit again as we quickly exit. I block out the sounds behind those closed doors as we silently make our way out of the castle. The other Councilors and attendants leave us in the care of Prince Nyall, who once again escorts us out.

I barely made it to the labyrinth of the garden before falling to my knees and vomiting up dinner.

"We ate a Dragon. We—oh my god. W-we ate Dragons." Mirielle loses it, sobbing openly.

I want to weep.

I want to weep, scream, and tear stars out of the fucking sky. But instead, I am numb.

"I'm so sorry. I had no idea he was planning that. I should have known." Nyall is furious, surprising me.

"You didn't know?" I whisper,

Nyall looks at me, eyes wide. "No, I swear on the Morrigyn Herself, I had no idea that would happen. I tried to warn you when I felt the magyk in the desert, but Achan raised a ward, suppressing magyk in the room so he could work the compulsion on Os."

"Is that why we suddenly couldn't talk? You weren't responding and I thought maybe you heard me, but couldn't reply."

"Yes. When you began trying to distract him, I tried to tell you to stop but there was nothing." Remus replies, surprising me.

Gods, the pain and anger in his voice make my vision go black for a second.

"I'm getting the hell out of here," I say, stumbling as I take off toward the Dragon Pit. Everyone follows, but Remus hangs back. His pupils dilated as he zones out.

We all process grief in different ways.

He and I are more alike than I realized.

Nyall sneaks back to the Dragon Pit with us, using some advanced magyks to make himself invisible. He follows us back to the dorms, where we grab Dyana before heading to Remus's room. We go over the plan a few more times. Dyana asks questions about what happened at dinner, but none of us can answer. The hurt on her face that no one will tell her what happened is a palpable pain in my chest.

After Nyall feels satisfied, that we all know our roles, and that we're ready for what's to come, we separate.

But there's anxiety and hopelessness in the air.

Tonight rattled everyone, even Nyall. We're all tense and shaky, unable to believe what just happened.

"Amalia?" Mirielle whispers after Nyall bids us good night and we all go our separate ways. I go to follow Remus, but Mirielle stops me with a hand on my arm.

"What?" I snap. Instantly, regret fills me at my sharp tone, but I can't help it. I feel like I'm about to explode and implode simultaneously, and my magyk struggles to stay under control.

Mirielle is silent as she wrings her hands nervously.

Ah. I see why Nyall picked her as a rebel.

"Ask it, Mirielle. Ask me the question that's been eating at you. I'm too godsdamn tired for word games." Her gray eyes meet mine, and there's a new fear in them. We're still in Remus's rooms, but Mirielle is about to leave to head back to her dorm. Dyana left the moment she could. I'm still deciding whether or not to stay, but...I don't think I can face Dyana and her questions right now.

Mirielle is hesitant, "That story you told. Is that real? Or did you just make it up?"

Remus growls from his spot by the fire, "Worried she'll eat your heart, rebel?"

"Of course not," Mirielle snaps. "It was a strange story and I was curious." Mirielle snaps, but her words are shaky. She shakes her head, "Gods, you two are so difficult. I'm done."

She's halfway out the door when I call. "Mirielle?" The redhead pauses, looking back at me as I smile, "Achan Drayven is not the only monster in this world, but right now, he's the only one you need to worry about."

CHAPTER 59
MIRIELLE

Amalia's words repeat over and over as I walk on numb legs.

Achan Drayven isn't the only monster here.

Monster. Such an interesting choice of words. She's hiding something, I'm sure of it. What that means for us, for our plans, for whatever kind of afterward might or might not happen? I'm unsure—but it's not good.

I know I shouldn't, but I walk straight to Dyana's room and knock. There's no answer, so I enter. She's still up, but barely, her eyes are bloodshot and swollen as she sits, half asleep and reading a worn book.

"Hey—" Dyana looks up and pauses. "Oh, it's you. What are you doing here, Mirielle?"

Her disappointment burns, but I shake it off. "I think Amalia is staying with Os tonight."

"Right, of course." Dyana sniffs, setting her book down. "I wanted to be alone anyways."

I hesitate. In my two centuries, I've never hesitated. Until her. Until Amalia. Until all of this.

"I know I shouldn't be here," I whisper.

Dyana glances at me before looking back to fluff her pillow. "You shouldn't. I have not and do not in any way, shape, or form forgive you."

"I know. I know. I'm sorry. But—" my words get choked as emotion takes over, "tonight didn't go well."

My eyes close as the adrenaline from the evening comes crashing down on me. Everything in my chest gets tight, and it's hard to breathe. Dyana's instantly up and out of bed, her white cotton nightgown transparent from the candle on her nightstand, showing the outline of her beautiful curves, I slide to the floor, head between my knees, and take great gasping breaths.

"Oh gods, oh gods, oh, gods."

Dyana slides to the floor beside me, "It's alright, Mirielle. It's ok. Right now, you are safe."

"None of us. Are safe. None." I push the words out in between my hysterical gasps, my tears now falling in earnest.

Dyana doesn't move. She just gently puts a warm hand on my back, rubbing small, slow circles for Gods knows how long until my breathing starts to even out again and the tears begin to ease.

"Amalia gets them too." At her name, I go stiff and look up.

"Panic attacks," Dyana clarifies. "Ones so bad she sleeps for days on end afterward. Sometimes, I think it's just a result of feeling so much in an already painful world. I get them occasionally, too, although I think I just pour all of my worries and heartache into dancing. The exertion, the sweat, it always felt like it was a way of releasing the pain, in a way. Not all, but some."

I hiccup and sniff, rubbing my running nose with my arm.

"It's only ever happened once before. When...when my mom died," my voice is hoarse as I look up and meet her warm gaze. There's still so much pain there, but the empathy makes my heart break all over again.

After all I've done, after all the lies. Even if she doesn't like me, she still can be kind, which makes Dyana Arkos stronger than any being I've ever known.

I suddenly realize we're awkwardly sitting on her floor. It seems Dyana has the same realization, too, as she clears her throat and stands, holding her hand to pull me up. I eagerly grasp her palm as if she's my lifeline. But the second I'm up, she lets go, and I immediately mourn the loss.

I sit on the end of her bed. Dyana just watches and sniffs, crossing her arms. "You' re only allowed to stay if you tell me what the ever-loving fuck happened tonight."

"He—" my voice gets choked up again, and I bury my face in my hands, "He served us Dragon, Dyana. We didn't know; none of us could tell it was in the pudding. After we had taken our first bite, he—" I pull my hands away, my palms soaked with tears, "he told us. I ate Dragon, Dyana. I ate a godsdamn Dragon."

All of the color has leaked out of Dyana's face as she stumbles and sits beside me, speechless. Her hands fly to cover her mouth as tears begin to fall.

"Nyall's right," I sniff. "The Gods are gone. They've abandoned us to the fae, to that son of a bitch Constantyn. It's all a lie." Then the sobs start, and I'm unable to stop as the words simultaneously vomit out.

"Amalia and I got really sick, we threw up right there at the table." I choke out, "The pain of its magyk is like nothing I've ever felt. Our bodies instantly rejected it. Then Os refused, and Achan...forced him to take a bite."

Dyana inhales sharply, her eyes wide with horror, "No!"

"Yeah," I whisper, my voice hollow, "But Amalia stopped it before he took the bite."

Dyana does not look at me. She doesn't move, but I notice every muscle in her body going still. "She stopped it?"

"Yes. She asked the High Councilor his opinion on some legend about a wytch."

The silence is heavy until Dyana asks, "What exactly happened with this story?"

She knows something.

I shrug, "She asked if he knew whether the wytch was real."

"And? What did he say?"

"He said the wytch wasn't real. That wytches have never existed. But it..." I break off, and Dyana turns to look at me,

"What?"

"It rattled him, Dy. Threw him off so much that he let us leave when Nyall suggested it."

Dyana clicks her tongue, "Did Amalia say anything else?"

"She told me Achan Drayen isn't the only monster here."

Dyana stands, facing away from me. She doesn't explain anything, and while that hurts, I'm not surprised.

Then she turns, clearing her throat and twiddling her hands, "Os is...what I think he is, right?"

We've never talked about it aloud, even with all of our planning with Nyall. But it seems we have all come to the same conclusion.

"I think so, but I'm not completely sure."

Dyana bites her lip, worrying, "We'll find out soon enough."

"Hmm," I nod my head in agreement.

We're silent for a few minutes as my tears dry for good, and sad exhaustion is left.

"I know you hate me, and I respect that. I'm not asking for anything. But after what just happened, I-I don't want to be alone tonight." The last word is barely whispered.

Dyana sighs and glances over her shoulder. "You can take my bed, and I'll take Amalia's. But this means nothing. Only that I'm not fucking heartless and I know what it is to feel alone."

I fight a sigh of relief as Dyana walks to the small dresser in the corner of their room, throwing a spare shirt my way, "You can sleep in this."

"Thank you," I whisper and turn around as I slide out of the dress. I can't get it off my body fast enough. I want the memory of this evening to fade away with the sands of time. The large tunic is loose and comfortable despite the fact that my feet and legs are freezing. But when I turn around, my heart stops as I catch Dyana watching me.

My heart is yours. How I yearn to repeat the words. How I yearn to tell her she's never looked more beautiful than she does right now—and yet, I say nothing as we crawl into bed. Hers is still warm from her body heat.

Dyana reaches over to blow the candle out, her dark, silky hair falling across a bare shoulder.

She's a marvel; and she will never be mine.

"Thank you," I whisper, and our eyes meet. For a single moment, I swear there is warmth reflected back at me, but it's shuttered a second later.

"You're welcome," Dyana breathes.

As I try to fall asleep, my dreams are delayed as Amalia's words replay in my head.

If she's a monster, what kind of monster is she?

# CHAPTER 60
AMALIA

Achan Drayven should say his prayers to Sol Constantus and consider himself lucky he's still alive. After the stunt he pulled tonight, it's taking every ounce of my willpower not to just say 'fuck it' and burn this world to the ground.

For the Dragons. For me.

For this scarred, tortured male in front of me who somehow managed to heal a small piece of my shattered heart. Somewhere along the way, Remus Ostia stole a piece of my heart and now holds it in his bloody hands.

I never planned on opening my mouth tonight.

But it was too much, too far.

What happened tonight is an unraveling. The others can feel it. I could see the nervousness written all over Mirielle's pale face. I'm sure she must have gone right to Dyana to talk about it.

No matter how my friend—my sister—feels, I've never once worried that she will spill the secrets that aren't hers to tell.

Secrets. So many years of secrets.

So many years of hiding.

I sigh and realize Remus is oddly quiet. I used to think he was a male of few words, but it's strange to realize how much he actually talks around me. He sits on the stone floor, elbows on his knees, staring into the crackling fireplace, unblinking.

Unraveling.

On silent feet, I walk over to Remus and slide down onto the cold floor next to him.

We sit there, side by side, silent. He leans his head over, onto my shoulders, but I stop him gently.

"Hold on," I whisper before leaning over to the loveseat, grabbing some cushions and tossing them to the floor along with a fur blanket. I roll around a bit, arranging the spot that reminds me so much of the place I, for many years, called home. Once everything is correct, I scooch onto the pillow and hold a hand out.

Remus's golden gaze is surprised and painfully vulnerable as he looks at my outstretched hand, before grabbing it. I tug him gently over to me and then, using my magyk, show him what I want him to do. He ducks, emotional, and crawls over to me, laying his head in my lap as I begin to run my fingers through his shoulder-length brown hair.

That's when Remus Ostia, Dragon Beastkyn, Magyka Prime, begins to cry. I don't falter or pause. Nor do I pity him or try to say I understand.

It took a while to figure out Remus's beast form. I didn't consider Dragons because Beastkyn are so rare. The only beings that can shift into a Dragon must be born a Dragon.

Remus isn't an actual shifter. A shifter is born as person. Even when they take the form of an animal, their soul remains mortal.

Instead, Remus shoved the righteous glory of his Dragon soul into the form of a mortal. But his soul is all *Dragon*.

Whatever caused him to end up here, whatever happened in the years since the fae turned him into their slave, it's broken him.

Maybe that's why we can't stay away from each other, like calls to like. Separate, we are broken.

Together...perhaps we're a bit more whole.

"When I was young, I decided I wanted to shift," Remus starts, his voice is hoarse from crying. "Much of Dragon magyk cannot be described accurately in mortal words, but I could only shift my arms at first. The other hatchlings beat me so bad I couldn't stand. My mother lost it. Near took out half of Elysium with her rage. But they all just stared and whispered, disgusted that I could, and would choose to, shift to human. I cried myself to sleep for a whole month, unable to understand why something as simple as curiosity would bring such hate. Why did they hate me for desiring to change shape? They always assumed it was out of shame. The last thing I felt was ashamed."

I'm quiet as Remus pauses. My hand trails through his hair as he watches the fire, the bright orange reflecting off his molten eyes.

"Eventually...she would come to resent me for it. But when I was still young, my mother would hold me each night and sing me to sleep. It was the only thing that could calm my thundering heart."

We're quiet as Remus's tears start to dry. An idea pops into my head as I think about his words, and before I can talk myself out of it, I close my eyes and begin to sing a song that hasn't been heard in this world for a very long time.

Our Queen, our pride,

Mother, be our guide.

We are the land, the sea,

the triumphant skies.

We'll fight with all,

mighty and strong,

till we hear the call.

What was lost,

shall yet be found,

when we reclaim

our sacred ground.

Our Queen, our pride,

Mother, be our guide.

We are the land, the sea,

and triumphant skies.

We are Arkaydia,

and still, we will rise.

The room is silent as I finish and catch my breath; the crackling fire and Remus's breathing are the only sounds.

"That was beautiful. I haven't heard that song for an age."

I blink, "You've heard it? I just—I've always assumed no one knew of it anymore. My mother loved to sing, and that was her favorite."

Remus *hmms*, rubbing his head into my lap and pressing a kiss to my calf muscle on top of my leggings.

"It was a lonely life. My only real friend was a small white mouse I rescued from a trap."

"What was his name?" Remus asks.

I snort, "At age six, I felt confident that the name Puff was perfect. He loved the name, though. He had the smallest, pink toes."

Remus hums thoughtfully as we continue to sit, each caught in our heads.

"I know it's not my fault, so I won't say I'm sorry. But I hope..." I swallow, nervous. "I care. That's all I want to say."

Remus is quiet but he reaches up and back, grabbing my hand to pull it down in front of him until it's right atop his heart. I curl around his shoulder, leaning my head on his arm.

Thump, Thump.

Thump, Thump.

Thump, Thump.

"I'm the one who is sorry, A gahrá. While you are comforting me and my pain, I can feel your own. Yet all I could do was sit there like a worthless welp as magyk prevented me from helping you, from protecting you. I failed you, I failed us. You should not want me as a familiar, Amalia. You should be angry, not sorry."

I yank my hand from him and stand up, walking around to his front so I'm framed by fire. I raise my finger and point, leaning down to his face, "Don't you dare pull that bullshit with me, Ostia. Don't you dare. You are the farthest thing from a failure. You cannot save me from every evil in this world. There was nothing you could do, so get that nonsense out of your mouth."

I pant, having shouted despite all efforts not to. My knees bend as I lower to kneel in front of him, grasping his scarred face between my pale hands.

"Let someone else save you for once, Ahavah."

"What does that mean?"

A small smile appears on my face as I lean down and press a slow, soft kiss to his stubbled cheek.

"My heart. Ahavah means my heart in the language of my father's kin. I learned it because my father called my mother Ahavah every single day."

Remus smiles, his eyes warm. He looks happy.

"You were the first Beastkyn, weren't you? Your magyk feels like a Prime," I murmur, taking a moment to finally ask him some of the questions that have been on my mind for so long.

Remus nods lightly, "Yes. For many years, I was the only one. When I decided to shift, I also shifted down to the genetic level. My magyk began to differ from that of the other Dragons."

I blink, trying to understand.

"Don't try to understand it; it'll hurt your head. Dragon laws do not adhere to mortal science. What you think of as impossible, I guarantee, isn't actually impossible. It's just impossible for mortals."

"I'm not mortal," I protest, but Remus just huffs,

"I am over a thousand years old, Amalia. You are longer-lived and slower aging than a human, but you are not immortal. The only beings on this earth that are immortal are Dragons and elves, and look what it did to the latter."

Wait—

"Are you saying Dragons really are Gods?"

Remus purses his lips. "A God is another mortal concept, A gahrá. No, we are not what you could call Gods, but we are beings of higher existence. However, there is no other word equivalent in your languages, so, I guess, yes. You can consider us Gods."

Remus is still beneath my hand, worried at how I'll react, so I do what Dyana would do.

"So since we're familiars, does that mean I'm holy?" I joke.

Remus rolls to his back and laughs.

Holy Gods, he's so beautiful when he laughs.

"Why thank you, A gahrá."

I blush furiously, having forgotten he was listening to my thoughts.

"Don't let the compliments get to your head, Beast," I say coldly, but I know my eyes sparkle with amusement. I run my hands across the planes of his face, fingers tracing his cheekbones and down his nose with featherlight touches. Remus closes his eyes, lips parting slightly when I run my thumb across them.

"Whatever form you take, Remus Ostia, you are good," I whisper the words as he blinks slowly, staring at me like he's just seen the sun for the first time in his entire life. It's overwhelming, the emotion in his gaze.

"Yours is the only opinion that matters to me anyways, A gahrá," he says softly. We stand and look at each other for a while, memorizing every line and mole and scar. Just in case tomorrow doesn't go well. I fought it for so long, but my heart had other plans, it seems. "I know you don't believe it, but you are good too, Amalia Roth. Never have I met someone with a heart as big as yours."

I look away, unable to face the compliments head-on while dealing with the immediate disagreement at his words happening in my head.

"Look at me." Remus grabs my chin gently with his large hand and pulls my gaze back until we're face to face. "You are good, Amalia. A little bloodthirsty, a little prone to violence, but you are good. You defend the voiceless and love those who would normally go unloved and forgotten. When you love, A gahrá, you give all of yourself. You are a rarity, and for what you did tonight, I owe you a debt that can never be repaid."

I shake my head, "There is no debt, Remus. It was worth it." I pause, swallowing again, chest tightening with nervousness as I hesitantly continue, "You are worth it."

Suddenly the room is too small and I can't breathe because my heart feels like it's too big for my body as Remus looks at me with such longing, I might actually spontaneously combust.

I clear my throat and lean away as I take a deep breath. "Right, well, we do have one other thing to do tonight."

Remus just looks at me, "Are you ready for this?"

I smirk, "It's not me I'm worried about." There is a piece of chalk on the table next to the loveseat, and I grab it as I turn back to Remus. "I'll start drawing, you start getting naked."

Time to break Remus's warding.

I just hope he's good with pain.

CHAPTER 61
AMALIA

My heart drops out of my chest as Remus strips in front of me, his movements slow and calculated, his skin illuminated in the warm firelight. I've seen him shirtless plenty but I've never allowed myself the chance to look at him so intensely. To see every bump and ridge of his muscular abdomen, every scar and mole.

I survey him like my own personal work of art, watching as his pants fall and I get my first up-close look at the rest of his warding tattoos. I've always been too...distracted to fully notice the way the warding continues all the way down his hip and leg.

"Remus, how many times did they ward you like this?" My voice is hollow with shock as I step closer, looking at the overlapping wards riddled with scars.

He just shrugs, "I stopped counting at 50."

"50? They redid your warding over 50 times? Gods above. That should have killed you."

And yet, 50 times over, Remus's magyk was so strong it continually degraded the integrity of the wards.

I knew he was strong, but this is insane.

Remus just smirks at me, "Nothing is a match for Dragon magyk. Mine is just different enough that the Archmage was never able to fully lock it down." He gestures down to the ink along his side.

Remus Ostia is a God among men. That much has always been perfectly clear. The news that he really is one is frankly comforting, because it's the only way to describe his otherworldly, imperfectly perfect beauty that is only enhanced by his scars.

But the scars. So many scars.

"What did they use in the ink?" I murmur.

Remus just sighs, "I have no idea. But it was made by the Elves; that much I know simply because theirs is the only magyk that could ever be strong enough to trap me in a single form. The imperial fae are powerful, but not like that."

I look him up and down as he stands, patiently waiting for me to finish. His eyes are alight with pleasure and what can only be described as purely male pride.

He's certainly well...equipped.

So I stalk him. Prowling closer, until we're toe to toe. I lift a bloody hand and trace a line with the edge of my nail all the way from his abs to his neck before lifting to my toes, pressing my body against him, and cupping his cheek.

"Remus?"

He meets my eyes and I fight a shiver at his golden stare. "Yes, A gahrá?"

"Make them pay," I reply.

Remus blinks, and his eyes are draconian again, the pupils narrow slits. His *true* eyes.

"With pleasure," he growls.

I fight a smile, "Remus?"

"Yes, A gahrá?"

"You're hard."

He chuckles, "I am Dragon, Amalia. I like it when you get a little bloodthirsty."

His voice turns to a purr in my head and all of a sudden it's as if an invisible tongue darts out, licking my core and making me jerk so hard the chalk is quite literally flung out of my hands.

This male is going to be the death of me.

Remus just watches me, gold eyes alight with amusement. I've never been one to back down from a challenge—something which has always annoyed Dyana to no end and resulted in days of grumbling from her. So I casually slide off the tunic Remus gave me, flashing him an innocent look over my shoulder. A low snarl fills the cavernous stone room, and I fight a shiver.

"Behave, Beast, or you'll see just how bloodthirsty I can get."

I face him across the elaborate warding circle I'd drawn onto the floor. "Enter the circle and stand in front of me."

Remus walks over to me, his thick, muscled thighs flexing in the firelight, and suddenly, I don't give a rat's ass about the warding spell; all I want is to put my hands and mouth on every bit of his gorgeous body.

"Who is the distraction now, A gahrá?"

My cheeks flush with embarrassment that he heard that particular thought, but I just glare, "No eavesdropping."

He just winks at me, and I let out a shuddered breath.

Remus steps into the circle, and I bend down, brushing two chalk lines together to completely close the circle. With a pulse of my magyk, the white chalk catches fire, burning with a flame darker than the midnight hour. Once the flame burns down the chalk, there's another bright white pulse and a small snapping sound as the circle activates.

It's like a curtain is lifted. I can see Remus's magyk in the air. Strands of gold and copper cover every single surface.

Remus's eyes have always been a brilliant gold, but now they glow as if lit from behind, growing bigger until they're just black diamond pupils amongst a sea of molten gold.

His features grow more prominent. Everything about him becomes more, even down to the way he's standing.

Then it stops.

The real Remus faces me now. Untethered and unleashed.

The Beastkyn.

The *Dragon.*

My Father's black and silver dagger burns in the firelight next to the swords Remus gave me a few weeks ago. Neiman and Macha. The beginning and the end. Morrigyn's blades. Hidden deep within the Dragon Pit where Remus found them centuries ago; and kept them hidden, until now.

I'll use my Father's dagger for this, but it feels right to have Neiman and Macha out. They are all that's left of the old world—of the days of Arkaydia.

They should be here to see Ur Daoine's end.

The reflection of the crackling fire makes it appear to almost glow as I drag the sharp blade down my arm, pressing just hard enough to slice open my skin.

Remus growls, and I struggle to keep my hand from trembling at the Dragonfear that fills me. His jaw clenches tightly, watching as my blood drips down to my palm.

The warding circle has two purposes. It will keep my magyk contained, but it also acts as an amplifier, making it easier to wield and giving me a safe place to do it.

Father didn't have time to teach me everything he knew, but this was one of the first things we practiced.

It's a memory and a curse twined with unending pleasure as I raise my other hand and watch as black smoke grows within my palm before winding through my fingers like snakes.

The feeling of letting more of my magyk free is euphoric as if I'd drunk too much wine. The shadows twirl along my body, cold and soft against my freckled skin.

I almost fall into the trap of power, almost forget why we're really here, so with a flick of my wrist, I turn the shadows into a cup, concentrating and solidifying them just enough to hold the dripping blood.

The strain is heavy, and my body twitches, trembling under the weight of my true magyk after years of keeping it locked up.

Remus doesn't move, but his eyes glow as if lit from behind. The shadows react to me, dancing against my skin and brushing against my senses with gentle touches as if greeting a lost friend.

I blink away the tears that come at knowing I chose this.

I chose to leave this part of me behind.

I had to.

The room is suddenly so dark that the only light to be seen is the crackling fire and Remus's golden gaze. His eyes pulse with light again, and his magyk brushes against me, making me shiver. A tingle begins in my arm, and I watch with awe as my wound begins to close.

We stare at each other for a few moments, letting our magyks mingle. With a deep breath, I dip two fingers into the cup of blood and smoke and begin to paint. Remus's eyes fall closed with a groan as I draw a long line down the center of his face, pressing my blood onto his lips. He growls under his breath, more beast than man. I draw sigils across his forehead as more smoke floods into the room. Everything grows hazy, and for a moment, I can hear drums, rhythmically beating in the distance, the sound everywhere and nowhere all at once.

"What language is this?" Remus says, his voice low.

I smile, sad. "It's the language of my Father's kin. I only know a handful of words, and I can pronounce a few. We didn't get very far in my training before they..."

Remus places a hand on my arm, squeezing gently. "Someday, I would like to hear you say every single word, my spark."

I nod, biting my lip as I concentrate on painting him.

We both begin to breathe heavily as I move down his neck and paint sigils on his chest, tracing his warding. I can't help but lean in and kiss his sternum, my tongue darting out as I taste him. Remus groans and fists my hair with his large hand.

"If you keep doing that, A gahrá, this is going to be over before it even begins," he protests, but he doesn't pull me back. I look up at him beneath my dark lashes and smirk as I dip my fingers in my blood again and continue drawing the sigils.

It's a few minutes before I finish painting. My mouth kept getting a bit distracted when painting his hip and thigh.

My new favorite sound is Remus groaning my name. But I stop teasing and torturing him as I use the last few drops to finish the design.

He's a maelstrom of red, black, and gold as the tattoos contrast against the dark red paint.

"You look good in my blood, Beast," I murmur as I push to standing.

"Finish the spell, Amalia," Remus snarls.

I grab my dagger and make another cut, this time on my other arm. Remus frowns, "I do not like you hurting yourself, A gahrá."

A buzzy feeling hits me at how upset he is.

"Then it's a good thing you're here to heal me, Beast."

Remus just looks at me, his eyes shockingly tender.

"Ready?" I slice my hand and let the blood pool before presenting it to him.

Remus meets my eyes without hesitation, placing his hand in mine.

"Do it."

"Right. Try not to scream." I advise before yanking open those iron doors deep inside me and letting all of my walls crumble to dust.

I am *unleashed.*

Dark blue flame explodes from me, surrounding us as Remus falls to his knees with a groan. I grunt, concentrating as I shove my fire into his body, sending it to all of that magyked ink.

Like a virus, it fights me, so I place my hands on Remus's shoulders and feed more magyk into his system. He groans again, trembling, coated in sweat as my blood begins to glow, and his warding begins burning right off his skin.

The smell of burnt honeysuckle and sour apple fills the air as my magyk continues to pummel him, as my fire traces the path up his body, right where I drew my blood.

He never screams. Even though I'm burning him alive. His arms tremble, and he moans under his breath, but he never cries out.

My fire burns through the remaining warding, the Elven magyk pushing back hard. I close my eyes and drop my head back, feeling lightheaded as I drop even more magyk and will behind the spell. I tremble and sweat under the weight of my power, unable to hold it for much longer. Then my fire goes out, plunging us into darkness.

It's gone.

There's no more magyked ink to burn away.

I feel like I just ran ten laps.

We both pant heavily as my shadows retreat, and my magyk goes back behind those barely standing iron walls deep within me, content and exhausted.

I freeze as I see the ash on the ground.

Ash made of my burned-up blood. A low growl begins to build as Remus pushes to stand. He gets up, cracking his muscular neck left and right, and—holy shit. He's even taller and larger than he was before.

Gods.

He walks out of the circle, facing away from me as he stretches his wings out, his fingernails shifting to viciously sharp black claws.

"It's been so long," his low voice vibrates as he relishes his freedom, "so long since I felt my magyk. Since I felt the scales beneath my skin."

His magyk tastes so strong now. The sweet, smokey taste almost burning my tongue.

"How do you feel?" I whisper, suddenly nervous, although I'm not sure why. Will he seem like the same male?

Remus is a blur as he moves, grabbing me and carrying me over to the bed. He tosses me and I bounce hard but he's already there, fisting my still bloody hair and flashes me a smile full of white fangs that set my heart galloping.

"I feel hungry, Amalia. So very hungry," he purrs, leaning down and licking up my neck, making my toes curl. "The only words I want coming out of your wicked little mouth right now are 'yes', 'more', and 'harder, please'." He yanks on my ankle, pulling me down the bed until I'm underneath him.

His shoulder-length hair falls on my face as he leans down and kisses me.

Kiss isn't a good enough word. Instead, with every touch and swipe of his tongue, he claims me, body and soul. He licks my body clean, caressing my scarred, sun-worn skin with reverence. I'm panting and moaning wantonly by the time he makes it back to my mouth.

Remus pulls my legs apart with his large hands, trailing hot fingers up and down the lips of my core, spreading my wetness all over.

"Gods, look at you. You're so fucking beautiful. My *familiar*. My other half," he growls. He's a blur, and then he's between my legs, spearing me with his tongue. I cry out as he sucks on my bundle of nerves, my back bowing as he works me with his lips and tongue.

Pleasure hits me with the weight of a ton of bricks as my orgasm shatters me. He continues to lap me up, growling with pleasure at my reactions. "You're mine, Amalia." He pauses and lifts one of my legs so it sits on his shoulder. "And I, Amalia Roth, am all yours." Then he thrusts into me with a growl, stretching me so much I might actually explode. I scream as he pushes in all the way, his pelvis grinding against mine.

"Look, A gahrá, look at how well we fit. Look at how perfectly you take me."

I grip his biceps and look down, moaning at the sight of him thrusting into me."Oh fuck...Remus," I cry and he just pulls back before slamming into me again. I meet his gaze and glance down, seeing my lips enveloping him fully as he thrusts in completely.

"You were made for me," he mutters almost to himself and I moan as he thrusts again, making me see stars. But I'll be damned if I make this easy for him.

I blur, using what little enhanced speed I do have, and flip him to his back sliding him inside of me in a single move. His cock is huge and stretches me to the limit but Gods, it's so good.

"And you were made for me, Beast. Say it again. Say you're mine." I hiss, clenching my abdominal muscles, thanks to years of horse riding. His whole body tenses as his hips jerk without conscious effort.

"Holy Gods, what are you doing, woman?"

I smirk, beginning to ride him, clenching my inner abdominal muscles in a pulse.

He snarls and grabs my hips, holding me still while he hammers into me from below. I go limp in his grasp as the pleasure becomes too much, and I detonate like a newborn star, my shadows exploding outward, coating the room in darkness.

He flips me over, yanking me back by my hair so I'm bent like a crescent moon and entirely at his mercy.

"I've always been yours, A gahrá."

"Remus," I mewl his name. He picks up a brutal pace, slamming in and out of me so hard I see stars.

This is not fucking. This is not sex. This is a *claiming*.

I am lost, and I am found, all within the arms of a beast wearing the skin of a man. There is no beginning or end to our bodies, and we spend the remainder of the evening learning each other.

In the dead of night, when we finally tire and are almost asleep, I whisper into the darkness. Whisper the words that have been in my heart, but that I've been too afraid to utter aloud, and I swear that for a moment the world stops, waiting and watching. I repeat the words, this time in a language long since forgotten.

"You know what needs to be done?"

"I do," I reply, although I know Kydis can hear my heart racing. The suns aren't even up yet, and despite the exertion—magykal and otherwise—I couldn't fall asleep.

I know Remus was calculated in trying to tire me out before bed. Genuine, yes, but it was also to help me sleep and to distract me from spiraling into oblivion within the confines of my mind.

There are no doubts about the path forward and what it will require, what it will change. But I have this sinking feeling, like a weight on my chest that gets heavier every minute.

We all can't make it out alive. Each one of us knows it.

Remus and I went down to the Pits during the morning guard change to meet with Kydis one last time.

"Let all from here to the shores of Elysium know: Amalia Roth is the friend of Dragons." Kydis gently presses her snout into my hand through the bars, her scales cool and smooth despite the many scars and bumps.

"Soon you'll be free," I caress her scales, stepping closer to the bars so I'm leaning against her. I maneuver my arms to wrap around her nose in as much of a hug as I can manage.

"Your debt is paid, Remus Ostia," Kydis says in our minds, pulling back from me gently. Remus closes his eyes and clenches his jaw as he leans forward and presses his hand to the other side of Kydis' snout as emotion catches him. I back up, allowing him to have this moment without me overwhelming it.

No words are exchanged, and neither open their mouths, but I hear the lilting tune of their voices, their true voices, echoing throughout the cave. Remus's is the loudest, his layered voice strong and powerful.

He looks at Kydis before kneeling and bowing, one fist over his heart. *"Thank you, your highness."*

"Do not thank me; just stick to the plan and be careful. May Livyathin protect you, may He protect us all."

I step back, chest tight with fear, and grab Remus's hand as I meet Kydis' gaze for the final time.

Dragons will be slaves to no one ever again.

CHAPTER 62
KYDIS

The clanging of armor and dozens of footsteps vibrating through the floor wakes me. The Gauntlet doesn't start until tonight, so it's best to conserve our energy until then. But I was barely nodding off; too nervous to do otherwise.

"My Queen, are you awake?"

"I hear it," I respond to Vesimyr, suddenly smelling rotten apples.

He's here. Achan Drayven steps into view as he strides down the aisle, heading towards me. So, he's not as stupid as he looks.

"Butcher."

"Murderer."

"You killed my son!"

"Where are my babies?"

"Where did you take my babies?"

My mind is a storm of shouts as we all watch as Evil himself, dressed in the skin of Achan Drayven, walks down the aisles of the Dragon Pit.

His skin is turning dark, almost purple, and shriveled as if he's rotting from the inside.

Achan Drayven is running out of time, regardless of any plans to quicken his end.

The poisonous monster walks straight toward my cell.

"Hello, lizard." Achan Drayven licks his lips as I lean back into my stall, curling up as far from the bars as possible. "Ah, no, no, come here lizard. No running away.

We need to talk." Red magyk that burns my scales wraps around me as he closes his fist and slams me against the metal door, stretching one of my talons through the bars. He grabs one of my long black claws and snaps it in half, blood coating his palm. The pain threatens to make me pass out.

"My queen, do you need assistance?" Vesimyr snarls in my head.

"No! No." I pant, *"Do not interfere. Whatever happens today, you must keep to the plan, Vesimyr."*

A pause. *"As you wish."*

"I've been hearing rumors of some rather...rebellious behavior lately." Achan muses, tapping his horrid black, misshapen nails on my broken claw, sending bolts of pain up my leg. "Something needs to be done about that. Did you forget, beast? You survive at my behest. Take her to the labs. We have business to attend to," he orders, and a dozen fae attendants come swarming. My stall is quickly opened, and I stumble as they quickly electrocute me, prodding me again with their sharp and pointy sticks. Manacles go around my four ankles and that damned muzzle goes around my snout as I'm led into a section on the far side of the Pits.

"Vesimyr," I say suddenly, *"you will lead in my stead, should I not return."*

I feel his shock rather than see it. *"My Queen, you will return—"*

"May Livyathin guide you, my friend. Get our people home; whatever the cost. Save as many as you can." I call one final time before the lab doors shut behind me, cutting off all sound and all communication. Blood stains the walls, and a giant stone table stained nearly black sits in the middle, with big straps and chains.

"You know the drill. Get on the table."

Shame weighs on me as I scooch onto the table awkwardly.

Another set of feet approach, "Flip over, Dragon scum."

The Elf. The one who calls himself the Archmage.

I flip over and allow them to chain me down, strapping me to that horrid, bloody stone.

Achan's beady red eyes come into view as he leans over me, smirking. "Now, I think we should have a little talk, don't you? The tip about the little Arkaydian bitch was quite useful, but I think you know more about your little gray-haired friend, don't you? She and that demis whore are up to something, and you're going to tell us what that is."

The Archmage moves into view behind him, holding a small, wiggling bundle in his arms.

"Fine," I say into their minds. Achan flinches slightly and punches me in the snout, embarrassed that he still fears me. *"I will tell you what you want to know. Just don't hurt her. Please."*

I tell them what they want to know and then retreat from their minds, exhausted.

"I'm so sorry," I whisper, but the lab is warded too strongly. Amalia cannot hear me.

There is no response.

There is only betrayal. *My* betrayal.

CHAPTER 63
AMALIA

"Repeat it to me," Remus demands as I finish snapping on the leather ties locking in my forearm guards. Mirielle stayed over with Dyana, and they showed up this morning, dressed and ready to go. Dyana watches me carefully, hurt and fear flashing equally behind her dark eyes.

Remus sighs, snapping his fingers, "Dyana, pay attention. Repeat the plan."

Dyana blinks. "Don't be a dick and I will. Gods," she mutters, clearing her throat and glaring at him, "When you two enter the bout," she nods to me and Mirielle, "Os and I will go down to the Dragon Pit. Nyall will send a signal when the battle starts, and you three distract Achan, warding him off so he doesn't feel the magyk. Which reminds me, how are you going to do that again?"

"I'm gonna put on a damn good show," I start sheathing my various daggers, hiding them everywhere I can.

"Right, you and Mirielle will handle that as the Prince charges up his magyk and preps for siphon weaving. Then, when Os and I get into position, we'll send the signal, and Ama, you'll use your magyk to break the warding around the Dragon Pit, which Nyall has spelled to automatically trigger all of the stable doors to open. Then, and for the record, I do not like this part and want it noted that I think this is a horrible idea," Dy clears her throat, her pupils wide and her face pale. "I will...hitch a ride from one of the Dragons as they escape through the cave. But before we do that, the Dragons are going to catch the hatchlings and use the slings Os built to carry the littlest ones as the others break through the Pit walls, and after that, we'll just...figure it out."

"You forgot something," I mutter.

Dyana wrinkles her nose, "Oh yeah, and after we get the hatchlings secured, you, Mirielle, Os, and Nyall will, uh, kill the entire High Council and Nyall will trigger his siphon spell so that all of their stolen magyk is injected back into the land, theoretically healing the damage the imperial fae have done to our land and then we can all live happily ever after. The end."

I swat her on the back of her head.

"Ouch! Rude!"

"Then don't be an idiot. We'll figure it out after...after."

Dyana just glares, "Great motivational speech, captain. What's next, a song?"

"What are you doing if something goes wrong?" Remus asks, throwing questions her way. We've all been doing this for days. Memorizing everything so that it was second nature when the time finally arrived.

"Get out, stay hidden, stick to the forest. Meet north of Eahmond by the small lake at the base of the Ulster Wald."

"Good," I mutter, adjusting my armor.

This morning, Remus asked if he could braid my hair. I nodded, shocked at the request. He then pulled me onto his lap, sitting behind me in bed as he brushed the comb through my hair and wove my hair into three different braids in the style of my people. I projected the image of the braid I wanted into his mind, and he copied it. Once he was done, he wrapped his arms around me, and we sat. Silently holding each other as we took in what very well might be our last moments together.

The memories fade as I continue to take in the image in the mirror.

A symbol of three triangles separated by lines, almost like a snowflake is on my cheek, drawn with Remus's blood. The...collection process, of course, lead to biting in other, more southern places, which lead to even more. But the symbol is something my Father always drew for me.

In the language of his people, the symbol means 'courage.'

"It's time to go," Remus says. He's always been able to tell what time it is, even without a clock to read. Part of his magyk, perhaps. Dyana coughs, and I catch the glance she throws Mirielle.

"We'll meet you outside. I need to talk to Mirielle about...um...something." the former mutters as the two of them hustle outside. Remus doesn't even turn to me. The second we're alone, I feel the words on the tip of his tongue.

"I can't, Remus. I can't do this.

"A gahrá—"

"No!" I exclaim aloud, "I'm not saying it!" He walks over and cups my cheek, leaning down until our foreheads touch. "I am not saying goodbye," I whisper. "I refuse."

"I'll see you on the other side then, my spark. But no martyr bullshit."

"I would never."

"Fuck that, promise me, Amalia. I need you alive. Don't be stupid unless it's literally the only option left."

My only answer is to press my lips against his. We sigh into each other and forget just for a moment. His dark brown hair is wet and loose, falling around his face and making him look more feral than usual.

Remus pulls back, holding me steady, his large hand hot against my throat. My magyk brushes against his, intertwining like the braids of my hair. Tingles break out across my entire body, and I shiver as the shadows waver.

"Give them Hell, spark."

Oh, I plan to.

Life isn't fair. This is a truth I know all too well.

As I watch Dyana and Mirielle awkwardly say goodbye, I send out one last plea to the Morrigyn to intervene.

Give them the chance to be happy, Mother. Give them the chance to live, please.

"FUCKING DO SOMETHING!" I scream in my head. At her lack of response, my prayers quickly turned to curses.

My parents always insisted She was the one who made my creation possible. Made my parents able to get pregnant at all. Whether that holds any truth or not, I'll never know, because the Mother is ever silent as my prayers remain unanswered.

Who knows if those two would have worked out if they met in different circumstances? It's clear they each care, but there are things we simply cannot come back from. We might be able to forgive, but to forget is another matter entirely.

Dyana won't forget. She's as stubborn as a ram, despite the fact that she always calls me the stubborn one.

Mirielle finally nods, donning her helmet. Her red curls are loose and wild, the helmet not doing a single thing to take away from her wild, untamed beauty.

"Make it quick; they'll call our names soon," Mirielle mutters as she passes me, giving us a tiny amount of space, not that there would be any hiding whatever is said.

I take a step forward, "Dyana, I—"

"I know, Ama. I already know," Dyana sighs.

"I'm sorry, Dy. I told you I would always keep you safe, and I meant it."

"I understand. I'm still pissed, but I get it." We're silent for a moment, and then she's in my arms, squeezing the air out of my lungs as I'm wrapped up in a tight hug.

Don't break. Don't you dare break.

~~*I am shattering.*~~

Silent sobs shake her body, threatening to shatter my steely resolve.

"Promise me you won't do anything stupid," Dyana whispers, her voice hard.

"I don't know what you mean—"

"Bullshit. That's bullshit, and you know it. I know you, Amalia Roth, which means I know you have some hair-brained, unhinged scheme planned that will likely get you killed. But you are all I have, too. Please don't take a risk unless you have to," she pauses. "Please don't make me watch you die."

Oh, Dyana.

I can't make that promise, and she knows it. I pull back and grab her tear-stained face with my hands, using my thumbs to gently wipe the tears from her cheeks. "I don't say this enough, but I'm so proud of you, Dy."

Dyana closes her eyes, crying openly into my hands as I push to my tiptoes and kiss her salty, damp cheek. "We will find each other again, in this life or the next," I whisper. "Because family sticks together, and you, Dyana Arkos, are my sister in all the ways that matter. You are my family."

I sniff and step back, taking her in one last time as I curse the Fates and rage at the Gods, at the Morrigyn for weaving us this fate. Damn you.

"Many years ago, you saved a lost, broken girl and gave her purpose. You saved my life; now it's time I return the favor." I don't bother wrapping my scarf around my head this time. Instead, I adjust it to cover my mouth and nose, exposing only my eyes.

Mirielle knows who I am, obviously, but Mirielle isn't who I'm here for.

Dyana watches me, tears falling openly and her face tense with pain.

"CITIZENS OF UR DAOINE! WELCOME TO THE FINALS!" The announcer calls, and the stone ceiling of the tunnel vibrates, dust falling all over us as the crowd of tens of thousands explodes in raucous cheer.

"MAY I PRESENT MIRIELLE FROM SUD AZYL AND AMALIA FROM TWYN FELLS—YOUR GAUNTLET FINALISTS!"

I turn, sparing one last glance at the person who has kept me on this side of sanity for the last eighteen years. Dyana's brown eyes meet my own, and for a moment, time stops.

"Stick to the shadows," I whisper in her head, forcing myself to turn away and meet Mirielle.

We each take a deep breath.

"You ready?" she asks.

I glance at her as I finally start to let loose the rage that's been simmering deep within me for weeks. Mirielle swallows shakily at whatever she sees on my face.

"I think the real question is, are you?"

I lift the hood of the gray cape that covers my armor, the hem trailing in the dust behind me.

"Achan Drayven doesn't leave here alive," I say, my voice low.

"Agreed," Mirielle responds, and together, we step onto the Arena sand.

CHAPTER 64
AMALIA

Fae, demis, and magyka alike are packed into the dusty Arena stands. The overcast winter weather is surprisingly tepid, but we're protected from much of the wind anyway.

The rows of seats are packed, with no empty space to be seen.

They curse and shout, screaming as we walk into the center of the Arena. Ready and eager for their daily entertainment.

The High Council's private box is fully transparent today, and everyone's dressed to the nines. Prince Nyall's eyes meet mine from where he sits behind his father. He's devastating in a simple, unbuttoned white shirt that shows off his tattoos, rolled up to his elbows and baring the black veining along his inked forearms.

I reach out with my mind and activate the network I made earlier, connecting everyone's minds. It was harder the first time, but now the connection is already there, so it only takes a small pulse of magyk before we're in each other's heads. Well, before I'm in their heads.

"We're in position." I share. *"Dyana, are you ready?"*

"Uh, hold on," she says nervously.

"What's wrong?"

"What's happening?" Mirielle hisses between barely moving lips.

I grab onto the light of her mind and merge the connection so she can hear too.

"60 seconds away from the guard rotation." Remus's voice grounds me, his calm instantly helping my worries.

"You better be right about all of this, Prince," I hiss as Achan Drayven stands, and the crowd goes quiet.

Here we go.

"My friends! I have a treat for you today. But first, let us congratulate the two candidates for getting this far." False words and pretty promises, as usual.

"One of you will die today, perhaps even both of you!" Everyone cheers at his grotesque words. Lovely.

"I put together an extra special final bout just for you both in honor of this momentous occasion."

"Uh, Nyall? What the fuck is he talking about?" Mirielle hisses. Achan just motions to the far wall of the arena.

"I don't know—fuck, the Council's minds are blocked. Something's wrong." At Nyall's anxious, vicious words, something settles deep within me.

I knew something was going to go wrong. There's almost a comfort in knowing we're going to get it over with.

"What's going on?" Remus demands.

"I don't know. Achan has some godsdamn surprise for us, which is never good news." I respond, and Dyana lets out a series of shouted mental expletives.

The ground wobbles as the Arena floor descends without warning. The crowd cheers as we struggle to maintain our footing. It drops fast and stops, tossing us both to our backs. We scramble to stand up as the crowd jeers. But then, they go quiet.

Too quiet.

Mirielle and I look at each other, panting as the sound of a stone door sliding open reaches us. We turn in sync, both stopping at the wall of pitch-black smoke billowing out of the door like a tsunami wave.

Then a snout emerges; a giant, scarred, crimson snout.

A snout I know all too well.

I just touched it this morning.

A snout belonging to a Dragon who is supposed to be in the Pits.

Yet, she's here.

Everyone begins shouting in my head as Mirielle frantically conveys what's happening. But I have nothing. There are no words I can form as I stare into Kydis's orange and yellow eyes as she steps forward, emerging in her giant, terrifying glory.

"I GIVE YOU, THE CRIMSON QUEEN!" The announcer roars as Kydis fully emerges from the dark, led by fae attendants carrying her chain confinements. A gold stone sits between her eyes, and as the attendants remove her muzzle and shackles, it flashes red and her pupils dilate in response.

~~*This isn't real.*~~

~~*This can't be real.*~~

"We have a serious fucking problem," I say, and everyone goes quiet.

"Nothing else matters on the sand, A gahrá. Nothing." Remus's voice is hard and unforgiving.

Nyall cuts in, *"Achan knows something. She wasn't the Dragon originally picked for this event. I checked this morning and another was listed. What the fuck happened?"* Now it's his turn to pause and let out expletives. He snarls, sounding more Dragon than Remus. *"Amalia, Os is right. You cannot care about her now. Nothing else matters but making sure you live long enough to finish through on the plan. In 15 seconds, you need to move. The distraction has to happen. You cannot hesitate."*

"Kydis?" I prod at her mind, but it's locked down tight. I push harder and funnel more magyk into it, but it's useless. The compulsion is too strong. I could break it but...that's last-resort level magyk. My mind races as I try and think of a solution here but come up blank. *"Please, Kydis. Please hear me."*

Nothing. As I search for her mind, search for a way in behind the warding, there is nothing but perfect silence.

My breath comes faster, blood pumping as my adrenaline rises and my vision tinges red. Slowly, one vertebra at a time, I turn from Kydis and look up right into the eyes of Achan Drayven.

"A gahrá...I'm so sorry." Remus says. His voice leaves little to interpretation. He's sorry...because now I have to kill her.

"We proceed as planned," my voice shaky even in my thoughts, *"and I'm breaking that godsdamn compulsion."*

But there's only silence. No one responds.

"Dyana? Remus?" I call.

Mirielle hisses at me, getting my attention. "Everything went quiet. I can't hear anyone!"

A slow laugh echoes around us, everywhere and nowhere, all at once. "It's no use, Arkaydian whore," Achan Drayven hisses at me as if he were standing at my back. "Now, we'll finally be done of your kind once and for all."

The fae attendants unlock Kydis's chains, and they drop to the ground with a large thump before sprinting out of the Arena, giant stone doors closing behind them—locking us in with a giant, deadly, poisoned Dragon.

Wait—

"She's not wearing the chain around her neck," I mutter.

"BEGIN!" the announcer yells, no warning, no countdown, when it dawns on me.

"MIRIELLE, WATCH OUT!" I scream as Kydis takes a deep breath and the air seems to get sucked out of the room as she explodes with a mighty roar, unleashing a torrent of flame so hot it could melt iron, right in our direction. We both leap out of the way. I hit the ground hard, and my ribs scream in protest. Mirielle shrieks as the Dragon flame singes part of her hair, but we're otherwise unharmed.

"Kydis, hear me! Please!" I push harder, funneling more magyk against her compulsion warding. The magyk slapback is painful and I grimace.

There's a snapping noise in my ears and I flinch.

"Amalia, can you hear me?" Remus asks frantically.

"Yes," I huff, sprinting across the sand.

"Trigger the damned spell! We can't wait any longer!"

"Uh Amalia, your boyfriend killed some people...er, uh, a lot of people actually...and some of the Dragonguard..." Dyana says casually.

"DO IT NOW!" Remus shouts, ignoring her.

With a growl, I release the spell, funneling all of my magyk into Neiman and Macha. Then I slam them into the Arena sand, sending a pulse of magyk down into the ground and right into Remus. My skin goes cold as the magyk burns right out of me.

Shit, did it work?

It's so subtle I'm not sure I'd even notice if I wasn't sure what to look for. But an electric shock zaps me, and Mirielle reacts the same as we stand quickly and pick up into a sprint, avoiding another jet of flame directed right at us.

Thanks to the magyk I funneled Kydis earlier, she's much stronger than she should be. Something I'm now deeply regretting.

Tears wet my face as we avoid another torrent of flame. Even though I'm not burnt, the heat is so immense that it feels as if my lungs are on fire.

Please, don't make me kill her.

I can't kill her. She's my friend.

As per usual, my prayers go unanswered.

"I need to get to the wardstone!" I shout to Mirielle, but Kydis leaps into the air with a great flap of her giant crimson wings as she uses them to pounce on top of us. Mirielle, who is closer to her legs, rolls out of the way, but gets a claw to the back, tearing right through her armor. She screams in pain as I hit the ground, Kydis's front claw almost crushing me.

"It worked. Holy shit, it worked. Amalia, the spell worked. The stalls are open."

I almost drop my swords in shock.

"Nyall? Can you hear this?" Remus asks.

"Yes," Nyall says.

"Drop the barrier. The stalls are open and the Dragons are beginning to dig. Now is the time for that distraction, spark!"

"Oh good, now the real fun begins," the Prince says happily. I feel him trigger the barrier wards he wove onto the Arena stands this morning. The ward bounces into existence, invisible to all but blocking all outside magic from being felt.

Whatever happens outside of the Arena—or beneath it—won't be heard.

"I'm beginning the Siphon weaving. At my signal, disarm Achan." Nyall replies, and everything goes quiet in my head as my thoughts shut off. Nyall just made the entire arena into a void field. No telepathy or psychic magyks.

"Whatever you're planning? Make it good."

Kydis whirls, tail almost decapitating me as I roll across the sand and withdraw my magyk from the swords, sending a wave of it right at Kydis.

Kydis's compulsion wavers for a moment, and her pupils narrow. She flinches, and it takes over again as her pupils dilate once more.

Damnit.

I sprint at her, dropping my sword and grabbing two daggers from my belt instead. Kydis leans back, ready to unleash another torrent of fire at me as she swipes Mirielle with her spiked tail. Mirielle jumps out of the way as I hit the ground, avoiding the flame. Sort of.

I slash both of my palms, and despite the fact that my heart feels like it might explode out my chest, run beneath Kydis, dragging my bloody hands against her scales.

Blood sigils would help more, but my blood alone will have to do.

The moment my magyk touches hers, I smash the compulsion with my magyk, shoving everything I have at the spell. The compulsion shatters, and I scream at the recoil as the Elven magyk burns me from the inside out. A clink sounds as the gold stone that was in between her eyes retracts, falling to the ground.

It's too much magyk.

My hands grow colder, and my heart races as I groan and roll for cover as Kydis stumbles.

"Kydis, please hear me." We're almost done. I whisper to her, directing all of my magyk to her burning red mind.

"MIRIELLE?" I scream.

"Yeah?" A voice shouts, panting. Kydis isn't going to like this part, but there's no other choice. I'm sick to my stomach as I turn to look at Mirielle, who pants in half-singed armor.

"HIT HER TAIL!" I shout. She doesn't stop to ask me what I mean, she simply unsheaths her staff and separates it into two, wickedly sharp ends, bringing both points down right into the meat of Kydis' tail, staking her to the Arena sand.

Kydis screeches in pain, distracted briefly as her eyes go back to normal. She writhes, trying to get the staff out of her tail.

"Kydis, I'm so sorry. We have to make this look real."

She interrupts me, *"It's too late. You need to kill me."*

"No. I won't do it." I run underneath Kydis as she struggles against Mirielle's staff blades. She swipes with her talon and misses me on purpose, trying to keep up the compulsion ruse.

Mirielle, however, doesn't know Kydis is back and under no power but her own. I watch in slow motion as she yanks her staff out of Kydis' tail, blood bubbling from the wounds as soon as the staff is removed, as she runs past me, preparing to slit Kydis's throat.

"MIRIELLE, NO!"

Yelling suddenly enters my head.

Oh shit. The ward is down.

I suck in a deep breath.

Nyall has his plan.

But I, too, have a plan.

The second the imperial fae declared us the Gauntlet candidates, I began formulating another plan.

My plan.

The one I've had all along.

I meet Kydis's flaming gaze as Mirielle watches, confused. I didn't exactly lie to Remus, but I didn't tell him the whole truth either.

My power is empathic, yes, but my power is not empathy. My power is *will*.

I cannot remove another's will, but I can force mine upon them. Mirielle grunts as I push my magyk on her, making her stumble and fall. Then I stop her heart—almost, at least. I slow it to the point of beating so slowly, it's inaudible. I press my will against that beating organ, and the rush of her blood responds to my command.

Kydis watches me, panting as I shift my magyk and toss it onto her and coating her like a blanket. I push my will onto her with nothing more than a thought, shoving her to the ground and causing her limbs to go limp. A long time ago, my parents told me the story of the Morrigyn, and of her earthly servants. Beings imbued with her power, chosen by the Mother herself to protect her world and her creations.

With Her left hand, the Mother protects and guides. With Her right, the Morrigyn punishes.

"Amalia, you need to let me go. If you don't, Achan will kill—" I stop Kydis mid-sentence, reaching a hand out in front of me. I snap my fingers and magyk wooshes out of me, threatening to make me pass out, but Kydis and Mirielle stop breathing as I shut their bodies down nearly to the point of no return.

The effort it takes is staggering. The crowd goes silent, confused as to what just happened. Whispers sound throughout the Arena, followed by angry shouts.

"What's the meaning of this?" Achan roars as the Arena shoots up in the air, bringing us back to ground level and closer to the audience.

"The Dragon and the girl are dead. I poisoned my blades, knowing it would mean a long, slow death." I say without shouting, knowing perfectly well Achan Drayven and all in his booth are able to hear me.

"The meaning of this, High Councilor, is that I win."

I unsheathe my two clean swords and stab them into the sand.

He doesn't feel the burst of magyk I send Remus or how I heal all of Kydis's wounds.

"How exactly did you poison them, Miss Roth? Why should I believe anything you say?"

I shrug, letting my gray cape fall. "I coated the blades in Nightbane I foraged in the Annag. It was just a matter of timing." I look up, seeing Achan Drayven's angry, flustered face. He clicks his tongue as Nyall catches my gaze, his mismatched eyes hard and suspicious. He's right to be, but not for the reasons I'm sure he's currently stewing on. His eye twitches lightly as he stands.

"I suppose you're right. No matter, you're coming with me for testing after this anyway. Let's find out what secrets you've got in there." Achan snaps, and the doors to the Arena begin to open.

Kydis's still body is prone, but I can see the quiet movement of her heart. Not dead. Just asleep. I take a deep breath and look up at the man who murdered my parents.

"No," I say.

Achan scowls, "What did you just say to me?"

I smile, "I said no. I refuse."

The crowd gasps, going silent again as Achan Drayven's eyes go wide and his face goes red with rage.

"How dare you! Who do you think you are?"

I smile behind my red scarf, "I know exactly who I am. But you don't. At first, I was worried you might recognize me, but that was before I met you and realized how fucking dense you are."

"Why would I remember a useless worm like you? Guards, seize this treasonous little bitch." Fae attendants and guards begin to enter the Arena, tentatively eyeing the still-asleep Kydis.

"I wouldn't do that," I say casually, and Achan hesitates. I release my hold on Kydis and Mirielle, letting their will become their own once more. Both groan and begin moving as guards flood around us. The crowd starts shouting as they realize they're not all dead. *Fuck. I need to hurry up.* "You see, Achan, the Gauntlet wasn't the only game being played here. There was another game, one hidden in the shadows. A game you've just lost."

The crowd gasps, and the High Council all surge to their feet, shouting.

"Amalia Roth, you're under arrest for treason against the High Council and Kingdom of Ur Daoine," Achan calls as guards surround me.

I smirk and lower my scarf, baring my entire face.

"My name is not Amalia Roth," I spit and a guard goes to punch me. I lean back, avoiding it easily before flicking my hand and pushing with my tired magyk, grabbing onto their mind and squeezing. They scream as blood bursts from their eyes and ears.

I keep squeezing until their dead bodies fall to the ground, their minds crushed to the point of decay.

I glance up at a shocked and enraged High Council, look Achan dead in the eyes, and say, "My name is Amalia Asteroth, daughter of Jhonathan and Ophiya Asteroth, Scion of the House of Morrigyn, Guardian of Arkaydia, Gray Wytch of the Ulster Wald—" I pause and look back at Kydis, whose eyes are open and looking at me with such emotion it threatens to tear me in half as I add my newest title, "And friend to all Dragons."

Achan Drayven's eyes go wide, "You."

The crowd starts to get nervous as many quickly try and exit, clamoring over each other. I pay them no mind as I smirk at the imperial fae who has resided in my nightmares for far too long.

"You told my father you wanted a weapon," I flash him a wicked smile. "Congratulations. You made one."

"GUARDS! SEIZE HER!" Achan screams, but they all lay prone on the ground.

I tsk. "You should have killed me when you had the chance." With that, I snap both of my fingers and let my iron walls finally dissipate after decades of holding back, as my Magyk explodes, covering the Arena in a blanket of shadows.

Everything goes completely dark, even blocking out the sun's distant glare.

But the magyk at my core, the magyk that makes me burn with righteous fury encases my arms, in a fire not of this world, but of the end and the beginning.

CHAPTER 65
MIRIELLE

Darkness greets me as I pry open my sandy eyes. It digs into my palms as I shove up to standing.

I knew Amalia was lying.

A loud groan next to me lets me know the giant crimson Dragon is also waking up, and despite the fact that Amalia claims she's friendly, I scurry away, hands in front of me as I try to see where I'm going. But it's pitch black. Even with my more powerful eyesight, I can't see anything.

A cold laugh fills the Arena, as a small light appears in my periphery.

No, not a light—it's a person.

Amalia Roth is *glowing*.

Not with a light, but with a flame as dark as midnight and as blue as the Midheym Sea. It spreads from her palms, covering her arms until it encases her all the way up to her neck. She doesn't burn, despite the wicked heat I can feel coming off the flame she wields—flame not of this world. The flame suddenly grows cold, and the air begins to turn icy with the smell of burnt lavender.

Oh, fuck me.

That's Hellfyre. Amalia Roth can wield Hellfyre.

She turns to look at me briefly, winking in my direction with eyes that glow pure silver, as her hair begins to smoke like ash-burnt coals.

Then she looks up, where I imagine Achan Drayven is panicking in the stands.

I hit the sand at the sight of her smile. The Hellfyre explodes with a great *BOOM*.

But there's no heat. No ice against my back. How—

Holy gods.

Turning over, I'm faced with a shield of hellfyre encasing me. Outside, Hellfyre circles the entire Arena. I glance to the side, and Kydis is similarly protected.

Amalia Roth. *Aste*roth.

Everything clicks into place as my heart turns to stone. She's from the Morrigyn's own line. A descendent of the Mother herself.

Amalia is *God* touched.

And she can wield Hellfyre. We've all been played by a woman with the power to destroy the world.

Mother...save us from your daughter.

The blanket of flame dissipates until it's just her again, burning against the cold night.

The metal armor covering her glows like a hot forge.

"I am the Right Hand of the Morrigyn, and you, Achan Drayven, have been found guilty." Amalia raises her hands, clapping them together with a scream. A massive burst of black flame explodes from her hands in a tight stream, shooting towards the High Council's private box.

At that exact moment, a giant white light explodes from the stands as Nyall launches Achan Drayven into the air with a bolt of magyk so intense it should have turned him to dust. Bright, glowing white symbols with intricate strands of magyk appear on columns around the entire Arena.

Nyall has been laying the symbols for weeks now, all in hopes that we would make this plan work.

The siphon spell is almost primed.

Despite the shadows blanketing everything, my sight has adjusted, and I can see just enough to note Kydis is now standing.

The fact something that large can move that quietly is terrifying.

There's some shouting and then another boom of white magyk as the symbols around the arena dim slightly.

Nyall is distracted.

Achan spins midair, landing on his feet like a cat as screams erupt from the Council box. I can't see a single thing but there's a loud crunch followed by three bodies falling to the ground. Bolts of magyk and explosions follow as Nyall fights the remaining Councilors. But Achan is already standing up. There's no time.

Nyall leaps into the air and lands on the Arena sand with a wave of white magyk erupting out from his landing. It hits me like a cool breeze, smelling of fresh forests and honeysuckle.

Nyall shucks off his coat, now covered in blood, and rolls up his sleeves to show off his tattooed forearms.

I'm both scared and excited.

It's been a while since I've seen him in a real battle. Nyall Drayven at full power is fucking terrifying. But we've never fought together like this.

Centuries of resentment and anger change a person, and the Heretic Prince is finally claiming long-owed vengeance. Achan stands slowly, spine cracking, the bodies of the dead High Councilors next to him.

"My own son betrays me; how poetic. I should have killed your mother when you were still in the womb," he sneers, brushing dust off his coat and turning to Amalia with glowing, horrible red eyes. "You should be dead, you little waste of flesh. Let's remedy that."

"Hello, Achan. You're looking rather upset. How does it feel to know your only kin betrayed you?" She smiles darkly and grabs her swords, lighting them up with hellfyre."I've been waiting eighty years for this."

Wait—*what?*

I knew Arkaydians had longer lifespans than humans, but not that much longer. She looks 28, 29 maybe. But she's nearing 100?

How many lies did she tell?

Nyall slaps his hands together with a roar, white ropes of magyk wrapping around his forearms as he begins to move his hands quickly. He pulls the magyk right out of the other Councilors as streams of it flow back into him. The black veins on his arms grow darker as their tainted magyk begins to destroy him.

"Enough of this," Achan waves his hand and red magyk floods the room, chasing the shadows away but tinting everything in red.

"Nyall?" Amalia asks calmly in my head and I flinch.

"A little busy right now..." Nyall grunts, concentrating on the weaving.

*"Finish the spell. **NOW!**"* Amalia screams in our heads just before everything explodes, and we're all knocked to our backs. The entire back half of the arena collapses, caving into a giant hole as the ground opens up.

An arm drags me up as Amalia yanks me to standing, "Get Dyana and get the fuck out of here. We'll handle Achan."

"No! We said it would be us," I protest, but Amalia just shakes her head, smiling sadly.

"It was never going to be you. You have a more important job. Get her out of here safely. Get her out of here alive. Now, **GO!**"

Kydis pushes to stand, stretching her great wings until they almost reach either side of the now-destroyed Arena. Her neck turns left and right as she rights herself and sets her sights on Achan Drayven with a growl that makes me feel lightheaded.

There's another loud noise—the sound of talons scraping against stone and the thump of something really large as a huge cloud of dust and smoke bursts from the hole in the floor. We cough, hurrying to the side as Nyall tails us, hands still working the weaving.

Two, gold eyes appear in the dust. Then wings, almost as large as Kydis, appear in a great shadow, spanning nearly the whole width of the Arena as a giant black claw with razor-sharp black talons slams to the ground, and a giant black Dragon emerges from the depths.

Its head is lined with black horns and as it growls, I notice fangs as large as my fucking staff.

But the gold eyes say everything I need to know.

Os is here. Os is a Dragon.

A *huge* Dragon.

"Gods, I forgot what a big bastard he is. Has he gotten bigger, somehow? How is that even possible," Nyall mutters, and he's right.

Os in his true form is *huge*.

Unlike Kydis who has four legs, he only has two, but his wings are tipped in sharp claws that he uses for balance as he steps out of the cave-in, allowing the remaining Dragons to start crawling up towards the ceiling.

A few smaller ones emerge and for a moment, there's nothing.

Then, a giant explosion as the hole widens and a Dragon bigger even than Os emerges.

Steel gray scales cover the Dragon's huge body. Sharp green eyes survey us, clear and fierce. A scar slashes through his right eye but it doesn't mar the pupil. White horns emerge from silver ridges lining the Dragon's face. This one is like Kydis. Four legs and clawed wings....wait.

As he emerges from the shadows, I see two sets of wings.

Two. That's not...that's not possible. *Two sets of wings?*

The silver Dragon must be another of the old ones because it's almost the size of Kydis. All of my thoughts come to a halt, and my jaw hits the floor as I see Dyana clutched in one of the Dragon's huge claws, her eyes wide with fear. But the Dragon is shockingly gentle as it carefully lowers Dyana to the ground before lowering its huge bulk to the sand.

"HURRY!" She screams, motioning for us to get on before climbing up herself, using the Dragon's spinal spikes to pull herself up.

"Get on the fucking Dragon, people!" Dyana screams, getting comfortable on his back.

"Go!" Amalia shouts, snapping me out of the stupor.

"What about Nyall?" I shout, but there's no time. A beam of magyk heads our way, and Amalia shoves me forward, throwing up her arm and creating a shield of pure Hellfyre to shield us. She grunts under the weight of the spells that are thrown our way. Nyall is still working on his weaving, sweat dripping down his face as he draws the remaining magyk from the three dead Councilors. He trembles, full of too much magyk. We all turn as a figure appears next to Achan Drayven in the distance.

Oh no.

The Archmage and his sycophants appear out of thin air, their gray robes dragging along the dirt floor. More fae guards shout and run in now that they can see us.

Os lets out a roar so loud we all hit the ground as he charges, jumping the Archmage. Achan and the Archmage disappear, reappearing to the side as the latter raises a hand and shoots a beam of purple magyk at Os, slamming him down onto the ground.

Amalia snarls, lowering her Hellfyre shield. Guards swarm Os, but he quickly gets up and begins tearing them limb from limb. They have weapons, but they might have left them with how he ignores them. Blood and screams fill the air as Os tears everyone to pieces.

The Archmage turns his attention on Nyall, his strange violet eyes bursting with stars. I never expected the Archmage to be so gorgeous.

"Amalia!" I shout, "The Archmage can't get Nyall. The spell can't stop!"

She looks at me, eyes still glowing, and nods, turning her attention to protecting the Heretic Prince.

"You've been a failure since birth," Achan sneers in disgust at his son as both he and the Archmage shoot huge bursts of magyk at us. Amalia throws up another shield, but I watch as it begins to crack under the weight of their combined magyk.

"Come on, get on!" Dyana screams, and I'm caught. I want to help Amalia, I want to help Nyall, but I also want Dyana to get out of here alive.

Fuck.

"The dark magyk is killing you, you fucking idiot. You're going to send the entire kingdom to the bottom of the ocean if you don't stop!" Nyall shouts at Achan, throwing a spell made of white light that turns into spikes that rain down on Achan, who cries out and tries to shield unsuccessfully. "Then what comes next, Father? When you've destroyed everything in this world, what's next? Will you go to another world and do the same thing, never satisfied with the power you were born with? Why is it never enough for you?" The magyk bursts towards Achan's shield and begins planting hooks in him. Nyall yanks both of his hands, and dark red magyk begins to stream out as Nyall starts siphoning his father.

"Go, Mirielle! Get Dyana out of here!" Amalia screams at me.

There's no other choice. I curse and sprint towards the huge steel colored Dragon still lying down, awaiting the rest of its passengers.

I take a great running leap and use my extra strength to easily jump on the Dragon's back, mounting just behind Dyana.

"Amalia, come on! We need to go!" Dyana cries, but I know the truth. Amalia isn't coming with us, because she doesn't anticipate surviving.

"Vesimyr, get them out of here." A voice so powerful and ancient it's a physical weight on my spine sounds in our minds.

"Is that—" Dyana gasps. We both turn and look at the crimson Dragon staring right at us.

"Yeah," I answer, voice hollow with shock.

The Dragon is speaking to us.

"Keep them safe. You know what to do." The voice says again, and the Dragon underneath us grumbles, the sound vibrating my legs, as it pushes to standing and joins the dozens of other Dragons climbing out of the hole in the Arena floor.

Most sport terrible old injuries, their wings torn and filled with holes, fangs broken, bodies worn and weary.

But their eyes all glow as freedom sits just on the horizon. The first Dragons begin taking flight, unsteady, but the sky is theirs. It knows them. Soon, dozens get into the air, some holding bundles of wiggling fabric containing the hatchlings.

"Wait, no! We need to go back! Amalia!" Dyana starts screaming as she realizes what's going on. I hold her tightly to the Dragon as it begins climbing out of the Arena.

On the ground, guards surround Amalia, but she unleashes more Hellfyre, turning them to ash.

Dyana begins hyperventilating and struggling in earnest, but I hold tight as we reach the top of the Arena and emerge into the sky. We both look back at the ground as the Dragon pants, slightly winded.

Os stands among the dozens of mutilated bodies, blood soaking his snout. But his gold eyes are alight with a fury that makes me shiver.

Wait, where is my staff? Where is Forsaken?

At the thought, the Archmage appears next to Os, with my staff Forsaken clutched in his spiny little hands. Then he stabs Os right in the chest.

My heart stops and we watch in slow horror as Os falls to his knees. Amalia screams bloody murder as if she was stabbed as well.

Os roars, Dragon body blurring for a moment, and suddenly, he's a man. A very naked and bloody man who yanks Forsaken straight out of his own chest, blood spurting everywhere.

My jaw hits the floor, and I watch as he cranes his neck, spitting fire on the wound and burning his own skin to cauterize it and stop the blood flow.

It doesn't work.

He continues to bleed out, wobbling and barely hanging on as he fights off the Archmage with every ounce of strength left in him.

Amalia Asteroth's rage is a thing to behold as she screams again, pushing to her feet and charging Achan Drayven, only to get thrown into the air with a vicious bolt of magyk. But she just gets up and charges again, over and over, still screaming with such gut-wrenching pain it makes me start to cry.

Nyall sneaks up behind Achan and continues siphoning. The black veins on his hands get darker and more visible as Achan cries out and falls to his knees, gasping for air as his skin begins to crack like dry paper. But the Archmage appears next to Nyall, blasting him with a spell that almost ruins the siphoning completely. Achan is momentarily safe but Amalia charges, letting out a roar of pure rage and shooting him with a metric ton of hellfyre.

When she's done, she pants as the Hellfyre disperses. But there stands Achan Drayven.

Still alive.

The Archmage watches, an amused look on their face. Something isn't right here.

Nyall yells, roaring to the Gods in the Heavens as the siphon spell dies within his hands, the ribbons of white light he's been weaving dying out completely.

It didn't work.

Our plan didn't work.

Centuries of careful execution, and it didn't fucking work.

The Arena is empty. The other Dragons have been crawling out, some with small bundles in their talons. The babies.

Kydis growls, prowling towards Achan and the Archmage. But the Archmage just smiles, purple eyes amused as he snaps his fingers, and one of the baby Dragons appears at Achan Drayven's feet, a little red one with copper eyes. The hatchling sits up, its small wings thin and light pink.

Kydis jerks back, trembling with fury. Amalia's knees hit the sand, her eyes wide.

"Submit, or I will kill your child," Drayven says simply.

"Go, Vesimyr! Get out of here!" the Dragon roars in our heads,I flinch, ears ringing.

The Dragon underneath us grumbles, hesitating.

It hits me like a lightning bolt to the chest.

Her child.

Gods, it's her *child.*

"Save them. Get our people home, Vesimyr."

The Dragon underneath us lets out a horrible roar, the sound full of pain and sorrow as his wings expand and they take a great leap into the air.

She snarls, and the sound is pure terror in my veins. Amalia's eyes glow as she falls to her knees, looking upon what is clearly the Dragon's child.

"You will not hurt my child." A booming voice echoes throughout the ruins of the arena. Kydis never opened her mouth, but the voice is clearly her. She sounds old, but the power in her words makes my skin feel like it's peeling right off my bones. The Archmage smiles.

"Hello, Dragon. See something you want?" Achan Drayven sneers.

Amalia just looks up at us, tears streaming down her face as the Dragon beneath us gets into the air, hovering slightly. Dyana screams.

"WE HAVE TO GO BACK!"

"I love you, Dyana." Amalia whispers, but her voice travels as if she was right next to us. "Always."

"I will keep them safe, I swear it." the Dragon beneath us responds as it continues the ascent to freedom. Dyana continues screaming, frantically trying to turn around and look at Amalia.

"NO! TAKE ME BACK! TURN AROUND!" But the Dragon doesn't stop.

"YOU PROMISED. TAKE ME BACK. TAKE ME BACK!" she screams bloody murder, but the Dragon doesn't stop.

"Look, Dyana!" I gasp, and Dyana follows my gaze. Dozens of Dragons wait by the horizon, heads bowed in unison. "Gods, look at them." Wonder and joy fill my heart for the first time in a long time as tears fill my eyes.

Dragons in the skies once more.

But Dyana doesn't respond. I look down with a smile, ready to comfort her during what I know is the worst moment of her life.

It quickly becomes the worst moment of my life, save losing my mother, as I watch in slow motion as a bolt of purple magyk shoots into the sky, hitting Dyana right in the chest. Blood sprays me in the face as a hole the size of my fist is blasted through her chest. My ears ring, and a scream releases in the distance. It takes a moment to realize the scream is coming from me.

Dyana's terrified brown eyes meet mine.

"I-I-" She gasps, blood bubbling out of her mouth.

"No, no, no, NO, NO!" I grab her, trying to hold her up, pressing my hand to her wound. But there's so much blood, and it's so slippery. Still, I press hard, trying to somehow keep her together. I watch with horror as the light fades from her eyes, and Dyana takes a final, gasping breath before slumping against me.

Dead.

CHAPTER 66
AMALIA

Year 420 PBM

The howling wind shakes the small cabin. The old wood walls rattle and the roof groan, every worn shingle barely hanging on. The wind shrieks and moans, sounding like the screams of a thousand miserable, tormented souls in the depths of purgatory.

Suddenly, the wind stops, and the forest goes silent.

"Son of Shadow, did you think you could really escape? Did you think we wouldn't find out about the child?" Achan Drayven asks, everything about him evil even down to the sound of his voice.

I know his name.

I've always known his name. Mother and Father made sure of it.

And now he's here, after all this time. Ten years of running that began the day Mother found out she was pregnant with me.

Ten years later he's finally here. Just meters away from the cupboard I'm hidden in.

I feel like a child, small and scared as I watch through the small hole in the cupboard wall.

Father laughs, dark and emotionless.

"Did you really think I would let you anywhere near my child, Achan?" he taunts. "There has never been a reality where you ended up with my daughter."

"Hand her over and I won't tie you to a pole in the Pit," Achan responds, his black horns so scary I can barely look.

"Never." My mother's voice is violent and angry as my parents walk out, meeting the fae males.

"You can't escape me, Asteroth. There's nowhere to run," Achan calls.

"I love you, my darling." Mother whispers into my mind.

"You and your mother are the best things to ever happen to me. Never forget that little spark."

"I love you too. But what's going on, Daddy? You're coming back, right?" I ask, but they don't respond. There is only silence and darkness. I squeeze closer to the hole in the wall, trying to see what's happening. Puff squeaks quietly in my ear, burrowing into my hair. Poor thing is trembling in fear—but I'm afraid his fear is justified.

The cabin begins to rumble and the floor wobbles. A tiny hole of light opens up from a can falling over.

My parents stand together, hands clasped, facing the horned fae.

"What the fuck do you think you're doing?" Achan snarls as they begin to glow.

One with shadow and one with light.

"Stop them!" He shouts, and the wind picks back up, blasting them, but they both stand still.

They glow brighter, until I can barely watch.

Then a huge BOOM sounds as a wave of energy explodes outward, and everything goes dark.

I have no idea how much time has passed, all I know is the ground is rough and something sharp is poking at my legs.

My eyes feel like sawdust as I pry them open.

Stars.

Why am I looking at the stars?

I push up and realize why.

The house no longer has walls.

The house fell in a perfect circle around me, but broken slats of wood line the circle's edge. I was too close to the outside of it and they started scratching me. I groan, pushing to standing, when something hits the floor.

It's a soft sound.

I cough at the ash falling in the air, looking down at my feet.

No.

No, no, please.

Puff's dead, crushed body sits at my feet, a blood trail beginning to form at his open mouth.

A scream builds in my chest, but another noise stops it.

A noise to the side of me. I turn slowly and stop when I see the source of this new noise.

My mother is on her knees, clutching her throat as Achan Drayven stands over her and laughs while she chokes on her own blood thanks to the dagger he has stabbed through the middle of her throat. He doesn't remove the dagger, he just stands there, smiling as she drowns, coughing up the blood now filling her lungs.

My Father screams, tackling Achan to the ground, roaring like one of the mighty Dragons in my stories.

Something else roars then, too.

Something buried deep within me.

As I watch the life fade from my Mother, my Father screams bloody murder next to her seizing body, something within me wakes up. Something I didn't even know was sleeping.

The wind picks up, this time at my back, like a cosmic nudge.

My legs move before I make the decision to walk. I gingerly make my way through the broken boards as Father holds his hands out in front of him, using his shadow magyk to attack Achan.

Nothing works.

Achan easily waves off the shadows with a pleased grin.

I try to go faster but trip, cutting open my shin.

The pain is nothing as I scrape my hands, pushing up to stand again, blood now dripping down my leg.

In the time it took me to fall and get up, a lifetime passed.

All I see is falling, as my Father hits the forest floor.

*"Get up," I wail. **"Daddy get UP!"***

But he doesn't move. His body remains still as his chest stops moving and his violet eyes go dark.

Achan Drayven sniffs, kicks my father's body and turns toward me.

"Such a rare little girl. Come here, girl. Let us leave." Achan Drayven stands there, waiting.

I continue climbing out of the broken boards of the cabin until I meet unmarred ground. Then I pause, looking around again.

"Don't think of running. It's no use." He holds out his hand, a sinister smile on his face. "You belong to me, little girl."

I look at his hand for a moment, then back to my parents.

My mother gasps, blood trailing down the side of her mouth, and reaches a trembling hand out towards where my father lies prone.

Then her hand falls and her chest stops moving.

So I turn to Achan and stare into his horrible red eyes and say, "No."

Then I let that feeling, that something newly awoken, explode as I let my head fall back and scream.

Everything goes black yet again as magyk surges out of me.

After a moment I look around and see a wave of fire so dark it's nearly black covering every surface.

Something falls on my head and I wipe my cheek, looking at the black staining my hand.

Ash.

Not snow, but ash.

Achan Drayven is nowhere to be seen.

He fled.

He actually ran.

Beneath my brow, I watch as my hair burns like a coal ember, all of the white fading away.

Charred, half-frozen bodies lay around the entire clearing along with the broken trunks of ancient trees.

Shadows wrap around my hands as if to comfort me, but I ignore it.

"Daddy?" I ask, voice trembling as I walk over to where my parents lay, now covered in flakes of ash. "Daddy? Please." I cry, falling to my knees at the sight of his cloudy eyes. "Wake up, Dad. Please, you have to wake up."

I sniff, curling into a ball and tucking my legs against his still, cold side. "You're reading to me later, remember? The story of the Wytch and the Prince. You need to stay awake so we can read."

But there is no response.

The tears come, then. Sobs so loud, so violent that my entire body shakes. "Daddy, wake up."

But he doesn't answer. His eyes don't open and his chest doesn't move. Air no longer fills his lungs.

"Mom? Please." I look over at the body of my mother, but there's no answer.

They're gone.

"Please don't leave me alone," I whisper, tears streaming down my face. The fire bursts from me again, surrounding me with a flame that is both hot and cold.

They're gone.

They're all gone.

"Please don't leave me alone. Please come back," I beg. "Come back, Daddy. Please come back."

I don't know how long I sat there.

But I won't leave them.

Even as my body gets cold and my muscles get achy as my stomach burns for food, I won't move.

There is only them, and they are gone.

I wish I was gone, too.

So I close my eyes, my hand around my mother's cold, limp palm, and my head against my father's chest, and go to sleep.

Hoping never to wake up.

I do wake up, though.

But I'm so cold and so hungry that everything is a blur.

I just see black fur walking through a wall of fire. It parts for the creature, allowing it entrance. Then something nudges me with a cold, wet nose.

I mumble, "Puff?" and the creature pauses.

Something fuzzy pushes me, lifting me off the ground and rolling me onto another of the creature's backs.

But I do not care.

The beast then begins to move and I bury my hands and face in its warm fur, hoping that maybe this time I won't wake up.

Weeks later when I finally woke up, I realized I got my wish. I did die alongside my parents.

Amalia Asteroth did die that night in the forest. The little girl who went into that cabin was not the same one who came out.

The Dyre Wolf who saved me leans his giant black head into my side, now my only companion.

From ashes and death, amongst the forest and the beasts, Amalia Roth is born.

A monster of the world's making.

NOW:

I thought I knew what it meant to break.

To feel true pain.

I didn't see the Archmage until it was too late. I scramble for my magyk as I watch in horror as that beam of purple light heads straight towards her.

I'm not fast enough.

Now I'm staring at Dyana, a giant hole in her collarbone, as the light leaves her eyes.

Her eyes close and she slumps against Vesimyr, the giant silver Dragon's scales now marred with streaks of red blood.

It's a physical thing when Mirielle screams.

The sound pierces me right through the chest as if I too was shot with a bolt of magyk.

Her scream pierces through the fog of shock and cracks me in two.

Then there's another sound, and I turn in slow horror, watching as Remus falls to his knees to my right. His chest is covered in bleeding wounds, including a large spot where the Archmage's arrow stabbed him.

His gold eyes meet mine as Mirielle's screams fade into the distance.

"You should've come with me, little Asteroth. Now you're all alone again, no help and no one to save you but me," Achan smiles, blood smeared over his face as he appears in front of me, the Archmage beside him, their white and silver robes covered with blood.

They killed her.

Dyana is dead. They killed her.

The world halts and everything goes still as my mind begins to break. Noise fades into the background as my ears begin to ring.

"You killed her," I stare at the Archmage.

"It was His will," they reply calmly.

Vesimyr keeps flying like I made Kydis promise.

"Your God is a fraud, and you are a blight upon this world," a deep voice booms.

Kydis approaches from behind me, but I can't move, even as her wings brush against me, almost like a hug.

Then she roars and pounces, her great, crimson wings flaring as she leaps into the air and comes crashing down on Achan Drayven and the Archmage.

They simply sidestep, but Achan uses the moment to jump onto Kydis' back.

Kydis takes one look at me as Remus falls to the ground, choking.

There's another noise, then, as Achan abandons the red hatchling. It squeaks, scared.

Kydis's eyes shut in pain as Achan stabs her in the back with a dagger.

Then her eyes open, and she looks right at me, "The Left Hand protects, and the Right punishes. Balance the scales, Amalia Asteroth. Be who you were born to be."

Something in her words triggers my rage.

All of my pain and grief disappear, reforming into a fury that burns me from the inside out. The air goes cold again as my skin gets hot and I begin to glow.

Everything goes sharp as Remus groans, lifting his head to look at me, his gold eyes filled with pain and pride.

"You're glorious, A gahrá. You are everything I could have ever asked for, and I am glad we had this time. Thank you for showing me one last slice of happiness; thank you for making me remember what it is to fly."

I blink, unable to form words beneath the weight of the magyk forming within me.

"Keep her safe, Daughter of Shadow," Kydis roars out loud and a bright red burst of magyk explodes from her, then a weight is falling on my chest.

The hatchling squeaks in fear, wiggling violently, *"Shh, sweet one. She will keep you safe."* Kydis whispers, and the hatchling calms down.

I feel like my heart is being ripped from my chest. Kydis looks at me again, *"Teach her what it means to be kind."*

"I will," I whisper, the shards of my broken heart tearing up my voice.

Achan stabs Kydis in the back again and she screams in pain.

With a groan, I shove a heaping ton of magyk through my bond and into Remus, whose head falls back against the sand as he begins seizing.

But we didn't complete the bond.

Why didn't I complete the fucking bond? My magyk tries but I'm so tired and there's not much left, and still, his wounds remain.

I can't stop this.

Across the sand, Nyall Drayven catches my eye.

His white hair is soaked in blood and he pants, exhausted. But I'm surprised to see my own rage mirrored in his mismatched gaze.

"Whatever the cost," I say quietly, to him and to all who can hear. Nyall nods and Kydis extends her wings and takes to the air, a complete vertical ascent, something a much younger Dragon would never be able to do.

Achan Drayven is yanked into the air, shouting and blasting her with bolt after bolt of magyk in an attempt to get her back on the ground.

The Archmage however does nothing. He just glances at them before disappearing, leaving Achan to his fate.

Achan hangs on for dear life as he continues battering away at Kydis, her scales burning right off her body.

Nyall sprints across the sand towards me, a weaving started between his hands, roping around his arms and neck.

But I don't care.

I don't care about any of that as I stare into Remus's golden eyes as life fades from them.

The magyk building within me explodes out in a wave of heat and ice so intense the stone of the Arena begins to melt and break. The entire building shudders and begins collapsing on itself. At the same time, I try to funnel as much magyk into Remus as I can. I don't know how to heal but I just picture him whole and fucking pray it works.

In the sky, Kydis disappears into the clouds.

Then she reappears, only this time, she's heading straight for the ground at full speed.

A death fall.

One she will not recover from.

A small red snout nudges me as Kydis's hatchling trembles in fear, unsure what's going on, all while her mother plunges to her death.

My fire doesn't burn her, nor does it burn Remus or Nyall. I chose who it burns and who is left standing. But the floor begins to quake as the Arena crumbles into the earth.

Kydis shoots toward the ground, a brightly burning red star who now clutches Achan Drayven within her talons.

It's the silence that follows as we watch her spear toward the ground, Achan Drayven screaming in her hold. He stabs at her legs, trying to break free, so I divert all of my rage at him, using my Hellfyre and shadows to trap him in her claws.

Nyall does the same, white ribbons of light shooting off him to wrap around Achan, holding him in place.

There we stand, Remus dying, Nyall and I holding Achan Drayven prisoner, as Kydis, the Crimson Queen and the bravest Dragon I've ever known, a true Queen in every way imaginable, dives towards the ground, taking Achan Drayven with her.

This is breaking; this is what it means to shatter.

The hatchling in my arms cries but the numbness within me is so great, it feels like I'm struggling against the weight of the world. I hold the wiggling, scared Dragon, begging my brain to move my body. To do something.

But there's nothing.

When they land, the weight is so immense that it finishes the job I started. The ground cracks and begins to cave in as the Arena starts disappearing into the Dragon Pit, collapsing into the earth.

I look at Remus, expecting his gold eyes to be on mine despite the void of a much different kind hidden within my heart. A void that started the second his heart stopped beating. He blocked me from feeling it, but his gold eyes are dull and lifeless as I look upon his dead body. My magyk didn't heal him.

I didn't get to say goodbye.

Suddenly, Nyall is at my side, activating a huge magyk circle that was hidden in the sand. It lights up with his white magyk and he spins it faster and faster.

"THINK OF HOME," he screams, wrapping his arms around me as portal magyk erupts and the ground beneath our feet starts to crumble. But there is nothing.

I don't have a home. I never did. My home died a long time ago, and I've just been floating aimlessly ever since. I am alone in this world and there is nothing or no one to anchor me.

"FUCKING PICK SOMEWHERE, AMALIA!" he shouts and I think of the only place that has ever felt safe in the last five decades of my life.

The stadium groans, the caverns below sucking everything into the earth as the screams of Castael Laryn erupt in the distance.

I hope the entire city gets sucked into the godsdamn abyss. I don't care if it takes us with it.

Fuck the imperial fae. Fuck all of this. What is the point of bringing justice if there's no world left on the other side? Why bring justice to a world that doesn't exist?

"HANG ON!" Nyall screams and the portal activates. I clasp Kydis' child to my chest as a wave of ash hits us and the ground disappears beneath our feet. Remus's limp body falling into a dark abyss is the last thing I see as I stretch my hand out, hoping he will grab it.

He doesn't.

Then something sucks me away, pulling me from him. I scream, fighting my way back, but it's no use.

He disappears as Nyall's magyk teleports us somewhere far away.

We land hard, my ribs protesting the hard ground. The smell of frozen forest tells me where we are, but I don't care.

I don't care where we are or what happened.

They're gone.

"No, take me back," I croak. "Take me back!"

Nyall gets up and looks outside. I don't even bother, I simply lay on the cave floor, the small Dragon crawling on top of me.

"Amalia...I can't take you back," he says gently.

"I DON'T CARE! TAKE ME BACK!" I scream. He just looks at me with sad eyes. "TAKE ME BACK!"

Howls sound from outside. Nyall's magyk is depleted, like mine, but he grabs two wickedly sharp daggers anyways.

"Don't," I say numbly. The hatchling crawls to my front, bringing its face to mine. It's a baby but under a year old. Dragons age slowly for their first year of life, and then they go through rapid maturation, becoming full size in a matter of months.

This one was so small, only a few months old. Its scales remind me so much of Kydis that it's a physical pain.

Her brilliant copper and silver eyes are wide as she wiggles closer, pressing her scaled snout into me.

Howls sound again, only this time they're closer. The sound of large paws approaches us.

"Holy shit," Nyall whispers, as the pack of Dyre Wolves descend on the cave. "Amalia, I don't think this is a good—" I ignore Nyall, tuning him out as one of the wolves moves closer, and a large cold wet nose smooshes against my cheek.

"Ah. I see you know each other," he muses.

But all that fills me is pain.

I turn over slowly, the little hatchling curling into my side as I gaze into the eyes of my oldest friend, and the being who was my only companion for so many decades.

"They're all dead. They...they're all dead," I gasp, at the giant black Dyre Wolf, his eyes just as yellow as the day I said goodbye. The wolf licks me, pressing his forehead into mine as a wave of love washes over me.

Full body sobs explode as I shatter completely, crying so hard it eventually turns into screams. Virgyl whines, licking my face as he lays down next to me. The rest of the pack whines and cries, tails between their legs as they crowd around. All pressing against me. None protest the presence of the hatchling. Instead, they lick her and nudge her, treating her instantly as one of their own. That only makes me cry harder.

"Take me back," I sob. "Please, take me back."

Someone nudges through the bodies as warm, large hands cradle around me. Virgyl growls lightly but lays back down, his eyes on the person pulling me against a warm hard chest. Nyall Drayven tucks me and the hatchling into his arms as the pack surrounds us, using their furry bodies to absorb our grief as Nyall too, begins to cry, tears falling from his mismatched eyes, silently grieving the Father he should have had but which Achan Drayven never was. We don't move for a long time.

A small mind touches mine as we lay there and I turn to look at Nyall, his eyes watching me with heartbreaking sincerity, causing my tears to flow anew.

"I'm so sorry, Amalia. I'm so fucking sorry," he whispers, his voice choked. "You were right. It didn't work. We failed."

"Are you mama?" A small voice asks. I bridge the minds around me so Nyall and Virgyl can hear, although I have a feeling Virgyl can hear whatever he likes regardless.

I sob into Nyall.

"She's not your mother, little one. Your mom was so brave and she loved you so much," Nyall whispers gently, pressing a soft kiss to my forehead as the hatchling curls between us, her snout pressed against my face.

"Then who are you?" The little hatchling asks, her voice like twinkling bells.

The pain is too much and I'm unable to answer, but a loud, deep voice answers for me. Day turns to night and the world is coated in darkness.

"We are friends, and friends are family. You are our family now, little one, you are safe." Virgyl's old voice booms, powerful yet gentle, leaving no question as to why he is the Alpha of all Dyre Wolves and God of the Forest.

But her question remains.

"What is your name, sweetling?" Nyall asks, using his magyk to gently hug her within his mind. I cry harder at the touching gesture, unable to do the same even though I wish I could. I can't even move let alone feel and it's all too much.

As I burn out emotionally and fade into sleep, a small voice answers.

"I don't...I don't know...but one of the big ones called me Ryu."

"It's nice to meet you, Ryu."

The voices fade as sleep finally sinks its claws into me and I fall into the abyss.

Days pass, fading into weeks. And still, I sleep.

"Who are you?" the baby Dragon had asked.

Who am I?

Finally, I become aware of my senses.

Who am I?

As my eyes peel open and consciousness returns, I finally have an answer to her question.

I am death, the destroyer.

I am the beginning and the end.

I am the Right Hand of the Morrigyn.

I am the Gray Wytch of their worst nightmares.

I am Amalia Asteroth, and I will make them pay.

THE END
IS ONLY
THE BEGINNING

xoxo, ECG

EPILOGUE

Somewhere Across the Midheym Sea...

Wakefulness comes slowly. My eyelids feel as if they're glued together and underneath heavy stones. Every muscle aches as I stretch, groaning beneath my breath.

Voices sound in the distance. I finally pry my eyes open, using all my strength to try and blink. The world is blurry but full of bright, shining light as the white and gold room comes into focus.

Where am I?

The bed beneath me is soft and sumptuous. Where everything in the Black Citadel was clinical and cold, this room was soft and bright, similar in color yet the complete opposite. This feels warm, and there's a cool breeze in the air that smells faintly like jasmine. There's a strange sound in the distance. I force myself up to sit, surprised at how shaky my arms are with such little effort. But I'm barely able to sit up. Still, I swing my legs to the edge and stand, although it does take three more tries before I can actually do it.

I have to lean against the wall as I walk to the large open windows, panting at what feels like an impossible task. My legs tremble so hard I worry my knees might give out with every single step.

I'm dressed in a simple white shirt and my hair trails all the way down to the small of my back.

Huh. My hair isn't that long, is it?

I shake off the confusion, I'm misremembering and it's fine. I tentatively step towards the window ledge, grasping tightly on unsteady legs. A gasp falls from my lips as I take in the scene before me.

Clear, turquoise water as far as the eye can see, with sandy white beaches and a lush, green forest greet me. The building I'm in seems to be a part of some large structure, but when I lean forward to look more, my legs do give out. So I promise myself I'll investigate more later. For now, I lean into the wall of the window awning and watch the Dragons soar.

Amalia must be loving this... My thoughts come crashing to a halt. Wait—*Ama.* Where is Ama?

Flashes of memories assault me. Blood and burned bodies, ash in the air and screams in my ears, the sound of great flapping wings in the breeze.

"Dyana? Oh, my Gods, Dyana!" Mirielle cries, running into the room. I turn, blinking at her strange outfit. She's dressed in loose green pants and a matching green tunic that bares her midriff. Her hair is loose and she's barefoot, carrying only a book. She grabs me, wrapping me in her arms, her soft scent enveloping me. But, where is Amalia?

"Oh my Gods, how are you awake? I can't believe you're awake!" she gasps, pulling back to clasp my face between her pale hands. Her gray-green eyes are full of tears but, why? I blink, trying to process but my brain is moving slowly. Mirielle guides me back to the bed as I try to process her words.

"Aw-ake?" I choke out. My throat feels like I've just swallowed shards of glass. I sound as if I've been smoking windweed everyday for the past decade! Why is my body so weak and why do I sound like this? "Mirielle, what is going on?" I manage, panting at the effort it takes to merely form a sentence.

What the fuck is happening?

"Vesimyr! Send for help! Dyana is awake!" A voice calls, but I fall back into the warm embrace of numbness. "It's ok, Dyana. Rest. You're safe," Mirielle mutters but it's far away as sleep reclaims me once more.

Days pass and I try again. My eyes finally cooperate this time when I open them, I know where I am. That same room. This time the other details come into focus. Carved, graceful designs decorate the stone ceiling. The stone almost looks as if it's made of diamonds but it's not fully clear, rougher somehow. I turn over and am surprised to see Mirielle in a similar outfit, this time in a dark shade of blue, sitting in a chair, asleep with a book in her lap. The bed groans as I sit up and she bolts awake.

"You're awake," she says, a smile on her face. She moves to sit next to me on the bed, wrapping me in a huge hug. She cries into my hair, her soft body trembling with emotion.

"I'm fine, I'm fine," I say. Mirielle pulls back, grabbing my hands as she looks into my eyes. Up close I can see the dark circles under her eyes.

"I thought I'd never see your eyes again, let alone hear your voice," she gasps, tears falling as she hugs me again.

I pull back, "What do you mean? How long have I been asleep?"

Mirielle, normally up front and calm, surprises me when she gets up and goes to the window, unable to even look at me.

"Mirielle, answer me! How long have I been asleep? And where the hell are we?"

Mirielle turns, wringing her hands nervously. She slowly walks over to me and kneels on the floor, grasping her hands in mine as she looks into my eyes.

"Dyana you—" she breaks off, taking a deep breath, "You've been in a coma for two years."

Wait, what?

"No, that's...that's not possible. We just left Ur Daoine, why would—" More flashes assault me as memories play behind my eyes.

Something's wrong.

"Mirielle, where is Amalia?" I demand as my heart begins racing. "Where is she?" Mirielle just looks down and I pull my hands from hers. "Answer me! Where is Amalia? Where is my sister?" With my shriek, something else happens.

The air goes still and my skin tingles, warming as something bursts from me, throwing Mirielle across the room.

I look at my hands, shaking, "What the hell?"

Mirielle coughs, pushing herself up to her feet. "The plan worked, Dyana. Parts failed but...it worked. Amalia killed him. Achan Drayven is gone."

I scooch away from her, "I don't give a fuck about the fae. Where is Amalia and...and what's wrong with me? What the hell was that?"

"The Arkaydian stayed behind to finish the job," a deep voice echoes and I turn to see a giant gray Dragon head in the window of my room. Clearly, sleep has addled my brain because the screech that comes out of my mouth is extremely embarrassing but holy shit, there's a Dragon! Right there! One did not expect to see a fucking Dragon in their bedroom right after waking up!

"What do you mean, she stayed behind?"

"She made the Dragons promise to get you to safety. We...we left her behind, Dyana. She stayed in Ur Daoine and killed the High Councilor. Amalia, Nyall, and the Crimson Queen finished the job," Mirielle says carefully.

"Then why do you look like someone died? Why are you staring at me like something is wrong?" I ask, tired of these word games. Mirielle glances at the Dragon...Vesimyr, I think. I remember that name.

I turn, looking at him. Two sets of great white horns curl atop his head. Scales of pure steel, albeit covered in scars, cover his gigantic body.

"Are you Vesimyr?" I ask

The Dragon shocks me by nodding. *"I am."*

"Some of it, it's all in pieces. But Vesimyr, please tell me what's going on. I'm tired of word games and whatever it is you're both avoiding telling me. Please just tell me the truth. If it's been two years, why isn't Amalia here?"

The Dragon blinks, *"The Arena is gone. Amalia and Kydis brought the entire thing down, sacrificing themselves to do it. They brought Achan, the Prince, and the Beast with them."*

"Bullshit," I say, despite the way my heart wonders if it might be true. "That's bullshit. You saw what she could really do. She's not dead, Mirielle. Don't you fucking say that."

Mirielle bites her lip, holding her hands up as if I'm a feral animal, "We've had two years to consider all the possibilities. There's been no word, no communication or anything. She's gone, Dyana."

It's comically slow, but I push to my feet and struggle over to Mirielle. She tries to help me but when I get to her I shove her hard. It barely moves her but I keep trying, swinging my fists into her chest. She grabs my hands and tries to stop me, "Dyana, stop—"

"No, you stop! Stop saying she's dead! She's not dead." Mirielle just guides me back to the bed. I writhe and try to escape but I'm too weak. Vesimyr watches, his bright green eyes keen and observant.

"You're a godsdamn liar!" I wrench myself away from her and off the bed, falling to the floor. She goes to help me but I slap her hands away. "We're leaving tomorrow and we're going to find her. She is not dead, I would know."

"Well, that's...uh, hmm, so that's going to be a bit of a problem..." Mirielle trails off, looking nervously at Vesimyr.

"I honestly do not care. We're leaving, we are going to get Amalia, and there's going to be no discussion on the matter. I am not abandoning my sister, although apparently abandonment is just fine in your book seeing as you went right along with her plan, no issue in leaving a teammate and my family behind. You say you care about me, Mirielle? What the fuck kind of caring is that?" I fall to the bed, exhausted. Mirielle steps back, hurt in her gaze.

I turn to the Dragon, seething and confused as my heart refuses to believe the words being said. Amalia can't be dead. "Vesimyr, please. Where are we and what the hell is Mirielle talking about?"

"Your friend is right. We cannot leave, because we're in Elysium, child. My home-land, Kingdom of the Dragons." My jaw drops, unable to comprehend the Dragon's words. Yet, the view outside my window confirms it's true.

"But if we're in Elysium then..."

"Then you're never allowed to leave. No humans are permitted to gaze upon the Kingdom of Elysium, but all who are lucky enough to be granted entrance promise in exchange that they will never leave, and never speak of what they see to another soul. The way out is locked, the promise has been made."

"But I never made any promise, nor did I enter Elysium of my own will. I was unconscious, clearly. So why am I not permitted to leave? Just put a damn blindfold on me so I can go get my godsdamn sister!" I scream at the Dragon who huffs a cloud of smoke at me.

'It's more complicated than that, Dyana." Mirielle grimaces.

"Then uncomplicate it for me already!" I shout, and suddenly my hands begin glowing. "What the hell is happening?" I cry.

"Dyana, you should sit down," Mirielle says with worry. There is something in the tone of her voice that is so wary, so scared that it makes me pause. I sit down even though I feel frantic.

"Just tell me what's going on so we can get out of here."

"Look you should get back in bed, this must be really confusing for you, and it's been a long time since you've been up. Let me go get one of the healers—"

"No. Don't you dare try and shut me up and pretend like nothing happened. You left her BEHIND!" I scream, sitting as far away from her in the bed as possible. Hurt covers Mirielle's face but I don't care. I don't care about anything other than getting Amalia back.

"I just think you're tired, and we have a lot to talk about. Why don't we continue this when you've rested?"

"Tell me to rest," I seethe, "and I will throw that fucking water jug at your head!" I grab said jug and smash it against the wall, glass shattering everywhere to make a point.

"Gods, Dyana, calm down!" she says but I'm done with her.

"No, you know what? Get the fuck out. Get out."

Mirielle pulls back, confused. "But Dyana I—"

"No," I silence her, "I don't want to see you again, Mirielle. You let my only family, the only friend I've ever made get left behind and now you're just trying to ignore the fact that she's out there, alive and alone, thinking that I've died? Are you kidding me?" I look at her, feeling as if I'm seeing her for the very first time in all of her lying glory. "You never loved me. Not really. I was just convenient and naive.

Love isn't this. Get out, Mirielle. Get out and stay out." I look away, disgusted with myself for ever feeling anything for her.

Where are you, Ama?

"Dyana, please—"

"You're certain she's alive. Why?" the Dragon asks.

I turn and look at him for a moment, then turn back to Mirielle. "Get out. I will only speak to the Dragon."

Mirielle jerks back as if I hit her. Tears start to fall but she swallows and leaves, quietly closing the large white stone door on her way out.

"She sat with you, you know. Every single day for the past two years, she was here, never missing a moment. The demis sang songs, read to you, did everything she could to wake you up. It might not be what you think of love, but the demis does care for you, Dyana. That much is clear, even to an old Dragon."

I sniff, "Right now, I don't care. I just want the truth and she still doesn't believe I can handle it. I know I'm younger than all of you, but I'm not a child."

"No, you're not," the Dragon pauses, watching me. *"You are very brave. The weakest of the group, and yet such bravery. I'll make you a deal. If you answer my questions, I shall answer yours."*

I take a breath, pushing to standing and walking on trembling legs until I'm next to the Dragon. Before I can think better of it, I lean against his scales, surprised at how warm they are. I tremble with exhaustion and fear but somehow Versimyr feels like my only connection to Amalia, so the desire to find her is overriding my gut-wrenching terror.

"Amalia's not dead because I would...feel it. We're bonded, too." I confess. I've never told another being alive of this, but I suppose a Dragon is a whole other type of being entirely.

"Hmm. I thought I smelled an echo of another bond on your gray-haired friend when we first met."

"Yes. She said it was like a familiar bond but not quite that."

The Dragon huffs, *"Crude terms, but yes."* He moves so he looks into my eyes which puts me a little too close to those extremely large fangs. I may or may not lose control of my bladder slightly but damnit, I'm too weak to run away and since I was stupid enough to come over here, my stubborn ass is staying.

"If you had been born with magyk, I suspect it would have been another familiar bond like Amalia had with the Beastkyn. But since you were human, it was diluted. You wouldn't feel her die, Dyana."

I pause, looking down. "No, it's still there. The bond is still there... but it's darker, fainter. Almost like an echo. It's never felt like that before. I thought maybe...maybe it was just the distance between us but now...I don't know." My legs give out but Vesimyr moves quickly for a creature so large, catching me on his neck and allowing me to lean on his horns. "Wait," I gasp, holding on for dear life as I use his scales to right myself. "If I can feel the bond, Amalia must too, right?"

"One moment," Vesimyr says calmly. He adjusts and okay, yes, I do scream bloody murder as I dangle outside the castle window, but Vesimyr quickly silences me as he grabs me with one of his claws, gently grasping me and leaning back in the window to deposit me near the bed. I fall onto the mattress as he reaches into the room.

The Dragon continues watching me, hanging off my window and looking oddly comfortable. He's terrifying but actually quite gorgeous. Thick plates line his spine and whiskers almost like a cat trail along his snout.

"If you feel the bond, then she's alive. But Dyana, she thinks you're dead."

"That's—no, that can't be true. If I feel the bond, she must too, right?"

The Dragon goes quiet.

"Vesimyr, please. We just put our lives on the line to set your people free, and look where we are?" I gesture around the room, "We did it. The Dragons are free. So please, please help me find her. She's all I have left."

Vesimyr watches me carefully, silent for a few minutes. I almost fall back asleep when he finally moves, bending into the room in a way that I would think is impossible for a creature of his size, yet his head is right next to the bed.

He nudges me slightly until we're eye to eye and I try not to breathe, let alone have a heartbeat as the giant Dragon looms just a meter away.

"I will help you find your sister, Dyana Arkos. For all she did to help us, and for the future of Elysium."

"Um, for the future of Elysium?" I sputter, confused, and clearly out of my damn mind if I'm questioning a man-eating Dragon.

"Yes. I've been hoping Amalia was alive because that means the heir to the Elysium throne is alive too."

My eyes go wide, "The hatchling."

Vesimyr nods. *"That hatchling is the last of the royal bloodline. We must find her."*

"Okay. Okay. Let's go find them. Let's bring my sister, and your Queen, home."

"There is one more thing, Dyana Arkos."

I sigh, bringing my hands up to rub my aching eyes. "Gods, please tell me there isn't," I mutter.

"The thing is, child, you actually did die. That's why Amalia thinks you're dead. When you died, so did the bond."

My hands fall and I look at the Dragon, confused, "If I died, then how am I here?"

"You died, Dyana. The bolt of magyk that hit you was too strong. There was no other option. So, I gave you some of my blood, which is an act of treason the Dragon Council is currently debating whether or not to execute me over."

I blink. "You gave me your blood? I d-drank your blood? Dragon blood?"

"Yes."

I look down at my chest, but there's only a small scar. My thoughts are sluggish as exhaustion hits but I try desperately to keep up as my heart races behind.

"Okay, right. Well, clearly I owe you my life. Thank you, Vesimyr," I reach a hand up and place it on his smooth snout, trying to express gratitude through my eyes. He rubs his snout into my palm lightly.

"Dyana..." the Dragon says carefully, as if I'm still not understanding. Clearly I'm not. The Dragon continues, *"With my blood came my magyk."*

I go still, pulling back to look into his green eyes.

"Magyk? But then..."

"You are no longer human."

Everything comes crashing to a halt as I realize the truth in his words.

"If I'm not human then why am I so weak? I feel human," I lift my hands to inspect them but everything seems the same.

I look inward, searching for something-

Wait. What is that?

Deep within me, something glows. I touch it and open my eyes to see that my entire body glows as if sunlight rushes through my veins instead of blood.

"Vesimyr, what's happening to me? What is this?" I ask, confused.

And yet I know what he's going to say.

The Dragon looks me in the eye and takes a deep breath, *"That, Dyana Arkos, is magyk."*

<u>IREYNA:</u>

Miles away, deep within the dark dungeons of the Black Citadel, there is a beast chained in silver and confined in a cage.

A beast who I thought was my friend. A beast I once *loved.*

Os is drawn out in a metal muzzle built to shift with him, as the heavy chains circling his ankles drag painfully behind each step, making it nearly impossible to walk. He is led to a windowless room, the same as the day before, where he's tied to a metal chair and forced to stare at the wall for hours.

I watch from my vantage point, behind the magyked mirror that separates us. He doesn't know I'm watching.

It's been months since the Arena collapse, but his healing took up a large part of that.

His body was crushed nearly to death.

How he survived, I have no idea.

Every day I've watched as the man I once, naively thought I loved is tortured.

It's certainly torture seeing the betrayal in his eyes when I walk inside the room, shutting the stone door behind me.

"I wondered when you'd show your face. I know you've been watching, Ireyna. I can smell you," Os hisses, flashing wicked fangs.

His hair was shaved, and dark stubble now covers his head. His muscles are more pronounced as the fat burns away from starvation.

"Os, please," I beg, squatting down to look him in the eyes. "This doesn't have to continue. Just tell us where Amalia is and we can pretend like this never happened. There's a room in the Citadel ready for you with a hot bath and all the food you could imagine. No more being confined to the city, no more wards and stupid false promises. The path to your salvation is there for the taking. You can fly again, Os. All you need to do is," I pause, reaching for his hand and clasping it, "tell us where you think Amalia and the Prince disappeared. The Father will forgive you, He is patient and kind, and He knows we are imperfect."

There's a large cracking sound, and pain shoots up my arm. Os lets my crushed hand go, the bones pulverized.

My screams nearly shred my vocal cords.

One of the Elven healers rushes in the room, grabbing me and helping me out. Which is when Os breaks the chains strapping him down, bending the metal so hard it snaps right in half and roars.

"You will never find her, you fucking traitor!" he snarls. The man is gone, only the beast remains.

The Elven healer drags me out of the room so fast I can't track it, even with my heightened senses.

"Guards!" the Elf screams, and Imperial fae guards flood the room, forcing the door open and tackling Os to the ground.

My heart tightens in fear and sorrow as I watch as Os is beaten. He laughs, spitting blood on some of the fae dragging him. None of the torture is working. Many of the soldiers bleed from wounds, despite having managed to subdue him. He's killed many fae and Elves in this process.

New chains are strapped on as he's hauled out to a different room, past all of us, where the Imperial fae strap him to a stone table.

"Anything?" the Archmage asks, suddenly beside me. I jump, startled. His purple eyes are so beautiful. When I look at him, I can't help but tell him the truth.

"Nothing, your holiness. But I haven't given up hope. He will see the light soon and submit to The Father, I'm sure of it. We will find the Asteroth girl." My words come out confident but on the inside...I doubt.

The Archmage just nods, smiling in a beatific manner. A crown of black iron rests upon his head, something the fae could never do, Imperial or otherwise. A message to all who doubt their power. The Elves control Castael Laryn now. They were beautiful and kind, but almost to the point of being unnatural. Another gift from the Father, surely.

However, as the Archmage approaches Os and the torture tools are pulled out of their storage spots, and as the screams begin in earnest, I can't help but feel like maybe this...isn't right.

Os is a traitor, but...I'm not sure he deserves this.

I tuck the thought away, shunning it. Pretending it never happened as I send a quick prayer to the Father for forgiveness.

But thoughts are difficult to destroy.

BONUS CHAPTER

Twelve Years Before The Events of The Forgotten and The Feared

(Year 488 PBM):

"I've decided I'm ready to be kissed," I announce, making Amalia choke on the water she was sipping. Virgyl lets out a wolfy cough before covering his face with his paws and whining.

"What he said," Amalia mutters, turning to me. Dirt smudges all over her face and her hair is in matted braids. "You're too young to be kissed, Dyana."

Anger fills me, "I am not! I'm twelve years old. Many ladies are married by now, and I've already started my monthly cycle. That means I'm a woman, and women get kissed."

Amalia rubs her temples, closing her eyes.

"Does that make you mad?" I ask, confused.

Her eyes flash open, "No! No. I'm not mad, Dyana. This is just...new."

"Oh. You've never been kissed either!"

Amalia's face turns bright red, "I've been kissed."

"Prove it."

She just glares at me, but Virgyl's mate, a white Dyre Wolf almost as big as he is, walks over to Amalia and gently licks her cheek.

"Ah, see?" Amalia says, "I've been kissed plenty."

"But not by a real person?" I ask.

Amalia stands up and exits the cave, looking up at the night sky. The suns just set and the stars shine brightly through the thick tree branches. I follow her outside, shivering against the cold.

I need a new jacket soon. This one has started falling apart.

Amalia wears worn clothes too, various leathers and furs that have seen better days.

Our clothes are either stolen or made from the, uh, leftovers from the wolves.

"No, I've never been kissed either, Dyana." she says quietly.

"Then let's go to town!" I say cheerfully. But her fists tighten.

"No." she says.

"But that's not fair. I want to live life, Amalia. I don't want to hide away in the forest forever. I want to kiss and dance and laugh!" I twirl with my hands out to either side of me, imagining music playing in the background.

Amalia sighs, "I said no."

"You're being so mean!" I blurt, stomping back into the cave, grumpy and frustrated.

It's a little while later when Amalia comes back inside. I'm curled up by Virgyl's side as he licks my hand with his rough tongue.

Amalia paces briefly before standing in front of me, her hands on her hips. "How about this. When you're thirteen, we will spend a few days in Eahmond. It's the town nearest south of here, and there will be plenty of cute girls and boys for you to dance with—and maybe kiss."

I jump to my feet, bouncing around and shrieking in happiness. "YES! YES! Thank you!" I wrap my arms around her, burying my face in her abdomen.

"But," Amalia pulls back, looking me in the eyes. "One wrong move from anyone and we're out of there. Okay?"

I sigh, "Fine. Yes. Anything suspicious and we'll leave."

"Okay, good." Amalia says, before we sit by the fire and enjoy the root vegetable stew she's been cooking all day long.

Ten Moons Later

"Would you like to dance?"

My heart falls from my chest as butterflies take residence in my stomach. The girl is around my age, with gorgeous pale blonde curls pulled off her face to show off sharp cheekbones and wide hazel eyes.

I thought Amalia might have forgotten our deal, that we could come to Eahmond for the Autumnal Equinox after my thirteenth birthday.

My birthday was 7 moon cycles ago, and yesterday morning Amalia announced we were going into town.

"Sure," I say, breathless not from movement but from the stunning person in front of me.

"What's your name?" the girl asks, taking my hand.

Her palm is so soft. I clasp it gently and let her lead me into the dance circle in the town square. My dress unfurls as I twirl. This is the first time I've worn a dress since I stumbled into the forest six years ago. When we got to town last night, Amalia disappeared and when she came back, she had a gorgeous red dress for me, with black leather laces up the back.

Flowers decorate every visible space of the village to celebrate the Fall Equinox. It's beautiful and the smell of honey and cinnamon in the air is heady and pungent.

"Dyana," I respond, finally finding my voice. "My name is Dyana."

"Dyana," the girl repeats, rolling my name off the tip of her tongue, "I'm Mara."

Mara.

Mara, Mara, Mara.

We dance for hours, twirling and laughing until the wee hours of the night.

Amalia isn't here. She said it wouldn't be a good idea to come. But I know she's watching from the window of the room she rented us in the small inn.

Our room faces the town square, something which I know was a purposeful choice on her part. But I don't care. Tonight isn't for worrying. Tonight is for *dancing*.

As the townspeople stumble away, drunk off forest mead, the dance circle thins.

Then it's just the two of us.

Mara.

"Where are you from?" she laughs, catching her breath. She's close to my age; maybe a few years older. There's an air of confidence about her that is hypnotizing.

I pause, "The Westlands. We're moving North for the winter."

Mara blinks, "North for the winter? That's strange."

Crap. Crap!

"It's for my sister's job. She...works with animals."

"Oh, that's cool." Mara says, smiling.

Her lips are so plump and pink.

I wonder if they're as soft as they look, or if she tastes like the honey mead we've been sipping all evening long.

The bonfire in front of us crackles, and I realize it's spinning lightly.

How much mead have I had?

I stumble, tripping, but Mara catches me easily. "Hehe, I think we've had enough mead."

"Yeah, I think so," I laugh. She helps me up and we stare at each other for a moment.

"Will I see you again, Dyana?" Mara asks, her big brown eyes hopeful.

"Maybe," I say with a sly smile.

Her fingers brush mine and I realize we're standing so close, the skirts of our dresses tangle. Drunk with happiness and wine, I reach up and trace her cheek with my hand.

"You're so pretty," I whisper.

Then I'm teetering forward and my lips just a breath away from hers.

We breathe each other in. She smells like a campfire.

"I want to kiss you," I breathe.

Mara smiles and closes the distance between us. Stars burst behind my eyes as she presses her soft lips against my own. She gently sucks on my lower lip before teasing my mouth open with the tip of her tongue.

I don't know how long we're there. Only that it seems like a lifetime. I want to stay lost in her kiss forever, but we're soon interrupted.

"Dyana, it's time to go," Amalia says gently from a few feet away. Mara and I break apart, panting.

"Your sister?" Mara whispers, still looking into my eyes. I nod, unable to look away from her. I'm not done yet. I want more.

But I say nothing.

"Dyana," Amalia says again. I press another kiss to Mara's lips before pulling away.

"I need to go," I whisper.

Mara frowns, sad, and turns to where Amalia stands near the outskirts of the circle. Mara goes still, her eyes wide as her pupils dilate and her breath comes fast.

"You," Mara gasps.

Amalia is next to me before I can blink. "Let's go," she says with a hurry.

"You're the Gray Wytch," Mara asks, her voice trembling. "I saw you! When I was just a child I-I saw you kill those men!" She scampers backward. "Wytch! It's the Wytch!" she screams.

"Shit," Amalia hisses. "We need to go, NOW."

"What? Why?" I ask, confused. I turn, trying to find Mara. "Mara, wait, I—"

"Don't touch me, freak!" she screams. "She's evil, and if you're with her...you're evil too."

My jaw drops and I half wonder if I look down, if I would see a knife stabbing my heart.

That's how it feels to see the disgust fill Mara's eyes as she watches us.

"It's the Wytch! She's here! Quick!" Mara screams.

But Amalia is next to her before I can track the movement, slapping her hand over Mara's mouth.

"Shut up." Amalia snarls. Mara moans and screams behind Amalia's hand, fighting her off. But Amalia stands firm.

She leans down to whisper something in Mara's ear, and the girl goes still.

Amalia lets go, and Mara backs away, panting and wiping her mouth, erasing every trace of me.

"It's the Wytch! She's here! Quick!" Mara screams, and in the distance I hear the townspeople wake.

Amalia sighs, grabbing my hand and tugging me away.

By the time the townspeople rally, we've disappeared into the darkness of the forest. Amalia dumps me on one of the Dyre Wolves waiting for us a safe distance away. Amalia gets on Virgyl as we take off.

The wolves move faster than normal wolves, so what would normally be a three day ride on horseback or by foot is just a few hours for us. I burrow down into Syska's thick white fur, using it to hold on as they begin the steep ascent up the mountain.

Syska is Virgyl's mate. I finally learned her name a few weeks ago.

But I don't care about Syska. I don't care about anything. As I close my eyes against the dark of the night, all I can think about is the feel of Mara's warm lips—and the terror in her eyes afterwards.

Amalia is silent when we return to the cave, but the rest of the wolves howl and yip happily at the sight of their pack leaders.

I stomp away, feeling too much, and plop down on my bed, using the curtain Amalia hung for me to close off my space.

I want space.

Lots of it.

"I'm sorry," Amalia says from the other side of the curtain. Her voice is a whisper but I hear it clearly. "I'm so sorry, Dyana. I...hoped that wouldn't happen."

My tears start to fall, soaking my pillow. "Why do they hate you, Amalia? Why can't we live a normal life?"

Amalia sighs.

"I just want to be normal," I say into my pillow.

The curtain squeaks as Amalia moves it, but I don't look.

I just listen as she crawls into bed next to me, tucking me in tightly against her chest as her arm wraps around my middle.

"I know, Dyana. I often wish for a normal life too." She breaths into my hair.

"Why did she say those things? That you...killed people?" I ask, hiccupping.

Amalia buries her face in my thick hair for a moment and the curtain squeaks again as Syska and Virgyl join us. Virgyl lays across our feet, his nose facing me, and Syska curls around our heads, merging with my pillow.

We're surrounded by wolf fur.

But it feels safer somehow.

Protected.

Soon, the excitement of the day leads to exhaustion, and sleep makes my eyes heavy. I close them, fading away, when Amalia finally responds. "She said those things because they're true. I am a murderer. But...not in the way she thinks."

I mumble sleepily, "You're not a bad person, Ama."

She sighs, pressing a kiss to my cheek, "I'm glad you got your kiss, Dyana. I promise, it won't be your last."

I hope she's right.

I hope I'm right, too.

WANT MORE DRAGON QUEEN?

Return to the world of The Dragon Queen in

THE BROKEN AND THE BRAVE.

486 years ago, a Dragon met a Prince.

200 years ago, a Prince became a Rebel.

80 years ago, a Wolf found a Wytch.

2 years ago and their world shattered.

The Broken and The Brave is a collection of never-before-seen stories from the characters you've come to know and love in EC Garrett's Dragon Queen series. Part novella, part prequel, and part alternative-pov to The Forgotten and The Feared, this book features POV's from Remus 'Os' Ostia, Prince Nyall Drayven, the Dyre Wolf Virgyl, the Dragon Vesimyr, and more.

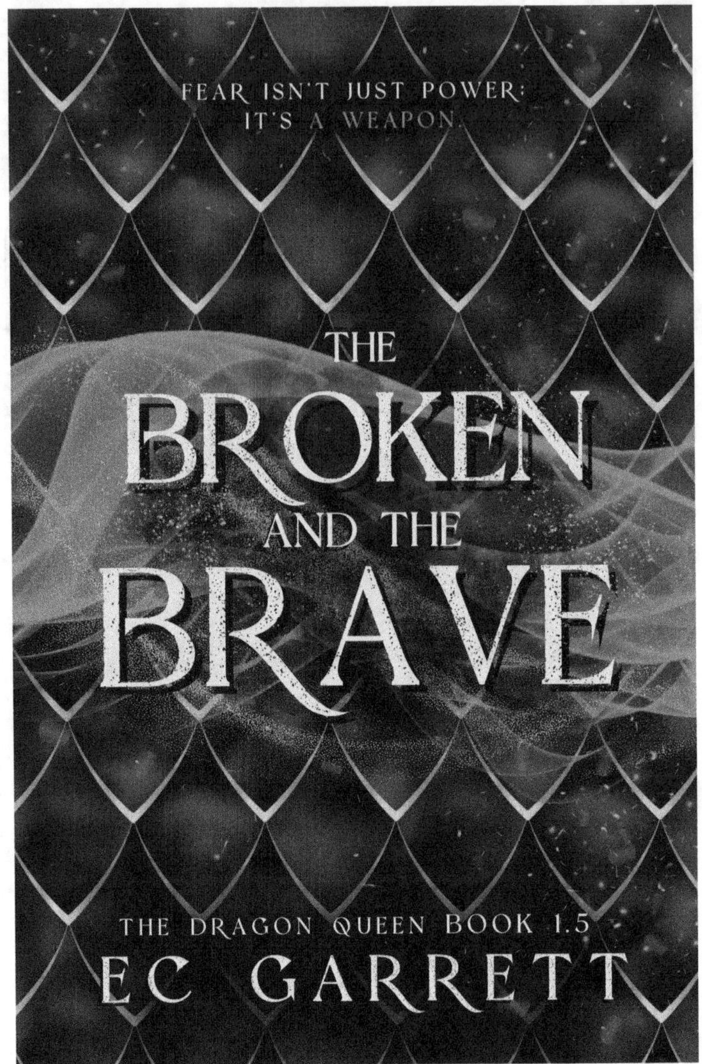

The Dragon Queen (Book 1.5)

Available now everywhere books are sold.

THE GAME HAS ONLY JUST BEGUN

Amalia Roth is dead. She died alongside the Crimson Queen in the arena two years ago. Donning her Gray Wytch persona, Amalia and the Dragon Ryu have spent the past year hunting down the Fae who wronged her. All the while, Amalia struggles not to crumble under the weight of grief.

Across the Midheym Sea on the isle of Elysium, Dyana grapples with her new-found magyk under the guidance of the ancient dragon, Vesimyr. She quickly learns that Elysium isn't paradise - it's a prison. Trapped under the claws of the Dragon Regent, she cannot leave. But Dyana knows Amalia is alive and will stop at nothing to get back to her sister - even if it means taking on the Regent alone.

The rebel Mirielle has lost everything. Her life's goal was to take down the High Council, but doing so only made things worse. Lost and alone, Mirielle begins plotting a way back home, regardless of the risk.

With the High Council gone, the Archmage has risen. Storms shake the continent as the situation grows more dangerous by the day. Ur Daoine lies on the brink of civil war. In secret, the heretic Prince Nyall Drayven leads the growing rebellion. After Nyall convinces Amalia to join him at the front, a divide grows within the rebel factions, and the Prince's carefully built control begins to crumble. When one of the rebels' carefully planned missions goes wrong, a familiar face steals Ryu and reveals a truth that will change everything; someone from Amalia's past is alive.

FROM ASHES AND PAIN, AMALIA ASTEROTH HAS RISEN.

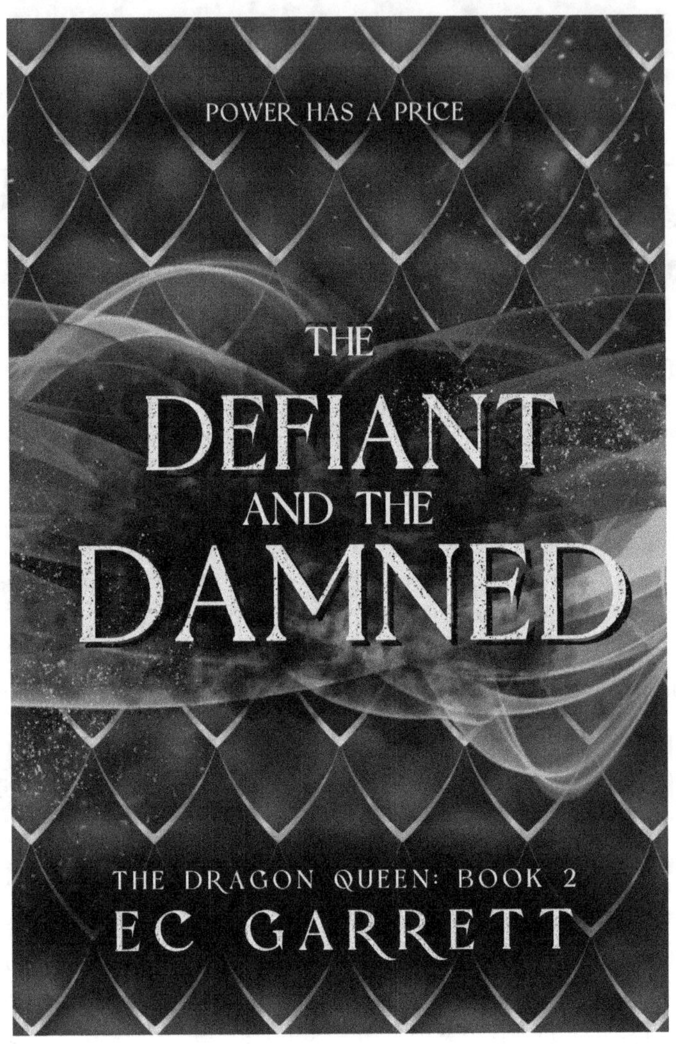

The Dragon Queen (Book 2)

Available now everywhere books are sold.

GLOSSARY

Abhaynn Gheal: A large river just south of Castael Laryn, the capital city of Ur Daoine.

ABM: Ante Bellum Magni, which means Before Great War. The years prior to the Fae taking control of the Kingdom.

Achan Drayven: High Councilor and leader of all Fae. Age is unknown. Was present when the Fae arrived 600 years ago.

A gahrá: Means "my beloved" in the language of the Dragons. There is no true translation because Dragons have three vocal cords and their words are made up of sounds Os cannot make in human form.

Ahavah: Means "my heart" in the language of Amalia's father and his kin.

Ains Selle: Arkaydian for "One Soul," a term for those who identify with the gender of their birth.

Alle Selle: Arkaydian for "All Souls," a term for those who identify with no one gender.

Amalia Roth: A woman who seems to be in her late 20s. Amalia lives in Twyn Fells, a town in the far north of Ur Daoine, where she passes for a human. Amalia hides her true identity but she is the last living Arkaydian, an ancient breed of magical being with powers that relate to living things and nature.

The Annag: A small forest to the West of Castael Laryn.

Archidna: A spider-like monster with sharp pincers and eight legs. They vary in size from a small pony to a full-size horse.

The Archmage: The position of High Councilor Achan Drayven's right hand. Filled by a powerful Fae.

Arkaydia: An ancient, magykal kingdom that has since disappeared.

Beastkyn: Animals with the ability to turn into people. Not shifters, but true animals that just change shape. Very rare.

Beide Selle: Arkaydian for "Both Souls," a term for those who identify with all genders and fluidly live between them.

Black Citadel, The: The High Council's fortress, in the center of Castael Laryn.

Castael Laryn: The capital city of Ur Daoine and seat of power of the Imperial Fae.

Dark Magyk: A forgotten, evil type of magyk practice first created by the elves thousands of years ago. The reason the elves destroyed their homeland and went extinct. Dark Magyk users should be avoided at all costs.

Demis: The offspring of a human or other magyka breeding with a fae. Demis simply means part fae.

Dragons: Four and two-legged creatures widely regarded to be Gods. They're made of magyk. Dragons first originated in their homeland, Elysium, which lies to the far west, across the Midheym Sea.

Dragonfear: A biological phenomenon that occurs in lower beings such as humans, demis, and magyka when they lay eyes upon a Dragon. The more magyk a being possesses, the easier it is to shrug Dragonfear off. Dragonfear causes heart palpitations, high blood pressure, anxiety, and panic, as it instigates a fight or flight response.

Dragonguard: The personal Dragonriders of the High Council. The Dragonguard is made up of a dozen or so tamed, lab-bred Dragons that have been domesticated. Only Imperial Fae have been able to ride Dragons, as the rest were eaten upon attempt. The Dragonguard patrols the borders and carries out assignments from the High Council, including the rounding up of Gauntlet candidates.

Dyana Arkos: A human orphan, adopted sister of Amalia Roth. 24 years old and is a professional dancer at the Birdcage.

The Dragon Pit: The caverns that house the dragon stables.

The Eastlands: The Eastern district of Ur Daoine. Known for being a big fruit and vegetable producer in the country.

Eahmond: A northland town.

Elves: An extinct group of highly magykal beings who wielded dark magyk, a type of magyk that can suck the life out of anything living. There are rumors of some elves that are still alive, but the ages of the elves have centuries passed.

Elysium: The legendary kingdom of the Dragons. Thought to be a myth. Elysium is surrounded by a giant wall of clouds that hide the most complex, advanced ward that has ever been woven. This ward keeps everyone that isn't a Dragon out. Only a Dragon can grant passage to a lower being, but once you enter, the wards will never let you out.

Fae: A powerful race of supernaturals who appeared within a portal 600 years ago to take control of Arkaydia. After 100 years of war, they emerged victorious and now rule. Fae possesses heightened strength and hearing, and the royals hold magyk.

The Fray: A monthly tournament where the top fighters in the kingdom fight each other and dragons, for the entertainment of the fae.

The Gauntlet: A tournament to the death held every 25 years where 30 candidates, two humans from every town in the Kingdom, compete for a prize and the right to live.

Grynte: Slang for a grunt.

The Gray Wytch: A legendary figure used to scare children into behaving. The Gray Wytch is thought to be dead, now, but she lived deep within the Ulster Wald with her pack of wolves, hunting down bad Fae and misbehaving children.

The High Council: The Imperial Fae rulers of Ur Daoine, made up of four councilors and a High Councilor. Highly skilled magyk users.

Humans: The bottom species of Ur Daoine, a race with no special abilities

Mrs. Hunton: Innkeeper and bar owner where Amalia rents her room. Wife to Mr. Hunton, owner of Taran the horse. Amalia gets a discounted rental rate in exchange for caring for and riding Taran at the stables.

The Infinium Sands: A large desert to the southwest of Ur Daoine.

Ireyna: Unknown species. Gauntlet trainer.

Kydis: The Crimson Queen, a great red dragon and the rightful ruler of Elysium. Ancient and very powerful.

Lir: The Arkaydian God of the Sea. Believers of Lir lived in the area that is now called the Eastlands. Few pray to Lir openly.

Macha: One of the two swords of Morrigyn, gifted to Arkaydia over two thousand years ago and hidden deep in the caves, only to be found by Remus Ostia five centuries ago. The pair to Neiman.

Magyka: Non-Fae magykal beings including shifters and vampires.

The Midheym Sea: The sea to the west of Ur Daoine.

Mirielle Zenyth: Unknown species. The candidate is from Sud Azul in the Eastlands. Her partner ran away the first day, so she has no partner.

The Morrigyn: One form of the Mother. The Arkaydian Goddess of War and Wisdom. Formerly had the world's largest temple devoted to Her. Few pray to her anymore.

The Mother: One form of the Morrigyn. The Arkaydian Goddess of Creation. She has two sides to represent the duality of being. For all light, there is dark. The Mother is the light, the Morrigyn is the dark.

Neiman: One of the two swords of Morrigyn, gifted to Arkaydia over two thousand years ago and hidden deep in the caves, only to be found by Remus Ostia five centuries ago. The pair to Macha.

Nyall Drayven: Crown Prince of Ur Daoine.

The Northlands: The Northern Territory of Ur Daoine. The biggest land wise but the least populated due to the Ulster Wald. Colloquially called the "North."

Oryx: A rare breed of warhorse with a swirling black horn, eyes like rubies, and sharp fangs for teeth. Oryx are 25% bigger than a normal warhorse and have twice the speed and endurance. Oryx hasn't been seen in the Infinium Sands, their hibernation grounds, for centuries.

The Pass of Brón Mór, The: A narrow and dangerous pass between the mountains of the Ulster Wald. Between the falling rocks, unstable ground, and cliffsides, it was extremely difficult to make the pass alive.

PBM: Post Bellum Magni, which means After Great War. The years following the Fae taking control of the Kingdom.

Puggō: A slur for humans.

Remus Ostia: Unknown species, likely shifter. Head trainer of the Gauntlet. Extremely dangerous and powerful, approach with caution.

Shifters: People with the ability to turn into animals.

Siphon: A higher level magyk user with the ability to drain the lifeforce from any living being as well as the earth itself, and transfer it to themselves or to another source. They can literally siphon and move magyk. Siphons are almost always of Elvish descent.

The Southlands: The Southern district of Ur Daoinc, which includes the Infinium Sands.

Sol Constantus: The national religion of Ur Daoine, of which they pray to the Father, Constantus. It wasn't illegal to pray to one of the other Gods but only allowed in private.

Sud Azyl: A port town in the Eastlands, and a large supplier of food for Ur Daoine.

Taran: Originally the horse belonging to Mrs. Hutton's husband, Taran has been cared for by Amalia for years and now belongs to her. Taran is a large white horse with gray dapples and a black mane and tail.

The Father: A version of Sol Constantus. A side sect of Sol Constantus believers pray to The Father. They believe that Sol Constantus and The Father are separate but equal.

Twyn Fells: The Northernmost town in Ur Daoine.

Ulster Wald: A sprawling forest that takes up most of the Northern territory.

Ur Daoine: A large country ruled by the Fae. Ur Daoine is divided into four territories; The North (composed mainly of the massive Ulster Wald forest), The Westlands, The Southlands (with the Infinium Sands), and the Eastlands.

The Westlands: The smallest territory of Ur Daoine to the West of the Abhaynn Gheal and South of the Ulster Wald.

Weaving: A term used by some to describe magyk castings. Weavers use a combination of incantations and hand movement to pull visible magyk from the air. It's one of the few types of magyks that are always visible, outside of shifters.

Wytch: Humans, fabled to have fae-like powers.

THANK YOU

Where do I even begin? First and foremost, I want to thank the animals who have saved my life time and time again. When the depression makes everything seem hopeless, and when my anxiety makes me too scared to move, the love of animals always brings me back into the light. **Boomer, Luca, Flynn, Beau, Blue, Xena, Stanley, Tosh, Artemis, Sophie, Lady...** I could go on. **Frankie,** thank you for being my best friend, even if it ended up that I'm your Emotional Support Human instead of you being my Emotional Support Animal. I never thought I could love something as much as I love you. Thank you for always licking up my tears and loving me more than anything on this planet.

The animal industry is incredibly cruel. I cry when I pass giant trucks stuffed with terrified, screaming animals on the highway headed to slaughterhouses. Everything in this book is inspired by real situations that happen to animals in this world every single fucking day, and it's disgusting. The Forgotten and The Feared poses a question; why do we care only if it's some mythical creature? Why do we care if a baby dragon dies, but not a chicken? I hope this book sheds some light on the ways animals are suffering; and how, even in the face of cruelty, they have so much love to give us. They deserve our respect and care in return. Even the smallest of creatures, like a little mouse.

Secondly, but not least, thank you to my parents. **Mom and Dad**, thank you for always supporting me, even when I announce I'm going to completely change careers and give writing a real chance. Thank you for keeping me afloat and giving me a support system I can rely on, even when I feel lost and alone. **Dad**, you taught me that stories are joy. When life gets low and things get tough, stories are what saves us. Thank you. I am so proud to be your daughter. Thank you for telling me the Bunny Story for three years, thank you for your endless patience and for always encouraging me to play and be creative, and most importantly thank you for always encouraging me to read. **Mom,** thank you for being the mom

I always wanted but didn't have. You took an angry, lost teenager and molded me into a (sometimes) capable adult who actually knows how to do laundry. More importantly, you've taught me to pause and listen. I am so grateful to have you in my life and that I get to call you mom. To my **biological mom and my grandparents**, who aren't here to see this—we had our differences, but I wish you were here to see this. I lost far too many family members during the early COVID-19 years. In the span of less than 36 months, I lost my biological mother, my last living biological grandparent, and my beautiful cousin Lauren. **Lauren,** you are remembered and loved. You made this world a better place—and me, a better person. Thank you for loving animals so deeply. It was your funeral and your love of horses that made me get back in the saddle. Puff, the magyk mouse, is for you.

To **Audrey and Katherine** – thank you for your constant support and love. You have given me the joy of feeling like I have siblings, which is such a gift for an only child. You both are so smart and so strong; thank you for pushing me to be a better person and make this world a better place for you. The entire **Schaeffel Clan, Wolski Clan, and Garrett Clan, t**hank you for making me feel like I'm not alone in this world. Moving back to the Midwest and being able to see you all on a regular basis is such a joy.

To my best friends. **Tiffany, Annie, Lyss, Corrine** – I love you all so much. It is your friendship and love that inspired the incredible female friendships in this book, and the strong female characters. Thank you for making long-distance friendship possible. Distance and time will never push us apart.

Finally, a book is a team effort. I have so many to thank who have made this book what it is. To my **writing partners and supporters** who got me past that first 10k word hump. I literally couldn't have done it without you.

To my amazing editor **YarnWyvern**; infinite thanks and gratitude for your friendship, mentorship, and your keen eye. You improved this story so much, and I am so thankful.

To my **Alpha and Beta readers; Julia, Jacqi, Dara, Harper, Becks, Corrine, Reina.** Your feedback made this book what it is. Thank you for always answering my 2:00 a.m. insane questions with no context. Thank you for the honesty and thoughtfulness behind every opinion and answer. I am beyond grateful for all of you.

To my **Kickstarter backers.** You made me believe in myself, which is no easy feat. Thank you for taking a chance on me and showing me that my ideas are worthy. I'm still in shock at your generosity and am endlessly grateful. All of you have a permanent place at my table.

To the authors who made me fall in love with books and storytelling in the first place; **Tamora Pierce, Christopher Paloni, J. R.R. Tolkien, Tahereh Mafi, Leigh Bardugo, Meridith Ann Pierce, Mercedes Lackey, P.C. Cast, Stephen King, Sierra Simone**... I could keep going here, too. But thank you for creating worlds so lush, so captivating, so thrilling, that I wish I could physically JUMP into the pages and transport to another place.

To the **University of Nevada, Reno, and the College of Liberal Arts.** The History, Philosophy, and English classes that I took molded me into the person I am today. Liberal Arts degrees are incredible and I hope to see more funding for Liberal Arts colleges in the future. Thank you for fueling my desire to learn and how to ask the right questions. To the Professors and teachers who molded me, I owe my success to you. Thank you for your patience with my endless questions.

To **Reina.** Seeing this world come to life has been the greatest gift; thank you.

And you, dear reader. Thank YOU for making it this far and for giving my book a chance. I can't wait for what's next—and there's a **LOT** coming up next.

Are you ready?

<u>**REPUBLICA HELVETORUM**</u>
gothic monster romance
Here There Be Monsters
Here There Be Witches – *coming 2026*
There Are Monsters Beneath – *coming 2026/2027*

<u>**THE DRAGON QUEEN**</u>
dark epic fantasy
The Forgotten and The Feared
The Broken and The Brave
The Defiant and The Damned
TDQ3 – *coming 2026*

<u>**THE HOME FOR WAYWARD CREATURES**</u>
paranormal romantic sci-fi
Vol. 1
Vol. 2 – coming 2027

<u>**SHORT STORIES & SERIALS**</u>
Rescue Me – *contemporary fiction*
FERN – *sci-fi horrormance*
DARKMOOR – *gothic why-choose romance*

EC Garrett is an Alaskan transplant now living in Kansas City, MO who writes fantasy/sci-fi speculative fiction. She received her Bachelor's Degree in English Literature with a focus in Early Modern and Medieval Literature and a minor in Medieval History from the University of Nevada, Reno in 2016. ECG is currently attending the University of Missouri-Kansas City where she is working on her Masters in English literature. In her spare time, she's either reading or watching the latest fantasy releases, riding horses at the barn, spending time with her family, or playing with her very cute but extremely ornery dachshund mix, Frankie.

She dreams of becoming a dragon rider.

Follow ECG on social media to get all the latest updates.

www.authorecgarrett.com

Instagram: @authorecgarrett

Tiktok: @author.ecgarrett

Threads: @authorecgarrett

Facebook: @authorecgarrett

Midnight Pages

indie publishing house + bookish candles

handmade in kansas city, mo